1c signed

MW00709325

DEMONS

OF THE GREAT

SACANDAGA

LAKE

To Kathy

Enjoy

Steve N. Long

DEMONS
OF THE GREAT
SACANDAGA
LAKE

IRENE H. POUGH

TATE PUBLISHING
AND ENTERPRISES, LLC

Demons of the Great Sacandaga Lake
Copyright © 2013 by Irene H. Pough. All rights reserved.

No part of this publication may be reproduced, stored in a retrieval system or transmitted in any way by any means, electronic, mechanical, photocopy, recording or otherwise without the prior permission of the author except as provided by USA copyright law.

This novel is a work of fiction. Names, descriptions, entities, and incidents included in the story are products of the author's imagination. Any resemblance to actual persons, events, and entities is entirely coincidental.

The opinions expressed by the author are not necessarily those of Tate Publishing, LLC.

Published by Tate Publishing & Enterprises, LLC
127 E. Trade Center Terrace | Mustang, Oklahoma 73064 USA
1.888.361.9473 | www.tatepublishing.com

Tate Publishing is committed to excellence in the publishing industry. The company reflects the philosophy established by the founders, based on Psalm 68:11,
"The Lord gave the word and great was the company of those who published it."

Book design copyright © 2013 by Tate Publishing, LLC. All rights reserved.
Cover design by Rodrigo Adolfo
Interior design by Mary Jean Archival

Published in the United States of America

ISBN: 978-1-62510-054-2
1. Fiction / General
2. Fiction / Romance / General
13.03.08

DEDICATION

To my daughter, Virginia, thank you for your words of encouragement and believing in my ability to turn a dream into reality. You are by far God's greatest gift to me. I love you.

To my sister, Lynda, there are not enough words to adequately express my love and gratitude for all that you have done for me through the years. Thank you for sharing my dream.

To my dear friends: Arlene for your words of wisdom, Queen for being my shoulder to cry on, and Sue for the special memories and times we shared in our youth in the Adirondacks.

Prologue

August 1979

Driving in the mountains on an ordinary day can be quite treacherous if one is unfamiliar with the road. Amanda Callison did not fit into that category. She knew the twisty and hilly one-lane road she was traveling on like the back of her hand. It was the way she had gone countless times during her younger years. Her leg muscles had become strong as she peddled her simple one-speed bicycle up these hills. Now she made her journey to her grandmother's cabin in her 1968 dusty-blue Chevy Chevelle 4 speed. As usual, the radio was cranked up playing the latest rock and roll of the '70s. Amanda usually enjoyed riding with the windows down so she could enjoy the breeze and sweet smells of wildflowers. Today was a different matter.

The late summer storm forecasted for the lower Adirondack Mountains blew in quicker than Amanda expected. As she turned onto the gravel road leading up into the mountain, the skies opened up. Amanda huffed as rain pelted against the windshield. Decreased visibility and gusts of wind were making it necessary for Amanda to keep two hands on the wheel in order to maintain control of her car. She slowed down to negotiate the one-lane bridge as lightning streaked against the sky, and thunder bounced against the mountains. Amanda sighed in relief as she saw her grandmother's cabin.

Mary Freeman, Amanda's maternal grandmother, a Mohawk Indian, had lived in this cabin on this ridge up in the mountain for as long as Amanda could remember. Amanda had a special bond with Mary. During summer vacation, Amanda would spend her days with Mary learning the ways of the Mohawks. Amanda liked to believe that her chocolate-colored eyes and facial structure were from her native heritage passed from Grandma to her mother and down to her. Growing up, Amanda had always considered Mary to be a beautiful woman. That beauty was not only evident externally. As Amanda matured, she came to appreciate her grandmother's character traits. This is where Amanda saw her beauty truly shine. She frequently called Mary by her native name, Gentle Spirit. That is how Amanda had always known her—gentle in spirit. Even when as a child her grandmother had disciplined her, it had never been harsh like when her father disciplined. In years past, the old woman's home had always been a refuge for Amanda. Many times she had escaped the wrath of her father and his violent temper. Today she sought refuge not from her father as he is now deceased. Amanda has troubles that have been piling up to become what seems like an insurmountable mountain. Her heart is consumed by grief.

Amanda parked her car near the front porch. She was dressed in a sleeveless turquoise pullover blouse, pale-blue shorts, and thong sandals. Looking at the rain steadily hitting the windshield, Amanda gazed at her attire. She removed her sandals to allow her to run without slipping on the wet grass. Opening the door, she sprinted across the yard hoping to avoid getting too wet. No such luck! She spitted out some words that were lost with a rumble of thunder and pelting of rain against her body. Much to Amanda's dismay, she dashed onto the porch soaked to the bone.

Mary heard Amanda pull into the yard. By the time Amanda reached the porch steps, Mary was standing just outside her door. Her long dark hair with streaks of gray hung limp around her face and cascaded down her shoulders. The lines on her face revealed years of hard living. Her dress was worn from too many years of service. She patiently stood on the porch with a towel. Amanda scowled and sputtered as she shook her hair. The old mutt of a dog that lay on the porch interrupted from sleeping raised his head.

He let out a whoof of discontentment as he received the drops of water from Amanda's hair. Amanda bent down and apologized to the dog while rubbing his head. Satisfied, the dog dropped his head onto his paws and returned to his nap. She stood up and faced her grandmother. Mary looked deep into Amanda's eyes. The older woman saw a storm brewing in her granddaughter that could be more dangerous than the one currently pummeling the mountains.

A tear escaped and trickled down Amanda's already wet cheek. Mary reached out and gently pulled Amanda into her arms. As she did, Amanda breathed in the scent of her grandmother. She smelled of herbs, earth, and all that is good. For the first time all summer, Amanda felt totally safe. Amanda sighed and then choked back the urge to cry. "You are the only one I trust at this point in my life."

"Amanda, you go on inside child and dry off. Take off those wet things and put on my robe. You lay those clothes out by the fire so they will dry." Mary gave her a gentle nudge inside. "I'll fix us a glass of my special iced tea. Then you sit here on the porch with me and tell me what brings you up here today."

Amanda did as the old woman instructed. As she dried off her hair, she heard the soft melodious tune her grandmother hummed. It was the song of her people the Mohawk's. How many times had Amanda heard her grandmother sing that same song? Somehow the old woman always knew what Amanda needed in her life. Amanda knew she had made the right decision in coming here.

When Amanda came out onto the porch, Mary sat on the glider. Her eyes were closed as she continued to hum. Without opening her eyes or missing a beat of the song, she patted the seat next to her. Amanda took the cue and quietly sat down next to her. Two glasses of iced tea sat on a small table roughly made of pine. Quietly, she picked up a glass and took a sip. Mary stopped her singing, however, continued to keep her eyes closed.

"'Too eager to wait,' that is what your mother should have named you," Mary stated with frankness. "You were always the one who was in a hurry." Amanda respectfully sat quietly and waited for her grandmother to continue. "I never saw impatience to match yours in your brothers. You, Amanda, were a different child. As if you had to prove yourself, always in competition with Samuel and James. No"—she shook her head—"not with Samuel, with James."

"Not anymore, Grandma. The competition is over. James and the people I considered to be my friends have won. I have lost." Amanda slowly lifted her gaze and looked at her grandmother. Pure raw pain and sadness consumed her eyes, face, and entire body. "You know, Gram, as we talked earlier this summer, I was hopeful things would work out for all of us. How could I have been so wrong?" Amanda did not wait for a response. "The way it stands now, I must leave these mountains. It is no longer safe for me to be here." Mary placed her hand on Amanda's and gently squeezed.

"Tell me, Amanda, as you have throughout this turbulent summer. What has happened during the past two weeks to add to your troubles?"

Amanda once again took her grandmother into her confidence, sharing all the sordid details of how her life had most recently unraveled. Her saga ended with great sadness. "So you see, Grandmother, Jim has chosen to believe his friends over me. I thought family was supposed to mean more than friends. I thought he loved me." Mary drew her deeply into her arms. Amanda now breathed in the scent of her grandmother as if to last her for her lifetime.

"Oh, my dear child, he does love you." Mary continued to hold Amanda who made no attempt to leave her arms.

"But, Grandmother, this time I'm afraid you are wrong. He abandoned me. I will never forgive him for what he has done. In my eyes, he's now as good as our Samuel...dead."

"Your wounds are deep Amanda and with good reason. Running from here will not solve the problem between your brother and you." Amanda pulled back from her grandmother's embrace. She began to respond when Mary raised her hand to silence her. "Family has always been important to you. You inherited that from your mother and me. Your brother James is in many ways like your father. He has not yet learned the value of family. Your brother is a good man. Give him time to see the errors of his ways. Amanda, in time, you must forgive him in your heart. Do it not for him, but for yourself. And, child, do it before it is too late."

Amanda took a sip of the iced tea. She looked out over the meadow up in the side of the ridge. Her grandmother began to hum another song. As she hummed, Amanda listened to the sound of the brook that ran behind the cabin. When Grandmother finished the song, Amanda quietly spoke.

"I love you, Gentle Spirit. Please do not tell Jim about our conversation. I hope that someday I can forgive him. Right now, I'm defeated. It's time for me to leave, to start over, to find healing and peace of mind. Gram, I'll contact you when I'm settled. All I ask is that you keep our conversations to yourself. I don't want anyone looking for me." With that said, Amanda stood. She went inside and changed into her now near dry clothes. When she emerged, Mary stood and walked with Amanda to the porch steps. The dog still lying in his original spot on the porch raised one eyebrow to take in what was happening. He immediately closed his eye to return to peaceful sleep. The two women hugged. Tears crept to the edges of both sets of eyes. Amanda let go of her grandmother walked down the steps and made her way to her car. The last rumble of thunder was heard in the distance as Amanda drove away from the place she had once called home.

CHAPTER ONE

PRESENT DAY

Amanda Newman stood alone on the shore of the Chesapeake Bay watching the tide roll in from the sea. In the distance, she saw the Bay Bridge spanning across the water from Annapolis to the eastern shore. The sun shone bright in the sky, a light breeze reminded her that soon the air would soon turn raw as winter set in. Being near the water always had a calming effect on Amanda. The water had been her major source of refuge for the past thirty years. She drew in a deep breath and sighed as she caught sight of a seagull soaring overhead.

So much had happened in her life to bring her to Baltimore. Thanks to the help of her friend Jeff Hashbroke, FBI agent out of Manhattan, New York, Amanda Callison had successfully disappeared from her past in 1979 by becoming Amanda Newman. At the age of twenty-four, she had come to Baltimore. Her master's degree in social work had immediately opened doors, allowing Amanda to secure a position as assistant director in the Second Chance Center and Shelter for Battered Women.

Within the next two years, Amanda had secured her certification as a licensed certified social worker, allowing her greater opportunities within her field. Through the years, Cassidy Serenelli-Phillips, LCSW, director of the Second Chance, had become more than just a boss to Amanda. A month after being hired, Amanda discovered that her nagging feeling of being tired and queasy in the stomach was more than simply a bout of the flu. Amanda was pregnant. She knew that the new life forming within her womb could be grounds for dismissal from her position; however, Cassidy had proven to Amanda that the staff also deserved a second chance in life.

Amanda had her second chance and then some. In a relatively short period of time, Cassie had become Amanda's best friend. Cassie, being pregnant herself, was involved in every aspect of Amanda's pregnancy, insisting that Amanda take Lamaze classes with her and that she would be Amanda's coach. Together they had cried and laughed as Amanda gave birth to her daughter Summer Brooke Newman. Cassie had insisted that Amanda take six weeks maternity leave with full pay, followed by being allowed to bring Summer to the center. Amanda was thrilled and assisted Cassie in her visionary thinking by establishing a small day care center within the agency for her employees. As the years followed, Summer spent her days in the child care with Cassie and Andrew's sons, Nathan and Ryan.

Over the years, Cassie and Andrew had become more like sister and brother rather than friends. Their children treated one another like cousins, loving and hating and everything in between. The holidays, birthdays, and major milestones in life were celebrated together. Summer is now married and living with her husband in Colorado. Nathan, Cassie and Andrew's eldest son, lives in Baltimore and is in a relationship with a NSA agent. Ryan, their youngest, is currently living in Chicago.

Now, at the age of fifty-four, Amanda found herself in inner turmoil. It is this new turmoil that led her to the Bay to think. The waves of the tide rolling in usually were soothing for her troubled soul, not today. While dining with Cassie and Andrew on Thanksgiving, they had extended an invitation for Amanda to join them on vacation. Their adult children would not be a part of the vacation; however, another friend of theirs would be joining them. Amanda had felt a twinge of panic as Cassie and Andrew regaled her with the story of their friend Dr. Kevin Wentzel. They assured her that this vacation was not a setup. They simply wanted to share their time with the both of them at their vacation home during the week of Christmas and New Year.

The doctor whom they had told Amanda about sounded like a decent guy. She understood that he too had some unresolved issues in his life—a twenty-five-year marriage that had disintegrated into divorce. Amanda could empathize with Dr. Wentzel being single and alone during the holidays that emphasized loving relationships with a significant person, gay or straight. That was as far as she was willing to go. Amanda definitely was not interested in a winter vacation romance or a long-term relationship. Through the years, Amanda had chosen to remain single and safely barricaded from the potential land mines of relationships. If she accepted an invitation to vacation with her dear friends Cassidy Serenelli-Phillips and her husband, Dr. Andrew Phillips, Amanda could run headlong into the demons of her past. She could land on a mine that would blow apart her well-protected world.

Three weeks after Amanda's walk along the Bay found the weather to be considerably different in the city of Baltimore, Maryland. Darkness increased in the sky over Baltimore. The low-hanging clouds were oozing with precipitation. Amanda Newman, assistant director at the Second Chance Center and Shelter for Women, paused from her work. She listened. The latest winter weather advisory was broadcast from the radio. *This is definitely not good*, she thought, *for the National Weather Service and the local weather stations to issue another severe winter storm weather warning.* She sighed and unconsciously raised her hand to her cheek as she processed the weather alert. *They are saying that now all of Northern Virginia, the Eastern West Virginia Panhandle, and all of the state of Maryland is under the warning. Perhaps I should stay home?* She continued to listen as the announcer went on to say that the storm originating from the Carolinas is continuing its steady march northward toward Baltimore. This storm is expected to produce wind, rain, sleet, and ice. Amanda's heart went out to the people in the state of Virginia who are already experiencing power outages. Yes indeed, this storm is dangerous and was only going to get worse.

There had been hope that a second storm now being reported on coming east out of the Northern Ohio valley would stay north of Maryland. No such luck. According to the latest announcement, the storm is moving southeast through western Pennsylvania bringing with it strong winds and heavy, wet snow. Drivers are being warned to stay off the roads as sections of the Pennsylvania Turnpike from Pittsburgh to Harrisburg are now impassable. *People could be stranded out there and in life-threatening conditions*, Amanda thought as she realized the severity of this announcement. She rubbed her arms and drew in a deep calming breath as she was beginning to experience the early signs of panic.

"The mid-Atlantic may well be shut down by morning. Both storms are expected to converge on the city of Baltimore by five o'clock that evening as sleet. Then as temperature drops, of course, it will change to snow. This is going to be disastrous," she said out load as she listened to the radio. The warning continued setting the expectation of wind gusts exceeding seventy miles per hour and blowing snow producing whiteout conditions throughout the night. Amanda already knew before the announcer made the statement that drifting snow and power outages are sure to follow. She had experienced and lived through worse storms than this while growing up in the mountains. Maybe it was a good thing that she was leaving the city tonight.

The emergency broadcast announcement continued on. Amanda, no longer listening, let out another heavy sigh. Her mind shifted in another direction as she wearily lowered the blind on the office window. Darkness would come earlier than usual tonight. Darkness, night, the holidays, and an uncontrollable storm; Amanda sighed. These were all powerful ingredients in domestic violence and rape. Amanda was overwhelmed with grief. Right now, a woman was being beaten and or raped.

Since Amanda's early days in social work, she had always prided herself on being able to remain empathetic with her clients. It did not matter how heinous the abuse had been perpetrated against them. That was until today when she met Janelle Calitano. In thirty years of counseling abused women, this one shook Amanda to her core. For forty-five minutes, Amanda had listen attentively to Janelle reveal a full account of the abuse she sustained at the hands of her husband. All the sordid details of Janelle's abuse and the psychological implications were compiled for the case notes.

As Amanda read through the text, she noticed something odd and began crossing out the inconsistencies. *Where did this come from?* "Ran the smooth blade of his knife over them. They were too strong for me. I gagged and began to vomit. Junior." During the counseling session, Janelle had not mentioned a knife. She did not mention anyone other than her husband being there during the abuse. There was no vomiting, and she certainly did not mention anyone by the name of Junior. An ominous darkness hovered over Amanda's heart. She rose from her chair, walked over to the cabinet, and took out a bottle of water. Amanda wished it were something stronger. There was a storm developing within her. This emotional storm was threatening to be more violent than the one brewing outside.

Amanda was startled by the quiet knock at the partially opened door. Glancing at the clock on her desk, Amanda noted the time to be 4:45 p.m. Her colleague Liz Rullison stood in the doorway. Liz quietly waited for Amanda to invite her into the office. Amanda attempted to disguise her uneasiness with a smile but to no avail.

"Amanda, are you okay?"

"Oh, yes, Liz. I'm just finishing up last minute things before heading out. Here is the file on Sarah Bayman. She's afraid Richard is going to come after her. Please keep an extra close eye on her. It may be a good idea to call metro police and give them a heads-up. Although it probably won't do any good considering he's one of theirs." Amanda felt weary and sighed. "Just keep her safe. Also, the intake notes are now in the new file on Janelle Calitano. I told

Janelle that if she wants to talk specifically with me, it is all right for you to call me. You have my cell phone number."

"Amanda, let me ask you a question." Amanda had an ominous feeling that like a quarterback who held on to the ball too long before passing, she was about to be sacked. And she was right. "If I were going on vacation and I told you to have a client call me regardless of what our agency policy is, would you make the call?" Liz had hit her hard.

"Noted. Thank you, Liz." A smile tugged at the corners of Amanda's lips, refusing to make its way to her weary eyes.

"You are welcome." Liz sighed. "Now please get yourself together. Give me the keys and get out of here before the storm blasts into the city. Go. Have some fun! The center will be here when you return and in good condition. I promise!"

The sidewalk was already congested with pensive people hurrying to reach their destination. "Great! Just what I don't need!" Amanda mumbled to herself as she slipped on the slick pavement. Having regained her balance, she then adjusted her stride to compensate for the change in texture of the sidewalk. "Oh, how nice it would be to drive to Fells Point to my own apartment. How nice to curl up in front of my fireplace in my favorite sweats with a good book and a glass of wine. Ah, now that would be the perfect ending to this day." But that pleasure would have to wait for another stormy evening. It had taken Amanda two weeks to reach her final decision regarding the invitation to vacation with Cassie and Andrew and their friend Dr. Kevin Wentzel.

On this particular Monday night, Amanda was driving to BWI airport to leave on her winter vacation. Amanda was heading to New York. Cassie Serenelli-Phillips and her husband Dr. Andrew Phillips had invited her to join them at the vacation home in the Adirondack mountains for the Christmas and New Year's holiday week.

As she journeyed to her car, a foreboding feeling hovered over Amanda. She silently scolded herself, "If you really didn't want to spend time with Cassie and Andrew at their cabin, then you should have been honest with them. You should have declined the invitation. But no, you had to keep your mouth shut. You know from past experiences the trouble that gets you into. Hmm... The trouble that gets me into. Actually, being quiet has caused no more trouble than when I speak up for myself." Amanda let out another heavy sigh. "Isn't opening my mouth and defending myself to no avail what led me to Baltimore in the first place?"

BWI was busy with holiday travelers and rush hour commuters. All were hoping to get out of Baltimore before all madness break loose with the storm. Amanda was pleasantly surprised by how quickly she was able to make her way through the check-in process at Southwest. Her flight was leaving from gate A6 at 7:09 p.m. Much to Amanda's relief, the weather was not having an effect on flights at this time. She had time to relax and prepare for the flight to Albany International Airport in Latham, New York.

Coffee...She had time for coffee! Starbucks happened to be an easy walk down the concourse from Amanda's gate of departure. As she walked toward the coffee shop, her mind was on all the choices in coffee. Perhaps she'd have a tall caramel latte. No. On a cold winter night like this, a tall holiday mint coffee with whipped cream was in order. Yum! She could taste the sweetness gliding down her throat already.

As Amanda walked back to the gate with her coffee in hand, she sensed something was amiss. It was as though she was being watched by someone. However, as she looked around, she didn't notice anyone in particular who seemed to be watching her. Perhaps this heightened sense of awareness came from her past and recent conversation with her ninety-nine-year-old grandmother. Amanda knew in her heart how fortunate she was to still have Gentle Spirit in her life. Her mother's early passing caused Amanda to deeply appreciate her grandmother's longevity of life. Having grown up in the mountains, Amanda had learned at an early age to be aware of her surroundings. Her grandmother and uncles had taken great care to teach her the ways of the land. One always was to respect nature, especially a black bear.

Sitting down to wait for her flight to be called, Amanda sipped her coffee and recalled the day she met danger head-on while walking on a path up in the mountain. Her family had also warned her of the wrath of a scared skunk. By the time she saw it, it was too late. The spray caught her on her right leg. The stench that resonated from her body indicated that it may have well sprayed her from head to toe. Upon arriving on grandmother's porch, she was stopped by her family. It was off to the shed for grandma's home remedy bath to be "de-skunked." An announcement interrupted Amanda's thoughts. The boarding of Amanda's flight to New York was about to begin. She looked around at the people sitting and standing near her. Sitting in BWI airport, she certainly did not have to worry about skunks. Still something was causing her to feel uneasy.

CHAPTER TWO

C assie Serenelli-Phillips had accomplished much in her fifty-six years of life. Professionally, she is the director of the Second Chance Center and Shelter for Women in Baltimore, Maryland. She is passionate about her work, family, and friends. Now two of her dear friends, Amanda Newman and Dr. Kevin Wentzel, would be spending the week with Cassie and her husband Dr. Andrew Phillips at their vacation home.

The cabin at Sacandaga Lake has been a family vacation spot for the past twenty-five years. This New Year, Cassie and Andrew came to the cabin without their sons, Nathan and Ryan, in tow. Their son's young lives were taking them further from their parents. Cassie donned in a big sweatshirt, blue jeans, and fluffy socks curled deeper into the oversized chair by the hearth. The great room of the cabin she owned with Dr. Andrew Phillips, a cardiologist at Johns Hopkins Hospital, was filled with warmth from the blazing fire. The two-story structure stood on the shore of the Great Sacandaga Lake located in the lower Adirondack Mountains in New York State. Without a doubt, this cabin served as the backdrop for many fond family memories. The late afternoon sunlight was rapidly fading from the winter sky. Shadows were forming outside the ice-frosted window. Cassie, deep in thought, took a sip of hot coffee. She then looked out the window toward the frozen lake. The vacation Andrew and she had planned was supposed to be relaxing. It was already showing signs of derailment. For the past hour, her mind was bouncing between two situations.

Cassie loved the three men in her life. Andrew, her husband, is her soul mate. They had met during their undergraduate years at UMD. In no time, their friendship blossomed into undying love for one another. A phone call earlier in the day from their youngest son, Ryan, had left Cassie ill at ease. She knew all too well that Andrew, a rather peaceful man, may well not accept the news she had to share with him. The question was how to broach the subject without enflaming Andrew's temper. She sighed again. If only life was free of bumps and bruises along the way, especially this one, but it isn't.

Andrew sat in a large chair across the room from Cassie. He was busy reading and responding to e-mails on his laptop. He paused as he heard her let out another heavy sigh. Andrew looked up from his computer. Cassie is his soul mate, his friend, and his lover. He could not imagine life without her. He studied her for a brief moment. Her eyes indicated that something was definitely troubling Cassie.

"Whatever is on your mind must be quite disconcerting, my dear."

Cassie turned her gaze from the window toward Andrew. She gave him a pained smile. "You know me too well. I do have some things on my mind."

"Do you care to share?"

"I've been reflecting on two entirely different situations. I'm afraid neither has a quick fix. Both have the potential for turbulent times ahead for all parties involved, including you and me."

"This sounds serious. Does either situation involve Amanda?"

"Oh, yes. However, right now, Amanda is the least of my concern."

"My goodness, you're not prioritizing a crisis or potential crisis with Amanda as first on your worry list. Then you must be in full mother mode and dealing with something regarding one or both of our sons. So, Cassie my love, what is going on?"

"You do know me too well!" Cassie was usually in command of her emotions. It was something she learned many years ago as she trained to be a social worker. She was always the one who knew the right thing to say at the ideal moment. She was the one who guided others to express themselves when words abandoned them. Now as she looked into her husband's eyes, she struggled to find the right words as she began, "Earlier this afternoon while you were napping, Ryan called. He wanted to talk with me about some things happening in his life."

Andrew's eyes smiled as Cassie spoke of their youngest son. Andrew was proud of both of his sons and their accomplishments thus far in life. Ryan, equally intelligent to their eldest son Nathan, graduated magma cum laude in the top 5 percent of his class. This was quite an accomplishment to be celebrated and recognized especially considering it occurred in both high school and during his undergraduate studies at the University of Maryland. Now he was pursuing his medical degree at Northwestern University in Chicago, Illinois.

"Ryan called? How come you didn't wake me? You know I would love to have talked with him. Is he heading back east to visit?"

Cassie saw the disappointment in Andrew's expression. A knot twisted in her stomach. Her voice was tight as she choked back emotions that sought to rush out of her. She hoped for the power, the wisdom to ward off a potential argument between them. She knew how passionate Andrew is about his beliefs, and her news was sure to rock his core convictions.

"I'm sorry, honey. I know how much it means to you to talk with him. Ryan asked me not to disturb you."

"This has to be something major in his life to specifically seek your counsel."

She turned back to gaze out the window as her voice drifted off. "It is."

Cassie dreaded continuing. Andrew took in Cassie's body language as well as her words. She was genuinely distressed. He rose from his chair and walked over to Cassie. Reaching down, he gently pushed her legs over on the ottoman. He took a seat.

His hip touched her leg. With ease and familiarity, he then rested his hand on Cassie's leg. His touch sent a sudden spark of warmth through her troubled body. She swallowed hard with dreaded anticipation.

"Ryan would like for us to come and visit him and..." Cassie struggled for the words. She was fairly certain as to how Andrew would react to Ryan's news. What she wanted to do was to protect both of the men in her life. But how could she spare any of them pain at this juncture in life? Andrew's eyes narrowed as he waited for her to finish her sentence. "And get to know his roommate."

"Oh. So he has a new girlfriend? Well, it's about time."

"Andrew," Cassie spoke with her quiet I have something terrible to tell you voice. Andrew's previous joy was suddenly replaced with impending doom. He was certain he had to brace himself for the worst. Andrew watched her take a deep breath before continuing.

"Ryan doesn't have a girlfriend."

"Oh?"

"No. He has a partner. His name is George." Cassie exhaled. She now realized just how tight her chest had been as she was speaking to him. Andrew looked as though someone had just sucker punched him. He was gasping for air. His face reddened.

"George." For a moment, Andrew wasn't sure he was processing this information correctly. Andrew was at a loss. His world was suddenly spinning out of control. Cassie saw the physical changes coming over him as she steadied her voice.

"Yes, his name is George. Ryan and George have apparently had an on-again and off-again relationship for some time. Now the two are pledging their love to one another. It seems that our son has finally decided to fully accept his gender identity. He has also decided it's time to inform the rest of the world that he is gay."

Andrew's whole body resonated with his shock as he quietly found his voice. "Gay. You say our son is gay and in love with George. He can't be gay."

Cassie had feared the worse, and it was happening. She nodded while she watched Andrew respond. Andrew was filled with disbelief and struggling to accept Ryan's life. Before too long, he was going to erupt in rage and anger. Cassie's heart was breaking. She watched her husband attempting to begin to process the news of their youngest son's new gender identity. Right now, she too was struggling with her own pain. Her own dreams for their son had been shattered in one phone call.

"And I take it by your calm demeanor that you have somehow known about this for a while," Andrew continued as he ran his fingers through his silver-streaked light-brown hair. His words became cold and icy as the speckles on the windowpane outside. "How long have you known, Cassidy? Why didn't you bother to share this knowledge with me?" Andrew's voice was raised. His face was flushed, and the veins on his neck were protruding. "For heaven's sake, Cassidy, I've trusted you! Now I find out you've been keeping secrets. You've been lying to me about one of our children. I thought we didn't keep secrets from one another? Isn't that what we always claimed as a fundamental strength of our marriage, honesty and trust?"

Cassie had expected anger disbelief but not this. She was appalled by Andrew's verbal attack. Usually in control of her emotions, something began to snap in her. "Andrew, do you hear yourself? How can you sit there and accuse me of betraying your trust? I haven't been lying to you, Andrew, nor have I intentionally kept this as a secret from you."

Cassie felt her world closing in around her. Their once orderly world has been thrust into sheer chaos. Andrew's voice was becoming louder than his normal conversational tone. He glared at Cassie as he stood and began pacing the room. He reminded her of a caged-in overstimulated animal at the Maryland Zoo. This was not good. Fear was rising in her for the first time in their marriage. The social worker in her desperately sought to gain control. The last thing she wanted was a shouting match between them. Yet it seemed as though her rational thought process was suddenly powered down. She felt her own emotions beginning to unravel.

"Andrew, perhaps if you would sit back down with me, we can regroup. Then, together we can quietly process our feelings and what Ryan's coming out means for our family."

All six foot two, 195 pounds of lean muscles of Dr. Andrew Phillips radiated dismay as he growled, "I'm not sitting with you…you the Benedict Arnold."

For a brief, very brief, moment, Cass wanted to laugh at the absurdity of Andrew's statement. Then something in her snapped. It was as if she was being thrust into the abyss. Darkness came over her, and she roared with anger. "Benedict Arnold…I'm the infamous Benedict Arnold you say!" Cass rose to her feet to level the playing field between them. Her stance and deadly fix with her eyes informed Andrew that the match was on. She looked as scary as a gunslinger from the old West that had just rode into town ready for a shootout. He had good sense to worry. "Oh, buster, you have no idea what you've just said and done. I've tried to carry on a rational conversation with you. But now my heart bleeds, Andrew. However, it does not bleed for me but for you."

"Me?"

"Yes you…You idiot! For such an intelligent man, sometimes you can be downright stupid!"

"I can't believe you're insulting me at a time like this. This is so out of character for you, Cassidy."

Fury sparked in Cassie's eyes. "No, it's not…I have feelings too and, Andrew, I have every right to attack you just as you have attacked me. I tried to have a calm and rational conversation with you. You're the one who chose to go on the defense. So I'm working my offense. Now before I get any more riled up by stupid remarks from you, perhaps you'd better explain to me how I have betrayed you?"

"You chose our son and—"

"What? Oh, Andrew, is that what you think I've done?" Cassie was emotionally raw. She needed Andrew to wrap his arms around her and hold her. He only stood there and glowered at her. The situation was rapidly unraveling. Over the years, they had had their share of arguments. Cassie had never experienced this type of rage in Andrew. Emotionally, she was uncertain where their words would eventually lead them.

"Cassidy, what did you mean when you said, 'He finally decided to accept his gender identity'? That sounds to me like you have known about his being gay for considerably longer than this afternoon."

"I observed subtle indicators while Ryan was growing up. Throughout his years of high school, I saw the signs and perceived that his gender identity is homosexual rather than heterosexual."

"Since high school...You've known all this time." Andrew looked down at his clenched hands. For the first time in his life, he became afraid of his emotions. He took a step away from Cassie and closed his eyes as he listened to her speak.

"Honey, until now, I only had mother's intuition to go on. I am processing this revelation just as you are. I'm bewildered. I'm grasping to find stability and fearful as you are. I need you to comfort me and allow me to comfort you. At this moment, I feel absolutely alone. Right now, my heart is breaking, and I am grieving for all of us."

Andrew did not respond as Cass had hoped. He continued to keep his distance as he spoke, "Perhaps you had better enlighten me on how you have perceived that Ryan is gay."

"I don't want my words to be twisted by you. I don't want it to sound like I'm accusing you of anything." She could see Andrew processing her words.

"Go on, I'm listening. But I'm not promising you anything, Cassidy." Listening was a start if only he would actually hear what she said. Cass took a deep breath.

"Some of the signs I observed through the years are considered classic signs. Ryan had a lack of interest in dating young women. While Ryan always had female friends, he was more comfortable hanging out with the guys. There were plenty of other signs as well through the years. Are you aware that our son was honored by his graduating high school class for his contribution to the AIDS Awareness Walkathon and his involvement in FLAG?"

"I do recall the AIDS thing. I just figured he was being compassionate and helping others as we had taught him through the years."

"At first so had I," Cassie quietly added.

"What's this FLAG that you mentioned?" Andrew's voice was strained.

"FLAG is an acronym for Friends of Lesbians and Gays."

"And you know this..."

Cassie sighed. She felt drained but continued on, "As director of the Second Chance, I have dealt with women with AIDS and frequently deal with lesbians. The abuse some of these women have experienced at the hands of men who claimed to love them at one time is unconscionable. When approached by Ryan's senior class, the center financially supported the AIDS walkathon. Some of the members of FLAG sent us notes of thanks while others did community service for us at the center. As a concerned mother, I then helped them make cookies and posters for their FLAG rally."

"Cass, I thought I knew you. I apparently don't know you any better than I know my children. Did you and those kids make cookies in our kitchen?"

"Yes, Andrew." Tears trickled down Cassie's cheeks. "One of those kids, as you put it, is our son." Cassie brushed the tears from her cheeks with the back of her hand. "I'm sorry, Andrew. I'm sorry that our family is not what we envisioned it to be when we first married. Perhaps if you had been home more and taken an active role in Ryan's life—"

"Don't say it, Cass!" Andrew was clenching his fists at his side.

"Yes, dang nab it! I'm saying what you need to hear. You always made time for Nathan but not for Ryan! Perhaps if you had been more attentive, you would have realized on your own that Ryan is gay." The words were out of Cassie's mouth before she had time to sensor them.

"Oh, so let me get this straight…You're saying I'm the reason Ryan is gay. It's my fault for not being home and spending time with Ryan. That's the reason why he is claiming to be gay. Is that what you're saying, Cass?"

"No, Andrew, that's not what I mean." Cassie head was whirling like a cyclone. She was feeling the strain and needed a break. "We need to cool off…I'll make us some coffee."

"Don't bother. I don't want any coffee. I'm through talking with you…I've gotta get out of here."

"Andrew, please…Don't go." Andrew turned to the hall where he gathered his coat. With his hand on the doorknob, Andrew looked down at Cassie. Without saying a word, he shook his head in disgust and walked out into the cold dark night.

Andrew returned to the cabin a little before midnight. He was surprised to find the front door unlocked. What was Cassie thinking? Just because they were out of the metro area of Baltimore did not mean they were safe. She's an intelligent woman and should have realized this. After all, this wasn't the first time they'd been to the mountains. As he removed his outerwear, he again reflected on how the evening progressed. Guilt rose from his inner being. His stomach twisted into knots. No. With all they had said to one another, she undoubtedly hadn't been thinking about safety. Cassie would have been too distracted to think about securing a door. With a heavy sigh, Andrew stepped farther into the cabin. The only light he saw was coming from the great room. The light was still on by the chair Cassie had been sitting on earlier that evening. She now lay curled up and asleep in the same oversized chair. The blanket that had been covering her was hanging half on the floor. The fire he noticed was down to a few remaining coals. There was a chill in the air. Andrew then saw the discarded tissues soaked with Cassie's tears lying on the pine board floor next to her chair. He knew that 99 percent of her tears had been the result of his rather boorish behavior, and he needed to apologize.

"Cassie," he spoke quietly as to not startle her. She stirred at the sound of Andrew's voice. However, she did not wake. Since the boys had grown and moved out of their home, it seemed as though Cassie could sleep through just about anything; however, this was far too important to allow her to continue to sleep. So he spoke a bit louder, "Cassie, wake up."

Cassie stirred disoriented as she opened her eyes. "What's wrong?"

"We have to talk," Andrew said as he sat down on the ottoman he had occupied a few hours earlier that night. In all the years they had been married, even during his grueling years and hours in med school, they had never gone to bed with cross words spoken between them. He was not going to break their record tonight if he could help it. She yawned, stretched, and looked him dead in the face. He saw anger in those tired eyes. Then she hissed.

"Andrew, I'm not talking about anything else of importance with you tonight. I'm too angry and hurt by your accusations. Given my current state of mind, I may say something I will later regret." Leaning over, Cassidy reached down and pulled the blanket closer around her. "We'll talk when I'm ready and not before. Now make yourself useful and stoke the fire. It's getting cold in here. Oh, yes, and don't expect me to share any bed with you anytime soon or anything else for that matter. Right now, I'm in no mood to be near you." With that said, Cassie snuggled under the blanket and closed her eyes.

Chapter Three

The sun peered in through the cracks in the drawn curtains, which Amanda had intentionally left that way. Amanda woke and yawned to a sliver of sunlight peaking through the window. Wiping the sleep from her eyes, she rose out of bed. Amanda stretched and did a modified workout in the hotel room. Satisfied with her repetitions, she showered and prepared for the next phase of her journey. The continental breakfast of donuts and coffee at the hotel provided Amanda with the sugar and caffeine jolts she needed to complete her jump-start for the day. Amanda stood and bundled up to prepare to face the frigid winter morning outdoors.

She grumbled to herself. The temperature was nine degrees above zero. Overnight precipitation had caused a thin layer of ice to form on the car. Amanda had to pull with some force to open the frozen door. Living in Baltimore, she didn't miss this! Still muttering to herself, Amanda threw her bag on the backseat. She then got in the driver's seat to start the engine. Amanda turned the key in the ignition. The car was not sluggish. She remembered there was a time when on a morning like this a car wouldn't start for anything. *Ah, those were the days. Thank goodness they are gone.* Amanda lost no time in setting the car temp on high. The defroster blasted out heat. Amanda smiled. She knew it had been the right move to pick up the scraper last evening. The windshield was scraped in minutes, and Amanda was back in the driver's seat heading for the NYS Thruway.

She reached in her purse for her cell phone. Amanda remembered that New York State is a hands-free state. Talking with Cassie was not an option. So Amanda did the next best thing. She turned on the radio. It wasn't long before she found a classic rock station. Cranking up the volume, Amanda drove while jamming to the tunes of days gone by. Each song conjured up images from her past. The familiar roadway also gave way to memories. Many of the memories opened old wounds. Amanda choked back a cry that longed to escape and snapped off the radio. Amanda remembered how when she left New York in 1979, the NYS Conservationists and land owners had spent the '70s engaged in battle over the Adirondack Park. The legislation had finally been passed regarding land development and use in the Adirondack Park. Everyone involved knew it was a fragile balance between economic development and conservation protection. She had taken up the fight along with her friends and older brother, Jim Callison, for the cause of the "little people."

While Jim and Amanda were growing up, they had been what you might call "as thick as thieves." When one would be in trouble with their mother or father, they both suffered the consequences. In their household, it was sheer guilt by association with the accused. When push came to shove, Amanda and Jim knew they could count on each other to have their back. "Well," Amanda snapped out, "that was until the summer of seventy-nine when everything changed. Jim turned on me. Jim had proven that there are times when blood is not thicker than water."

Now thirty years later, Amanda was returning to the scene of the crimes. During this trip, Amanda had no intention of seeking out her brother. As far as she was concerned, her attitude toward Jim hadn't changed since 79. He was as dead as all the other people whom she had once loved. Well, that is, everyone except her very old grandmother, Gentle Spirit. The day Amanda left her grandmother had been one of the most challenging days of her life. Through the years, she had kept in touch with her. Together they decided that Amanda's moving to Maryland had been a wise decision for her. Amanda thrived in the position of assistant director at the Second Chance for Women working side by side with Cassidy. She smiled as she drove on while recalling her life in Baltimore.

Andrew awakened to the chirp of his cell phone. In the light of a new day, Andrew was suffering from a stiff neck and kink in his lower back. Upon returning to the cabin late last night, he had settled into the chair opposite from Cassie. The chair he now rose from was not conducive to a good night's sleep. The cabin was far too quiet. Andrew was mobile checking through the downstairs for any sign of Cassie. There was no smell of fresh brewed coffee permeating the air. The pot was cold and empty. Perhaps she had gone up to their bed at some point during the night to sleep. Andrew made his ascent up the stairs to their room. Cassie had not slept in their bed. She was not in the shower.

As Andrew was turning toward the stairs, he heard the porch door open. He bolted down the stairs as Cassie was coming inside. She had on her winter running gear. Her cheeks and nose were red from the cold. Cassie's eyes met his, sending a chill through Andrew. It appeared to be more frigid than the cold air that had come blasting in from outside. She didn't speak until she had closed the door and removed her coat.

"Morning." Her tone was curt and as icy as Andrew had anticipated it would be. Cassie did not smile or pursue any further conversation with Andrew. She walked past him into the kitchen. In silence, she opened the cabinet and got out the supplies for making coffee. She ran the water and filled the coffeemaker. In silence, Andrew counted the spoons of coffee Cassie added to the coffee filter. This morning's coffee would be strong, extra strong. This was a good indicator of her mood. Well, at least he had an idea where he stood with her.

"Did you have a good run?"

"I power walked today, Andrew." Cassie slightly turned her head to reveal her scowl. "I do this every Tuesday morning before I go in to work. Put your arms down, Andrew. We're not kissing and hugging this morning. You'll get a cramp and then whine about pain for the rest of the day."

"Cass, please, my dear. Come and sit down with me so we can talk." Andrew's voice was strained. His hair was sticking out in all directions, and his clothes from the previous day clung to him in a wrinkled mess.

"Andrew, sitting down with you is not a good idea," Cassie said in a curt tone.

"Fine. Then you stand. All I ask is that you listen to me."

"I'm listening." Cassie drew a bottle of water out of the refrigerator opened it and began to drink.

"Cassie, I've thought long and hard about what you and I said to each other last night. I'm sorry. I'm truly sorry about everything I said to you before I stormed out of here."

Cassie did not make eye contact with Andrew as she continued to go about the morning rituals of preparing breakfast. "I don't know if I believe you, Andrew. I will take what you said into consideration and get back to you."

"What? Cass…How can you say something like that? After all these years, you know I stand by my words. I said I'm sorry. Da—" He bit off his frustration while raking his fingers through his hair. "Woman, what do I have to do to prove my love to you?"

"Oh, Andrew, I believe you're sorry. I'm just not sure what you're sorry about. You see, I believe that if Ryan were here, you'd have been all over him. Your precious son isn't the son you imagined. Now you have to figure out how to accept and love him for who he is rather than whom you want him to be. Since he's not here, thank goodness, you took your shock, your shattered dreams, your grief and anger out on me. In some ways, last night when you accused and verbally attacked me, you proved to me that you are no better than the men who abuse the women who come in to the center. Last night you spoke of trust and honesty. Right now, you've broken my trust. I believe you'll say whatever you want to keep up the facade that we're a happy family."

For the first time since they had been married, Andrew felt genuine fear. The expression on Cassie's face caused him alarm. He realized that if he were not careful, he could lose the one who was most precious in his life.

"Cassie, I love you. I'm sorry. I wish I could take back my words. I should never have thrown that in your face about trust and honesty. There is no one on earth more trustworthy and honest than you. I want to work with you to rebuild our marriage, our life. You are my best friend, my lover. Like the old song we used to listen to, 'You're my'"—his voice choked with emotion—"'my everything.'"

Cassie fixed her coffee and turned to Andrew. Picking up her coffee, she locked her sight on him. Andrew stared into her raging sapphire-blue eyes. "At least you figured something out. Let me know when you figure out the rest. I'm not hungry. Fix your own breakfast."

Amanda sighed as the exit for Amsterdam, New York, came into view. After paying the toll, she pulled on to Route 30 north. Negotiating a detour through Amsterdam proved to be an interesting distraction during the drive. As Amanda made her way through the city, the stark reality of the economic disparity confronting the nation hit her yet again. In years past, the factories had been a bustle of activity. She recalled how during the 70s the unions called for strikes against the plant owners. So many men and women would have been standing out there on the sidewalk with their signs on mornings equally cold as today. But as Amanda looked, she mused, *There are no people, no signs, no cars, and no trucks…only empty deteriorating factories. It's almost as if you can hear them saying, "Does anyone care about me?"* But then Amanda had to ask herself, *Is the economy any worse here than in Baltimore or anywhere else in our country?* In the midst of these depressing thoughts, Amanda spotted a glimmer of hope. Jo's Route 30 Diner was still open for business. Ah, and none too soon for Amanda—more coffee, hot food, a bathroom. Turning into the parking lot, Amanda was surprised to see how full the lot was. Quickly finding a parking space, she immediately pulled out her cell and hit speed dial to make her first call.

"Hey, Cass, good morning."

"Good morning, Amanda. You sound very wide awake. I wasn't expecting to hear from you this early."

"Did I wake you?"

"No, not at all. As a matter of fact, I've already completed an hour of yoga, been out for a power walk, and now I'm sipping a hot cup of coffee before I head to the shower. So where are you? Please tell me you are not sitting in our driveway here at the cabin. I really need a shower before you get here." The laughter she heard coming through the receiver eased some of Cassie's tension.

"Relax, Cass. I've just gotten off the Thruway. I plan to get some breakfast before driving the rest of the way to your cabin. Have you ever tried Thruway coffee? It is horrid! Those people should be arrested and shot for cruel and inhumane treatment of travelers."

"Amanda, knowing how much coffee you consume on a regular basis, perhaps you should try decaf this time."

"What decaf? Oh, Cassie, I can't believe you suggested that to me. There is no way I am doing unleaded. I need the real thing."

"Honey, you really don't need any more regular coffee."

Amanda chuckled. "How about this? I'll only have one cup with breakfast in anticipation for your delicious coffee."

"Fair enough, Amanda. But let me warn you, it's a bit strong this morning."

"Oh no," Amanda gasped. "May I assume there's trouble brewing in the North Country in the Serenelli-Phillips cabin?"

"Could be, my dear. In the meantime, be careful. It's been rather icy up here. I don't want anything to happen to you on these local roads."

A foreboding feeling crept across Amanda as she approached Mayfield. Within a matter of minutes north of the town, she was going to be vacationing in the town of her childhood with Cassie and Andrew at their cabin. Through the years, Amanda had chosen to not share this part of her life with Cassie and Andrew. She had carefully tucked away all the pain associated with this place. Perhaps that had been a mistake. Now she questioned herself and the choice she had made to not share what had occurred at the lake thirty years ago. Why, she wondered, had she chosen to withhold information about Gentle Spirit? What harm would it have done for them to know that over the years she had returned to the mountains and met her grandmother? She had made her choice; Grandma, while not agreeing with her, had respected it. Amanda now had a feeling that this week was going to be a time for more counsel with the wise old woman whom she trusted with her life.

Driving out of Mayfield, Amanda noticed that the gas gauge read less than one quarter of a tank of gas; she should have filled up while in town. Amanda found a Quik Mart and gas station was now at the corner of Route 30 and Stony Notch Road. Scanning the area, Amanda noted two pickups, along with a couple of cars, were parked along the side of the building. A state police cruiser was parked at an angle for easy exit. Amanda pulled up to pump number 2 and shut off the engine. She smiled as she noted the freedom she had to fill up her vehicle and then pay for the gas. That would never be the case in Baltimore. *How different city and country life is*, Amanda thought. Inside the store, Amanda noted that the majority of the men were standing by the coffee machine with coffee in hand and lively conversation. Their style of dress was basically the same—well-worn jeans, work boots, flannel shirts tucked into the jeans, down vests, while others chose to let their shirts hang out from under their unzipped jackets. Most, but not all, were wearing knit caps on their heads.

As Amanda approached the checkout counter to pay for her gas, she heard a distinctive male voice. An unexpected shiver of fear went up Amanda's spine. "Oh why did it have to be him?" With that question, one of Amanda's favorite scenes from the old movie *Casablanca* sped through her mind. *Well*, she thought to herself, *this isn't a classic romantic movie. This is real life and their local hangout...their convenient store.* She was simply passing through. Still, she asked, "Why did he have to be here at this precise moment?" Amanda was on the verge of a panic as she listened to the men speaking to one another. She felt like she couldn't breathe as she listened to the congenial conversation taking place around her as she waited to pay for the gas.

"Well, guys, I've enjoyed this coffee break," she heard him say with a crisp commanding voice. "Duty calls."

"Hey, Jim, can you stop by the bait shop later? I'd like your input on the conclusion of the ice fishing contest," one of the men asked.

"Sure, Wes. Mel gave me her 'honey do' list. I have to make a couple of stops on the way home from work. By the time I get to the shop, it should be around five or six p.m."

Amanda wanted to die right there on the spot. Her worst nightmare was coming true. She knew, without a doubt, both of the men. Her brother, Jim Callison, the police officer, was now standing a few feet away from her. She had inconspicuously caught a glimpse of him. His dark hair now peppered with gray was considerably shorter than when they were last together. His chiseled face with high cheekbones revealed the wear and tear of the years. He was still in good shape with no excess weight from what Amanda could tell. From what she could hear by eavesdropping on his conversation with the other men, Jim still was recognized as the leader of the group. Apparently, not much had changed in thirty years.

"Hey, Callison, you giving your boy a ride home today or am I?"

"Well, Johnson, I suppose since I'll be at your place at about quitting time, I won't make him walk home...Yeah, I'll give my son a ride home."

Amanda coughed in order to disguise her gasp. The day had begun with such high hopes. Now it was turning into a nor'easter before her eyes. *Of all the guys who could own the old bait shop, it had to be Wesley Jones and Stephen Johnson.* Jones for the most part was all right; however, when it came to Stephen Johnson that was an entirely different story. In Amanda's eyes, he was nothing more than a slimy slug. James Callison wasn't much higher on the food chain. Until this moment, Amanda had not realized how much unresolved anger she had toward each of them. As Amanda waited for her turn to pay for the gas, she remembered a conversation she had with Gentle Spirit many years ago. Could Jim have changed as Grandma said he would? Should she talk with him? Had too much time passed for them to reconcile their differences?

Amanda, lost in thought, had no idea how long the cashier had been speaking to her. "Will that be cash or credit?" Becky Jones cheerfully asked her. Her voice sounded familiar to Amanda; however, she couldn't place how she knew her.

"Ah, credit." Amanda was already pulling her card out to pay for the gas, only to replace it. "No, wait, I changed my mind. I'll pay with cash instead. May I have a receipt?"

With that, Amanda dropped her purse on the counter as she fumbled to pull out a twenty. Amanda did not realize that Jim Callison had been casually observing her since she had pulled into the gas station. He made no indication to the others that he had noticed her when she entered the store. With his well-trained eye, he had observed her hairstyle and makeup. He noticed her style of dress as well as the slight limp. When she first got out of the car, he thought the stiffness may have been caused by a long drive. As Amanda had walked into the shop, he realized the limp was not from simple driving fatigue. She had appeared a bit distressed as she waited to pay for the gas, looking around as if to make certain she was safe. With two strides, Jim was alongside Amanda. When he spoke, Amanda gasped for air.

"Excuse me, ma'am." Jim's casual smile revealed the ever-present dimple to the right of his lip. "I'm Officer James Callison. I couldn't help but notice you seem to be a bit flustered. Are you all right? Do you need some help?"

Amanda couldn't breathe. Her chest was tightening up. She was close to shaking. Tears were forming in her eyes. Amanda engaged herself in deep breathing. She felt the nearness of Jim's body. He was in her space. After all the years that had passed between them, this was disconcerting. Amanda commanded herself to smile even if it killed her.

"Why, thank you, Officer Callison, aren't you just the sweetest to be concerned about little old me?" Amanda looked up at Jim and lightly patted his arm. "I'm fine, really." She poured on acquired Southern charm. "I must say you Yankee cops sure are nicer than we've been led to believe down where I'm from. Ya'll sure could give our local officers of the law some pointers on how to treat a lady."

Jim's smile didn't quite meet his eyes. She saw something in them. It was a look she had seen many years before as Jim was processing information. Amanda had an uneasy feeling he might not be buying her story.

"And where might home be?"

"Baltimore, Maryland."

"You're a long ways from home. What brings you up here in the dead of winter?" His eyes stayed fixed on her.

"I'm on my way to visit friends. They have a vacation home at some place called the Pines."

"The Pines is a real nice community. I'm sure you'll enjoy your stay."

"Oh well, if I had known it was going to be this cold, I may have reconsidered accepting the invitation."

Jim kept his gaze on Amanda. "Don't stay outside too long, and you should be fine."

"Why, thank you, Officer, you sure are kind. It's been real nice meeting you. Now if you'll excuse me, I'll be on my way."

"Be assured the pleasure is all mine. May I help you to your car?" A look of concern had crept back into Jim's expression.

"It's not necessary, you have a nice day." Walking out the door, she took her time and did not look back. She already knew that each one in the store was watching her leave and had plenty of speculation as to what her story was. What she didn't know was that Jim had decided to further investigate her.

Jim had paid for his coffee and was picking his hat up off the counter when Stephen and Wesley came to his side. Becky Ann Jones, Wesley's wife, had just handed Jim his change when Stephen approached them.

"Did you get a load of her?" Stephen asked while nodding toward the window and continuing to share his thoughts about Amanda's physical appearance.

"I should have known that you would thoroughly check her out." Becky sighed while shaking her head in disgust. "Will you ever change?"

"Probably not, Beck," Stephen said to Becky as he rounded the corner of the counter. "But I must say that I don't look at your body like that."

"I should hope not!" she exclaimed.

He affectionately put his arm around her shoulder. "I do love you though," and with that, Stephen tweaked her cheek.

Wesley Jones was now standing on the other side of his wife. He pushed Stephen's arm away. Grabbing Becky around her waist, he piped up, "Johnson, leave your sister alone." The others in the convenient store chuckled as they listened to the light bantering between brothers-in-laws.

"Jones, you can keep my sister with my blessings! I experienced living with her for eighteen years. That was enough to last a lifetime." Stephen and Wesley cracked some more jokes all at Becky's expense before Wes asked him.

"So, Johnson, she said she's staying at the Pines, not too far from your place. Are you lookin' to a—you know—maybe try and have some fun?"

Stephen winked at Wesley. "Trust me, I definitely have some thoughts about that woman." He then glanced out the window toward the now empty gas pumps. "I'll be sure to not let you people know if I score." The men laughed. Becky rolled her eyes then, without warning, smacked her brother in the arm. "Ow, Beck." He sheepishly smiled while rubbing his arm.

Jim cleared his throat. "Guys and gal"—nodding to Becky— "this has truly been an enlightening morning. As my kids would say, 'TMI.' I'll see you around. Oh, and Johnson just make sure looking at the lady is all you do. I think she just might be out of your league."

A mile south of Palmer's Lane, Amanda saw the Bait and Tackle Shop on her right. It sat not far from the edge of the lake and appeared to offer more than just bait and tackle. She slowed down to read the sign. It appeared that during the winter they offered ice fishing and ice skate rentals. Good for them! An ice fishing contest was being held between Christmas and New Year's Day. *Hmm,* Amanda thought, *now wouldn't that be a hoot to enter the ice fishing contest and walk away with first prize. No. The interactions a few minutes ago had been more than enough excitement for this trip. It would be too risky to go anywhere near the Bait and Tackle shop. But what if Cassie wanted to go ice skating...*

Deep in thought, Amanda missed her turn onto Pine Lane, the entrance to the vacation village. About a half mile on up the road, she was able to safely pull over. Perhaps it was a blessing to have gone past the entrance. Now she was only a mile from the road to her grandmother's. With how distressed Amanda was feeling, she knew she needed to visit Gentle Spirit first and then go to Cassie's.

The road up the mountain was plowed, revealing that the gravel had since been replaced with blacktop. It had been widened as well. Amanda felt the tension in her body begin to ease the closer she came to her grandmother's cabin. After she came across the small bridge, she had to slow down for a doe to make her way across the road. Amanda chuckled and said to the deer, "Don't look so shocked, I once roamed this mountain too!" One more turn and the cabin came into sight. A tear welled up in Amanda's eyes. Smoke poured out of the chimney. Wood was piled on the porch for easy access. At the age of ninety-nine, Gentle Spirit keeps her home as in years gone by. A random tear that had been pooling in Amanda's eye trickled down her cheek. Reality began to set in. Amanda sighed. She should not be living here alone. What if something were to happen to her? Would someone find her in time?

As Amanda parked the car, the door to the cabin opened. She shook her head as she took in her grandmother's attire. Mary Freeman had slippers on her feet and an old dress under the sweater she wrapped around her as she stepped onto the porch. The mountain air was frigid, way too cold for her elderly grandmother to be outside wrapped only in her sweater. Where was her heavy coat? Another tear trickled down Amanda's face as she hurriedly got out of the car and made her way along the snow-packed path.

"Well now, Amanda Kathryn, aren't you a sight for old eyes! To what do I owe this surprise?"

Amanda stepped into her grandmother's open arms. "Hello, Grandma, oh how I've missed you. It's too cold for you to stand out here talking with me. Let's go inside, and I'll tell you all you want to know."

Still holding on to one another, the two women walked into the cabin. A fire blazed in the fireplace providing the only heat in the two-bedroom cabin. A pot of water hung over the fire on a hook that had hung there for as long as Amanda could remember. Amanda smiled as she listened to her grandmother bustled around regaling her with stories of how the winter had been thus far. Over hot tea, Amanda brought Gentle Spirit up to speed on her life and her encounter with Jim and the others at the Quik Mart.

Before leaving the cabin, Amanda was given some of Mary's special tea for tension. She did not ask what her grandmother used to make the tea. For all she knew, there could be some bark from one or two trees, a root of something, dried flowers, and goodness knows what else. History had taught Amanda some things are best unknown. As she made her way down the mountain, Amanda realized that she felt less tense. She had done the right thing visiting with her grandmother before going to her friend's vacation retreat. No matter what the outcome of the week, Amanda was here and was going to enjoy her time with her friends, Cassie and Andrew, and her grandma. This week she would set things straight with Cassie and Andrew about her past and introduce them to her grandma, Mary Freeman. The verdict was still out on whether she'd see Jim.

The drive on Route 30 took few minutes before Amanda turned the car into the entrance of the Pines. With directions in hand, Amanda turned down one lane after another. Finally, she came to the end of the road and the lake looming in front of her. "Let's see…Cassie and Andrew's place should be here on the corner lot of Lake Front Drive." Sure enough, "Wow!" Amanda exclaimed. "Now this is a vacation cabin!"

Just as Amanda got out of the car, the front door of the cabin burst open. Cassie was dressed in faded jeans and dark-blue turtleneck sweater. She came outside while wrapping her wool cape around her. "Amanda, you made it!" Amanda smiled as they threw themselves into each other's arms. As they pulled away from the hug, Amanda saw the sadness in Cassie's eyes. Soon she would have to investigate what was amiss between Cass and Andrew.

"Cass, this place is gorgeous. I see why you and Andrew have been after me to come up here. I'm glad I'm finally here."

"I always knew you'd love it here. I hope this will be a time for you to relax and unwind." Cassie paused and then continued, "From what Liz told me, yesterday was busy at the center. Do we need to debrief in order for you to truly relax?"

"So she called you…" As Amanda was pulling her bags out of the car, she heard a familiar voice. Ah, spared for the moment from having to discuss the intake session that chilled her to the bone.

"Hey, stranger, does your favorite guy get a hug?" Andrew's voice sounded strained to Amanda. She quickly observed his disheveled look. Something was definitely wrong with her favorite couple. Amanda smiled at Drew and teasingly licked her lips.

"Mm-mm-mm, you sure are luscious to look at." Andrew grabbed Amanda into a hug. Amanda casually placed her hand on Andrew's shoulder while attempting to lighten up the tension. "I'm into this rough mountain man persona you seemed to have acquired. If your wife wasn't—"

"Go ahead hug him all you want."

With that, Cassie turned and walked into the cabin, leaving Amanda and Andrew standing where they were. Amanda looked at Andrew for a comment. His eyes spoke of great pain. She nodded in understanding and quietly handed Andrew her bags. A major storm was brewing in the mountains, and it wasn't only inside of her. A cup of Gentle Spirit's tea may be needed for all three of them before this day was over.

CHAPTER FOUR

Andrew heard the sound of tires crunching on the snow-laden gravel drive. Looking out of the side window, he saw Dr. Kevin Wentzel getting out of the car. Andrew and Kevin had met while both men worked at Johns Hopkins Medical Center. Andrew is a respected pediatric cardiologist, and Kevin is an emergency trauma specialist. Ten years ago, Kevin left Hopkins to take on the position at Maryland Shock Trauma hospital as chief of shock trauma. Through the years, Andrew and Cassie had enjoyed social outings with Kevin and his wife, Megan. During this past year, Megan left Kevin and filed for divorce. It had been a difficult time for Kevin. His children—Kyle, age 26; Nicole, age 24; and Brian, age 21—had abandoned him and defended their mother. Both Andrew and Cassie were worried about Kevin and had invited him to join them for the holidays. Andrew hurriedly threw on his jacket and opened the door. Walking out onto the porch, he saw Kevin reaching in the backseat for his bags.

"Hey, Kevin, good to see you," Andrew called out while making his way down the steps. Kevin stood up with his bags and closed the door of the car. He pressed a button on the keypad. The *bleep, bleep* noise indicated that the car was locked. He turned and made his way up the path to the cabin.

"Hey, man, nice place you and Cassie have here in the woods. You weren't kidding about the views. I have been in awe of the countryside here in New York ever since I hit the open road out of Albany." Kevin took in a deep breath of air and felt the sting of cold hit his lungs. "Ah. Smell that?"

"Smell what?"

"Well, there's chimney smoke, pine, and the absence of common city pollutants. And listen to this." Andrew nodded and with silent amusement listened to Kevin as he continued, "Do you hear the birds?"

Andrew patted Kevin on the shoulder. "Man, if you're this hyped up about nature on this side of the cabin, just wait until you see the lake. Come on in. Let's get you settled in and then go out and join the ladies on the front porch."

"Ladies?"

"Yes. Cassie's friend and colleague Amanda Newman is also spending the week with us." Andrew watched Kevin's reaction to his statement.

"Let me guess, she's someone who Cassie has rescued and just happens to be single."

The temperature for the day was still hovering in the low thirties. Andrew and Kevin found Amanda and Cassie bundled up in their winter gear sitting on the lake side porch sipping decaf coffee. As Andrew and Kevin came out through the door, Cassie and Amanda's conversation ceased midsentence.

Amanda was glad to hear a relaxed tone in Andrew's voice. Obviously, the visitor was a welcome relief for the poor guy. She was certain that in time she would certainly discover what was muck in her friends relationship. Cassie let out a glee of happiness. She was on her feet and threw her arms around Kevin.

"Oh, Kevin, I'm glad you're here. I've been concerned about you traveling these roads by yourself."

Kevin reciprocated Cassie's hug with one of his own. It was then that his eyes fell upon Amanda. Smiling, Kevin released Cassie from his arms and stepped around Cassie and approached Amanda. She was glad when Cassie stepped in to make introductions.

A twinge of panic caused Amanda to take a deep breath to calm down. So this is the friend they had told her about. Dr. Kevin Wentzel, as her daughter would say, was some nice eye candy—sweet! His dark brown hair had a touch of gray over his ears. He was taller than her by a couple of inches. His smile and blue eyes could melt the lake for sure. Kevin was casually dressed in blue jeans, a navy-blue turtleneck shirt with a cream-colored pullover cable-knit sweater. Some people Amanda had found were unable to either dress up or down. Kevin was not one of them. My goodness he looked good. As she took in her surroundings, Amanda began to feel that all too familiar floating feeling. It was as if she was having an out-of-body experience. This was the panic that frightened her. It was the one she had difficulty controlling. Amanda didn't realize she was starting to pace on the porch. She knew she needed to get away so she could breathe and regain control. Now as the panic pricked her skin like tiny needles, she incessantly rubbed. She was afraid she would hyperventilate. Amanda was no longer conscious of where she was or what she was saying; she blurted out, "Excuse me. I need some air."

With that, Amanda was making her way down the front steps and on down toward the lake. Fortunately, there was not too much snow on the ground as it was protected by the pines. All three remaining on the porch were temporarily stunned by what just transpired before them.

"Oh dear!" Cassie breathed out in concern. "This is not good!" Kevin, used to stepping in to take charge of emergency situations, started to follow Amanda when Cassie reached out and grabbed his arm. "Give her a few minutes to herself."

"Does this occur on a regular basis?" Kevin asked.

"Yes, they do. Some panics are so mild that only Amanda knows it is happening. Then there are these. Actually, this one is not as bad as some have been since she had the accident."

"Oh really, how long ago was her accident?" Kevin looked from Cassie to Andrew, waiting for one of them to respond.

"Ten years ago," Cassie quietly said.

"Was she at shock trauma?" Kevin turned his gaze from Cassie to watch Amanda as she walked by the frozen lake.

"Yes, Kevin," Andrew responded. "Come to think of it, I suppose it was about the same time you went to shock trauma. Kevin, do you think you worked on her?"

"I believe there is ninety-nine point nine, nine percent probability that I attended to her in the trauma bay. I will know for sure after I talk with her. Now if you both will excuse me. I think I'd like to venture down by the lake." With that, Kevin was making his way down the path Amanda had made to the lake.

Amanda knew she would have to apologize to her friends for abruptly fleeing from them. The latest panic caught her by surprise. She had felt so calm after sipping her grandmother's tea earlier in the day. Whatever the old woman put in the tea sure did work. Well, at least for a while. Then this latest panic hit with a vengeance. So what had set her off? Could it have been the lake, the fresh air, a smell, no it came after she was introduced to Dr. Kevin Wentzel. But why him? He had nothing to do with the lake and Amanda's past. Or did he somehow have a place in her past? Her past was here, in this community, in these mountains, at this lake. What was that song Grandma used to sing to soothe her rattled nerves? Amanda remembered with little difficulty and began to hum the native tune of her childhood. The sun was warm, and calmness began to engulf her as she reconnected with the land of her past. Amanda heard footsteps on the crust of snow on the lake's edge. Without turning her face from the sun, Amanda took in a long deep breath of air.

"Be careful! On those rocks there's black ice on some of them, and you could fall and hurt yourself."

"Thanks, Amanda. Oh my..." Kevin's foot slid as he stepped down. "You definitely are right. I noticed you didn't have any difficulty negotiating the stones."

"Ah. So you've been watching me from afar." Amanda glanced down at him. "Did you find it odd I couldn't breathe out here in all this fresh air?"

"Yes, but then Cassie told me about your panics."

"I'm sorry you had to witness one of them. I'm usually able to conceal how annexed I am."

"You don't have to be sorry. I must say that I am a bit concerned. May I join you up there?" Amanda shielded her eyes from the glare of the sun reflecting on the snow and ice. She saw concern in Kevin's eyes. Not pity, as so often happened to her, but concern. Amanda tentatively smiled.

"I'd like that."

Kevin looked at the boulder Amanda sat on. "My dear, how did you get up there with such ease? From a distance, it hadn't looked difficult to climb. However, up close, it is a different story."

"Years of practice. I'll walk you through it. Now, give me your hand." Kevin paused and looked at Amanda as if she were nuts. "Oh come on! I'm stronger than I look! Jeez, you men need to get past your egos and let a woman assist when it's needed."

Kevin couldn't help but laugh. At age fifty-seven, recently separated, he decided she was definitely a breath of fresh air. He extended his hand. In a matter of seconds, Kevin found he was safely sitting beside her on the rock.

"Thank you, Amanda." His eyes seemed to smile at her.

"You're welcome, Kevin."

She felt a giddiness within her that had lay dormant for many years. They sat together and chatted for some time before comfortable silence crept between them. As they sat together, Amanda felt safe. This was something that did not readily happen with her. Time and experience had taught her to not trust men. There was something different about Kevin. Lost in thought, she felt the gentleness in his gloved hands approach her cheek. He had replaced the scarf that had fallen from her shoulder. His finger lingered on her check and traced her jawline. Amanda shivered from his touch.

"Are you cold, Amanda?"

"No…well, maybe…perhaps…I don't…" Amanda could not think clearly. Kevin was eliciting a response from her that had been asleep for decades. Her thoughts were all muddled up inside her. Could she be like an old volcano about to erupt back to life? It was then she felt Kevin lower his finger to her chin. He raised her chin up so their lips were almost meeting. Time seemed to stop for Amanda. The sun's warmth and the bite of late December north wind seemed to go unnoticed. It was only her and Kevin sitting there on the rock. Amanda came to realize that Kevin had raised his other hand to frame her face in his hands. She was becoming like putty in his presence as he caressed her cheekbones and ran his thumb beneath her ear and down her neck. Amanda felt the heat rising in her. "Kevin," Amanda whispered. She knew she should tell him to stop, after all, they hardly knew one another. But there was something about him that drew her in.

"Shh, my love," and with that, Kevin lowered his lips onto Amanda's. She tasted sweet and earthy at the same time. Kevin had ignited a fire in Amanda, and she was ready for what he had to offer her. Then in an instant, the mood was broken.

"Oh gross! Dude, if you're gonna do 'er, go inside!"

Amanda abruptly came back to time and place as she heard the *swish, swish, swish* of the skate blades against the ice. Then as she pulled away from Kevin's embrace, she saw the two teenage boys. They were well-built, fairly tall, and in command of their skating while shooting the hockey puck between themselves. Regaining composure from the unexpected kiss, and being caught by teenage boys, Amanda finally spoke up.

"We're sorry to have offended you both. Please accept our apology." Amanda's eyes twinkled as she found herself beginning to spar with the teens. "And might I add in our defense that what you saw is not gross. I bet you don't think anything of making out with your girlfriends out here by the lake." The two boys started to snicker while giving one another a knowing look.

"Ah, so I'm right." Amanda felt a bit of triumph having put them in their places. She noticed that the one young man briefly hung his head. His dark hair was well cared for, obviously his parent or parent's required regular haircuts. Then when he raised his head, his eyes met Amanda's. An eerie feeling crept over her. She had seen those eyes before.

"So you boys—" Both skaters glowered at Amanda, and she realized her misstep. "Excuse me…you young men appear to be quite the skaters. I assume by your sticks and puck you're hockey players or avid wannabes."

Both teens let out a hoop of laughter. "Wannabes? Lady, we play varsity hockey. I hope to be able to go on and play professionally."

Amanda smiled and encouraged the two teens to share with them their love of hockey. It quickly turned to a time for regaling them with stories of the exploits of two older men they called Mr. C. and Uncle Steve. As it turned out, Mr. C. is none other than James Callison Sr. and Uncle Steve happens to be Stephen Johnson. Amanda felt light-headed. She was talking with her nephew, James Callison Jr., and his best friend Peter Jones. His dad Wesley Jones owns the bait shop with Peter's uncle, Stephen Johnson. Amanda was about to speak when JJ looked at his watch.

"Oh man, your dad and uncle are going to kill us. We have two minutes to skate back to the shop."

Amanda leaned against Kevin. She couldn't help but chuckle to herself as she watched JJ and Peter skate their hearts out toward the bait shop. "Oh yeah, those two are dead ducks."

CHAPTER FIVE

The bait shop and the lake were busy for a Tuesday in late December. Usually during winter the smell of dead fish was almost nonexistent. This year, the ice fishing contest being held at the bait shop changed that. Now the smell of dead fish along with charred wood from the bonfire prepared daily for ice skaters permeated the air.

Stephen Johnson listened to the chopping of wood and the hoops of laughter. He looked out the window and watched Peter Jones and JJ Callison chop and chuck wood. This brought back many a memory of his days gone by. Stephen remembered how Jim Callison had always been the one to organize the traditional bonfire and night hockey game for New Year's Eve. Amanda or "Calli" as they all called her and Becky would be right there alongside the guys chucking wood. *Ah, those were the days*, Stephen thought with a smile.

Turning from the window, Stephen prepared himself a cup of coffee. As he sat down behind the counter to review the list of inventory, his mind wandered back to the events a few hours before. JJ and Peter working at the bait shop had allowed Stephen the opportunity to run into Mayfield. On the way back from town, he stopped off at the Quik Mart. It had been a normal uneventful morning until the woman had appeared in the store. Stephen could not get her out of his mind. Her voice was haunting him. She hadn't exactly sounded like a northerner. With all those scars he had seen on her face and the limp, she didn't look like anyone he knew. Still, there was something unnerving about the encounter. It was like a ghost of his past had come to haunt him. "Oh great," Stephen muttered to himself. "I'm not Ebenezer

Scrooge and that woman is not a ghost of my past or present. Get a grip, Johnson!" He felt a bit better after lecturing himself. Stephen stood up and walked over to the coatrack and grabbed his jacket and cap. He made his way outside to get some fresh air and clear his head of whatever was ailing him.

The bait shop continued to have a steady stream of customers throughout the day. By midafternoon, Stephen was refilling the coffeepot and hot water pot for hot cocoa. He looked up as Wes came in from outside. "Do you know those two crazy boys skated almost to Cooper's Island and back during their break?"

"With the time we give them for break and the way they skate, they should have made it all the way up and back here with time to spare."

"Yeah, Steve, you'd think. But you know those two, they are always up to something."

"Thank goodness they're nothing like what we were at their age." Stephen seldom allowed himself to reminisce even with Wes, his dear brother-in-law and friend. Seeing that the coffee was now ready, he filled a fresh cup for Wes and one for himself. Shaking his head, Stephen smiled and sighed. "It's a wonder any of us lived past high school!"

Wes returned a smile and, while rising the cup to his mouth, commented, "Remember how Jim and Calli would light into each other on the ice? She was an amazing woman." With the words spoken, Wes realized he had gone there too quickly. "Sorry, man, I was lost in the moment."

Stephen reached out his hand and grabbed Wes's shoulder. "It's all right, Wes. Since this morning, I've been thinking a lot about our past—that is, my past and Manda."

"Really, would you care to share these thoughts with me? You know I won't go telling your sister. As hard as it may be for you to believe, I do manage to keep some conversations out of her reach."

"And here I thought my sister had you on a tighter leash than that. Becky must be slipping!" Stephen and Wes enjoyed their private jokes about Becky. As quickly as the conversation had turned lighthearted, Stephen returned it to being serious. "I've decided that this New Year is going to be one of change. I can't change the past, only the present. For too long I've allowed the past to dictate my present. Well, my friend, not anymore and this time I mean it."

"What brought this on?"

"The woman we saw this morning at the Quik Mart."

"Oh, so you're planning on looking to get..." He cleared his throat. "Have you seen or spoken with her since then?"

"No, this isn't about that. I just have been thinking about how she looks and walks and how she has to keep going. She reminded me that I have to keep going and that thirty years is too long to grieve over Amanda Callison. I gotta stop comparing other women to her. It's time to move on."

The bell rang as the door to the bait shop opened. Wesley and Stephen continued drinking their coffee as they saw four strangers enter the store by the fishing gear. Wes and Stephen exchanged greetings with the patrons welcoming them to the Great Sacandaga Lake. Andrew and Cassie were in the lead. As they walked up the aisle toward the counter, Cassie glanced over to her left where she saw lures and rubber worms for sale.

"Oh that is disgusting!" she exclaimed. Andrew and Kevin both chuckled at Cassie's squirming. Andrew by now had reached his arm around Cassie to comfort her in her temporary distress over rubber earthworms. Cassie would rather have choked at that moment than have Andrew touch her. She was still madder than a wet hen but refused to air even a hint of her family's dirty laundry in public. "This is not funny at all," she huffed. Amanda, who was behind Cassie and had not yet caught sight of the lures and worms, wanted to know what was wrong. Cassie grabbed a pack of rubber worms. "Look, Amanda, did you ever see such a thing?"

"Sure." Amanda chuckled at Cassie's displeasure. She then reached out and touched the rubber worms. She shook her head in what could be interpreted as disgust. "Real worms or minnows are far superior." Cassie's mouth flew open.

Andrew grinned. "Really, Amanda, what makes you say that?"

"Well, when I was a young girl, my granddad and I would go fishin'. He taught me to fish by using minnows and worms." Amanda made a slight upward curl of her top lip. "Not these rubber things! Grandpa used to say that if you have a big old earthworm you can snip it in two. That way here if you're lucky, you can catch two fish with one worm."

Amanda smiled to herself as she remembered the times when on that very lake they would go out in his canoe and do just that. They'd spend hours sitting patiently waiting for a trout or pickerel to come along and grab on to their hook. When they got hungry, Amanda would unwrap the sandwiches she had made for each of them. Grandpa always wanted liverwurst with mustard on pumpernickel bread. Yuck! But in the spirit of the day and their tradition, Amanda would make his sandwich along with her peanut butter, banana, and strawberry jam on white bread. One of the things she always appreciated about her grandfather was that he never drank alcoholic beverages in front of her. He probably figured she had enough of that with her father. So they each would have a bottle of Coke and, in keeping their tradition, would clink their bottles together as a toast for a good day of fishing. It had been years since Amanda had last thought of fishing with her grandfather. She was glad that particular memory had been tucked away and resurfaced now. It was one of the good ones she would cherish forever. Amanda picked up a pack of rubber worms. She rubbed the worm between her fingers, thought for a moment, and then looked at her friends.

"In my opinion, these rubber worms definitely are not worth the money you pay for them."

Both Wes and Stephen heard Amanda's crisp authoritative voice and were glad no other patrons were in the store at the moment. This opinionated woman could be bad, very bad for business. Where did she come off saying that the rubber worms were for the squeamish? Stephen caught a glimpse of her. He recognized her from the Quik Mart; however, it was Wes who spoke up.

"Excuse me, ma'am, is something wrong with the merchandise?"

"Oh no, sir, I know there are plenty of people who prefer these rubber things to real worms and minnows. I, on the other hand, prefer the real deal, nature's best." Amanda smiled at both Wes and Stephen the most innocent smile her body would let her conjure up at the moment.

Stephen asked, "And what is the problem with rubber worms?"

"Well, as you can see, this rubber worm doesn't have good action." Amanda noted the angling of his brow. Stephen looked like he was ready for an all-out challenge. *How amusing to have the power to rile him after all these years*, Amanda thought.

"I'm lost by all this." Amanda noticed that Cassie did look as bewildered as she sounded. "Amanda, how do you know so much about worms?"

"Really, Cass, we live by the Chesapeake and have inlets all along the coast feeding into the bay. Now why shouldn't I know something about fishing?"

"Yes, well, it's just that you've never mentioned fishing before this."

"Yes, well, Cass, we all have our secrets, don't we? Now here's what I know about worms." Amanda's gaze momentarily fell upon Stephen and Wesley who were watching them. Removing her gloves to better handle the rubber worm, Amanda showed her friends the action in the rubber. Her eyes sparkled with mischief as she regaled them about the positives and negatives of rubber and real worms.

Stephen immediately noticed Amanda's hands as she pulled them from the gloves. Her nails were tastefully done with a French manicure. He listened to her speak with authority of one who had spent time in the water. However, he had to wonder if she really would dirty those beautiful long fingers with worm guts to go fishing. Something about her sent a chill through him. She may just be one of those women who deceive you by their looks. He was taken in by her and had the urge to continue conversing as long as possible.

"Hey, Wes, do you hear this lady?"

"Yeah, I do. It seems we've got ourselves a patron who might just be interested in our tournament. What do you think, miss, interested in trying your hand at ice fishing while you're here?"

Amanda laughed and looked up at Kevin then back at Wes and Stephen. Her smile, Stephen noticed, didn't quite meet her eyes. There was something haunting in them. Stephen felt a chill run up his spine again as Amanda continued to speak.

"No, I'm not interested in ice fishing. I came here to ice skate with my friends."

The topic of fishing was quickly forgotten as the vacationers made their way to the lake. Sitting on a log, Amanda removed her hiking boots and pulled on a second pair of wool socks. She then slid her feet into the skates and laced them up. As she stood up, her legs felt a bit wobbly. It had been so long since she had been on the ice. Over the years, she had had many opportunities to skate, just not the desire. Today, she needed to skate. She needed to conquer this frozen lake. Getting her bearings, Amanda took a ginger step toward the ice. In an instant, her legs responded as if to say, "What's taken you so long to do what you enjoy most?" As she put her first skate on the ice, everything in her began to come alive. Step, glide, step, glide—the pattern was as familiar to her as the back of her hand. Amanda skated along with her friends, rested with them, and returned to skating all the while being in total command of the ice. Something inside of her was being set free.

The blast of cold arctic air brought both Wes and Stephen to attention as Peter and JJ burst in slamming the door behind them. Wesley enjoyed having his son with him and knew that all too soon he would be out on his own.

"Dad, Uncle Steve, you won't believe it!" Pete was winded from running in the cold.

"Slow down, son, what's wrong?" Wes was concerned that Pete's asthma was rearing its ugly head. The bitter cold had a habit of doing that. The very fact that Becky had allowed Peter to work at the bait shop had been a major milestone for all of them. Now if he had an attack, their working together would be finished.

"He's okay," JJ piped up. "Just excited about what he saw out on the lake." Knowing that he had full attention of both men, JJ continued, "There are four new people out on the lake this afternoon. We recognized a man and woman from when we were skating past the Pines earlier today."

"This old couple was kissing on the rock. It was really disgusting, kind of like watching you and Mom."

"Or my parents, Yeesh!" JJ made a disgusting face to accompany his comment.

"But then the lady talked with us. Dad, she was really nice. We saw her again out here on the lake. Have you seen her skate?"

Wes had not seen her skate. He had rented out the skates and knew Amanda Newman had requested a size 10 women's skate so she could wear two pairs of wool socks on her feet in the skates. He had a strange feeling as he recalled another woman who had skated that way but chose to say nothing.

"Stephen, I'm telling you this lady's...well... I've never seen anyone skate like her." JJ was busting with enthusiasm. "For an old lady with a limp when she walks, she's hot on ice!"

"James Matthew Callison Jr., what have I told you about being disrespectful of your elders?" No one had heard Jim enter the shop, and all were taken quite by surprise when he spoke. He proceeded to walk toward them with a commanding presence. JJ knew the look all too well and expected to be chewed out during the entire ride home. Oh he hoped his father would not take the long way home tonight!

"Sorry, Dad, but you should see her for yourself!" All three men followed JJ to the window to get a good look at Amanda. "See she's got on the bomber jacket, tan scarf, no hat, and gloves. Watch her skate. She's awesome!" The three older men watched for a moment. Then all exchange glances at one another. No one said a word. Each knew the other was thinking of a woman who had shared their lives so long ago. Jim's younger sister, Amanda "Calli" Callison could be this woman's twin.

Stephen, Wes, and Jim refilled their coffee cups and returned to the window as they waited for Peter and JJ to complete their evening chores before closing shop. All skate and ice fishing rentals had been returned for the day. It was Stephen who resumed the conversation on the four who had been skating.

"JJ's right about the woman with the limp." That was the way they distinguished Amanda from the others. "She sure is something, isn't she?"

"I swear the woman could well have been my sister. It was creepy to watch her." Jim rubbed his chin while deep in thought.

"Remember how Amanda loved to skate and play hockey? I have to say that if the guys on our HS team had taken hockey as seriously as Mandy, they would have made the all-star team with us," Stephen added.

Jim started to chuckle. "Remember the day in late winter as the ice was beginning to thaw on the lake when Amanda encountered the moose?"

"Oh yeah…" Wesley snorted out a chuckle and then continued with the story they all knew by heart. "Like usual, something was gnawing at Amanda. She was in one of her moods that afternoon and already skating when we got here. This cow moose should have been warned." They all let out a laugh. Jim shook his head with a smile while Stephen removed his cap and ran his fingers through his hair. Wes continued, "That moose came out onto the lake a ways south of where we were going to be skating. The moose was moving on, and Amanda continued to skate toward her."

Jim wiped a tear from the corner of his eye as he laughed and remembered Amanda's tangle with the moose. "The ice cracked, broke with the moose hitting the frigid water. Amanda started, gasping as she realized what was going to happen. The ice continued to crack and break. I can still picture it in my mind as Manda splashed into the water with the moose. The moose is bellowing, Amanda is yelling...For a moment, all we could do was laugh." And the men did just that as they looked out the window toward the empty frozen lake. "It's a good thing you were with us, Wes," Jim said, "If it hadn't been for you realizing the seriousness of the situation, we might have lost my sister."

The men stood silent as memories flooded them. It was Stephen who spoke. "When we finally got her out of the water, she cussed us all out. She was still spitting words at me when we got back to my place. It took a lot of bourbon and hot bath water to begin to warm her up. Later that night, I finally got her calmed down and totally warm..." Stephen's faraway look and smile said it all.

"I take it you had a whole lot of fun that night!" Wesley roared.

"Hey now, that's my sister you're talking about and—"

As if on cue, Peter and JJ opened the door and stepped into the bait shop. The conversation came to an abrupt end. The men gathered up their gear and headed to their respective homes for the night.

While Wesley drove home to Becky, Stephen had no desire to head home to the empty cold space where he lived. After this day, Stephen had to acknowledge how lonely his life had become. It was as he had told Wesley time for change. Calli had been the love of his life. They were supposed to grow old and ornery together. Then everything fell apart in the summer of '79. Without a word, Amanda Callison walked out of his life. Glancing at the dashboard clock, Stephen knew it was far too late to go make a visit. For that, he'd have to wait until tomorrow. Now he would find comfort in other ways.

Stephen pulled his pickup into the crowded parking lot of Mike's Pub. As he was getting out of his truck, Junior McGrath and Shannon Green came stumbling out of the door. It was obvious to him that both men had consumed too much alcohol and probably should not be out on the road. Tonight with the mood he was in, he really didn't care if anything happened to them. Fortunately, neither one saw him therefore he was able to avoid conversation with them. The friendship they had all had while growing up had diminished to the point of Stephen now simply tolerating their existence. In fact, he loathed them and their obnoxious behavior toward people in general, but especially toward those whom he loved and cared about. So why, Stephen had to ask himself, had he been unwilling to see the truth years ago? Should he chalk it up to age and experience? Why hadn't he listened to and believed Calli when she had turned to him for help? Even if he had, Stephen now had to wonder if she would still be in his life. The answers to his questions would never be known. So again, Stephen counseled himself it is time to move on and live in the present.

Opening the door, Stephen could see that all the tables were occupied and only one bar stool was vacant. He sauntered over and took a seat. Tom Baxter was tending bar and nodded when they made eye contact. He knew Stephen's preference for drinks and filled a glass of Sam Adams from the tap with a low head. "Looks like you could use more than a drink tonight, my friend."

"That obvious?"

"I've known you a good many years and have come to understand your moods. How about a burger and fries on the house to go with that brew?"

"Yeah sure…It's been a long day." Steve looked around at the crowd. It was rather busy for a Tuesday evening in December. Some of the regulars nodded a hello to Stephen, and he returned the gesture. "Looks like things are going pretty good around here. I saw Junior and Shannon leaving as I pulled in."

"Yeah, they were here. I can't complain about the night now that they're gone. You know if it weren't for you and Wes hosting the Annual New Year's Eve Festival and having that ice fishing contest, there'd only be a handful of regulars in here."

"Me included." As Stephen spoke, he tilted his empty glass toward the tap. Tom took it from his hand and turned to fill Stephen's glass.

"Yeah, you included, my friend."

"How about two fingers of JD to go with the beer? Tonight I could use the comfort of another old friend."

Tom snapped his head up and looked intently into Stephen's eyes. It wasn't too often Stephen Johnson ordered Jack Daniel's. When he did, it was for a very good reason. Tom knew well enough to not ask. He'd simply comply with the request and pour. Placing the glass in front of Stephen, Tom stepped away to attend to his customers at the other end of the bar. An hour later, Stephen got up from the stool he had been sitting on and laid a twenty on the bar and left.

CHAPTER SIX

B y the time Cassie, Andrew, Kevin, and Amanda returned to the cabin, they were chilled to the bone. The smell of the pot of vegetable beef soup that had been simmering all afternoon greeted them as they walked through the door. Cassie, in her gentle way, commandeered the men to build a fire for them to relax to while Amanda assisted her in the kitchen.

"You're quiet, Amanda. It's almost as if you've mentally gone some place far up into the mountains. Do we need to have a therapy session?"

Cassie's comment and question startled Amanda. She realized that the silverware she was to be placing at each place setting was still in her hands. How long had she been standing there staring out toward the lake? Amanda sighed as she turned her gaze from the lake back into the kitchen. She strained a smile while briefly making eye contact with Cass.

"Sorry, I was just thinking."

"I can see that. You should know by now that you don't have to smile and pretend with me. It is obvious that something is bothering you. Is there anything you'd like to talk about?"

Amanda sighed and began to busy herself by setting the table. "No. Not right now. Let's just enjoy the remainder of this day."

The fire continued to crackle in the fireplace. Amanda had taken a chair close to the hearth. Her legs were stretched out toward the fire. She could feel the warmth of the flames easing the effects from skating. What had she been thinking? As she listened and watched her friends attempting to discretely yawn, it became apparent that they all were feeling the effects of the day in their fifty-some-year-old bodies.

"Oh my goodness." Cassie yawned as she lazily stretched. "My muscles certainly had a workout this afternoon. I do believe they are informing me I am no longer a spring chicken. I hope you won't consider me a rude hostess. I feel I must excuse myself to indulge in a hot bath. Hopefully that will relax my tight muscles."

Without a word, Andrew stood and walked over to Cassie's chair. "Let me help you, my love." As Cassie came to her feet, she threw a glare at Andrew while he brushed a lock of hair back from her face. "After your bath, I'll give you one of my special back rubs."

"Thanks but no thanks. After my bath, I'm going directly to bed." She paused then added, "And to sleep." Amanda heard the strain in Cassie's voice. She grieved for them.

"Good night, Cass. Andrew, thank you for a lovely day." Amanda yawned as she burrowed deeper into the chair. "I think I might just stay here for a while and enjoy the fire. I'll make sure it is fully out before I retire for the night." Without another word, Amanda returned her attention to the fire.

As Cassie and Andrew made their way up the stairs, Kevin closed his eyes as he reflected on the time he had spent with Amanda. He had enjoyed himself with her out on the rock. She had felt good in his arms. Kevin could feel his body respond to the memory. Amanda was the first woman in quite some time to ignite this type of response in him. They had enjoyed one another's company skating on the ice at the bait shop. During the time they had spent together, Kevin sensed that Amanda was holding something deep within her. He saw it in her eyes. It was as if she had a protective shell around her. Kevin heard Amanda yawn. He watched her eyes becoming heavy with contentment. She appeared less guarded and safe as she snuggled lazily in the chair by the fire.

A while later, Kevin got up from the couch and quietly knelt in front of the fire and chair that Amanda now appeared to be asleep in. Taking the poker in his hand, he began to stir the fire.

Just one more log, just a little longer in her presence, and then Kevin would retire for the night. The crack and pop of the log as it became engulfed by flame startled Amanda. Surprised and now awake tangled in the blanket Kevin had laid across her Amanda was on her feet. Looking up at her, Kevin couldn't help but smile. Standing up and easing Amanda into his arms, Kevin brushed her scrunched-up hair from her cheek. "You're all right, Amanda. It was only the fire."

Disorientation was now leaving Amanda's mind as she realized where she was and in whose arms. She automatically did her breathing exercises to fully regain her composure. Amanda clung to Kevin as she continued to calm herself.

Kevin spoke quietly as he lowered his lips to brush Amanda's lips. She didn't pull back. A tentative dance of passion had begun as Amanda melded into his arms. He pressed his lips to hers. His touch of his lips and the gentle caressing of his hands was about to undue her. It had been so long since she had last allowed herself to be vulnerable with a man. Amanda heard a soft moan. It took a moment for her to realize that the moan she heard had come from her. Unexpected heat was surging through Amanda's body. This was no hot flash. Her breathing was becoming erratic...This was no panic attack. She had to catch her breath.

Kevin eased himself away from her mouth far enough to speak. "I want to know you, Amanda, really know you in every sense of the word."

She tensed with his words. "It's too soon. I'm...I'm not ready for this." The relaxed moment had disappeared as true panic had risen to the surface in her.

"I'm sorry, Amanda, I'm not usually this forward. I don't know what came over me. Please don't pull away. You're such an amazing woman. I don't want this night to end. Here, let's sit down by the fire, and we'll just talk. Whatever you do, please don't shut me out."

Amanda looked deep into Kevin's eyes and found something she didn't expect. He had vulnerability about him that she had never seen before in a man. For whatever reason, she felt as though she could trust him not to pressure her. Fighting the panic inside her, Amanda took deep breathes.

"Give me a minute please..." Another breath in and slowly out.

Kevin silently watched her regain her composure. He was certain that this had taken all the energy she could muster at that moment. Taking her hand, Kevin guided Amanda to the rug in front of the hearth. Seconds turned into minutes, and minutes would soon turn into hours. What Amanda appreciated most was that Kevin had an uncanny ability to make her relax and laugh. Through their unguarded conversation, they continued to discover that they had more in common than either had previously fathomed. Amanda hadn't realized that at some point they had moved closer, and they were now leaning up against one another as they looked into the fire together. Without consciously thinking, she had slid her hand onto Kevin's leg. Kevin in turn laced his fingers with Amanda's. Kevin drew his face in close to Amanda's so their lips brushed one another's.

Amanda tentatively slid her free hand up on to his chest. Did she want to try this again? Could she afford to let her guard down and invite him to go all the way with her? A few hours before, they had been mere strangers, now they sat before a warm fire on a cold winter's night. It definitely was romantic. His kisses were gentle yet inviting. Her body was fully awakened to desire.

Kevin felt the apprehension in Amanda's body as he held her against his chest. This time he would advance with caution as to not spook Amanda. "We'll go as slow as you like, Amanda. I'm in no hurry. You feel so good in my arms. I like holding you close," he whispered. She sighed. Kevin could feel Amanda begin to relax in his embrace. Amanda moaned. She tilted her head back to look into his eyes. Her words were barely audible.

"I think I'd like you to really kiss me." With that invitation, Kevin smiled then lowered his lips onto hers.

The creaking of the stairs brought Kevin and Amanda back to the moment. Like two teens being caught by a suspecting parent, they were sitting up as Cassie entered the room. Pleasantly surprised by what she saw, Cassie smiled. "I thought you two had gone on up to bed. Sorry for the intrusion."

Pulling herself away from Kevin, Amanda got up from the floor. "It's fine, Cass. After all, it's your cabin. You do have a right to come downstairs any time you like."

"Well, since we're all up, how about joining me in drinking a cup of hot cocoa?"

Cassie was well aware of just how much her friends had been enjoying one another's company. She appreciated that neither had attempted to try to hide the fact from her; their swollen lips and flushed cheeks were a dead giveaway. At the moment, the jury in her mind was out as to which one was more fortunate, Kevin or Amanda. While Cassie prepared the hot cocoa, Kevin stoked the fire. Settled back around the hearth, the three quietly chatted, sharing stories of their past. Kevin noted that Amanda continued to be evasive about her past even with Cassie. Then an idea hit him.

"So, Amanda, earlier this afternoon while we were ice skating, I shared with you where I learned to skate. I do believe you omitted in sharing with me exactly where and when you learned to skate."

Cassie watched Amanda's expression turn from relaxed to pensive. Kevin had riled something in her. Cassie was now intrigued to find out what Amanda was guarding about her past. She glanced down to see Amanda's hand intertwine with Kevin's hand that was resting on Amanda's thigh. This was a pleasant surprise for Cassie to see. As Cassie watched her friends' silent interaction, she saw a subtle change came over Amanda. It seemed that Amanda was drawing strength from Kevin.

"Well, Kevin, if you really must know. It really wasn't as grand as your skating in a club in Reisterstown." Kevin raised an eyebrow. "Not that a club is bad, mind you, it's just that…I learned to skate out in the open like here at the lake." Kevin smiled as he recalled their time on the lake. As she skated, she flowed with ease on the ice as if it were a part of her.

"Really." This was news to Cassie. "That sounds nice."

"Oh yes, Cass, it was great to learn to skate out in the open as well as difficult." Amanda got a faraway look in her eyes.

"And how is that, Amanda? How was it nice and difficult?" Kevin asked.

"Being outside in nature is always great. You do, though, have to pay attention to weather and the condition of the ice. Sometimes it's just not safe to be on the ice. Then there is the issue of whom you skate with. Having an older brother, I was expected to learn how to skate so I could play ice hockey with him and his friends. Sometimes the guys forgot that I was made different from them. They simply did not understand that there were days when I did not feel up to playing." Amanda closed her eyes for a moment.

Cassie was about to open her mouth to speak when Kevin, upon making eye contact with Cass, shook his head no and quietly asked, "How did that make you feel?"

Cassie sat in awe of how quietly Kevin was guiding Amanda in the conversation. He was gently opening the windows into Amanda's soul. In all the years Cass and Andrew had spent with Kevin and Meg, she had never seen this side of him. She had to wonder if Andrew knew this about him.

Amanda continued, "It was tough being the only girl playing with the guys feeling like a beached whale and you can surmise the rest. You guys just don't understand the crap women go through."

"Amen, Amanda, they certainly don't!"

"Well, ladies, despite your solidified opinion of the male species, I'd like to believe that I am sensitive to what you women go through in life."

Amanda gently squeezed Kevin's hand. "I believe you do care, Kevin. However, the idiots I played hockey with were in a totally different league."

"Are these the ones you were bluntly referring to earlier this evening?"

"Yes, and occasionally, I'd have to adjust their attitudes."

"Oh, and what did your attitude adjustment include?"

"Well, let's see through the years my brother James had a couple of black eyes and lost some teeth when I nailed him with the hockey puck. Phil also ended up with a huge black eye, Johnny had a split lip, and the others fortunately for them they knew enough to duck or simply run when I was in a mood. I guess you could say I was a force to be reckoned with."

Cass was nearly in shock. In all the years she had known Amanda, she had never heard this about Amanda's life nor about this more aggressive aspect of her personality. Hockey, her friend played hockey. Who would have guessed? Now thinking back to the story in the bait shop, she had to wonder what else Amanda knew about fishing. What other secrets was she hiding? Then again, perhaps she didn't want to know.

"So, Amanda, did you have a nickname to go with your attitude?" Amanda heard the humor in Kevin's voice.

"Oh yeah!" Her smile reached her eyes as she laughed and said, "On and off the ice, they called me Calli the Crusher."

"That's quite a nickname," Cassie said.

"Yes well, as I told you, some of the guys experienced the results of my swing of the hockey stick in unkind ways. I was known to play my heart out on the ice and not afraid to do what I had to in order to win."

Kevin noted the sadness that crept into Amanda's voice and facial expressions. Amanda fought to contain a yawn as she nestled herself against Kevin. When had he drawn her into him? She couldn't remember; whenever it was, Amanda wouldn't complain for she enjoyed being in his arms. Kevin quietly stroked her hair as she found it increasingly difficult to keep her eyes open. Finally, Amanda gave way to sleep with Kevin's arms wrapped around her. Cassie tucked a blanket around Kevin and Amanda before turning down the light and returning upstairs to nestle herself in bed with Andrew.

CHAPTER SEVEN

Andrew awakened with the light of early morning. He thought that he was first to emerge from sleep. He had not been sleeping well since Monday night when he and Cass had fought. The battle lines had been drawn, and there was no crossing them in the bed. Last night or early this morning, he had felt Cassie slip out of the bed and then return sometime later. This impasse had to be dealt with soon. At fifty-eight years of age, he considered himself to be a strong man; however, his wife freezing him out was killing him.

As he came downstairs, he discovered that Kevin lay asleep on the coach and snoring quite loudly. The smell of fresh brewed coffee indicated that someone had indeed risen before him. He looked out the window and saw that Amanda was sitting out on the front porch looking out toward the lake. Andrew watched her take a sip of hot coffee. He could see the steam rise from her coffee cup and the vapor come from her mouth as she exhaled. He glanced at the thermometer and found the temperature outside was a balmy nineteen degrees above zero.

Only Amanda would chose to sit outside on a cold morning like this. Smiling and shaking his head, Andrew quietly poured himself a cup of coffee. He watched her as he sipped his coffee. She was one of the strongest women he had ever known. Perhaps the strongest; however, given the current state of his marriage, he knew better than to admit that to his wife. Things were tense enough these days. As Andrew observed her, he saw a frown or perhaps angry expression on her usually smiling face. He decided to bundle up in his winter gear, brave the cold, and join her. Perhaps she, as much as he, needed a friend to talk with; only time would tell.

Amanda was indeed deep in thought. It seemed that no matter how she played out a meeting with Jim or Stephen in her mind, the ending was the same. Old wounds would be reopened, and lives would possibly be further destroyed. Even though Grandma had yet again counseled her to forgive, in Amanda's eyes, there was no room for forgiveness toward the men who had once been such a vital part of her life. As happy as she was to spend time with Gram, it had been a mistake to come back to the lake. Amanda decided that it would be best for everyone involved for her to leave, to go home to Baltimore. Kevin and she could meet when he returned to the city. They could resume a relationship of getting to know one another. After all, there definitely is chemistry between them. Amanda breathed a sigh of relief. After she finished her coffee, she would go up to her room, call the airline to book an earlier flight, and pack. Then she would broach the subject of her early return with Cassie. After saying her good-byes here at the cabin she would drive up to Gram's.

Amanda jumped as she heard the door open. She saw Andrew step out onto the porch. He was bundled up from head to toe as if expecting a blizzard to strike at any moment. Amanda lazily removed her feet from the railing and sat up in a more dignified manner. She laughed to herself. Years ago, she would have thought nothing of continuing to slouch in the chair. Now she gave way to proper etiquette; she lowered her feet so Andrew did not have to walk around her to sit in the other chair.

"Good morning, Amanda. What a glorious day! I hope you don't mind my intrusion on your solitude out here."

"Not at all, Drew, I'm always glad to share in your company. Is Cass up yet?" Amanda was well aware of the conflict between them. Exactly what had occurred before she arrived, Amanda did not know. Regardless, the strain between her two friends was obvious to her.

"Not as far as I know. Were you aware that Kevin is snoring on the couch? Apparently, he didn't make it upstairs last night."

Amanda sheepishly grinned as she thought about how she spent last night with Kevin. Then her expression sobered as she momentarily laid her hand on Andrew's arm.

"Drew, I'm sorry."

"About what?"

"Yesterday morning when I spoke with Cass on my cell, I thought I had detected something was amiss. Then when I got here, I noted her icy tone when you greeted me. I've known you both for too long. Whatever is happening between you two is quite serious. I must say you're both doing a fairly good job of pretending everything is all right between the two of you. But you know you don't have to keep up the happy appearance on my account. We've been friends for far too long." She saw the unmasked pain in Andrew's eyes. "Would it be better for me to leave so you and Cassie can work this out?"

"Oh no, Amanda, no, I'm sure that neither one of us want you to leave." Andrew clasped his hand over hers. She felt his gentle squeeze. "I'm glad you're here, and I hope that as my friend you will help me figure out how to resolve this impasse with Cassie."

Amanda's heart was heavy. Earlier while she had been sipping her coffee and meditating, she had made up her mind to leave. And now her friend needed her and asked her to help. The last thing she wanted was to triangle her friendship and end up in the middle. She had been down this road before. Trouble was sure to follow. Amanda pulled the coffee cup to her mouth only to discover she had already consumed all of its contents. Darn, she could use more coffee. That would obviously have to wait. Looking into Andrew's eyes, she saw his fatigue and desperation.

"What do you need from me, Drew?"

The two settled back into the Adirondack chairs. For a moment, Andrew simply looked out onto the frozen lake. Amanda quietly waited. She knew from her years of experience as a social worker to not rush him. She'd allow Andrew all the time he needed to find his voice. It didn't take long for him to begin. She listened to him and guided their conversation. At one point, Amanda noticed that he fought back a few tears. As the conversation wound down, Amanda could see his demeanor had begun to change. The sheer desperation was no longer present. Through Amanda's counsel, he now had a plan of action.

"Thank you, Amanda. At least now if nothing else I have some idea as to how to beg and grovel at Cassie's feet for forgiveness."

"Andrew." Amanda sighed.

"Seriously, I do appreciate you listening to me. You know, Amanda, you are very good at what you do. I imagine the women you work with must truly benefit from your compassion and your straightforwardness with them."

"Thank you for your kind words." With that said, Amanda stretched, yawned, and looked out toward the lake. Andrew's gaze followed hers. The sun was peeking out of a series of puffy clouds. Blue jays were heard fussing about something in the pine trees overhead. A male cardinal was heard whistling to his mate. The frozen lake shimmered in the sunlight yet hiding its residents down deep below the surface.

"It sure is a beautiful morning, isn't it?" he said filled with awe.

"Yes it is, my friend. We sure don't get mornings like this in Baltimore." Amanda felt a tugging at her heart. A lump of emotion was in her throat. As if on cue, her eyes began to fill up with tears. No, she commanded herself. Whatever has brought this wave of emotion on will simply have to abate itself.

"Now, Amanda, would you care to elaborate on what happened after I turned in last night and Cassie returned downstairs to join you and Kevin?" Amanda abruptly turned to face him. Surprise was written all over her rosy cheeks and smoky-brown eyes. A twinge of sadness covered her like a sheet of ice. She shivered. "Yeah, you guessed it. I was awake when Cass joined you downstairs. As you probably guessed by now, I haven't been sleeping too well."

"Well, Drew, before I fell asleep in Kevin's arms—" Andrew smiled.

"So that explains why he's still on the couch."

"Oh yes it does." Amanda's own smile turned coy. This pleased Andrew. "I wish you had joined our late-night gab session. I missed you."

"Thank you, Amanda. How about you bring me up to speed on the conversation so if Cassie refers to something that happened when you all were talking and she expects me to already know, I'll be able to respond correctly?"

Andrew watched Amanda as she enlightened him. Amanda didn't realize that in looking out over the lake as she regaled him about the late-night adventures she had opened a door for Andrew to glimpse inside her. Andrew and Cassie both knew Amanda was from New York and sometimes made visits to see her aging grandmother. Through the years, she had always successfully managed to skirt around the subject of her hometown until now.

"Amanda, where was home? Where was the lake you skated on?" Andrew watched Amanda's whole body process his question. She was quiet. He noticed that her breathing had changed. Her hands began moving and then she sprung to her feet. Andrew was on his feet as well and now stood with his arms encircling her. "You don't need to flee from me. Amanda, you are safe. No one is going to hurt you." He quietly asked, "Was this lake area your home? Is that why you have avoided coming to vacation here with us for so long?"

"Yes." The emotional levy Amanda had tended to and repaired over the years gave way. Amanda melted into tears, heart-wrenching-from-her-toes kind of tears. Andrew's arms tightened around her. This was not a panic attack as previously thought but a long overdue crying jag. He became a safe haven for Amanda to bury herself into.

"Go ahead, Amanda. Cry your pain out." Amanda cried as Andrew had encouraged and held on to him for dear life. She was afraid that if she let go she would not have the strength to stand on her own. As they shared that intimate moment, Andrew cried as well. His were tears for both of them. Right now he was thankful to have Amanda as his dear friend and grateful he could be her friend as well. Neither of them knew that Kevin and Cassie had awakened. They each had fixed a cup of coffee and were watching them from inside the cabin. Cassie turned to Kevin and quietly spoke.

"After all these years, I still don't know how my husband does it. Andrew has gotten Amanda to open up about something mighty powerful. You know, Kevin, he will treat this time as if he were talking with one of his patients. He will not share one speck of this new knowledge with me."

"Oh?" Kevin sighed with a twinkle in his eye. "And here I thought you two were joined at the hip so tight that one knew what the other was thinking." A smile that never reached her eyes came to Cassie.

Stephen could smell the coffee brewing as he opened the door to the bait shop. It was a good thing. With how he was feeling, it would take a lake full of coffee to make a dent in his latest hangover. With a headache the strength of Niagara Falls, Stephen stepped into the shop. Wesley took one look at him. He winced with pain for Stephen. He had seen that look many times before. There was one problem. The last time Wes saw Stephen look this bad was about twenty or so years ago. He took a deep breath and slowly exhaled.

"So, Johnson, where'd you go last night to be looking like the walking dead this morning?"

Wes doubted if Stephen had looked in the mirror. The stubble on his face indicated that he hadn't touched his razor. *Probably a good thing*, Wes thought. The smell of old booze permeated the air.

"Do you by chance want to go out and breathe on the kindling the boys have laid and get the fire going for them?" Wes said with a flat voice.

Stephen removed his gloves and unzipped his jacket. From the looks of him, it appeared that Stephen had put back on the same clothes he wore the day before. He pushed his sunglasses up the bridge of his nose and lowered his cap on his forehead. The light of day was killing him where he stood. Not saying anything, he stumbled past Wes and reached for a cup.

"It's not ready yet. Sit your sorry self down on that stool, and I'll get it for you when it's done." Stephen didn't speak. He simply sat down as Wes had directed him to do.

"Man you're a mess."

Wes shook his head in disgust. He hoped for Johnson's sake that he sobered up real soon. There was a strong possibility that Becky would stop in to the shop on her way home from work. It would do no good for Becky to see him like this. She would be all over her brother like a fly on molasses. Stephen made a grunting noise, which Wes assumed to be meant as agreement with his observations thus far. The coffeemaker made its final gurgling noise indicating that the coffee was ready and not a moment too soon. Wes poured a cup and handed it to Stephen; black the way he needed it this morning.

"What happened last night?"

Stephen sat the coffee cup on the counter. He then took off his sunglasses, rubbed his eyes, and replace his shades to cover his red swollen hungover eyes.

"I stopped at Mike's for a burger and brew. I was thinking about stuff that happened yesterday and you know." Stephen fell silent then took a swallow of coffee. It burned going down his throat. Wincing from the hot coffee, a stabbing pain shot through his head. He raised his free hand to his head and moaned.

"Johnson, a brew and burger didn't do this to you." Wesley kept his tone even as he studied him. "What else did you have to drink?"

"I had a couple of shots of JD at Mike's and then drove home." Stephen took another slug of coffee. It was still hot enough to scorch his throat. "Jumpin' bullfrogs that's hot!"

"Serves you right, Johnson." There was no sympathy in Wesley's voice.

"Will you shut up!" Stephen growled as he pushed his sliding glasses back up his nose.

"No, not yet. You come in here to our business drunk as a skunk, and I want answers. How much and what did you drink after you got home last night?"

Wes was angry with Stephen for allowing himself to wallow in his sorrow. More than that. He was angry as all get out with a woman. There was only one particular woman who had this much power to mess with his best friend's mind. At one time, he had loved and cared for Mandy like she was his own sister. Now he watched his friend suffering in pain brought on by memories of her. He'd give anything to have a go around with Amanda Callison and tell her what he thought of her.

"Oh man, I'm too old for this crap. I just overslept that's all." Stephen ran his hand across his chin and then through his hair.

"I'm waiting for an answer."

Stephen growled. "A half a bottle of wild turkey, some Old Grand Dad, and I don't remember what else." With that, Stephen was off the stool and heading to the bathroom. Wesley remained standing by the counter, shook his head, and took a sip of coffee. It was going to be a long day, even longer he mused for Stephen Johnson.

It was late morning; the remnants of breakfast had been cleared away. Andrew and Kevin sat at the table lingering over their last cup of coffee. Cass sat curled up in a chair in front of the fire with crewel embroidery in hand. Her fingers worked fast as she kept one ear on the conversation at the table. She reflected on how Andrew had attended to Amanda earlier in the day. Jealousy was subtly weaving its way into her stitches. She needed time alone with Andrew to work through their differences. But now it seemed as though he would rather stay as far from her as possible.

Was that her fault? Whether it was or not, Cassie decided that they would resolve their impasse one way or the other before the New Year, and it was now only two days away.

Amanda came bounding down the stairs with a heavy sweatshirt on over her turtleneck sweater. She wore faded jeans with a slight hole in the knee, which revealed insulated leggings better known as long johns in the north country underneath. On her feet were hiking boots with wool socks sticking out of the top. With gloves and earmuffs in hand, Amanda stopped at the doorway between the great room and kitchen. Both Kevin and Andrew simultaneously put down their mugs of coffee as they looked at Amanda. Her eyes shimmered with a smile as she spoke.

"Kevin, if you'd like to join me on my walk, I'd welcome the company."

"Yes I would, Amanda. Give me a minute to change into warmer clothes, grab my jacket and gloves." He took in her attire. "Are you sure you'll be warm enough dressed like that?"

"Sure. I have on other layers you don't see." Amanda smiled. She then turned her attention to Cassie and Andrew as she waited for Kevin to get ready to accompany her outside. When Kevin remerged downstairs, Amanda provided Cassie and Andrew with a rough route for their walk. "FYI, we'll be walking along the lake. My doctor has recently prescribed fresh air and the lake as part of my therapy." Cassie and Kevin both noticed the winks and smiles exchanged between Amanda and Andrew. "We should be back around lunchtime," Amanda added.

The quiet of the cabin was unnerving as neither Cass nor Andrew would look at the other. Andrew knelt down in front of the fire and began moving the partially burned logs and rebuilt the fire to continue to warm the cabin. There was a knock at the door. Cassie got up from the chair and opened the door to find a delivery of flowers. "Good morning," she said to the young man standing on her porch. She beamed, imagining that Kevin had ordered flowers for Amanda.

"Good morning. I have flowers for Cassidy Serenelli-Phillips. Would you be her?"

"Yes I am." Moisture filled Cassie's eyes as she looked at the box of flowers she was now holding.

"Ma'am, you might want to put them inside as there are more for you."

"More, flowers?"

"Oh yes, ma'am. You have three dozen flowers in all. You must be some pretty special lady."

Cassie stepped inside with her first box and returned to wait for the two remaining boxes. Upon wishing the delivery man a nice day, she entered the cabin carrying her long boxes of flowers. Andrew remained by the fire where he watched Cassie enter the kitchen and open her three boxes of long stem red roses. She found the note in one of the boxes. "Red roses for my blue lady. You are my life. I need you now more than ever. Please forgive me. All my love, Andrew." Cassie completely melted into tears. She did not hear Andrew enter the kitchen. She felt his hand on her shoulder, turned, and sunk into his waiting arms. He quietly spoke what was in his heart and asked for her forgiveness. Cassie fumbled around and found a tissue in her sweater pocket, wiping her eyes and blowing her nose before she spoke.

"Oh, Andrew, of course I forgive you. These flowers must have cost you a fortune. They're beautiful. You know I'm a sucker for sentimental things...your note, your holding me in your arms. The words you've just shared with me will last in my heart far longer than the flowers. I, in turn, need to ask for your forgiveness. Yesterday and this morning I've been...Well, I guess worse than when I hit the onset of menopause."

A deep chuckle rose from within Andrew. "Oh no, my love, you're wrong on that one! Nothing you can ever do will compare with what you were like during that time in our life. The boys and I were miserable."

"You never said anything about my mistreating you…not you or the boys."

"That's because we treasured our lives! I do love you, Cass. Now that the cabin is quiet, let's sit in front of the fire and talk."

The impasse was lifted. Cass and Andrew each fixed a fresh cup of coffee that they intended to sip on while conversing. As the two grieved and reevaluated their life together, the coffee grew cold and remained untouched.

"Cassidy, why do you suppose Ryan waited until now to disclose his sexuality with us?"

"Because, my dear, he needed time to figure out who he is. He trusted us to allow him time to do just that."

"When you were involved with the AIDS and FLAG rallies with Ryan, did you ever have the urge to confront him?"

"No, Andrew, I didn't want to confront him. I wanted to protect him from the cruelty I knew he would encounter in this world we live in. I knew in my heart that it was not the time for me to broach the subject with him, that when Ryan was ready we all would talk. You remember how difficult high school was for each of us as heterosexuals. Imagine what it was like for our son…He was so young, vulnerable, and gay. If either of us had broached the subject with him and expressed any displeasure, think about what that would have done to our relationship with him. Ryan needed to see that our convictions about accepting others for who they are and not judging them by their choices begins at home. Andrew, we can be proud of our son."

Andrew was quiet. Then with intense admiration, Andrew spoke, "Cassie, both Ryan and Nate have no idea how fortunate they are to have you as their mother. You, my love, are a phenomenal woman."

Andrew leaned over to Cassie and drew her into his arms. Their lips touched and without pause opened. Tongues played together the dance of love with sweetness of longevity and, yes, even trust which rocked by grief had been questioned a few nights before. Holding on to one another, Cassie and Andrew cried in grief over their past, the present, and what the future may now be for them. Their love for one another once again proved it was; it is able to withstand the test of time. Together they would make it through this new chapter in their life. They would be united in their love for one another and their love for their son and his partner, George.

CHAPTER EIGHT

Amanda was making her way over rocks by the edge of the lake with confidence like that of a mountain goat. She took for granted walking on the rocks and snow-covered shore of the lake. For her it was like revisiting an old friend or perhaps as comfortable as a well-broken-in pair of shoes. Her steadiness continued to amaze Kevin. Every few steps, it seemed that he found the loose or slippery rock. Amanda was keeping a brisk pace as they made their way north along the west bank. When she heard a wheezing noise, she slowed down. Amanda looked at Kevin and stopped dead in her tracks.

"Oh my, Kevin, I'm sorry. I was lost in thought as we were walking, and I didn't take into consideration that you are not used to this type of exercise. Please forgive me."

"Apology accepted." Amanda noted the twinkle in his eyes as he spoke. "So did Andrew suggest you take a power walk around the lake?"

"Power walk, no. Normal pace, yes. I suppose"—she paused for a moment, taking in a deep breath of frigid air—"that you're wondering what we were talking about earlier on the porch."

"You knew we were watching you?"

The sound of surprise in Kevin's voice caused Amanda to chuckle. "Ah, so Cass was there with you...With the shadow on the glass, I wasn't quite sure if I saw her standing by you or not."

"You are good."

"It's something you learn out of necessity growing up in the mountains and have a weasel for an older brother."

"Tell me about it."

"Which one are you referring to, the mountains or the weasel?" There was an edge to Amanda's voice. The lightness that previously existed had suddenly been replaced by sarcasm.

"Either of them and anyone or anything else you'd care to share." Kevin raised his gloved hand to touch Amanda's jaw. A lock of her hair had fallen against her cheek. The gentle brushing of his hand sent sparks of heat through Amanda. If he were to kiss her again, there was no telling what might happen between them.

"Let's walk." Amanda didn't wait for a response and set herself into motion. Kevin stepped in stride. Her voice was quiet as she spoke. The crispness was gone. "Last night when we talked about ice skating, I told you I learned to skate on a lake." Kevin nodded.

"This lake and area was my childhood hometown." She gestured to the land and lake surrounding them. "Although, that is probably quite obvious considering how you've seen me skate on the lake, negotiate over the land from the cabin to the lake, climb the rock with ease, and now this morning as we have been walking together here by the lake."

"I also noticed that being here is causing you internal pain. Your panic attack as well as your interactions with the two young skaters and the proprietors of the bait shop were indicators for me that something is amiss."

"For years, I have been able to side step Cassie and Andrew's invitations to come and stay with them. This year I could not come up with a valid excuse to decline the invitation. So here I am in a place that encourages memories to flood over me without warning. Right now as we stand here together I am fighting the panic within me. Time has not healed all the wounds of my past. My grandmother is still living and has remained a part of my life. We've been able to have brief visits throughout the years. I must say sometimes it was very tricky to keep the information of my existence from my brother." Kevin's expression appeared to Amanda as shock. She had expected it would.

"We, my brother and I, had a falling out thirty years ago. Being here and encountering him in the Quik Mart yesterday morning has opened up some of the old wounds." Kevin gently brushed away the tear that was escaping down Amanda's cheek. He took her hand in his. Together they walked on in silence for a bit.

"Amanda, what happened between you and your brother to cause you to leave and not want to contact anyone from your past other than your grandmother?"

Amanda paused. Continuing to hold on to Kevin's hand she gazed out over the frozen lake. When she spoke, Kevin could barely hear her whisper. "He betrayed my trust when he chose to believe people whom I had considered friends over me." Abruptly returning her fix on Kevin, Amanda continued, "Kevin, I really don't want to go into it right now. It's complicated. Besides, nothing will change what happened here in the summer of '79. It's best to leave it alone." Amanda looked out to the lake and pointed toward the other side of the lake and abruptly changed the conversation. "If we were to walk across the lake and head up the mountain to the north of here, we'd get to my grandmother's cabin." She looked deep into his eyes. It was almost as if she was challenging him. "Are you game?"

"Perhaps another time." Having said that, Kevin turned to face Amanda. He looked deep into her dark-brown eyes. This morning in the bright sunlight by the lake they seemed to shimmer with anticipation as her smile danced into her eyes. Kevin gently ran his finger down her jaw. Neither one spoke. They held one another's gaze as if drawing the other into their souls. He lowered his lips to meet hers. His gentleness encouraged Amanda to let down her barriers. Amanda's arms circled Kevin's neck. Just then, a gust of cold north wind sent a shiver through Amanda reminding her of where they stood.

Amanda lay napping on her bed. Cassie and Andrew, now at peace, set out for an afternoon of walking by the lake as they continued rebuilding their life together. After Cassie and Andrew left for their walk, Kevin wrote Amanda a note and then he too quietly left the cabin. Kevin headed down the now well-worn path to the lake. He climbed on the rock; their rock where Amanda and he had shared their first kiss. Kevin let out a heavy sigh.

"Well, old man, if Amanda can bravely face her demons, don't you think it's about time you faced your own?" Kevin took in a deep breath. "There was something about this place," he mused. "It is almost spiritual."

Kevin lay back on the rock and allowed himself to reflect on his relationship with his three children. They each had brought joy into his life. Kevin had always considered himself to be a good dad, a good provider. He certainly was proud of their accomplishments at this point in their respective lives. Things abruptly changed this year not long after Meg walked out. Hateful words had spew between Kyle and him. Kyle ranted at him about all the times when Meg had been there for him and his siblings. Meg was the one who shouldered the burden of raising three children on her own. Kyle was right. What did Kevin have to be proud of? As both a husband and father, he was a failure. Kevin continued to reflect on his life. If he was going to build a new relationship with Amanda, he had to take accountability for his actions—past, present, and future.

"Okay, so I can't change the past. It is done. I have to accept this and learn from it so I don't make the same mistakes with Amanda. I can and will live without Meg but not without Amanda." Kevin opened his eyes he smiled into the sunshine, gazed around at the pristine beauty of the lake, and whispered, "Thank you."

The day continued to creep along for Stephen. Whatever had been left in his stomach had been lost upon arriving at the bait shop. Some aspirin and a hand full of vitamin B had finally kicked in. His head was no longer throbbing. Now Stephen had to contend with the cotton mouth. He knew one beer would take care of it. Instead, he downed his last slug of yet another cup of coffee.

"I'm too old for this foolishness. Wes, the next time I contemplate or do something this stupid, just shoot me. Put me out of my misery."

A lazy smile crept across Wes's face. "My friend, I learned a long time ago when to keep my mouth shut. When you get something this stupid and destructive in your mind, there ain't no changing it. It's quiet around here today. Go on home, take a shower, and sleep this off. You'll feel better tomorrow."

The sunglasses were still upon Stephen's nose protecting his eyes. He rubbed his face now ripe with stubble. A gander at his clothes revealed he had put on yesterday's shirt and jeans. He couldn't remember if he had changed his underwear. Stephen raised his arm and smelt himself.

"Oh man, you're right. I don't just stink, I reek! I guess I do need a shower."

He patted his pants pockets, cussed under his breath, and looked at Wes. "Where the blazes did I leave my keys?"

Wes brought Stephen's keys out from behind the counter. "Peter brought them inside a while ago. Apparently, you dropped them by the door of your truck when you slid out of it this morning."

Stephen scowled and cussed under his breath. "Tell your boy I said thanks." Stephen made his way to the door opened it and turned back toward Wes. "And Wes…"

"Yeah, Steve."

"I owe you."

"See you tomorrow, Johnson, and you better be sober."

"That's for dang sure!" With those final words, Stephen walked to his pickup and gingerly slid in behind the wheel. His head gave a wicked pounding for just a moment to remind him of his recent foolishness.

Stephen had started home and then changed his mind. He headed up Route 30 and turned into the community cemetery. At the fork in the road, Stephen went left and parked over the hill by his parent's grave site. He spent a few minutes with them as he always did and said a little prayer. From there, he walked up over the hill through the hemlocks to the oak grove. The snow was considerably deeper than Stephen had anticipated. As he trudged along, he realized that he should have taken the road. Laughing out loud, he recalled how his mother had always declared that her son would never choose the easy way to do anything. For a moment, he wondered if perhaps his mom was looking down from heaven and laughing along with him. Looking at the mounds of snow before him, Stephen knew he had taken the correct way. He needed the physical challenge of trudging through the snow. He needed to feel the bite of the sting of cold against his legs and the wet of snow melting in his work boots. He needed to feel again.

Stephen made his way to the grave marked Rose Amanda Johnson. He lost track of how much time he spent crouched down and touching Rose's gravestone. He told Rose all about the winter festival and celebration that was planned for tomorrow night. Stephen continued, "I love you, Rose. I wish things had turned out different for all of us. You know your daddy was a real jerk back then. Your momma needed me, and what did I do? The same thing I did last night. I went out drinking. I left her alone night after night. She'd beg me to stay. Sometimes I would only stay long enough to take care of my own needs. Then I'd go out like an old Tom cat on the prowl. I didn't treat her better than any of the—" Stephen did not complete his thought. He sighed heavily. "Girl, listen to me talk to you about your mother this way. You should be ashamed of your old man. I know I'm ashamed of myself. But perhaps it's better this way. At least with you here in the ground, you're safe. I can't hurt you." Stephen stood up removed his sunglasses to wipe his tear-laden eyes. "Bye, sugar, I'll see you soon." And with that, Stephen made his way up the hill to the path through the hemlocks.

Kevin was dusting off the seat of his pants as he stood in front of the rock. Amanda paused for a moment to watch him. When he caught sight of her, he waved and hollered, "Hello." Amanda thought that she felt her heart skip a beat. She was feeling rather giddy. There by the side of the lake stood a warm, caring man. He was in many ways the total opposite of her. He was born and raised in the city. She on the other hand was country gone city. Well, Amanda considered, they do say that opposites attract. Could she actually have met her soul mate?

It seemed like eternity until she stood before him. Kevin drew Amanda into his arms as he leaned against the rock. At first, they simply stood together holding on as if afraid the other would disappear. Amanda quietly encouraged Kevin to share what he was feeling. His revelation touched her. Yes, there is something almost spiritual about these mountains. Something was occurring within her as well.

He stroked her jaw. Without hesitation, Amanda raised her head. Her eyes locked on Kevin's. Their mutual desire was evident as he lowered his mouth to Amanda's. She realized that she could easily get used to this man kissing her be an everyday occurrence. Kevin drew his mouth back from Amanda. Looking intently into her eyes, he drew in a breath.

"Woman, you are going to drive me crazy. Please, come with me to the cabin. Make love with me, Amanda." Amanda nodded in agreement. Hand in hand, they walked back to the cabin in quiet anticipation of what was to come.

Sometime later, Amanda lay wrapped in Kevin's arms with her head on his chest. It had been years since she had last given herself to a man. He had been so gentle, so caring, even remembering to provide a condom for their protection. Unfortunately, an ominous feeling crept over her. With regret, Amanda began to question her actions. Should she have trusted him and given herself to him? Would history repeat itself with her? Would he hurt her? It was then as she was drifting off to sleep in Kevin's arms that she thought she heard him say, "I love you, Amanda."

Still feeling the effects of a delightful afternoon, Amanda made her way to the door of the cabin. She had shared more of her story with Kevin and asked for him to respect her privacy. If they were going to stand a chance at having a future together, she needed to take a drive by herself to deal with part of her past. Kevin helped Amanda into her jacket before slipping her a kiss. Cassie continued to express her concern about Amanda being out by herself. Amanda gave Cass a reassuring hug before she opened the door. Andrew had been privileged to some of Amanda's story and knew she was quite capable of handling herself in the mountains. He winked at her as he gently squeezed her shoulder.

Kevin walked Amanda to her rental car. He opened the door for her and then pulled her into his arms. Holding her close to him, Kevin said, "I told you I respect your need to go off by yourself. I hope that later you will trust me enough to share where you've been."

Amanda looked into Kevin's eyes. "Thank you for understanding my need to be alone. I'm learning to trust you and will at some point share this with you. All I ask is that you don't pressure me to do it before I'm ready."

"Fair enough. Be careful."

Kevin helped Amanda into her car and then closed the door for her. Amanda let out a heavy sigh as she turned the key in the ignition. She backed out of the driveway and onto the lane. The starkness of winter sent a chill through Amanda. She had to be nuts to be going to the cemetery during this time of year. However, if she is to move forward with her life, this visit is necessary.

The drive north of Route 30 to the community cemetery took Amanda about five minutes. She turned on the left directional signal as she slowed down to turn into the cemetery entrance. The main road was plowed far enough to enable a car to be parked and one to pass through. At the Y in the road, Amanda turned to the right. She drove up the hill and stopped by the oak grove.

After turning off the engine, Amanda took a deep breath. She opened the door, stood, and was clipped by a gust of north wind. It chilled her to the bone. Amanda got out of the car, shut the door, and stepped into the snow. With each step, she sank about halfway up to her knees. Having come this far, there was no way Amanda was turning back. She had family in that cemetery, and she needed to spend some time with them.

By the time she reached the Callison grave site, Amanda was out of breath and in need of wiping her teary eyes and dripping nose. She had an uneasy feeling this was just the beginning of many tears before she left here. The first stone she came to was that of her brother Samuel Callison. Sam graduated from high school in 69. With his draft number coming up, Sam went ahead and enlisted in the army. He was proud to serve his country. Right out of basic training, he was shipped off to Vietnam for his tour of duty. Six months later, he came home in a plain box draped with the American flag.

Amanda reached in her pocket for a tissue as a tear trickled down her cheek. She recalled how Rev. Johnson sat with her parents listened and consoled them for hours. The service Rev. Johnson conducted at church was beautiful. So many people turned out to show their support. "I miss you, Sam. You were a good brother. After we lost you, Dad's outlook on life changed. Before your death, he had been such a gentle man. Folks in town would seek him out to help them in time of need. He was dependable. But then after we lost you, he took to the bottle. He turned selfish and mean. One day, he simply disappeared. No one ever heard from him again. I don't know if he is still alive or if he too is dead." There was faraway sadness in Amanda's eyes as she looked at the stone. She turned from Sam's gravestone to her mother's stone.

"I miss you, Momma. You were the center and strength of our family. Sometimes in the quiet of the night I would hear you praying out loud to God. You drew your strength from your faith. I'm quite ashamed to tell you this, but somewhere along the way, I seemed to have lost my faith. I'm bitter, and don't know how to get it back. Oh I still believe in God, but not the same as when I was younger. Perhaps if you hadn't died that winter of pneumonia, I might have stayed by the lake. You would have believed me and stood by me in 79."

Amanda allowed herself time to grieve. She openly cried and wiped her tears. Then she turned from her mother's grave to that of Rose Amanda Johnson.

"My little Rose, I often wonder what you would have been like had you been born alive. The day my doctor told me your heart had stopped beating only two weeks before your due date, I wanted to die along with you. That was the moment when my life began to change forever. I will never forget being able to hold your lifeless body in my arms after the C-section. You were so beautiful." Amanda swiped back a tear. "I hope you are happy in heaven."

She cast her eyes down to the snowy ground. It was then that Amanda saw someone else's footprints. She knelt down as her eyes were taking in other indicators as to who may have been there. "Hmm…I'm positive these impressions in the snow and tracks are from a male. Yes indeed, he knelt here for a while, and from the looks of it, he was here not too long ago."

Amanda brushed her hand over the loose snow. Then she returned to a standing position to quickly scout the area. Something caught her eye. She focused her attention on the hemlocks. Amanda had a feeling she was being watched. "It must have been a shadow." Looking down at the packed snow and footprints, Amanda shook her head. "Oh yes, someone was definitely here earlier today." And in her gut, she knew who had been there.

CHAPTER NINE

Morning at the bait shop was abuzz with activity. A new load of wood had arrived for the New Year's Eve bonfire. Peter and JJ were busy with unloading the wood. There would be no slacking off today for these two. They were on a mission to have their work done early so they could head home to get ready for tonight.

Wesley and Stephen were working alongside Peter and JJ swapping stories of their adventures as young men growing up at the lake. Well at least they told the stories that Wes deemed fitting for his son's ears. Wes was hoping that Steve's and his presence was viewed by Peter and JJ simply as preparing for the celebration that was happening there in a few hours. He knew it would be heartbreaking for Peter to know he was keeping close watch of him due to an asthma attack that had landed him in the county hospital for a treatment late Tuesday night.

All four men looked up and stopped their work to watch the police cruiser pull in the lot. Jim Callison got out of the driver's side while his partner Charlie Simpkins got out of the passenger side. Charlie was the senior partner. He always rode shotgun and said he had done his time in the rookie position of speeding after the ruffians in town. Now it was Jim's turn. Everyone in town knew it had been Jim's turn for the past twenty years that they rode together. Jim didn't mind. Charlie was more than a partner for him; he had been a mentor, friend, and father figure guiding him through a rocky time in his life. Other than Jim's wife, Melissa, Charlie was the only one he truly trusted.

As the two state police officers made their way to the men, Wesley suggested that Peter and JJ take a break. "Peter, you and

JJ go on inside and get a cup of coffee. You know how important it is to keep your lungs open. I know you're looking forward to being here tonight. So, Peter, you do as I say. Besides, if you come home wheezing and coughing tonight, I'll be catching it from your mother." The last thing Wes wanted was to have it out with Becky on New Year's Eve.

"Dad, I'm all right! Hey, Mr. C. Good morning, Mr. Simpkins."

"Peter." Wes gave his son a look that spoke volumes. Peter knew that if he wanted to be allowed to be anywhere close to the shop tonight, he had better listen and follow directions. The last thing he needed was for his dad to go home and discuss him with his mother. After his episode on Tuesday night, he knew Becky and Wes were sure to side up against him.

"Dad." JJ nodded to his father who in turn nodded back.

"Son, are you working hard or hardly working?"

"Of course I'm working hard." JJ smiled as he regaled his father with his tale of woes about his work. "You know these two old guys act like they do all the grunt work when it's really Peter and me. Slave labor I tell you!" Charlie Simpkins roared with laughter at the wise mouth on JJ Callison. Stephen picked up snow, forming it into a ball, and hurled it at JJ. After a few more lighthearted comments were exchanged between all gathered in the parking lot, Jim nodded at his son to inform him that it was time for him to leave.

Light jovial bantering continued to be exchanged between the men. Coffee was suggested, and they began to casually make their way to the shop. When almost to the door, Stephen quietly asked Jim if they could have a moment for a private conversation. Jim knew all along that was what Charlie and he had stopped in for. From previously hearing Stephen's voice on the phone, Jim knew this was going to be serious.

Stephen and Jim had stepped away from the entrance. He scuffed the gravel, looked up to see Jim watching him, and waited for him to speak. "Jim, when I tell you what's on my mind, you're going to think I'm crazy and need to be shipped off to some psych ward someplace."

"How about you let me hear what's got you so uptight. Then we'll decide if you need psychiatric care."

Stephen nodded. "Do you believe in ghosts?"

Jim Callison had known Stephen Johnson for close to fifty years. During that time they had played tricks on their sisters, been social deviants, came darn close but never broke the law that they could remember, laughed together, suffered broken hearts together, got drunk too many times to tell about so, Jim figured he knew his friend fairly well. But never in his life did he expect his good friend to be asking about ghosts.

"Um...Well, I..." Jim looked at Stephen with left eyebrow raised. "Are you talking about spirits like your dad used to preach about when we were kids or an actual apparition?"

"I'm talking the real thing." Stephen was stone-cold serious. Jim paused for a moment to allow himself time to process the seriousness of their conversation.

"Well, Steve, I've seen television programs with people swearing that there are paranormal encounters at certain haunted places. I myself have never personally encountered a ghost." Jim intently studied Stephen. "Johnson, you don't look so hot...Do you think you have seen some sort of ghost?" Jim attempted to make light of the situation. "So do you think your daddy is coming down from heaven to chew you out for your drinking binge?" Stephen shifted an eye toward Jim. "Oh, yeah, I heard all the details from Wes when I stopped by last night to pick up JJ."

"This isn't about my dad. Jim, I know this is going to sound totally absurd. Man I think... I think Calli is back in town."

Jim had that same feeling that came across him Tuesday afternoon as he watched the woman skating on the ice. "Let's go for a walk, and you tell me what you know."

Stepping out of the shower, Amanda could not remember when she had enjoyed a more relaxing New Year's Eve day. Tonight she had mixed emotions. When the fireworks went off at midnight, she would be with Kevin, Cass, and Andrew. She was falling head over heels in love with Kevin. Her mother would have warned her not to haste into this relationship. But hey, Momma was no longer here on earth to hound her about the proper ways for a woman to behave; and besides, at fifty-four years of age, Amanda didn't have any time to spare! Then there were Cass and Andrew. It had broken Amanda's heart to hear each of them share with her their pain and grief as they struggled with the news of Ryan coming out of the closet. She was so grateful they had begun to work through their grief and reconciled their differences. This would be a New Year to remember! Drying herself off, Amanda considered her choices of clothing for the evening.

"Let's see. We'll be outside for fireworks and then inside for dancing. Hmmm…decisions, decisions, decisions! Long johns would be good for outdoors however too hot once we're inside, so I'll go with my khaki corduroy jeans and this long-sleeve burgundy scoop-neck cashmere sweater. My hiking boots, and oh, I think one pair of wool socks will be sufficient." Amanda dressed and fixed her makeup and hair in record time. She stepped in front of the mirror for one final look and approved. Now she couldn't wait to see what Kevin thought. With that, there was a knock at her door.

"Come in." Amanda smiled as she saw Kevin come through the open doorway.

"Wow." Kevin's heart skipped about four beats he surmised as he smiled and took in the sight of her. "Amanda, you are beautiful." He stepped over and took her hands in his. Kevin then raised her hands to his lips and gently kissed each one. "Are you ready, my love?"

"I guess so, Kevin." Amanda continued to mentally lecture herself that she had nothing to fear. It wasn't working. "You know, I'm apprehensive about going to the fireworks and then the celebration at the bait shop."

"Yes, I know. And I also know that you would not in a million years ever dream of ruining Cassie's expectations for the night."

"You already know me too well." Amanda squeezed Kevin's hands but not too hard. After all, he is a surgeon, and she wouldn't do anything to jeopardize his career.

"Amanda, I want you to know that Andrew and I have discussed with one another our concern for you. Now don't look at me that way. We both care about you. If at any time while we are at the bait shop you feel a panic attack coming on and you need to leave, we expect you to tell us. We are both here to take care of you no matter what. Oh, and don't worry about Cassie. Andrew will handle her." When Kevin spoke of Cassie and the thought of Andrew handling her, Amanda burst into laughter. Goodness it felt good to laugh even though her stomach was aflutter with nerves.

The countdown had begun—ten, nine, eight, seven, six, five, four, three, two, one, Happy New Year! Kevin wrapped his arms around Amanda and lowered his head so their lips met. While the fireworks exploded over their heads, warmth and desire sent tingling sensations through both Amanda and Kevin. Right at that moment under the nighttime sky with fireworks overhead, Kevin moaned as Amanda responded to his need and slid her tongue into his mouth. She was warm—no, hot—and tasted like honey. Oh how he wanted to skip the dancing and take her back to the cabin and make love to her; for now, he would relish in anticipation of what was yet to come.

Cassie and Andrew stood near Kevin and Amanda lost in their own thoughts as they watched the fireworks. Andrew had been standing behind Cassie during the fireworks display. Now she was turned toward him. Holding her in his arms, Andrew lowered his mouth to her ear, and he whispered, "I love you,

Cassie, and I can't wait to go back to our cabin and make some fireworks of our own."

"I love you too, Andrew. I have a bottle of champagne on ice in our room and something special just for us. With how this year has ended and the new one is coming in, I'm counting on our own fireworks!" Cassie settled back in her husband's arms to watch the rest of the fireworks show.

The festive feeling of the night lingered in the air as the steady stream of people young and old made their way up from the shore of the lake. Some families with children were making their ways to their cars to head home and to tuck their little ones into bed. Others were descending on the bait shop for the New Year's party. When Amanda stepped through the doors with Kevin, she felt like she was a time traveler making a journey back thirty-some years. The people dancing to the music playing on the dance floor were strangers to Kevin, Cass, and Andrew, however, not to Amanda. Some of the men she recognized as having played hockey with her here at the lake. Other men had played hockey with Jim and Stephen on the high school team. Many of the women also shared her past.

Amanda felt the familiar tightness creeping into her chest and squeezed Kevin's hand. Kevin was quickly becoming keenly aware of Amanda's body language. Before the squeeze of her hand, he had already been observing the early signs of panic. With a slight turning down of his head, he whispered, "Breathe, my love. You are in control. Just breathe."

Amanda gave Kevin a pitiful smile as she exhaled a third time. She saw through the crowd of people that Cassie and Andrew had found a vacant table. Andrew made eye contact with her and Kevin. He waved to them to come on over. Keeping Amanda's hand in his, Kevin guided her across the room to their table. Amanda breathed a bit easier as she felt his other hand gently resting against her back. Kevin had no idea how that small gesture was easing her distress.

Within a few minutes of sitting down and getting acclimated, Kevin asked Amanda to dance. Amanda was thrilled to find that Kevin was light on his feet and commanded the lead regardless of the song being fast or slow. After having danced the jitterbug to a number of oldies, Amanda was glad to be gently embraced in a slow dance to the Righteous Brother's "Unchained Melody." Amanda rested her head on Kevin's shoulder while he rested his chin on the top of her head. With Kevin towering at 6'3" and Amanda at 5'10" they molded nicely in each other's arms. They danced flawlessly as one in fluid motion. Kevin quietly spoke the words that Amanda knew she would treasure in her heart for as long as she lived, "I love you." Amanda slowly raised her head so her eyes met Kevin's. There on the dance floor it seemed as though they were one. He had said the words to her that she thought she would never hear again from a man. Did she dare totally give herself to him?

Stephen knew in his mind that he should be in a good mood, after all it's New Year's! The fireworks had gone off without a hitch; people from the community were here having a good time dancing and celebrating the New Year. And with the ice fishing contest that Wes and he had held, the local economy had greatly benefited as well. Johnson had a knot in his stomach and felt miserable while others he noticed were having a real good time.

Wesley, Becky, and Stephen were engaged in conversation with the mayor and her husband when Stephen noticed Cassie and Andrew on the dance floor. It was then his heart sank even lower than before. Stephen figured that if one couple from the Pines was there, the other couple probably was as well. Stephen knew he should be glad that tourists felt welcome to join community events, but he wasn't. These people were major contributors to his foul mood. Actually, one member of the quartet in particular:

the woman named Amanda. He blamed her as the cause of his hangover the other day and his foul mood for tonight's festivities. Then he caught sight of her. She wasn't seated or simply standing; no, she was out there with one of the local men on the dance floor. She was smiling and in conversation with Matt Quinblatt. Matt was a large guy who usually had a scowl on his face. Not tonight. Amanda and Matt were dancing to an old disco favorite. Johnson moaned. "Oh man, the broad not only is a smooth skater, she can even dance like a pro." Without warning, his thoughts cruised down memory lane.

Jim Callison's wife, Melissa, was called out as EMT for a woman who had gone into premature labor. The New Year had come in with a bang as the team assisted a healthy baby boy ring in the New Year. Mother and son were now resting in the county hospital. Riding back to the barn in the ambulance with Butch and Mark, Melissa was glad for the joyful diversion in her night. Her daughters, Caitlin and Elizabeth, were out of the house now. Caitlin was married and mother of a beautiful little girl whom she had named Calli in honor of the aunt whom she had never met. Mel smiled as she remembered how taken back Jim had been by their daughter's act of love.

She knew that Jim still grieved over the loss of his sister. Amanda had disappeared from their lives thirty years ago. Mel also hoped that someday Amanda would hear about her family and how her nieces cherished her from afar. Elizabeth, the free spirit of their daughters, who was more like Amanda than either she or Jim cared to acknowledge, was making her mark on the world as she put it before she'd consider settling down. Their daughter Samantha who was still living at home was soliciting the entire family's assistance in planning for her upcoming wedding this year. A twinge of sadness filled Mel as she realized that this will leave daughter Jordan and their son James Jr. still at home. Soon, all of Jim and her babies would be fully grown. She hoped they'd find happiness that was comparable to what she and Jim had shared through the years.

Melissa smiled as her mind wandered to when she and Jim Callison were high school sweethearts. Through the years, they had witnessed family and friends come together. Some they saw drift away from one another or ripped apart by circumstances. Jim and Mel had triumphed. Their love for one another had never faltered. They were a team and understood that sometimes one had to make sacrifices for the other. Tonight they both were making sacrifices. Melissa knew in her heart that Jim was as disappointed as she that they were not together. Melissa looked out the ambulance window at the stars glistening in the frigid winter sky. She silently breathed the words, "Happy New Year, sweetheart, wherever you are. Be safe and come home to me soon. I love you."

Jim Callison's mood was not festive for New Year's Eve. He was grumpy. Out of all the younger men on the force, none of them had been called in to work the late shift. His last shift had been the 7:00 a.m. to 3:00 p.m. shift on New Year's Eve. Now he was ringing in the New Year by working. He didn't give a tinker's toot about the overtime money he was making. Mel and he had made plans for a festive night together. The evening had begun quiet at home with just the two of them dining together by candlelight. Then the mood was abruptly ended when he was called in to cover the late shift 11:00 p.m. to 7:00 a.m. Jim was tired, and he was running on no sleep since 5:00 a.m. In years past that would not have mattered, but Jim knew his age was beginning to catch up with him. Plus, every time he remembered taking the call from his captain, Jim had to contend with seeing Melissa's sullen face flash in his mind. All week Melissa had talked of nothing else but New Year's Eve. Jim let out a heavy sigh. At least if he had to work he lucked out and was patrolling tonight with Natalie Hashbrook. Natalie is a younger cop transferring in from NYC.

She already had been out on a couple of dangerous calls and proved she has what it takes to work up north in the mountains.

"So, Jim, you've obviously dealt with plenty of New Year's festivities up here. Do you think the night will get busier when the party ends at the bait shop?"

"Oh"—Jim yawned—"I imagine we might have a DWI or two. Hopefully, nothing more than that. I've worked plenty of New Year's that have had devastating consequences. As tired as I am, it would be nice to have a quiet one." The words we no sooner off Jim's tongue when the second call came in, and they were on their way to the first accident of the night.

"Whew." Cassie breathlessly collapsed onto the chair. "It's been a while since we've danced like that." Cassie's face was flushed a rosy pink; her eyes danced with joy as she loving looked up at Andrew who was still standing.

Amanda smiled as she watched her two friends. She let out a sigh a little louder than she had expected. Kevin raised his hand to Amanda's cheek, brushing her hair back from her face so he could have a better look at her. Quietly he asked, "Are you all right? Do we need to leave?" Amanda surged with warmth as she looked into his eyes. His concern for her well-being was evident in his words and gestures. She caught his hand in hers.

"No, we don't need to leave. I am deep breathing to reduce my anxiety and reminding myself I am in control. Nothing is going to spoil our first New Year."

Kevin had already learned in their time together something very important about Amanda. She spoke the truth and meant what she said. Kevin had to wonder if Amanda realized that her control was about more than her panic attacks.

JJ Callison had made it to the New Year's festivities as his parents had promised him he could. This was something special for him to be there without adult supervision. Even though Stephen, Wes, and Becky would be keeping close watch, to JJ they didn't count. They weren't family. JJ had watched Amanda enter the bait shop and had been thinking about their encounter at the lake. Even though she was much older than him and obviously had a man in her life, something was drawing him to her. JJ knew it was unrealistic for a seventeen-year-old male to have a secret wish like he had about Amanda. But there was no harm in pretending for a little while. So from the shadows of the side of the room, JJ watched Amanda and Kevin dance together. He had seen her dance with other men from the community as well. Now his gaze followed them as they left the dance floor and walked to the table they occupied for the evening.

With all the courage he could muster, he walked over to table where Amanda and Kevin sat together. JJ took a deep breath to calm his nerves. Standing in front of Kevin and Amanda, JJ cleared his throat hoping a sound would come out before he totally lost his nerve.

"Excuse me." Amanda and Kevin ceased their conversation and turned their attention to him.

"Yes." Amanda smiled. "JJ, right?" She knew perfectly well her nephew was standing there in her midst. She wondered if he knew just how much he mirrored his father's likeness. How often did he hear that his looks and his mannerisms are like Jim? She wondered does he resent people's comparison of them.

"And what can I do for you, JJ? Do you want to sit down?" JJ shifted his weight from one leg to the other. Amanda could see his internal struggle. She wondered where this predominately one-sided conversation was going. He cleared his throat, sounding like what she remembered of Jim. This young man had no idea what power he held at this moment.

"Well, ma'am, the DJ just announced the next dance. This is New Year's as you know." Amanda watched JJ again shift his weight from one foot to the other before continuing. "And we have a tradition here. Since it's a small community, everyone dances with each other. It doesn't matter if you're part of a couple 'cause everybody knows that at the end of the night you'll go home with your man or woman." Amanda bit the inside of her cheek to keep herself from smiling.

"Oh my pop would skin me alive if he knew I was doing this." JJ nervously sifted his weight yet again.

Amanda tilted her head and raised an eyebrow. No doubt Jim would have words with his son if and when he knew about this encounter. JJ, she mused, is definitely his father's son. Undeveloped charm oozed from him. He looked so serious. Amanda understood how important it was for him to ask her to dance. His cheeks revealed a darker shade of pink. He was embarrassed. Amanda suddenly realized that she wanted to hug her nephew. She couldn't, not yet, for JJ didn't know who she was. This emotion was something new and unexpected. Amanda continued to sit quietly waiting for JJ to make the next move. As he reached out his hand to her, Amanda felt a tear trickle down her cheek. Jim's son, her nephew, was an amazing young man. Then he spoke with poise and certainty in a commanding voice.

"Miss Amanda, may I have this dance?"

"I'd be honored, young man." Kevin had stood with them. Amanda turned to him and gently kissed his lips. "I'll be back. Miss me."

"Oh I will." Amanda did not see Kevin smiling as he sat back down and watched them.

JJ and Amanda fell into step with a song by Jay-Z. Amanda noticed that when the song ended, JJ had a look of disappointment. He thanked Amanda for the dance. Then as JJ began to turn away, Amanda placed her hand on his arm. She watched JJ's expression change as she spoke.

"JJ, would you do me the honor of dancing with me to another song?" JJ's smile was bright enough to light up the whole bait shop. The next song was "Music Again" by Adam Lambert.

When the song ended, it was Amanda who suggested to JJ that they continue dancing. This time, the tune was a bit slower. Aunt and nephew joined hands. Amanda felt a surge of pride as she felt JJ take the lead in the dance. When the song ended, JJ escorted Amanda back to her table. After a brief conversation, JJ returned to the festivities with the younger crowd. A smile of pride brushed Amanda's lips. Jim had obviously taught him well.

Junior McGrath and Shannon Green pulled into the bait shop parking lot. Both Junior and Shannon had grown up here in the mountains. They had gone to high school with most of the folks who were celebrating at the bait shop. Junior was a mechanic at Frank's auto shop in Mayfield. Shannon had sustained an injury while working in forestry and was now collecting disability. Ten minutes before their arrival at the bait shop, they had been drinking at Mike's Pub and hitting on the women. Tom Baxter had thrown both of them out and banned them from returning for the night. The two were fully loaded and were looking for a good time. After all, it was New Year's Eve, and they both needed a woman to celebrate the New Year with.

Amanda had been in the ladies room when Junior and Shannon first arrived on the scene. Groups of people conversing and dancing made it a challenge for Amanda to negotiate through the crowd. Amanda quickly discovered that her path was blocked by two rather large males. They smelled of too much liquor and too little soap. She shivered as the new smell triggered fear within her. She felt herself tightening in the chest. Her breathing became rapid. Panic was soon to follow. Amanda had been in control of herself and her surroundings thus far into the night. She was determined to make it back to the table and the safety of her friends.

"Excuse me. Y'all seem to be blocking my way. May I please get through?"

Amanda suddenly recognized them. She gasped for air. It didn't feel like any air entered into her lungs.

"Breathe—keep breathing as hard as it may be. Keep breathing. I am in control," she told herself. "They don't know who I am. This is to my advantage," she counseled herself.

"Hey, Shann, sounds like we found ourselves a southern bell to celebrate the New Year with." Junior was closing in on what limited personal space Amanda had at that moment. Flashbacks to that night long ago ripped through her memory. He touched her shoulder, and Amanda jerked away. Thoughts of Junior touching Amanda thirty years ago raced through her mind. Her whole body tightened. Panic was rising in her.

"Now, little lady, that's no way to treat my friend here. He's just trying to be friendly." Shannon slurred out his words as he ran his finger through the side of Amanda's hair. The whiff of his breath about knocked her over.

"Please don't do that." Before Amanda had time to further react, she heard an all too familiar voice.

"Hey, Junior, Shannon, didn't you hear the lady? She asked you nicely to not do that and leave her alone." Stephen had come to stand between the two men and Amanda.

She breathed a momentary sigh of relief. For once in Johnson's life, he had done the right thing. The look she saw in Stephen's eyes chilled her to the core. He reminded her of a renegade dog growling and ready to attack. *Too bad it took him thirty years,* Amanda thought. Stephen's scent also filled her nostrils with memories. These memories were different than the one's evoked by Junior and Shannon's presence. Amanda realized that even though it had been a while since Stephen had showered and shaved, a woodsy pine-scented aftershave lingered on his body. How she used to love his scent. She noticed a hint of gray in his hair and slight wrinkles of age near his eyes. Stephen's face revealed that the years between them had been difficult for him as well. He had a few scars. *No doubt,* she thought from barroom altercations.

Amanda attempted to slip past Stephen as he lectured Shannon and Junior. His size and the congestion of people at that particular moment made it impossible for Amanda to leave. Then when it seemed she might be able to get by, she felt Stephen's hand on her arm. As she began to pull away, she felt his grip tighten. She remained still. "Breathe, Amanda, just breathe," she commanded herself. Stephen finished speaking to the men. Amanda watched Junior and Shannon wander off like a couple of shamed old coon dogs with their tails between their legs.

"I'm sorry, miss, and do apologize for those two. They really are harmless."

Stephen was filled with a sense of familiarity. She smelled of earth and a hint of rose petals. He could breathe her in all night. Stephen studied Amanda's face. Her makeup was beautiful. However, he noticed the scars that were not hidden. No amount of makeup would totally disguise the fact that she had been through something horrific. He had watched Amanda dance with Kevin, Andrew, some of the locals, and yes even JJ Callison. He'd listened to her talk and laughing with her friends. He had watched her skate and was certain he had seen her at the cemetery. Stephen, now drawn by her scent, knew he had to dance with Amanda. He had to feel her in his arms. This woman was a bit shorter than his Amanda and walked with a limp. Stephen knew in his heart he would know the truth if he held her and danced with her.

Amanda wanted to grab a hold of Stephen and shake some sense into him. She fought to keep control of herself. Revealing her identity to Johnson was not part of her plan. In her mind, she was screaming, *Harmless? Johnson, how can you still think they are harmless?* Amanda's blood was beginning to boil. After all this time, he still was just as blind as he had been in '79. Amanda looked down at his hand holding on to her arm.

"Well, Mr...Ah, Stephen, I do appreciate you coming to my aid just now. Would you kindly let go of my arm so I may return to my friends?" The music had begun. Firmly holding on to Amanda's arm, Stephen piercingly looked into Amanda's eyes as he spoke.

"Amanda, honor me with this dance."

It was not an invitation or a request. Amanda knew she was being commanded. She also knew that she was treading on very thin ice. The music was familiar to both of them. How many times had they previously danced to the Bee Gee's "Too Much Heaven?" In moments, their feet were in sync with one another. Amanda, lost in the moment of dancing with such familiarity, didn't notice people stopped dancing. They stepped aside and gave over the dance floor to Amanda and her partner. Realizing that they were making a scene on the dance floor, a chill ran up her spine. She was in Stephen's arms. The ice was breaking, and she was sinking. Memories were flooding over her.

Another slow song began. Stephen had not let go of Amanda. Her quiet protests had been ignored as he swept her into motion. Again, people cleared the way for them as they glided along to Steven Tyler singing "I Don't Want to Miss a Thing." Every step was in perfect alignment. Together they flowed as one on the dance floor. Amanda knew she not dared to look up at Stephen. She could feel his breath upon her head and knew he was looking down at her. His right hand was placed on the small of her back; his left hand held her close to him. It took everything in Amanda to keep her composure. After all these years, how could something that had gone so wrong now feel so right?

When the song ended, Amanda was one fraction away from a full-blown panic. Tears were seeping from her eyes. Not raising her eyes to meet Stephen's, Amanda sniffled and choked out, "Thank you, Stephen, that was very lovely. Now if you'll excuse me, I must be getting back to Kevin."

She slowly raised her chin so their eyes met. What she saw in Stephen's eyes frightened her. Amanda racked her brain to try to remember a time in which Stephen Johnson had looked at her with such concern. Where did that tenderness come from? She stammered as she spoke.

"I...Ah...I'm sure he's concerned about me." Much to Amanda's dismay, she realized that Stephen still had a hold of her. Now for a brief moment, she looked again into his eyes. "Please let me go. I can't do this," she softly pleaded. His hand dropped from her arm. He didn't move from the spot where they had just been dancing. Stephen simply watched as Amanda fled across the room.

Amanda had made eye contact with Kevin who was making his way to her. She pressed on knowing that in a few steps they would be together. Kevin would hold her, Amanda assured herself, and sooth away her fears. Then her worst fear came true. Junior and Shannon were back.

"Surprise, sweetheart, now don't you look pretty." The stale stench of liquor mixed with coffee on Junior's breath permeated the air as he belched in Amanda's face. The smell nauseated her.

"We've been watching you and Johnson. You know our good buddy don't dance too much anymore."

"Yeah." Junior belched. "On the account of that Amanda Callison, she broke his heart." Junior was unsteady on his feet and bumped into Amanda.

Amanda was on an emotional roller coaster. First Stephen had taken her down memory lane with painful memories of their love for one another, and now these two were again reminding her of all the darkness and bitterness of her past. At that moment, something snapped in Amanda. It wasn't panic. No, this time it was pure unadulterated anger. With her index finger poking into Junior's chest, Amanda went on the attack.

"You moron, get off me! Never! Do you hear me? Never again! As everyone here is now my witness, never again!" As Shannon drew his arm around her shoulder, Amanda turned and brought her knee up into his crotch as hard as she could. Shannon let out a moan of pain that caused everyone in close proximity to stop dancing and chatting to observe him doubled over in pain.

"You idiot," Amanda hissed through clenched teeth. "I tried to be nice although I don't know why. But you wouldn't listen. You certainly haven't changed over the years."

It was then she felt Junior reaching out yet again to touch her. His words were lost somewhere in Amanda's thoughts. Now Amanda was fully charged. Her anger was hot enough to melt a hole in the polar ice cap. Without warning or hesitation, she spun around, deflecting Junior's arm with her right hand and planted her left hook alongside of his nose. Blood spew everywhere, sending people away. As Junior grabbed his now broken nose, he cursed out words Amanda had not heard in a very long time. Falling to the floor, a dazed Junior looked over at Shannon who was crumpled in pain.

Amanda bent down so they would hear her words intended only for their ears. "You two pigs had me once," Amanda hissed. "You destroyed my life, my family, and my friends." The muscles over her eyebrows drew together. Then with total calmness, Amanda made her declaration. "I swear on my Rosie's grave that if either of you two slugs ever again attempts to touch me, I'll kill you two worthless puddles of pond scum with my bare hands." With that Amanda stood up, turned, and fled out the door of the bait shop into the cold of the New Year.

CHAPTER TEN

Kevin was close enough to hear and see the entire altercation between Amanda and the two sorry excuses for men. He couldn't reach her before she fled the shop in the dead of winter. Andrew and Cassie already on their feet headed toward Kevin with coats in hand.

"What happened to cause Amanda to bolt?" Andrew asked with a raised voice to be heard above the noise of the crowd.

"Two guys whom I assume are from Amanda's past were pressing in on her. She appears to have had a flashback to something that happened to her," Kevin continued on to share what he had witnessed before Amanda bolted.

"Flashback...past...oh no!" Cassie's voice quivered with distress.

"Cass," Andrew quietly spoke, "there's a lot we need to explain to you. However, now is not the time. I suggest you fix a cup of coffee and have a seat. I have a feeling it's going to be a long night." Andrew placed a gentle kiss on top of Cassie's head. "Kevin, you should go look for Amanda. She's going to need medical attention. I think I had better go see how Mutt and Jeff crumpled up over there on the floor is doing."

Andrew made his way through the crowd of onlookers that had gathered around Shannon and Junior. Some he noted were regaling one another with accounts of Amanda decking the two men who were now sitting in chairs. What he saw amazed him. Amanda had brought down these two rather large men. Andrew shook his head. "Still water runs deep so they say, and it is obvious that when truly riled, Amanda is a force to be reckoned with. I do believe we all have underestimated our girl!" Andrew stepped closer while assessing the situation. "Excuse me, I'm a doctor. Is there anything I can do to help?"

Becky Jones was holding ice on Junior's nose as he whimpered. "Oh shut up, you big baby. You got what you deserve." Becky applied more pressure than necessary to make her point while looking over at Andrew. "You're a doctor?"

"Yes, I am. Dr. Andrew Phillips, cardiologist at Johns Hopkins in Baltimore, Maryland. My wife and I have a vacation home at the Pines." Andrew stood next to Junior and caught a whiff of his breath. Becky, still holding the ice to Junior's nose, looked at Junior with disgust then back at Andrew.

"Thanks for taking a look at them." Becky scrunched her eyebrows together. "Are you sure you want to get your hands dirty with this lowlife?" Andrew nodded.

"Do you happen to have any latex gloves? There's a lot of blood here." Wes went into the kitchen and produced a box of gloves that were used in food prep. "Great, these will do fine. Your name is Wesley, right?"

"Yeah, that's right. Becky, my wife, here has already called for the rescue squad to come, you know, since we didn't know the extent of their injuries."

"Good judgment call." Turning with a scowl, he looked at Junior. "You are fortunate to have friends who obviously care about your welfare. So, slugger, what's your name?"

"Junior, Junior McGrath—Ow! That hurts!" Andrew continued working his fingers on Junior's swollen bloody nose.

"How many fingers am I holding up?"

"Two dang nab it."

"Good, now do you remember what your nose connected with to receive a break like this?" Becky had appeared with a basin of warm water and towels to clean up Junior's bloody face.

"Ow! That crazy woman broke my nose?" Junior's deflated ego hit the floor.

"Afraid so, slugger. Becky, if you wouldn't mind, after cleaning him up, fill a bag with fresh ice for Junior here and make sure he doesn't pass out."

"Sure doctor, Andrew, thanks."

"Now let me see to our other victim."

Stephen was surprised to discover that one of two doctors attending to the injured men. Right now, Stephen wasn't sure Junior and Shannon deserved such kindness from a stranger. A short while ago, Johnson had thought of Amanda to be like a brittle flower. She certainly had proven she could take care of herself. For some reason, the thought of her knuckle colliding with Junior's nose made the hair stand up on Stephen's neck. He shivered as he heard Shannon exclaim, "She had this crazed look in her eyes and went wild on us. I'm not going to be able to stand for a week."

"You got what you deserved," Becky snipped. "At least now you won't be screwing any women for a while."

"Well at least you didn't have your life threatened tonight!"

Becky, Wesley, and Stephen froze for a moment and turned their attention to Shannon. Andrew, still kneeling next to Shannon, let out a slight chuckle. "Surely you jest, and now who'd want to threaten a big man like you?"

"That"—He decided not to hold his tongue—"crazy woman who attacked us and then flew out of here that's who!"

Andrew knew Amanda was capable of many things; however, murder was not something he could fathom. "I beg to differ with you. The woman you and your friend were sexually harassing is one of my dearest friends. I know for a fact that she would not seriously threaten to take someone's life."

Shannon yelled, "I'm not making this up!"

Stephen had known Shannon for too many years to count. He knew that Shannon was one to fabricate about many things; however, this time Shannon was dead serious. Stephen lowered his voice so Shannon had to listen.

"Shannon, besides beating the crap out of you, what did Amanda say to you?" Stephen saw genuine fear rise in Shannon's eyes.

"I don't feel so good." Andrew immediately swept into action, checking Shannon's pulse. "She's going to kill me, Johnson. Calli's ghost has come back to kill me for what I did."

"Calli, what do you mean? Shannon, what exactly did the doc's friend Amanda say that makes you believe she's Calli?" Stephen felt he had just stepped on a loose piece of shale and was sliding down the mountain.

Shannon took a deep breath and began, "She yelled at Junior and me."

"That's because you deserved it you," Becky snarled.

"Beck, please, let him go on." By now Wesley had wrapped his arms around Becky. He could feel the tension in her body, and if not careful, she herself might strike out against Shannon. The women in these mountains sure could get angry in a hurry.

"So before my sister cut you off you were saying Shann…"

"Oh, yeah, Johnson, she said, 'You two pigs had me once. You destroyed my life, my family, and my friends.'" Stephen's heart was racing fast, and his mind was swirling. He was certain that was no ghost any of them had seen.

"Shannon," Stephen swallowed hard, "what else did she say?"

"I don't know if you want to hear this, Johnson."

"Yes I do. Now spill."

"She said, 'I swear on my Rosie's grave that if either of you two slugs ever again attempts to touch me, I'll kill you two worthless puddles of pond scum with my bare hands.'" A hush fell over the bait shop following the collective gasp of onlookers. Becky was the first to recover.

"Amanda's back. My prayers have finally been answered!" Stephen hadn't realized that Becky had broken out of Wesley's hold and had placed her hand on his arm until she gently squeezed it. "She's outside in this frigid weather. Oh my…Steve, you have to go…You have to find Mandy."

Andrew had been gazing around the room. Unfortunately, he did not see Kevin or Amanda in their midst. She was still outside, and now Andrew was concerned as well. He knew the possibilities of hypothermia were high considering Amanda had fled without her coat. His eyes met Cassie's. Cassie knew by Andrew's expression that it was time for her to join him at his side in the chaos of the night.

"Stephen, you should know that Kevin took off after Amanda when she bolted out of here."

Stephen sighed. "Oh great, now we'll be looking for two instead of one." He yelled out, "Wes, we need to contact my brother Phil and let him know we need a sheriff's patrol for a possible search and rescue."

"Already on it!" Wes had his cell phone, Becky's cell, and the bait shop phone all going at once. "Mel is already on her way to pick up Junior and Shannon. I'll fill her in on the rest when she gets here." Stephen looked at the two beat up men.

"They'll live. We need Mel for Amanda." Stephen was raw with pain. "And, Wes, when you get through with your calls, you better call into the State Police Barracks. According to JJ, Jim is working this morning. Whatever you do, don't tell him that Calli is outside somewhere. We don't want to give the man a heart attack!" Stephen added under his breath, "At least until he gets here."

"Calli," Cassidy gasped. "Did you say Calli as in Calli the Crusher?" Everyone stopped and looked at Cass.

"And how do you know about the crusher?" Stephen ran his fingers through his hair his face drawn as he was processing this news.

"Amanda was regaling Kevin and me with a story about ice skating with her brother and their friends." Cassie looked at Stephen, then at Andrew, and then back at Stephen. "Oh my goodness, Amanda grew up here, didn't she? You Stephen are one of the guys she skated with. Andrew?"

"Yes, Cassie, this is Amanda's hometown. Let's go sit down, and we'll sort this out together. Stephen, let me know if there is anything we can do."

JJ and Peter had headed out as soon as they saw Amanda flee from the bait shop. The two were tracking her until she cut up the lakeshore and into the woods. Without flashlights, they could not follow her footprints. The bitter cold was aggravating Peter's asthma and JJ's hands and feet were feeling the cold. Kevin had met up with the teens and was circling back with them. They definitely needed more help in finding Amanda. As the three came to the bait shop door, Stephen stepped out into the cold. He looked first at Kevin.

"I take it you didn't find her out here waiting for you to come to her rescue?" Stephen's tone was as icy as the lake.

"No, I didn't, and I am gravely concerned for her well-being. Perhaps it would behoove you to cut the sarcasm and listen to what JJ and Peter have found. Actually, Peter, you go on inside. You're wheezing mighty hard there. My friend Andrew is also a doctor. I'd like him to make sure you're okay." Peter did not hesitate to follow Kevin's directions. JJ remained outside with the men.

"Stephen"—frustration radiated from JJ's voice as he spoke— "if you two are going to stand there acting like jerks, then we'll never find my aunt." JJ was tired, cold, and sorely afraid of what might happen to Amanda.

"All right then, JJ, you tell me what you know." Stephen's patience was wearing thin rather quickly. The last thing he wanted to do was take his anger out on the boy. JJ proceeded to tell Stephen how far up the lake they were when they lost a visual. Amanda had slipped into the woods, and they couldn't see to track her.

"Good work. Now here's what I want you to do for me. Becky and Wes are working out coordinates for search parties. You tell them what you just told me." JJ was listening intently to everything Stephen said. "Then when your dad gets here, you tell him to stay here until I get back. You are not, and I repeat, you are not to tell him that your aunt Amanda is out here. I will tell him. Do you understand me?"

"Yes, sir." JJ looked at Stephen and then at Kevin. "Don't worry, Kevin, we will find my aunt Amanda. We can't lose her again."

When the door closed, Stephen faced Kevin. "Look, Kevin, I know you're worried about Amanda, but really, you're not prepared for searching for her up here in the outdoors."

"Stephen, you need me with you. I specialize in trauma emergency care. Right now, Amanda is in the first stages of frostbite, perhaps heading into secondary frostbite and hypothermia. You don't know her medical history and I do. She will need medical attention stat."

"All right, you can come." They walked for a while in silence with the flashlight on Amanda's tracks. "So I hear Amanda told you about growing up here at the lake and the nickname we gave her." Kevin could hear the tension in Stephen's voice. He pitied the man walking beside him and what he had lost.

Static was heard on Stephen's pager. "Stephen, call the shop on your cell." Then there was more static.

CHAPTER ELEVEN

Deputy Phillip Johnson and his partner Mike Thompson walked through the door of the bait shop pavilion. Becky ran across the room and flew into Phil's arms. "Gee, sis, Happy New Year to you too!" Becky was quickly unwrapped from her brother's body by Wesley. "Thanks, Wes. From the looks of this place, there's been quite a party here."

"Oh you don't know the half of it. I'll tell you over coffee." Wes continued, "This is a New Year's Eve that will go down in this town's history. I can guarantee you that. First there was the brawl involving these two drunks over here"—Wes motioned to Junior and Shannon—"and now a search and rescue."

Phil and Mike followed Wes over to the coffeepot. Phil sniffed for freshness. "It's a fresh pot." Wes nodded.

"Mike, I was going to have you escort Melissa and the team to the hospital with Junior and Shannon. From the sounds of it, we need the rescue squad for more pressing matters than those two over there. Get some coffee and babysit them for me until we can get another rescue company to come get them."

Phil and Wes were just sitting down with Andrew and Cassie when Stephen and Kevin came in. Everyone looked beyond them in hopes that Amanda would come straggling in behind them. With another round of introductions out of the way, they got down to serious business: saving Amanda. Phil called into dispatch for more assistance in the search and rescue they were now conducting at the lake. Many of the town's people, who had left the bait shop soon after Amanda disappeared, had now begun to return with winter clothing on and flashlights.

Sirens could now be plainly heard from the approaching rescue squad and the state police cruiser. For a moment, everyone inside of the bait shop was silent and looked around at one another.

"So who's going to tell Jim and Mel about Amanda?" Becky quietly asked.

Phil stepped away from the area Wes and Becky had set up as command post. He came over to stand at Stephen's side and responded, "We both will."

Quietness filled the bait shop as Jim entered through the door. People who had stayed or returned to help in the search watched Jim as he surveyed the room. He saw Phil standing with Stephen. Becky and Wes were at the command post they had set up coordinating and communicating with search parties already out looking for Amanda. Jim also took a mental note of how many people whom he surmised had attended the festivities were still there. Melissa had also arrived and was now standing next to Jim. They briefly hugged before Jim turned his full attention to Phil Johnson.

"Phil, I see things are well underway."

"Jim." Phil looked deep into Jim's tired eyes. He cleared his throat. "I asked for you to come and assist us because I knew you'd want to be a part of this search. The last thing I need is for you to be mad at me on the first day of a new year."

"Phil, you know I always will do what I can to help you." Jim took in the seriousness of Phil's voice. His face was grim. "Why should I be upset about you searching for a fifty-four-year-old woman from Baltimore, Maryland?"

Stephen cut in, "Well, Jim, these folks here"—nodding toward Cassie, Andrew, and Kevin—"are her friends from Baltimore. Dr. and Mrs. Phillips have a vacation home at the Pines. Our missing lady and the other gentleman here are staying with them for the week. They were all having a nice time when Shannon and Junior here came in. Then she bolted out to the lake."

"So you're saying that the lady fled because of these two?" Everyone was silently nodding in agreement. "Okay. So who did Junior and Shannon get in a fight with to look like death warmed over?"

"Well"—Stephen rubbed his chin—"remember the other day when I asked you if you believe in ghosts?"

Jim scrunched his eyebrows, a trait of his when he was figuring that what he was about to hear would be disturbing. His eyes appeared smoky with confusion. The color immediately drained from his face. Melissa took charge. "Sit down, Jim, before you pass out." She placed her hand on his shoulder for support. "Continue, Stephen."

"My gut was right, Jim. Calli is back in town. She's staying with those folks over there." Stephen pointed toward Cassie, Andrew, and Kevin. Everyone could hear the pain in Stephen's voice. "I talked with her. I danced with her and didn't know." Stephen's voice cracked. "Mandy…she's out there somewhere on the ice all because these two jerks! They could not keep their stupid mouths shut or their slimy hands off her yet again!" Stephen didn't realize how loud he had become until he saw the onlookers' expressions. It was then Stephen felt the gentle touch of his sister. "Oh, sorry." Becky hugged her brother to console him.

Color was gradually returning to Jim's face much to Melissa's relief. She continued to hold on to his shoulder. She could feel the tension rising and knew it would not be too long before Jim would again be on his feet.

"My sister." His voice caught with emotion. "Oh no, not Manda!" He raked his fingers through is hair. The pain in Jim's voice shook like a thunderstorm sashaying against the mountains. Jim was now rising to his feet. With a visible shiver, Jim in an instant changed from disoriented brother to state police officer in charge. He looked at Phil and Stephen. "She'll die out there! We have to find her. Let's go!"

Amanda was exhausted and freezing cold. As near as she could figure without being able to see land markers, she had traveled about a mile north on the western edge of the lake. Another mile and she would be able to start making her trek northeast toward the eastern mountain ridge. Then when she came to the lakeshore, she would climb up the mountain to her grandmother's cabin. She had to get to Gentle Spirit.

The cold has a funny way of taking over one's body. Amanda was no different in thinking she could make the unrealistic journey up the mountain in the dark. Looking back toward the bait shop to the south, she could see people with flashlights. It appeared that many were heading south or east out onto the lake, looking to see if she was held up in an ice shack no doubt. "Really, Johnson, you and Jones should have figured I'd be too smart to go that way. Ah, but it was a good try." Amanda could at least smile to herself for being one step ahead of them in that regard. Now her nephew and Johnson's nephew were proving to be quite the trackers. She'd have to keep an eye out for them. Blowing on her hands that now had minimal feeling in them, Amanda shook her head in concern. "I'll have to have Kevin take a look at my hand." Pain from her altercation with Junior and Shannon and the severe cold radiated throughout her body. Amanda tripped and fell. "Oh my, my legs hurt. This is not good. My feet feel like someone has put them in quick-hardening cement." Using her right hand, Amanda was able to steady herself as she got to her knees and then on to her aching cold feet. "Oh my, I need strength. I have to make it to Grandma's."

Jim and his partner Natalie Hashbrook were heading south on the lake in their patrol car. He knew this lake like the back of his hand. Anything out of the ordinary heightened his senses. Jim had been studying the movement he had seen up ahead for a while.

"Natalie, tell me what you see in the shadows there on the ice to your left? Do you see that movement going from the west in toward the northeast side of the lake? Shine the searchlight over there. Is that a person walking out there?"

"Oh yeah, Jim, you're good."

"I do believe we've found our missing fifty-four-year-old woman from Baltimore, Maryland, also known as my missing sister. Keep your searchlight on that spot and continue at your present speed. I have to contact Phil Johnson." With that, Jim reached over to the mic to contact Phil at base control.

"BC 15, this is car 381, come in. Over."

"Car 381, this is BC15, read you loud and clear. Over," Phil responded.

"Phil, will you contact the rescue squad to be standing by? We have a visual on our missing woman. She's heading northeast on the lake near the western edge by Saile's landing and appears to be heading northeast. At this point, we have yet to make physical contact. Over."

"Roger that, 381. Melissa informs me she'll be standing by. We hear you're heading out to meet a real wildcat. Let us know if you need any backup. Over." Jim opened the mic as he laughed.

"Phil, if I need backup for this one, I'm in serious trouble. Over."

Amanda yawned. She felt sleepy. Her legs were tired. Everything about her was slowing down. She saw the light. "Oh, the light, it's coming closer. Oh my, I'm really dying. I just know it! Oh please. God, if you're listening, I don't want to go to hell—anything but hell!" Amanda stumbled as she heard the voice.

"Amanda Callison, or as I hear you prefer to be called, Amanda Newman, this is the state police, and we are authorized to bring you in for emergency care. Manda, if you treasure your life, stop where you are this minute!"

"Who the…" Amanda knew that voice. "He called me Manda…Oh no, I'm not dying. This is worse than hell…It's Jim!" Amanda couldn't breathe; she was gasping for air. "Oh, God, I don't like your sense of humor. I think I'd rather be dead and seeing you right now atoning for my sins…anything but this! Of all the people who could be working tonight, it has to be him, just my luck!"

Amanda's legs were not moving as she was commanding them to. Every part of her body ached and felt as though shreds of glass were stuck in her. Amanda kept walking at a slower pace than what she intended. With every step she took, she slipped and almost lost her balance. The cold was having its way, and Amanda knew that frostbite and hypothermia was a distinct possibility. Perhaps if she moved out farther onto the lake she could shake him.

"Amanda, you thickheaded twit, stop where you are!" Jim's voice was loud and seemed to be echoing in her head. *He sounded mad*, she thought. *Now what could he possibly have to be mad about? Was his vacation ruined?*

"Natalie, stop so I can get out and corral my sister." Natalie heard what she thought was anger in Jim's voice and was hesitant to stop. She slowed down and kept inching the car forward. In her peripheral vision, she could see Jim glowering. "Stop the car! That's a direct order!" Natalie stopped as commanded. Jim flew forward. He fortunately was able to firmly grab the dash before plowing head first into the windshield.

"Sorry," Natalie squeaked. Jim gave her a look of disgust before softening.

"I'm sorry too, Nat. I shouldn't have yelled at you. You've done a great job. My sister who is freezing to death out there deserves my wrath not you."

"Noted!" Nat smiled and breathed a bit easier now. "So what is our plan of action?"

Jim smiled back at her. "Here's how this is going to play out. I am getting out and will join her on the ice. You stay here in the cruiser. I don't need you getting frostbitten as well. When I have secured my hold on her, I will escort her back here. When I'm in the car with her, we will make contact with base camp. You will be bringing us in. Got it?"

"Yes."

"Oh, and one more thing…Nat, roll down the window so you can hear what we say to one another. I may need you to collaborate my story that I have not attempted to murder my sister." With Natalie laughing and shaking her head, Jim stepped out onto the ice. It took him a moment to gain his footing. He was amazed that Amanda was still upright after all this time.

"Amanda Kathryn Callison!" Jim's words stung as Amanda listened to the commanding voice. Much to her dismay, Jim sounded like her parents had sounded when chastising her for something reprehensible she had done. "Didn't I tell you to stop where you are?"

Amanda took a painful step, slipped, and recovered, never turning to look at Jim. "I guess lost I was and didn't hear you— lost in my own thoughts." Amanda was obviously becoming disoriented. She yawned and giggled.

Jim was annoyed. "Oh, you heard me all right, little sister, and you chose to ignore me." Jim reached out to touch Amanda's arm.

"Shh…quiet. They'll hear you. Now go away before I hit you with this hockey stick." Jim looked at Amanda in her hiking boots sliding on the ice as if skating; she was holding her left arm in her right hand. "Now go away, Cop, this doesn't concern you. I'll fight my own battle. Thank you."

Amanda was not making any sense now. Jim had a heightened sense of urgency. "Natalie, radio Melissa in rescue 33 and tell her we have probable case of early hypothermia." Natalie didn't respond to Jim. He heard her talking with Mel as Amanda slipped and went down. She hit her head and saw stars.

"Oh, Momma, that hurt!" Jim knelt down alongside of his sister. It was then he got his first good look at her.

"Oh my...Oh, jeez, Manda. It's you, the woman at the Quik Mart! We talked and you pretended you didn't even know me." Amanda was trying to get up; however, her strength was almost gone. She yawned and lay back on the ice.

"Go away. I'm too tired to make it to Gentle Spirit. I'll rest, you go ahead." Amanda began to laugh; she rambled on saying something Jim could not understand. This was rapidly turning into a desperate situation. Jim removed his backpack. He pulled out an emergency blanket for trauma for Amanda. Now near frozen, Amanda did not struggle as the instant warmth surrounded her. Jim gently lifted her into his arms. Amanda yawned and attempted to move. "Put me down!"

"No, Amanda, you're coming with me." Jim walked over to the cruiser to find that Natalie had the rear door open for him. He briefly looked at Nat, nodded in thanks, and placed Amanda in far enough so he could join her. Wrapping his arms around Amanda, Jim quietly spoke. "Manda, we're going to get you help."

Amanda sat quietly next to Jim. She couldn't look at him. Her mind was fuzzy. Panic hit like a blast of arctic air. Her voice came out as a whisper, "Let me out!"

"Not on your life, little sister, not on your life. I'm not letting you go. You have to stop running. I know what Junior and Shannon did to you thirty years ago, and I know what they did to you tonight. Now, when we're both warm, we're going to sort this mess out together." Jim had leaned forward to speak with Natalie as she drove. She held the mic open for him.

"Rescue 33, this is car 381. Come in."

"Car 381, this is rescue 33. We read you loud and clear. Is it a pleasant family reunion?"

"Rescue 33, I'll give you commentary about the family reunion later. Now for the record, we have found and are bringing in a fifty-four-year-old Caucasian female who was reported missing.

Preliminary physical finding in poor lighting include frostbite, probably early hypothermia, abrasions, and swelling to the left hand as well as severe limping of the right leg. She appears to be somewhat disoriented to time and place. I went ahead and wrapped her in the emergency trauma blanket."

"Car 381, thank you for your report. Good call with the blanket. We are standing by waiting your arrival. Rescue 33 over and out."

Amanda was shivering so hard her teeth were chattering. Jim kept his arm around her to prevent the emergency blanket from falling away from her. Amanda yawned. Jim softly encouraged her to stay awake. He began to explain what was happening and why she was in the squad car. Amanda looked at Jim with confusion as she attempted to process what he was saying.

"Manda, you're not being arrested. We're taking you to Mayfield Community Hospital. See, we're at the bait shop, and we have the ambulance waiting for you."

Amanda's teeth were chattering as her body shivered. "Kevin," she whispered.

"I'll find Kevin for you, sis. I promise. But first we have to get you to the hospital."

"Don't promise me. You let them hurt me. They came back." Amanda clumsily slapped at her arms under the blanket. "I can't wash it off." Amanda had melted into tears.

"Go ahead, sis, cry your heart out if that will help. This time I will protect you."

Natalie quietly opened the door slight way so that Jim could get out with Amanda when they were ready. Melissa was standing by with the stretcher positioned against the side of the cruiser. Melissa's gentle touch to his cheek and quiet tone brought him back to the task at hand. His sister needed emergency care.

CHAPTER TWELVE

"Ouch." Amanda was disoriented to her surroundings. The sounds pounded in her head like native war drums. She turned slowly in the bed focusing on the room and then like a clap of thunder reality set in. "Oh…God help me I'm not dead! This has to be a nightmare." No. Amanda's mind was becoming clearer. She was awake, and she had been through a horrific experience. Smacking her chapped lips together, Amanda decided her mouth was also dry and pasty. "Oh crap, morning breath." Amanda felt her face with her right hand to discover she was on oxygen. "Great." She sighed as she gently laid her arm and hand back on the bed. She gently raised her throbbing left hand to discover it was wrapped in gauze bandage, and an IV was attached in her arm. "Oh, ow, ooh…What did I run into?" Amanda's whole body ached and still felt chilled even though unbeknownst to her for the past five hours she had been in a hypothermia blanket. Amanda felt the tube lying across her thigh. "Oh wonderful plumbing to boot…How humiliating!" Amanda lifted her head to scan the room.

"Kevin," she croaked in a strained voice. Amanda was devastated to see that Kevin was stretched out as much as possible in the upright chair not designed for sleep. "Are you awake?"

He yawned, stretched, and smiled in just that order. "Yes I am. Welcome back, honey." Kevin stood, moaned, and stretched again before coming over to the side of Amanda's bed. He leaned down to kiss her on her forehead. Then he gently stroked her cheek with his finger. Amanda saw tears in his eyes. His voice choked with emotion. "I thought I was going to lose you last night." He ran his fingers through her hair above her ear while studying her features. It was if to imprint her into his memory. "How are you feeling today?"

"Peachy," she croaked with a smile that was attempting to hide her pain. Her voice sounded worse than an old bullfrog in the marshes of Van Loan's pond. Amanda began to weep. "I'm sorry, Kevin," she whispered.

Kevin lowered the bed rail and sat down next to Amanda. "Shush." He touched his finger to her lips. "You have nothing to be sorry about."

"But I ruined everything for you, Cassie, and Andrew." Kevin gently brushed a lock of hair from Amanda's cheek and gently kissed her close to her ear. Amanda felt a surge of warmth radiate through her body; she shivered.

"Amanda, you didn't ruin anything." She saw pain in Kevin's eyes. If she only knew how he had been blaming himself for not protecting her from Junior and Shannon and her ordeal on the ice. *If only*, Kevin kept repeating in his mind, *if only*. He had kept a silent vigil by her side through the early morning hours and would continue to keep his vigil. Amanda had once again come near to death in her life and now lay there in the hospital bed in pain. "I love you," he whispered. Kevin was leaning close to brush his lip against Amanda's while he was massaging her shoulders. Amanda moaned in sheer pleasure. Kevin's touch was relaxing and exciting her at the same time.

The clearing of a throat brought Amanda and Kevin back to the moment. They both looked up to see Amanda's nurse standing at the end of the bed. "Good morning, Amanda, I'm your nurse for the day. My name is Danielle LaVoni." Her smile was warm and caring. "I'm here to take your vitals."

Kevin stood glanced at the wall clock to see it was now 8:30 a.m.; he lightly squeezed her hand. "Honey, while you're being attended to, I'm going to step out to speak with Cassie and Andrew. I know they are anxious to hear of your status. "

Jim Callison and Natalie Hashbrook ended up working overtime on New Year's Day. Their hair-rising shift had left both drained and in unpleasant moods. After securing their statement from Amanda, they were heading back to the barracks where Natalie would submit the formal statement and then she and Jim would go home to their respective families. On the way to the hospital, they had discussed who would take lead in ascertaining the statement. Since Jim was definitely emotionally involved, Natalie would question Amanda.

They entered the hospital main entrance at 8:45 a.m. on January 1, 2010. With coffee cup in hand, they stopped at the information desk for their law enforcement visitor's pass. Natalie observed Jim's demeanor, followed his cue, and remained quiet as they took the elevator up to the third floor. She couldn't imagine what it must be like to discover that your sibling had returned home and you were the one responsible for saving their life. The elevator stopped, the bell rang, the door opened. Jim extended his hand indicating Natalie was to exit the elevator first. She waited for him to be at her side then the two state police officers proceeded onto the third floor for official business.

As Jim and Natalie approached Amanda's room, they heard laughter. Tension eased in Jim's tired body. "Nat, do you hear that? That's a good sign!"

"Yes, it sounds like a party is going on in there." Jim stopped about five paces from the door. Looking down at Natalie, he put his hand on her shoulder.

"Nervous?" Jim waited for a response.

"A little bit." Natalie then let out a heavy sigh. Jim smiled and nodded.

"Nat, you're a good cop. You certainly proved yourself last night."

"By almost putting you through the windshield!"

"Yeah, well, I'm still here, so we'll forget about that for now." Jim winked and could see some of the strain easing from Natalie's face. "Right now, we have a duty to perform. You are going in there as lead officer, and I am your backup. Although I don't expect too much resistance…On second thought, we are dealing with my sister." Natalie was now smiling and chuckled.

"Thank you, Jim. I'll do my best."

"I know you will. Let's go!"

The conversation in Amanda's hospital room ceased with the knock on the partially closed door. As soon as Cassie, Andrew, and Kevin saw Jim and Natalie, they excused themselves from Amanda's side and promised to be in the waiting room. Kevin stopped by the door, reluctant to leave.

"Natalie, will you escort Kevin out into the hall and wait there with him for a few minutes while I speak with my sister in private?"

Natalie nodded and escorted Kevin from the room. Jim walked over toward the bed Amanda was lying in and placed his hat on the windowsill. Then he turned and gazed down at her banged-up body lying in the bed. Jim's emotions were raw. In the early morning hours, he had found his sister and at the same time had almost lost her for a second time in his life. For a moment, neither one spoke. They only stared into one another's eyes.

"Amanda, you look like the lake got the better of you." Jim could not continue due to his churned-up emotions.

Amanda was not smiling. "Are you here to interrogate me?" The rough sound of her weak voice hit Jim harder than he expected. Jim pulled up a chair and sat down as it was evident Amanda was not going to extend the invitation to do so.

"Manda." Jim blinked and sniffled back what Amanda thought was perhaps tears. She hadn't been called Manda in more than thirty years; it had always been Jim's pet name for her. She remained silent while intently watching Jim.

"Tell me the truth. Were you planning on contacting me before you left the lake?" Amanda turned away. She could not look at

Jim. How could she explain to him her motives? "Amanda, you weren't going to contact me, were you?" When she was finally brave enough to look at him, a chill ran through her. Jim glowered at her with such anger that made the hair stand on her arms. All Amanda could do was whisper.

"No, I wasn't going to contact you." She swallowed hard. "I didn't want to cause you any more pain."

"Any more pain? What in the world are you talking about? How would you contacting me have caused pain? Don't answer that!" Jim's face was beet red with rage. "Did it ever cross your mind, little sister, that for the past thirty years—including this week, I might add—I tried to find you? You do remember talking with me in the Quik Mart, don't you?" Amanda nodded afraid that if she spoke tears might fall. "Manda, I have worried about you. I have grieved over you not being a part of my life and my family's life. You are here and were going to leave without contacting me." The scornful look in Jim's eyes penetrated into the depths of Amanda's soul. "My sister used to care about people's feelings. Obviously, you're not that sister I remember."

Amanda closed her eyes. When she opened them, what Jim saw was alarming! Amanda's mood was equally as changeable as Jim's. Anger came shooting out of her like deadly lightning bolts, and when she spoke, her voice about sliced him in two. Amanda's voice cracked as she strained to speak.

"How dare you! How dare you throw it in my face that I do not care about people's feelings! You, my own brother, swore on our mama's grave that you would watch out for me. You, my own flesh and blood, abandoned me just as Johnson did! Yet you have the audacity to sit here acting like some pompous self-righteous big-time state police officer babbling on about how I don't care." Amanda's voice cracked again. With the energy Amanda had left, she huffed, "Oh go suck an egg!"

Amanda turned her face away from Jim as if to dismiss him. Much to Amanda's displeasure, Jim remained seated in the chair by her bed. They both sat in silence. Footsteps drew Amanda and Jim's attention to the door. Seeing Natalie quietly enter, Jim turned to Amanda; his expression instantaneously transformed from angry brother to professional doing his job. "Natalie is here to take your statement for our report on the events at the bait shop and lake this morning."

Amanda's steely eyes locked with Jim's. The hair on the back of Jim's neck stood up as he heard the sharp tone in her voice. On Tuesday, she had used a sweet lilt in her voice to make Jim believe she was from Maryland. Now even as she lay in the bed looking ravaged by a fierce battle, her tone reflected her family roots. "Are you staying or are you going?"

"Staying," Jim replied in a commanding voice.

"Great." Amanda rolled her eyes. "You may want to go. After all, what I have to say may disillusion you about your friends. Oh, wait a minute. What am I thinking? It doesn't matter what I say, I'm your sister, not one of the good old boys. It's too late for you to care. You better leave, so Natalie can do her job!"

Amanda overexerted herself and began to cough. She turned onto her side and moaned in pain as she reached for her glass of water. As she sipped, allowing the coolness to ease the discomfort in her throat, she concentrated on finding a calm place in her ravaged mind. Returning the glass to the tray, she turned to Natalie. "I'm sorry you have to work with him!"

Natalie calmly spoke to both of the siblings about what she expected of them while she took Amanda's statement. Jim stood and walked to the window in silence. He leaned against the sill listening and watching as Amanda made her statement about the events of New Year's Eve. When she finished, Natalie thanked her and wished her well. Natalie exited the room into the hall. That left a silent Jim still leaning against the sill. Amanda refused to look at him or be the first to speak. She was certain he would look at her with pity. She was embarrassed that Jim had heard all the gory details of the night before and the event in '79. Why couldn't he have simply believed her thirty years ago? He had betrayed her trust. Now he could stand there all day for all she cared. Finally, Jim straightened up to full standing position and picked up his hat. It was then he spoke to Amanda. His voice was quiet and direct.

"I'll be going now, little sister. Before I do, let me remind you that this isn't over between us. We're going to resolve this one way or another." With that said, Jim walked out of the room. She closed her eyes and listened to the succinct footsteps of Jim and Natalie as they made their way down the hall from her room.

Jim, now dog tired, dragged himself into his home to find Melissa and three of his five children lounging in the family room in front of the television. Popcorn that had not found its way to someone's mouth was on the floor and being consumed by the dog. The cat curled up asleep by the hearth didn't move. This is his family, the home he and Melissa had created. How fortunate he was to have the solace of his loving family to come home to after horrendous shifts like his last one. Mel rose up out of the chair. She met him and folded herself into Jim's arms.

"Happy New Year." Jim lowered his mouth onto Melissa's lips. His often playful, gentle, arousing kisses were not there today. Melissa slightly pulled back and quietly commanded Jim to go upstairs to rest. Jim nodded and turned to make his ascent.

"Samantha," Jim's tired yet authoritative voice brought his daughter to attention.

"Yes, Dad."

"Pour me a double shot of bourbon and bring it upstairs to me." Samantha was on her feet heading toward the liquor cabinet when Melissa stopped her.

"I'll get it and take it up with me. Sam, you're now in charge down here. Please prepare dinner and don't wait for your father and me. We have a lot to sort out, and he desperately needs to sleep." Having said that, Mel lifted out of the cabinet two glasses and a bottle; Jim would not be drinking alone. Melissa looked at their children who still lived at home. She counted her blessings as she headed up the stairs to be with Jim. Samantha; her sister, Jordan; and younger brother, James, all settled back down to finish watching the movie. From upstairs, they heard water running in their parent's bathroom shower and music filtering down from their parent's room.

Stephen and Wesley were running on no sleep for about twenty-four hours. A catnap at the bait shop didn't count. Both men were exhausted and heading for another cup of coffee. After Amanda was found and transported off to Mayfield Community Hospital, Junior and Shannon were arrested for disorderly conduct and sexual harassment. Stephen and Wesley decided that no charges would be filed against Amanda. It was the least they could do given the circumstances. Neighbors who had participated in the search effort continued to congregate at the bait shop for what seemed to Stephen like eternity. All he wanted to do was to go home and crash for a couple of hours before opening up for the ice fishermen; much to his dismay, that never happened.

It was now midafternoon. Wesley was assisting a family that had come into the shop to rent skates. Stephen desperately needed a few moments alone. He knew that if he went outside, someone was bound to find him and start talking about last night. The events of last night were still too raw in his mind. He decided that the best spot to be alone would be downstairs in the pavilion. It was quiet and now quite cool as the heat had been shut down. Stephen made his descent, turned on the overhead lights, and surveyed the scene. He began to pick up soda cans for recycling and garbage that had not found its way to the trash bins. As he made his way around the room, the events of New Year's Eve flashed through his mind in Technicolor. He remembered how Amanda had smiled at Kevin, how she danced with her nephew JJ. Stephen's breath caught as he recalled how it had felt to hold her in his arms. The look in her eyes as they danced and his attempt to talk with her would haunt him for some time. Her spunk of youth had been replaced with a fragility that he supposed had come from too much trauma in her life. "Why?" he asked himself. "Why had he been so stupid and let her walk out of his life? Calli had been his everything. What could he say to her to ever repair the damage that had been done to her so long ago?"

Lost in his thoughts, Stephen walked over to the broom closet. He hauled out the large push broom and dustpan. Pushing the dirt and garbage along the floor, Stephen came to the spot where Junior's blood had turned the cement floor rust colored. Holding the broom in one hand, he squatted down and ran his finger across the now dry floor. "Junior, you finally got what you deserved. I hope Calli presses charges against you two jerks and that this time they stick. With what you both put her through, neither of you deserve to see the light of day ever again." Stephen shook his head and stood up. He picked up the broom and continued to make his way around the room.

CHAPTER THIRTEEN

Melissa, who had now changed her outfit for the third time, let out a heavy sigh as she looked at herself in the mirror. Jim was sprawled out on the bed where he was enjoying watching Melissa scrutinize her appearance. A devilish smile had made its way into Jim's eyes. Over the years, this scrutiny is one of the things he had grown to love about his wife. Regardless of the occasion, Melissa always put great thought into her appearance. In Jim's eyes, Melissa always looked beautiful whether in her Sunday finest or in work clothes with her hair disheveled while chucking wood from the back of the truck to be piled.

"Oh for goodness' sake, Mel, what may I ask is wrong with this outfit? Do you honestly think Manda is going to care how you are dressed when you meet her?" Seeing the first spark of fire in Mel's eyes, Jim took defensive action. "On second thought, don't answer that!" Mel smiled.

"Smart man, Callison, that's one of the many reasons I love you." Jim scrunched his eyebrows as he always did to brace himself for the rest of Mel's comments. "You usually know when to shut up. Yes indeed, smart man!" With that, Jim was on his feet and wrapped his arms around Melissa's waist.

"Since I was rather exhausted yesterday, perhaps later I can show you just how much I love you?" A devious gleam was in Jim's eyes, and a lazy smile tugged at his lips. Melissa gently brushed her lips against his.

"Perhaps you might."

Andrew knelt in front of the fireplace, moving partially burned logs and added some kindling, which quickly ignited in the hot coals. As the fire began to blaze, Andrew added a couple of more logs. Cassie came in with a fresh pot of coffee and treats for them to munch on. She placed the items on the table in front of the couch where Amanda rested and walked over to where Andrew knelt by the fire. Andrew stood up and folded Cassie into his arms. Neither one of them appeared to be concern about showing affection in front of their friends; after all, they had a lot to celebrate this year. The preceding year had come to a rocky end. Their love had been tested and proved that theirs is a love to last forever. A knock at the door broke the intimate moment. Amanda, who had been resting on the couch under Kevin's watchful eye, stirred at the sound of the knock. Andrew and Cassie, hand in hand, went to answer the knock at the front door of the cabin.

"Jim, Melissa, how nice to see you." Andrew stepped aside. "Please, by all means, do come in." Cassie's warm smile and gracious welcome that followed Andrew's touched both Jim and Mel's hearts. Andrew and Cassie made them feel as though they had all been friends for years rather than meeting for the first time around forty hours ago.

"I'd like to introduce you both to our grandmother, Mary Freeman." The old woman nodded. Her smile revealed a gaping hole where teeth used to be. "Gran has been hounding me to get her down here to see Amanda. We hope we're not intruding on you folks. If this is a bad time, we'll be happy to come back later." Jim held his grandmother by the elbow to steady her.

"Oh my goodness, you certainly are not intruding. Of course you're all concerned about Amanda. Mrs. Freeman, it is nice to make your acquaintance. Please do come and visit with us for a while. Amanda is in here resting on the couch. We were about to have coffee, would you all care to join us?" Cassie asked as she looked around at their three guests. "I will be happy to make tea or hot cocoa if you'd rather have one of those."

"Coffee is fine," both Jim and Melissa asked for Cassie to not put herself to any extra trouble on their account. Their sole purpose for the intrusion is to see Amanda. Cassie excused herself to go into the kitchen to acquire three more mugs while Andrew escorted their guests into the great room.

When Andrew entered the great room with Mary, Jim, and Melissa, Kevin sat on the couch with Amanda's head resting on his lap. Even though the fire was giving off plenty of warmth in the cabin, Amanda was covered with a blanket. Amanda's left hand continued to be bandaged and held close to her chest. Her cheeks, nose, and right hand were still discolored from the frostbite. Snuggled under her blanket, she had a hot water bottle on her feet as they had sustained second-degree frostbite. The effects of hypothermia still lingered, causing her to be very drowsy. She was fortunate to be alive given the fact that when Jim found her it was two degrees above zero with a wind chill of ten below.

Jim escorted their grandmother over to the couch. Andrew hurriedly moved the coffee table and brought over a chair for Mary to sit in. After being helped into the chair by Jim, Mary bent down, reached over, and drew Amanda's hand up to her lips. Her wrinkled thin lips were soft and warm against Amanda's cool skin.

A tear managed to find its way to the surface and fell down Amanda's cheek. This did not go unnoticed by the old woman. With the pad of her thumb, she traced the line of the tear down granddaughter's cheek. Amanda didn't know what to attribute her wave of emotion to as the tears began to stream down her cheeks. She only knew that at that moment as much as she loved being close to Kevin, she wanted to be in the arms of Gentle Spirit. It seemed as though everyone else understood that need at the same time and accommodated the two of them. Mary took Kevin's spot on the couch, and Amanda lay in her arms. Then the others quietly excused themselves to the kitchen to allow grandmother and granddaughter time alone.

It didn't seem as though the tears and heart wrenching crying would ever stop. Amanda, now exhausted, looked up from Mary's shoulder. "I love you, Grandma, thank you for coming," Amanda whispered and then returned her head to Mary's shoulder.

Mary ran her fingers through Amanda's hair. "Child, I hear you had some wild notion that you could walk to my cabin from the bait shop dressed for summer in the dead of winter."

Amanda began to speak, only to be hushed by Mary. The old woman spoke quietly. Her voice was only to be heard by Amanda. Her words were soothing. All the years of running, hiding, and avoiding were coming to an end whether Amanda was ready or not. Another tear attempted to escape.

"No more tears. You are a strong woman. You draw your strength from your momma and me. Now it's time for you and your brother to put aside this feud and start being family again. I'm getting to old for this drama between the two of you." Again Amanda attempted to insert her thought only to be silenced yet again by Mary. "Here's the way it's going to be. I know Jim wants to have it out with you this afternoon." Amanda made no attempt to conceal her alarm. "Don't you fret. I've already put the brakes to his ideas. I'm inviting your friends to join our family for a meal at my cabin. You, your brother, and his family will be there tomorrow, and then we are going to settle some things that have gone on for too long. Having your friends there may just help keep you two civil with each other." Amanda, now exhausted, once again dropped her head to her grandmother's shoulder. "James Matthew," Mary called out, "I know you've been doing your best to hear our conversation. You come along in here now and see your sister. We won't be staying much longer as Amanda is plum worn out."

Jim came in as commanded and sat down next to Amanda. A lump the size of Lake Champlain lodged in his throat. He wasn't usually at a loss for words; however, taking in the sight of Amanda slumped against Mary looking so helpless was more difficult than he had expected.

"Manda." Jim smiled in hopes that she wouldn't see how unnerved he was at this moment. "I must say you look a sight better than you did yesterday."

Amanda didn't attempt to smile; it simply was too exhausting. As she began to speak, she made a croaking sound followed by a round of coughing. It was becoming a joke between Amanda and her friends. The cold, her yelling at Jim out there on the ice followed by hysterically crying had done its toll on her. When she finally spoke, her tone was one of politeness as if they had once been good friends rather than being siblings. "Thank you. You look a lot better yourself. I also want to thank you for bringing Grandma here to see me. It really means a lot to both of us." Weariness resonated from Amanda as she coughed and moaned again. Years of unresolved tension resonated between sister and brother.

"Manda, I hoped that we could talk about some stuff. That is, if you're up to it."

"I told you this visit is not for too many questions. Can't you see your sister is exhausted?" Mary scowled at her grandson. Jim paid no attention to the look he had received too many times to count in his life. He was watching Amanda's eyes. Her eyes didn't sparkle as they had on Tuesday at the Quik Mart. The pain associated with her injuries was evident. How had the old woman known this would not be any more than a social call? Oh how he hated it when she was right, and that was most of the time.

"It's all right, sis, we can wait until you're stronger. In the meantime, let me introduce you to my wife, Melissa." Melissa, who had been standing with Cassie just inside the great room, came over to join Jim by the couch. She too knelt down beside Amanda.

"Hello, Amanda, it is a pleasure to finally meet you. I must say I'm looking forward to hearing your side of some of Jim's stories about our family. I also hope we can get to know each other and become friends. I never had a sister and would like for you to be mine."

Amanda didn't have the energy to speak more than a whispered, "Melissa, although I don't remember anything after getting to the bait shop, I owe you a debt of gratitude for caring for me at the shop and on the way to the hospital."

"I'm just glad we both were able to come to your aid. After all, Amanda, that's what families do." Mel gently placed her hand on Amanda's hand. "You look like you need to rest."

Amanda smiled with gratitude for Melissa's astuteness in assessing the situation. Her head was pounding, and she ached all over. To her surprise, Jim leaned over and hugged her before he stood up to assist Mary to her feet. She smiled as Mary leaned, over whispered in her ear, and planted a small kiss on her cheek. Amanda's past had finally caught up with her. There would be no more running. At that moment, she felt a sense of calmness come over her. She let out a sigh as Kevin attended to her needs while Andrew and Cassie accompanied the guests to the door.

The festivities of the ice fishing contest had come to an end. Floyd Parkers Jr. was awarded the trophy for first prize and a new Polar Therm Extreme Tip-Up Kit. Chester Tompkins came in second and received an Arctic Fire Tip-Up and a twenty-dollar gift certificate toward any item in the bait shop. Twyla Hancock beat out her brother Otto for third place. She won an Arctic Fire Tip-Up Light and two free cans of worms to be received at any time for fishing on the lake.

"On behalf of Stephen Johnson and me, Wesley Jones, whom most of you already know, we would like to thank you for your participation in this year's ice fishing contest. Twyla I especially want to congratulate you on holding your own against all us men. How about next year you round up some more women to make the contest even more exciting?" Twyla beamed for the recognition she was given and gave Wes a thumbs-up. "Hey, folks, give yourselves a round of applause for a great contest."

As the hooping and whistling erupted, Becky Jones took a long hard look at her brother Stephen Johnson. Like Wes and her, Stephen was exhausted. While Stephen smiled along with the others, his eyes conveyed a dark, troubled mood. Becky quietly picked up a package of fish hooks lying on the counter and sauntered over to the end of the counter where Stephen stood. She did not make eye contact with him but simply lay the hooks on the counter and quietly stood beside him. Stephen glanced down at his sister. He draped his arm over her shoulder. Becky in turn slid her arm around Stephen's waist and gently squeezed. It was then that they made eye contact. Stephen kept his voice quiet as to not allow others to hear their conversation. "What was that for?"

"Thought you just might need to know I love you." Becky squeezed Stephen again.

"I love you too, Beck. Will you do me a favor?" Stephen was now withdrawing his arm from Becky's shoulder while Becky cocked her head a bit concerned about what the request might be.

"Sure, you know I'll do whatever I can for you." Her tone was intent.

"Help Wes close up the shop for me. I have to do something." A flash of alarm shot out of Becky's eyes. Stephen knew from his recent behavior of excessive drinking that Becky had reason to worry. He squeezed her shoulder for reassurance. "Don't worry." He then gently brushed his knuckles against her cheek with brotherly affection. "This something doesn't include wild turkey or old grand dad. I'll call you later." Becky nodded and watched Stephen quietly slip on his coat and head out the side door to his pickup.

CHAPTER FOURTEEN

The room was quiet when Amanda stirred. Cassie was sitting in the chair next to the couch with knitting on her lap. Her eyes were closed. Guilt shot through Amanda as she watched Cassie peacefully rest in the chair. Her actions and the actions of others from the lake had caused undue pain and worry for her friends. Somehow, Amanda had to make it up to Cassie, Andrew, and Kevin. Amanda realized that before she thought of a plan to thank her friends, she needed to get up and attend to more pressing needs. She tried to do it without disturbing her.

"And where are you going?" Cassie had already put aside her knitting and was by Amanda's side as she was still attempting to steady herself.

"Bathroom…Ah, Cass, I may need some help."

Cassie had her arm around Amanda. "I already figured that and am here to help."

"Where are Andrew and Kevin? Don't tell me they have abandoned ship." Cassie laughed at Amanda's attempt for humor with her situation.

"No, they haven't abandoned us. Andrew and Kevin decided it would be best to get rid of one of the rental cars. You are obviously in no shape to return your car. So our amazing men drove down to Mayfield to drop off Kevin's rental car."

"They both are pretty amazing, aren't they?"

"Yes, indeed they are."

A smile crept across Amanda's face as she looked at Cassie. The journey to the bathroom and back was taking its toll on Amanda. Still she was getting tired of lying on the couch. Making their way back into the great room, Amanda paused. "Cass, would you mind helping me into the chair by the fire? I think I would like to sit up for a while, and hopefully, we can have a chat that is long overdue."

"No problem. I think that is an excellent idea." As the two women were busy getting Amanda situated in the chair, they heard footsteps on the front porch followed by a loud knock. "I wonder who is here now."

"Cass, please, you be careful. We're here alone, and I am not exactly in the best shape to defend us." Cassie chuckled as she looked at Amanda attempt to wave her bandaged hand in the air. She looked out of the window to see Stephen Johnson standing there. She hastily opened the door, welcomed him, and invited him to come in out of the cold. His smile and nod were returned to Cassie with guarded politeness.

"Hello, Cassie. I heard that Amanda was discharged from the hospital earlier today and hope that I might see her."

"Actually, Stephen, Amanda is just settling down again to rest. It's been a rather busy afternoon with her family visiting. Let me see if she is up to a short visit with you." Cassie's loyalty and protectiveness of her friend was clearly made known in her tone of voice and body language. Stephen remained standing in the foyer of the cabin. He could hear the muffled voices of the women as they spoke. The soft squeak of a floorboard indicated Cassie's approach. Her smile didn't reach her eyes as she spoke. "I'll take your coat for you and then show you in for a short visit with Amanda. If you'll follow me, our patient is sitting up in a chair near the fire." As they entered the great room, cheerfulness replaced the guarded tone Stephen had heard only a few moments ago in Cassie's voice. "Amanda, I bring you company. I've already informed Mr. Johnson that he is not to stay too long as you are quite tired." Cassie shot Stephen a look that was easily understood as "and I mean business buster."

Stephen walked over to the chair that Amanda was seated in. She noticed that his face looked rather haggard. After hearing various accounts of the New Year, she attributed it to lack of much needed sleep. Amanda whispered a thank-you to Stephen for the flowers he had brought her. She smelled them before laying them on the table alongside of her chair. A coughing jag hit her again. Cassie attended to her need and then excused herself to give them some privacy. The two sat quiet for what seemed to Stephen like eternity. He watched her avoid making eye contact with him as she had done on New Year's Eve. Amanda paused and then glanced at him.

"Stephen I…" Her voice cracked as she strained to be heard. "I guess I should have been expecting you. Becky was at the hospital to see me last night." Amanda noticed a worried frown creep over him. "Even through all the pain medication that was making me drowsy, I could tell she had an ear full for me. Then, shortly after she left, your brother Phil showed up for a brief visit. It seems the Johnson family has not lost their touch for berating people." Amanda's eyes were glistening as tears trickled down her cheeks. Another coughing jag struck, and her voice was now barely a whisper. She was afraid that before too long she would be reduced to writing notes to communicate.

"Amanda," Stephen's voice drifted off as he appeared to be at a loss for words. His head hung down. Amanda could see that he had his eyes closed as he so often had done when they were younger. She could tell that Stephen was carefully choosing his words before speaking again. And then as she expected, he raised his head and looked her straight in the eyes. "This isn't how I wanted to begin our conversation. However, if it makes you feel any better, I will apologize for my meddling sister. You remember how protective Becky was of me when we were younger. As for Phil, I have no idea what would cause him to speak unkindly to you. He was a vital part of your rescue."

"I just bet he was." Amanda now wished she had returned to the couch. She was uncomfortable—her hand ached, her feet throbbed, and she longed to lay her pounding head down. "Stephen, please get Cassie for me." Amanda laid her head back against the softness of the chair and closed her eyes. The distress in her voice sent a stabbing pain through Stephen's breaking heart. She looked so helpless, so fragile, not at all like the spitfire young woman he remembered who had left the mountains so many years ago. In the past few days, Stephen had come to realize his own accountability in the story of his life with Amanda. He knew without a doubt that he was just as much to blame as Junior and Shannon for Amanda's condition. He was the one who was ultimately responsible, yet it had been so convenient for him to blame her leaving so many years ago. Somehow he had to make amends with her. If only she would forgive him. Perhaps then he could begin to truly live again. She felt the slight pressure of his hand on her arm as he quietly stood. He walked over toward the kitchen only to be met halfway by Cassie. Together, the two of them assisted Amanda back to the couch. Cassie was suggesting to Stephen that perhaps he should leave when Amanda interrupted her. Again, Cassie excused herself, leaving Amanda and Stephen alone.

"Stephen," Amanda's eyes revealed her fatigue as she whispered, "you and your family can rest assured that as soon as I am well enough, I am out of here. I have no intention of further intruding in your lives."

"I'm sorry you feel that way, Amanda." Stephen chose his words carefully as he quietly spoke. "I guess I was…am hoping that we can try to make some sense out of what has happened between us."

"Us." The weariness in Amanda's voice stabbed Stephen in the depths of his soul. He watched her close her eyes as if to blink out a tear and let out a very heavy sigh. "Stephen, after we buried Rose, you were not the same man I had fallen in love with. I needed you, and all you did was push me away."

Stephen's voice caught. "I didn't mean to. I just didn't know how to reach out to you. Calli, please believe me." The sound of her old nickname rolling off his tongue sent goose bumps over her. The look of yearning in his eyes was almost too much for Amanda to bear. "You meant the world to me. You were the bright spot in my life. You were my—well, for lack of better words—my everything."

"It didn't seem that way to me," Amanda whispered. "Your words and actions said otherwise. Do you remember what you used to say to me?"

"Yes." Stephen blinked as moisture stung his eyes. "I told you I would do anything for you."

"But you didn't, Stephen. If you loved me, truly loved me as you proclaimed, then how could you abandon me first when we lost Rose and then when Junior and Shannon…" Amanda's strained voice cracked as she dropped her thought. She paused. "You were supposed to protect me. You were my best friend!" Amanda felt herself on the verge of a crying jag and intentionally drew in a deep breath to regain control. "Do you remember the day when you swore on my mother's grave? Do you remember exclaiming that you would always be there to take care of me? Stephen, where were you when I needed you most?"

"Calli, I expect what I'm going to say to you here and now will sound kind of lame. All I ask is that you listen. Please give me a chance." Amanda nodded. "I was scared. I didn't know what to do to help you. I'm ashamed to say that I was afraid to let you see me for my weakness." As Stephen continued to speak, his revelation shed a whole new light for Amanda on their past. Her years of bitterness toward Johnson were rapidly melting like a warm spring thaw. The heaviness that had enfolded her heart for all these years was lifting. Her own accountability along with Stephen's was smacking her on the back of her head as she listened.

"When you left, Calli, I was beside myself. My world was totally shattered." Amanda saw raw pain in Stephen's eyes. He wasn't holding anything back. "Calli, the day you disappeared something in me died. You didn't even say good-bye, and I think that is what hurt most. You were my best friend, and you just left."

Amanda began to open her mouth only to have Stephen reach his calloused finger up to her lips to silence her. Amanda felt his gentle touch linger against her lips. Her emotions were coming unglued, but she knew she needed to listen. Stephen deserved to have his say. She at least owed him that much. "I haven't been able to love another woman as I loved you. Oh, I've tried to love again." Stephen paused. Amanda swallowed hard as she waited. "I simply couldn't trust a woman to not rip my heart apart as you did. Believe me, I haven't lived in celibacy all these years." A smile crept over Amanda. "You can ask your brother." Amanda raised a brow wondering where he was going with this. "I was checking *all*"—he emphasized *all* with a hint of a smile in his eyes—"of you out while you were in the Quik Mart."

As Amanda opened her mouth to respond, a piece of wood in the fireplace exploded into fire. She gasped and jumped, pulling her bandaged hand in a protective position over her chest. For a moment, Stephen thought he saw genuine fear in her eyes. Without hesitation, Stephen placed a protective hand on hers. The feel of his hand on hers was too much to bear. Why was he being so gentle so caring? Tears spewed from her eyes uncontrollably.

"Calli, that day after you left the Quik Mart, Jim warned me you were out of my league. Your brother is right. You have always been out of my league. You are a better person than me. I am sorry for not comforting you and for not sharing my...our grief with you. I'm sorry for not protecting you and for not believing you. I should have trusted you over Shannon and Junior. I only hope that someday and somehow you will forgive me."

"Forgiveness." Amanda's voice cracked yet again as she sniffled and wiped aside a stray tear from her cheek. "Forgiveness seems to be the theme of this vacation. You know, a wise old woman has been counseling me on forgiveness. As usual she's right! Stephen, it's beyond time for both of us to let go of the past. Yes, I forgive you. Will you also forgive me?"

What happened next came without any further words being exchanged between them. Amanda and Stephen were in each other's arms hugging, hanging on to one another for dear life, as they wept together the tears they had forbidden to share with one another thirty years ago. Their lips met in haste, plundering and consoling one another as they grieved over their past. When they were finally quietly holding one another, it was Stephen who broke the silence.

"So, Calli"—Stephen brushed a piece of hair from her cheek—"where do we go from here?"

Amanda sighed. "I don't know. As you know I have begun a new relationship with Kevin. I'm learning to trust again and ready to take a chance with him. He may not be too keen on sharing me with my former boyfriend." Amanda entwined her fingers with Stephen's.

"I know how much he cares about you. It was pretty obvious while we were out looking for you on the ice. Don't worry, I won't try to steal you back from him. I guess I just want to know if we're still friends…if we can be friends."

"I guess we should start by taking it one day at a time. Down the road, we may discover that we really don't like one another."

Stephen laughed, reached up, and cupped Amanda's chin in his hand. "This day has ended much better than I anticipated. I look forward to seeing where the future takes us." Cassie cleared her throat as she came into the room. Shortly thereafter, Stephen took his leave.

It had been a long day. Amanda was exhausted and did not hesitate to accept Kevin's invitation to assist her to bed. When Amanda returned to her room from the bath, she discovered that Kevin had prepared her bed for her. The bedside lamp was on and provided a gentle glow to the room. On the nightstand was a glass of water accompanied by the appropriate doses of her prescriptions. Amanda walked over to the side of the bed where Kevin waited for her.

"So, my dear doctor, what drugs are you expecting me to take and what are the side effects?"

"How perceptive of you. Yes, you are expected to take the meds I have laid out for you. One pill is your antibiotic and the other is your pain reliever. Now the flexoril will make you very relaxed. You should feel it begin to take affect within twenty minutes. Having said that, it is time for you to get in bed. Amanda, before you give me any kind of argument, let me state that both Andrew and Cassie, in that order, have informed me that if you resist your meds I am to tell them." A defeated tired smile was produced on Amanda's lips as she extended her palm for her pills. Amanda did not protest, which pleasantly surprised Kevin. She even allowed Kevin to make sure the pillows were comfortably under her head and her left wrist rested on another pillow. Amanda yawned as Kevin dimmed the bedside light to night-light.

"Kevin?"

"Yes, Amanda."

"Please stay with me. I don't want to be alone."

Amanda had not known that Kevin was already planning on staying whether she wanted him to or not. Amanda's request just made his life a bit easier. He walked around to the other side of the bed and gently sat down to not cause Amanda unnecessary discomfort from moving the bed. Kevin kicked off his shoes and picked up the extra blanket Cassie had provided for him. "Just in case Amanda doesn't want to be alone," she had said. He lay on his side facing Amanda. Kevin took her right hand into his. He bent over and tenderly kissed Amanda. She sighed and yawned in contentment.

"Amanda, I will take care of you. Now, my love, close your eyes and rest. I'll be here when you wake up I promise."

Her breathing was hypnotic, making it easy for Kevin's mind to wander and wander; it did. In a matter of days, Kevin had fallen in love with the woman who had cheated death not once but twice in her life. Perhaps most amazing for Kevin is the fact that he was to be a part of her life both times. In the quietness of the night with a hint of light glowing in the room, Kevin allowed his thoughts to return to the first time they met.

July of '99 was brutally hot. The average daily temperature was hovering between 95 and 105 with an oppressive heat index. For three consecutive weeks, the health department had issued code oranges and reds in Baltimore City. The sultry nights were not much better dipping down to a balmy 85. Kevin a practicing trauma reconstructive plastic surgeon had recently been hired at shock trauma as assistant director of trauma emergency. He was working on that Saturday when the call came in. "A forty-four-year-old woman who was riding her '85 Harley was sideswiped by a passing T-Bird heading south on I-95 one mile south of the 695/95 interchange. The driver of the T-Bird was in serious nonlife-threatening condition. She was being taken to South Harbour Hospital via ambulance. The woman riding the Harley had not faired too well; that was an understatement. Due to her injuries, she was being transported via medivac in to shock trauma. Kevin remembered how amazed he was to hear that the EMT had talked with her before she slipped into unconsciousness. When the team brought Amanda in to shock trauma, Kevin was flabbergasted by what he saw. Even with the helmet she had on, there was no way this woman could still be alive and not have brain damage.

As trauma team leader, Kevin positioned himself next to Amanda's head. He assessed Amanda's immediate needs and directed his team into action. She faintly moaned as Kevin lightly touched her bloody, fractured face. "Amanda, I'm Dr. Wentzel. If you can hear me, squeeze my hand." Amanda immediately responded and attempted to speak. He looked in disbelief as she tried to speak through broken teeth and swollen lips. She had strength he had never before witnessed in a trauma patient. This could be both an advantage and hindrance for her recovery. Her neck had been stabilized at the scene for transport. "Amanda, you need to relax for me. We're going to take this collar off now. I need you to lie very still. We need to work on your throat, just a little pinch." Kevin felt a tear form in his own eyes as he remembered how brave Amanda had been as they locally anesthetized her neck, cut, and inserted the trachea tube. "This should help you breath better." He remembered how she opened her eyes for a brief moment, making eye contact with him. Fear radiated from her. Yet as he held her eyes in his, Kevin knew in his heart that somehow Amanda trusted him. "Amanda, I'm going to take good care of you."

Kevin's thoughts returned to the present. He looked over at Amanda as she stirred in the bed only to reposition herself in her sleep. Then he allowed himself to return to their previous encounter. He remembered how he progressed from the ER to the OR with her. A neurosurgeon was called in to assist Kevin as he began the arduous task of trauma reconstructive plastic surgery to her face. His procedure was specifically intended to stabilize Amanda. Then when Amanda was out of critical condition and had begun to heal, Kevin's reconstructive plastics colleagues would continue on with countless other surgeries she would require. Following Kevin's trauma surgery, the orthopedic team picked up with reconstructing her legs. Her left leg was broken in three places, and her right hip was shattered. Kevin smiled as he remembered how through it all Amanda's heart continued to beat strong. Her brain waves indicated that she had the will to live.

Amanda amazed most of the staff at shock trauma. She had become his star patient. Kevin recalled how when he would check in on her she would attempt to smile through her wounded lips. He knew in the past and now from the New Year's Eve altercation that Amanda was in great pain. Kevin smiled as he lovingly listened to her steady breathing. She was at peace lying in the bed next to him. Strength—Amanda could teach the world a lesson or two about strength. Kevin gently raised her right hand and rubbed his lips over her knuckles. "Rest, Amanda. I love you, and I will take good care of you." Having said that, Kevin settled in and shut his eyes.

CHAPTER FIFTEEN

Wesley was surprised to find that Stephen was at the bait shop ahead of him. He noticed that Stephen had parked his pickup down near the woodpile. It looked to Wes like Johnson was planning on loading on some of the wood they had left. *Hmm...looks like great minds think alike.* Wes laughed to himself. As he entered the shop, the music of Waylon Jennings was blasting out of the speakers. "Storms never last..." This was a good sign. An unopened box sat on the floor in the middle of the aisle. As Wes looked toward the end of the aisle, he saw a pair of legs and two arms around two stacked boxes.

"I sincerely hope my business partner is behind those boxes and not some new ghost."

Startled by Wes's voice, Stephen dropped the boxes midstep. "Jumpin' bullfrogs, Wes, that wasn't nice to sneak up on me like that. You about scared the crap out of me."

"Yeah, well, you would've done the same thing to me so, I guess no harm done." There was a hint of laughter in Wes's voice as he continued to speak, "So you got the coffee on?"

"Oh man, I knew there was something I forgot to do. Since I had a cup of coffee with your wife and brought one with me, I plumb forgot. Sorry."

"You were over to see Beck? Did she call you, or did you go on your own?"

"I went on my own. I...um...had to finish a conversation we had started here yesterday afternoon."

"I saw you two talking and then you disappeared. Becky was tight-lipped about your conversation. You know that's not like her. So are you going to tell me what was going on?"

"Man, you're getting to be as nosey as my sister. Living with her all these years must be rubbing off on you! Ah, what a shame! Another good man taken down by Becky Johnson."

"You know, partner, we wouldn't be the good men we are if it wasn't for your sister." At that moment, both glanced toward the speakers as they heard Waylon belt out another one of their favorites, this one about good-hearted women. Wes turned serious for a moment. "You know Becky, she is a good woman. I'm glad you didn't object to my marrying into your family. With how rough my past was and all…"

"I did object. You forget I tried to bribe her not to marry you."

"What? Johnson, you are a poor liar! You know dang well you were happy when Beck told you we were getting married." Stephen sheepishly grinned at Wes. However, he did not respond. "I gotta tell you I never knew the love of family could be as good as it is with yours. Beck, Phil, and you are the only family I got and that means something to me."

"Yeah, you're all right too. Now before someone comes in and catches us doing this here male-bonding crap, let's get that coffee going. I'll tell you about my visit with Calli, that is, Amanda Newman."

"So you saw Calli. This I've got to hear."

The sound of a noisy, hungry woodpecker tapping in the pine tree just outside the bedroom window woke Cassie from a sound sleep. Andrew apparently had not yet been wrestled from his slumber by the inconsiderate bird. Looking at the clock on the nightstand, Cassie decided that 7:00 a.m. was late enough. She rolled over and slid her hand upon Andrew's chest and lightly rubbed her hand on his warm skin. She loved to feel his muscles on his lean body. Andrew captured her hand in his and raised it to his mouth. "Good morning, Cassie my love, waking up to you lying here with me is much better than the dream I was having."

"Oh and did that dream include this?" She giggled as she kissed his chest.

Amanda's cell phone rang. Kevin reached over to the bedside table, picked it up, and read the caller ID. "It's a 518 number. Would you like for me to answer it?" Amanda nodded. She was still lying in bed in Kevin's arms and feeling very relaxed. Kevin had stayed with her all night as promised and assisted Amanda during the night when she woke.

"Hello." For a moment, there was a pause and then Kevin heard Jim's voice.

Amanda saw Kevin's smile reach his eyes as he looked at her. "Well, Jim, I'm pleased to report that she's on the road to recovery, and yes, she is behaving herself."

Amanda did a funny little thing with her lips to indicate she was not thrilled with the conversation that the two were having at her expense. Still, it warmed her heart to hear Kevin laugh and chat with Jim. After what they had all been through during the past few days, it really was not that odd. Amanda hoped that in time Jim and Kevin would become dear friends. Perhaps her family would fill a void left by Kevin's estranged ex-wife and children. Her thoughts were interrupted as she felt Kevin brush her hair back from the side of her face.

"Well, Jim, let me see if she wants to talk with you. She's smiling and nodding her head yes. Looks like this is your lucky morning."

Kevin enjoyed holding Amanda in his arms as she chatted with Jim. He noticed that as Amanda talked with Jim, her face took on a glow that had not been there at any other time during the past week. He watched her eyes light up as Jim spoke words that only she could hear. Then he heard Amanda say, "They're worse than a Mafia hit team...Don't you worry, they'll be with me. See you later...Bye."

Mary's cabin came into view as Kevin came around the corner. Cassie and Andrew were seated in the backseat. Both let out sighs of wow in unison as they caught sight of Mary's home nestled in the side of the mountain. For Amanda, this was an anxious time. In a sense, she was finally coming home. She would be sharing a meal in her grandmother's home with the remnants of her family for the first time in thirty years. The other part of her wanted to run again. She wanted to avoid the discussion she knew needed to take place between Jim and her. Amanda closed her eyes for a moment and let out a heavy sigh. Kevin's hand slid onto her leg and gave her a slight squeeze. She looked at him. Without saying a word, she knew that somehow their time at Mary's would be all right.

Jim's pickup was parked up close to the old shed, allowing for Kevin to pull his rental car close to the path leading to the cabin porch. Andrew assisted Cassie from the backseat of the car and then came around to assist Kevin with Amanda. As Andrew closed the door behind her, Amanda drew in a deep breath of the cold mountain air. "Do you smell that?" she asked all of them.

"All I smell is wood smoke from the chimney," Kevin said.

"Obviously, we're missing something," Andrew added as he looked into Amanda's eyes. With the sunlight bouncing off the snow, her eyes looked as dark as coal and sparkled with mischievousness. As they made their way to the cabin porch, Amanda pointed out the different evergreens distinguishing each for its particular scent. She spotted and pointed to a doe and her fawn by the edge of the woods and some wild turkeys all getting ready to come out for the treats Mary had carried out for them earlier in the day. So engrossed in conversation, Amanda had not seen Jim come out of the door. The clapping of hands from the porch startled all of them. Amanda looked up to see her brother standing there leaning against the post by the top step.

"You always did have a keen sense of smell and eyes like a hawk." Amanda noted the turned-up corner of Jim's lip. Was that pride she saw in his eyes? Amanda took a step and faltered a bit; Kevin instinctively grabbed her elbow. Her limp was more pronounced today. Her whole body still ached from her recent escapades on New Year's Eve and Day. With only one useable hand to grab the rail, Kevin and Andrew assisted her. Amanda was thankful for their strength. Jim held out his hand for Amanda as she came onto the porch. She took his hand and in one swift motion was embraced in a bear hug. With one arm still around Amanda, Jim used his other hand to open the door and escort her inside. Melissa met them at the door and welcomed the others, taking coats and seeing to making all feel at home.

"Hey, Mary," Jim hollered, "look who I found sneaking around outside, your long lost granddaughter!" He pulled his handcuffs out of his pocket. "I thought about cuffing her to me to make sure she doesn't run again. But then seeing how she's hobbling around here today, I guess she won't run." Amanda scowled at Jim. She quietly placed her foot on top of Jim's and stepped down.

"Ow!" Jim let go of Amanda before putting the cuffs back in his pocket.

"Don't push it with me. I've had thirty years to hate you. If I walk out of here now, it will be for the last time. Is that what you want for Mary?" Amanda's eyes were like simmering coals, dark and full of unseen danger. The lines drawn around her mouth and eyes showed of a woman who had experienced and survived a hard life. Jim did not know the woman Amanda had become. He realized that he obviously had been out of line with his jesting. A stabbing pain of guilt shot through him. His sister had every right to hate him.

Mary came in from the kitchen carrying a plate of warm bread. Her long gray hair pulled back with what looked like a piece of rawhide. Her well-worn sweater had patches on the elbows. At her waist, an apron was tied to cover her old dress. Sitting the plate on the table, she came over to greet her guests. Mary gathered Amanda into her arms and spoke to her in Mohawk.

Amanda responded and carefully walked out into the kitchen area with Mary.

Jim was left standing with Melissa and the others. The significance of their conversing hit Jim. "How do you like that?"

"What is it, Jim?" Melissa asked as she laced her fingers with his.

"Through the years when I would stop in to visit with Gram, I would sometimes find her speaking in Mohawk to someone. She would always have a faraway look, say the person on the other end of the line was an old friend, someone whom she deeply cared about. It never crossed my mind that the old woman would have taught Amanda to fluently speak her native language."

"Seeing them together again confirms my initial observations. It is quite apparent that they have a special bond. They share many of the same traits, or as we say at the center, they mirror one another. I'm glad Amanda and your grandmother had a private way to communicate through the years. They obviously draw strength from one another," Cassie continued as she looked directly at Jim. "Your grandmother has taken a bold step bringing the two of you together here in her home. The love and respect you and Amanda have for her is evident. I do hope Mary's actions are not in vain and that you and Amanda will be able to begin to reconcile some of your differences here today. Your sister truly is a good person."

The conversation around the dinner table was light and jovial. Cassie tried the venison stew with "long teeth," only to discover the flavor and tenderness far exceeded the finest cut of beef. Amanda smiled to herself as she noted that all of her friends helped themselves to seconds. For Amanda, this was comfort food, food she had not enjoyed in a very long time. As she smashed a piece of potato on her plate and drizzled the gravy over top of it, her mind journeyed down memory lane. Many a Sunday afternoon had been spent during her youth assisting Mary in preparing the venison and vegetables for the stew. Today's stew somehow tasted far superior to that she remembered of her youth. Amanda looked at her grandmother. Their eyes met. No one heard or acknowledged the few words uttered between them.

Mary may be an old woman, but her mind was sharp as a tack. At one point, she turned to Jim to remind him of his manners while sitting at her table. Amanda had to bite her tongue to keep from laughing out loud. Respect for one's elder was expected at that table. She too would be chastised if Mary saw fit. As the meal progressed, Mary wanted to know all about her guests and didn't mind asking some rather personal questions that caused Amanda, Jim, and Melissa to blush with embarrassment. To Amanda's friends' credit, they handled the pressure of Grandma's interrogation quite well.

As the coffee, tea, blueberry pie—which happened to be Amanda's favorite—and cherry pie—Jim's favorite—were passed around, Mary took a hold of her grandchildren's hands. The once plump soft hands were now boney and arthritic; however, her strength cautioned them both against defying her. Amanda and Jim exchanged looks to signal they knew what was about to happen. Quietly, they turned their attention to Mary. Amanda drew in a calming breath. Kevin became aware in the change in Amanda. He turned to her questioning whether she was heading for a panic. Amanda slightly shook her head while drawing in another slow breath. As Amanda exhaled, the time of reckoning appeared.

"Well, now that everyone is full, it's time to get down to business." Mary's voice was stern, her expression serious. "Melissa, you go in by my chair and bring me my 'spirit stick.'"

"Yes, ma'am." Mel excused herself and gathered the stick as Mary explained the rules. Mary took the stick and then spoke.

"As you all know, I have called you here today so this family can begin to straighten out this mess that happened thirty years ago. Anger, bullheaded pride has dominated Amanda and Jim for too long. My days are getting shorter. Before long, the two of you will only have each other. I have waited far too long for the two of you to settle this. Today, we will begin to take the first step in the journey toward peace." No one spoke as Mary continued to hold the stick. She began to hum. Amanda and Jim made eye contact and immediately looked away. As Mary came to the end of her song, she handed Amanda the stick.

Amanda sat quietly with the stick in her hand. She slowly made eye contact with Kevin, Cassie, and Andrew. First she thanked them for their friendship, love, and support, and then she apologized for drawing them into her family drama. Amanda then turned and acknowledged her family, Jim, Melissa, and Mary. "Grandma is right. It is well past time for necessary words to be said. This will not be easy for any of us. What I am about to say I expect for everyone in this room to keep to themselves. If you cannot respect my request, then I ask you to leave before I begin." Amanda paused, no one moved, as she nodded and continued.

"I will begin with the most important events that transpired in 1979 since that is the year I left." She did just that. Some of the events in May through August of that year had directly involved Jim. He had forgotten and immediately requested the stick so he could speak in his own defense. Amanda again resumed possession of the stick and spoke. "It was open knowledge around here that Stephen Johnson and I were very much in love. We were excited about the fact that we were going to have a child together. Our plan was to marry in the fall. That obviously never happened." Amanda was quiet; everyone waited for her. "Our love child was not to be born." Amanda swallowed hard. "A few weeks prior to her due date, my doctor could not find a heartbeat."

Tears streamed down Cassie and Melissa's cheeks as Amanda shared her pain-filled story. Andrew drew his arm around Cassie. Jim slid his hand over Mel's, locking his fingers with hers. Kevin slid his hand on Amanda's thigh. His leg touched hers. Mary very quietly began to hum. The tune was the same one her grandmother had hummed as she sat on the porch swing thirty years ago. Amanda drew in a deep breath. She made eye contact with her grandmother who slightly nodded. Amanda continued.

Jim held out his hand for the stick. Amanda reluctantly gave it up. "Johnson was a total jerk. He started seeing other woman claiming that Manda had thrown him out. I warned him not to do it. I told him he better find some way to make it back into your life or there'd be pain and suffering for all of us." He spoke a few more words before Amanda stretched out her hand. Her eyes were filled with heat and fire. Jim stopped midsentence and handed his sister the stick.

"Speak for yourself, you were a major jerk as well." The quiet sound of humming drifted over to Amanda. A spirit of calmness came over her. Amanda reminded Jim of things he had said to her during the month of July. "Besides being angry with Jim and Stephen, I was on the warpath with most of the young men in our county that summer. They were all sticking together like a bunch of thieves and getting on my nerves. By the beginning of August, Stephen and I had completely broken off our relationship. He was spending his free time with Jim, Junior, Shannon, and our other supposed friends, drinking and who only knows what else."

Melissa held out her hand requesting the stick. Amanda obliged her. "Jim and Grandma told me that you didn't leave until the end of the month. Neither of them has ever spoken about what made you leave." Melissa looked at her husband then at Amanda. "Jim always gets the same look he has now, pain almost too great to bear. He will only tell me he should have believed you. Amanda, please put an end to this family secret. What happened to make you run?"

Without waiting for Amanda to reach for the stick, Melissa held it out to her. Amanda took the stick and then turned to Jim. Had he honestly kept her secret all this time? "That's right, he should have believed me. Instead, he chose to believe Shannon and Junior." Her expression held the pain of being betrayed by one she loved.

Mel watched the interaction between Amanda and Jim. She sat up straighter, and forgetting all about the stick, she spoke. "Tell me, Amanda, what did they do, and what did my husband choose not to do?" Jim began to speak. "You, James Callison, you need to be quiet." Everyone sitting at the table was taken aback by Melissa's forceful voice. "I have known Junior and Shannon for many years and know that sometimes they are less than upstanding. Let's not forget how they ended this past year. As I'm listening to Amanda, I'm beginning to have a good idea of what may have transpired in August of 1979."

In that moment, there was an unspoken sense of solidarity between the Callison women. Amanda maintained eye contact with Mel as she began to speak.

"It was late August. Stephen and I had been fighting yet again. In the early evening, I had gone down by the lake to one of the old hangout spots to sit and think." No one said a word or requested the stick as Amanda shared the story of how Junior and Shannon gang-raped her by the edge of the lake. "After they left, I went to the police to report it. I went to find Jim and Stephen, but by then, Junior and Shannon had told their own version of what happened. I packed up my car, said good-bye to Rosie, and then said good-bye to Gram before I left town. No one but Grandma believed me. She is the only one who I kept contact with for all this time." Amanda closed her eyes and took a deep breath. "There's more to tell. When I left here, I did not go alone."

Jim didn't reach for the stick. His look reminded Amanda of someone in shock. Then he spoke, "What do you mean you weren't alone? I don't remember anyone else disappearing the same time you did. Who went with you?"

A tear had formed in Amanda's lid and escaped rushing down her cheek. Her voice was now strained. "At that time, I didn't know I was pregnant. Nine months later, my daughter Summer Brooke was born."

Melissa gasped. Jim was unable to move. Andrew drew Cassie into his arms. Kevin leaned over and whispered into Amanda's ear before brushing her cheek with a kiss. Amanda turned to Cassie.

"Sorry, Cass, I should have told you a long time ago. I just couldn't. You know what shame does to a woman." Amanda turned away, unable to look at anyone; she then excused herself from the table with the pretense of needing to use the bathroom. In truth, her nerves were shot. What she needed was a moment alone to regroup. Stunned silence hung over the cabin.

Mary surveyed the group that remained at her table. She cleared her throat. "My Amanda did more than survive being raped. She has survived betrayal of the worst kind." It was then that Mary drew her attention to her grandson. "It broke my heart the day Amanda came here and told me she was leaving. I couldn't make her stay. Only one person had that power, and he chose to walk away from his sister when she needed him most. The shame Amanda talks about doesn't lie at her feet anymore." James swallowed hard as Mary spoke directly to him. "Do you remember the promise you made to your mother before she died?"

Jim flinched as his own grandmother had gone for the jugular with her guilt trip. "Yes, ma'am, I do."

"What was it?" The old woman's eyes had that same dark tone that he had recently seen in Amanda's. Underneath the darkness lies scorching heat that could take him out at any moment if he wasn't careful.

"I promised Mom that no matter what I would look after Amanda." Jim was unable to make eye contact with anyone. He looked down at his empty coffee cup as he spoke. "Thirty years ago, I had a lapse in judgment. I forgot that above all else family comes first." He looked up at the eyes that were focused on him and cleared his throat. "Will you all excuse me? I think I had best check on my little sister. We have some things we need to further discuss, and if you don't mind"—he looked at Mary—"I'd like to talk with her in private."

A light knock on the door drew Amanda from her meditation. "Yes?"

"Sis, are you okay?" The concern in Jim's voice was overwhelming.

"I just need a little," Amanda sniffled and whispered, "time."

"May I come in?" His voice was filled with concern.

"Yes."

Jim opened the door took one look at Amanda who stood leaning against the vanity. He grabbed a hold of her as she melted into a puddle of tears. Continuing to hold on to Amanda, he lowered both of them to the floor as gently as possible. Jim cradled her in his arms as she wept, and he quietly spoke what was in his heart.

"Manda, you'll never know how sorry I am for all that has happened to you and between us. I have been wanting to and have placed all the blame on you. After we rescued you from the lake, I had planned to rip you apart for all the heartache you caused Mary only to discover that the two of you have had your secret rendezvous over the years. We'll talk about that another time. Right now we need to clear the air about '79." Amanda sniffled as she sought to gain control of her tears. She tightened her grip on Jim with her right hand as he continued. "Unfortunately, I can't change what I did or didn't do that summer. When you told me about the rape, I guess I was in shock. I didn't want to believe that something that horrific could happen to you. After all, you had always been able to take care of yourself. I just couldn't picture them hurting you in such a violent way. So like everyone else, I went into denial. This sounds so lame."

He hugged Amanda closer to him. "I was supposed to look out for you and failed miserably. I chose the friendship of two rapists over the love of family." Jim's voice cracked. "I'd give anything to change the past, but we both know that is impossible. All I can do is ask, perhaps even plead with you, to please find it in your heart to forgive me. I love you, Amanda Kathryn Callison." Amanda began to speak. Jim placed a finger over her lips. "Sis, no matter what you change your name to, you will always be a Callison. We are family, and our family sticks together. I've missed you more than you can imagine. Amanda, I hope that you will chose to once again be a part of my life. Maybe you'll even allow me to be a part of yours."

Amanda sighed as she looked at Jim. She thought that he looked as exhausted as she felt. "I forgive you," she whispered. Amanda lowered her head onto Jim's chest. Together, they held on to one another as if they were afraid the other would disappear. Their tears freely flowed. It didn't matter; this was their moment and theirs alone. Amanda fell asleep cradled in Jim's arms as he leaned against the vanity. The floor was hard and cold, but Jim didn't seem to mind. He held on to his sister, relieved to finally have her home where she belonged.

Jim listened to the quiet conversation taking place out in the living room as he sat cradling Amanda in his arms. After a while, he heard quiet footsteps approaching. Melissa came to the door and quietly entered. She held out a cup of coffee, which Jim gladly accepted. Then Melissa sat down next to them and whispered with Jim as to not awaken Amanda.

When Mel left the bathroom, Kevin came in. He sat down next to them with medication for Amanda. Together, the two men awakened her. Amanda was disoriented at first and startled to find herself sitting with them on her grandmother's bathroom floor. Jim kept his hand on Amanda to steady her as she sat up straight. Kevin handed her the medicine and a glass of water. Upon taking the pills, Amanda stretched and was then lifted to her feet by Kevin who kept his arm around her for support.

"I guess it's time for us to face Gram and everyone else," Amanda said as Jim came to his feet.

"Yes it is, sis, and we have more to talk about." He patted her hand and winked. "At least the hardest part is behind us."

"Yes it is." And with that, the Callison siblings walked back into the living room to join the others.

By now, Mary, Melissa, Andrew, and Cassie had made their way to more comfortable seats in the living room. As Amanda sat down on the couch with Kevin, Mary got up from her chair. She shuffled out into the kitchen only to return with a cup in her hand. She came over to Amanda and handed it to her. "You drink my tea to calm your nerves."

Andrew shot to attention and leaned forward in his chair. "Mrs. Freeman, you should know that Amanda has taken a prescription drug before she came out of the bathroom. Whatever home remedy you have in that tea may cause her to have an adverse reaction."

Amanda saw the devastated look in her grandmother's eyes. "Gram, thank you for the tea, I'm sure that after a while I'll be able to drink a little of this." She brought the cup up to her nose and smelled the aroma of the tea. "For now, I'll simply inhale the delightful smell."

Her action was enough to appease the old woman. She glanced over at Andrew with a stare that warned him to keep his mouth shut. Jim had been sipping his fresh cup of coffee and observing the interactions between Amanda, Andrew, and Mary. He had to hand it to his sister, she knew how to tactfully deal with the old woman. In the days, weeks, and months to come, Jim felt certain that Amanda would be a vital source in the decision making regarding Mary's care. Jim took another swallow of coffee, crossed his leg over the other to get more comfortable in the old chair. He looked around the room. It was becoming apparent that full stomachs, the warmth of the fire, and the drama of Amanda's story had tired everyone.

"So, Manda, are you up to talking some more or should we call it a day?" Amanda appreciated Jim's concern. As much as she would have preferred to not deal with anymore family matters, she knew it had to be now. In the morning, she would be returning to Baltimore and then it would be months before she returned to the mountains.

"I guess it depends on what you want to talk about." Jim smiled and raised a brow. Both Amanda and Jim were surprise to hear Cassie speak up.

"I'd like to hear some more stories about your family. Amanda told Kevin and me some stories about your days of skating on the lake and playing hockey. I'd like to hear of some of your other adventures in growing up." From there, the conversation turned jovial and lively as Jim regaled the group with stories of their childhood. At one point, Amanda picked up a pillow and hurled it at Jim's head only to be caught midair and tossed back. Mary shook her head and smiled as she listened and watched her grandchildren come alive before her eyes. Her family had weathered the storm, dealt with the heartache, and remembered their bond of love.

Chapter Sixteen

Morning came early for Amanda as she awakened to the sounds of cardinals whistling for their mates, blue jays directing morning traffic in the woods, chickadees cheerfully greeting one another. They all seemed to be beckoning Amanda to visit with them for one last time. Amanda stretched and yawned as she lay next to Kevin who was still soundly asleep. Her body was stiff and sore. Yet she didn't want to miss this opportunity.

As quietly as possible, Amanda got out of bed; her bandaged left hand throbbed with pain, every muscle in her legs and lower back reminded her of the events she had participated in during the past few days. Amanda winced as she awkwardly dressed and descended the stairs. When Amanda finally reached the bottom of the stairs, she smelled the coffee beginning to brew. Thank goodness Cassie had a pot that was preset to perk at a given time. Fixing a cup to enjoy during her morning walk, Amanda slipped into her hiking boots, which she left unlaced and unzipped bomber jacket. Opening the door, Amanda gingerly made her way onto the front porch. She smiled as she stood looking out over the lake. Taking a sip of steaming coffee, she listened to the birds continuing to sing and chatter. It was almost as if they joined in song to greet her. Taking in a deep breath of cold mountain air, Amanda eased her body down the steps. She then quietly walked to the frozen lake shore.

A week ago, Amanda had been sitting in her office listening to totally different morning sounds of rush hour traffic and sirens. On that Monday with the impending storm front moving in, she was dreading the thought of coming here to vacation with her friends. The demons of her past had been suffocating her for thirty years refusing to allow Amanda to fully move on with her life.

Amanda gazed out onto the lake and stepped on the sheen of ice. Many of the demons had been slain; peace and reconciliation united the Callison family. The New Year had begun with quite a bang and promised to be filled with more adventures. A smile graced her face as she thought of Kevin and how he was to be a part of that adventure. He probably was still asleep in the bed they had again shared. His tenderness, his strength, and his love had already helped her begin the healing process.

As Amanda's thoughts were turning to Cassie and Andrew, she heard footsteps. She slowly turned to find Cassie with coffee cup in hand making her way on the shore of the frozen lake. "Good morning, Cass. I hope I didn't make too much noise when I got up this morning."

"No, Amanda, you're fine. It sure is a beautiful morning."

"Yes, it is." Amanda drew in a deep breath as she looked out over the lake.

"How are you feeling this morning?"

"Stiff, sore, and surprisingly okay. I've been reflecting on the events that have transpired during the past seven, actually now eight days. You, Andrew, Kevin, my family, old friends, and enemies have been through enough drama to last a lifetime." Amanda turned and looked into Cassie's eyes. Tears sparkled as they clung to Amanda's lashes. "I will never be able to thank or repay you and Andrew for what the two of you have done for me. My gratitude not only includes this week but all of the almost thirty years we have been a part of one another's lives."

"Oh, Amanda, this certainly has been quite a week for all of us. I too owe you a debt of gratitude. You listened and were able to help Andrew and me work through our impasse. Now together as the team we are, we're making progress with our accepting Ryan openly acknowledging he is gay. You'll never know how much I appreciate your friendship and being here for us in our time of need."

Amanda's eyes misted as she recalled that chilly morning sitting on the porch with Andrew. He was distraught. "Andrew loves you, Cassie, with all of his heart and soul. I'm glad I could help." Amanda turned back to look out over the lake. "This lake holds much power to heal and to destroy. I'm glad its healing powers are at work in your lives."

Cassie watched as Amanda closed her eyes, smiled, and drew in a deep cleansing breath. "Well, my wise friend, I don't know about you, but I'm getting chilled. Andrew and Kevin are making breakfast. Let's go see what damage has been done to my kitchen by our men."

Laughter filled the quiet morning air as they returned to the cabin. As they stepped onto the porch, smells of bacon, eggs, and a whiff of cinnamon buns permeated the air. Opening the door, each was greeted with a sensual kiss from their mate. From that moment on, the morning flew by. Before Amanda had any more time to process the events of the week, Kevin was loading the last of their luggage into the rental car.

"You're quiet, Amanda."

Amanda let out a sigh. The lines of fatigue were evident upon her face as she turned her gaze from looking out the window to Kevin. "I'm sorry, Kevin, I'm just thinking."

"So I noticed." The softness of his voice touched Amanda's weary heart. Removing his hand from the steering wheel, he gently took hold of Amanda's hand. "Do we need to make any stops as we head back to Albany?"

"No, Kevin…No stops today. I'm ready to go home to Baltimore and begin my life with you."

No sooner were Amanda's words out of her mouth when she heard the siren. Her body tightened. Kevin also heard the siren and had begun calming techniques with Amanda. While doing so, he glanced in the rearview mirror and saw a state police car with lights flashing rapidly approaching them. Kevin knew he was not speeding and pulled over to allow them to pass. Much to both

Amanda and his dismay, the state police pulled in behind them. Both officers got out of the patrol car and came up to opposite sides of their rental car. Officer Charlie Simpkins tapped on the driver side window.

"Roll down the window and then place your hands on the steering wheel where I can see them." Kevin immediately complied with the older officer. There was something about him that caused Kevin to believe that regardless of this officer's age he was a force to be reckoned with. Leaning down, Officer Simpkin's looked across Kevin to address Amanda. "Ma'am, step out of the car. We have some unfinished business to attend to with you."

Kevin was alarmed. He could see the anguish on Amanda's face. A panic attack was on the horizon. "Sir, please don't make her get out. She has not been well and—"

"Sir, keep quiet, or I'll have to take you in for impeding a police matter that does not include you."

"Oh yes it does…" Amanda saw and heard the tension rising in Kevin. Oh how she loved him for wanting to once again come to her rescue. She was scared that if he said anything else he might just end up in the county jail.

"Kevin, please be quiet. We don't need any trouble with the NYS police. I'll be fine." Amanda refused to give in to the panic that was welling up inside of her. She commanded herself to stay calm. Right now, she had to keep both of them out of trouble with the police and perhaps out of jail as well. Later she would be making a call to Jim to complain about the rude cops and a few other things. Stepping out of the car, Amanda was temporarily blinded by the bright sunlight reflecting on the snow. Because of this, she did not immediately see the face of the officer whom she was now standing next to by the side of the road. She heard his voice. The panic within her immediately subsided and turned to annoyance.

"So, Amanda Callison"—she glared up at him—"oh, excuse me, Amanda Newman. I see you're sneaking out of town yet again." Working devilishly hard to maintain a straight face, Amanda responded.

"No, sir, I've learned my lesson. This may be hard to believe... you know, given my past track record and all. But honestly, I'm not sneaking out of town. My family knows I'm leaving this time, and I'll tell you, near hypothermia must have done something to my brain cells because I've even given my brother my cell number and e-mail address. I've promised to keep in touch and even return later on this year."

"Is that so?" It was becoming increasingly difficult for Amanda to maintain a straight face with Jim grinning at her.

"Yes, sir, and if you don't believe me, I suggest you contact my sister-in-law Melissa Callison."

"And why not your brother?"

"Because you fool you're standing right here, now why on earth did you pull us over and about give Kevin a heart attack? Not to mention I almost went into a panic?" They laughed together. Then Jim turned serious.

"I know we said our good-byes last night. I just need a few more minutes to talk with you, Amanda. You see, I've been thinking, mulling over all the information I now have."

"Oh." Amanda had been so engrossed in her conversation with Jim that she had not heard Kevin get out of the car and come alongside of her. He protectively slid his arm around her. She leaned against Kevin as she listened to Jim.

"Unfortunately, as you know, the statute of limitation is up for your being raped in '79. So we can't lone convict Junior and Shannon for raping you. Just so you know, sis, I went into records and pulled your '79 statement. Thirty years later, your statement matches almost verbatim. The DA and I have spoken. We are confident that we can use your current testimony and past report as collaborating testimony in two other recent cases of sexual assault. Plus, on your behalf, we're filing sexual harassment charges against Shannon and Junior with the intent to inflict bodily harm on New Year's Eve."

"Sounds good." Amanda paused. "Jim, you know you didn't have to do all this. But I'm glad that you have. Shannon and Junior need to be held accountable for their actions."

"Manda, before you go, there's something else that's been on my mind." Amanda waited as Jim cleared his throat. "How much does Summer know about your past? Did you ever tell her about being raped?"

"Goodness, Jim, you really have been thinking about stuff. Actually, she does know that her father is from here. She also knows I was the victim of a sexual crime and that the man who impregnated me was never prosecuted."

Amanda watched Jim's expression; she had seen this same one when he was deep in thought so many times when they were younger. Now she waited for she knew he had something else equally important to say to her.

"I think it would be good for you to petition for a paternity test and sue for back child support for Summer. I know, I know, you don't have to tell me. I know you made it without either one of them helping to raise your daughter. However, sis, they need to be held accountable for their actions. This is one more way to hold them accountable for raping you." Jim reached over and brushed a piece of hair that had fallen into Amanda's face. Leaving his hand on her cheek, he added, "Think about it, and when you reach a decision, let me know what you want to do. If you decide to determine who the father is and press for back support, I'll do whatever needs to happen on this end to make sure justice prevails on your behalf."

Amanda looked up at Jim. "I love you. You're the best brother anyone could ever have."

Amanda and Jim laughed as he engulfed her into his arms. Amanda felt a tear escape from her lid as Jim spoke, "I love you too, sis."

Letting go of one another, Amanda reached for the door only to have Jim open it and help her back in. "Take care of yourself."

"You too, Amanda. Call me when you get home."

CHAPTER SEVENTEEN

FOUR MONTHS LATER

Amanda anxiously sat in the county courtroom waiting for the day to begin. She knew in her heart that on this day the lives of family and friends would be changed forever. After lengthy conversations with Jim, Kevin, and her lawyer, Amanda had decided not to press charges against Junior and Shannon for New Year's Eve. She reserved the right to press charges after today's proceedings. Two young women who had been raped by Junior and Shannon had come forward to file charges of sexual assault against them. Now, thirty years after the fact, unable to file her own case against them for rape, her voice would be heard for the benefit of the other women as she gave testimony in the trial of Junior McGrath and Shannon Green. The prosecutions intent was to show the court that Junior and Shannon had a history of predatory behavior against women. Amanda drew in a calming breath as she waited. Even though her testimony would not be used in convicting Junior and Shannon, she would finally have the opportunity to slay the demon that had been holding her and significant people in her life hostage for all these years. Amanda glanced over at her friends Cassie, Andrew. They along with Kevin, who sat beside her, had made the trip north with her. Summer had flown in from Denver to be with her family during the trial. Her daughter's love and poise in the midst of this situation was humbling, to say the least for Amanda. She allowed herself to exhale a heavy sigh. Kevin gently squeezed her hand as he whispered words of encouragement in her ear. Amanda drew in a calming breath and smiled as her thoughts returned to her daughter and the day before them. When the trial was over, Amanda and her family would meet with the judge in closed session to hear the results of the DNA tests. At that time, Amanda and Summer would finally know if Junior or Shannon was the biological father of Summer. Amanda's stomach did a flip flop as she waited. Oh how she wished she could find out now which one of the two jerks had impregnated her. The waiting in finding out the truth was driving her crazy. Taking a deep breath, Amanda laced her fingers with Kevin's. He already knew the story of Amanda's life. As vulnerable as she felt at that moment, Amanda had no doubt that Kevin is her new strength and would help her get through this day.

As Amanda gazed around the courtroom it seemed as though nearly everyone from her past had gathered to view the trials of Junior McGrath and Shannon Green. For the morning session, Summer chose to sit behind her mother with her cousin Samantha, Uncle Jim, and Aunt Melissa Callison. A year ago, her family had lived as strangers to one another. Then on New Year's Eve, everything changed with all the turmoil Junior and Shannon had caused in their lives. Amanda had seen Stephen Johnson enter and take his seat with Becky and Wesley. On this particular morning, no words had been exchanged between them. Perhaps this is just as well, Amanda thought, as she decided Stephen looked as if he was ready to string someone up as bear bait.

Her breathing was shallow and forced; her grip on Kevin's hand was tighter than she realized. Kevin leaned over and whispered to her, "Amanda, my love, I need that hand."

"Oh, sorry." Amanda dropped her death grip and patted his hand, now turning red. Kevin showed Amanda the indentation her fingers had left in his hand. "I guess I'm a little nervous." Kevin drew his arm around her shoulders. Amanda breathed deeply as the doors to the judge's chambers opened.

"All rise. The Honorable Judge Janis Van Talen now presiding."

The morning seemed to fly by as testimony was given by a number of women who had filed complaints and accusations against Junior and Shannon. Amanda listened to the women and was appalled by what she considered to be the irresponsibility of the judicial system in the past for not listening to the other women who had come forward. She and the others had not only been violated by Junior and Shannon. They also had been violated by the legal system that was supposed to protect. At various times during the proceedings, Judge Van Talen had to rap her gavel calling order to the court. Finally, the assistant DA David Donaldson after reminding the court that testimony was for information only, called his star witness Amanda Newman to the stand. Amanda was shaking and her breathing was shallow as she stood. She looked at Kevin who met her gaze. He smiled and mouthed the words, "Breathe, honey, just breathe." She took a hesitant step, slightly turned, and looked first at Summer and then at Jim. With Jim's slight nod, Amanda took in another deep breath and made her way to the stand.

After being sworn in by the bailiff, she sat down and silently fought the butterflies that were seeking escape from her stomach. Amanda decided that if the DA didn't hurry up, she could not guarantee that what was left of her breakfast would not make a grand entrance into court. Oh how embarrassing that would be. Another deep breathe was in order.

"Miss Callison or do you prefer Newman?"

"Legally, my last name is Newman. However, Amanda is fine."

"All right, Amanda, tell the court in your own words what occurred between you and the two defendants on New Year's Eve at the bait shop party." Amanda told her version of the story of the reunion with Junior and Shannon. The DA entered into evidence the collaborating statement that Amanda had given while in the hospital on January 1.

Vanessa White, attorney for the defense, cross-examined Amanda. "Miss Newman, your account of New Year's Eve is quite dramatic. What were you drinking while you were at the celebration?"

"I was drinking diet coke. I make it a policy to not drink alcoholic beverages when I'm in a place with people who are strangers."

"Ah, but the people you were with were not all strangers, were they? You knew most of the people there. However, they did not know you." The color was draining from Amanda's face.

"Objection, Your Honor, badgering my witness."

"Sustained, Ms. White. Where are you going with this?"

"Sorry, Your Honor. Miss Newman, you accuse my clients of intending to harm you when it is you who harmed them. Junior sustained a broken nose that required surgery, and Shannon has had medical issues following you kneeing him in the groin. Isn't it true that you were the violent one and not them, that you were afraid they would expose the truth of your identity?"

Amanda's face was absent of expression, her lips drawn into a thin line. "Ms. White, you are very good in your attempt to rattle me. My fear was not in my identity being exposed by them." Amanda turned her deadly stare toward the two defendants. "I know too well what their hands feel like. I was protecting myself." Amanda turned back to their attorney. "You can accuse me of being the aggressor, but you know the truth, as well as I do. I'd like to believe that if you had been in my position with the two of them, that you too would have defended yourself."

Amanda breathed a slight sigh as Vanessa White returned to her seat next to Junior and Shannon. The court was in a buzz as Amanda had taken down the defense attorney.

Rap, rap, rap. The judge's gavel brought the court back into order, and the assistant DA resumed questioning Amanda. "Ms. Newman, Amanda, I know this is difficult for you. I'd like to apologize on the behalf of the defense's attorney for her lack of regard for your feelings."

"Thank you," Amanda quietly responded while maintaining eye contact.

"Now, Amanda, are you aware that the statute of limitations is up for filing rape charges against a perpetrator?"

"Yes, sir, I am."

"My next questions are for information only regarding the night of August 28, 1979. The information you provide will support the other women's rape charges against the two defendants. Are you willing to proceed?"

"Yes, I am." Amanda nodded her head as she took a deep, cleansing breath. Tears pooled in her eyes as she considered the enormity of what she was about to do. She held the power to help change the lives of two women. Silence filled the room.

"On August 28, 1979, did Shannon Green and Junior McGrath gang-rape you?"

"Yes."

"In your own words, tell the court what happened." Amanda took a deep breath, looked at Kevin, Jim, and Summer. She drew her strength from their love.

"On August 28, 1979, Stephen Johnson and I had exchanged harsh words earlier in the day. I had gone down to the lake to one of our favorite spots to sort out my thoughts. Since it was now dusk around 7:30 p.m., I thought the initial sounds in the brush were just normal evening in the mountain noises." Amanda stopped and took in a deep breath to help her not panic. "I heard their voices and realized it was Junior and Shannon coming down to the lake. At that time, I really didn't care if they were there with me by the lake. We were all friends. So this was not out of the ordinary." Amanda took another pause. "After we greeted one another, they invited me to party with them. Junior offered me a beer, and I refused. Shannon had rolled a joint bragging about how it was Columbian Gold, and I should take a hit. I refused him as well. My stomach had been out of sorts, and I just didn't feel like partying with them. I asked them to leave me alone."

A tear rolled down her cheek. She took in another deep breath and continued.

"They didn't leave me alone." Amanda had begun to whimper. "They overpowered me, knocking me to the ground. It was Junior who overpowered me first. He pinned down my shoulders and arms so I could only kick, which did nothing to stop him..."

Gasps were heard from the spectators as Amanda continued to relive in her mind and share what they did to her. Amanda made eye contact with Jim who slightly nodded his head. Then her eyes met Kevin's; he too was slightly nodding with encouragement. Oh how she loved him and longed to be finished so she could melt into his arms. The assistant DA continued, "You're doing great, Amanda. And then—"

"Objection! Leading the witness—"

"Your Honor—"

"Sustained."

"I'm sorry, Amanda. I'm sure this is very difficult for you. Please continue."

Amanda then turned her face to look both Junior and Shannon head-on. She was no longer going to be their victim. Drawing in a breath of confidence, Amanda continued conveying every intimate detail of what their hands felt like when they touched her, where they touched her, and how dirty they made her feel.

"I begged Junior not to touch me. He laughed and said..." The court gasped and mumbled to the point that Judge Van Talen once again rapped the gavel. Amanda noticed that Shannon was now unable to look into her eyes. Along with Junior, he hung his head in shame. With gentle encouragement from the assistant DA, Amanda continued.

"I was sobbing and pleading with Junior to stop and let me go. He laughed at me and declared it was his turn to have what Johnson threw away. I was crying and pleading for them to stop. They didn't. When they finally were done, they got up, spit on me, and left. I lay there for a while before I got up and went to the police. By then, they had both told a different story to my brother and friends. No one, not even the police who I had thought were supposed to protect me, believed me that they had raped me. A week later, I packed my car and went to the cemetery to say good-bye to Rose. I went to the bank withdrawing all my money. I said good-bye to my grandmother and drove away from here. Nine months later, my daughter, Summer, was born."

Vanessa White, attorney for the defense, cross-examined Amanda. The questions came, and Amanda answered unwavering. Two strong women questioned and answered, neither one intimidated by the other. Then the defense's final question left the court in shock.

"So, Amanda, thirty years after your alleged rape and this morning you shed only one or two tears. Tell us in your own words, was it real or simply for show?"

"Objection—don't answer that, Amanda."

"Sustained."

"Withdrawn. No further questions, Your Honor."

During the lunch break, Amanda noticed that Jim had mentally distanced himself from the others. She admired his dedication and wondered what he might be working on in his police brain. Perhaps, Amanda thought, Jim might simply be considering all the possibilities of the verdict in the case of the people against Shannon Green and Junior McGrath.

When the announcement came for court to be called into session, Kevin helped Amanda from her chair and seized the moment to give her a kiss. "Mmm…Thank you for that nibble of dessert. I look forward to more dessert with you later."

"Come along you two. Playtime will have to wait."

Amanda smiled at Jim as they walked back into the courtroom. "My goodness, aren't we cranky! Must be you didn't get any promise of dessert. Too bad, brother. If you'd like, I'd be glad to plead your case with Mel. I'm rather liking this testifying stuff, real law and order-ish. Don't you think?"

Before Jim could rebuttal his sister's statement, the honorable Janis Van Talen reentered the court. Then the moment they had all been waiting for came. Judge Van Talen gave her ruling in the cases against Junior and Shannon. For the recent rape of a local women the judge declared Junior and Shannon were both guilty and would be sentenced to fifteen years in prison. Justice was being served.

The judge looked at the two defendants. "Before you are escorted to your new home, is there anything either of you would like to say to the court?"

Amanda was breathing heavy as she waited with the rest of the court to see if either Junior or Shannon would accept the judge's invitation. She squeezed Kevin's hand in anticipation. Kevin unclasped her hand and laid it on his thigh. He slid his hand on top of hers. Shannon hung his head and shook it back and forth so all could see he was silently saying no; then to everyone's shock, Junior stood.

"Yes, Your Honor, I would like to have a word with ah"— Junior choked on his words—"ah, Amanda if I am allowed."

"You are, Mr. McGrath. Turn to face her and then speak. But I'm warning you, if you say anything out of line, you will immediately be removed from my court. You will not be allowed to return to hear the results of the DNA testing that is next to come before the court. Do you understand?"

"Yes, Your Honor."

"All right then, turn and speak your mind."

"Amanda"—Junior cleared his throat—"I've known you all of my life. When we were young, you were the one who would stick up for me when kids would tease me because I stuttered and was slow at math. You are a good person, and no way did you deserve what we did. I mean, what I did to you in '79. Hearing you tell everyone what we did"—Junior choked on his words—"I had forgotten how it happened, but you didn't. What you said to me on New Year's was true. I am a slug, and you breaking my nose is far less pain than what I've caused you. Before I go off to prison, I just have one thing to ask you." Junior turned to Judge Van Talen. "Judge, can she answer me if she wants to?"

"Yes, Junior, you may ask your question, and Amanda you may answer the question if you'd like." Amanda was reeling from Junior's confession and wasn't sure she could handle any more and then it came.

"Amanda, I'm really sorry for what I did to you. Is there any way that you can find it in your heart to forgive me?"

The courtroom was abuzz with noise as people whispered and spoke out loud in disbelief at what they had just heard Junior ask of Amanda. Amanda stood and all eyes were on her as she spoke up. "Your Honor."

"Yes, Amanda."

"I'm sure what I'm going to ask is probably out of order in some way since I don't know how the New York court works, however, I have to ask."

"Go ahead."

"Your Honor, may I approach Junior?"

The judge was cognoscente of the displeasure in her court. She also saw something unusual occurring in her court between Amanda and Junior. A rap of the gavel brought the court to order.

"Ladies and gentlemen, let me remind you that this is my court, and I will deem what is appropriate and inappropriate. Keep your thoughts to yourself or you will be told to leave." Looking between Amanda and Junior, she continued, "It seems to me that Amanda and Junior are seeking to resolve their differences, and we should accord them this opportunity." Turning her attention to Amanda, she said, "Now, Amanda, I have to advise you that contact with a felon is not allowed. However, this is my court, and I am the one who interprets the law, and so in this case you may approach the convicted."

Amanda walked up to the front of the court and turned toward Junior. She was glad a table was between them and took advantage of leaning against it to support herself. "Junior, I have to admit I'm as surprised as everyone else here today by what you said to me. I know that it wasn't easy for you to man up and take accountability for your actions. As you reminded me, we do have a history, and it isn't all bad… Junior McGrath, as God is my witness, I forgive you. And I hope that someday you will find it in your heart to forgive me for breaking your nose."

The courtroom of onlookers erupted in laughter; only the judge, Kevin, Cassie, Andrew Jim, and Melissa saw what happened next. Amanda extended her hand to grab a hold of Junior's. They shook hands without another word spoken between them.

With just enough time to use the ladies room and grab a drink of water from the fountain outside the courtroom, Amanda found herself between Kevin and Jim as they entered to take their seats. This was a closed session and therefore only immediate family and selected friends were gathered along with Amanda, Summer, and Junior to hear the DNA results.

"Ladies and gentlemen, this has been a long day for all of you, and I am sure you are all anxious for the results of the DNA testing to be read. Amanda, your attorney has informed me that you are in counseling. From what I observed earlier today here in my court, you are obviously making great progress in dealing with your past. You are a strong woman, and I encourage you to continue working toward further healing. Summer, my dear, today has no doubt been difficult for you to hear graphic details of the violence perpetrated against your mother. Regardless of what you hear in the next few minutes, remember, child, that above all else your mother loves you. The choices she made thirty years ago and has made over the years since then were what she felt were right at the time."

Amanda and Summer looked at one another. The judge's words had struck a nerve in both of them. In a few minutes, their lives would again be changed forever. They would have proof that Junior is Summer's father.

The old feeling of wanting to flee so she could breathe and not feel as though the world was spinning out of control was descending upon Amanda. Her erratic breathing and fidgeting were indicators that both Kevin and Jim picked up on. Jim took a hold of her hand and squeezed. Kevin laid his hand on Amanda's leg to steady her. She was safe. They would be her strength to get through the moment. But Amanda thought, *What about Summer? How can I help her when I can't even help myself?* Then she heard the honorable judge Janis Van Talen speak.

"The DNA of Junior McGrath and Summer Newman is not a match."

Amanda gasped in shock. "Oh my!"

Everyone else was equally stunned and sat in silence looking at the judge.

"Amanda, I'm sorry that this came out for all the court to hear rather than in the privacy of my chambers. There is no doubt that someone else fathered your daughter." Judge Van Talen said and then she turned to Summer. "Summer, this is obviously a shock for you as well. I'm sorry, my dear, that you have to further wait to find out the identity of your biological father."

The courtroom remained silent so you could have heard a pin drop. Tears were forming in Amanda's eyes. She briskly brushed then aside while cursing under her breath. Then her voice was clearly heard. "Your Honor."

"Yes, Amanda?"

Shock and disbelief had rushed over Amanda. The room was closing in on her; she couldn't breathe. "There's no possibility that test was wrong?"

"No, Amanda, there is not a mistake. Junior's blood type is O- and Summer's—"

"Is AB+," Amanda completed Judge Van Talen's sentence as tears were now streaming down her cheeks. She squeezed Kevin's hand as she looked at Jim. Jim nodded and Amanda then realized that this is what Jim had pieced together and was thinking about during lunch.

"Amanda, given your reaction, I take it that you know who the father is?" The judge looked at Amanda with tenderness.

"Yes, Your Honor." Amanda's voice quivered.

"We will allow you time to talk with him in private." The judge quickly adjourned the court. Amanda collapsed onto the chair. Sensing she was being watched, Amanda looked up past Jim who remained by her side. She found Stephen Johnson's eyes dead set on her as if looking through his rifle scope ready to shoot her dead where she sat.

Cassie walked out of the courthouse with Andrew and Kevin. She sat down on the bench next to Summer. Cassie gently laid her hand upon Summer's hand that was resting on her leg while quietly speaking, "Summer, I know you are in shock with the news you have just received. We all are. Your mom has held much about herself locked away for thirty years. Only this year along with you, Andrew, and Kevin have I learned who she really is." Cassie continued to talk in a calm soothing voice, "One thing I am absolutely sure of is that until today your mom did not have any idea that Stephen Johnson is your biological father. Remember, Summer, that no matter what your mom has done or not done, the one thing that has remained constant in your life is that she loves you."

"So let me get this straight—being that I'm a country bumpkin and all..." His words stabbed Amanda with guilt. "In thirty years, it never crossed your mind that I might be Summer's father? Jeez, woman, I thought you were brighter than that!" Amanda felt the hair on her arm raise from the sting of Stephen's words. He glared at her as he took a slug of coffee. Amanda recognized that the tiny muscles twitching by his eyes; his voice, glare, and twitches were all warning sign that Stephen Johnson was like a trigger on a rifle ready to be let go. She too was ready to fire off and did without hesitation.

"Johnson, I don't appreciate your insult regarding my intelligence or lack thereof in discerning who among the mighty men of the lake provided the sperm to create my daughter." Amanda's index finger was shaking at Stephen, a sure sign she was royally pissed. "Honey, don't you think for a minute that you have a right to sit there in judgment of me. When I discovered I was pregnant, my thoughts immediately went to that night when Junior and Shannon raped me. In case you have forgotten, it was close to four weeks prior to that night of the rape that we had last been together. We had sex, we fought, and then *you* left." Amanda made sure she emphasized *you* for impact. "In my mind, you were not even considered to be a possibility to be my daughter's father."

The coldness in Amanda's voice shook Stephen. Every day he mourned the loss of his and Amanda's child who had died thirty years prior and now today he has discovered that he has an adult daughter with Amanda. This is a miracle. Somehow he had to get a grip on himself. He had to reach out to her so that they could resolve their differences. Somehow he had to speak without shouting at her and driving her further away from him. Awkward silence fell between them. Amanda refused to look at Stephen as she took deep breathes to work on regaining her control. All the signs were there. No way was she going to have a full-blown panic attack in front of him.

Stephen's voice was quiet. "That hurt you know." Amanda looked up as a tear splotched onto her napkin lying on the table. She remained silent. "You didn't even consider that I may have planted my seed in you...My gosh, Amanda, if you had come back...we could have...it's...I don't know what to think...It's like you demonized me along with them."

Amanda's whole demeanor was unnerving Stephen. She looked shattered. The heaviness of her voice revealed a vulnerable Amanda, one he was unfamiliar and uncomfortable with.

"I'm sorry for our past. What we've said and did, what we didn't say or do. I take full accountability for my actions and the pain it has caused both you and Summer. As we both agreed earlier this year, we can't change the past. I hope that at some point in time you will find it in your heart to forgive me." Amanda stood up, and as she did, she held out her hand to signal that Stephen should remain seated. "Stephen, I'm exhausted. I can't process anymore of this right now, with you or anyone else. Perhaps in the future we can again attempt to talk but not for a while. I need time. If you want to contact Summer to work on building a relationship with her, I suggest you contact Cassie or my brother, Jim."

Chapter Eighteen

"I thought I might find you here at the lake." Stephen had been lost in thought and had not heard the car drive into the bait shop parking lot or the door slammed shut.

"Don't feel much like company." Stephen continued to look out onto the water. Dusk at the lake was one of his favorite times of the day...The peace and tranquility it usually brought to him was avoiding him tonight. All the events of the past week kept running continuously through his mind.

"I figured as much since Becky and Wes said you once again refused dinner at their place and drove by the Pub and saw you weren't sharing your sorrows with JD."

"No...no bourbon tonight. That's the last thing I need. Although your sister is a good excuse to tie one on."

"I know she's a pain sometimes." Both men nodded in agreement. "My feelings won't be hurt if you don't want to talk with me since I'm Manda's brother and all..."

"You didn't have any choice in that matter of being her brother." Stephen looked over at Jim. His face was drawn in pain, eyes bloodshot from lack of sleep. "Even though I said I don't feel like company, I'm glad you're here. Right now I can use all the friends I can get. Let's walk." The two friends walked down by the lake to a spot where an old oak tree had fallen and sat on the trunk. As the light of day faded, Stephen talked, and Jim listened for well over an hour. The peepers along with the other familiar sounds of evening in the mountains provided nature's music in the background. "Amanda told me that if I want to contact Summer I should ask you to set it up for us. Don't worry, I'm not going to put you in the middle of this."

"I'm afraid I already am in the middle and not by my choice. Amanda informed me that I'm the go-between. Take note that I didn't get to offer or anything. I was simply told this is what I'll do."

"You know, Jim, this bossy sister of yours is the same woman we both missed for thirty years. What are we going to do with her?"

"That's a good question." Jim slightly grinned. "I've been working on my relationship with Manda, and right now, the question is what are you going to do, Johnson? What are you going to do with her and now Summer?"

"Summer, believe it or not, is not as complicated as Amanda." Jim raised a brow in question. Stephen smiled with a sense of satisfaction. "Today, Summer and I had lunch together, so you're off the hook on that one."

"Oh, I wasn't aware that you had been in contact with Summer."

"I'm not the one who initiated the contact, and I don't think Amanda knows about it yet 'cause if she did, I probably would have heard from her by now."

"Are you saying Summer called you?"

"No. She came here around 11:30 a.m. and said she wanted to look around at the infamous bait shop where her mother broke Junior's nose on New Year's morning. At first, Jim, I was so nervous. You know I didn't quite know what to say to her. She's a woman, my daughter, and don't you know she put me at ease." Jim smiled as he listened to Johnson continue on. "I gave her the nickel tour of the place, we talked, and one thing led to another and then I was taking my daughter out for lunch. Callison, she's amazing!"

"Yeah, I agree, she's pretty special." In the midst of twilight, Jim saw genuine happiness in Stephen's eyes. He heard it in his friend's voice. The years of pain and sorrow were being replaced with joy and expectation of new promises of life. His friend finally had family to call his own.

"You know she lives in Denver with her husband." Jim nodded. "Has she told you about her work with the National Park Service in Colorado? Do you know of the work she did while living in Wyoming? My daughter—boy I like saying that." Jim could not help but smile as he watched and listened to his friend. "Summer was involved in mediation between Yellowstone and the private citizens over wolves coming out of the park and attacking their stock. She's quite a spitfire—so passionate about her work." Stephen continued to relay insight and knowledge about Summer to Jim. "You know what struck me even more than Summer's work with the National Parks is her interest in our situation here in the Adirondack's. She wants me to go hiking with her into the interior of the mountains and visiting some of the small communities. My daughter is so amazing. She is a passionate and caring woman, smart, articulate, humorous, and strong—oh for cryin' out loud, listen to me. In one day I've turned into a braggin' dad just like you!"

Jim chuckled. "Here's to being a dad and all the bragging rights that come with the title. You deserve it, my friend! We'll drink later..." Silence feel between them as they listened to an old bullfrog croaking from somewhere in the marsh.

"You know, I am really looking forward to getting to know more about Summer. She wants a relationship with me." Stephen paused; his voice cracked as he spoke, "Amanda did a fine job raising her, didn't she?"

"She did." Jim gave Stephen a few moments with his thoughts. "Johnson, you need to remember some of what you see in your daughter is a reflection of you as well. Don't cut yourself short, you're a good man." Jim placed his hand on Stephen's shoulder and rose to his feet. "Listen, I gotta get going before Mel organizes a search and rescue for me. Just so you know, Manda's been spending time by herself up on Goodman's Ledge. She mentioned something to Mel about tomorrow morning hiking up by the waterfalls. Kevin won't be with her." Stephen didn't say anything; his look asked the question to which Jim responded. "He had to go back to Baltimore for something urgent that came up."

The sun was bravely peaking out of the clouds in the early morning sky. Amanda parked her rental in the Goodman Park lot and got out her gear. Logging in the registry, she noted that for her route up to the waterfalls she would be using an old deer trail rather than the state-approved trail for most of her hike. Amanda cut through the woods, walking by the old foundation of the Goodman homestead. As she walked, her mind wandered to childhood. So many memories of family gatherings of the good times and the sorrows they had shared. As children, she, Jim, and her cousins had romped through these woods. They picked wild berries and hoped to never have to share their bounty with a black bear.

Bearing off to the right, Amanda made her ascent up a small ledge covered with moss, and to her amazement, she found honeysuckle. Since she was now on state land, it was illegal to pick the honeysuckle, so Amanda took pleasure in bending down touched and drew in a deep breath of the sweet fragrance. Farther up on the top of the next full ledge, Amanda found herself immersed into a thriving patch lily of the valley. The fragrance filled her senses with the sweetness of everything that is good. Taking a long slow sip of water to keep well hydrated, Amanda continued on her way. Following the deer path, which Amanda noticed is used on a regular basis, she came out onto the state-marked trail about a half mile down from the water falls.

Later in the season, this trail would already be noisy with hikers discussing their adventures. Today she relished the solitude of the mountain as the sound of water tumbling over the falls and down the gorge was beckoning her on. Still Amanda paused, assessed her surroundings, and took another sip of water while listening to the mountain speaking to her. About a mile into her two-mile hike, Amanda had felt a presence and thought she heard someone following her. The density of the forest had prohibited her from seeing anyone. Here on a groomed path, Amanda only heard silence; however, she was certain that if someone was following her, she'd know in a few minutes.

Amanda let out a heavy sigh as the falls came into view. "I guess it's true you really can't take the country out of a mountain girl." Amanda scanned the area. Near the edge of the stream not far back from the top of the falls, Amanda found the perfect spot to sit and relax—a flat rocky surface now in full sunlight. The clouds that had been looming overhead earlier had dissipated. The warmth of the sun's ray felt good upon her shoulders as she removed her sweatshirt. Sitting down, Amanda removed her hiking boots to enable her to wiggle her toes. Later she may even get brave and dip her toes in the stream. It was a thought, but for now, her stomach was grumbling so Amanda began scrounging through her day pack for her nourishment. Taking a sip of water, Amanda slowly lowered the bottle to the ground. She didn't turn but continued to gaze upon the water as she spoke; her voice cool and crisp as the late morning air. "Whoever you are come on out of the trees and make your presence known."

The sun was behind him as he stepped out of the tree line so his body cast a shadow. She recognized his silhouette and knew her gut feeling had been right all along. "I came up here to be alone. If I had wanted company, I would have invited someone to come along."

"Would you have invited me?"

"Probably not, since you're one of the people I came here to think about. How did you know I was coming up here anyway?"

By now he was squatting down next to Amanda to take a place on the rock. He didn't respond to her question just yet. Instead, he pulled his thermos out of his pack as well as two cups. Opening the bottle, he poured two cups of hot coffee with cream. "There's no sugar. I brought some packets in case you're taste has changed over the years."

It was then that Amanda finally gazed over at Stephen Johnson. "No, my taste hasn't changed. I still drink it the same way I used to. Thank you. This is very kind. So who suggested you track me up here?"

"Suspicious, aren't you?" Amanda tilted her head down and looked up at Stephen. It still had the same effect as when they were younger. "Now, Amanda, don't go getting ready to spew porcupine quills at me. Last night I had a conversation with Jim, and he may have mentioned where I might find you."

"Well, my brother sure has been busy and—"

"And before you continue to run your mouth sputtering about him interfering or saying whatever else is on your mind, let me tell you he is deeply concerned about all of us, that includes you, me, and our daughter, Summer."

Amanda sat quietly and took a sip of coffee before looking into Stephen's eyes. Warmth and compassion unexpectedly met her. Finding her voice, she quietly asked, "Did you come to appease my brother, or were you concerned something might happen to me?" Much to Amanda's dismay, an unrecognizable look came upon Stephen's face as he spoke with unnerving gentleness.

"Mandy, Jim has nothing to do with my sitting here on this rock with you." Amanda raised an eyebrow, not quite sure she believed Stephen. These two men in her life seemed to have this pact between them, especially where she was concerned. "Granted, he did tell me where you probably would be hanging out today—Okay, will you stop glowering at me? I hate it when you do that."

"Sorry, old habit...You know, they die hard."

"Yeah, don't I know it...I'm sitting next to mine." Amanda huffed in feigned disgust. "At first, I was simply going to see if I could meet up with you before you began your hike. My original plan was to see if we could hike up together on the marked trail. When I saw on the registration form that you had left fifteen minutes before I got here, I was going to leave. Then I read the route you intended to use to come up here to the falls, and I was concerned about your safety."

"Why? You know I'm an experienced climber, and besides, the route is not all that challenging."

"Yes, you certainly are experienced. Now, Mandy, don't look at me that way. I didn't mean it sexually...although if you want we could—"

"Stephen Johnson, you are disgusting." Amanda leaned over, bumping her shoulder into his. "You planned to get my goat with that remark, didn't you?"

"I did not. You're the one who twisted my words, and if memory serves me correctly, you had a habit of doing that when we were younger."

Amanda chuckled. "Guilty as charged. Shall I walk to the edge of the falls and throw myself over to—" Stephen grabbed a hold of Amanda's arms. His abrupt words, fierce expression, and firm hold caused Amanda to gasp.

"Don't you ever threaten to do something so stupid, do you hear me? I don't care if you were jesting with me. There is nothing funny about what you just said." Amanda realized she had gone too far.

"You're hurting me." Stephen immediately released his hold on her. Amanda rubbed the red marks on her arms from his finger imprints. Stephen gently laid his hand on Amanda's hand. She stopped rubbing but did not pull her hand away from his.

"I'm sorry, Amanda, it seems we keep on hurting one another no matter what we do." She looked up so that their eyes met.

Neither one spoke as Stephen removed his hand from Amanda's arm. Comfortable familiar quietness settled over them as they sat and looked at the water making its way to the falls.

"You know, Mandy, what I said before is true. When I signed in the registry and saw the route you took, I was concerned about you being up in the mountain alone and with some physical limitations." Raising his hand to stop Amanda from commenting,

Stephen continued, "Call it chivalrous on my part or whatever you want. I had to follow you. I couldn't let anything happen to you. You see, Amanda, whether you want to believe it or not, you have a family and friends who care about you. I still care about you. That is why your comment about jumping over the falls angered me so much. You are too important to too many people. What would we do without you? I've tried to live without you for thirty years, and at times, it was nearly unbearable."

"Oh, Stephen, please don't complicate things."

But he did as he leaned over and brushed his lips against hers. Amanda was an emotional train wreck. The collision she had been avoiding for so long had just hit her head on. His lips felt warm like the sunshine. Amanda felt herself being drawn in all the while she knew in her heart she shouldn't respond to his invitation. She is now in a relationship with Kevin and that is what she wants, isn't it? But this man now nibbling on her lower lip is Stephen Johnson, love of her youth and her daughter's father. Amanda responded to his kiss. Her fingers found their way to his jaws and into his hair as when they had been together. Then much to her surprise, Stephen pulled away from her.

"I'm sorry, Amanda. I shouldn't have kissed you. You're with Kevin and I...I just—" Amanda put her finger to Stephen's lips.

"Shh...Don't say anything else. Yes. I'm with Kevin, and that is not going to change. I love him with all my heart, and I still care about you. If we hadn't kissed, we would always have wondered. Now we know."

"Yes, we do."

"Stephen, you were the love of my childhood. And as hard as it may be for you to believe this considering everything I've said to you and about you, as much as I have tried to hate you for all these years, I never could. As the old Dolly Parton song goes, 'I will always love you.' With you I conceived two children. One died and one by the grace of God lived. I've already told you how sorry I am that I believed Junior to be Summer's father. You will never know how grateful I am that you are her father. Stephen, you are a good man. I know years ago I said mighty mean and spiteful things to you. You said some rather nasty things to me as well. Who knows perhaps if I had stayed and we had stayed together, maybe we would have separated and then caused great emotional pain for Summer. One of the benefits of my not being here is that I've had Summer through all her tumultuous years of growing up. Now you get to enjoy the harvest."

"I guess I should thank you for giving me the finished product of our daughter."

"Oh, don't thank me just yet! I wouldn't say she's finished by any means." They laughed together knowing full well that their daughter in her early thirties has a zest for life stronger than theirs combined. "Stephen, as my friend, will you do one thing for me?"

"If I can, you know I will."

"Please appreciate and don't hurt our daughter."

"I'll do my best. And, Calli, may I be bold and ask something of you in return?"

"I guess it's only fair."

"Will you go out for dinner with me tonight? I'd kind of like to hear what my best friend has been up to for thirty years." Amanda nodded then smiled a sigh of relief. By the grace of God, they were working it out. Her prayers were being answered. Stephen stood up and stretched. "How about we head back down the mountain? I have some work to do at the bait shop."

EPILOGUE

It was now Sunday night. The week filled with its moments of intense drama had flown by for Amanda. The gathering at Cassie and Andrew's cabin was a festive one with both family and friends gathered together for a spring barbeque. The smells of wood smoke and steak on the grill filled the air with a tantalizing odor. Amanda expected that any time now an old black bear may come meandering through the woods to see if any food was left for it. A smile filled Amanda's heart as she listened to the chatter and laughter of her family and friends. Her grandmother Mary Freeman sat in a cushioned chair listening to Summer. Mary's expression was one of pride as she listened to her great-granddaughter regaling everyone with excerpts of her life as a national park ranger. Amanda then turned her attention to Jim as he listened to Summer speak. What she saw brought joy to her heart. Jim Callison was proud of his niece as if she was one of his own daughters. *Family*, Amanda thought, *it's a good thing*. Sighing to herself, she added, "And it only took me thirty years to figure it out. Well, I guess it's better late than never."

As the coolness of evening in the mountains in spring settled in, Amanda stretched. "Oh goodness ya'll this food was amazing. I do believe I ate too much." Those sitting around the table concurred with her on her observation. Standing up, Amanda added, "If you all will excuse me, I feel the need for an evening stroll down by the lake." Her eyes fell on Cassie's as she walked toward the steps. The two friends spoke without words both knowing that this time there was no fleeing from but drawing to for healing and renewal.

Amanda, fully aware of the boisterous conversation around the picnic table on the front porch of the cabin overlooking the lake, made her way down to the shore. She listened to the sounds of evening as the light of the evening sky was slipping away. Shadows loomed all around her. Tonight Amanda felt no fear. No one or nothing could hurt her. Junior and Shannon were now behind bars serving time for their crimes against her and other women. Stephen Johnson now had a new place in her life, one that she was beginning to like.

Amanda took in a deep breath as she found the rock she had sat upon with Kevin when they had first met back in December of the previous year. Now four months later, she climbed up the rock and took a seat, dangling her legs over toward the water. Without realizing it, a smile came upon her lips as she recalled their first interrupted kiss that had taken place on the rock. Tonight there would be no kiss interrupted or otherwise. Plain and simple, Amanda missed her man. Kevin had returned to Baltimore on Wednesday to handle some unexpected issues with his divorce from Meg. That ugly mess was a stumbling block in their relationship moving on to their exchanging of marital vows. She would have gladly gone with Kevin so he didn't have to face the barracuda alone; however, he suggested that she stay and spend time with Summer, family, and further resolve her past with Stephen Johnson. With a kiss that could have melted more of the polar ice cap and tears, Amanda had said her good-bye. Amanda sighed; she knew Kevin had been right in suggesting she remain behind. It had been a good week for her to work through more of her past. Now as Amanda listened to the frivolity of her family and friends, she missed her man.

Amanda looked up into the dark sky to take in the first stars of night. "How does that saying go? Starlight, star bright, first star I see tonight," Amanda quietly said aloud only to be startled by a quiet voice. Amanda gasped. She had not heard a car drive up to the cabin nor had she heard a car door. She also had not heard approaching footsteps.

"I hope I'm what you're wishing for. May I join you on your rock?" Amanda looked down from the rock to find Kevin smiling up at her.

"I'd like that. I've been waiting for you here on *our* rock."

Kevin climbed up onto the rock and sat next to Amanda. He took her hand into his and leaned over, brushing his lips against hers. Smoldering heat shot through Amanda as their kiss intensified. Oh how she cherished this man. Kevin slowly pulled away from Amanda and looked intently into her eyes. Tears were forming.

"Amanda, what's wrong?"

"Nothing really. I love you so much, Kevin. You knew exactly what I needed to do this week even before I did. Thank you for being with me during the trial and DNA disclosure, thank you for trusting me to deal with Stephen on my own, and for now being here with me. I could not have made it through all this new drama without you."

"Oh, my love, you're welcome." Kevin gently pulled Amanda into his arms. Amanda let out a heavy sigh and rested her head on Kevin's shoulder. They sat together in silence looking out onto the lake at dusk. It was peaceful for both of them. Kevin could feel Amanda's body grow more relaxed in his arms. "Amanda, I've been thinking."

"Oh."

"Yes, my love. I've had plenty of time during car rides and flights to and from Baltimore to reflect on our relationship." Amanda tightened in Kevin's arms. He rubbed her arms. "Shush, relax, Amanda, breath. We're okay. Just listen and hear what I'm about to say." Amanda nodded. "Last year ended and this year began with significant turbulence in both of our lives. I think it's time for us to change that." Amanda looked at Kevin with skepticism. She was tired and had no idea what he was thinking. "Amanda, I love you with all my heart, and I can't keep waiting for crises to end in our lives to ask you this." Amanda's heart started to race...She was panicked, but this felt like a totally different panic...one unfamiliar to her. Kevin pulled a ring out of his pocket and began to place it on her significant finger of her left hand. "Amanda, will you marry me?"

Amanda was in shock. "What about Meg? Your divorce isn't final. How can you ask me to marry you?" In the moonlight now shining down on them, Amanda saw something of mischief in Kevin's eyes.

"As of this past Friday, the divorce is final. Honey, I would have flown back on Friday night, but I had to wait until this morning to pick up your ring." Amanda began to cry. "Oh, sweetheart, please don't cry on me. Let me ask you once again. Amanda Newman, I love you and would be honored if you would spend the rest of your life with me. Will you marry me?"

Amanda felt light-headed. "Yes."

As they brought their lips together, an eruption of cheers was heard from the porch of cabin in the Pines. Jim and Melissa stood with Cassie and Andrew they raised their glasses of wine for a toast. The old woman leaned over toward Summer and was heard saying, "I was beginning to think I'd have to do one of my interventions again and bring them together over venison stew. I just may live to see her married yet!"

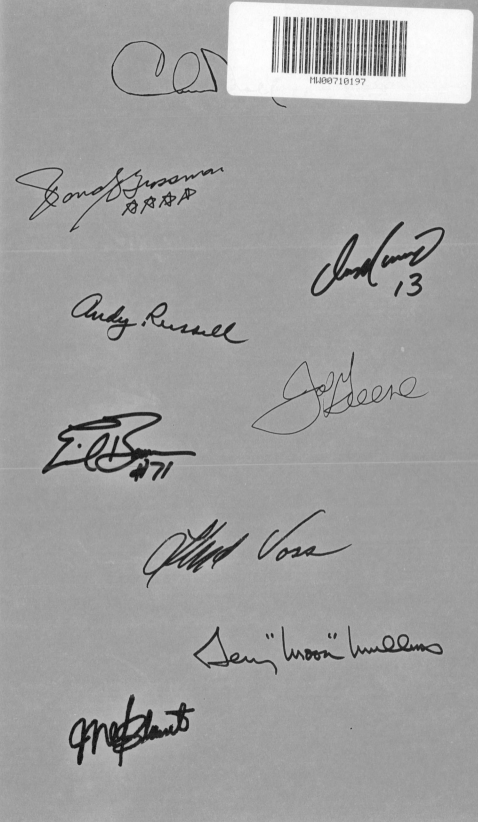

MW00710197

Merry Christmas 2004

To Denny,

Always a Stuler!

Hope you enjoy my
stories and your
own memories. Esther,
Bria, Lindsay, Kristin
and Brennon offer
this to you with love and
pride.

Best wishes,

Jim O'Brien

11-13-2004

ALWAYS A
Steeler

By Jim O'Brien

George Gojkovich

*"Once a Steeler,
always a Steeler."*
— Terry Bradshaw

Books By Jim O'Brien

COMPLETE HANDBOOK OF PRO BASKETBALL 1970-1971

COMPLETE HANDBOOK OF PRO BASKETBALL 1971-1972

ABA ALL-STARS

PITTSBURGH: THE STORY OF THE CITY OF CHAMPIONS

HAIL TO PITT: A SPORTS HISTORY OF
THE UNIVERSITY OF PITTSBURGH

DOING IT RIGHT

WHATEVER IT TAKES

MAZ AND THE '60 BUCS

REMEMBER ROBERTO

PENGUIN PROFILES

DARE TO DREAM

KEEP THE FAITH

WE HAD 'EM ALL THE WAY

HOMETOWN HEROES

GLORY YEARS

THE CHIEF

STEELERS FOREVER

ALWAYS A STEELER

To order copies of these titles directly from the publisher, send $26.95 for hardcover edition. Please send $3.50 to cover shipping and handling costs per book. Pennsylvania residents add 6% sales tax to price of book only. Allegheny County residents add an additional 1% sales tax for a total of 7% sales tax. Copies will be signed by author at your request. Discounts available for large orders. Contact publisher regarding availability and prices of all books in Pittsburgh Proud series, or to request an order form. Some books are sold out and no longer available. You can still order the following: Doing It Right, Dare To Dream, Remember Roberto, We Had 'Em All The Way, Hometown Heroes, Glory Years, Keep The Faith, The Chief and Steelers Forever. E-mail address: jpobrien@stargate.net.

George Gojkovich

Jim O'Brien

Author's mother, Mary O'Brien, enjoys meeting Rocky Bleier at Asbury Heights, an assisted-care facility near his home in Mt. Lebanon.

This book is dedicated to the memory of
my dear mother, Mary M. O'Brien.
She helped me with these books, magazines and
newspapers in earlier years to make sure I got it right.

Cover photo by George Gojkovich

Copyright © 2003 by Jim O'Brien

All rights reserved

James P. O'Brien — Publishing
P.O. Box 12580
Pittsburgh PA 15241
Phone: (412) 221-3580
E-mail: jpobrien@stargate.net

First printing: August, 2003

Manufactured in the United States of America

Printed by Geyer Printing Company, Inc.
3700 Bigelow Boulevard
Pittsburgh PA 15213

Typography by Cold-Comp
91 Green Glen Drive
Pittsburgh PA 15227

ISBN 1-886348-09-X

Contents

6	Acknowledgments	251	Dr. Joseph C. Maroon
9	Preface	263	Rick Druschel
13	Comeback stories	270	Merril Hoge
16	Mike Webster's funeral	284	Pete Duranko
28	Chuck Miller reflects	294	Bob Milie
29	Mike Webster	310	Ron Shanklin
54	Former NFL players	314	Life's work
56	Johnny Unitas	319	From the '50s
59	Ray Mansfield	327	Joe Greene
62	Leon Hart	337	Art Rooney Jr.
66	Clark Hayes	349	Mel Blount
80	Lou Curinga	366	Roy Jefferson
84	Jon Kolb	373	Ernie Holmes
91	Terry Bradshaw	379	Jack Lambert
106	Snapshot: Boomer Esiason	385	Rocky Bleier
107	Mike Webster tribute	394	Looking after the children
120	Night to remember	402	UPMC Sports Center
126	Steve Courson	403	Tom Clements
139	Snapshot: Johnny Majors	416	Tommy Maddox
140	Brother Pat Lacey	434	Snapshot: John Elway
147	St. Vincent College	435	Charlie Batch
152	Harry Carson	448	Antwaan Randle El
161	Snapshot: Donnie Shell	455	Kendrell Bell
162	Dick Modzelewski	461	Amos Zereoue
174	Snapshot: Matt Bahr	471	Dan Marino
175	Marvin Lewis	474	Art & Terry
184	Hayes family	476	Jim Clack
186	Robin Cole	482	Dinosaurs
196	Cliff Stoudt	484	Revisiting Steelers
214	Andy Russell	499	Sojourns on South Side
224	Mike Wagner	508	The real ironmen
236	John Banaszak	512	Author's page

Acknowledgments

"The past is never dead.
It's not even past."
— William Faulkner

The year 2003 got off to a difficult start. There was more snow and then more rain than Pittsburgh experienced in many years. There were too many gray days. The economy and stock market were in their third year of a precipitous slide. Two friends, both in their 60s, died of cancer. My mother, Mary O'Brien, died in March. She was 96 and I was fortunate to have her so long, but it hurt just the same. There was a time when she did the proofreading for my newspapers and magazines and, at the very beginning, some of my books. At the end, she had dementia, so I know what it's like to have a loved one lose her mind.

So Mike Webster was not just another story. Terry Bradshaw was a story of ups and downs, and so was Tommy Maddox. Their comebacks in Pittsburgh helped soften the blow of the stories and the death of Webster. They offer hope to all of us who are willing to work hard and persevere. There were other inspirational stories that caught my attention. We can learn lessons from all of them. Many Steelers, past and present, were challenged in different ways.

Family and friends and faith are so important to all of us. We can't survive without them. I'm grateful for those who were there when I needed them. I appreciate the patrons who support my writing and publishing efforts. Books like this one and the others in the "Pittsburgh Proud" series wouldn't be possible without the support system I've had over the last 20 years.

Loyal patrons include Anthony W. Accamando, Jr. of Adelphia Cable Communications; Tom Kehoe of Affordable Car & Truck Rental; J.T. Thomas and Larry Brown of Applebee's Neighborhood Grill & Bar; John Zanardelli of Asbury Heights; Louis Astorino and Dennis Astorino of LD Astorino Associates, Ltd.; Pat McDonnell and Jay Dabat of Atria's Restaurant & Tavern; Ronald B. Livingston Sr. of Babb, Inc.; Bill Baierl of Baierl Automotive Group; Rich Barcelona of Bailey-PVS Oxides LLC; Andrew F. Komer of Bowne of Pittsburgh; Boys & Girls Club of Western Pennsylvania; the National Baseball Hall of Fame and Museum; Robert Seiden of Bryan Mechanical/SSM Industries; Ralph Papa of Citizens Bank; Howard "Hoddy" Hanna of Hanna Real Estate Services.

Don Carlucci of Carlucci Construction Co.; Kenneth F. Codeluppi of Wall-Firma. Inc.; Tom Sweeney and Joe Reljac of Compucom, Inc.; Tom Snyder of Continental Design & Management Group; James T. Davis of Davis & Davis Law Offices, Armand Dellovade of A.C. Dellovade, Inc.; Don DeBlasio of DeBlasio's Restaurant; Suzy and Jim Broadhurst of Eat'n Park Hospitality Group; Everett Burns of E-Z

Overhead Door & Window Co., James S. Hamilton of Federated Securities Corporation; David J. Malone of Gateway Financial; John M. Kish and Todd L. Cover of Great American Federal; Dr. Ken Melani and Jack Shaw of Highmark Blue Cross & Blue Shield.

John E. McGinley Jr. and John R. McGinley of Wilson-McGinley Co.; Steve Fedell of Ikon Office Solutions; Lou Grippo of the Original Oyster House; Frank Gustine Jr. of Armstrong Gustine Development, Inc. Fred Kienast of Limbach Company; Ed Lewis of Oxford Development Co.; Paul Walsh of Pittsburgh Athletic Association; Jeffrey Berger of Heinz, U.S.A.; Mike Hagan of Iron & Glass Bank; William V. Campbell of Intuit; Jack Mascaro of Mascaro Construction; Joseph A. Massaro, Jr. of The Massaro Company.

F. James McCarl, Robert Santillo and Danny Rains of McCarl's, Inc.; David B. Jancisin of Merrill Lynch; Thomas W. Golonski, Anthony J. Molinero, Angela Longo, and William S. Eiler of National City Bank of Pennsylvania; Jack Perkins of Mr. P's in Greensburg; Dan R. Lackner of Paper Products Company, Inc.; A. Robert Scott of Point; Joe Browne Sr. of National Football League; Joseph Piccirilli and Tony Ferraro of Pittsburgh Brewing Company, Andy Russell of Laurel Mountain Partners, LLC.

Lloyd Gibson and John Schultz of NorthSide Bank; Pat and John Rooney of Palm Beach Kennel Club; Patrick J. Santelli of Pfizer Labs; Sy Holzer of PNC Bank Corp.; Pennsylvania Sports Hall of Fame, Pro Football Hall of Fame, Fred Sargent of Sargent Electric.

Jim Roddey and Michael J. Fetchko of SportsWave, Inc. (International Sports Marketing); Daniel A. Goetz of Stylette, Inc.; Vince Locher of Sky Bank; Dick Swanson of Swanson Group Ltd.; Robert J. Taylor of Taylor & Hladio Law Offices; Jim, Barbara and Ted Frantz of TEDCO Construction Corp.

John Paul of University of Pittsburgh Medical Center; John Lucey and Alex J. Pociask of USFilter; Thomas J. Usher of USX Corporation; Clark Nicklas of Vista Resources, Inc.; Stephen Previs of Waddell & Reed Financial Services; John Seretti Chevrolet Inc.; Judd Gordon of Western Pennsylvania Caring Foundation; Ray Conaway of Zimmer Kunz, PLLC; Gordon R. Oliver of Steeltech, Inc., Bill Shields of McCann Shields Paint Company, Bob Randall of TRACO, Inc.; Bill Tillotson of Hefren-Tillotson, Inc.; Mike Wagner of Capital Markets-HT.

Friends who have been boosters include Aldo Bartolotta, Mel Bassi of Charleroi Federal Savings Bank, Jon C. Botula, Judge John G. Brosky, John Bruno, Miles Bryan, Dave and Frank Clements, Art Cipriani, Beano Cook, Joseph Costanzo Jr., Ralph Cindrich of Cindrich & Company in Carnegie, Tony and Ronnie DeNunzio of DeNunzio's Restaurant, Jim Godwin of J. Allan Steel, Joe Goldstein, Joe Gordon Dave R. Hart, Harvey and Darrell Hess, Mrs. Elsie Hillman, Zeb Jansante, Dr. Dan Kanell, Zundy Kramer, Jim Lokhaiser, Fred J. Mackaness, Gregory L. Manesiotis, John Marous, Paul Martha, Ron Maser of Maser Galleries, Robert F. McClurg,

7

Dennis Meteny, George Morris, Mark Nordenberg, Andy Ondrey, Ed Prebor, Art Rooney Jr., Len Stidle, Dr. Edward Sweeney, George Schoeppner, Steven A. Stepanian II, Ron Temple, W. Harrison Vail, Tom Volovich, State Senator Jack Wagner, Dorothy Weldon, John Williams, Jr., Bill Wolf, Gene Zappa, Rudy Zupancic of Giant Eagle.

Friends who have offered special encouragement and prayer and those who have opened up doors for our endeavors include Bill Priatko, Rudy Celigoi, Herb Douglas, Bob Shearer, Jim Kriek, Foge Fazio, Bob Friend, Stan Goldmann, Ed Lutz, Pete Mervosh, Joan and Thomas J. Bigley, Mike Ference, Phillip Monti, Art Stroyd, Bob Lovett and Debbie Keenan of Reed Smith Shaw & McClay, Patrick T. Lanigan of Lanigan's Funeral Home, Art Rooney Jr., Tom O'Malley Jr. of the Bob Purkey Insurance Agency, Sally O'Leary, Chuck Klausing, Nellie Briles of Pittsburgh Pirates. My heartfelt thanks to Mavis Trasp, my "Christmas angel" and her daughter, Sherry Kisic, and their friends at Century III Mall for all their kindness.

Another of my angels, Gerry Hamilton of Oakmont, handled the proof-reading for this book, and provided kind assistance at many of my booksignings. I do all my work with Pittsburgh firms. All of my books have been produced at Geyer Printing. Bruce McGough, Tom Samuels, Charlie Stage and Keith Maiden are great to work with each year. Denise Maiden, Cathy Pawlowski and Rebecca Hula Fatalsky of Cold-Comp Typographers did their usual outstanding job.

The *Almanac* newspaper in the South Hills, for which I have been writing a man-about-town column for the past 12 years, has promoted my book signing appearances through the years, as has *The Valley Mirror* in Homestead-Munhall. I have always appreciated the efforts of Pittsburgh photographers George Gojkovich, Michael F. Fabus, Bill Amatucci, Ted Thompson, Jay Nodianos and Mike Longo. Ron Wahl and Dave Lockett of Steelers' public relations staff were particularly helpful.

My support team begins with my wife of 36 years, Kathleen Churchman O'Brien, and our daughters, Dr. Sarah O'Brien-Zirwas, Rebecca O'Brien and Rebecca's dog, Bailey O'Brien. My son-in-law, Dr. Matthew Zirwas, is also a point of pride. They make it all worthwhile. Sports author Dick Schaap said his favorite sport was people. I agree.

As this book was going to press, Marie Ellen Rooney McGinley died at age 84. Mrs. McGinley was a sister of late Steelers founder Art Rooney Sr. and the wife of Jack McGinley, a minority partner in the pro franchise. Mrs. McGinley hosted family and friends in the family's suite at Heinz Field and Three Rivers Stadium. She was a sweet lady. She, too, was always a Steeler. The Steelers, ironically enough, opened training camp for the 2003 season on the same day she was buried. This book is in her honor as well.

— Jim O'Brien

Postcard to author from Art Rooney, Jan. 21, 1970:

"We don't know what to do with our first choice. Whatever we do, I hope we guess right. Good luck, Art."

Preface

*"This was the greatest landing
I ever made."*
— **Dan Rooney**

Iknew the Steelers were going to have an interesting season by some of the reported events at the outset of the summer of 2002. I thought there might be a good book in it, so I'd better pay attention. I had no idea how much more interesting it would get.

The stories were about Marvel Smith, Dan Rooney and Jerome Bettis. They pointed up how one day — when you just happen to be at the wrong place at the wrong time — can change your life forever. Or even end your life, if you're not lucky.

Steelers' founder Arthur J. Rooney, a great handicapper at the race tracks, used to say, "I'd rather be lucky than good."

The two Steelers, Smith and Bettis, both did something without giving a great deal of thought to it that hurt their images, and Rooney, the president of the Steelers, showed a cool head and a veteran air pilot's savvy to save the day and enhance his sterling image.

Years ago, when several Steelers were involved in auto accidents around the same time, with one rookie losing his life in a collision not far from St. Vincent College in Latrobe where the Steelers have their summer training camp, Rooney had remarked, "Now you know why auto insurance rates are so high for young people."

In mid-July, just before the Steelers were to report to training camp, Marvel Smith, a starting offensive tackle, was arrested in Tempe, Arizona for smoking marijuana in public. He was charged with one count of possession of marijuana, a felony in Arizona.

This was not the first time Smith got into trouble with marijuana. As a junior at Arizona State University in that same community he tested positive for marijuana in routine tests conducted by the school's athletic department. What struck me was the brazenness or stupidity of Smith, but 23-year-old athletes don't always think about the consequences of their actions. Somehow rules don't apply to them. Consider Kobe Bryant of the Los Angeles Lakers.

Dan Masters, public information sergeant for the Tempe police, said that around 11:45 p.m. on July 12, an officer on horseback was patrolling outside the Tempe Mission Palms Hotel when he smelled marijuana coming from an open window. The hotel is in downtown Tempe, next to the police station. Get the picture now?

Two other officers who were patrolling the area on bicycles contacted hotel security and were told that several guests had complained about the smell. The officers knocked on Smith's door and asked him who was with him. "Just my wife," he replied. Masters said Smith admitted to hiding some marijuana in his shoe. "It was a usable quantity," reported one of the police officers, whatever that means.

The Steelers managed to get Smith out of this jam. They have lots of practice. He apologized and seemed contrite enough when he came to training camp. Smith, a 6-3, 315-pounder, was the Steelers' second round draft pick out of Arizona State in 2000. He became the first rookie offensive lineman to start his first game for the Steelers. He became the full-time starting right tackle midway through his rookie season. He has yet to show star talent or consistency.

I remember meeting Smith for the first time, along with his fiancee, when we were both booked to appear on "Sportsbeat" and we said hello to each other in the Fox Sports studios at Allegheny Center on Pittsburgh's North Side.

Smith was wearing one of those doo-rags popularized by NFL players. They wear them under their helmets during games. They were first popularized by fashion-setter Deion Sanders. It was a gray one and was color-coordinated with the Oakland Raiders jersey he was wearing. I thought it odd that Smith would show up for a TV appearance in Pittsburgh wearing an Oakland Raiders shirt. He had no idea how much Steelers' fans hate the Raiders. Smith and I were both interviewed by Guy Junker. His co-host Stan Savran was off that night.

I learned that Smith grew up in Oakland, California, the same as the Pirates' Willie Stargell and so many other great athletes.

I thought about Gertrude Stein, the author who once lived in a brownstone row house in the same neighborhood as the Rooneys on the North Side. It's a home, by the way, that was up for sale in the summer of 2003. Gertrude Stein once observed of Oakland, California that "there's no there there."

That explains a lot about Marvel Smith, too, I think.

"Only in America."
—Harry Golden... and Baldy Regan

Now for the story about Dan Rooney...

On Wednesday, July 31, 2002, Rooney was flying his airplane from the Arnold Palmer Airport in Latrobe, just across Route 30 from St. Vincent College, to the Allegheny County Airport in West Mifflin, just southeast of Pittsburgh. It's a 40-mile trip. Rooney's plane had a mechanical problem, and he couldn't get the wheels down. He was forced to make an emergency belly landing.

Rooney, then 70 years old, had nearly 2,000 hours of piloting experience. As he was approaching the airport in West Mifflin he realized that his Cessna had no electrical power. He attempted to lower the landing gear manually, but the hand crank jammed.

Rooney was unable to reach the control tower at the airport, so he used his cell phone to call 911. "The fellow at 911 did a great job,"

Rooney related a few days later when he spoke to reporters at training camp. "He contacted the tower and was relaying the messages between the tower and me. I got the instructions of what they wanted me to do." Rooney circled the airport a few times to burn fuel. Then his cell phone went dead.

"So I just shook my wings and came in and landed," said Rooney, choosing to land on the grass rather than the runway to prevent the possibility of sparks igniting a fire. "I kept going forward, no spin or anything like that, and then finally I hit the markers that say which runway it was. And I hit that, and that put the plane in a turn and the plane came to a stop."

Rooney got out of the plane, and walked to a waiting emergency medical crew. Charles Lindberg never looked so good. Paramedics checked him out. He was fine. He telephoned his wife, Pat, at their home on the North Side, telling her with boyish enthusiasm: "This was the greatest landing I ever made." Rooney said he wasn't afraid. "I really was fine flying," he said. "I did not panic."

Coach Bill Cowher was concerned about his boss' wellbeing and was glad to hear he was okay. "I told him there's a road with the No. 30 on it that's not a bad way of going," said Cowher. "I'd rather see him just drive up here, but he loves to fly. He said it was the best landing he ever had and he got right back on the bike. To his credit, he handled it like we knew he would."

Rooney returned to the training camp the following day, flying a new plane, and he brought his wife Pat along for the ride. That points up Pat's faith in her husband, and that both are confident individuals. That's how they raised nine children. Rooney's dad, Arthur J. Rooney, also did a little flying in his day. He was taking lessons to be a pilot, and legend has it that he flew a plane under some of the bridges of Pittsburgh and buzzed the City-County Building where some of his friends had offices. He was a bit of a daredevil. His wife, Kathleen, then pregnant with Dan — the first of their five sons — begged her husband to cease his craziness. She said she wanted her child to have a father. And Rooney gave up piloting airplanes. Chuck Noll has a pilot's license, but no longer flies his own plane.

Just as training camp was about to end in late August, Jerome Bettis got into trouble. He was hanging out with some of his teammates at Bobby Dale's Restaurant and Bar, a popular watering hole on Route 30, not far from St. Vincent College.

A woman approached him. Bettis had no idea it was a setup. She had been advised by a teacher at Penn State's McKeesport campus to do this. Bettis, a bachelor, was fair game. He was one of the most popular of the Pittsburgh Steelers, one of the best paid, the one with the most endorsements.

Bettis had been named the NFL's Man of the Year for his community service. His record was impeccable. He was one of my favorite Steelers. He had given so much of himself to the Steelers and their fans. He had taken his family everywhere with him to share in his good fortune. As a rookie, one of the first things he did was buy his mother and father a new home in Detroit. Former Steelers' publicist Joe Gordon says, "Jerome Bettis and Mark Bruener are on my all-time Top Ten list of good guys with the Steelers."

The woman would later accuse Bettis of forcing himself on her. She went to the Greensburg police with her charges. Bettis was later cleared of all charges when police learned of the conspiracy involved.

The bad press soiled the squeaky-clean image of Bettis, but it shouldn't erase all his good actions and efforts through the years. Men just get stupid once in a while. When Kobe Bryant became fodder for sports talk shows the following summer, Bettis was often mentioned in the same conversation.

Look what happened that same summer. On Tuesday, June 24, Marvel Amos Smith signed a contract extension with the Steelers. Smith was being switched from right tackle to the more important left tackle position — where protecting the quarterback's blind side from the rush is critical — and was considered a key factor in the team's future prospects. The 24-year-old Smith signed a five-year, $25.5 million contract extension that included a $6 million signing bonus. They offered him more money than they had offered to 32-year-old left tackle Wayne Gandy, who left as a free agent to sign with the New Orleans Saints. Smith's $5.1 million average salary put him among the league's elite at that position. He turned 25 on August 6.

When I heard about Smith's signing, I thought about the late Bernard J. "Baldy" Regan, a wheeler-and-dealer who was known as the "Mayor of the North Side" and organized and coached the Steelers' basketball team. He was always one of my favorite Pittsburgh characters. He held an annual Christmas party in his magistrate's offices near Perry Traditional Academy, and the crowd there one night prompted his friend Larry Werner to observe, "Baldy has the only parties where judges and criminals are in the same room."

Baldy had a favorite phrase that he stole from Harry Golden, the editor and publisher of a newspaper called *The Carolina Israelite*.

Golden had a collection of his philosophical feel-good columns published in a book called *Only in America*.

When Baldy Regan saw someone he knew who enjoyed some success, he'd say, "Only in America." Whenever he'd see me, for instance, he'd say, "From Hazelwood to New York . . . only in America!"

When Regan, a life-long friend of the Rooney family, recognized how far Marvel Smith had come from smoking marijuana next to the police station in Tempe, Arizona to signing a contract for over $25 million in Pittsburgh, surely he'd have screamed, "Only in America!"

This then is about one extraordinary team's journey through the triumphs and tragedies of pro football and life.

"The Irish cry at card tricks."
— Jimmy Cagney

Comeback stories
Duranko is a Steeler at heart

"I'm still smiling and praying."

Pete Duranko has always been the life of the party. He likes to entertain people, keep them laughing. He was always a blast at a wedding reception, urging the band or deejay to play a polka. He loved to sing and dance. He'd tell the audience he was going to sing the Notre Dame Fight Song in Polish. And then he would. Only he doesn't speak Polish. He'd just make it up as he went along, pure gibberish, like Sid Caesar used to do, he'd tell you.

On Karaoke Night, anywhere, Duranko was dangerous. My wife has always told me I'm dangerous with a microphone in hand, and the same is true of Duranko. He doesn't know when to quit.

"I can do it in Hawaiian, too," Duranko declared, still talking about the Notre Dame Fight Song. "Anything for a laugh."

The days are often difficult for Duranko. When he's not dancing or singing, or telling stories and jokes, he has time to dwell on what's gone wrong with his health and his life. It's serious stuff. Of all the people I interviewed for this book, Duranko stays with me the most. It wasn't just an interview. Pete Duranko is a person with a big problem and it's not going to go away. He gave me a big hug the last time we parted. His story goes beyond sports to reveal an understanding of life. He didn't sign up for such a story.

Duranko didn't play for the Steelers. But he was a teammate of Jack Ham at Bishop McCourt High School, he still lives in Johnstown, and he should have been a Steeler. Instead, he played for the Denver Broncos from 1967 to 1975. He was a teammate of Rocky Bleier on Notre Dame's national championship team in 1966. He comes to meetings of former Steelers in Pittsburgh. He's one of them.

Back in 1999, Duranko was diagnosed with ALS — amyotrophic lateral sclerosis, the silent killer better known as Lou Gehrig's disease. Gehrig, the Yankee Hall of Famer, found out he had this disease when he was 36. He died two years later, at age 38. Most people live three to five years after they are diagnosed, but treatment has improved and some are living longer. There is no cure for Lou Gehrig's disease. Duranko believes that someday they will find a cure.

"If we can send someone to the moon, surely we can conquer this," he says, hopefully. "With today's technology breakthroughs, they can find a cure."

There are days he has difficulty combing his hair. Or knotting his tie. Or tying his shoes. It takes him an hour-and-a-half to get dressed to go anywhere. This is a man who used to walk around the football field on his hands, or do the same thing on the dance floor at a wedding.

Now he's sitting across the table from me at Fathead's, a restaurant bar on the South Side of Pittsburgh, and he's holding a glass of raspberry iced tea with two hands.

"It gets frustrating," he confesses, "and I swear a lot, but you learn to deal with it. I don't want any sympathy."

There's much bravado about Pete "Diesel" Duranko. He puts on a good front. No one knows how he really feels.

Johnstown is 30 miles north of the town of Quecreek, Pennsylvania, where they rescued nine coal miners who had been trapped 240 feet underground for three days. It was a story that seized the nation's attention in late July, 2002.

Johnstown is even closer to Shanksville, where United Flight 93 crashed on September 11, 2001. That flight carried 45 passengers and several of them rushed the terrorists who had taken over the plane and were going to reroute it to Washington D.C. to do more damage that day. The plane instead crashed in Shanksville, killing everybody aboard. Duranko believes the brave men who charged the hijackers were real American heroes. "When we hear 'America the Beautiful' and 'God Bless America' now, it means more to us," he said.

Duranko also has a cousin who is a policeman in New York and was personally affected by 9-11. After discussing these events with Duranko, my wife and I paid a visit to Shanksville later in the summer.

"I think what we have gone through at home shows the steadfastness of Pennsylvanians," said Duranko. "That mine disaster showed how good and tough people are. I wake up and I'm miserable and it's tough getting going. It takes longer, but once I get going, get around people, then I get excited." Pete Duranko doesn't know what's ahead of him. When he first learned of his disease, he admits he cried out at times, "Why the hell did this happen to me?"

Lou Gehrig's disease causes the motor nerve cells to stop functioning and begin to die. Eventually, all the muscles, including those controlling swallowing and breathing, become paralyzed. This could be depressing, but Duranko's story rescues the spirit. He confesses to human feelings and emotions.

"At Notre Dame, I learned how to get knocked down and get back up again," he says. He goes everywhere he can help these days to spread the word about Lou Gehrig's disease and to cheer up others. He hugs Down Syndrome children at a Special Olympics. "When they see me, they smile," says Duranko, "because they know I have something, too. I feel good making them feel good."

He worries about his wife Janet and their sons, Greg and Nick, and how they will deal with his difficulties when they worsen. "I thank God for my family," he says. "It's a lonely disease, it really is. People love you and want to do something, but your spouse ends up taking care of you. I believe in the Blessed Mother and she helped me through high school, college and the pros. She helped me when I thought about leaving Notre Dame. She'll get me through this. I am religious, but I'm not a religious freak, you know? I think you have to pray and that helps get you over the hump sometimes."

He said he would gladly accept your prayers and your jokes. "I'll keep living every day," he said with a smile, blinking his dark eyes.

This book is about comebacks, and battles with different kinds of afflictions and adversities. It's about some aspects of professional football we don't hear a lot about. It's about a situation that keeps some former pro football players awake at night.

It's about Mike Webster, trying to find his way when he had suffered brain damage. It's about Terry Bradshaw, battling with lifelong depression and self-doubts. It's about Tommy Maddox, dealing with repeated rejection from teams throughout the National Football League. It's about Merril Hoge and Jim Clack teaching us how to deal with cancer. It's about Steelers dealing with separation from the game and the spotlight and the money and adulation and, too often their wives. Just as I was finishing this book I learned of the breakup of the marriages of former Steelers Jim Sweeney and Mike Tomczak. In earlier books I've written, both spoke enthusiastically about their wives and families. What went wrong? It's about the challenges they have faced and overcome, for the most part.

"They came from different backgrounds, different parts of the country," as Stephen Ambrose wrote of the Men of Easy Company in his World War II book, *Band of Brothers*. "They were farmers, and coal miners, mountainmen and sons of the Deep South." The same was true of the Steelers. They had, as Bradshaw said, "a bond that could not be broken."

When Bradshaw came back to Pittsburgh, a prodigal son straight out of the Bible that has always been more important to him than his playbook, he announced, "Once a Steeler . . . always a Steeler." Like it or not, they were Steelers forever. They were talented young men and they were well coached. They became a family of sorts.

This book is about challenged people like Pete Duranko and, most of all, it's about some of our favorite Steelers through the years. Some of the stories weren't easy to write. I'm hoping it will help others deal with difficulties and come through a winner. These Steelers can show us the way. Their stories are somber and provocative and illuminating. They've given us even more to cheer about. I'm grateful to all of them for their time and graciousness and, most of all, their stories.

"Comeback stories, examples of tenacity under pressure, provide a model for beating the odds. They become part of the collective imagination, and they are drawn on in countless situations by people in all walks of life. The stories tell us never to give up — that failure can turn to success, that misfortune can be overcome, that the human spirit is indomitable, and that all of us are stronger working with one another than we are working alone."
— **Bill Bradley, From** *Values of the Game*

Mike Webster's Funeral
Saying goodbye to a good man

"It was a strange scene."

I wasn't sure whether I should go to Mike Webster's funeral. There seemed to be a lot of anger with the Websters toward the Pittsburgh Steelers, the Rooneys and anyone they felt had done Mike Webster wrong. This anger had been building up through the years like lava in a volcano, and was now spewing forth from the mouth of Mike's 18-year-old son Garrett.

Garrett was a big guy, at 6-8, 335 pounds, so people listened when he spoke. He was bigger than anybody who had ever played for the Pittsburgh Steelers. Garrett got the attention of the Pittsburgh media and railed against those he felt failed to help his father when he needed their support. It wasn't a pretty picture. It was disturbing.

I thought Mike Webster would be upset at some of the stuff his son was saying. It had never been Webster's style to behave that way. Garrett had been looking after his father the previous two years at a house in Moon Township. They slept on mattresses laid on the floor. The place was a mess. It's not a scene that would be shown in a spread in *Good Housekeeping.*

Garrett was going to the local high school, playing on its football team and coming home to take care of his father. Their roles had been reversed and Garrett, big as he might be, was only 18 years old. He was cast in a role he wasn't ready for. Mike and his wife, Pam, had split up several years earlier. His personal difficulties divided them.

"My father would go out sometimes and call home," related Garrett, "and tell us he didn't know where he was. We'd get him to describe his surroundings, and go get him."

Stories like that were unsettling to those who had played ball with Webster, but didn't know all the details of what was going on in his life. Most knew Webster had gotten into trouble, faking drug prescriptions, that he wasn't himself, and that he had been avoiding most Steelers' social functions with former teammates. It was difficult enough to deal with the fact that Webster was only 50 years old when he died of a heart attack. Pittsburghers pause and shake their heads ruefully at the mere mention of Mike Webster's name.

I was at the Ray Mansfield Memorial Golf Outing at Diamond Run in the North Hills on Monday September 25, 2002, when the word got out that Webster had suffered a heart attack. He would die at the outset of the following day at Allegheny General Hospital. So many of his former teammates were there, along with Chuck Noll and Art Rooney II, when they learned of Webster's heart attack. Many of the same Steelers were reassembled for the funeral service. Former Steelers' publicist Joe Gordon, who coordinates this golf tourney each year, pitched in to help the Websters with funeral arrangements.

"It seemed like a dysfunctional family," said one of Webster's former teammates who attended the funeral service. "It was a strange scene. I mean having an 18-year-old as the family spokesman. What's that all about?" Everyone, it seemed, had more questions than answers about what became of Mike Webster after he quit playing pro football. What happened to him alarmed his teammates and left them examining their own lives.

Garrett was positively growling in some of the TV interviews, and he may have succeeded in scaring some people away from his father's funeral. What was he so angry about? Personally, I was worried that I might have written something about his father's sorry state in his post-retirement years that may have, unintentionally, wounded the Websters somehow. After all, I had interviewed Webster before he was inducted into the Pro Football Hall of Fame in August of 1997, and he had told me about all his problems. I didn't want Garrett to give me a hard time when I offered him my condolences. I didn't want him slaying the messenger. I didn't want a bad scene.

I felt sorry for him and his family. Mike Webster was one of the greatest Pittsburgh Steelers there ever was. He was a good guy, too. He was humble, low-key in conversation, so dedicated to his profession and the people around him, especially his family. That's what was so tough to figure out about what went wrong with Webster. His family and his faith seemed to be the rock upon which he stood so tall. During his football playing days, Webster was eager to talk about his family and his faith more so than his football heroics.

He seemed like one of the team's most solid citizens, a farm boy from Tomahawk, Wisconsin where his father grew potatoes and raised some cattle and a kid who became one of the strongest linemen in the history of the National Football League. He was so proud yet so humble. Mike was never a flashy fellow. His clothes and cars were modest. The only time he stood out in a crowd was on the football field, where he always bolted out of the huddle and hustled to line up over the football. That was his trademark. The other time was at the Steelers' 50 Seasons Celebration in 1982.

All of the former Steelers showed up in dark suits, some even wore tuxedos for the special evening at the David L. Lawrence Convention Center. Webster showed up in a burnt-orange corduroy suit, and then sat in the center of rows of Steelers for a team photo. He stood out like a country bumpkin or pumpkin. It was so Mike Webster. Yes, there was always a bit of hayseed about Mike Webster.

In the end, I had to go to his funeral. Art Rooney, the founder and long-time owner of the Steelers, was the one who taught me why you should go to funerals. You weren't going to see the dead, he said, you were going to offer comfort to those they left behind. He also said it was more important to go to a funeral when a friend or family member lost a loved one than it was to go to your friend's funeral. In other words, it was more important to go to Kathleen Rooney's funeral and

> *"I'll ride off into the sunset*
> *with you anytime."*
> **— John Wayne**

offer condolences over her loss to her husband, Art Rooney. It was more important to offer condolences to Jack McGinley and his family when his wife, Marie Ellen Rooney McGinley, died in late July. It makes so much sense, like most of what Marie's brother — she always called him Arthur — related to you through the years you were around the Steelers. He was the wisest of wise men. He liked Mike Webster. Webster was one of his favorites. He was a throwback to another era, like so many of the Steelers from the '40s and '50s. Webster was always friendly and cooperative with the media, and did his best to answer any questions directed his way.

It looked like it wanted to rain when I left my home in the South Hills on Friday, September 27, 2003 to pay my respects to Mike Webster. It was a dreary day in Pittsburgh. I wanted to be there, too, because it was part of the Steeler story. I am fascinated by these people.

I had attended funeral services for Art Rooney, Ray Mansfield and Steve Furness, as well as Joe Zombek, who had played at Pitt and with the Steelers in the the early '50s. I found that I learned so much about the Steelers that you never learned watching them play or talking to them in the clubhouse, or on the fields or in their rooms at the summer training camp at St. Vincent College in Latrobe. Frankly, I wanted to see the Steelers in such a serene setting. I thought it provided real insights into the real Steelers. This showed what a true family they were, warts and all. Like most families, they weren't perfect. The Rooneys were Irish and they knew better than most that Irish wakes were good times, but often tumultuous. There were feuds in the best of families. As an O'Brien, sorry to say, I'm an expert on that subject. As Simenon writes, "When someone is dead, you feel guilty, even if for a smile you did not smile."

I took my camera with me, but wasn't sure there'd be any appropriate opportunities to use it. The early morning mist remained and it was drizzling by the time I drove into the parking lot behind the Joseph M. Somma Funeral Home in Robinson Township.

The first thing I noticed when I pulled into the parking lot was a cluster of TV cameramen encircling Mel Blount and Terry Bradshaw. They were the tallest and most recognizable of the bunch. Blount always stands the tallest of the Steelers. Mike Wagner jokes that Blount cheats because Blount is always wearing high-heeled cowboy boots and a big white cowboy hat. Bradshaw's blond balding head makes him easy to spot. He's on TV so much that everybody recognizes Terry Bradshaw when they see him on the street, or passing through an airport. According to one national survey, Bradshaw is still one of the ten most popular sports figures in America.

Bradshaw and Blount had embraced, and then they embraced every former teammate and their wives as they approached the funeral home. It was a little after 9 a.m. and the services were to start at 10 a.m. There was time to talk.

Steve Courson stood out, too. He was the only one wearing black leather slacks. His sport coat was form fitting, snug to his body. "I never thought I'd outlive Webby," he said to me when we exchanged greetings. No, Courson had been on the endangered list the previous

Terry Bradshaw and TiAnda and Mel Blount meet outside Robinson Township funeral home where Mike Webster's memorial service was conducted. Mike's son, Garrett, below, is interviewed by John Shumway of KDKA-TV regarding his father's death of a heart attack at age 50.

Photos by Jim O'Brien

20 years, suffering from a weak heart, ruined, he thought, by 15 years of steroid use. Now Courson looks better than most of his teammates.

"This guy was strong."
— Harry Carson
New York Giants

Marianne and Chuck Noll came walking toward the funeral home on Steubenville Pike. I spotted Art Rooney II, the oldest son of Steelers president Dan Rooney, and heir apparent to the team's throne. He was with his beautiful wife, Greta. Ralph Berlin, the team's trainer in Webster's day, and Paul Uram, the conditioning coach, were talking to Courson. There were Bryan Hinkle, Emil Boures and Gary Dunn. Ron Blackledge, who had been one of Webster's line coaches, came as well. Kathleen and Art Rooney Jr. were there.

J.T. Thomas and Larry Brown were there, as were Randy Grossman, Mike Merriweather, Tunch Ilkin, John Rienstra, Craig Wolfley, Jim Clack, Moon Mullins and Matt Bahr.

I saw Dave Robinson, a former Penn State and Green Bay Packers star defensive lineman, whom I'd see each summer on induction day at the Pro Football Hall of Fame. He lived in Akron. Robinson was a big favorite with my friends, Bill Priatko and Rudy Celigoi, who'd go with me to the Canton ceremonies each summer. Harry Carson, the former middle linebacker for the New York Giants, flew in for the funeral.

"Going up against him, there's a certain respect level you establish," Carson said outside the funeral home. "I respected him tremendously. Oh yeah, he was very intimidating. There were guys who were bigger, but this guy was strong. He definitely hit you. A lot of athletes now, they talk a big game; he just played."

I spoke to many of the players in the parking lot, and took some photos. I didn't stick out in that regard because so many members of the news media were there doing the same. I spotted Bob Pompeani of KDKA-TV, retired sportscaster Sam Nover of WPXI-TV, Chuck Finder of the *Pittsburgh Post-Gazette.*

Late arrivals were Lamar Hunt, the owner of the Kansas City Chiefs, and Carl Peterson, the team's general manager. Webster had played center and coached with the Chiefs in his last two seasons in the NFL. They had both attended Art Rooney's funeral at St. Peter's on the North Side, I remembered. I had once played tennis with Hunt at an NFL Owners' Meeting and hit him in the groin with an overhead slam. I thought he had vacated the area where I hit the ball. It brought him to his knees on the court, as I recall. That was no way to treat one of the richest men in the country and one of the founding fathers of the American Football League, the man who gave the Super

Former Steelers colleagues, left to right above, Paul Uram and Steve Courson, greet Terry Bradshaw outside funeral home in Robinson Township. Mike Webster's last NFL employers, owner Lamar Hunt and general manager Carl Peterson of Kansas City Chiefs, pay their respects.

Photos by Jim O'Brien

Bowl its name. I spent a year in the military service at the U. S. Army Home Town News Center in Kansas City, Missouri and spotted for TV announcers Charley Jones and Paul Christman for Chiefs' games at the old Kansas City Municipal Stadium. That was in 1965. Hunt had always treated me well. It was good to see him again.

Once inside, I took my place in line to pay my respects to the family. There was Pam Webster, her daughters, Brooke and Hillary, and sons, Colin, and Garrett. Colin was in the Marines and was stationed at Camp LeJeune in North Carolina. He would soon be shipping out to an assignment in the Mideast as the United States prepared for a war with Iraq.

When I shook hands with Garrett and he thanked me for coming, I said, "Make your dad proud of you." Garrett looked down at me, and said, "Don't worry, I will."

Then I went over to the casket. It was surrounded by baskets of flowers. The room was full of flowers. The first thing that caught my eye was the sight of a neatly pressed and folded bright red Kansas City Chiefs football jersey with No. 52 on it. There was something wrong about that. Wouldn't Webster always be remembered as a Steeler? He had concluded his career with two seasons in Kansas City, but wouldn't he always be regarded as a Steeler?

There was a dog-eared copy of *The Wit and Wisdom of Winston Churchill*, and a book with Mark Twain's most memorable sayings. Mike Webster used to like to quote those guys, as well as John Wayne and Gen. George S. Patton. There were long-stem yellow and red roses laid horizontally across Webster's body. That looked strange.

Then I looked at Mike Webster. His color had been bad in recent years. He always looked jaundiced. His cheeks had sagged. He didn't look good. He looked the same way in the casket. Art Rooney used to say, "No one looks good in the box."

Dan Rooney and the Steelers were paying for this funeral, yet the Websters snubbed Dan Rooney when he made an effort to pay his respects in the receiving line. He was visibly shaken by the experience. "They wouldn't shake my hand," he told his family members with a quivering voice when he came away from the Websters. It had to hurt.

"You didn't know you were going to be a gatekeeper."

After I said a prayer, I retreated to the area where seats had been set out for those in attendance for the funeral service. I saw a friendly face sitting on the aisle of the second row of the second group of seats, just beyond where the family and closest friends were seated. It was Bob Milie, who had been a trainer with the Steelers and at Duquesne

> "Fans must realize this: No matter how much you know about an athlete, you really don't know them."
> — Terry Pluto, *Akron Beacon Journal*, July 13, 2003

University, and someone I'd always liked. There was an empty seat next to him. I asked him if anyone was sitting there and he said no and invited me to sit there.

I didn't realize, at first, that I would have one of the best seats in the house for the funeral service. The front row seats directly in front of me were empty when I sat down. They were reserved, I later realized. Sitting to my left was John Banaszak, with his wife Mary. She was holding his hand to comfort him. I remembered that she had done the same thing at the Beinhauer Funeral Home on Washington Road in Peters Township at the funeral for his close friend Steve Furness.

I often can't remember where I put my car keys, but I remember stuff like that. Next to the Banaszaks were Debra and Jon Kolb. Jon was wearing wire-rimmed glasses down at the end of his nose, and he had his head bowed. He didn't say a word. He appeared deep in thought. He is fond of saying, "Life is deep, life is shallow."

Sitting directly behind me were Joy and Dwayne Woodruff, and to their left, were TiAnda and Mel Blount. Someone from the funeral home asked Bob Milie and me if we would hold the seats in front of us for Terry Bradshaw and Lynn Swann. That's when Joy Woodruff tapped me on the shoulder and whispered, "You didn't know you were going to be the gatekeeper, did you?"

Swann had snubbed Bradshaw in his remarks when Swann was inducted into the Pro Football Hall of Fame two summers earlier. Swann had mentioned Steelers who made a contribution to his career and — how could he? — purposely omitted Bradshaw in his acceptance speech. As players, surely, they had contributed to each other's success. This was a rare instance when Swann's timing, always one of his greatest attributes, failed him. They shook hands when they sat down together at the funeral home, but hardly spoke to each other. That's some picture, I thought, but I knew better than to take my camera out in such a situation. I found myself drawing a simple sketch in my notebook, showing the two of them sitting there together. It was as if I had to preserve the moment somehow.

Then Franco Harris came into the room with his wife, Dana, and they sat in seats just ahead of Bradshaw and Swann. Franco looked over his shoulder and smiled and nodded. Franco's face was still like a theatrical mask. He transformed every room into a stage.

I felt like I was in the midst of a huddle with the Steelers of the '70s, still the greatest Steelers of them all. It was always Webster who started the formation of such a huddle, racing to a proper spot and holding his right hand overhead. There was something surreal to the whole scene. I was surrounded by greatness and sadness. There was a sense of melancholy in the room.

As a youngster, playing center and linebacker for a midget football team called the Hazelwood Steelers, I never thought that someday I would be writing the story of the Steelers, that I would be, indeed, documenting their deeds. That I would be in their midst, in their huddle. That I would share their pain. I wasn't living on Sunnyside Street anymore.

"We were like sidekicks."
— Garrett Webster

There were about 200 who came to say goodbye to Michael L. Webster. A partition was closed in the room so that only family members could be with the deceased just before the casket was closed. Those familiar with the words to the song, "The Dance," by Garth Brooks, could appreciate its appropriateness as recorded music that was played to start the service.

> *"Looking back . . . all the memory of the dance we shared beneath the stars above . . . For a moment, all the world was right. How could I know you'd ever say goodbye? The way it would end . . . the way it would go."*

I thought about moments spent with Mike Webster...speaking at dinners with him, mostly on behalf of Spina Bifida. I remember him telling inappropriate jokes or stories. But he was so sincere no one minded too much. I remember a woman who was waving a cigarette holder in the front row at a roast for the offensive linemen on behalf of the local chapter of the American Diabetes Association at the Allegheny Club at Three Rivers Stadium. I remember she started coughing when Webster made an off-color remark. Larry Brown and Ray Mansfield made a mock move to crawl under the table so they wouldn't be associated with Webster's story. My mind wandered through memories like that. Crucial moments of everyday life contain great drama and substance.

Then the partition was opened and The Rev. Hollis Haff of New Community Church offered a welcome to all in attendance. Haff used to conduct Bible study sessions and served as one of the chaplains for the team during the '70s. He and Webster were close. He wanted to celebrate Webster's life, and to try to comprehend what lessons we learn about life and death from such a personal loss.

Mike's older daughter Brooke read Psalm 23 from the Old Testament ("The Lord is my shepherd, I shall not want . . .) and his younger daughter Hillary did a reading from John 14:1-3 from the New Testament ("Do not let your hearts be troubled. Trust in God . . .")

Then several in attendance offered remembrances. Al Seretti, a friend of Mike Webster since 1996, began the service by saying, "I'm glad I didn't know Mike Webster as a football player. I knew him as a friend. Some people you know all your life. I've known him for six years, and I didn't cry as hard when my brother died. Mike was like a brother to me."

Another friend, Sunny Jani, who owned a small supermarket in McKees Rocks and promoted sports card and memorabilia shows that often featured Webster, was too emotionally distraught to speak as scheduled in the program. Garrett embraced Jani and held him tight.

"The first step to eternal life is you have to die."
— From *The Fight Club*

Colin Webster said, "It would have meant so much to my father to see everybody who is here in this room. He loved you so much and so deeply. I talked to him frequently about his teammates and he thought they were all good men." He urged those in attendance to reach out to other teammates who might need to hear from them as well. "Don't let it go by," said Colin Webster. "Don't let another day go by. Tell them you love them."

Garrett Webster took that a little further. His dad's number — No. 52 — was on his left sleeve. "He'd tell us war stories," said the biggest Webster child. "He loved you guys. Your presence here today proves to me that you're true friends. In the end, we were best friends. We were like two thirteen-year-old kids talking to each other sometimes. We'd talk about girls; we'd talk about Arnold Schwarzenegger. We'd watch some of my dad's favorite movies, like John Wayne and Dean Martin in *Rio Bravo*. Dean Martin called him 'Dude.' That's how our relationship was. We were like sidekicks. "When Colin was in the Marines, my dad was so proud of my brother. He was so proud of his two girls. We'd talk about Brooke and Hillary.

"He had problems, but he tried to overcome them. He said all the right things. He didn't want me to see John Wayne in any kind of pain. I hope you will share some of those stories you know about my dad. I hope you will tell those tales, and Mike Webster will never die."

Lynn Swann and Terry Bradshaw were the only Steelers who spoke at the service. Some former Steelers wondered why they were chosen to speak, especially Swann. They knew Bradshaw had a connection with Webster, as quarterback with center. They thought that some of the linemen like Tunch Ilkin and Craig Wolfley, who had remained involved with Webster during his difficult times, should have been asked to participate in the program. Like Swann, they were comfortable in front of a microphone, but they were more personally associated with Webster through the years. Swann did a fine job, though, to his credit. Lynn Swann said, "We were drafted together in 1974, and were rookies at camp the same summer. I think about Mike and how people will remember Mike. Number 52. Iron Mike. The man in the middle. He was so dedicated to the team. It didn't matter how cold it was, or if it was snowing. You'd see him with those bare biceps. It was a signal to the other team. He was telling the whole world that nothing was going to stop him or the Steelers.

"In the locker room, he was a teammate. He was part of the family. Yes, the players in that locker room became our friends and our extended family. There's always a place in your heart for them, no matter where they go. Mike was so funny at times.

"He was a roommate my first year. We were born 18 days apart. Mike didn't say much. But when he was in a huddle and he spoke up

> **"Sports tells anyone who watches intelligently about the times in which we live: about managed news and corporate politics, about race and terror and what the process of aging does to strong men. If that sounds grim, there is courage and high humor, too."**
> **— Roger Kahn, author**
> ***How the Weather Was***

people paid attention. Franco and I and John would be chattering. We all wanted the ball. Mike would quiet us down. Then Terry would give us the play. Then Terry would ask Mike what play he had called.

"I remember hunting for birds with Mike," Swann continued. "He'd shoot them before I could. I said, 'How are you beating me to the bird?' He said, 'Swannie, you have to learn how to move.' On the field and in the locker room, he led by example. There wasn't a day that went by that you didn't see him working full blast to get better."

Terry Bradshaw offered the final eulogy. His appearance was described as "a command performance" because he had missed the funerals of Art Rooney, Ray Mansfield and Steve Furness. "It's not easy to say goodbye to a friend, one I know so well — especially his butt," he said, and allowed time for everyone to laugh about that opening line.

"I made my living by placing my hands under Mike Webster's butt. You know, that's not natural. More seriously, Mike was one of those players who were committed to the team, not just himself. He thought about those around him, not just himself. That's what made the Steelers a great football team.

"How many times, Moon (Mullins) and Sam (Davis), did we go to the line and Webby would go, 'No, Brad, no,'" Bradshaw went on. "We didn't rehearse that. We didn't practice it. Webby saw something I definitely didn't see, and he was telling me not to run the play called.

"He loved it when people criticized me in the papers. And he was the first one to keep it going. 'They think you're stupid and dumb. I call all the plays,' he'd say with a laugh. Now I have to come clean and tell everybody: He was right. He did call all the plays.

"It's scary to know today it ends," and he had to pause here to collect himself and wipe away a few tears. "We should never allow the passing of a loved one to be the drawing card to keep our family together."

In the closing eulogy, the Rev. Haff mentioned that Webster never missed a service or Bible study that he conducted when he was the team chaplain. He said Mike's devotion touched his teammates in a positive manner. "Whatever happened after his career — and we may never understand what happened — there's a sense of comfort and hope where he stood with God."

There was a prayer of thanksgiving, and Jamie Wright, a vocalist, sang "I Can Only Imagine," with Jeremy Olsen at the keyboard in accompaniment. I thought it was a well-planned service, but strange just the same. I didn't go next door to a luncheon at a neighborhood fire hall. I just thought it was time to leave and go home.

It was Friday. Friday in the fall is high school football night in western Pennsylvania. It would turn out to be a nice day, with temperatures rising to 70 degrees. Garrett Webster went ahead and played defensive tackle for the Moon Area High School football team

> *"The key to success is sincerity and if you can fake it you've got a chance."*
> **— Dick Schaap**

in its 42-8 victory over Ambridge High at Moon Stadium. When he sacked the opposing quarterback early in the fourth quarter, Garrett got off the ground and stood and pointed his right index finger toward the sky. He said that was for his dad up in heaven.

He said his dad wouldn't have wanted him to miss the game. His dad never missed a game when he was with the Steelers.

"I never understood that I had a family here," said Garrett after he got a warm welcome from the crowd and his teammates at the game. "Until now."

Jim O'Brien

Garrett Webster, 6-8, 335 pounds, embraces one of his father's closest friends, Sunny Jani, owner of Blue Eagle Market in McKees Rocks and a promoter of sports card and memorabilia shows in Pittsburgh area. Mike and Sunny were an odd couple.

"Just a sense of loneliness..."

Chuck Miller, a 57-year-old fan of the Steelers, was wearing a black leather jacket and his dark brown mustache seemed to be drooping like the weeping willow trees at the end of the practice fields where the Steelers train at St. Vincent College, as he discussed Mike Webster, his favorite Steeler, and what it was like to attend his funeral.

"I used to go to Three Rivers Stadium about once a week to watch them practice. I was a friend of Tony Parisi, the team's equipment manager, and he'd get me out on the sideline. I loved those Steelers, especially the ones from the '70s. You always felt close to those people.

"I guess that's why I felt it was okay for me to go to Mike Webster's funeral. I felt like I knew him. There were lots of flowers from other teams in the National Football League at the funeral home. I noticed that.

"I saw Gerry Mullins and his wife in the funeral home when I was there. He was a great player, too, and he lined up right alongside of Webster. I saw some other ladies and some older guys. This was during an afternoon viewing. I have a big picture of Mike and me and a friend's little boy. We had it blown up this big. He posed for us; it was no problem.

"I can still see that scene at the funeral home. You got a sense of loneliness. Like he shouldn't have been there. It wasn't his time. He was only 50 years old; he was too young. You remember the guy you used to see Sunday after Sunday . . . running out, leading the troops. Nah, he shouldn't have been there. His shirt wasn't new, either. It looked like it had a few miles on it. That wasn't right.

"He was a good guy and he always came to play. He deserved better.

"Rocky Bleier was one of my favorites, too. He was just happy to be there. And he wouldn't have been there at all if he hadn't been an Irish Catholic from Notre Dame with a bad foot from what he went through in Vietnam. And Mr. Rooney said, 'Give him a chance.' So Noll gave him another chance. And the rest is history."

28

The two individuals who set the tone for Steelers' offensive and defensive units were Mike Webster (No. 52 above), checking with Terry Bradshaw on call, and Jack Lambert (No. 58 below), looking for cues from opposing offense.

Photos by Jay Nodianos

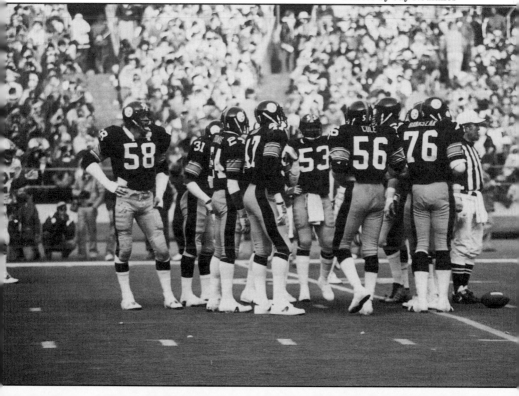

Mike Webster
Strongest man no more

*"All I did was go to work every
day and do the best I could."*

I remember how excited I was when I managed to line up hour-long interviews with Mike Webster and Bill Cowher at Three Rivers Stadium late in the 1996 season. I'd be talking to both of them within a few days of each other. Webster was experiencing mental, physical and financial difficulties, but they were mostly rumors, second-hand tales, and he hadn't talked much about his sorry situation for publication. Cowher seldom did one-on-one interviews with writers. So I was pleased that they had agreed to meet with me and talk. I was looking forward to it.

Webster didn't look well when I met with him. Something had gone wrong. Sometimes he didn't make sense when he was talking to me. He'd be talking in circles. But he told me what had been happening to him, and was as honest and sincere as he'd always been. He looked jaundiced. His skin was loose on his neck, like a turkey. I didn't feel comfortable hearing some of the stuff that was going on in his life. He was visiting the Steelers' offices, seeking some old photos he wanted to use in plaques he planned to sell. He said he would be back the following week and we could sit down and talk.

I was writing a book called *Keep The Faith*, and none did that any better than Webster when he was playing center for the Steelers. He seemed like one of the team's most solid citizens, on and off the field. No one seemed better grounded. His family, faith and football were so important to him, and he seemed to have struck a sensible balance among them. He had been the anchor on the Steelers' ship.

"Everybody has tough times," Webster said. "That's a part of life. It's not something that's unusual." Webster remained modest, self-effacing and polite.

He gave me a good story, but it bothered me. My book was on the presses at Geyer Printing in Oakland, and I thought I had an exclusive on his tragic story. There hadn't been much in the local papers about his situation. He had been generous with his time and remarks in our interview. Writers love to have exclusives, usually, but I was uneasy about this story. I wasn't eager to be among the first to get his tragic tale on the streets. One day, in early July, 1997, I was sitting in my family room, watching ESPN-TV, when they had a special interview with Mike Webster, just a few weeks before he was to be inducted into the Pro Football Hall of Fame in Canton, Ohio. I was planning on going, as I do each year.

Mike Webster was on TV, saying many of the same things he had told me in our interview a half year earlier. I felt a sense of relief that

Pittsburgh Steelers were represented in 1983 Pro Bowl game in Hawaii by six of their stars, from left to right, Jack Lambert, Donnie Shell, John Stallworth, Mike Webster and Larry Brown, posing with local hostess. It was Lambert's eighth Pro Bowl appearance and Brown's sole appearance.

Mike Webster and Chuck Noll were both all smiles at press conference following the 1982 season to announce that Webster was retiring after 15 stellar seasons as a Steeler. He took a position as an assistant coach with the Kansas City Chiefs for the following season, and was coaxed out of retirement to play center for two more seasons.

his story was out. His wife, Pam, was interviewed in one segment. I called my wife, Kathie, into the room to watch it.

"Things got so bad," said Pam Webster, who had split up with her husband, "that we didn't have enough money to buy toilet paper."

"Why didn't you get a job?" said Kathie, talking to the TV.

That's exactly what Kathie did when I lost a job as editor of a national magazine in 1992. That's why I love that girl. That's why I was able to start writing and publishing books on my own that year. Kathie provided a bridge rather than blame.

"He meant so much to us."
— Dan Rooney

All seemed right in Mike Webster's world on Saturday afternoon, July 26, 1997, as he was inducted into the Pro Football Hall of Fame in nationally-televised ceremonies in Canton, Ohio. That was at the start. Then Webster started unraveling, and one had to wonder whether he would ever quit talking. After awhile, it was evident his thoughts were scrambled. Steelers' fans dominated the scene as they always do whenever one of their own is so honored, only 110 miles of interstate highway west of Pittsburgh.

Webster smiled when he heard the familiar chant of "Here We Go, Steelers…!" The fans yelled out to him by name. He squinted into the sun to see all the black and gold costumes, many of them wearing No. 52 on their authentic NFL-licensed jerseys, and the signs and banners that hailed him as "Iron Mike" and "The Iron Man" of the Steelers. Surely, some of those fans had been pumping Iron, or Iron City beer, in the parking lots around Fawcett Stadium to get into gameday form. The Pittsburgh Brewing Company, in fact, had already signed a deal with Webster to issue a special commemorative beer can in honor of "Iron Mike" for the 1997 season. They had honored three of his former teammates, Andy Russell, Ray Mansfield and Rocky Bleier, by having their likenesses on Iron City beer cans the year before. It's not the Heisman Trophy, but in Blitzburgh it's close.

The fans in Canton were doing their best to make Webster feel like he was back at Three Rivers Stadium when the Steelers were the greatest team in the National Football League, and Webster was hailed as one of the greatest centers ever to play the game.

Webster was one of four enshrined that day, but his reception from the home crowd was greater than that afforded Don Shula, the

"Announcers and pundits always like to say that near tragedies help to put sports into perspective, remind us that they are merely a diversion. They've got it backward. Sports puts tragedy in perspective; life is the diversion."
— Joe Queenan, author
True Believers: The Tragic Inner Life of Sports Fans

Photos by Mike Longo

Mike Webster posed with his Hall of Fame bust with teammate Terry Bradshaw, who introduced him at Canton ceremonies, and, left to right below, with the 1997 HOF Class of Mike Haynes, Wellington Mara and Don Shula.

winningest coach in NFL history with the Baltimore Colts and Miami Dolphins; Mike Haynes, a hard-hitting cornerback with the New England Patriots and Oakland Raiders; and Wellington Mara, owner of the New York Giants, and son of Tim Mara, the founder of the Giants and a charter member of the Hall of Fame.

Going to Canton for the Hall of Fame enshrinement ceremonies has become a rite of summer. I love to see all the greats of the game on that special weekend, and many Steelers' fans make the pilgrimage there each July or August no matter who is being honored. Many Hall of Famers show up each year, and it's like seeing your boyhood bubble gum card collection come to life when you see the likes of Pete Pihos, Y.A. Tittle, Arnie Weinsmeister, Lenny Moore, Sam Huff, Dante Lavelli, Chuck Bednarik and Otto Graham, and guys you met and got to know as a young sportswriter such as Larry Csonka, Larry Little, Bob Griese, Joe Namath, Gale Sayers and so many legendary Steelers such as Ernie Stautner, "Bullet Bill" Dudley and John Henry Johnson. It's great to rub shoulders with those outstanding individuals at different social events. When I go to Canton, I feel like a kid again.

Jack Lambert looked at it that way, too. He loved seeing the old uniforms and those flap-eared leather helmets, going there often during his youth from nearby Mantua, Ohio. Webster didn't share our enthusiasm in that respect, but said he was glad to be honored. He just never saw himself as important enough to have his bronze bust in the same building as Vince Lombardi, the coach of his favorite football team, the Green Bay Packers, during his youth in Wisconsin. Mike Webster didn't see himself in the same light as Art Rooney, his friend and former boss with the Pittsburgh Steelers, his favorite team as an adult. Webster starred at center for the Steelers in the '70s, and was a pivotal member of the fierce offensive line — they with the bare biceps — that intimidated other teams and won four Super Bowl titles. He was with the Steelers from 1974, their first Super Bowl year, to 1988, and finished his pro career in Kansas City with two more seasons with the Chiefs. There was an appealing simplicity about him. He had a relentless pursuit of perfection.

Lamar Hunt, the owner and founder of the Chiefs, and Carl Peterson, the team's general manager, were in the audience in Canton. Webster had, in fact, asked Peterson to present him for the Hall of Fame, but Peterson declined, advising Webster to get someone from the Steelers to do that. The Steelers were playing an exhibition game in Dublin, Ireland that same weekend, and were not well represented. Two former front office employees, Jim Boston and Jim Kiely, were there on their own. Art Rooney Jr. and Chuck Noll, who could have been there, did not attend. Noll should have been there for Don Shula as well as Webster. Art Rooney Jr. now admits he should have been there.

Webster put in more seasons (15) and played more games (220) than any player in Steelers' history. He was known for dashing out of the huddle to get things going.

34

Photos by Mike Longo

Mike Webster looks back to Terry Bradshaw during his acceptance speech at Pro Football Hall of Fame ceremonies, while Bradshaw checks in with Webster, as the two former Steelers, sat between honorees Wellington Mara and Don Shula as well as Frank Gifford, at right, who introduced Mara.

"I'm just excited," he explained back then. "I can't wait for the play to start. I'm like that all day before a game. The alarm rings in the morning and I sprint to the breakfast table."

Webster called out signals for the offensive linemen and spearheaded the offense as much as Terry Bradshaw. Altogether, he missed only four games in a 17-year career and his 177 consecutive games played (until an extended elbow sidelined him) is second in the Steelers' record books only to his predecessor and mentor, Ray Mansfield, who played in 182 straight games. Webster, Lambert and Joe Greene may have personified the Steelers of that era more than any one else.

Webster went six seasons without missing an offensive play.

Webster was joining a distinguished list of former teammates who had already been inducted into the Pro Football Hall of Fame, namely Greene, Lambert, Bradshaw, Mel Blount, Jack Ham and Franco Harris. That made seven Steelers from the '70s who had been so honored. Lynn Swann and John Stallworth, as well as club owner Dan Rooney, have since been honored by induction into the Hall of Fame. L.C. Greenwood, Donnie Shell, Jack Butler and Andy Russell remain on the outside looking in.

"I was surrounded by great athletes," said Webster. "All I did was go to work every day and do the best I could. I'm not sure I'm a Hall of Famer. I was there every day and did everything I could to be as good as I could be. This is more a reflection of what happened to me in the '70s. It's beyond what you could hope to experience. It's an all-consuming award for the organization and the fans."

Bradshaw was picked by Webster to present him at the Hall of Fame induction ceremonies, which guaranteed greater TV exposure since Bradshaw was one of the stars of the Fox Sports team. By contrast, Shula had his two sons introduce him. "If Terry's there, I won't have to say much," Webster said in advance of the big day. Nobody could play to a crowd better than Bradshaw and he said the same sort of things about Webster that have drawn laughs before. During his stay in Canton, Terry told the people what a thrill it was to stick his hands under Webster's backside on every offensive play. Bradshaw swears that Webster had the perfectly shaped posterior, and that it warmed his hands on those cold winter days in Pittsburgh, Cleveland, Cincinnati, Buffalo and other NFL outposts. Of course, Bradshaw once said the same things about Mansfield. So it was fun in the sun for Webster. His wife, Pamela, and their family and friends were seated in a reserved section in front of the steps of the Hall of Fame, and his loyal and boisterous fans filled the hillside in the natural bowl setting at George Halas Drive. All appeared to be in place, so it seemed anyhow.

"Giving Bradshaw a forum and a microphone is like giving Visine to a peeping Tom."
—Mike Webster
at his Hall of Fame induction
July 27, 1997

Mike Webster rubs Terry Bradshaw's bald head for good luck during Hall of Fame parade in Canton, and complies with Bradshaw's request to put his hands under his butt one more time for one more snap on the steps of the NFL shrine on Saturday afternoon, July 27, 1997.

Photos by Mike Longo

"I was never good-looking."

When Mike Webster learned of his selection to the Hall of Fame, he was in Pittsburgh, staying at the Holiday Inn in Green Tree. His former teammate and good friend, Tunch Ilkin, was picking up the tab for Webster's stay in Pittsburgh.

Ilkin, of course, did not tell me that. Ilkin was reluctant to even discuss Webster's personal situation at all, which was true of most of Webster's former teammates and insiders with the Steelers. Earlier, the Steelers had picked up a $6,000 tab for Webster during a lengthy stay at the Hilton Hotel in downtown Pittsburgh. Webster had not left the team on the best terms — he had regrettably said some critical things about Noll and Rooney when he departed Pittsburgh in a huff — yet the Steelers still tried to help him. He later stayed at the Red Roof Inn. He was, indeed, a lost soul.

The Steelers, sad to say, had gotten phone calls from officials at Amtrak saying that Webster was seen hanging around and even sleeping in the waiting room of their railroad depot in downtown Pittsburgh. "I slept in a car for a year and a half," admitted Webster. "Yeah, I spent some time at the railroad station, too."

Ilkin and the Steelers were picking up the tab for Webster because he was virtually broke. It was difficult to comprehend. Why was he so down and out? Six years earlier, he was making $350,000 to $400,000 a year with the Chiefs. He made over $100,000 a year most seasons in the second half of his 15 seasons with the Steelers. Most of it was gone. He went broke. He lost his home. He was reported to have sold his four Super Bowl rings, but he denied this. The Steelers were lining up Webster for paid appearances after his Hall of Fame selection, trying to help him make a comeback. There were reports, however, of Webster being a no-show for autograph signings and personal appearances. And he kept money he was paid in advance even when he failed to show.

Webster was suing his former agent, Greg Lusteg, and investment counselors who had gotten him (and other former Steelers) into limited partnerships that went bust. Webster had lost his money in a series of bad investments; some as esoteric and ill-conceived as worm farms or worms as fishing bait in coin machines. Webster was hardly unique for losing money on limited partnerships — the great tax-saving investment of the '70s — but worm farms? He and his wife had separated, but he would visit his family often in Wisconsin, sleeping in the basement, and then taking a train back to Pittsburgh where he was scuffling to put together some business ventures. He and Ilkin were looking into teaming up on some sports marketing efforts. Webster talked about a desire to create and sell some sports plaques, autographed prints and memorabilia. He mentioned big names like Kodak, Muhammad Ali, Dan Marino, Art Rooney, et al, in the same breath, but whether he had the contacts to deliver on it seemed vague. Too many people were already attempting to mine that field, and Webster had not shown he had the business savvy to make something like that succeed.

38

Photos by Mike Longo

Cathy and Steve Courson, above, sat with the crowd at Canton, Ohio ceremonies as their friend Mike Webster was inducted in summer of 1997. Pam
Webster comforts her children in front row seat during induction ceremonies
on the steps of Pro Football Hall of Fame. Soon after, the Coursons would take
Mike into their home in rural Fayette County.

His health also was suspect. The word on the street was that he was ill. He didn't look good. He had lost a lot of weight; his ruddy complexion appeared withered and paler than one remembered. "I was never good-looking to begin with," Webster said. He had been to Allegheny General Hospital for check-ups and treatment. Rumors were making the rounds that he was having more physical problems associated with anabolic steroids he had taken — before their damaging side effects were known and before their use was banned by league officials — during his manic body-building developmental days with the Steelers. Webster said he tried steroids, but didn't continue to use them very long. Dr. Jerry Carter, a psychiatrist at Allegheny General Hospital, was treating him. Webster said he was waking up at night with convulsions and spasms. He had blackouts, and what Webster called "small heart attacks." Dr. Carter said Webster suffered from depression, which Webster blamed on abuse in his childhood. He denied that he had any serious health problems.

Hospital records said otherwise, however. He had been treated for symptoms of congestive heart failure. He passed out twice in 1992, once while jogging and once at a swimming pool. He said he might have Parkinson's disease. That sounds like serious stuff.

Dr. Carter said he was planning more tests to determine what was wrong with Webster. "He doesn't get much enjoyment out of anything. He's not able to enjoy his accomplishments, and he's acknowledged that he's had difficulty concentrating at times."

One of his former teammates and fellow weightlifters, Steve Courson, had crusaded against the ill effects of steroids that he blamed for heart problems that had threatened his life. Courson was a candidate for heart transplant surgery at one point, but managed to miraculously correct his health problems with medicine, rigid diet and training regimen. Courson was suing the NFL for looking the other way, insisting the Steelers had been among those who ignored the players taking pills and drugs to enhance their performance.

Webster cursed those who were saying steroids were at the root of his distress, and felt this rumor is what kept him from being voted into the Pro Football Hall of Fame a year earlier, when he first became eligible five years after his playing career was completed. He insisted then that he had never used steroids, but he hedged on that claim years later. Webster had been thought to be a shoo-in by most NFL observers. Coaches can be elected within a year of their retirement, as Shula and Noll were.

The Hall of Fame looked like a possible life raft for Webster. He needed to set sail on a new life. Shula and his wife were millionaires in their own right, as was Mara. Haynes had a good job. Webster was in worse shape, in every respect, than everyone else in the Class of 1997.

Ilkin was in the crowd at Canton. A congenial man, Ilkin was doing well as an analyst on WPXI-TV's Steelers coverage and in a suburban construction business, and had settled in with his family in

40

Upper St. Clair. Ilkin is a good man, a devout Christian who practiced what he preached, and he wanted to help an old friend. Ilkin came to the Steelers in 1980 and stayed till 1992, and missed the best days of both Noll and Bill Cowher. Ilkin was one of Webster's proteges, and he genuinely loved the man. "He was the hardest-working guy that I've ever played with," Ilkin said of Webster. "He outworked everybody. He was such a resolved competitor and played hurt. He was just the best."

Soon after he retired from football, Ilkin had attempted to start a sports promotion and marketing business with another former teammate and offensive lineman, Craig Wolfley, but it didn't pan out. Wolfley and Courson were both in Canton for Webster's big day.

Wolfley was as reluctant as Ilkin, understandably, to discuss Webster's situation. Like Ilkin, he did not want to betray or embarrass a buddy. It was the way most Steelers of that era, and front-office officials of the Steelers, clammed up when anyone asked about Webster or Sam Davis, a great guard on those Super Bowl teams who lined up next to Webster. Davis was beaten to a pulp in his Gibsonia home in early September of 1991 for failure to pay off a business loan from the wrong guys, and had spent recent years in personal care homes in McKeesport. Teammates said he was beaten with a baseball bat, or some such instrument, and kicked senseless. It was white-washed in local media reports that Davis had suffered head injuries in a fall down a stairway in his farmhouse.

Many former Steelers have been quite successful since they retired from the game. People point with great pride to Andy Russell, Mike Wagner, Dwight White, Rocky Bleier, John Stallworth, Randy Grossman, J.T. Thomas and Larry Brown et al. There are, however, still some worrisome situations that give anyone who cares about those guys some pause for thought. Mike Webster should have been doing better. There wasn't a dishonest bone in his body. He was never accused of being a slacker. You had to like this guy. He had no guile. And he gave all he had to give. But he seemed lost and disoriented without football, without the demands and structure football offered and demanded. His life's work was football. Doctors determined that he had brain damage. That's all anyone needs to know to help explain his odd behavior.

"My talent was God-given."

Mike Webster learned of his selection to the Pro Football Hall of Fame on the eve of Super Bowl XXXI. Members of the media panel who pick the individuals for induction meet each year at the Super Bowl site, which was New Orleans this time. They get together Saturday morning for their discussions and balloting. Many felt Webster should have been selected the year before when the Steelers were playing in Super Bowl XXX at Tempe, Arizona.

41

"It would be awful selfish to think I've done that on my own," Webster said when he learned of his selection. "First of all, I wasn't really a good athlete by professional standards. Second, my talent was God-given. He put me in this situation — to be able to play with great players on a great team."

The players so honored are first introduced as a group at half-time of the Pro Bowl in Honolulu, Hawaii. Mara missed that party, but Webster posed for photos with Haynes and Shula, with leis around their necks.

Webster said he was sorry Ray Mansfield would miss his induction into the Hall of Fame. He and Mansfield had shared the position when Webster first joined the Steelers in 1974. Mansfield confessed that he had problems withdrawing from football, and missed the limelight. Mansfield had died at age 55 in November, 1996. "It's sad," said Webster. "I haven't dealt with what happened to Ray yet. He was a tough, tough football player."

Webster was also named to John Madden's All-Time Super Bowl team that weekend of Super Bowl XXXI. No one liked tough, tough football players more than Madden. They didn't come any tougher than the kid from Tomahawk, Wisconsin.

As a youngster, Webster had admired the tough guys in pro football, such as Packers center Jim Ringo and linebacker Ray Nitschke, Bears end Mike Ditka and linebacker Dick Butkus.

Webster was joined by former teammates Stallworth, Swann, Blount, Ham, Lambert and Greene and by Joe Namath of Beaver Falls on the team selected by Madden, who was the analyst to Pat Summerall for the Super Bowl XXXI telecast.

"Got to get back to work."

On the surface, Webster seemed to have so much going for him. He had made some bad decisions, though, and was no longer employed by any pro team, and had lost most of his money in business ventures gone sour. "Pro football players tend to think everyone wants to help them get rich," said Ilkin. In early July, 1997, just weeks before his Hall of Fame induction, ESPN revealed Webster's financial and family problems. Extensive newspaper stories followed that coming-out interview.

"I don't think it's anybody's business," he'd say to anyone who asked too many questions about his situation.

"I'm not destitute. I'm not in grave danger or anything else. In no way, shape or form am I down and out. I have a cash-flow problem. I handle my own problems and situations just like everybody in life. I can handle them, and I don't need an outpouring of sympathy because that's not the situation. And I have read a lot of things that are untrue, but there's nothing that I can do about that but overcome it," he said in an interview with Jonathan D. Silver of the *Pittsburgh Post-Gazette*. Webster always expressed great pride in his family and his Christian beliefs as a ballplayer, so one had to wonder what had gone wrong in his life. He had never blown money on clothes, cars or appearances. Webster always looked like a farmer. He was football smart, but life dumb. When he was playing with the Steelers, Webster lived in McMurray, a suburb about 12 miles south of Pittsburgh. His home was the only one in the community with a blocking sled in the yard next to the swing set. Webster never stopped working at his game. It consumed him. It was his life. In truth, it was his wife. It was the farmer in him. Going to work every day is its own joy and reward.

He was the first player to report back to work at Three Rivers Stadium after the players' strike in 1982. I remember him passing Joe Gordon and me in a hallway at Three Rivers Stadium, telling us, "Got to get back to work." He sued the Steelers for failing to pay him what he thought he was due him in salary that season. When players went on strike in 1987, Webster crossed picket lines, and took a lot of heat from veteran teammates. I remember seeing him after games where his knees hurt so much he had great difficulty moving around the clubhouse. He moved in a crab-like manner. I thought he was on his way to becoming another Jim Otto, the former Raiders' Hall of Fame center, who had to get artificial knee replacements in order to be mobile again. Webster held the football in his hand to start every offensive play, but in a sense the football held him. Steve Blass, a former Pirates pitcher who lived in Upper St. Clair, recognized that he was obsessed by his sport. In an interview for a book about Bob Prince, the Pirates' legendary broadcaster, Blass once told me, "I thought I was holding the baseball, but the baseball was holding me."

Tim Green, a former ballplayer with the Atlanta Falcons and at Syracuse University who had served as an analyst on Fox Sports, offered some insight in *From the Dark Side of The Game*:

"It comes down to a total lack of sophistication," wrote Green in his book that was published in 1996. "Most NFL players don't have advanced education in law or finance, and they don't have the business experience to survive in the world outside football. They think that because they are big and tough, that no one would dare rip them off. They don't know that the real world can be more cruel and more treacherous than even the football field. The adage is true more times than not: A football player and his money are soon parted."

During the family's stay in McMurray, Webster seemed to know what he wanted for his family. When his kids were pre-schoolers, he used to take them to a nearby farm. "They feed carrots to the horses and feed the chickens," Webster said. "I'd like to buy some acreage, and get some animals. We had pigs on our farm in Wisconsin. We used to ride them around the yard, and have a lot of fun."

He expressed a desire to get a farm of his own, like two of his teammates, Jon Kolb and Tom Beasley, who had spreads in Washington County.

43

Webster seemed best suited to be making his living in football or farming. He could always get others to work hard.

"Habits," said Kolb, now an assistant football coach at Grove City College, explaining why Webster succeeded in pro football. "I used to tell players that the only time you have to be working is when Mike's working; which means you work all the time."

Football players respected Webster's zest and know-how. His football credentials were impeccable. Along the way, however, he had waffled on invitations to be an assistant coach in Pittsburgh, Green Bay, Cincinnati and had gone to Kansas City, in the first place, to serve as assistant coach to Marty Schottenheimer. He ended up playing instead simply because he was still better than any centers in the Chiefs' training camp.

Webster had gone on record saying he didn't like the way they were playing pro football these days. Like Lambert, he hated wholesale situational substitutions. He stated publicly that he couldn't coach in modern-day football. Ouch! That's not the way you apply for future employment.

"My father was the reincarnation of Vince Lombardi."

I had a lengthy interview with Webster when he made a rare visit to the Steelers' offices late in the 1996 season. We sat down in Art Rooney's old office on opposite sides of The Chief's old desk. I was sitting in The Chief's chair, a sacred spot.

"I used to look in here a lot to say hello to Mr. Rooney," Webster said. "I didn't stay long; I didn't want to overstay my welcome.

"When I first got here, Mr. Rooney was coming down the hallway for lunch. I got nervous talking to him; I waved my hands. I knocked coffee all over him. I thought I was gone."

Webster looked around the room, where there were photos on display from when Art Rooney held court there, pictures of pro football icons like Lombardi, Halas and Bert Bell. And team photos from nearly every Steelers' seasons.

"This is only the second time I've been in here (the Steelers' offices) since I left the team. Last Friday was the first time."

He was looking for help from the Rooneys.

Art Rooney remarked at the team's 50 Seasons Celebration at the David L. Lawrence Convention Center in 1983 that, "I never had a player I didn't like. I never had a player I didn't think was a star."

Webster had worked in that environment. There was a photo on the nearby wall of all the former Steelers who attended that dinner. All wore black or dark business suits save for Webster. He wore a burnt orange corduroy suit with matching cowboy boots.

"Pride is developed from a winning tradition."
— Vince Lombardi

Mike Webster

Bill Amatucci

Mike Webster is out front for the 350-yard "gassers" to be run around the practice field at St. Vincent College in 1984. Lining up with Webster, left to right, are Pete Rostosky of Bethel Park, Craig Wolfley, Gary Dunn and Terry Long.

"I sure stick out; I didn't know we were supposed to wear black," Webster apologized once again. "No one told me to wear black. Every time I see that picture . . . those cowboy boots, I say, 'That's the idiot! What a hick!'" Webster was wearing a light green and white jersey, an off-white Panama hat and a chagrined smile as he said this. He had some good moments, some good thoughts — so heart-felt and pure — and I'll never forget that session for several reasons.

Webster knew Art Rooney Sr. was special and missed his presence. He missed football the way it was when he was playing for the Steelers when they were winning Super Bowls.

"I'm a helpless romantic," Webster said. "When they tear down Cleveland Stadium, I'll be heart-broken. As bad as that place was — like an indoor cattle facility — some powerful ghosts are in there. I left some skin and blood on that ballfield. Those locker rooms were awful, but you felt like you were playing football. If they ever tear this place down, I'll feel the same way.

"I loved to play at Lambeau Field in Green Bay. I grew up idolizing the Packers and Lombardi. You always felt he was there. My father was the reincarnation of Vince Lombardi. He wanted to be just like him. My father was very intolerant. But he could motivate us. He loved the Packers and Vince. My dad felt that type of discipline was essential for the development of character. That was Lombardi's trademark. His charm. I would love to hear him speak today. He was so charismatic.

"As a kid, I never went to see the Packers play. We couldn't afford it. In 1961 (December 31), when I was 9, I listened to the NFL championship game on the radio. The Packers clobbered the Giants, 37-0. My dad and his brothers were all there listening to the game on the radio." The year before, the Packers lost to Norm Van Brocklin and Tommy McDonald and the Philadelphia Eagles in the 1960 championship game.

Thinking about those days reminded Webster of his youth on the farm in Wisconsin. That's where he got his work ethic. Farmers never take a day off, either. It's a killer occupation. The life is one of pervious resolve. Farming is a character-building endeavor. Farming requires the kind of dogged determination that is its own reward.

"We had a crop farm, and hogs and beef cattle," Webster said. "We had plenty to do. My dad frequently worked 18 to 20 hours a day, getting fields ready for planting.

"My older brother and I did a lot of work. I rode on tractors at age 7. You'd start talking to yourself because you didn't always want to be working. You had to do it. Back then, no one talked about child abuse. You'd get a boot in the ass or a strap if you got out of line. I didn't do the same things with my kids. I remember during the summer we'd get up at 7 in the morning and, when I was 7 years old, I got to drive the tractor. Plowing the field was a real thrill to us. I think a farm is the only place to raise kids."

Photos by Jim O'Brien

Mike Webster said his father, Bill Webster, was a lot like Vince Lombardi, the legendary coach of the Green Bay Packers, when it came to discipline on their Wisconsin farm. The photos were taken during a visit to Green Bay and Milwaukee.

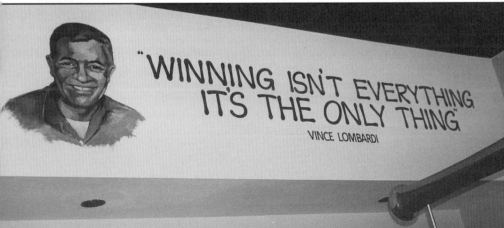

"WINNING ISN'T EVERYTHING IT'S THE ONLY THING"
VINCE LOMBARDI

Quite a contrasting reflection, huh? Wonder what the real story is. Was Webster telling the truth in 1981 or was he telling the truth in 1997? What happened in the interim that changed Webster's story?

We're back in Art Rooney's old office in 1997, and our most recent interview:

"If my dad could have lived his life all over again, he would have been a football coach," Webster was saying. "When I was growing up, he was the kind of guy like Vince Lombardi, a real butt-kicker. He was a tough disciplinarian, and he taught me good values, and how to be mentally tough. He was affectionate, but strong and tough, too."

Most successful people were ones who were able to experience positive things in their childhood. Those subjected to trauma or abuse seem to carry scars. There are exceptions.

"But I wouldn't trade those days for anything," Webster said. "My dad taught us how to work..."

Back in 1981, Webster had said, "It was always a struggle. There were five of us kids and my dad sometimes worked two jobs. He'd have a night job to make extra money. But he never complained. We always had something to eat and clothes on our back."

Back then, his father felt he had made a bad choice in trying to make a living on that 640-acre potato farm. "It was the biggest mistake of my life," Bill Webster said when we spoke at Three Rivers Stadium. "When we'd have a good crop, so did everyone else and the price would be down. But we never had a crop failure."

He said it with the same sort of pride that motivated his son to excel on the football field. At heart, Webster was a potato farmer forever.

"I didn't play to be a legend or a hero."

Being in Art Rooney's office reminded Webster of the way it used to be, and way it was different today. Even in his day, Webster was a throwback to another era. In practice, for example, he wouldn't take water, no matter how hot it was.

"There are different types of training today," he said. "These guys are already bigger and quicker. We had a great weight program. We had a lot of maturity. It was a joke. We built up the image of it, the strongboys, the bare biceps business. We bared our biceps, in truth, so defensive linemen couldn't grab our jerseys so easy. Then they had those 'strongest man' contests."

And Webster won such contests, and so did Jon Kolb from that same club. Webster was asked what drove him to do it.

"To keep from failing, more than anything else," he answered. "There were lots of other reasons I was so driven, but that's kind of personal. There was definitely a fear of embarrassment. Everything we did was on film. Everything you did, others judged. You did all this

48

to prepare to be successful. I didn't want to miss any games; it was great to go to work. I don't feel that way about football anymore. I have no desire to be involved. I don't even watch football."

That sort of remark won't help you get a job in the NFL, either.

To hear Webster, it sounds like he should have stayed with the Steelers. It was never as good elsewhere. "I should not have gone to Kansas City," he said. "It was definitely a mistake. I got caught up in making big money. I had been on the greatest team you could ever have. It would have been the final impression of me as a player.

"Mr. Rooney and winning Super Bowls . . . that's what was special about playing for the Steelers. I wouldn't trade that for zillions of dollars. Today, I wouldn't give you two cents for the way they play. How can you get into the rhythm of the game if you play two or eight plays? You're not a football player anymore. You just do everything as you're told. Coaches have so much control now. I don't like the West Coast offense. It's a piece of crap."

That's not the way it was with the Steelers of the '70s. "I have to go into the locker room here to feel the ghosts," Webster went on. "Chuck (Noll) was so disciplined. He was so focused. I see him now and I can't believe it. He's gotten 15 years younger since he retired. He looks like a young man. You had respect for him. You listened. You have to work for a guy like that. He demands it and you want to anyhow."

Webster wasn't easy to understand when I spoke to him about the split in his family, and how he and Pamela had parted ways. They seemed to have a lot in common. During their days in Pittsburgh, Pamela called herself "just a housewife and a mother and I really enjoy it." She said their move from Pittsburgh was stressful for the family. Why didn't she get a job when times got tough? (By the time Mike died, Pam was doing housekeeping work.) Webster's thoughts were somewhat disjointed. He rambled on, trying to sort it out, trying to make sense of it all. His commentary was frequently confusing.

"People change," Webster said. "It was very traumatic. Now there are questions about who dad is? Where's our home now? I'm not going anywhere. What am I doing in Weirton? I have a friend there. I'm trying to get something going. I'd like some security. I want to be working for someone. You can't go back. There's just been a lot of changes. I spend a lot of time talking to people, trying to get something going. It's still traumatic. I missed 22 years in there somewhere.

"My kids are in Wisconsin. My wife and I get along great. She's a wonderful lady. I live in the basement when I visit. I want to be there for the kids. I see them whenever I can. Right now, I just want to be home. This is past and future business here. I don't like to be looked at. I didn't play to be a legend or a hero. I stayed too long. I played too long...

"My life is taking a turn. There are a lot of things I want to succeed at. I was never afraid to work. I'll straighten this out."

> *"In life you'll have your back up against the wall many times. You might as well get used to it."*
> **— Paul "Bear" Bryant**

"I enjoyed the challenge."

Seeing photos from his past in the Rooney office may have prompted some more stream-of-conscious thinking:

"I remember how great it was to work out with guys who were similarly motivated, who wanted to improve themselves, who wanted to get stronger, who wanted to succeed, who wanted the Steelers to be something special," Webster said, surveying the scene. "We used to get together a few days a week to lift weights. I miss that. I loved to do that. We had Steve Furness, Larry Brown, Ted Petersen, Jon Kolb, Steve Courson and Jim Clack. Craig Wolfley and Tunch Ilkin came along later. We worked out together at the Red Bull Inn in Washington, Pa. Lou Caringa, an avid weightlifter, owned the Red Bull, and had a gym in the basement. The players ate at the restaurant as well. Lou and his friend, a big coal miner named Clark Hayes, worked out with us.

"Lou and Jon were more dedicated and tougher than I was and more stubborn to a fault," Webster went on. "We challenged each other. I enjoyed the challenge. That's why I used to run the steps at Three Rivers Stadium."

Webster skipped around in his reminiscences. Often his thoughts would take him back to the farm. He was like one of those shiny steel balls in a pinball machine, bouncing here, there and everywhere, lights flashing, bells ringing.

"My mom's name was Betty and my dad was Bill. I had two brothers and two sisters. People had lots of kids in those days to work the farm. That's the way my dad grew up. My parents split up. My dad was married and divorced three times. It was a stormy situation. It was an alcoholic-dominated environment. Us kids were always shuffling around in rural northern Wisconsin. There were a lot of problems. One of my brothers did hard time in prison. After my parents split up, my two sisters lived with my mother, and my two brothers and I lived with my dad. It was a difficult childhood."

He spoke of attempts to kiss and make up with the Steelers after he went to Kansas City, but said he was unsuccessful.

"I wrote to Chuck (Noll), but he never responded. I had a proposal for him, an idea for a video tape production. It was pretty traumatic at the time not to hear back from him. Maybe he's still pissed at me for going to Kansas City."

Just as Mansfield knew that Webster was going to move him out, Webster recognized that Dermontti Dawson would be a better center than a guard, where he was originally slotted for the Steelers.

"I'm the one who said, 'Put Dermontti at center. He can hold his own,'" Webster said. "He's a big Dwight Stephenson."

Webster was with the Steelers when they played the Hall of Fame game to begin the pre-season schedule in 1983. They defeated the New Orleans Saints that day. So he had seen the Pro Football Hall of Fame.

> ## "Nobody in the world really knows anybody else in the world."
> ## — From Thornton Wilder's *The Matchmaker*

"I have no desire to go there," Webster said, not knowing he was going to be selected for the next class. "I walked through the building quickly, I remember. I'm not into that. I'm not worrying about whether or not I'll be elected. I'm already in there. There are photos of the Steelers of the '70s, the four championship teams. I don't need a bust of myself. I'm not the only former Steeler who should be in there. L.C. Greenwood should be in there, and so should some others I played with. Maybe you can't have too many Steelers. Al Davis is in there; it's funny who gets in and who doesn't.

"There's got to be something more important in your life than running helmets into each other. The ultimate joy is the people working together and doing something successfully with other people.

"There's only one Hall of Fame I want to be in. That's the Kingdom of Heaven. I'm not really interested in getting recognition in the secular world. It was enough for me to be looked upon as being dependable when I played here."

Webster squirmed in his seat, changed the position of his legs and made a face. "Can't sit too long," he said.

"I have good days and bad days. My knees hurt most all the time. My problem is calcium buildup, arthritis. My feet, they're totally ruined. My elbow. I've got big bones, cow joints.

"About 6-2, 265 pounds was the biggest I was. Today, they wouldn't even look at me. Lot of teams play 6-5, 6-6 offensive linemen now. And everybody weighs 300 pounds. In some ways, that's a mistake. They don't move. They don't really block. What's allowed now doesn't require any technique. A lot of teams just get the biggest guys they can possibly get.

"I was always dependable. I always showed up and I never quit. I just kept going until the end. Just keep at it until you can't go on any more. Physical collapse is your only excuse. I was never satisfied. I've never been satisfied with myself.

"Chuck Noll . . . he never offered many compliments. Maybe he complimented me and I missed it. To him it might have been a compliment, but I didn't recognize it as such. The biggest compliment he paid me was keeping me that long.

"Noll never gave anyone that personal attention. Terry (Bradshaw) needed that. I'll tell you why Terry was so good. He had the ability to make the big play in the big games. In the third Super Bowl, Dallas covered our guys real close and Terry just threw the ball by them. In Kansas City, they always wanted me to tell them stories about the Steelers."

Webster announced that he was retiring from the Steelers several times, and then changed his mind.

Back then he said, "I could never put on any jersey but a Steelers jersey. My special feelings for Pittsburgh will always be there."

He should have listened to himself. He never was that comfortable in Kansas City. "He had a hard time out there," Ray Mansfield said during Webster's stay in Kansas City. "He's not happy. He misses that era when he played with great teams."

51

Webster played in nine Pro Bowls, more than any other offensive lineman in NFL history. Through the years, Webster offered some thoughts about his approach to playing football and to life.

Webster's work ethic — report early, leave late, play hurt — is the major reason he earned the name "Iron Mike" and a reputation as one of the hardest-working guys in the league.

"No matter what you're up against, the No. 1 ingredient to life is that you continue to fight with everything you have. You have to fight the word 'can't.' You have to fight the word 'failure.' You can never give in to that. I'm on the way up, on the way back up. All I have to do is finish the game. As John Wayne said, 'I'll finish up, maybe not standing up.'

"I didn't do everything right. But I always tried to do everything the best I know how. I liked our approach to football in Pittsburgh. If you go back and check the tally board, the guys who ended up winning the most ran the football and played the great defense."

"I grew up on a potato farm."

Mike Webster watched John Wayne movies and memorized some of his lines. He'd say things like, "You owe it to God, Mom and Dad."

The family farm was actually in Harshaw, an old logging town with a population of 39 people, about 17 miles from Tomahawk.

"I grew up on a potato farm, lifting sacks of potatoes — hundreds of them — after school. We went to school and worked the farm before and after school. There wasn't much time for recreation and games and cartoons on TV. We were happy to just play a game of baseball on Sunday. Kids don't do that anymore. Once in a while we played a pick-up football game, three or four to a side.

"I was a running back, quarterback and wide receiver back when we played in the hayfields of northern Wisconsin. If you asked me back then, I would have said I had a heckuva lot better chance to become a farmer than a Super Bowler.

"My dad kept me working so hard that I wasn't able to play football until my junior year in high school."

At Rhinelander High School, Webster played football, wrestled, threw the shot and discus. In his senior year, he started lifting weights. The football season ended in mid-October. There was too much snow after that to play.

"If we didn't have the crops out on the first of October, we'd lost them to frost," Webster said. "And usually the ice doesn't come off the lakes until the first of May."

From there, he went to Wisconsin where he was a three-year starter and all-Big Ten as a senior. The computer rejected him as a high draft choice. The Steelers selected him on the fifth round in 1974. Pamela grew up in Lodi, a small resort community near Madison.

Pamela worked in the athletic department at the University of Wisconsin, which is where she met Mike.

"There is more pressure and emotion involved in our family than in a normal family," she said when the Websters were living in suburban Pittsburgh. "When that happens, you have to give more of yourself to make the situation normal. We're quiet and stay home a lot. Everything we do is centered around the family."

Being the wife of a well-known professional football player had no special charm for Pamela Webster. Her thoughts might help explain why Pamela parted with Mike, and why she filed for divorce in 1996.

The Websters tried to distance themselves from the limelight in their Pittsburgh days. They both expressed a Christian attitude toward life and football, and Pamela promoted Mike as a terrific father and man.

"It might have been better if I had been born a century ago," she said. "Sometimes, I don't feel ready for this day and age. I can see myself having a log house, a big horse farm and living outdoors most of the time.

"It would have been fun to be born in the horse-and-buggy days because it was a romantic, practical and very enjoyable era. I just can't see the glamour in this world of pro football."

Jim O'Brien

Jane Greenwood and Pam Webster are former wives of Steelers' stars L.C. Greenwood and Mike Webster. Both appeared at Dapper Dan luncheon to pay tribute to the late Mike Webster

Former NFL Players Fear For Their Lives

Len Pasquarelli, who grew up in the Bloomfield section of Pittsburgh, wrote an extensive report on "The Price of Pro Football," and ex-players' concerns about their well-being and life expectancy. It was published in *The Atlanta Journal and Constitution* in January, 1994.

There was a strong perception that their life expectancy was shorter than the average male in America. Many players opted to take a reduced pension at age 45 rather than a full pension at age 55.

Ron Mix, a Hall of Fame tackle for the San Diego Chargers, was 55 at the time the article was published. He was working as an attorney in San Diego. He said he could hear his knees when he'd get up out of his chair, and he worried about what they were telling him.

"Football can take years, maybe 10 to 15 years even, off your life," said Mix. "You see young men who played in the league keeling over at my age . . . and it keeps you up at night."

Pasquarelli mentioned some cases that were on players' minds at the time. Richie McCabe, a defensive backfield coach for the Denver Broncos, and a former player with the Buffalo Bills and Pittsburgh Steelers, had died of cancer at age 49. McCabe had grown up with the Rooney kids on the North Side and played with Dan at St. Peter's Grade School and North Catholic High School. There is a ballfield named for McCabe near West Park, not far from St. Peter's Church.

Bobby Layne, who had been a star quarterback with the Detroit Lions and Pittsburgh Steelers, was felled by a heart attack at age 59. Matt Hazeltine, a linebacker for the San Francisco 49ers, died at age 53 of Lou Gehrig's disease.

Another celebrated case was that of Doug Kotar, who died of a brain tumor at age 33 in 1983. Kotar was from Muse, Pennsylvania and had been a star athlete at Canon-McMillan High School. He was signed as a free agent out of the University of Kentucky by the Steelers and then traded to the New York Giants. The Giants' starting center at the time was Jim Clack. Kotar and Clack had been at the same summer training camp with the Pittsburgh Steelers before the 1974 season. Kotar was a fine running back with the Giants for eight years, and is seventh in their all-time rushing statistics. Clack learned he had cancer in 2002.

When Kotar was ill at home, the Giants visited him when the team was in Pittsburgh to play the Steelers. Team captain Harry Carson rounded up the players to pay the visit. Giants' owner Wellington Mara picked up more than a million dollars in medical expenses after Kotar's benefits were exhausted. Carson and Mara are good men.

According to a report released then by the National Institute of Occupational Safety and Health (NIOSH) and the NFL Players Association (NFLPA), the early-death fears of Mix and many of his former NFL colleagues may have been dramatically overstated.

Pasquarelli polled many former NFL players for their opinions on a variety of subjects relating to life (or death) after football. Former Pittsburgh center Mike Webster once estimated he had gained and lost more than 200 pounds during his NFL career. Such dramatic weight swings, according to Dr. Harold Solomon of the Harvard Medical School, can take years off your life, no matter the occupation.

Players were warned that anabolic steroids could have long-term hazards to their health and wellbeing.

According to the poll taken by Pasquarelli, "Many players who left the game cited feelings of abandonment, loneliness, paranoia, helplessness, despair and loss of self-esteem. Some blame the awkward transition for failed relationships, unemployment, drug or alcohol addictions and other problems. Many players are forced into psychiatric counseling." The real world often overwhelms them.

"All of a sudden, you're out of the routine," said Atlanta Falcons' center Jeff Van Note. "You're not making money off your body anymore, so you're not into taking care of it like you were as a player. There's a real loss of identity, and I'm sure that contributes to it. The huddle is a comforting place, kind of like a safe womb. When you're yanked out of there . . . you lose friends and contacts. It isn't the same anymore."

Scene at Pro Football Hall of Fame in summer of 1997 showed strong support for Steelers' Mike Webster.

Johnny Unitas
Boyhood hero

"I knew I could play the game."

I felt a strange sadness on September 11, 2002 like one feels a few days after a family funeral. I wasn't sure what to do on the anniversary of the terrorists' attack on America, another infamous day we shall never forget.

Then, as if things weren't bad enough, the news came that Johnny Unitas had died. He suffered a heart attack while doing rehabilitation following surgery and died at age 69. Unitas, who had grown up and played schoolboy football in Pittsburgh, starred for the Baltimore Colts in the '50s and '60s and was regarded as one of the greatest quarterbacks in pro football history. He was my boyhood hero. We'll never forget that Johnny Unitas died on September 11. Talk about timing. It was like Willie Stargell dying the same day the Pirates opened PNC Park. It hits home, like the death of another Pittsburgh treasure, Fred Rogers or Mister Rogers.

Frank DeFord, one of the most famous sportswriters in America, grew up in Baltimore. Unitas was his hero, too. DeFord, who came to Pittsburgh to speak at the Town Hall South series in 2002, said during a television interview the next day, "The death of Johnny Unitas is like the official end of my boyhood." Indeed.

When I played sandlot football in the late '50s, I wore No. 19, high-top black shoes and a crewcut, just like Johnny Unitas. I practiced throwing the ball just past my right ear with a downward thrust on the follow through. It was a thrill to play on some of the same sandlot fields in Pittsburgh where Unitas had played for the Bloomfield Rams for $6 a game after the Steelers cut him from their squad during the 1955 training camp. I still think of Unitas when I pass those fields. His never-give-up story had great appeal. It was a rags-to-riches tale later adapted by Tommy Maddox.

Johnny Unitas was the embodiment of the children's tale about "The Little Engine That Could." He was deficient size-wise and school-wise when he came out of St. Justin's High School, a Catholic Class "B" School in the lower end of Mt. Washington. He was passed over by Pitt and Notre Dame even before the Steelers said he couldn't cut the muster in the National Football League. He ended up at the University of Louisville. He led the Colts to two NFL championships and was the star in the 1958 sudden-death overtime victory against the New York Giants that was billed as "the greatest football game" in history. He was seen on TV a lot in Pittsburgh because the Steelers and Colts had some kind of contract with the Dumont Network to televise their games in this area. The Colts as well as the Steelers were our team, and the Colts were a lot better than the Steelers in those days.

Johnny Unitas, who came out of Pittsburgh to become one of the greatest quarterbacks in pro football history, visits with Terry Bradshaw in Steelers' locker room at Three Rivers Stadium.

Three candidates for quarterback slot with Steelers at 1955 summer training camp at St. Bonaventure University in Olean, New York are, left to right, Jimmy Finks, Johnny Unitas and Vic Eaton. Walt Kiesling kept Eaton over Unitas because he could also play defensive back. Finks made it to Pro Football Hall of Fame for his administrative work with Chicago Bears, Minnesota Vikings and New Orleans Saints, and Kiesling as one of the NFL's pioneer players.

I spoke over the telephone with Unitas, at age 67, in late November of 2000. One day I came home and one of the messages on my telephone went like this: "Jim O'Brien, this is John Unitas in Baltimore. You called and said you wanted to speak to me." I received return phone calls from Unitas, Mike Ditka and Dan Marino in an eight-day period. It doesn't get much better than that. Forgive me, but I still get excited about stuff like that.

The message from Unitas sounded like a voice from heaven. I told my wife, Kathie, to keep it on the message system the remainder of the month. I wanted to hear it again from time to time. I wish I still had it.

One of his teammates was once asked what it was like to be in the huddle with Unitas and he said, "It's like being in a huddle with God."

"I never doubted my ability," Unitas told me over the telephone in that interview. "I knew I could play the game."

His father, who delivered coal, died when Johnny was four. Johnny was reared by his mother. She cleaned floors in downtown office buildings, worked in a bakery, and later went to business school to become a bookkeeper. "I learned more from her than any football coach," he said, "not about the game but about life, about being tough, about hanging in there. She was a tough, tough lady. She died about seven or eight years ago in a nursing home in McMurray.

"My sister, Shirley Green, lives in Bethel Park. I see her once a year. I have a brother, Leonard, who lives in Jacksonville. My other sister is Millicent, who lives in Gettysburg. I have a cousin, Joe Unitas, who played semi-pro football in Pittsburgh (Valley Ironmen). He has a photo studio in McMurray. I have a cousin, Bill Unitas, who lives in Gibsonia."

His sister, Shirley, also credits their mother for making a difference. "We all got our work ethic from her. They don't make them like her anymore. John never complained; he just went to work. I think we got that from our mother."

John Steadman, a sportswriter in Baltimore, told me once at Three Rivers Stadium, that you could sum up the success of Unitas in two words: "Beyond intimidation."

When that observation was pitched to Unitas, he said, "I never let stuff bother me. Just growing up the way I did in the street, or working at home. If you had a problem you looked it in the eye and resolved it. We did what we had to do in order to get along. We didn't panic."

I found myself throwing a football like Unitas the other day.

"There are always losses. We forget. That's part of the price of life."
— Rev. Jesse Jackson,
Evangelist and former quarterback

Ray Mansfield
Still remembered at smoker

"He was the keeper of the tradition."
— **Rocky Bleier**

Ray Mansfield was a really fine football player. He took great pride in never missing a game, in high school, in college and in the pros. He set endurance records during his 13 seasons (1964-1976) with the Steelers, playing in 168 straight games. His record was broken by Mike Webster, who succeeded him as the starting center, and played a record 177 consecutive games. Mansfield's parents were migrant workers and he worked with them in the fields before going to school each morning. He was an all-pro asparagus picker.

Mansfield was a most popular player, with his teammates and with the fans. He lived in Upper St. Clair and had an insurance business with Chuck Puskar in Canonsburg, and was always organizing get-togethers for the Steelers. He loved to drink and to smoke cigars and to tell stories. "He was the Ol' Ranger," recalled Rocky Bleier, who lives in Mt. Lebanon. "He was the keeper of the tradition and tales of the Steelers."

Bleier and Andy Russell headed the cast of former teammates who attended the seventh annual Ray Mansfield Memorial Cigar Smoker Spectacular at the Westin Convention Center on Sunday, November 3, 2002. Russell and Mansfield used to climb mountains and take on all kinds of physical challenges after they retired from the Steelers.

"I miss him like a brother," said Russell, who lived in Upper St. Clair when he played for the Steelers, but later moved to Fox Chapel.

"It's hard to believe it was six years ago yesterday that my dad died," said Jim Mansfield, now 31 and living on the city's South Side. "It seems like two years ago." Jim joined his Dad on a hike through the Grand Canyon where his dad died from heart failure. His family had a history of heart disease. Mansfield was 55 when he died.

"If the Ol' Ranger were here," his son continued, "he'd be having a great time, smoking these cigars, and telling stories. Plus, he loved to go up against the Browns. That was always special."

"He was always calling us to do something," recalled Gerry "Moon" Mullins, a guard on those great Steelers teams who now works out of Bridgeville. "He loved this kind of gathering."

"He was my dear friend; we were roommates during my seven seasons with the Steelers," said former guard Bruce Van Dyke, who lives in Peters Township and has a son, Brett, playing for his seventh grade football team. "Ray was a fun-loving guy who loved being a pro football player."

Among those in attendance at Ray Mansfield Memorial Smoker at Westin Convention Center in November, 2003, were, left to right above, Louis Lipps and Dr. Freddi Fu, one of Pittsburgh's most renowned sports doctors, and, below, former Steeler guards Bruce Van Dyke and Gerry Mullins.

Photos by Jim O'Brien

Other former Steelers such as Robin Cole, Craig Bingham, Louis Lipps, Dwight White, Mike Wagner, Emil Boures, Randy Grossman and Todd Kalis came to the Mansfield Memorial. About 400 fans paid $75 a ticket to attend the event. It was for the benefit of the *Post-Gazette's* Dapper Dan Charities, with proceeds going to the Boys and Girls Club among others. They watched the Steelers beat the Browns in a nail-biter by 23-20, cheering as if they were at Heinz Field, and enjoyed a pre-game tailgate party, a buffet luncheon, and a halftime question-and-answer session with the former Steelers in attendance. Many arrived in a good mood, buoyed by Pitt's upset victory over Virginia Tech the night before.

The death of Webster, at age 50, was still on their minds, which also rekindled stories of Mansfield. They were both considered "Iron Men" in their Steelers days. Their deaths reminded everyone, teammates and fans alike, of their own mortality.

It was ironic that the Steelers went into their critical encounter with the Browns not certain who could play center. Jeff Hartings was questionable and Chukky Okobi was probable. Mansfield and Webster were often listed that way, too, but there was never any doubt that they would play. They might be hurting, but you couldn't keep them off the field on game day. At the time, they were regarded as tough guys, old-fashioned pro football players. Today, some of their teammates wonder whether they gave too much to the game, whether they were too dedicated to their profession. Now they think their passion for the game may have contributed to their early demise."It definitely gives you something to think about," claimed Cole. "I address these topics now when I visit schools and speak to the kids. It gives you a new perspective on sports and life."

Jim O'Brien

Former Steelers' defensive lineman Dwight White chats with Jim Mansfield, who was hiking with his father, Ray Mansfield, in Grand Canyon when Ray was stricken and died of heart disease at age 55 in early November, 1996.

Leon Hart
The pride of Turtle Creek

"We knew he was going to be a great player."
— Johnny Lujack

One day after Mike Webster died, we learned that Leon Hart had died as well. Webster and Hart were from different generations of players in the National Football League, but they were both players who represented power and strength on championship teams. Hart, who grew up like no one else in the neighborhood in Turtle Creek, Pennsylvania, just east of Pittsburgh, died at age 73 on Tuesday, September 24, 2002. He had been diagnosed with prostate cancer four years earlier.

Hart had been a two-way star at Notre Dame in the late '40s when the Fighting Irish ruled the collegiate football world, and he won the Heisman Trophy in 1949 as the outstanding college football player in the land. He then starred with the Detroit Lions when they and the Cleveland Browns had the best teams in the National Football League. He was a member of three NFL championship teams in his eight seasons with the Lions.

Leon Hart's name was always synonymous with Turtle Creek. It was like a word association game. Mention Turtle Creek and people would say Leon Hart. He stood 6-4, and weighed between 245 and 260 pounds most of his career. He was a giant in his day. He was always a point of pride for football fans in western Pennsylvania.

He was one of several famous football people who died in 2002 who had a tie with Pittsburgh. Others included former Steelers running backs Fran Rogel, Byron R. "Whizzer" White, Joe Geri and Sam Francis and, of course, all-pro center Mike Webster. Johnny Unitas, a Hall of Fame quarterback from Pittsburgh, and two other former NFL stars, Dick "Night Train" Lane and "Bullet" Bob Hayes, who was also known as "the world's fastest human," died as well. Roone Arledge, the creator of "Monday Night Football," and Ray Downey, who had been the Steelers' public address announcer at Forbes Field, Pitt Stadium and Three Rivers Stadium, also died that year.

A Steelers' fan suggested to me that Art Rooney, the late founder of the Steelers, was putting together a new pro football franchise in heaven. He'd probably call his team the North Side Saints.

"Mastery of others is strength; mastery of yourself is true power."
— Lao-tzu

"He was a great act."
— Johnny Lattner

I was looking forward to seeing Leon Hart in October of 1998. He had accepted an invitation from my friend Bill Priatko to attend a testimonial dinner that Priatko and his pal, Rudy Celigoi, were putting together to honor their boyhood idol Fran Rogel. Rogel had been a star fullback and the Steelers' leading rusher for five seasons in the '50s. Hart was a contemporary. He had played for Turtle Creek against Rogel's North Braddock Scott High School team in some great neighborhood rivalries. I was emceeing the dinner and would be introducing Hart, as well as Jack Butler, Bimbo Cecconi, Dick and Ed Modzelewski, wonderful people like that.

I was hoping to get a more positive read on Hart, a legendary figure from my youth. I had last seen him at the National Football Foundation Hall of Fame banquet at the Waldorf-Astoria in New York back in 1984. I had shared a room with Cecconi for that event.

Many former Heisman Trophy winners were seated at one end of the banquet room that night in New York, starting with Jay Berwanger of the University of Chicago, the first Heisman Trophy winner in 1935. There were a lot of old guys in attendance at the dinner that night who had played football at Holy Cross, Fordham and Manhattan, and were on the small side. Hart was hollering at them, bullying them, I thought, making fun of their diminutive size — like they couldn't have been very good football players — and I thought it was a bad scene. That's not the way I wanted to remember Leon Hart. Maybe he was just having a bad night. I also recall "Baldy" Regan, the "Mayor of the North Side," shouting to me from a balcony overhead.

A few days before the dinner to honor Fran Rogel, I received a telephone call from Priatko, telling me that Hart had called him and said he would be unable to attend the dinner. Hart had just learned that he had prostate cancer. Priatko said that Hart was understandably upset by the bad news, and sorry that he wouldn't be coming to the dinner. He had always been a big admirer of Fran Rogel, going back to their days as high school rivals. He just wasn't up to it. Cancer doesn't care how big you are. Suddenly Hart was in a different league: men coping with dashed dreams, with truth, with life.

Hart died at St. Joseph Medical Center in South Bend, Indiana where he had once been the BMOC — the Big Man on Campus.

Hart had helped Notre Dame go undefeated in his four seasons as a starter at end for the Fighting Irish. They won three national titles during that time. They went 36-0-2 during Hart's four years at the school, winning national championships in 1946, 1947 and 1949, and finishing No. 2 in 1948. Notre Dame had as many fans in western Pennsylvania as the University of Pittsburgh football team.

The Irish whipped Pitt in all three meetings during Hart's stay at Notre Dame, by 33-0 in 1946, 40-6 in 1947 and 40-0 in 1948.

John Lujack, a quarterback from Connellsville, Pennsylvania who won the Heisman Trophy in 1947, said he knew Hart was going

"If you believe in yourself and have dedication and pride — and never quit — you'll be a winner. The price of victory is high, but so are the rewards."
— Paul "Bear" Bryant

Leon Hart
Notre Dame
1949 Heisman Trophy Winner

Courtesy of Notre Dame Sports Information Department

to be a great one when Hart first joined the Irish in 1946. I had last seen Lujack when he returned in mid-September, 1994 to his hometown to be honored with the 1941 Cokers' football championship team.

"He was a big freshman, he weighed about 260 pounds," Lujack recalled. "We tried to fool him on a couple of plays and he wasn't very foolable. We knew he was going to be a great player. He was second team to Jack Zilly, our regular right end, and he played an awful lot as a freshman. That didn't happen a lot at Notre Dame."

Hart was one of only two linemen to win the Heisman Trophy. Larry Kelly of Yale was the other, winning it in 1936. Hart and former Notre Dame quarterback Angelo Bertelli are the only players to win the Heisman Trophy and national championship in the same season and then become the first player taken in the first round of the NFL draft. Hart was named the Associated Press Athlete of the Year in 1949. "He was a great act," said John Lattner, who won the Heisman at Notre Dame in 1953 and was then the first draft choice of the Pittsburgh Steelers. Lattner was in Pittsburgh along with two dozen other Steelers from the '50s for a sports memorabilia and card show at Robert Morris University on April 19, 2003.

"I remember watching him in high school. He was a great athlete and had a great pro career. He was a nice guy, too."

Lattner added that Hart was an outstanding student at Notre Dame, obtaining a degree in mechanical engineering.

Hart, Lattner, Lujack, as well as George Gipp, George Connor, Tim Brown, Dave Casper and Frank Carideo are all members of the Notre Dame All-Time team.

Lou Creekmur, who played center for the Lions for ten years (1950-1959) and has been honored by the Pro Football Hall of Fame, said, "Leon was probably a little more intelligent than the average football player. He had a degree in engineering and he had an IQ that was a lot higher than the rest of us. Sometimes he'd flaunt it."

Hart helped the Lions win titles in 1952, 1953 and 1957. Bobby Layne was the quarterback of the Lions in those days. Hart earned All-Pro honors in 1951. During his pro career, Hart played offensive and defensive end and fullback. In his eight seasons with the Lions, Hart had 174 catches for 2,499 yards and 26 touchdowns. He ran for 612 yards and five touchdowns, all in 1956, and he had four interceptions, eight kick returns and twice returned fumbles for touchdowns.

After retiring from football, Hart lived in Birmingham, Michigan and ran a number of businesses, most of them associated with automobiles. He sold his Heisman Trophy for something between $150,000 and $200,000, at an auction conducted through the Internet in 2000. Hart said he wanted the money to help finance his grandchildren's education. He was married over 50 years to Lois, his high school sweetheart from Turtle Creek, and they had six children and eight grandchildren.

If you re-read this chapter you will see that it is chock full of famous football names. None was bigger than Leon Hart.

Clark Hayes
The biggest coal miner

"It was a manly place to work."

Clark Hayes has to be one of the biggest coal miners in the world. At 6-7, 350 pounds, he hardly seems suited for work in such a confined environment, but he wouldn't want to work anywhere else. "I'm the biggest," said Hayes with a warm smile, "the best looking, too. I whack myself in the head a lot when I'm moving through the mines. Those beams weren't installed with someone my size in mind."

Hayes was 47 when we first met, and he turned 48 in May, 2003.

Hayes became a good friend of many of the Steelers of the '70s and '80s when they lifted weights together at his good friend Lou Curinga's Red Bull Inn at 1050 Washington Road, or Route 19, in Washington, Pennsylvania, not far from the Meadowlands. It's now called Curinga's Inn, and the outstanding homemade chicken noodle soup will take the chill off your bones in the winter.

There's a room in the basement that bears resemblance to a blue prison cell out of a medieval period. The weights there — some resemble the black steel wheels of a train — are hardly state-of-the-art but Hayes, Curinga and a dozen or so of the Steelers turned that spare room into one of the most productive workout areas anywhere. Seeing the blue room was like doing an archaeological dig and uncovering a sepulcher containing sacred relics. The leather back braces, big punching bag, and sweat-stained Terrible Towel and the weights are still there. Even Steelers' insiders haven't laid eyes on this blue room.

"It's a bit of a dungeon," declared Hayes.

Several of the strongest men in the National Football League were forged in this blue room. Jon Kolb, Mike Webster, Steve Furness and Larry Brown were the ones who gained the most honors in so-called NFL "strong men" competitions. Others who worked out regularly, or at different periods, with that bunch included Ted Petersen, Steve Courson, Tom Beasley, Ray Pinney, Jim Clack, Tunch Ilkin, Loren Toews, John Banaszak, Mike Kruczek, Gary Dunn and Craig Wolfley. Their sweat, indeed their DNA, is still in the carpet runners.

Even with all those Steelers working out, Clark Hayes was still the biggest man in the blue room. Lou Ferrigno, the "Incredible Hulk" on the once-popular TV series, stopped by one day to check out the room. He was in the area for the grand opening of Stride, a state-of-the-art health and fitness club just north of the restaurant on Route 19. He said he had heard about this workout room in the Red Bull. His signed faded photo is still on the wall. So is a collection of Polaroid shots of some of the Steelers who were regulars.

"Lou came in off the street stone cold and started doing some presses. He said that one of the pieces of equipment was the same as he had as a kid, and that it brought back some good memories. Lou

Photos by Jim O'Brien

Clark Hayes, a 6-8 coal miner, lifted weights in basement workout room at Curinga's Red Bull Inn with Steelers' offensive linemen during the '70s. The scene and photo album bring back many memories.

Ferrigno said you got the best possible workout at our place," recalled Hayes.

There was a controversial story that appeared in *ESPN*, the sports magazine, soon after my initial visits to Curinga's Inn, relating to what became of some of the Steelers who used to work out there when it was the Red Bull Inn. It was an exposé story of sorts. The story pointed out that Furness had died at age 46, that Webster died at age 50, that Courson was being treated for a damaged heart, and had once been on a heart transplant list. There were suggestions that steroids and performance-enhancement drugs may have been taken by some of these Steelers strongmen. Such zealous behavior toward reshaping one's body seemed like a shortcut to the cemetery. The late Lyle Alzado of the Denver Broncos and Oakland Raiders was mentioned as another victim of such performance-enhancement drugs. The story, understandably, upset some of the Steelers and had reverberations around the NFL. It brought denials from some of the Steelers who were quoted in the article.

"Steve Courson was one guy who went public with his personal use of steroids and the damage he thought they did to his body," said Hayes. "He single-handedly brought steroids to the surface. When you see Steve today he's in phenomenal condition. He says he stopped taking steroids while he was still with the Steelers. The other players never spoke about steroids, and we never brought up the subject when they were here. Steroids was never a part of our discussion in the gym. No one was advocating that anyone else ought to try them. And they weren't a banned substance in the NFL or anywhere else at that time. People didn't know then about the negative side effects. We never gave a thought to taking steroids."

Hayes and Curinga joined me one day in mid-January, 2003 at Applebee's Neighborhood Grill & Bar in Peters Township, and sat in a booth where former Steelers linebacker Robin Cole had been sitting during an interview for this book. Steelers' fans in the room recognized Cole, but asked me as I was walking through the room to tell them who the other player was. They were referring to Hayes. He says he never played football, but did a little wrestling at Peters Township High School. "I'm not an athlete," he said with a smile. "I was just not that interested in sports."

He said that whenever he was in the company of any of the Steelers it confused people because they couldn't figure out who he was. He sure looked like a former football player. Hayes got a kick out of that. I heard about Hayes from his soulmate, Sis Haller. When she bought one of my books at a signing at Waldenbooks at South Hills Village, she told me about how her boyfriend and her brother, Lou Curinga, used to have all the Steelers working out at the family restaurant.

Clark Hayes was easy company. He and Sis had been together for 17 years. She had two children from a previous marriage, a daughter Nicole, 32, and a son, Richard, 31. "They're both great young

Lou Curinga and Clark Hayes are joined by former Steelers' linebacker Robin Cole at Applebee's Neighborhood Grill & Bar in McMurray.

Photos by Jim O'Brien

This is the home where Mike Webster and his family lived in McMurray during the team's glory days of the '70s. Webster had a blocking sled in the side yard where he would work out.

people," said Clark Hayes. He was as warm and fuzzy as the plaid flannel shirts he wore to our first two meetings. He was just a lovable giant teddy bear. It's easy to appreciate why the Steelers liked Lou Curinga and this big guy. These avid weightlifters weren't cozying up to the Steelers because they were famous football players, but rather because they were dedicated to getting a good workout every time out. "We didn't dote over them," said Hayes. "Our common link was we all enjoyed lifting weights. You couldn't find people who had more integrity or character than those guys."

When Hayes and I had lunch at Curinga's Restaurant on Wednesday, January 22, 2003, there was a front-page story in the daily newspapers about three coal miners who were killed a day earlier in a mining explosion at the McElroy Mine in nearby Cameron, West Virginia. The mine was operated by a subsidiary of Pittsburgh-based Consol Energy. It was a reminder of what a dangerous business Hayes had chosen for his "life's work."

The nine miners who had survived being buried beneath the earth in the Quecreek Mine were still on people's minds. "People remember them because they lived," said Hayes. "They don't remember all the men who have died in the mines." Hayes shook his head when the story was mentioned to him. "It's gruesome," he said. "People don't get killed in a nice way in the mine. It's all blood and guts."

He said it was real dry and dusty in the mines during the winter. He said the extreme cold or barometric pressure on the outside, and the dry and dusty interiors, force gas to liberate in the rock.

"It's a tremendous recipe for a fire or explosion," explained Hayes. "You take more gas tests when conditions are like this. This is the time of the year I'm not comfortable working in the mine. If there is an explosion it's even worse because of the conditions. It's a little scary in the mines at times in the winter. There's a sense of nervousness, but it goes away."

He was working for the Enlow Fork Mining Company, operated by Consol Energy. He had worked in coal mines for 28 years. He said he was a trackman. He laid track throughout the mines. He worked three different shifts, often changing from one week to the next. These eight-hour shifts are midnight till 8 a.m., and 8 a.m. till 4 p.m., and 4 p.m. till midnight. He says he gets up at 6 a.m. when he starts at 8 a.m. The mine where he was working is located in East Finley, eight to ten miles south of Claysville in Washington County. It's not too far from the Mel Blount Youth Home in Taylorstown.

"You go to work by riding in a cage down into the mine," said Hayes. "It's a miner's elevator. When I'm in a hurry to catch an elevator in a building, I still holler, 'Hold that cage!' It's just a habit."

He started to work in the coal mines in 1974, a year after he graduated from Peters Township High School. He had some friends whose fathers were coal miners.

"The average mortality rate for a vested NFL player is 56! It's a dangerous game."
— Steve Courson in his book, *False Glory*

Clark Hayes:

Lou Curinga and I were not really football fans. We worked out together in the basement of Lou's restaurant. Lou invited Jon Kolb to join us. Little by little, more Steelers started coming. We got a lot accomplished in that little blue room. I think Kolb did not agree with the training methods of Lou Riecke, who was the Steelers' strength and conditioning coach in those days. So he came here in the off-season rather than train at Three Rivers Stadium. Jon didn't like being under Riecke's watchful eyes; he wanted to be more creative.

When those guys started coming here, Lou and I watched even less of pro football on TV. It made us too nervous. Now we had a personal connection with those guys.

Those guys were more interested in what I did for a living than I was interested in what they were doing. These were championship people, but not one of those guys ever made you feel less. They uplifted you.

I was sitting here one day with Jon Kolb and Ted Petersen and Louie Curinga and a little boy came by and asked me for my autograph. The guys got a kick out of that, and I appreciate the way they handled it. The kid went away with a smile on his face like he was the butcher's dog.

When I went in the mine for the first time, there was just something about it that appealed to me. I just felt I had found my niche. There was something daring about it, challenging to a degree. It was a manly place to work. There's lots of testosterone in a coal mine.

I started out working at the Mathies Mine in Finleyville. It was on land owned by the Mathies family. There was a plaque there memorializing a World War II hero from the family. He was a bombardier who was shot down in Europe. That mine was one of the largest deep mines around here. Seven people had been killed at different times through the years while I was there. Five people were killed in a 15-month period in what we called the dark days of the late '70s. The authorities nearly shut down the mine. Some died by being electrocuted or in mine shaft accidents. Ghastly stuff. One guy died just around the corner from me one day. He was 62 and was talking about retiring. I had taken him to where he was working that day. I had told him to be careful, and he told me he had been working in those mines when I was just a gleam in my father's eyes, and that I needn't worry about him. His death was difficult to deal with.

> *"Some people are eating their dinner*
> *when they read our paper."*
> — Ike Gellis, late sports editor
> *New York Post*

One of the worst area mine catastrophes occurred around 1900 when 96 miners were killed in the Cincinnati Mine down near New Eagle.

Those stories stay with you, but I still like working in the mines. I suck down dust and I dodge rocks to make a living, to put a roof over my head and food on my table. Pro football players put up with a lot for the same reason. The Steelers were good at what they did. I consider myself good at what I do.

At the beginning of every season, I don't have some young guy who's after my job, someone who's bigger and faster. Somebody who takes steroids and wants my job. I swear to you, I don't know what I'd do in those circumstances. If I were placed in that situation, I think the answer is pretty clear. I'd want to hold my job.

"Mike always wanted to do more."

Some of the things I remember from Mike Webster's funeral are Garrett Webster, his younger son, giving his personal thoughts. I can remember when Mike was working out here. He was the youngest in our group at one point. Every one had to team up with a partner here, and I remember when Mike Webster was my partner. People who worked out here got the best workout of their lives. We pushed each other; that's why. I can remember when Mike and Steve Furness would work out in the morning. They'd come around nine or ten in the morning. It was rare when everyone was here at the same time. Mike would have his kids with him. Furness would bring his kids. Jon Kolb would bring Eric. The kids would play back there in the next room. Mike would load up every piece of equipment he could find. He always wanted to do more. It's called circuit training. He'd go from machine to machine. He'd wear his lifting gloves. He'd leave them on that shelf there when he wasn't lifting and they'd be absolutely soaked. I'd keep an eye on the kids while their dads were lifting weights.

Garrett was brutal as a little kid. He was just awful. He had so much energy. I don't know how Pam could handle him. He's pretty rough now, too. Mike admitted that Garrett was a handful. Mike used to say that if Garrett had been their first child he'd have been an only child. There's such an emptiness about the whole thing. There were a lot of mysteries about the way Mike was living. I didn't know all that was going on. Who knows what was the catalyst for the whole thing?

Every so often I'd hear rumors about Mike. I'd hear that he was sleeping in bus stations. A friend said he saw him in a bar selling a Steelers' football helmet he had autographed. He

Tunch Ilkin, wearing a University of Tennessee T-shirt, lifts weights at Curinga's Red Bull Inn during his early days with Steelers.

Young Mike Webster, wearing a T-shirt of Pittsburgh Fire Fighters Local No. 1, shows up for workout at Washington, Pennsylvania restaurant.

Photos provided by Curinga family

had brought some other Steelers' memorabilia with him, and was asking if anybody was interested in buying the stuff. He had a lot of people who really cared about him, yet he ended up in such sad shape. The guy who told me that — he worked on a different shift at the mine — was the same guy who told me that Mike Webster had died. You could have knocked me over with a feather when I heard that.

I have so many fond thoughts of Mike, and I'd rather hold on to those memories. I'll tell you the most dynamic story I know about Mike Webster from a personal standpoint.

I was going to this church in Washington. My minister asked me if I could get Jon Kolb to come to our church and speak to our people. He had heard me talk about Jon, and his strong Christian spirit. Jon is a wonderful man and a dear friend. I was closer to Jon than anyone else who worked out with us. I called Jon up and tried to make a date with him, but he was booked solid on the dates we had in mind. I didn't want to let the minister down. Jon said that maybe Mike Webster would do it.

Mike said he'd love to do it. Forgive me, but this story chokes me up a little. We set a date and put it in the paper. Mike Webster would appear at the Christian Church of North America, at 4th and Sherrill in Washington.

I picked Mike up at his house to take him to our church. He had a blocking sled in his yard, I remember that catching my eye. It was in his side yard. It shows you that he was always working to get better and stronger. I remember Mike wore a Navy blue jacket, gray pants and a yellow shirt. The shirt didn't seem to go with the rest of his outfit. He wasn't a fashion plate, I'm told, but then neither am I. I wear flannel shirts and jeans and I'll probably be buried in that. You see somebody like Mel Blount and he's always dressed so well. Same way with Franco Harris. Blount and Harris always look great. That wasn't Mike Webster. That's not Clark Hayes.

I introduced Mike to John DePaulo, our pastor. Pastor DePaulo introduced Mike to the congregation. He was so dynamic. He read a passage from Romans, Chapter 8, if my memory serves me correct. And he gave a moving testimony. His theme was forgiveness. He was a wonderful speaker and I was just taken by it. He stayed for an hour and signed things. He talked about fishing to the old men. I took him home. I got to stop here. It chokes me up. Today, when you confront an athlete, you better have a $10 bill for an autograph. Mike Webster didn't get a dime for what he did that day. Mike Webster thanked me for asking him to come to my church. He shook my hand, and thanked me for sharing my day with him. I didn't know how to thank him enough, and he took all the pressure off me by thanking me. That was a great and wonderful memory I have of him. The Websters were living in McMurray at the time, not far from where Steve Furness lived. I'll have to take you over and show you their homes.

The Steelers all can vouch for the way Mike Webster played. We kinda thought he worked out like no one else we ever knew. It was like he wasn't going to be here tomorrow. No one works out that hard. He had a mission to fulfill. He worked out two and three times a day.

I remember that Mike used to take these liver pills all the time. They were good for flatulence. Mike used to blow them out pretty good, and he cleared this room a few times. You couldn't stand to stay in here when Webster was at his worst. It's funny now; it wasn't so funny at the time.

Maybe Mike gave too much, or maybe he trusted too much. I don't understand how he got into such a predicament. Any of us would have given Mike the shirt off our backs. That brief moment on that Sunday when he came to my church comes back to my mind from time to time. I was sold on Mike Webster. Time has stopped there.

"Who's the big guy in the picture?"
— Zack Furness

When Jon Kolb met Louie, and saw the room downstairs he asked if it would be possible for him to work out here. Other Steelers followed him here. They became like thousand-year friends. Louie did not know, in the beginning, that Jon Kolb was a football player. It was later that Louie found out what he did for a living.

At one point, Jon said to Louie, "Do you mind if I bring a friend?" Louie said it would be all right. And Jon said, "Well, he's black." I guess he felt he had to ask because we were in Washington County. It's not the most progressive place in the world. We still have people here who'll burn crosses on lawns if they don't like you living in their neighborhood. Louie is a good man, though, and he said, "If he's your friend he'll always be welcome here." So Larry Brown joined us and it was never a big deal. They don't come any better than Larry Brown.

These guys used to work out at W&J before they met Louie. I think they wore out their welcome at W&J because, they say, Steve Furness used to get upset about something and he'd throw weights around in anger.

Steve would throw a temper tantrum if he failed to lift a certain weight. He'd lose it and throw a ten or twenty pound weight against the wall. When they came here, Jon told Steve,

75

"We like it here, so you have to control yourself." We got a towel and knotted it, and gave it to Steve. We told him he could toss the towel against the wall when he was upset.

He finally worked his way out of doing that stuff.

Louie understood all those things. He's a psychologist, too. It was Louie's idea to give Steve that towel to toss around.

I ran into Steve when Robin Cole was running for county commissioner on the Republican ticket. This was at a political rally at what is now the Holiday Inn by the Meadowlands. I admire Cole's courage. Again, he's running for public office in a Democratic stronghold in a county where they still burn crosses. Robin would have done a great job. He's a very sincere individual. And that's coming from a Democrat.

If they had given me $10,000 that night I couldn't have felt as good as I did. There was a roomful of Steelers. These guys all got up and they came over and hugged me. It was a great thing. I was just floating. Here were these guys who were such great people in the eyes of the public and they were making a fuss over me.

Steve said something to me, privately, that meant a great deal. Louie and I were just a couple of blue-collared stiffs. We don't think of people retiring in their 30s. We didn't take a lot of pictures from those days, and now we wish we did. We took a picture here and a picture there. These guys were all part of something very special in this area. We didn't think it would ever end. It was ten to twelve years and then it was gone. We should have taken a group picture. Steve Furness was always saying we should do that. Toward the end, Steve said that was one of his big regrets that we never did that. There were so many opportunities we missed. I was in one of the pictures we took. Jon Kolb was in it, too. And Steve's son Zack, who was just a baby when Steve used to lift with us, asked him, "Who's the big guy in the picture?"

I almost never changed clothes at the gym. One day I did, and I'm standing there completely nude when Steve Furness barges through the door. He had his mother and his wife with him. I'm standing there stark naked. I was somewhat traumatized by that. (I can only imagine what the sight of a nude Clark Hayes did to the Furness family.) They really surprised me. I have to laugh now about stuff like that. I have so many wonderful memories.

There are some scars on the pipes overhead where Steve Courson hit them while lifting. We had an arm-wrestling contest in here one day. You might be surprised who won it. Ted Petersen won it. He iced them all. One time Petersen left his third Super Bowl ring in there. He set it on the shelf and forgot it. We held it for him.

> *"All of us entertained the illusion that we could make events march in the direction we pointed, if we pointed clearly enough."*
> — Theodore H. White, *In Search of History*

Steelers' offensive linemen Larry Brown and Craig Wolfley, above and below, respectively, worked out with other teammates and friends at Red Bull Inn.

Photos provided by Curinga family

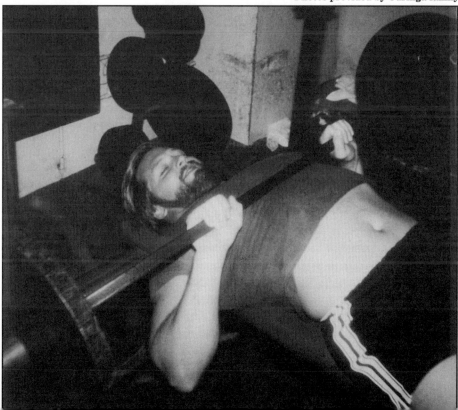

Seeing Mike Webster in the coffin at the funeral home was difficult to accept. When Terry Bradshaw started crying when he was speaking I started crying, too. I'm not made of stone. It was a pretty somber moment. I could see Mike holding his hand out for help. I was sitting next to Steve Courson. It reminded me of when we used to lift weights together.

I saw Dan Rooney there. I saw a lot of the Steelers that I recognized. I introduced myself to some of the ones I'd never met before.

Mike never looked like a young guy, but he looked 70 in that casket. He looked awful. It hurt to see him that way.

Photos provided by Curinga family

Ted Petersen and Steve Courson dined after working out at Curinga's Restaurant in Washington, Pennsylvania. Petersen was the house champion in arm wrestling. Now Petersen is athletic director at Upper St. Clair High School.

From Steve Courson in his book, *False Glory*:

"Sheer strength is more important to offensive linemen than any other position. Offensive linemen are more likely to use steroids to enhance their strength. During my time in Pittsburgh, 70 percent of the Steelers offensive linemen took anabolic steroids at one time or another. Other teams in the league called us 'The Steroid Team' during that time."

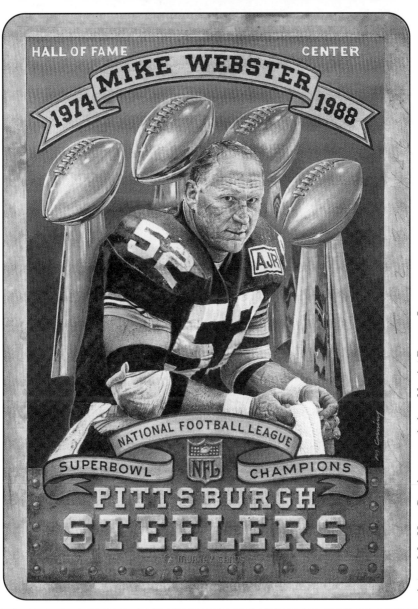

Artwork by Merv Corning, commissioned by Art Rooney Jr.

"There has never been nor will there ever be another man as committed, totally dedicated, to making himself the very best that he can possibly be. What good is a machine if you ain't got a center. And, oh, did I get a center. I just didn't get any center. I got the best to ever play the game, to ever put his hands on a football. And I said, 'Make sure he ain't as pretty as me,' and he ain't."
— Terry Bradshaw, introducing Mike Webster at Pro Football Hall of Fame ceremonies Saturday, July 27, 1997

Lou Curinga
Helped strengthen the Steelers

"What's it feel like to be 60?"

Lou Curinga is the president and principal owner of Curinga's Inn, at 1050 Washington Road in Washington, Pennsylvania. He always looks like he is about to burst out of his clothes, kind of like Superman. He stands 5-10, 205 pounds, and it's nearly all muscle. He has curly silver-gray hair, a perpetual tan and a warm smile.

It was Curinga, who turned 60 on June 5, 2003, who invited some of the Steelers to start working out with him in the basement of his restaurant on Route 19, back in the 1970s, when it was a Red Bull Inn. Most of them were offensive linemen and they became one of the most feared and respected forces in the National Football League.

When I told him I had turned 60 on August 20, 2002, Curinga came back with a question, "What's it feel like to be 60? Do you feel any different?"

I told him I didn't feel 60, but I was all too aware that I was 60. You go to more funerals, and you're more aware of the age of the deceased. Too many are now contemporaries.

"I worked out this morning," he said. "I try to pay attention to my body and my spirit. I appreciate every day. You never know. You're only on this earth so long. As you get older, I think you put your priorities more in order."

He said he liked helping people with their workouts. He thought it was a great way to relieve stress, and he thought he learned to be more patient. He said his father lacked patience — "he had a short wick" — and it was something he worked at so he wouldn't be that way. He said he enjoyed the camaraderie in the workout room.

"It looked like the land of the giants."

Lou Curinga:

I don't know what you thought when you saw the blue room. It's nothing fancy. But it's full of useful weight equipment that still serves its purpose if used properly, and that room is full of stories. There's a lot of memories there. It used to be a green room, by the way, an ugly green. We steamed up a lot of mirrors in that room.

80

I can still see Jon Kolb bench-pressing 550 pounds in that room. Those guys used to leave their shoes and boots at the door. I think size 14 was the smallest. It looked like the land of the giants.

I never worked in a coal mine like my friend Clark Hayes, but I had friends killed in a workplace incident that got me to change careers. In the late '60s, around 1966 or 1967, I was working for Equitable Gas. A team of our workers were busy in a building in Crafton-Ingram. I was working about four miles away. There was a big explosion and seven guys got killed. The building in Crafton-Ingram was flattened. There was nothing but rubble. Twenty-three more guys went to the hospital. Someone from Equitable Gas came by our work site, and picked us up and took us over to Crafton-Ingram. It was some sight.

A good friend of mine was among those who were killed. He was blown to pieces. My dad, Paul Curinga, talked me into quitting. He had the Red Bull Inn, and I went to work for him about four months later. I didn't want to quit my job at Equitable — I was there for about five years and they treated me right — but my dad thought it was dangerous. The first two years I worked for my dad, I was the janitor here. Now I'm the president. America is a great country, right?

I couldn't work in a coal mine like my friend Clark Hayes. It's not so much that it's dangerous, but it's unhealthy. It's bad air you're breathing down there and it can cause a lot of problems. Clark's a great guy, though, and we get along so well. I was training in a garage I had fixed up at my dad's place in Carnegie at the time. I was single and still living with my dad. Then I decided to clear an area that wasn't being used in the basement here. I put some weight-lifting equipment in there. I went through a lot of training partners before I found Clark. I'm demanding, and I want to do it right.

Before long, we added other sets of weights. Mike Webster was an interesting case. He trained so hard. He would floor most guys with his training ethic. He loved to work with heavy poundages, and he'd move from one set to another with hardly a break. When I think of Mike, I think of someone who was intensely dedicated to the team. He wanted to be the strongest Steeler. He was a very good man.

Sam Nover, the TV sportscaster, was standing in front of me at the funeral home. I was very sad, upset. I haven't felt so bad in a long time. Here was a guy who gave so much, and to be gone at such an early age was so sad. I remember the pictures of him and his kids on the swings behind their house.

"Winning makes you think you'll always get the girl, land the job, deposit the million-dollar check, win the promotion, and you grow accustomed to a life of answered prayers."
— Pat Conroy, author
My Losing Season

Jon Kolb was the first Steeler who started working out with me. He was very intense. He was very strong and a great person. That's how it started. I didn't know who he was when we first met. I didn't follow football. I didn't know him from a hill of beans.

He asked me if he could work out here after the season. I said, "What season?" He looked at me with a puzzled look, and he said, "I'm a Steeler." I told him, "If you work out, will you stick with it?" That's all I cared about. He could've crushed most men for speaking to him that way, but I was serious. He worked out that Monday morning, and we really clicked together. He's a true Christian. He walks the talk.

Then one day he says, "I got a friend who'd like to work out with us." He told me it was Larry Brown and that he was black. He didn't know if I was prejudiced or not. I said, "If he's your friend, I don't care what color he is." Larry started to work out with us. I loved the guy; he was great to be around. He was a big guy, but so mild-mannered and pleasant.

You can't find two better people than Jon Kolb and Larry Brown. They are both real gentlemen.

Mike Webster had built a place in Wisconsin where he could work out. Kolb told him about our workouts. He said I was like a little Mike Webster, the way I was so enthused about lifting weights. So Mike moved to McMurray, and bought a house here, so he could work out with us. Steve Furness was working out with us, and before you knew it we had 14 or 15 of the Steelers here.

I can't speak loud enough about their character. I remember when Jon Kolb saved two young kids who were caught at a fire in his home. One was his son and the other was his infant niece. Jon's first wife Sandy left something on the stove before she went out, and the house almost burned down. Jon was very tough. He could take a beating. Larry Brown used to say that after a game he was covered with ice.

We had some fun together. I remember a time when we agreed to help Tom Beasley castrate about 25 young steers. The pen was muddy in March. We jumped those steers and tried to get them in what they call squeeze chutes. In one instance, I got the head and Beasley's got the tail, and we're getting thrown all over the place. The first ones we got let out a yell, and after that the rest yelled even louder.

I was much smaller than the Steelers. I was more inventive about what to do with the weights. They'd see me do it and they'd say, "If he can do that, then I should be able to do it."

They never talked about themselves. They always talked about other guys. Jon was worried about Larry Brown losing his job after he was moved from tight end to tackle. Jon took

"Everybody is vying for center stage and everybody is trying to gain attention for themselves."
— **Mike Ditka**

it upon himself to help Brown get bigger. Brown was unbelievable the way he worked that summer to get bigger. He was a well-spoken guy, but he was something else in the weight room.

We've had some famous people stop in this restaurant through the years. We've had Perry Como, Mario Lemieux, Joe Montana, Lou Ferrigno and David Hasselhoff. We've got pictures of some of them in the lobby as you enter. We're proud that they wanted to come here. I just wish we had taken more pictures. We've had some pleasant times here more than 28 years. Our times with the Steelers will stay with us forever because they were such great guys.

Jim O'Brien

Lou Curinga was a championship weight-lifter who helped Steelers strengthen themselves for NFL combat.

Jon Kolb
Good Fit for Grove City

"He walked the talk."
— Mel Blount

Grove City College seems like the perfect place for Jon Kolb to be a football coach and a mentor for ambitious young men and women.

It is a beautiful, Christian-based 150-acre campus in an idyllic rural community of 8,000 just 60 miles north of Pittsburgh on I-79, just east of the popular Prime Outlet Shops complex. Grove City College has all these neo-Gothic buildings, 27 of them according to sports information director Ryan Briggs, and it always gets high marks in ratings in the annual *U.S. News & World Report* survey. It's always rated one of the "best buys" in the country, and the kind of school for those seeking one that holds its students to high standards in and out of the classroom. No alcohol or drugs are permitted on the campus.

Students are expected to attend chapel services on a regular basis at this Presbyterian-affiliated institution. It is one of the few schools in the country that does not accept any state or federal monies, because they don't want the baggage that comes with this largess, yet it keeps its tuition at an attractive rate for its 2,500 students.

I am most familiar with Grove City College because my wife, as Kathleen Churchman, was a 1965 graduate of the school. Her brother, Harvey Churchman Jr., graduated two years later, and he met his wife, then Diane Thomas, during his student days there. They are three of the nicest people I know, so I have always had the highest regard for Grovers.

Jon Kolb was one of the nicest people who played for the Pittsburgh Steelers during their glory days of the 70s. This is a well-chiseled man who was one of the strongest Steelers ever, in the weight room and at chapel services. He's got a chin that can hold its own in competition with Bill Cowher but he doesn't exercise it as much. Kolb was one of the Steelers who organized Bible study sessions for his teammates. He walks the talk, and has led others down similar paths. He was quiet most of the time, so when he spoke people listened.

I'll always remember that when my brother Dan died while I was covering the club in the early '80s that Kolb, Jack Ham and Mel Blount were the first Steelers to offer condolences to me for my loss.

Kolb, at age 55, was looking forward to his ninth season as a Wolverine assistant coach and seventh as a defensive coordinator when we spoke on January 15, 2003 during a break in his work at Specialty Orthopedics Rehabilitation Center in nearby Hermitage. He had previously worked in the same Mercer County community as

Courtesy of Grove City College sports information department

Jon Kolb
Grove City assistant football coach

*"Mike Webster was the consummate Steeler.
A guy who, in my mind, was the greatest Steeler
of them all."*
— Craig Wolfley

Director of Personal Fitness at the Regional Health System. He's also on the instructional staff for the Fellowship of Christian Athletes summer camp in Erie.

There is a sense of permanency at Grove City College. The football team's head coach, Chris Smith, and his highly respected offensive coordinator, Bill Jordan, were both approaching their 20th seasons on the coaching staff. Both played football and are graduates of Grove City College. Smith succeeded his football coach Jack Behringer, who'd been there forever, as athletic director in 1996.

While at Grove City College, Kolb has contributed to championship football teams in the Presidents Athletic Conference (PAC) in 1997 and 1998. Kolb was there when R.J. Bowers came to the campus after playing four years of minor league baseball to become college football's all-time leading rusher with 7,353 yards from 1997-2000. Bowers scored his first NFL touchdown as a member of the Pittsburgh Steelers in the finale of the 2001 season against the Cleveland Browns. A year later, ironically enough, Bowers was playing for the Browns. He, too, seems like a wonderful young man.

Grove City College plays football in the PAC against the likes of Thiel, Washington & Jefferson, Waynesburg, Bethany and Westminster. Carnegie-Mellon is also a traditional opponent, and should have remained in the conference.

Kolb was an offensive tackle for the Pittsburgh Steelers from 1969 through 1981. He and Joe Greene, Sam Davis and L.C. Greenwood were among the pillars on Chuck Noll's first team in Pittsburgh. Kolb was a starter for four Super Bowl championship teams, and was voted to the "All-Century" team by Pittsburgh fans. After retiring as a player, Kolb became an assistant coach on the Steelers' staff under Noll. He was the only coach who, as a player and a coach, was with Noll for his first 200 victories in the NFL.

Kolb was originally a third-round draft pick from Oklahoma State, where he had played center. He was a second-team All-America selection and two-time All-Big Eight performer. A native of Ponca City, Oklahoma, he completed his Master of Science degree in 1997 at Slippery Rock.

Kolb and his wife, Deborah, were sitting in the same row of seats as I was at the funeral service for Mike Webster back in September. Kolb was wearing eyeglasses that day, and had his head bowed during the remarks that were offered on behalf of his former linemate. His eyeglasses were perched at the end of his nose. He and Webster had worked out together for years, lifting weights in the basement of the Red Bull Inn in Washington, Pennsylvania. They had competed in and were the class of the NFL's "Strongest Man" competitions.

"Jon Kolb was strong before they knew anything about being strong in the National Football League," said former teammate Mel Blount. "He was also such a beautiful person, and a devout Christian. He walked the talk."

A woman who bought a book from me during a signing at Waldenbooks at the Crown Center in Washington asked me if I knew about Jon Kolb saving his kids in a fire when he owned a 100-acre farm in nearby Ninevah when he was playing for the Steelers. I was not aware of that story so I asked Kolb about it for openers in our interview.

"If I go back in, I'm going to die."

Jon Kolb:

I was out fixing a fence on the farm when I saw smoke coming out of the fireplace. It was April, but I wasn't alarmed at first. I had built a fireplace and had just put the first fire in it the night before. Then I saw smoke coming out of the windows, and it was the sickest feeling I had in my life.

My son, Eric, who was only one-and-a-half years old at the time, was in the house. So was my niece, Cindy, who was my sister's daughter. Cindy was 15 months old.

I did the dumbest thing I could do, something really stupid. I ran to the front door and opened it. A ball of fire shot toward me and burned off my eyebrows and sideburns. It was just solid flame, what they call a backdraft. I knew there were two kids upstairs, and I had to get in there somehow.

I was running around the house, trying to figure out how to get to the kids. I had fractured my left hand playing football, and my left hand was in a cast. I jumped up and grabbed onto a waterspout on the edge of the roof. I couldn't use the fingers on my left hand, but somehow I pulled myself up onto the roof with one hand. It's amazing what you can do under such circumstances.

It was a miracle. I knocked the window out in Eric's room, and it was easy to get him out. I got out on the roof with him and laid down on my stomach and held him. Then I dropped Eric into the hands of a neighbor who caught him. I went back through the window. It was so hot and it was so smoky. There was intense heat. It was burning underneath the floor. I went back in, but I got disoriented and lost. So I retraced my movement and got back in the window. I'm thinking, "If I go back in, I'm going to die. If I don't go in, my niece is going to die in the fire." I prayed about it. I did a short "God help me" prayer. I was trying to figure out the layout of the rooms, and exactly where the crib was where my niece had been napping. Somehow I found my way to the crib. I grabbed her ankle and I pulled her out upside down. I was probably rough with her. They say you can't worry about how you're handling them in a time like that. Just get them out, however you can. I was crawling on my hands and knees, and the floor was hot to the touch. I was trying to remember where I was. I did worry that we weren't going to make it. I thought we were going to die.

Then I saw the light in the window. Seeing that light in the window was the highlight of my life. Even more than winning the Super Bowls. When I got out on the roof, I just sat there for a while. I'm so happy. People who had gathered round the house were wondering why I was smiling so much. My house was burning down. But a few minutes earlier, I thought I was dead. My niece lives in Oklahoma now, and my son lives in Germany.

I don't think about that fire that much, but when I do it makes me realize that some of the things that get us down aren't worth worrying about. You remember what's really important. We were all lucky that day. Our prayers were answered. It was a fire that started in the kitchen, as we later learned, and thank God no one got hurt or killed.

"Mike loved John Wayne movies."

Mike Webster remains an enigma for me. I thought I knew someone really well. After what went wrong in his life, I realized I didn't know him that well. I can remember him and his wife Pam being in our house. They were a great couple.

To me, Mike Webster was part of a piece. The offensive line is one entity. It's very cohesive. We played together for a lot of years. Ray Mansfield and Mike Webster were splitting time in our first two Super Bowls, and then Webster became a fixture there. Jim Clack had gone to the Giants, and it was Webster there for every offensive play. We had Sam Davis, Moon Mullins and Steve Courson sharing time at guard, and Larry Brown and me at the tackle positions. We had six guys playing five positions for a number of years. The guys were real close.

I remember Mike at our training camp at St. Vincent's. Mike loved John Wayne movies. He memorized John Wayne lines from the movies. He knew General Patton's famous speech by heart. I remember Mike was always taking these iron pills, and he passed gas a lot. We wanted him to put towels under the door of his room so he didn't kill the rest of us.

He had a good sense of humor back then. Maybe there were two Mike Websters. The old Mike wouldn't have done some of the things he did over the past ten years or so. I'm not sure about what went wrong with him. Mike emerged as a real leader on our club. He was an All-Pro performer at his position in every way. That's the way I prefer to remember him.

Mike could dominate the best nose tackles in the league, people like Curly Culp, one-on-one. Mike didn't need help. That's unheard of. Centers always needed help with guys like that. One of the people who contributed to Mike's downfall was his agent, Greg Lusteg. Mike lost a lot of money with that agent. After that, Mike seemed to be focused on getting that money back. He got into some other deals that went sour. He'd have been better off if he had just banked his money. A lot of guys on the team got into bad investments, limited partnerships and stuff like that. Mike became bitter. I was not a *Wall Street Journal* subscriber, but I knew I wasn't smart enough to get as involved in investments as Mike did. I remember he got involved in a business deal where you got worms for fish bait out of this machine. It was like a soda pop machine, only it dispensed worms.

He was still losing money, but Mike wouldn't let it go. He wanted to get his money back somehow. The last time I communicated with Mike he was looking for money for more projects. I had given him money that had been earmarked for my son's college education. I told my wife I couldn't continue to contribute to Mike's business ventures. I was there to be supportive of Mike's family and my teammate, but he was destroying his life.

Mike wasn't in the best of situations his last few years. I heard those friends of his talking at the funeral — they'd become his friends late in his life — and they were saying they weren't his friends because he was a football player. But I don't believe that. I wondered what was going on. There are plenty of homeless people. Go find them and help them, if that's what you want to do. They were definitely excited to be keeping company with a famous football player like Mike Webster. I don't know all those guys, but they don't look like guys I'd pick as friends. I know there were people who think the Rooneys didn't help him. I know the Rooneys and I know they did try to help Mike. I know Pam Webster told me all the things that went wrong between them. Mike wasn't letting anybody really help him. I know that Tunch Ilkin and Craig Wolfley, in a kind and loving way, were trying to help Mike Webster get reestablished. Hey, life is not fair sometimes. But they were trying to get him back on focus. They were trying to get him to move ahead.

It hurts to see what happened to him. It hurt to see what happened to Sam Davis. I loved those guys. It just shows how fragile life is. There are deep and shallow aspects of life, and pro and con situations. I was aware of some of their struggles. There are other people who played in the NFL who have similar problems. We talk about these things.

Ninety-nine percent of professional football players had a football scholarship. It took me four-and-a-half years to get my degree, but I went back and finished my studies to get my degree. Later, I got my Masters (at Slippery Rock University) because I thought it would help me in my post-football career.

People should have their degrees and they should be able to apply that. The average pro football career lasts an average of 4.2 years. Pro football should give you a pretty good start on a professional career.

Some of us came away with physical problems that persist the rest of your life. I've often been asked if I had to do it over again would I play pro ball. The answer is yes. I don't think you have a right to complain when you had a free choice as to whether or not you wanted to play pro ball. It's inane for someone to think you can play and then blame somebody else for your physical problems. It's a game of collision. The team that wins the game wins the most collisions.

On Mondays after a game I always had a stiffness in my walk. I started getting stingers, or burners, in every game. There was sharp pain. I'd have tried to come back for a 14th year, but I knew it was best to quit playing. I know the kind of injuries Mike Webster suffered through the seasons. I could empathize with him. It never quits hurting.

When I was 28 and playing for the Steelers they put me through some x-rays and looked at my neck and back. They told me I had the neck and back of an 80-year-old man. I have mild spinal stenosis. Every football player is going to have it.

I'm in good spirits. I don't want to preach to anyone. I want to help others find their own way. I don't want to undermine Mike Webster in any way, or be critical of his family and friends.

I don't have all the answers. I'm offering this so that others might be careful, and watch what they are doing.

Courtesy of Grove City College sports information department

Grove City football coach Jon Kolb instructs defensive unit.

Terry Bradshaw
Comes back to embrace Chuck Noll

*"All I wanted to do
was play . . . and win."*

Beads of sweat formed fast on the expansive forehead of Terry Bradshaw. They glistened under the harsh lights of the TV cameras in a VIP reception room at the Hilton Hotel. Bradshaw was speaking to the Pittsburgh media. He was explaining his latest comeback.

Right from the beginning, Bradshaw was sweating silver bullets. It was a nervous night for the former Steelers quarterback and Hall of Fame star. He was like a cat on a hot tin roof.

He was back in town as the marquee attraction for a dinner and luncheon sponsored by Dapper Dan Charities. He was to be inducted into the Dapper Dan's Pittsburgh Sports Hall of Fame on Sunday evening, February 9, 2003, and he was to offer reflections the following day at a luncheon in memory of Mike Webster, who centered the ball to Bradshaw most of his stay with the Steelers. Webster had died in September.

Bradshaw had come back to Pittsburgh to pay his respects. It was all part of the process of getting back into the fold. He had failed to attend the funeral of his dear friend and former boss, Art Rooney, Sr., and people in Pittsburgh still remember that. They never bought Bradshaw's flimsy excuse that he didn't want to be a distraction, stealing attention by his appearance at the funeral home or St. Peter's Church on the North Side. They felt Bradshaw should have been there.

Starting the previous year, Bradshaw had been busy trying to make amends. He offered a eulogy at the Webster funeral service and hugged Marianne and Chuck Noll when he saw them outside the funeral home. The comeback has been a continuing soap opera.

Bradshaw saw the 67th annual Dapper Dan Dinner, one of the most respected sports awards dinners in the country, as an opportunity to make peace with Pittsburgh, the Steelers, the Rooneys, the fans and, most of all, his former coach, Chuck Noll. None of it was necessary, of course, as far as his perceived adversaries were concerned. For the most part, this was Terry's perception of the way things were, not their perception.

Most of the guys who covered the club during his distinguished stay had to love the guy. He was always there, usually full of fun and good cheer. You couldn't ask for a more approachable star athlete. He was more light-hearted and quotable and productive than any sports superstar in the history of Pittsburgh.

"Act like you've been there before."
**— Paul Brown, Founder
Cleveland Browns**

What amazed me was the public reaction to Bradshaw coming back to Pittsburgh and making peace with everyone. "Isn't it great that Terry and Chuck are getting together again," said so many people I spoke to at book signings in shopping malls throughout western Pennsylvania. People loved this Prodigal Son story. Personally, I thought Terry was protesting too much. With Noll, it was never a big deal. The young Bradshaw was guilty of misreading pass coverages, and the older Bradshaw was guilty of misreading Pittsburgh, the Steelers and, most of all, Chuck Noll.

Bradshaw has always been one of the most respected and popular athletes ever to grace a field in Pittsburgh. Sure, he was booed in the early days, and labeled as being dumb, and all that. At his appearances at the Dapper Dan events, Bradshaw admitted he didn't know what he was doing in those days, as far as reading defenses and being football smart. "All I wanted to do was play, and win," he said. "That's what it's all about. So I didn't like it when I was benched, or when Chuck criticized me, or called me out in front of the team. No, I didn't like that at all."

Bradshaw, at age 52, has forgiven those who hurt him back then, and now he was asking anybody he'd ever said anything bad about to forgive him as well. Bradshaw has regained his religious roots, and wants everybody to embrace him and know that he never meant any harm. He's written about his new outlook on life in his best-selling book, *Keep It Simple*.

Noll, now 72, was not exactly what he would have liked in the way of a coach back then. He wasn't patting Bradshaw on the back and assuring him that he was the man. He wasn't a warm, fuzzy type, like Sam Rutigliano of the Cleveland Browns. Teammates of Terry Bradshaw, especially quarterbacks like Terry Hanratty and Mark Malone, thought he got plenty of attention from Noll and everyone else. Attention has always been important for Bradshaw. That's just Bradshaw. He needs attention. I remember him, late in his stay with the Steelers, talking loudly on the team buses and charter airplanes. Bradshaw was a ball.

He had three marriages go bad. "Terry ought to ask himself what happened, and how he figured in the equation," said several of his former teammates, and even two of his opponents, Boomer Esiason and Harry Carson. "He's the last guy I'm going to get a self-help book from," said Esiason. "He's a good guy, but he's always been a little screwed-up with his personal life."

Noll was what Bradshaw needed back then. Noll was demanding and difficult, at times, but he taught Bradshaw all he needed to know to become one of the biggest winners in pro football history.

"Terry was always there when the chips were on the line," noted Noll in his introduction of his former quarterback at the banquet. "He was always at his best in the biggest games. He always came through when we needed it the most. That's why we won four Super Bowls."

Terry Bradshaw signs autographs for Steelers' fans following practice session at St. Vincent College in Latrobe, and sets the pace for "gassers" around practice field, followed, left to right, by Steve Furness, Ted Petersen, Joe Greene and Jack Lambert. They were truly the boys of summer in the '70s.

"Winning is not everything — but making the maximum effort to win is."
— Green Bay Packers coach Vince Lombardi

"Winning is not the most important thing, it's the only thing."
— Vanderbilt football coach Red Sanderson

"What an unbelievable ovation he received."

Basketball winners Ben Howland of Pitt and Swin Cash of McKeesport, an All-American at Connecticut and a WNBA star in Detroit, were honored as the Sportsman and Sportswoman of the Year at the Dapper Dan dinner, but Bradshaw was still the star attraction. He's the reason they sold out the dinner so early, and prompted them to add a follow-up luncheon to handle all the ticket requests. There were over 1500 for the dinner at $125 per ticket, and around 250 for the luncheon at $75 a ticket. Noll and Bradshaw both received long standing ovations at each of these events.

The dinner was five hours long, the luncheon lasted less than two hours. The luncheon program was more compact and easier on the backside. The marathon dinner had some special moments, though.

Howland said he had taken his son to see the Steelers play the Indianapolis Colts in a nationally televised Monday night contest at Heinz Field back on October 21, 2002. Bradshaw was an honorary captain for that night's game. "What an unbelievable ovation he received when he was introduced at halftime," said Howland. "It was impressive." Howland also said he loved Pittsburgh and planned on being here for a long time.

Bradshaw hugged everybody who was within reach, including Swin Cash and Greg Gattuso and, of course, Chuck Noll. The next day, he was hugging sportscaster Stan Savran, who emceed the program and confessed that Bradshaw had been one of his heroes. And this was coming from a guy who grew up in Cleveland. Bradshaw also hugged Pam Webster, the wife of Mike Webster, and Garrett Webster, one of Mike's sons.

They could have raised more funds for the Boys and Girls Club of Western Pennsylvania if they had charged money for hugs with Bradshaw.

Pittsburghers were so pleased that Bradshaw was coming back to town again, as he'd done during the Steelers' season, showing he had a change of heart, and wanted to be a part of the Pittsburgh sports family once more. "I'm home; I can't tell you how much that means to me," began Bradshaw in his remarks.

Bradshaw had been talking non-stop to Noll, who was sitting next to him on the dais. Noll was not comfortable about all this fuss. He was never comfortable in the spotlight. He never thought there was any problem with his regard for Bradshaw.

"There was no reason to respond," Noll said, when asked about the apparent feud with Bradshaw. "You don't get into those kind of contests. Life goes on. He's in something he obviously loves to do. He's having fun and enjoying it."

He thought Terry was just being Terry, the ultimate showman, saying anything to cause a buzz. He knew Terry often jumped back and forth in his reflections, apologizing from time to time for ill-tempered remarks, and then doing it all over again. He always admired Bradshaw's athletic ability, and was a bit bemused by his showbiz antics.

94

Terry Bradshaw consults with Coach Chuck Noll. That's Terry Hanratty behind Bradshaw.

Terry Bradshaw on being cool in the clubhouse:

"As a pro athlete you learn early to get your quotes down. When you talk to the press after a big play or big game, you need to sound a little hip, throwing in a few technical terms so that they never totally understand what you're saying. And always act humble while taking credit for something that you don't really deserve."

"Terry is obviously a man who enjoys life," Noll said of the guest of honor. "But I'd rather talk about Terry, the football player. Terry came out of Louisiana, and he was just a great athlete. He not only had great ability, but the ability to do it when the chips were on the line. To do it in the big games. Terry had great ability to throw the ball deep. He wanted to do it on every play, and that's where we differed a bit. But I looked up some records, and in the Super Bowl Terry averaged more yards per pass than any other quarterback. He threw nine touchdown passes in four Super Bowls. He had two receivers who were pretty good. John Stallworth averaged 40.33 yards per catch in the Super Bowls, and Lynn Swann averaged 40.25 yards per catch in the Super Bowls.

"If Terry has just thrown passes, the offensive line would have been at a real disadvantage. But we could run the ball, too. Franco Harris rushed for 354 yards in the Super Bowls. There were people who wanted to stop the run when they played us, but few of them succeeded. They had to respect our running and passing games.

"So Terry could go back and have time to throw the football. It all added up to us having four Super Bowl victories."

He introduced Bradshaw the way Ed McMahon used to introduce Johnny Carson on the Late Night Show. "As they say in show business . . . And here's Terry!" announced Noll, dragging the line out "here's Terry" as long as he could.

Noll was brief in his remarks. He knew it was Terry's show. Noll always preferred having his players in the spotlight.

"I'm still trying to please him."

Terry Bradshaw was every bit the TV evangelist in his appearance at the Dapper Dan dinner, but he seemed honest and genuine in his remarks. One never knows for sure whether Bradshaw is just being an actor. One night he showed up for Jay Leno's late night show by dressing as Santa Claus and he just took over the show. Leno became the guest. Bradshaw was more nervous about this assignment than being on TV with irreverent Jay Leno or with irascible Don Imus on his morning show. Bradshaw was sweating more than ever.

"Even tonight," he confessed about still being nervous around Noll, "sitting next to him, I'm still trying to please him. I've always been that little child around him.

"The problems I've publicized were never really problems," Bradshaw continued. "They were my problems, no one else's. For all I tried to make out a bad situation for Chuck, it wasn't a bad situa-

---

"Being a real fan is the stuff of life itself. It is the ongoing quest for the municipal Holy Grail. It is the implacable fight for justice. It is the honest belief that today will be better than yesterday and tomorrow even better than that."
— Joe Queenan, author
True Believers: The Tragic
Inner Life of Sports Fans

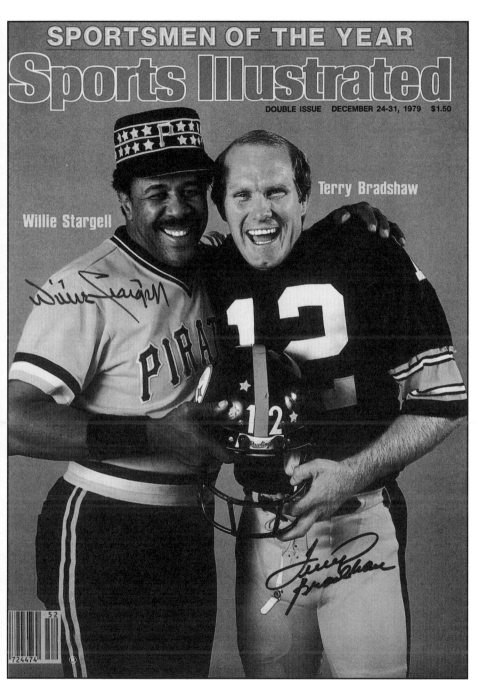

Sports Illustrated's year-ending 1979 issue featured Pittsburgh's Willie Stargell and Terry Bradshaw, leading citizens of "the City of Champions."

tion. He did the best he could do to test me to see if I was the guy who could get it done.

"In a greater sense, he became my father. He helped me in so many ways, I realize now. I guess I've finally grown up, and matured. He taught us and we listened and we executed. And we won. Hey, I'm so glad to be back."

Terry pointed to John Majors, the former Pitt football coach, sitting in front of him on the dais, and spoke about how they got to know one another in Terry's early years with the Steelers. "He was one of the few people in Pittsburgh who talked like me," said Bradshaw with a big smile.

"I remember being on the sideline at Pitt Stadium when Tony Dorsett rushed for 250 and some yards against Notre Dame. I was so lonely for people back home in those days. It's good to see you again, John."

Then Bradshaw showed that he can poke fun at himself for some of his shortcomings. He brooded when anybody questioned his intelligence when he started out with the Steelers. Hollywood Henderson of the Dallas Cowboys had said, "You can spot Terry Bradshaw C-A and he still can't spell CAT!" That stuff was all behind Bradshaw now.

"I'm just so glad to be back," he continued. "I would have liked to have written a speech, but I don't write very well.

"I was a smart boy because I always thanked my Savior and my mommy and daddy. They were always there for me. They're here with me tonight. My mom's pushing 74 and my dad's 75. He had a heart attack last year. He was just going to the lake to troll when it happened and he ended up in the hospital. I'm so glad they're both in good health.

"I've always been a mama's boy. Soon after I reported to the Steelers, I had to have an operation. John Best, the Steelers' doctor, did the operation on me. When I came out of the anesthesia they told me I was saying, 'I want my Momma.'" Bradshaw smiled and took out a handkerchief and mopped his wet brow, something he would continue to do from time to time.

"It's been way too long," said Bradshaw, getting back to his Prodigal Son song. "One of the good things about life is that, as we grow up and mature, we get wiser. I've never been one who has had all the answers.

"We were supposed to win Super Bowls. It wasn't easy. It was difficult. I came out of Louisiana Tech, and I wasn't too sophisticated, on or off the field. I couldn't read coverages. It was such a culture shock coming here. All of you were so different.

"I didn't know what you expected of me. I didn't ask to be the No. 1 (draft choice) pick. And you only paid me $25,000! My dad was there when Dan Rooney signed me to a contract on the 50-yard line at Three Rivers Stadium. The stadium wasn't even completed. I never had money like that in my life (Dan Rooney told Bradshaw the next morning that he had made a mistake. Rooney said the contract was for $26,000). I went home with $7,100 in the bank. Then I learned about a thing called taxes. I had a P.E. degree . . . what did I know about stuff like that? I had to sell cars on the side just to get by.

"As I settled in with Coach Noll, I had a lot to learn. I was about five years behind everybody else."

Then Bradshaw directed his remarks to Noll, sitting to his left. "I was just a little bit slow about all this stuff," he said, laughing aloud at his own remarks. "I'm sure I drove you crazy. You're trying to pass along your brilliance, but I just wanted to play football. I didn't want to read coverages — cover-four and stuff. I didn't want to audible. I sure didn't want to run the football. I just wanted to throw it.

"We were being taught the lessons to be successful. I learned something from football most quarterbacks don't — I knew more about defense than I did about offense. He made us study defenses so much. If you knew the opponent and their weaknesses you could attack it and win.

"I didn't like being benched. I didn't like losing my job. I didn't like it. You have a choice. You can blame somebody else, or you can accept the blame."

By now, Bradshaw had everybody in the vast audience in the palm of his hand, the way he once gripped an NFL football. He owned the room.

"I didn't want to be a failure in life. I just wanted to play and win. That's what it's all about. I went to his office one day, during our first Super Bowl year, and I wanted to be traded. But he told me how glad he was to have me, and he told me, 'You're my guy.' That meant a lot to me because he had been going back and forth between Joe Gilliam and Terry Hanratty and me. After that, he was really my father. In a greater sense, he became my father.

"Dan Rooney was learning how to run the football business back then. Chuck Noll knew what he wanted from us. He taught us and we listened and we executed. People say we had trouble. I created that. I wasn't mad at Chuck then as much as I was mad at me.

"I was steaming because I got hurt doing what I do best — throwing a deep pass in practice. When I was hurting, though, after my first divorce, or when something else was wrong, Chuck would ask me if I wanted to come and stay with him and Marianne for awhile.

"I forgot about that, I guess, when I was saying some of the things I've said in recent years, and when I was staying away from Pittsburgh. You'll never know how happy I am to be back. You'll never know how proud I am to be a Steeler. You'll never know how much my family roots for the city.

"I've been in the TV business for 19 years, and I stayed away from Pittsburgh except for a few visits most of that time. Now I realize that everything that I am, everything I have, everything . . . I've accomplished everything that matters right here in Pittsburgh.

"From now on when you see me, you don't have to ask me any more questions. Coach Noll, if I could reach down in my heart, I would

say I'm sorry for every unkind word and thought I ever had. It was
. . . my wrong, my childishness, my selfishness. God, it feels good to
say this. Having said that, it kind of cleanses me.

"I miss my coach. I love my coach. I miss Chuck Noll."

With that he slumped back into his seat next to Noll. He took out
a white handkerchief and wiped the sweat off his brow. His confession
was finished.

During an auction of sports memorabilia, conducted by KDKA
Radio's Larry Richert, a painting of Bradshaw by Pittsburgh artist
Johnno Prascak went for $10,000. The woman with the winning bid,
who wore a black sweater and a gold leather mini-skirt, said she had
a son named Steele R. A Steelers' helmet autographed by Bradshaw,
Noll, the late Mike Webster and Mel Blount, Jack Lambert and
Franco Harris, all Hall of Famers, went for $5,000 to construction
magnate Corky Cost.

"It was tough love."

Before the dinner, Ed Bouchette of the *Pittsburgh Post-Gazette* had
suggested they have a couch instead of a chair for Bradshaw at the
Dapper Dan dinner. Bouchette said Bradshaw was going to pour out
his long repressed feelings about a coach he had publicly criticized in
books and in TV and personal appearances the previous 20 years.

"I miss my head coach," Bradshaw had said prior to his appearance in Pittsburgh. "I'd love to be in contact with him. He's just a great
guy. He taught me the game of football, and it's just stupid the way
things went along.

"He's a good man. We all grow up. The picture becomes clear
when you retire. Chuck's plan for me, the way he coached me and
treated me, it was tough love. I didn't understand it, but I understand
it now and I appreciate it.

"We probably can all say things now we wouldn't dare say before:
I love him and care for him.

"He did it right. I may not have agreed with it, but a lot of
people say quarterbacks and their coaches don't get along. I got along
with him. I was afraid of him, which I guess is good. And I wanted to
please him. I was not as secure about myself as you would have
thought. I think I was trying to please him, trying for him to be happy
with me. And he was, as long as I was obedient and good. It's like with
your parents: When I was bad, I got punished. Same with Chuck.

"It's kind of like the final piece in the chapter. I want to try to
silence everything and show everybody that everything is fine with
Chuck and me, as it should be and as it has been. It just backs up
what I said. Hey, look, I screwed up.

"It'll all be good. I'll just straighten it all out once again in front
of everybody, let him know how much I love him and care for him and

TERRY BRADSHAW
STEELERS
QB

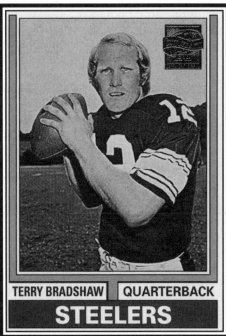

TERRY BRADSHAW | QUARTERBACK
STEELERS

STEELERS
Steelers 50 Seasons
TERRY QB
BRADSHAW

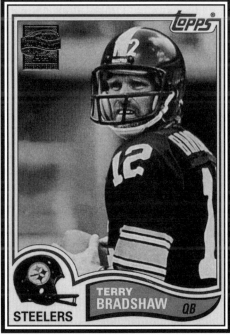

topps
TERRY BRADSHAW QB
STEELERS

how sorry I am that I caused such a ruckus. I'll make sure everybody knows that I'm sincere, let them know there's no hidden agenda.

"I want a relationship with him. I want him to know how great he was to me and how much I appreciate it. I might even break down and cry."

Bradshaw showed up in the Pittsburgh area in one of his rare appearances since his retirement as a player back on Monday, July 10, 2000, playing in the Sheetz Family Christmas Golf Classic at Treesdale. He met with members of the Pittsburgh media, including Chuck Finder of the *Pittsburgh Post-Gazette* and Stan Savran of Fox Sports Net Pittsburgh's "Sports Beat."

He addressed several topics, and here's some of what he said:

Terry Bradshaw:

The only reason I got into the Hall of Fame is because of my rings. You can't look at my statistics and say, "Those are Hall of Fame statistics." It's always been about the rings. The Pittsburgh fans, we won four, and what was the first cry out of their mouths? "Win one for the thumb." The dust hasn't settled yet. I mean, that's what you're measured by. That's what you play for.

I'll take the rings, and those other guys can have the yardage and the touchdowns. Plus, I called my own plays, Jiminy Cricket.

Now they have microphones in the helmet. They don't call the plays. Don't even think anymore. "Call timeout." "Got a bad microphone." It's just crazy. I say, get rid of that stuff.

You only find out what someone is all about when the game is in his hands. Let him make the crucial call. Especially with the money they pay these men, the amount of time they put in . . . you tell me they can't learn these plays and learn these defenses and what works against them? All they have to do is study and prepare and understand it.

As for my rocky relationship with Pittsburgh, it was the career. It was, like, unfinished business. I was just really starting to have fun. Then I got hurt.

You know, nobody knows what I was going through, and I wasn't going to say anything. Pressure from people in the organization — 'you can play hurt.' I had a torn ligament in my elbow. I couldn't throw, and I played the following year with a torn muscle. Had to get it shot up (with drugs). The reason I didn't play in Knoxville (in a 1983 preseason game) was because I tore the muscle . . . When (the doctor) shot me up, he found out that my ulna nerve split. The whole arm was dead, just flopping around. So we just kept it quiet.

> "There is a bond among us that cannot be broken, regardless of any differences."
> — Terry Bradshaw

Bill Amatucci

As rookie in 1970

Terry Bradshaw

Three Steelers who have gained Pro Football Hall of Fame honors are, left to right, Franco Harris, Lynn Swann and Terry Bradshaw.

I just went through so much. I was working out at a high school at night, turning on the gym lights, trying to come back without anybody knowing it. Lifting. Had a trainer. I mean, I was killing myself. You don't want to tell people: "Look how hard I'm working." That's not my style. I just feel like if they knew how hard I wanted to come back, and how much I wanted to come back.

If they had just left me alone and let me have (1983) off, I would have been fine. I would have been 100 percent. But, you know, they were constantly challenging me, and naturally I said, "OK" — tried to face up to the challenge.

I'm just angry. Angry that I had to leave like I left. Every time I'm not here, it's like there's more bad blood between us, and there isn't. I wish that never happened.

People ask me, "Why don't you come back?" Well, for what? I'm in the horse business in Texas. My kids live around the corner from me. My wife divorced me and remarried and moved next door, which is all right I guess. They asked me once (1999) for the Monday night (25th anniversary reunion) . . . I just couldn't flat do it. I already said yes to a TV committment. It wasn't my fault; it was Fox's fault. When they open the new stadium (Heinz Field), I pray to God that I can come. To show that when it works, it works. I'm fine with it.

You think I need to talk to someone about all this. You mean a therapist? The first time I saw a therapist, I was so embarrassed. I lied to him for three weeks. And the guy he healed is doing a hell of a job, but I'm still screwed up. That's a true story.

Talk to Chuck (Noll) or some others? It's nobody's doing. It's my undoing, if anything. I haven't really come out and had this definitive statement. I've made comments . . . everything's fine. Then people read something here or there. I don't show up for this, I don't show up for that. The truth is . . . no, I never have been mad at Pittsburgh fans; I've been upset at me. You know what I mean? It's never been them. If I had a problem, it's been an ego problem that I have to deal with.

I've just never made an effort to just wipe it clean. I don't have an avenue to do it. I don't do it on the Fox show. If you listen to me on the pre-game show . . . I don't ever say anything about them (the Steelers). I never have. That ought to tell you something. If I had an ax to grind, I'd be taking shots at them. I would love for them (Steelers fans) to know...we never had a problem at all.

Confession of an Ex-Presser

When I was working at *The Pittsburgh Press*, I remember getting a phone call one night from a woman who posed the following question about Terry Bradshaw's wife: "Is Jo Jo Starbuck any relation to Roger Starbuck of the Dallas Cowboys?" I responded, "Yes, Ma'am, they're first cousins."

Excerpt from *Looking Back*, Terry Bradshaw's 1989 book with Buddy Martin:

"It is far more important that the player develops some kind of support system outside of the football when he is still playing. So that when it's over, his whole world doesn't come crashing down on his head. He needs to be loved and supported emotionally. If he can't do anything but dig a ditch, his wife ought to say to him, 'I love you. Dig the best ditch you can dig.' If that player has built his support system around other athletes and has married a groupie, then he is in real trouble when it all ends. It's critical for these athletes to be loved by their families. Their value to their communities should not be measured by how many dollars they bring in."

Mike Longo

Terry Bradshaw embraces his former backfield coach Dick Hoak during return to Pittsburgh to serve as honorary captain of Steelers in 2002.

Boomer Esiason, former quarterback of Bengals and Jets, appearing on Don Imus Show on October 6, 2002, talking about Terry Bradshaw and his book, *Keep It Simple*:

"He's got a gazillion jobs, and those commercials, and he's making millions of dollars. And he has all these problems. Who's got his problems?
It's always about Terry. You got him on there ("Imus in the Morning") crying. The last person I'm taking advice from or want to know how to live my life is Terry Bradshaw. He won four Super Bowls and I haven't won any, but there's nothing I can learn from him. Keep It Simple — that's what they did when he was quarterbacking the Steelers."

REAL FANS — Station Square is a popular tourist attraction for Steelers' fans from all over the country when they come to Pittsburgh to see their favorite pro football team in action. This book's author has met Steelers' fans there from Wyoming, California, Arizona, North Carolina, Delaware and Illinois who did not grow up in Pittsburgh area. They simply adopted Steelers as their team as kids and have stayed with them. Many older Steelers' fans got hooked in the '70s. Younger fans Jason and Brad Quast of Fargo, North Dakota, and Cory Mannil and Karl Foisburg of Sioux Falls, South Dakota, came through during the 2002 season.   Jim O'Brien

Mike Webster Memorial Luncheon

It was an Irish wake

"Webster had a low butt."
— Terry Bradshaw

The Mike Webster Memorial Luncheon lived up to its name. "It was like another funeral service," said Pam Webster, his former wife. "It was good for our kids to hear all the good things about their father. They don't remember much about Mike before he was brain-damaged. They don't remember him from his good days. It's important for them to know he wasn't always moody and mean."

Those who were unable to attend Mike Webster's funeral service at the Somma Funeral Home on Steubenville Pike in Robinson Township back on Friday, September 27, 2002 were able to hear what his former teammates had to say in tribute to him. He had died at Allegheny General Hospital on September 24 after he had suffered a heart attack. He was 50 years old.

"It was a strange funeral," said Pam Webster. "We got the word that he wasn't doing well, and we were on the highway coming here (from Lodi, Wisconsin) when we learned he had died."

That news hit his teammates and all Steelers fans quite hard. Many knew that Webster had been going through a challenging time following his retirement from football. There had been reports that he had mental, physical, marital and financial difficulties. He had been known as "Iron Mike" during his days with the Steelers. He was what the Steelers of the '70s were all about. That's why his problems puzzled people who remembered him in his halcyon days.

Webster, born March 18, 1952, in Tomahawk, Wisconsin, had earned four Super Bowl Rings and played in nine Pro Bowls during a 17-year pro career and was voted to the NFL's all-time team in 2000. He played in more games, 220, than any other player in Steelers history and was inducted into the Pro Football Hall of Fame. He played every offensive down through one six-season stretch with the Steelers.

This luncheon in his honor was a bit of an afterthought. The demand for tickets for the Dapper Dan Dinner exceeded the 1500 capacity of the main ballroom of the Pittsburgh Hilton and Towers, so they added the luncheon to accommodate all those who wanted to see Terry Bradshaw get back in good graces with his coach, Chuck Noll, and make peace with Pittsburgh and Steelers fans on February 9-10.

Soon after the announcement that Bradshaw would be appearing at the dinner, to be inducted into the Dapper Dan Pittsburgh Sports Hall of Fame, with Noll making the introduction, tickets for the dinner at $125 a plate sold out within a few weeks. The Dapper Dan had never experienced such a demand for tickets. Bradshaw and Noll agreed to extend their stay so they could provide a program for those left out in the cold. The luncheon, at $75 a ticket, drew an additional 250 to the Hilton. Most of the proceeds were going to the Boys and Girls Club of Western Pennsylvania. It's a good cause.

"You were there for us."
— Garrett Webster

Everybody had a good view of the speakers and the program was more compact than the night before. In short, it was a better show.

Seated at the dais for the noontime program at the Hilton were former Steelers, left to right, Randy Grossman, John Banaszak, Louis Lipps, Tunch Ilkin, sportscaster Stan Savran who emceed the event, Terry Bradshaw, Chuck Noll, Andy Russell and Craig Wolfley. Sitting next to Wolfley, at the far right end of the dais, was Garrett Webster, the 17-year-old son of Mike Webster. At 6-8, 335 pounds, he was bigger than any of the other Steelers seated at the dais. He was wearing a black suit, and a black turtleneck sweater and his head was shaven bald. He looked like a member of the Oakland Raiders. He was a senior at Moon Township High School and expressed plans to go to Pitt as a walk-on candidate for the football team in the fall.

"What these Steelers meant to me was family," said Garrett, addressing the audience as well as those seated on the dais. "The town was proud of you. My dad didn't want you to know all that was troubling him — he was embarrassed — but he always felt you were like family. That helped our family when my dad died. You were there for us. Everyone gave us that feeling again."

Garrett's mother, Pam Webster was sitting in a front row table with her two daughters, Brooke, 25, and Hillary Webster, 15, of Madison. Pam Webster told me that her other son, Colin, 23, a corporal in the U.S. Marines, had been dispatched from Fort LeJeune, North Carolina to Kuwait during the buildup in the Mideast because of a looming war with Iraq. They were sitting at a table for ten with friends of Mike's from his latter days in Pittsburgh that I had remembered seeing at his funeral. Pam said she was concerned about Colin's safety. She was pleased that Garrett was going to Pitt. "He had some offers from some Division II schools, but he wanted the top level," she said. "He didn't do well his last two years at school when he was looking after Mike, and schools didn't understand what he was going through. If he has to pay his own way, maybe he'll work harder. I hope so." Bob Junko, a neighbor of mine and the associate head football coach on Walt Harris' staff, was doing his best to get Garrett accepted at Pitt. Garrett's scores on standardized tests were solid, but his grades were poor.

Savran did a superb job of introducing all the speakers, tossing zingers at first and then praise, roasting and toasting them all at the same time. Savran said he grew up in Cleveland, but has become a

---

"Don't give up . . . don't ever give up."
— **Jimmy Valvano**

Brooke Webster talks to, left to right, Steve Courson and John Banaszak during Dapper Dan luncheon in her dad's honor. Brooke and sister Hillary flank their mother, Pam Webster, at Hilton Hotel program.

Photos by Jim O'Brien

Pittsburgh guy. He confessed that Bradshaw had been one of his heroes. That earned him a warm embrace from Bradshaw at the close of the program.

Savran also introduced Dan Rooney, the Steelers' president, who made a brief appearance in the audience, and Steve Courson, one of Webster's teammates and closest friends. They spent a lot of time working together on the offensive line and in weight rooms. Courson showed up dressed like Daniel Boone, with a burnt orange outfit that had two-inch fringe along the sleeves and the seams on his slacks. He wore a snug-fitting teal-colored jersey. He sat at a table as a guest of Jim Rossero, who was one of Banaszak's assistants on the coaching staff at Washington & Jefferson College. Still the outsider, Courson was the only Steeler in the room not sitting at the dais.

Bradshaw stole the show, naturally, and kept it from becoming too maudlin. Terry can make you laugh and he can make you cry, and he did a little of both at the banquet the night before and at the luncheon. He was always so much fun at Steelers' practices and in the locker room, and it was great to see him cutting up again.

When Lipps got up to speak, he mentioned that he was excited when the Steelers made him their No. 1 draft choice in 1984 because he was going to be teaming up with Terry Bradshaw. He was a wide receiver and he couldn't wait to be one of Terry's targets.

"My home boys back in Reserve, Louisiana were excited, too," recalled Lipps. "They were eager to find out from me if Terry threw the ball as hard as they say he did. They'd say, 'Man, you're going to catch passes from Terry Bradshaw.' And I'd say, 'You got that right!' I told them I'd let them know what it was like, sure thing.

"I came up here and I see Terry Bradshaw in the locker room. He's sitting in a big chair, with his feet up, just relaxing. He'd just come back from seeing the team doctor. I learned that same day that his elbow was injured so bad that he wasn't going to be able to play any more. What a bummer. So much for my dream.

"I didn't want to go back home and tell them that. So when I went back I told them he sure did throw that ball hard. But I could catch it. The truth is I never caught a ball from Terry Bradshaw. I missed out on that."

Bradshaw is show business all the way, and he didn't miss a beat. "It's not too late," he said. He looked out into the audience, and asked, "You got a ball? I'll throw you one right now."

There was a football, baseball and hockey puck on a centerpiece at every table, it turned out. So somebody flipped a black and gold and white football, more of a spongy Nurf football, and Terry caught it. "Go down there," he directed Lipps. And Lipps moved quickly down the dais to the far left. Terry threw a pass with some zip on it to Louie who grabbed it cleanly. One pass, one completion. "That's what it's all about," shouted Bradshaw. Lipps laughed and hurried back to embrace Bradshaw. They both smiled. Bradshaw was having those kinds of embraces with everybody who got too close to him that weekend.

"Hell, I'd play for nothing. I love it."
— Bobby Layne
Hall of Fame QB

One of those who felt his warmth was Savran, but that didn't keep Savran from needling him in his introduction:

"It's good to have Terry back," said Savran. "If you wanted to find him in Pittsburgh in recent years, you had to look at the back of a milk carton. He just took a long vacation. He's back and he's back for good."

When it was Terry's turn to speak, he got more laughs describing the difference between taking snaps from Ray Mansfield and then Mike Webster when he played for the Steelers.

"Mansfield had a high butt, and you could stand up behind him tall and see everything out there," explained Bradshaw. "Webster had a low butt, and you had to bend down real good to get that ball. Chuck told me I had to ride him and stay with him so I'd get the ball cleanly. So I did. It was like riding a bull at a rodeo."

Bradshaw demonstrated how he did that, breaking up everybody in the audience with his antics. His mother and father were in front row seats and he even made fun of them. Referring to his three divorces, he said his mother had warned him. "She told me, 'You'll have trouble if you marry outside the family,' and she was right. So I'm seeing my cousin Anita now and my mother likes her. Hey, it's OK to make fun of your family." He mentioned that his 75-year-old father, Bill, was working as a greeter at Wal-Mart back home in Shreveport, Louisiana. "He says he's working," Terry said, "but he just goes there and hangs around all day."

Then he got to Mike Webster, and he led off with a line that left the audience in stitches. Just as calmly as can be, Bradshaw said, "Mike Webster liked to fart on my hands." When the laughter died down, he added, "This is something you didn't know. And he thought it was funny. You're in a two-minute drill and you stay down there and take it. His butt would be going up and down. That's because he was laughing while he was farting on my hands. I never could get the snap count right.

"I tried to keep it simple. You know, if he's open throw it and if he's covered throw it anyhow. I preferred to go on the first count. Mike was one of my most honest critics. He'd say, 'You stunk today.' We went to the sauna right after the game, to hide from the media, and we'd put a board across the door so (public relations man) Joe Gordon couldn't get to us. We'd sit in there and talk about the game.

"You have to get along with the center. Webby was one of those guys who commanded your respect. He was a high-energy guy. He was focused in on what we were supposed to be doing. And he was like that in all types of conditions. He thrived on cold weather. Chuck allowed us to run our own huddle. We called our own plays. I'd get a vapor lock in the huddle once in a while. I'd say, 'Fellows, I'm out of plays. Help me out. Anybody got something for me to run?'

Mike Webster on the Steelers' owner Art Rooney:

"He really made everybody feel special. He had a unique ability to make people feel special. My favorite memory of The Chief was allowing my daughter to interview him for a school project. He made an 11-year-old feel very comfortable and very important."

"Moon (Mullins) would never say anything. Sam (Davis) wouldn't say anything. Jon (Kolb) never said anything. Larry (Brown) wouldn't say anything. Benny Cunningham, our tight end, would be saying, 'Throw me a five-yard hook.' That never appealed to me, a five-yard pass. Webby would say, 'Shut up, Benny!'"

Then Bradshaw looked directly down at Chuck Noll, sitting in the seat nearby, and interjected, "I don't think you knew all about this, or what was going on out there at times." Noll just smiled and shook his head.

"But we couldn't have done any of this without Chuck. He trusted us. He let me do it my way. I wasn't a quarterback who yelled at the players."

(In a separate interview during his visit to Pittsburgh, Bradshaw said, "You are strong with your personality, but not overpowering. You don't embarrass people. I don't like the Dan Marino approach of screaming and hollering at people out on the field.")

At the Webster Memorial Luncheon, Bradshaw continued his story about his days with the Steelers.

"The only guy I ever yelled at was Mike Webster, and I'm embarrassed to say that," said Bradshaw. "I didn't see well at night. I never talked about that; I didn't want to sound like I was making excuses, but I couldn't see that well at night. I had a hard time seeing the game clock. I wear glasses now when I read.

"I was trying to kill the clock late in this one night game, and I knew that Webby was upset with the way I was taking so long to call signals. He called time out with two seconds left on the play clock. I went crazy. I called him every name I could think of and chewed him out on the field. He just took it.

"In truth, though, I never felt I was the leader of the offense. Mike was. He led by example. He would turn around, at times, and suggest audibles I ought to call. He knew everybody's blocking assignment. He was the quarterback of the offensive line, and called out all adjustments. He helped me through a few games, I'll admit that."

In his 1989 book, *Looking Deep*, written with Denver sportswriter Buddy Martin, Bradshaw reflected on a scary period in October of 1988 when he was hospitalized and there was concern that he had a tumor or a heart problem.

He said one of the former teammates that he heard from at that time was Mike Webster. "He told me he was gravely concerned and was praying for me," said Bradshaw. "Mike also told me he wished more than anything that someday Chuck Noll and I could get back together. I told him I would be glad to do it, but we'd have to have a mutual agreement. I told him I didn't know if it was going to happen."

With that in mind, maybe Mike Webster was smiling somewhere over what was going on in Pittsburgh between his coach and his quarterback that weekend.

"Seeing Chuck and these guys again is great for me," Bradshaw was saying at the Hilton. "I'm getting some answers that I needed.

Terry Bradshaw was embracing Chuck Noll and he was on his best behavior with both of his parents, Bill and Novis Bradshaw, in the audience at the Dapper Dan dinner and luncheon on February 9-10, 2003.

Photos by Jim O'Brien

This is therapy to me now. I'm so proud of what we did. The Rooneys
. . . Chuck Noll . . . the staff . . . all the people they put together. You
people. . .

"No one understands why God gave such special gifts to Chuck
Noll, and the players we had. My legacy is tied with Webby. He asked
me to introduce him at the Hall of Fame, and I was thrilled to be
asked.

"I'd heard about the trials he'd been going through. One thing
about Mike is that if he were down to his last breath, he wouldn't let
you breathe life into him. He was his own man. He didn't want help.

"I'll always love Webby. I'll always love you, Coach Noll. I'm
back. I love you, Pittsburgh."

"It's great to see these guys."

James S. Hamilton, a senior vice-president with Federated Investors,
was one of those who couldn't get tickets for the dinner, despite being
rather well-connected about town for such things. He had to settle for
the luncheon, and he felt like he hit the lottery. He was there with
some fellow Federated Investors people, and some clients.

"I thought it was really a special luncheon," he said afterward.
"I turned 61 this month, and everybody says February is a tough
month in Pittsburgh, with all the snow and little sunshine. A lot of
people get a case of the blues, so it's important to get out to things like
the Auto Show, or the Dapper Dan Dinner. You've got to push yourself a little.

"You know all those stories they told were terrific. Every one of
them had a different story or two about Mike. Each story was special.
They are the kinds of stories that should be preserved in books. These
are stories you want to retell. It's great to see these guys without their
uniforms, without their helmets and face masks. It's great to see them
and learn more about them, and how they're doing.

"There were two or three things that were really special. I
enjoyed hearing about Mike Webster's work habits, and how he
pushed himself in the weight room, how he was always the first one
there and the last one to leave.

"That's important in Pittsburgh. That's an old carryover from the
way people here would work in the mills or the coalmines. There's still
a good work ethic here. Even when I go to lunch at the Duquesne
Club, at 1:30 everybody stands up and goes back to work.

"I was among those pleased about Terry returning here, and how
he's changed his attitude about this town, the fans and his former
coach. That's a real issue. He should come here. This is a reinforcing
trip for him. People like to hear him tell those stories. He has a different attitude now and that's the way it ought to be. I thought it was
great that he brought his mom and dad. That was special.

114

"I was in the stands when he brought his two beautiful daughters with him the night he was an honorary captain for that game with the Colts. That's a homecoming. The crowd couldn't get enough of him that night. They let him know how they feel, how special he still is to all of us. I was standing there with tears in my eyes.

"Hey, I've been a season ticket holder for 30 years. We were there in the stands for the Steelers of the '70s. They're still special to us. So I loved listening to those guys. Each story was different and each story was personal.

"After I came back to the office I thought about what I had seen and heard. Think about this . . . when we pass on . . . Will our friends gather to reflect on our passing like that? Will they say things like that about us?"

"Mike was a hero."

Randy Grossman:

I'm here representing slow, small white guys. I thought Mike was that, too. He was so focused on what he was interested in accomplishing. He did it in a quiet way. I came to camp in Mike's rookie season of 1964. That's the same summer that Lynn Swann, Jack Lambert, John Stallworth and Donnie Shell were rookies. We were like the babies running around there. But Mike remarkably took charge of the offensive line, in a quiet, silent way.

You hear about receivers, running backs and quarterbacks — in a tough game — wanting the ball. Mike was like that in a way. When the game was on the line, Mike wanted them running the ball over him. He'd clear the way.

It's really hard to hold your position as a hero. Mike was a hero. He was amazing. From my perspective, being a contemporary of his, it's unusual to find a hero who is the same age as you are. We walked and worked together, but he was my hero.

John Banaszak:

I was born and reared in Cleveland, Ohio, but I managed to overcome that. Mike Webster was a roommate of mine for two years, during my rookie year and second year in the league. There's something unique about the relationship you have with your roommate, something special, a bond that lasts forever. I'll always remember what we went through, as a team, as individuals.

He relates well to Pittsburgh. Mike was blue collar, blue collar all the way. He had such an attachment to that phrase. You saw him on Sundays. You saw how he dealt with cold weather. It never seemed to phase him. You saw him, his powerful arms sticking out of short sleeve shirts. You didn't see him in other situations as I did.

You didn't see him when we were sharing a room on the eve of a game at Three Rivers when we stayed at the Sheraton (now Ramada) across from South Hills Village. I woke up about 4:30 a.m. on the day of a game and I was absolutely freezing.

I looked around and the window in our room was wide open, and the drapes were blowing in. Mike was in the next bed in shorts only. Mike was sleeping and snoring away. Like it was a summer day in Wisconsin. I'm hollering at him and he's not responding. Mike was a little hard of hearing. I don't think he could hear out of one ear at all. I couldn't wake him up. I just closed the window and hoped I didn't wake him up.

There were other times when I'd say, "So, Mike, where do you think we should go for dinner?" And he'd say, "What?" And I'd repeat myself and he'd say, "Huh?" He couldn't hear. That's the way our conversations went.

Louie Lipps:

These are the ones who made Pittsburgh what it is today. They just showed you the way. They're why I'm here. They paved the way, and showed us how to get it done. Mike showed us how to get it done.

It didn't matter how cold it was. Mike was ready to do battle. I remember a home game at Three Rivers Stadium where Mike had a dislocated elbow. He said he was going to play. Coach told him, "No, you're not."

If I had a chance to do it all over again, I'd do the same thing. The Rooneys, the best coach in the league . . . I wouldn't have it any other way.

Tunch Ilkin:

Webby was the absolute greatest zinger. He could really put you in your place with some sharp comment. Webby always had a sense of humor. You might not remember, but I came here as a center, so I got to know him right away. In my first day of practice, I snapped the ball to Terry and jammed his finger. I figured he said, "Chuck, get rid of this kid!" Mike wouldn't let me forget about that. Before long, I was cut.

I was lucky that some guys got injured and Chuck brought me back. This time I was a tackle, and that's where I stayed. For me, the most important legacy of Mike Webster is that he impacted my life tremendously.

Wolfley and I saw the best lineman in the NFL, and we just wanted to hang out with him and learn what he knew. He took us under his wing and showed us the ropes. He taught us how to be a man.

When we got to practice, Webby was always there. He'd be lifting weights on his own. When we'd leave we'd see him in a dark room watching film. We didn't take long to realize that this was the way to do it.

"He'd grade out so high every week. He'd be at 98 or 99. He probably could have been graded at 100. I think the coaches did that so the rest of us wouldn't feel bad. We'd be at 75 or 77. Mike Webster would check himself out of a hospital bed in order to play. We'd wonder whether he was going to play. When we were hurt, we'd ask ourselves, 'Would Webby play?' We knew the answer, so we'd suck it up and play despite injuries.

He was also an example for us when it came to community involvement. He was the chairman of the Spina Bifida campaign in this area. He'd get us to all those fund-raising affairs.

He was brutally honest, too. I remember once we were losing to the Lions about 35-0 in the fourth quarter. Cliff Stoudt got yanked at quarterback and Mark Malone comes into the huddle. Mark is all pumped up and he's giving us all this gung-ho talk. He says, 'C'mon, guys, we can do it!' Webby looks up and says, 'There's no way in hell we can do it!'

He taught me how to be a professional. He taught me how to be a father. He always gave a part of him away. He taught me — a Muslim who grew up in Istanbul — he taught me about Jesus. I'm extremely grateful for that.

Andy Russell:

Look what happened in the 40 years with the Steelers before Terry Bradshaw came to Pittsburgh. In the four years before Terry came, we won 12, lost 41 and tied 3. We had lost 13 in a row before he arrived. And I'm giving him advice when he showed up, since I was one of the team's veteran players. What the hell did I know? Terry was one of the guys who turned us around.

When Mike Webster came, we knew he was special, too. Ray Mansfield, my best friend who'd been our starting center, said to me, "I'm in trouble."

We had other great players. If there was only one linebacker on the field, then Lambert and I are on the bench behind Ham.

Ray Mansfield and Mike Webster passed away all too early. It's a shame. I played at Forbes Field, Pitt Stadium and Three Rivers Stadium, and they've torn them all down.

If I was a current player I'd be sick of hearing about the Steelers of the '70s. So I tell stories about the Steelers of the '60s. When our defensive unit came off the field back then we'd tell the offense, "See if you can hold them."

We were taught to get out and do things in the community, and it's important to carry on that tradition. It's important to give back to the community.

Craig Wolfley:

We were running laps around the field one day, and I fell down on the grass field. Mike Webster said to me, "Son, if I have to give you mouth-to-mouth resuscitation, you're dying."

One time we were playing against Bob Golic, and Mike Webster, Steve Courson and I all blocked him at the same time. Mike told Golic, "Sorry, Bobby, I'm surrounded by incompetents."

I remember how big his hands were. When you shook his hand, his hand would swallow yours.

To me, he was the greatest of the Steelers, and he will always be the greatest. He will always be missed by all of us.

Chuck Noll:

I'm going back to the beginning. I was scouting college football players in the East-West Game. The big thing is that Mike was too small, too slow, and ran a 5.5 40. Nothing special there. He was going up against a guy who was 6-6, 275 pounds. The more I watched the more intrigued I got. He dominated this guy.

One thing they never measure is what you have here (Noll tapped his heart). He had so much here, as do all of these gentlemen up here. He had great quickness and strength. He was a young man we were lucky to get to anchor the line.

The thing that separates people is not size and ability. It's your attitude. That epitomizes our players in the '70s.

118

Andy Russell, Craig Wolfley and Garrett Webster all paid tribute to Mike Webster at a luncheon held in his honor February 10, 2003 at Pittsburgh Hilton.

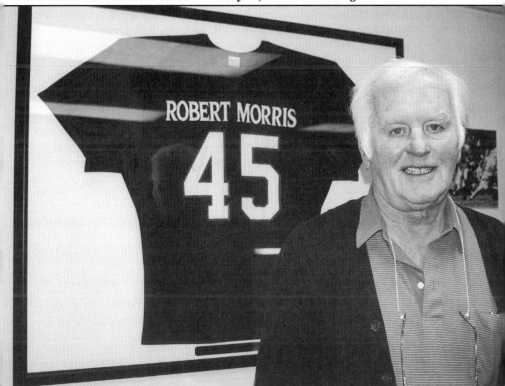

Dan Radakovich, former Steelers' assistant coach now on staff of Joe Walton at Robert Morris University, has always been one of Mike Webster's biggest fans. Radakovich said Webster was the best college center in the country as a senior at Wisconsin.

A night to remember
Bradshaw comes back to Pittsburgh

"It's good to be home."

It was a night Steelers' fans won't soon forget. It was the night Terry Bradshaw came back to Pittsburgh. It was the night Bradshaw served as honorary captain of the Black & Gold, giving more than 62,800 fans a lifetime thrill. It was a lovefest.

It was a Monday Night football game with the Indianapolis Colts at Heinz Field on October 21, 2002, and it marked the first time Bradshaw stepped on a football field in Pittsburgh since he retired as a player 19 years earlier. And that field was Three Rivers Stadium.

ABC-TV officials blew it by not showing the half-time ceremonies that honored Bradshaw because he was a football analyst and personality from rival Fox Sports. They didn't want to promote him on their air time. That's too bad, because the Steelers fans who watch each game with great enthusiasm in their homes or neighborhood bars should have seen it too.

It was an event that rivaled the Steelers' last game at Three Rivers Stadium, the implosion of Three Rivers Stadium, the first game at Heinz Field, the four Super Bowl victories and the passing of team owner Art Rooney Sr. as moments to remember. In Pittsburgh, the Steelers are a significant part of many people's lives.

Everybody but the concessionaires and vendors loved it. Few left their seats at halftime. They didn't want to miss a moment of this deeply moving homecoming. It was a bonus that the Steelers beat the Colts, 28-10, and that Tommy Maddox — another quarterback born in Shreveport, Louisiana — continued to play well. Bradshaw shook hands with Maddox at midfield and wished him well.

The night Terry Bradshaw came back to town touched the hearts of so many of us. Most of us could never quite understand what his spat with the city, Steelers' fans, Chuck Noll and the Rooneys was all about. But, for Bradshaw, it was real. In his mind, the disappointments piled up and pushed out all the good times, and he stayed away to vent his disapproval. Maybe this was his way to punish us for booing him or being critical of him. Bradshaw has been diagnosed as suffering from depression, and anybody who is similarly troubled can better understand Bradshaw's dilemma. People with depression often find it difficult to find anyone who truly understands what they are experiencing. Or why some days are just so gray or blue.

Ed Bouchette, the Steelers' beat writer for the Pittsburgh *Post-Gazette*, talked on the telephone to Bradshaw shortly before his comeback to Pittsburgh. "Hey, I'm back," Bradshaw said from his home in Dallas. "We've been through a lot, me and the fans. They've loved me, they've hated me, and I've driven them crazy. Through it all — what's that old song? — I've learned."

"I give hope to every average-looking, bald-headed person who ever wanted to make something out of his life in television, sports or whatnot." —Terry Bradshaw,
It's Only A Game

Photos by Mike Longo

Terry Bradshaw talks to Steelers' owner Dan Rooney and his fans, while his beautiful daughters, Erin, 13, and Rachel, 15, look on admiringly.

"I am so excited about coming back. I'm so excited to go out on that field. It's the highlight of my post-playing career. It's a chance for me to get back and talk to the fans and tell them how much I appreciated them helping me to grow up — what little I have grown up — and how much I love them. It's good to be home. When I say it's good to be home, that's pretty powerful. It makes everything good!"

No one has a better idea of what a great and deeply satisfying experience it was for Bradshaw than his friend and agent, David Gershenson, who has represented him more than 20 years. I met Gershenson when he and Bradshaw came back to Pittsburgh again for the Dapper Dan Dinner and follow-up luncheon program on February 9-10, 2003. Both affairs were sellouts and Gershenson had a front-row table for both.

Gershenson telephoned me from Los Angeles on June 26, 2003 to talk about Bradshaw and what that night at Heinz Field was like for him. It filled in some blank spaces in the Terry Bradshaw story.

When the idea was first introduced about having Bradshaw come back to be honored, Dan Rooney was reluctant because he thought Bradshaw might change his mind, and that would be embarrassing. Chuck Noll is not one who is comfortable in public appearances, or in showing his true feelings, so he had his concerns as well. He's not the showman Bradshaw is. In the end, however, Rooney and Noll knew that this was a good thing, something that needed to be done — if just for Terry's sake — but they and the team's marketing director, Tony Quatrini, also knew it would be great theater, and a real treat for Terry and his fans. It would be good for Steelers football. It was long overdue. "I didn't think he would show up," said one fan.

"It was beyond anything he dreamed of."

David Gershenson:

That Monday night was probably the most rewarding and thrilling night of Terry's career. On the plane on the way home, he said that emotionally it surpassed being inducted into the Pro Football Hall of Fame.

When you looked around that night, people were standing with tears rolling down their cheeks. And 60,000 people were all standing. For Terry, who had some trepidation about coming back and is a very sensitive man, he didn't know how the fans would react.

He made some bad choices, and he had told everyone that beforehand. He wanted to make peace with everyone; he wanted that dearly. He wanted to put it all behind him. He especially wanted to make peace with the Rooney family.

There were over 60,000 people standing and screaming.

And his two daughters, Rachel and Erin, were there with him. To have them witness it was great. He brought them along for protection — he didn't think anybody would boo his daughters — but from the look in their eyes they were so proud of him. They weren't born yet when he was playing for the Steelers. To get some idea of what he meant to that town . . . it was beyond anything he dreamed of.

On the plane home, he kept talking about it. He had such joy in his heart and in his eyes. Getting together with Chuck Noll was important, too. It was good to see them all reconnect.

When we made our initial plans for the Dapper Dan Dinner it was to be a one-night deal. But the demand for tickets was so great that they asked us if we would stay over a day and have a luncheon for the overflow. It was decided to have that luncheon pay tribute to Mike Webster. Chuck and Marianne Noll were scheduled to leave the day after the dinner for a vacation in Hawaii, but Chuck changed his plans in order to be with Terry at the luncheon. That meant a lot to Terry.

That was when he and Terry had a chance to really talk, and to enjoy each other's company.

Deep down, he had great affection for Chuck. It reminded me of the way some of my friends talk about their dad. They'll say, "I wish my father had done this or that . . ." But, most of all, they admit how much they loved them, or how much they miss them. He always had tremendous admiration for Chuck.

This all got started when I put in a call to Joe Gordon, whom I had gotten to know through the years. I knew he was no longer the team's public relations man, but I knew that he still had the ear of Dan Rooney and that Rooney respected his opinion. We had been looking for an opportunity to come to Pittsburgh.

The Steelers had wanted to bring Terry back for the last game at Three Rivers Stadium. For a while, we thought Fox would free him up to attend, but he ended up with a schedule conflict. He had a game to do for Fox that day, so he couldn't come. We sent a tape of his remarks that they played on the big screen at Three Rivers Stadium. The Steelers had wanted to honor him, and that was the genesis for us calling and trying to make a date. I saw the Monday night game on their schedule, and thought that would work.

Gordon thought it was a great idea and, in later conversations, Tony Quatrini thought it would be fabulous. They were more positive about it than even I was.

Joe contacted the Steelers after I spoke to him. It was all based on the Steelers wanting to do something initially for Terry. It wasn't something we cooked up on our own. We tried to figure out a way to do it.

This was perfect. Terry always respected the team's tradition, and took great pride in being part of it, in being the quarterback who led them to four Super Bowl championships.

I remember when we went back to Pittsburgh a few years earlier for a special reunion of the Steelers of the '70s. It was not a Steelers' function; it was something put together by an independent promoter. At the dinner, Chuck Noll spoke about the team and what made it special. He said it was the diversity of the individuals that made it work. He said it couldn't have been accomplished with 11 Joe Greenes or 11 Terry Bradshaws. The whole was greater than the sum of its parts. Chuck made Terry the best he could be, and it took Terry a long time to realize that. They brought out the best in each other. They achieved more than they could have on their own.

Terry was on such an emotional high when we came home after that Monday night game. It was such a perfect night for him. The only thing that could have made it better was if his parents had been there. But his dad had just had open-heart surgery and couldn't make the trip.

They were there for the Dapper Dan events.

This was a part of Terry's life that needed closure. He went back for the Dapper Dan events, and there will be more opportunities for Terry to return to Pittsburgh.

Terry has great affection for Dan Rooney and the entire Rooney family. This was one of the most gratifying things I've ever done in my life, being a small part of this. I know what it meant to Terry.

I think everybody wanted Terry to know how they felt about him and I think everybody wanted Terry to have an opportunity to let them know how he felt about them. It was a mutual catharsis.

There were over 60,000 of them standing, with tears coming down the faces of most of them. I was crying, too.

That town will always be important to Terry, and now he knows how much the fans still love him. It is a huge part of what he is.

"The difference between a successful person and a non-successful person . . . A successful person continues to do things he doesn't want to do."
— Provided by Pat Santelli, Pfizer, Inc.

"Inspiration is the act of drawing up a chair to the writing desk."
— Anonymous

Photos by George Gojkovich

Terry Bradshaw is cheered by Steelers' chairman Dan Rooney and Terry's daughters, Rachel and Erin, at his special night at Heinz Field.

Photos by Bill Amatucci

Terry Bradshaw of being calm, cool and collected:

"You may be scared to death, totally uncertain about the next few seconds of your life, but you don't ever admit it for fear of being branded a quitter, non-believer, and a lousy team player. I had to fake my coolness. I had my walk down to perfection, and could swagger in and out of the huddle like a showhorse. As long as the fans didn't see my knees shaking, they probably said, 'Look at that Bradshaw boy! He's in total control'"
— From *Looking Deep*, With Buddy Martin

Steve Courson
Always at war

"I like the peace and quiet."

Steve Courson is comfortable in his pad in a small cluster of modest homes out in Farmington, deep in the woods of Fayette County, just outside of Uniontown. It's a rustic hideaway, perfect for Courson. He has two black labradors, Rufus and Rachel, and they have the run of the place. His backyard and the fields that surround his property were all buried in deep snow in mid-February, 2003.

He said the dogs loved running through the snow. "They make me laugh," he said. "They're both characters and they're good company. I enjoy them. " He loved getting out in his snowmobile and traveling the roads on a neighboring state preserve. When the roads are cleared, he likes to ride his quad ATV. He kept an eye on the state-owned park and, in turn, he can wander over and do some target shooting or hunting there.

He likes to do some archery hunting.

His little community is carved out of the woods. He says he is surrounded by 1500 acres of hardwood forest.

"I can go out on my back porch and shoot into the woods," Courson said. "I like the serenity, the seclusion. I like the peace and quiet."

When he wants a break from his reclusive existence, Courson calls former teammates to come visit him from time to time, hosting them at cookouts. He says he can get to Pittsburgh or Morgantown or Uniontown when he needs to socialize. Ohiopyle State Park and Nemacolin Woodlands are both just down the road from his place.

"I'm 35 minutes from Deep Creek, 35 minutes from Morgantown, and 35 minutes from Seven Springs," he said. "It takes me about an hour and 15 minutes to get to Pittsburgh. I still like my entertainment. I just do it at a different pace. I'm single and I still date periodically."

He came to Pittsburgh during the 2002 season to attend a party that Franco Harris hosted at the Sheraton at Station Square to celebrate the 30th anniversary of his "Immaculate Reception." Courson always enjoys being with his former teammates.

He's not the social animal, or party hound, he was during his glory days with the Steelers in the late '70s. He's toned down his act considerably, and wisely. They still tell stories about Courson — an avid weight-lifter — pressing girls into the rafters at various bars about town. Just for the hell of it. Anything for a laugh. He was a wild-eyed, fun-loving bachelor in his Steeler days.

They still talk about some of the costumes he has donned through the ages. He's never dressed like anybody else in the room.

Steve Courson still cuts a mean figure during visit to sports card and memorabilia show at Caputo's, and brief stop at Waldenbooks at Century III Mall.

Photos by Jim O'Brien

It's as if he wears the outfits he saw his movie heroes wearing when he was a kid at the neighborhood theatre.

Since he retired as a player, he has done some coaching and provided strength and conditioning expertise on a volunteer basis with his former teammate Ted Petersen at Trinity High School in Washington and at Uniontown High School. He has done some motivational speaking at schools about the dangers of drugs. He's got a bad heart, and he has been on an NFL partial disability pension.

At the outset of 2003, Courson took a test to become certified as a personal trainer and planned to open his own workout facility.

His teammates say that Courson attended a team reunion at the David L. Lawrence Center back in 1999, accompanied by his wife Cathy. They reported that they both seemed to be having a great time. The following week, Cathy committed suicide, shooting herself. It was later learned that she was a manic-depressive.

"I went through my own depression for two years after Cathy's death," Courson said. "I was miserable. So I am enjoying my days now. I am taking my drugs as prescribed, and feeling better. If I started drinking I'd be dead. I'd also be miserable. I have to watch what I eat as well if I want to stay in good health.

"Losing Cathy was a real kick in the ass. I wondered at the time, 'Is this what life's about?' I'm OK now. I've been through so many different things. My life has been stable of late."

"No one could believe the guy."
— Dan Radakovich

When he was with the Steelers, he was a compelling sight at St. Vincent College. Fans and sportswriters alike used to gawk at him as he passed during practice sessions. He was unreal. He was always wearing jerseys with cut-off sleeves that showed off his enormous physique. He still wears stuff like that.

He was a well-sculptured 6-1, 275 pounds.

He had a 58-inch chest, 22³/₄-inch neck, 29-inch thighs, 18-inch calves, 38¹/₂-inch waist, and 20¹/₂-inch biceps. He could run the 40-yard dash in 4.65 seconds, he was one of the best on the ballclub at a standing long-jump. He could dunk a basketball. He was unreal.

"No one could believe the guy," said Dan Radakovich, who served two different stints as an assistant coach to Chuck Noll. "He was bench-pressing 600 pounds. He was flying in those 40-yard sprints. He was a physical phenomenon. He was also on steroids. I think some of the guys noted this. It might have influenced some of them to try steroids. They wanted to be able to do what he did."

He also had a demoniac look in his dark eyes. He was scary. He could wilt you with a stare, but he smiled a lot, too. He was popular with his teammates.

As a linebacker at the University of South Carolina, Courson weighed 230 pounds. He said he tried to gain weight through nutritional and weight training programs, but had little success. Finally, he said, a team physician prescribed steroids. Courson said he gained 30 pounds in 30 days. At his peak, he said he weighed 300 pounds, with just 8 percent body fat. He said he first started using steroids as an 18-year-old freshman, but gave them up because of side-effects until he was a rookie with the Steelers in 1977. He was a fifth-round draft choice, and spent his first season on injured reserve with an ankle problem.

He ended up with a serious heart problem. He retired after the 1985 season. He had played his last two seasons with the Tampa Bay Buccaneers, and learned he was suffering from cardiomyopathy. It is a rare disease that enlarges the heart and weakens the heart walls. His heart simply wasn't pumping enough blood anymore.

"Steve's heart is stretched and dilated," said Dr. Richard Rosenbloom, his physician back then. "It is flabby and baggy and doesn't pump as a normal heart should."

Soon after he quit playing, Courson could barely walk up a few flights of stairs without feeling winded. He blamed his health problems on his 15 years of steroid use, though he had no solid proof to back up his claim. He believed he had read enough on the subject to make a self-diagnosis.

There was a time when it was thought he would die if he didn't get a heart transplant. He wasn't a great candidate, though, because of other problems. Then, too, it would be difficult to find a heart that would be suitable for a man his size. "You usually have to be critically ill to get one," Courson said when he was 35 years old. "I'm praying for the heart of a 300-pound biker."

He dealt with bouts of depression. He went public with his claims. He became a controversial subject, an outcast of sorts. He was critical of Chuck Noll and team management in some of his charges. He became a bit of a pariah in the Steelers organization.

Courson, to his credit, followed doctor's orders and began a training regimen and diet to deal with his life-threatening problems. He attacked his illness with the same zeal that he once went to the weight room. He tried to help others. There was a two-year span, about four or five years earlier, when Courson visited prisoners around the country in an effort to boost their spirits. It was called the Prison Fellowship program.

Now, at age 48, he looked terrific. He was as sculptured as ever and he still dressed like no one else. Sometimes he showed up looking like Daniel Boone and another time like G.I. Joe or Jungle Jim. He was still marching to the beat of his own drummer.

"The media writes these stories in which they blame a lot of former players' health problems on steroids," Courson said. "That's not necessarily so. They mask the fact that there are lot more drugs out there that are far more dangerous to the players and their long-term health. Steroids can have positive effects when properly prescribed for people who have certain health problems. There's just a lot of misunderstanding, and the media contributes to it. I know as much about steroids as any person in the country. I've done my homework, believe me."

Courson is still an outcast. He doesn't get invited to many Steeler-sponsored events. He shows up sometimes, but is usually at the back of the room, or roaming on the fringe. At the Mike Webster Memorial Luncheon, for instance, he sat with friends in the rear of the room at the Hilton Hotel. His presence was acknowledged, however, by emcee Stan Savran. He was the only former Steeler in the room not sitting at the dais. He was the one wearing a buckskin jacket with the fringe on both sleeves.

"I thought it was a nice event," recalled Courson. "It was good to hear so many people say nice things about Webby. He was a good man. He had a positive effect on so many of us when he was at his best. It was good to hear what his son Garrett had to say.

"I'm glad Terry (Bradshaw) is back in everyone's good graces. When he came back for that Monday night football game with New England I thought that was a good start. He explained some of the differences he had with people here. I thought it was good to get it out in the open. I'm glad he did it. I think the fans feel better about him."

"Life is treating Steve Courson better than it has in a long time."

Steve Courson:

Pittsburgh's expectations for its football team, and the Steelers' expectations for the franchise, are different from other cities and NFL clubs around the country. Every season the Steelers are supposed to win the Super Bowl. Even Bill Cowher says every year that the team's goal is to win the championship. He paints himself into a corner, but he knows that's what the Rooneys expect of him and the team.

I think it's an unusual climate when you compare it to the rest of the NFL. Anything less than the Super Bowl is considered a bad season. It's not really relative to their actual chances of accomplishing this. There's a win-at-all-cost philosophy. Now it's even a bigger deal. The pressure today is bigger than ever. When you look at the finances, the Steelers' ownership has made a huge commitment to put this team over the top.

"People have to learn that you never throw the towel in; you'll never quit fighting."
— Mike Ditka

But in the first two games this year you could see that the other teams were prepared to stop the Steelers offense. They saw what the Patriots did to them in the AFC title game the year before. The first seven on our defense are pretty good. That defensive backfield would really be exposed if it weren't for the front seven. Their corners didn't cover that well.

You can't bank on an immediate fix in the draft. It's hard to find rookies who can break in and play in the defensive backfield right away. It takes time to learn the system.

But Steve Courson is not coaching the Steelers, so why worry? Life is treating Steve Courson better than it has in a long time.

It's been a long slow road to recovery, and there were some bumps in it that made you wonder if you could ever overcome them. There are a couple of therapies on the horizon that could bring me back to total recovery. At my last cardiology check-up, my numbers are so close to being normal that it's really encouraging. I have been very compulsive on following dietary plan. It was introduced to me by Craig Wolfley in the early '90s and it has changed my life. I take my medications, eat intelligently and do moderate exercise. It's been amazing. They were able to take me off the heart transplant list. I'm into preventative maintenance.

I was forced to do something when my weight went up to 330 pounds. I lost 70 pounds of body fat, and now I'm back to 255 pounds. I'm pretty lean. My strength levels are comparable to what they were when I was in college.

Things didn't look so good for me back in 1988 when I was diagnosed with heart problems. So I've come a long way. I've been fortunate.

I go to the best gym in my area. It's called Hopwood Fitness Center, just outside of Uniontown. There are a lot of guys in the gym. You should have seen when I was still "juicing." Now I just do training as a way to stay fit. I train differently these days. I don't train heavy (lifting heavy weights). I walk the treadmill a lot. I train more like a body-builder now. I don't train heavy and I don't use drugs.

"The blue room was a nice little sweatbox."

Yeah, I remember when we used to work out in the basement of the Red Bull Inn in Washington. Lou Curinga provided us with a great place to lift weights. He and Clark Hayes were good guys to work out with. The blue room was a nice little sweatbox. I worked out there with Jon Kolb, Mike Webster,

Larry Brown, Steve Furness and a few other guys who changed from time to time. Jim Clack was there my rookie year. Gary Dunn, Tom Beasley and Ted Petersen came in from time to time. It was an elite crew. There were six or seven of the strongest guys in the league all working out in the same sweatbox. It was fun. It was a great place to train and you just tried to keep up with the rest of them.

Webby used to take these supplements and liver pills, and he'd have gas attacks that would clear the room. Webby would wipe out the entire weightlifting area.

It hurt to hear that Webby had died, and to go to his funeral. That was one of the hardest funerals I've ever attended. I saw the death of my dad, and my wife's funeral was difficult to deal with. Especially the way she died.

Mike Webster probably had more of an impact on my life than anyone else. Webby was such a mentor to me. Most of what I learned technically came from Mike. He was a great teacher, and a great friend. It was really hard to deal with his death.

I got as close to him as he allowed me to be in recent years. He lived with me for a few months out here in the woods. Right after his introduction into the Pro Football Hall of Fame, he came to live with me that fall. He came for a get-together of the guys and just stayed on. We had a cookout for him to celebrate his Hall of Fame induction in October of 1997, and he just never left. He didn't have any place to go.

My wife was still alive and she took care of him like a lost puppy dog. He was lucid and clear on occasion; and other times you would wonder what was going on. It was like talking to a stranger.

Sometimes he was the same old Mike. Sometimes it was so difficult. Tunch Ilkin and Craig Wolfley would come up and they tried to help him, too, but they got frustrated. He had played 17 years in the National Football League, and people used to tell him, "Oh, Webby, you'll play forever." But even he couldn't do that.

He was just a guy who was unable to enjoy life after football. When you've played for a long time sometimes it's hard to convert to civilian life.

He stayed with Cathy and me for a couple of months. His problems, to me, were rather obvious. He had a number of problems he was dealing with. Not being coherent mentally had to be the most frustrating thing, for him and for his family. He didn't have a clear level of communication, and he did things it was hard to understand.

When he stayed with us, sometimes he was real lucid. Then there were times when he made no sense at all. He was in a vicious cycle. How do you help him if he didn't want

Mike Webster (52) checks with linemates Ted Petersen (66) and Steve Courson (77).

George Gojkovich

people to be helping him. He wasn't always willing to accept any assistance. Maybe he just didn't understand what was going on. The Mike Webster who stayed with me at my place wasn't the same Mike Webster that I played with. Parts of him were the same, but most of him was changed.

From a mental standpoint, and I'm not being critical of him, Mike was a shadow of himself. I remember how acute his mind was when it came to football. He understood every facet of the game of football, and he knew what everybody was supposed to be doing. He could recognize a defense faster than our quarterbacks. We had other guys on the offensive line who were intelligent, but Mike was far above everybody else when it came to know what we were supposed to do in every situation. It says a lot about him when you think of the quality of our other offensive linemen in that period. So it was really hard to understand how different he'd become.

One time Colin came out to our place and he and his dad would go for rides in the area. Mike would load his car and come back and unload it, and he'd do that over and over when it made no sense. So you knew he wasn't himself.

Cathy and I would watch him and just look at each other. Like what's he up to? We didn't know what to do. One day we went out and when we came back he was gone. He'd cleaned out his room and took everything with him and just left.

There was a time when he was staying at a Red Roof Inn in Robinson Township. Ted Petersen and I went to see him. This was when the guys were reaching out to him, trying to help him. He took us into his hotel room. The room looked like the room of a mad scientist.

There were little scraps of paper everywhere. He had all these ideas about things he wanted to do, different projects. It was scary. Right there, we knew he needed help. It's hard to help someone who won't let you help him.

Many of his teammates tried to help him, the way they tried to help me when I needed help. It was very frustrating, especially when it's someone you have an inordinate amount of respect for. If you look at Webby's life after football, he had problems with money. He had financial problems for quite a while. He had problems with his health. He had problems with his family. He lost everything that had been meaningful to him.

It was hard for me. My illness was almost the best thing that happened to me. I was really screwing up my life, and I had to find something to get grounded again. A depression smothers you. You miss the dressing room and drills and the games. You miss that environment, the camaraderie, the sense of purpose.

I've been doing some artwork. That keeps me busy.

Bill Amatucci

George Gojkovich

Steve Courson

Bill Amatucci

Steve Courson (77) leads the way for Franco Harris (32) on end sweep.

"I saw myself as a gladiator."

I went through a big change when I played football. I was one of those guys who was basically in awe of professionals and the incredible accomplishments that the Steelers had made before I got here.

I came after they'd won their first two Super Bowls. The Steelers were the power team in professional football. To a young college player, they were already legends. I was in awe of what I was getting into. I didn't have a mirror on myself, but I didn't see myself as good as they were. Seeing Franco Harris, Mike Webster, L.C. Greenwood and Joe Greene can give you a case of the shakes.

As I became an older player, however, I changed. I was less excited and in awe of my surroundings. I developed a more mercenary attitude. You go through a few strike situations, and you see it as less of a game and more of a business. You see friends go, getting cut or traded or retired. You play with injuries, and you take pain-killing drugs, and you learn things about yourself and the business.

That's why I wore the camouflage outfits, and started doing my unique thing. I saw myself as a gladiator and a mercenary. And I told myself I was going to do the best I could do to win. I've never been a real suit-and-tie person. I've always been a bit of a renegade. Basically, my attire was my suit and tie for what I chose to do for a living.

The whole way through, I asked a lot of questions. I came into a game that had win-at-all-costs models. I always have to question that. I saw steroid use in college, but a lot more in professional football. The players are older and require it more. They're playing for a paycheck. Steroid use becomes much more pronounced the older you get. You can bounce back faster, and do more physically with performance-enhancing drugs. Hell, when I first came up, amphetamines used to get passed out in the trainers' room like mints at a restaurant. They didn't know how dangerous they were in the long term. That doesn't happen these days. The first team to do it was the San Diego Chargers, and guess who was an assistant coach there when that was going on? That's right, Chuck Noll. So he's not dumb about this stuff.

After the '82 strike, it was less of a game to me. As far as I was concerned, I was going to war. I wanted to win to survive. They don't keep a guy who doesn't pull his own load. You are a marketable commodity and you can get hurt.

The problem with a lot of athletes, including teammates of mine, is that a lot of us wrap up our self-worth in that game. Jack Lambert took offense at some of the things I said in the article in *Sports Illustrated*. He wrote a letter. I think he misunderstood me. He was speaking to me through the media. Jack is a big anti-drug person. So am I. I've done research in libraries on this stuff. I have busted my ass to get the right information. I've forgotten more about drugs than most of the people who are criticizing me. Don't tell me about this state-of-the-art drug testing. In most cases, it's a waste of time. You can beat the system. I can tell a high school student in 25 seconds how to beat that testing. But the players association seems more open to doing things that will help approach the problem. Such drug testing is a way for organizations to morally absolve themselves of blame. There's also a lot of hypocrisy out there. Alcohol and cigarettes are drugs and they kill more Americans than American drugs. The difference is they are legal. You tell me why they're legal.

I know that Jack Lambert and Jack Ham, for instance, never took steroids, and that they trained hard and played hard. But I trained as hard as anyone. I spent ten times as much time in the weight room as most of the players on the team. So I wasn't looking for shortcuts. We all have drug prejudices. Some people think alcohol and cigarettes are OK because they're legal. One of the things that's underplayed in my problem is that I was also a heavy drinker. That couldn't have helped my condition.

There were good times, too, and I won't forget them. We had a real tight-knit offensive line group for one thing. My favorite years were when Rollie Dotsch was our offensive line coach. We had a real camaraderie. We had such an unusual group of dedicated guys. I played between Mike Webster and Larry Brown. That was a great privilege. I played behind Sam Davis and Moon Mullins and I learned so much. They were winning and took a lot of pride in what they did.

Mike Webster was still playing when the rest of us were finished. It was sad for me to watch him toward the end of his playing days. I respected him so much. Why the heck was he still playing? But I respected the fact that he was still playing. But I think so many of us have our self-worth tied up in being a pro football player.

I had physical ability, but I was a real raw talent when I first joined the Steelers. Playing against guys like Joe Greene every day in practice made me a better ballplayer.

I was popular. I was single. Gary Dunn and I were the talk of the dressing room. Most of the other guys were married. The other players took pleasure in hearing about our antics. Yeah, I know they told stories about my shenanigans at the VIP and the Green Tree Marriott, but I was having a good time. I wasn't serious about any woman. The NFL was my wife, my mistress and my girl friend. It was the most important thing in my life.

We used to go crazy. This is a shot and a beer town, and the fans liked to bump elbows with the players. Gary Dunn and I used to get a little crazy, anything to have fun. With the size of us, we could have been destructive. But we weren't; we just wanted to have fun. We wanted to blow off steam, and relieve the pressure that was on us to win. When I got traded, that put a damper on our program. Gary had been the only other single guy (along with Jack Lambert) among the veterans. His locker was next to mine. We lived near each other in the same apartment complex in Hunting Ridge, down in South Fayette. Ted Petersen was there, too; he still is.

I've toned down my act considerably. I can't do real heavy exercise. I have a beer once in a while, but that's it. Right now, I'm trying to channel my energies. I learned from my earlier athletic activities that if you get knocked down you have to get up and make the best of it. I got a lot of support from my teammates and my friends. That was important to me. When I first got out of football, I felt that everything was so unfair. I was a real frustrated case.

Now I have more hope. I'm ready to move on. Slowly, at a pace I can handle. I like working in my woodshop. It's pretty sedentary work. I've been feeling pretty good. I'm taking good care of myself.

Jim O'Brien

Road sign on George Blanda Drive in Youngwood, Pennsylvania

Jim O'Brien

Famous foursome of football coaches, left to right, Foge Fazio, Jim Render, John Majors and Don Yannessa, get together at Armand Dellovade's "Italian Day" party at his Lawrence, Pa. residence. Fazio and Majors, both former Pitt coaches, are now retired. Render remains at Upper St. Clair High School and Yannessa, who gained fame at Aliquippa High School and Baldwin High School, had recently taken the head post at Ambridge High School.

Snapshot:

Johnny Majors on Mike Webster:

"He was my favorite player of all the players I've coached in an all-star game. I coached in about a dozen of those games and I never saw anyone with his attitude. He was all eyes and ears, and he'd always be the first one in front of me when I said I wanted to talk to the players. I never saw a player try to please his coach more than he did. He was all-out in everything he did. I was coaching the East team along with Jackie Sherrill, and Barry Switzer was coaching the West team. So I was always a big fan of Mike Webster when he played for the Steelers."

Brother Pat Lacey
"Fire Chief" of St. Vincent's

*"Every time I'd cut the grass
I'd say a prayer to The Man upstairs."*

The Pittsburgh Steelers have been conducting their summer training camp at St. Vincent College since 1966. For 37 years, Brother Pat Lacey has been a part of that summer experience at the beautiful campus in Latrobe, just across Route 30 from the Arnold Palmer Airport.

The setting was the same for many years, but a recent renaissance has brought new buildings to the campus. The Massaro Company, owned by Joe Massaro of Oakmont, has been adding dorms to the campus skyline. One of the newer buildings is the Arthur J. Rooney dorm, and that's where the Steelers stay during their annual summer visit.

Brother Pat kept the grass cut on the practice fields of St. Vincent and, literally, put out any fires that occurred on the campus. He likes telling people he's been the Fire Chief at St. Vincent for nearly 40 years. He confessed ignorance when I asked him if there was any truth to the tales that there are priests and brothers buried in catacombs under those practice fields at St. Vincent College.

When the Steelers of the past reflect on their glory days they often tell stories about something that happened at St. Vincent College. They were together, often 24 hours a day, for five or six weeks, and it's where they really got to know each other and learned a lot about themselves as well. They practiced hard on the fields of St. Vincent and many of them drank hard afterward at various bars along Route 30. They tell tales about those who broke curfew to revisit those local bars, and some of their late night shenanigans.

Such stories abound in the wonderful book by Roy Blount Jr., *About Three Bricks Shy of a Load*, written just before the Steelers started winning all those Super Bowls.

St. Vincent College is where they found out that they were good enough to make it in the National Football League and where, at some point later on, they may have learned that they were no longer regarded as good enough to stay with the Steelers. There were happy times and sad times at St. Vincent. There was the heat, the humidity — when you couldn't see the hills in the distance at dawn you knew you were in for a rough day — the weeping willows, the grass fields, the climb up the cement stairway to the locker room after practices, the sound of cleats on concrete, the workout tents, the fans lining the walkways and covering the hillsides. The meals in the cafeteria, the dorm rooms, the Oklahoma drills, the 7-on-7 drills, the tedium, trying to get to sleep at night, worrying that "The Turk" might come calling, telling you to bring your playbook with you. Your days with the Steelers were behind you.

Even Chuck Noll came and went. So did Art Rooney Sr. and Art Rooney Jr. and Tom Donahoe. Dan Rooney is one of the few who's been there since the beginning. He remembers fondly when his kids were ballboys there. Dan Rooney remains a familiar figure at St. Vincent. So is Brother Pat Lacey.

He has been a worker on the campus and its surrounding fields since he first arrived at St. Vincent. He was responsible for overseeing the campus fire department. He was often seen driving a tractor across the practice fields, pulling a mower behind him. It was Brother Pat who kept the grass cut at St. Vincent. I remember seeing a photo of him doing just that which appeared in a Pittsburgh newspaper. No one can find it now.

In April of 2003, I asked Bill Amatucci, a photographer friend of mine from Latrobe, if he had any pictures of Brother Pat from earlier days at St. Vincent's. "No, I don't," he said. "But it's a real coincidence that you're asking me about Brother Pat. We're good friends. I just told him to let me know when he wants to go into the city. I told him I'd take him. He has early Alzheimer's Disease and he can't drive a car anymore."

This was news to me. I had spoken to Brother Pat at the completion of the Steelers' summer stay at St. Vincent in a grotto near the main buildings back on August 22, 2002. He seemed a little slow in his speech, bashful perhaps, when I had talked to him in the past, so I didn't notice any problems, and he was able to recall people and events relating to the Steelers from past summers.

I also recalled that Father Edmund Cuneo had died in August of 1990, and was buried on the hill above the campus. He had been the president of St. Vincent, and was known as "Mr. St. Vincent." He, too, had Alzheimer's Disease during his last five or six years at St. Vincent. "He had no idea as to what was going on," said a fellow priest.

Brother Pat would pay a visit to Three Rivers Stadium on occasion, and was always welcomed warmly by the players in the locker room. Brother Pat was popular with the players. He had a constant smile and made a fuss over them. He claimed that he's 5-feet 9-inches tall, but that's a fib he'll have to mention at his next confession. He's more like 5-6, more like Myron Cope in stature.

Brother Pat was a fixture at St. Vincent. He was a bit player on the scene each summer, but a constant. In recent years, he lived in a room in the school gymnasium. Sometimes he'd show up in work clothes, and sometimes in a white dress shirt and black slacks, with black suspenders holding up his slacks. Other times, he was wearing a black robe, his costume as a brother.

Marcy Canterna, a school teacher and one of the daughters of former St. Vincent's basketball coach and athletic director Oland "Dodo" Canterna, said, "I think Brother Pat is one of the most amaz-

---

"Nothing lasts forever. Nothing."
— Walter Payton, in his autobiography
Never Die Easy

ing, selfless, marvelous human beings who ever walked the earth. He has done so much for so many people — and most of it was done quietly and without need for any kind of recognition."

Brother Pat was there, though, like one of Myron Cope's celebrated "little birdies," and he got to know some of the Steelers, from owner Art Rooney on down, and he can provide some interesting insights on them.

Brother Pat liked to tell a story about how Jack Lambert had befriended Father Raymond J. Belko, one of the priests at St. Vincent. Father Belko is buried on the hillside above the campus. It's beneath one of the Benedictine crosses that line the horizon. He was born April 4, 1895, and died February 25, 1985, according to his tombstone.

"People came to see me play
and I wasn't going to let them down."
— Jack Lambert

Brother Pat Lacey:

It was for Father Raymond that Jack Lambert stayed in the pros. They became friends in Jack's first year with the Steelers. Father would see him walking around, looking like a bit of a lost soul, and started to talk to him. They got to be friendly, and Jack would go to his room to talk to him. Jack was thinking of quitting the team at one point, but Father talked him into staying. They were very close. Jack always went to Father's room and talked to him when he wasn't feeling so hot. Jack would be down and out, and Father would be an inspiration to him.

He believed in Jack. They went fishing together and . . . maybe I shouldn't say this . . . but they used to drink a few beers in Father Raymond's room. Jack came back to our school when Father died, and Jack read one of the homilies at the funeral service. Jack said it was more scary than playing in the Super Bowl. You should have seen Jack Lambert as a pall bearer for Father Raymond. Jack was a very feeling person.

He'd tell me, "Brother, on the field, I'm an animal. I'm giving 100 percent. People came to see me play and I wasn't going to let them down." He never did. He was very faithful to his word.

142

Jack Lambert liked to join Father Raymond J. Balko in fishing at the lake at the lower end of the St. Vincent College campus. Lambert returned to the Latrobe college to offer a eulogy at Father Balko's funeral service in late February, 1985.

Photos by Jim O'Brien

REV.
RAYMOND J.
BALKO
O.S.B.

BORN APRIL 4, 1895
DIED FEB. 25, 1985
R.I.P.

Jack was very humble. He wanted to prove to people that he was giving 100 percent. He's not dogging it. He'd say, "Hey, I'm getting paid. I'm not going to freeload!"

Jack would stop up here sometimes in the winter. Jack and I were like two books. He'd say, "Hey, brother, you're doing a good job in the fields." He was very supportive of my efforts. Jackie Hart, who was the Steelers' field manager, also helped me any way he could. Lambert liked Jackie Hart a lot, too. Lambert would get upset if any of the Steelers gave Jackie a hard time. Steve Furness spit on Jackie Hart one time when they were fooling around on the field after practice, and Jack Lambert would have liked to have killed Furness right on the spot. You have to give Jack Lambert credit. He was a special man. He had good feelings that he tended to keep inside. He'd slip into the chapel from time to time. In the sight of God, he was a different man, much mellower than the guy you saw at the Stadium.

I have all those good memories. I've enjoyed my stay here very much. That's why I say rosaries to the Blessed Mother and God that I have persevered. When I'm ready (for heaven), they can take me. I still do my divine office to make sure.

"We even had our own coal mine."

I was 17 and had just graduated from Carrolltown (Pa.) High School when I came here. I had played center on our high school football team. I came into the brotherhood and was trained in sheet metal and plumbing. I was very lucky because one of the brothers taught me a lot and I became very useful around here. I helped out on the farm here. We raised corn and wheat here, but that land has been leased out to local farmers in recent years. At one time, we were more self-sufficient here. We had our own electricity generators, our own reservoir for our water needs. We even had our own coal mine out on the road three miles from here. We kept cattle in the barn below the church. The nuns here used to do all the cooking and canning. Now a restaurant company (Parkhurst) handles all the meals served here.

I have a good vocation and every day I say the rosary three times to express my thanks. I've known about 160 to 200 priests here, and about 25 brothers, and they've all treated me well.

I've been here 39 years, so I've been here the whole time the Steelers have been here. I'm told they trained here once back in the early '30s. I think they came here because Art Rooney Jr. had played football here when he was a student. I think Dodo Canterna, who was the basketball coach and

Photos by Jim O'Brien

Brother Pat Lacey likes to pray to St. Vincent DePaul and in the campus church at St. Vincent College where the Steelers hold training camp each summer. Religious retreats for Catholic men are held there at the same time.

Brother Pat Lacey enjoys having lunch with Steelers' family, including head trainer John Norwig, in the dining hall at St. Vincent College.

later the athletic director, was friendly with the Rooneys and encouraged them to come here. Dodo loved it when the Steelers were here. We had retreats here in the summer for men, and they liked being here when the Steelers were training at the same time. I know the Rooneys were comfortable here, and Chuck Noll had gone to Benedictine High School in Cleveland. That's our order. So he liked it here, too. Our priests originally came from Germany. And Noll was German. I went to three Super Bowls as a guest of the Steelers. Mr. (Art) Rooney used to tell them, "You take good care of Brother Pat. He takes good care of us." I hope the Rooneys remain happy here. I hope they'll never leave here.

I'd cut the grass every third day. I loved doing it. I'd get a great sun tan. Every time I'd cut the grass I'd say a little prayer to the Man upstairs. I'd say, "Every blade of grass grows in Your glory."

I've been the Fire Chief here for 39 years. I'm the chaplain for the county fire departments. We had a bad fire here in 1963 that they still talk about. We almost lost the whole campus.

We've had a seminary here for years to train priests and brothers. After a war or national crisis, that's when all orders get a boost in new applicants.

There are changes going on here. There's talk that they're going to bring back a football team here. We had a good football team here once upon a time. Every so often, I get tickets to go to a Steelers' game, and I enjoy that. Mr. Rooney told them to take care of me. He was very generous to me at Christmas time. He'd send me a Christmas card every year, and there was always a check for $500 in the card. The Rooneys made me feel like I was a part of the Steelers' family.

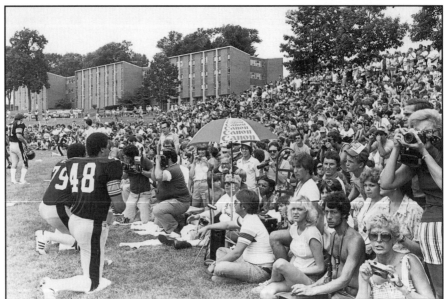

George Gojkovich

Steelers attracted larger crowds to summer training camp in 1979 when the team went on to win its fourth Super Bowl in four years. This was the scene on Photo Day, when the veterans joined the rookies for the first time and they posed for pictures for media and fans.

Steelers president Dan Rooney outside stu-dent dorm named in his father's honor. It's where the Steelers stay during summer camp at St. Vincent College.

Check out Bill Cowher's casual footwear as he conducts weekly press session at St. Vincent College.

St. Vincent College

St. Vincent photos by Jim O'Brien

Kimo von Oelhoffen is all smiles as he sits amidst teammates in portable whirlpool baths outside Kennedy Hall at St. Vincent College. Rodney Bailey is in the back.

Bill Cowher dons straw hat during summer camp as he appears with media for sideline interview following practice session.

Two young fans wear their favorite players' jerseys as they watch Steelers practice from hillside site. The highest paid player on Steelers, linebacker Jason Gildon, flashes a $7.5 million-per-year smile at St. Vincent College.

Kevin Colbert, director of football operations, provides update to Steelers' club president Art Rooney II as Steelers' defensive unit comes off practice field at St. Vincent. Steelers include, left to right, Chad Scott (30), Dewayne Washington (20), Brent Alexander (27) and Chris Hope (28).

White tent alongside practice fields is where Steelers lifted weights when they were at St. Vincent College. This gave way at the 2003 camp to an air-conditioned state-of-the-art weight room. Below, offensive players wear black and defensive players wear gold in intra-squad drills.

Quarterback coach Tom Clements comes away from pizza and other Italian entrees at special section of St. Vincent College dining hall, while Joey Porter and Hines Ward get around campus in Toro Workman vehicle.

Harry Carson
A classy competitor

"Learn how to take care of yourself."

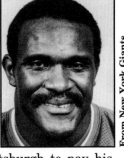

From New York Giants

Harry Carson was a surprise visitor to Pittsburgh to pay his respects at the funeral service of Mike Webster. He stood out in a crowd of Steelers standing in front of the Somma Funeral Home in Robinson Township on Friday morning, September 21, 2002. His face didn't register at first, as he stood there talking to familiar-looking faces from the Steelers past.

"I always admired him as a player," said Mel Blount. "When I saw him at Webby's funeral I told him, 'This even lifts my respect for you.' I was so impressed that he came so far for the funeral of an opposing player."

The only other visitors from another NFL team were Lamar Hunt and Carl Peterson, the owner and general manager of the Kansas City Chiefs, Webster's last employers in the league. They had attended Art Rooney's funeral as well.

Carson spent his entire National Football League career as a Pro Bowl linebacker for the New York Giants. He traveled to Pittsburgh for the funeral out of respect for a former opponent, plus he wanted to learn more about what Webster had gone through in his difficult days following his retirement from pro football. Carson was suffering from post-concussion syndrome and wanted to learn all he could about the problem.

"When Mike Webster was hitting his helmet against somebody else's helmet," Carson said, "I was one of the guys he was hitting."

They had been to some of the same doctors. Carson had suffered loss of memory in some situations, and it had proved embarrassing. He was even more concerned about its later ramifications. He had been doing radio and TV commentary and confessed there were times he forgot his train of thought, and had to back off a conversation.

Carson was concerned that it could cut short a promising post-football career. He was a well-spoken individual, smart and sensitive, and he had a gift as an analyst and thoughtful commentator on his sport.

Carson spoke at a symposium relating to head injuries that was organized by Dr. Joseph Maroon in Pittsburgh. Maroon is one of the Steelers' team doctors.

Carson was under consideration for the Pro Football Hall of Fame. He had been among the nominees when Lynn Swann and John Stallworth were on the ballot, but like former Steelers Donnie Shell and L.C. Greenwood he was still waiting for the call. He was a terrific 6-3, 245-pound inside linebacker. At the age of 25, he became the youngest captain in Giants history.

He had been a teammate of Shell in their schooldays at South Carolina State University, and had great respect for Shell as well.

Carson was a classy performer on and off the field for the Giants for 13 seasons, from 1976 to 1988. He and Lawrence Taylor teamed up to provide the Giants with two great linebackers during much of that span.

Carson was chosen to play in the Pro Bowl on nine occasions, and was named the NFL's top inside linebacker in 1980 by *Sports Illustrated*, and was named the NFC's Linebacker of the Year that same season by the NFL Players Association. He played in most of those Pro Bowls against an AFC team that usually included Mike Webster and Jack Lambert of the Steelers.

Before the merger of the rival two professional football leagues in 1970, the Giants were one of the Steelers' greatest rivals, right behind the Browns and Eagles.

Harry Donald Carson was born on November 26, 1953 in Florence, South Carolina and starred at McClenaghn High School in all sports, as well as serving as senior class president. He graduated from South Carolina State and had done some work on a Master's Degree in Business Administration (MBA).

Being responsible and self-reliant was something Carson learned at an early age. Carson was eight years old when his mother left the family's home in Florence. Harry says the separation wasn't as troubling as some might think because he still had a father and five older brothers and sisters to look after him.

"I come from a very caring family," he says. "We weren't really poor, but we went without a lot of things. My father worked on the railroad, the Atlantic Coastline Railroad it was called back then. He worked to a certain point, got laid off, then drove a taxi.

"My mother did domestic work, and there weren't a lot of job opportunities in South Carolina. When she found out she could make better money up here, she left the family and moved to Newark. Worked there for 17 years. There wasn't a dispute or anything; she left the family to take care of the family. We knew what it was all about.

"Before she left, I used to sit around and watch her cook in the kitchen. She was a great cook, so now I'm a good cook. My mom told me a long time ago, she said, 'Learn how to take care of yourself.' She instilled that in me. Well, I can take care of myself now. I clean, wash, iron, sew. I can do anything a woman can do — except have kids. I can take care of myself very well.

"In all, I've been blessed. I still have my friends and my family. I have my health."

He said it was an honor to be named the captain of the Giants. "That's what the players wanted," he said. "I've always been the kind of person to be there for a person. I was the same way in high school and college; guys sort of hung around me.

"I tried to be there for all the players if they needed me. I cared about them as human beings, but I couldn't get too close to anybody because football's really a business. New people come in, old people go out all the time."

He once said that every player should suffer an injury that would keep him out of the lineup for awhile because they would learn something valuable from the experience.

"You're like an outcast," he recalled. "People don't treat you the same, coaches don't talk to you, because there's nothing you can do for them. It's kind of like life. It has to go on, and just because you're out, they're not going to stand still."

Harry Carson, number 53, played the game with great pride. He was regarded as the heart and soul of the Giants. He once said that football is about hitting on every play, no matter the score.

Dave Anderson, a Pulitzer Prize-winning columnist for *The New York Times* and one of the nicest guys in the business, believes Carson should have aimed higher than being a broadcaster. "He has the smarts and the style to be a head coach in the National Football League," wrote Anderson.

Carson has spoken about his situation with me on several occasions by telephone from his home in Franklin Lakes, New Jersey in the early months of 2003.

"I think there are a lot of Mike Websters out there."

Harry Carson:

What prompted me to come to Mike Webster's funeral service is that I had the greatest respect for Mike as a competitor. I remember what it was like to play against him in the '70s and '80s. I'd crack the defensive huddle and I'd see him sprinting to the ball. I always admired that. I respected that. They'd break huddle and he'd lead the pack. He was eager to get on with it. He was always on the attack. Usually, quarterbacks set the tone for the offensive team, but it was definitely Webster who set the tone for the Steelers on offense, the same way Lambert did on defense.

The Steelers offensive linemen all wore their jerseys so snug, with short sleeves, and those bared biceps. Webster's biceps were impressive. They got your attention.

When he went into the Hall of Fame (in the summer of 1997) I felt badly that most of the publicity surrounding it was about the problems he was going through. It was all about his

Chuck Noll and his wife, Marianne, are met outside the funeral home where Mike Webster was on view by Paul Uram, a member of Noll's staff in Steelers' glory days. Below, Terry Bradshaw greets Mike Webster's parents.

Photos by Jim O'Brien

personal life, not his professional life. I thought that was very tragic.

Mike was probably no different from other players in the National Football League. Mike had a lot of pride, a lot of pride in his ability and in his team. That's the reason he got to be where he was as a ballplayer. The pride that he had was probably a detriment to him when things soured for him. One of the problems with professional athletes is that if you're hurting you don't tell people you're hurting. You don't want people to know when you're physically hurt, or when you're hurt emotionally or financially. You try to take care of it yourself. To me, that's part of having so much pride.

You try to take care of it yourself. That pride doesn't always permit you to ask for help. It can be looked upon as a weakness. That's one of the problems he had.

Mike went through a divorce. I went through a divorce. I've talked to other guys who've gone through this in the league. Things change when you're no longer playing pro football.

When you play against one another you might view one another as arch-enemies. When you retire you're all in it together. Once you retire you're all in the same fraternity. You put that other stuff aside. You see each other at golf outings and charity-related dinners, and there's a bond between you. It's nice to see each other and discuss things. You're dealing with the same thing.

I think there are a lot of Mike Websters out there.

From what I'm told, he made some bad business decisions, and he lost most of his money that way. A lot of guys have been scammed in some way. Like Mike, they don't want to alert anyone that they need help. If it hadn't been documented you wouldn't have known all the problems he experienced. I did see him as being well grounded when he was a ballplayer. You couldn't visualize Mike doing anything else but playing football. Maybe that was a problem, too. I'm told his teammates tried to help him, but he kept them at bay for the most part.

You don't really retire from football. You have to make a transition to another phase of your life. It's not like being an executive where you quit working and start relaxing and playing golf and going out in your boat. You've got to find something else that's satisfying and rewarding to occupy yourself.

Almost anything that comes along is very insignificant by comparison to playing football. If you've played in a Super Bowl only the birth of a child can match it. Ain't a whole lot you can do to compare to that.

You need something significant to keep you going. Otherwise, you're going to fall into a rut. There's nothing else to strive for. You have so much money, so much fame. Unless you're Michael Jordan or Willie Davis, there's no where to go but down. You're playing on a much smaller stage.

There are a lot of athletes, in general, and football players, in particular, who are sort of lost. It's the nature of the game. It's a very macho sport. It takes a lot for them to humble themselves when they're having some problems to seek help. It's the way football players are built. Sometimes you have to swallow your pride and reach out for help. Maybe someone can help you get a job, or a better job.

Mike was diagnosed with neurological damage. I have been diagnosed as having post-concussion syndrome. Did Mike have the same condition? That's why I'm intrigued with his case. When Mike was firing off the offensive line he was firing out at people like me. I'm hitting him in the head with my forehead.

After I was done playing, I was doing television and I'd lose my train of thought. I started checking around with doctors and that's when I learned about post-concussion syndrome. I went to see Dr. Julian Bailes, who used to work with Dr. Joseph Maroon at Allegheny General Hospital. Dr. Maroon is one of the Steelers' team doctors. He's a neurologist, specializing in head injuries. He's the doctor who looked after Tommy Maddox this year when he got knocked out at Tennessee. I saw that on TV. It didn't appear that he got hit that hard, but it's those quiet hits that nobody notices that do the most damage. I know Dr. Maroon was involved in the treatment of Mike Webster as well.

I was wheeled off the field in San Francisco and in Dallas, so I could relate to seeing Maddox taken off the field in Nashville. In Dallas, I was trying to make a tackle on Tony Dorsett, and I was hit in the head by a teammate. I didn't have any feeling in my arms and legs until I got to the hospital. I was able to return to the stadium and stand on the sideline in the second half.

Nobody wants to see anybody wheeled off the field. It gets to the players on both teams. They don't want anything like that happening to them. You don't want your opponent carried off the field. He has a family, too. We're all in the same boat.

I know Merril Hoge has had similar problems from the concussions he has suffered. I spoke on his behalf at a deposition when he was suing one of the team doctors of the Chicago Bears for letting him play too soon after he had suffered a concussion.

There are times when players should be sat down after they've suffered injuries, but they want to get back on the field as fast as possible. Many of the problems former players have may be attributed to head injuries they suffered during their playing days. I've learned a lot of things about my own condition.

I'm in the midst of writing a book about what I'm dealing with. I was working on "NFL Preview" on CNN and doing some work on the Big East Network. I have been employed by the Giants to do some of their pre-season games.

I think I was very anxious when I was going on the air. Sometimes while making a point, I'd mispronounce words or I was having difficulty retrieving words, finding the word I wanted. This led to the anxiety I was feeling. Since that time, I've been taping most of my stuff in advance. When I left the game I thought I'd go into television because I was always told I was good in interviews. It was always second nature to me. So I thought it would be a piece of cake. I still do some live television.

I don't know about the Pro Football Hall of Fame. I might make it . . . I might not. I have been a finalist for the last four years; I've been down that road before. There's a great deal of excitement about that. The first year I saw my name (on the list of candidates) I heard people talk about it. Just to be mentioned meant a lot to me. I was extremely honored to be a finalist.

When I was in college it wasn't a goal of mine to play pro football. It was my way of getting a college scholarship. But as I got better I started to hear that I might be drafted by the pros. Hey, it was a helluva way to make a living. I played in the mud, in the cold and rain, in the snow, but it was still a great way to make a living.

I initially wanted to go into the military and fly airplanes. Football put that dream into a back seat. I graduated with a degree in education. I've always thought of myself as a seeker of knowledge. I've used my experiences as a former athlete.

I've done a lot of speaking to athletes and corporate types about leadership and teamwork. I know something about that.

I was two years behind Donnie Shell in school. I came in 1972 and left in 1976. He was already in his second season with the Steelers when I was drafted. Donnie was an inspiration for me. He was a tough, hard-nosed, no excuses kind of player. I think you could say that of me, too. At South Carolina State, we took pride in the way we played defense.

Donnie was always involved in Bible study classes, in college and in the pros. On any team, you have some players who are very religious. You have some who aren't so religious. You have some who are in the middle. Donnie wasn't a Bible-toting player. He didn't push it on anybody. But you knew where he stood. You could tell the type of home he came from. You knew what Donnie Shell stood for, and a lot of younger players wanted to emulate him.

I respected him. He was one of the first players I met when I visited the campus to check it out.

"Most people don't realize how difficult it is."

I think many people — especially players — recognized Mike Webster for the player he was on the field. Many people recognized Mike for what he did off the field. The center position is not one of the marquee positions in football. But Mike was great at what he did.

It was documented that he was separated from his family, that he was sleeping in bus stations, that he was sleeping in his car, stuff like that. That stuff jumps out at you. Mike was never a big spender, a splashy dresser or a big fancy car guy. You'd never think he'd have the problems he experienced. Most people envision players retiring to a better life than that. Most people don't realize how difficult it is to make the transition.

There's such a stark contrast to your previous situation. I guess you could compare it to postpartum blues.

It takes a certain kind of pride to will yourself to be something you want to be. To battle, in every practice, and to hold on to it, you have to have great pride. But that pride can be a deterrent to reaching out when you need help, as I've said.

It starts with not communicating with your spouse. Your athletic career is over, and your personal life is in shambles. You get divorced. Mike Webster was a case study in what can go wrong.

Terry Bradshaw jokes around about having three ex-wives. I haven't read any of his books, but I'd like to know why does he have so many ex-wives. He should ask himself that question.

I don't know Terry personally. I saw him at the funeral. I think he might be in some pain the way he talks about his experiences in pro ball and in his private life. I've only been married once. I know how difficult it was for me to separate and divorce. As an athlete, you don't want to fail. There's a pain you carry with you. It's a losing thing. You feel like a loser.

As a player, I've seen players get married, and you think they have a great life. Then the marriage breaks up. And that

159

happens even higher than the national average among retired pro football players. Is the player stressed out by his separation from pro football? He has to adjust to a new role. He's not ready to give up the dream. Personal problems manifest themselves. Perhaps there's a crisis. Life is different. The wife says I didn't sign up for this. I was just there for the good times. Hey, it can happen that way. Or the guy just gets to be such a miserable soul, bad company, that she can't stand being with him any more.

She's part of the package. I've thought long and hard about this. When the player is released the family is released. The spouse had reserved seats at the stadium. She doesn't have the same clout in the community anymore. The kids are in school and their dad is a pro football player. Everybody respects the kid for that, and treats him or her special. The kid's expected to be as athletic as his father. That puts some pressure on them, too. There are pluses and minuses for the family during and after a player's career.

Phil Simms (the former Giants quarterback) and I are neighbors. His son Chris felt a tremendous amount of pressure. They look alike and the kid was expected to be a great quarterback just like his dad. When it comes to the spouse, there's an identification problem from the start. My ex-wife said, "I'm losing myself; I'm like a different being. I'm Mrs. Henry Carson." When you go into a restaurant, someone says, "Good evening, Mr. Carson, I have a great table for you." And there's no acknowledgment whatsoever of your wife or partner. That's a tough thing. She wants her own identity. At the same time, there are benefits from being the wife of a professional athlete. You have to live with the good and the bad.

I heard certain things about Mike Webster. He probably has gone through more than he should have gone through. He should have had more life to live. I was glad to see his ex-wife was there with the kids. You wouldn't have known they were divorced. I'm sure there was still love there, but things got out of whack somehow. It's too bad, no matter how you look at it.

> *"I live for Sundays. Sunday is a great day.*
> *If I had a wish I'd wish that every day*
> *was Sunday."*
> — Harry Carson, New York Giants

Jim O'Brien

Former Steelers, left to right, Craig Bingham, Greg Lloyd and Donnie Shell were happy to see one another at Mel Blount Youth Home Celebrity Roast.

Snapshot:

Donnie Shell,
Pittsburgh Steelers' safety (1974-1987)
Player Development, Carolina Panthers
At Mel Blount Youth Home Celebrity Roast
Pittsburgh Hilton, May 30, 2003

"Mike Webster was like family to me. We came in as rookies together, and we played a long time with each other. He was such a special guy and he worked so hard. I hated to hear all that had gone wrong for him.

"I thought it was great that Terry Bradshaw came back to Pittsburgh and made peace with everyone. I don't think he realized how much people here loved him and appreciated him. I knew that. This city appreciates what you've done when you played here.

"It's great to see all the faces in this room, and to have a chance to visit with so many old friends. Sometimes you take this city and the fans for granted. They loved their football and the way we played. Pittsburgh will always have a special place in my heart."

Dick Modzelewski
A long way from West Natrona

"I played with some great guys."

Dick Modzelewski played one season for the Pittsburgh Steelers. That was in 1955. His name still has special significance for older football fans from Western Pennsylvania.

He was traded to the Steelers by the Washington Redskins. The Redskins had made him a second-round draft choice in 1953 after he was an All-American at the University of Maryland. He had won the Outland Trophy as the nation's outstanding lineman in his senior season of 1952.

After one season in Pittsburgh, he was dealt to the New York Giants. "It was the best thing that ever happened to me, next to meeting my wife," Modzelewski says today.

In New York, Modzelewski became a part of the "Fearsome Foursome" that included Andy Robustelli, Jim Katcavage and Rosey Grier. Sam Huff played behind them. Modzelewski was with the Giants from 1956 through 1963. He was traded to the Cleveland Browns in 1964 and played three more seasons before retiring as a player in 1966. He was a player for 14 seasons. He was a coach in the NFL for another 22 seasons. He loves to talk about those days. He's fun company. He's modest and self-deprecating

Modzelewski was an All-Pro defensive tackle for several years for the Giants and the Browns. He played on six conference champions and two National Football League championship teams — the Giants in 1956 and the Browns in 1964. He went to the Super Bowl as a coach with the Bengals.

His older brother, Ed Modzelewski, an All-American running back at Maryland, was the No. 1 draft choice of the Steelers in 1952. He, too, only stayed one season with the Steelers. He was traded to the Browns in exchange for Marion Motley, damaged goods with bad knees, who played only one year in Pittsburgh. "My mind wants to do certain things, and I got it in my heart," Motley told Dick Modzelewski on a Steelers' charter plane flight in 1955, "but my knees won't allow me to anymore." It was a lucky break for Ed Modzelewski. He played with championship teams under Paul Brown in Cleveland.

Dick was called "Little Mo," even though he was bigger than his older brother Ed, who was known as "Big Mo."

I remember the Modzelewski brothers because I turned 60 in the summer of 2002, and I've been a football fan from my earliest days. The Modzelewskis came from West Natrona and played at Har-Brack Union High School, the same school that produced the legendary run-

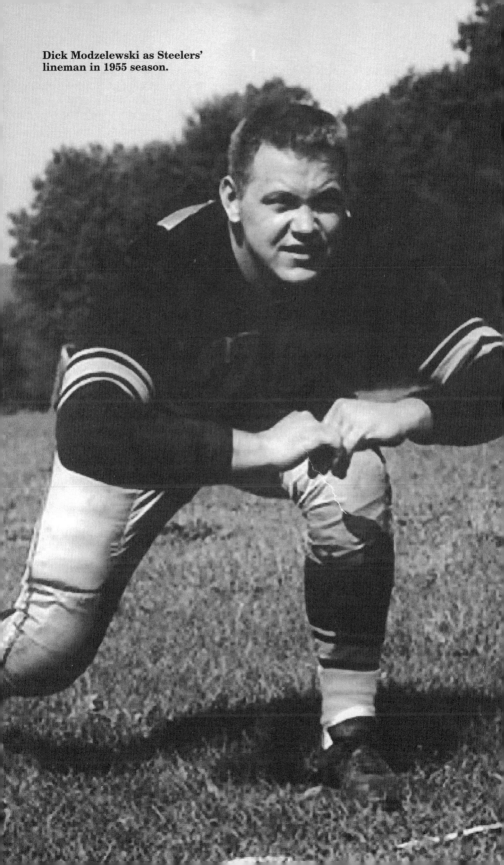

**Dick Modzelewski as Steelers'
lineman in 1955 season.**

ning back Carleton "Cookie" Gilchrist. Maryland was a national power when the Modzelewskis played for the Terrapins. Modzelewski remains a magic name in western Pennsylvania football history.

Their boyhood buddy, Dom Corso, drove the parents of Ed and Dick to every home game when they were at Maryland. They remain close friends to this day.

Neil Brown, his coach at Har-Brack, said that Dick could thank the Lions Club for his football career. "Dick couldn't see too well," said his coach. "Sometimes, Dick would be on the bench, and he'd ask who had the ball. The Lions Club came through and bought him a set of contact lenses."

"Once I got the lenses," recalled Dick, "the whole world came back to me. My brother Ed and I took a bus from our home to Pittsburgh — we didn't have a car — and we walked to the *Post-Gazette* Building to see Al Abrams. We read in his column about different charities he was involved with and we thought he had some contact with the Lions that he could help me get some lenses. And he got in contact with the Lions Club in my hometown, and they took care of me. Thank God for Al Abrams and the Lions Club."

Dick could see well enough to help lead the Big Green to a 23-6-1 record in his three varsity seasons. He was named all-state lineman in 1948. He helped the Har-Brack Tigers to the 1947 WPIAL Class AA championship game, where they lost to New Kensington, 28-0.

"We had busloads of fans at Forbes Field for the game," recalled Dick, "but we were beaten pretty good. I'll always remember that one."

When "Little Mo" followed his brother to Maryland, the Terrapins of Jim Tatum posted a 24-4-1 record in Dick's three varsity seasons.

The Modzelewski brothers were with the Steelers in the early 50s when I first started following the team. I helped my brother Danny deliver the *Pittsburgh Post-Gazette* when I was nine and ten years old, and then took over the 80-some paper morning route myself. I read the sports section each morning. I thought Al Abrams, the sports editor and columnist for the *P-G*, had a great job. He always seemed to be in nice places, met nice people and wrote about them. He was a sharp dresser and he went to every sports dinner in town. He frequented nightclubs, when there were bona fide nightclubs in Pittsburgh, not abandoned warehouses posing as nightclubs. He was always in the company of interesting characters. He knew Billy Conn and Ralph Kiner and Archie "Tex" Litman and Count Phil Petrulli, people like that. He always referred to one friend as the Japanese Ambassador. He was a man about town. I wanted to be Al Abrams when I grew up.

The Steelers weren't very good in 1955 when I was 13 years old and collected bubble gum cards when they were black-and-white images. I wish I still had those cards. I would become the sports editor of my hometown *Hazelwood Envoy* the following year.

Walt Kiesling was the coach. He's enshrined in the Pro Football Hall of Fame in Canton, Ohio, but it wasn't for his work as coach of the Steelers. "He was the worst coach I ever had," recalls Modzelewski, always candid in his comments. It may also explain why Modzelewski stayed only one season with the Steelers.

The Steelers finished that season with a 4-8 record. They played their home games at Forbes Field. They were still my Steelers. Modzelewski didn't care for his coach, but he was fond of his teammates. He loves to talk about them. Their names still stir the heart of anyone who followed the Steelers in those days.

They included Fran Rogel, Elbie Nickel, Jack Butler, Lynn Chandnois, Dale Dodril, Lou Ferry, Jim Finks, Ernie Stautner, Ted Marchibroda, Ray Mathews, Richie McCabe, Ed Meadows, John Reger, Bill McPeak, John "Bull" Schweder, Lou Tepe, Frank Varrichione, Bill Walsh and Joe Zombek. Johnny Unitas was at the Steelers' training camp that summer of 1955 at St. Bonaventure University in Olean, N.Y. Kiesling cut Unitas in favor of a rookie quarterback from Missouri named Vic Eaton. Unitas and Modzelewski would meet on another field later in their pro lives. More about that later.

It's a joy just to write those names again. They are so familiar. I flipped and sailed their bubble gum cards. I knew all their vital statistics. They played for the Pittsburgh Steelers and that was a big deal. I was playing for a sandlot team called the Hazelwood Steelers in the Greater Pittsburgh Midget Football League. We loved those Steelers, and they had never been in a playoff game let alone a Super Bowl.

The Modzelewski brothers both showed up for a testimonial dinner in Fran Rogel's honor in September of 1998. I emceed that dinner. I also emceed a dinner in the spring of 2000 when Dick Modzelewski was inducted into the Pennsylvania Sports Hall of Fame. I remember how "Mo" made fun of his Polish heritage with jokes that night at the Sheraton Hotel in Warrendale. He even poked fun at himself, no one is prouder of being Polish than Dick Modzelewski.

He was born February 16, 1931 in West Natrona. He and his wife, Dorothy, have four children — Mark, 46; Laurie, 44; Terrie, 44, and Amie, 40 at the time of our initial interview. Dick was nearing his 72nd birthday when we spoke several times at the outset of 2003.

"This place is a picture of retirement."

A visitor to New Bern, North Carolina can be captivated by the historic coastal community. It's where Dorothy and Dick Modzelewski were living in retirement for 11 years, in a suburb called River Bend. New Bern is located 105 miles southeast of Raleigh. It's a storybook town, one that invites a stroll through its streets. It was featured in a 2000 issue of "Where To Retire" as one of "10 Great Small Towns Near Big Cities."

My wife Kathie and I had to visit one of its most popular tourist attractions when we were visiting New Bern in the summer of 2002. As proud as the residents are of the area's pre-Revolutionary history, they appear equally proud that Pepsi-Cola was invented by pharmacist Caleb Bradham in New Bern in 1898. The "birthplace of Pepsi" at a drug store at the corner of Middle and Pollack streets, now a gift shop with a soda fountain, is a must stop. You just have to have a glass of Pepsi at the soda fountain. It's a trip back to a simpler time.

Modzelewski bought a home near the waterfront in New Bern after he retired from the NFL in 1989. He can walk to a pier and loves to do some fishing there with his friends. "This place is the picture of retirement," he said, almost smugly. "We get snow once in a while, but it's gone by the next day." His brother, Ed, lives in Sedona, Arizona and has a condominium apartment in Cleveland. "It's beautiful out there in Sedona," said Dick. "You have those pink mountains." It was rated the "best view" in an American city by USA today Magazine in 2003. The view from Pittsburgh's Mount Washington was No.2.

He has a souvenir on the mantle in his home from his last victory in his final game as a coach with the Detroit Lions. It was a 31-24 victory over the Falcons in Atlanta. Dave Hamer, an NFL official from Fair Hope, Pa., near Belle Vernon, was the referee for that game. "The Lions' quarterback took a knee on the final play, and flipped the ball to me," recalled Hamer in February of 2003. "I decided I'd give it to Dick Modzelewski. I had told all of our officials at a pre-game meeting that I wanted them to be sure to shake Modzelewski's hand before the game and wish him well.

"I spotted him walking toward the dressing room after the game, and I flipped him the ball. I said, 'Here's a souvenir from your final game. You get the real game ball.' He's told me since then that it's the only game ball he has on display in his home."

Modzelewski has been inducted into the Pennsylvania Sports Hall of Fame, and the western chapter of the Pennsylvania Sports Hall of Fame. He's a charter member of the Allegheny-Kiski Valley Sports Hall of Fame, the National Polish Sports Hall of Fame, the University of Maryland Sports Hall of Fame and the National Football Foundation Hall of Fame.

Dick Modzelewski:

I have many souvenirs of my days in pro football. I had my right knee totally re-done in April. I've got a new knee there. I've had two back operations, and two shoulder operations. I call my left shoulder Jim Brown and my right shoulder Jim

Taylor. My shoulders are the way they are from hitting those guys so much. I have some swelling in my left ankle. But I'm still breathing. I'm above ground and I can't complain.

I played 14 years in the National Football League and I spent 22 more years coaching. I loved every minute of it. I didn't make the money, but I'm rich in memories. I was the Redskins' second draft choice in 1953 and they offered me $3,200. Mind you, I had been an All-American two years in a row, and was voted the best lineman in the country. I told him I wanted to make more money than my dad who was a coal miner. I signed for $6,500, with a signing bonus of $1,500. I still have a picture of me sitting on the couch with my family in West Natrona after I heard the Redskins had drafted me. Draft day wasn't the big deal then that it is today. My brother signed a $10,000 contract, with a signing bonus of $3,000, as the Steelers' No. 1 draft choice in 1952.

I think I gave them their money's worth. I played in 180 consecutive games to break Leo Nomellini's record for consecutive games played. They stopped the game in Cleveland — we were playing the Eagles — and they presented me with a game ball when I hit 179.

The Redskins traded me because I signed a contract to play in Canada, and the Redskins' owner George Preston Marshall threatened to sue me. The CFL guys told me it wasn't worth a legal hassle. Then Marshall sent me to Pittsburgh.

Kiesling was the worst coach I ever had when I was with the Steelers in 1955. We scrimmaged 30 some days in a row. He killed us. We won four of our first five games, and lost the last seven. We were worn out by mid-season. We were so tired. He beat the hell out of us at training camp. They were throwing bottles at us from the stands at Forbes Field by the end of the season.

I asked to be traded. I didn't want to play for Kiesling. He was no head coach. He was a miserable bastard. It was a mistake on the part of the Rooneys to have him as a coach. I got lucky in New York. We won the championship my first year there. Tom Landry was our defensive coach and Vince Lombardi was our offensive coach; you can't do any better than that. Jim Lee Howell was the head coach.

Ernie Stautner was on our team when I was with the Steelers and he was the toughest guy I ever came across in pro football. When I was with the Giants, I remember our coach Jim Lee Howell saying that we'd gotten the best of Stautner after this one game. We double-teamed him with Rosey Brown, a Hall of Famer at left tackle, and Darrel Dess, our right guard. They bragged about how they took care of Ernie Stautner. Our two guys were both in the training room on Monday. They were both nursing wounds. They didn't look to me like they'd

167

beaten the hell out of anybody.

I remember the Steelers came to New York my first year there and they stayed at the Concourse Plaza out by Yankee Stadium where we played our home games. I went to the hotel to see some of my friends from the team, guys like Dale Dodril. When I was in the lobby I saw Walt Kiesling coming my way, but I just turned my back on him. I wanted no part of that guy.

They had a great end in Elbie Nickel, but you hardly ever hear about him. Art Rooney really liked Elbie Nickel; I remember that.

One day I reported for practice at Forbes Field. I get a phone call while I am getting dressed for practice that my wife is going to have our baby. I told Kiesling I had to be excused so I could be with my wife. This was our first child. Kiesling said, "If you leave I'll fine you!" I kept getting dressed in my football gear, and then I said, "Screw him!" I changed back into my street clothes and left for the hospital. My son Mark was born that day. I got there in time. When I came back to practice the next day, Mr. Rooney told me that Kiesling had no right to do what he did. He told me I wouldn't be fined. Kiesling was planning on fining me $500. Today, guys get out of practice whenever they want to for personal reasons.

It's all changed. They have too many players and too many coaches. We used to get by with 33 players and five or six coaches. Now they have 50 some players — everybody's a specialist — and they have 15 and 17 coaches. They got coaches to coach outside linebackers and coaches to coach inside linebackers. They've got to get in each other's way. They used to have about five or six coaches for a full team. When I was with the Browns, we had Lou "The Toe" Groza, and he was a great offensive tackle as well as a great place-kicker. We had Horace Gillom and he was a great defensive end and our punter.

You've got coaches trying to impress the owners by sleeping at the stadium. Dick Vermeil did that. We'd see his coaches on the sideline and they all looked half-asleep. They spend too much time trying to think up new things. They try to make it a 12-month-a-year job to justify their salaries. Now they've got team psychologists. They should just let them go out there and have some fun.

I know Chuck Noll didn't believe in overdoing it. He thought that you could get good work done in a certain time period. After that, you had diminishing returns. He came from the Paul Brown school. Brown believed that it was important to make sure you had a tank-full on Sunday.

I stayed on in Cleveland as a coach after I was finished as a player. I was there for a few years. Art Modell made me the head coach for the final game at the end of the 1977 season,

Maryland coach Jim Tatum joins Dick and Ed Modzelewski after Terrapins knocked off Kentucky in Sugar Bowl.

Ed Modzelewski sits between his father and mother at their West Natrona home after he signed a $10,000 contract, with a $3,000 bonus after being the Steelers' No. 1 draft choice out of Maryland in 1952. His siblings, from left to right, are Betty Lou, Joe, Dick, Florence and Gene, with their dog Minnie in the forefront. Dick would join the Steelers in 1955.

replacing Forrest Gregg, whom I had coached for in Cincinnati as well. I'm the only head football coach in NFL history who never won a game. There's a good trivia question for you. I could have stayed there, but they were bringing Sam Rutigliano in to be the head coach, so I went to the Giants for a year in 1978. I heard the Bengals were looking for a line coach the next season. I was still under contract to the Giants. I went to Wellington Mara, the Giants' owner, and asked him if he'd release me from the contract. I wanted to get back to Ohio. We had a great relationship and he let me go.

I still think of myself as a Giant. They say "Once a Giant always a Giant." You're telling me that Terry Bradshaw said, "Once a Steeler always a Steeler." No way, not with me anyhow. Blame Walt Kiesling for that. I loved Art Rooney. I love the Rooney family to this day. I root for them. But I don't see myself as a Steeler.

I went to the Bengals as an assistant coach for five years (1979-1983) and I was lucky enough to be with them when they played in Super Bowl XVI. Then I went to Green Bay for four years. We loved it there, believe it or not. Great people. Blue-collar people, just like in Pittsburgh. I finished up with two years with the Lions in Detroit.

In Cincinnati, I worked with three great coaches I know you know. We had Frank Ganz, who grew up in Pittsburgh, as our special teams coach, and Dick LeBeau, ol' No. 44 when he played, as our defensive backfield coach and then defensive coordinator. Hank Bullough was on our staff, too, and he later coached in Pittsburgh.

I used to sit in on some of Frank's meetings. He had been in the Navy as a pilot, and he'd talk to those special team guys like they were flying in the Navy. He'd talk about staying on someone's wing and protecting them. He was one of the best special teams coaches.

Dick LeBeau is a good friend. He also played 14 years in the National Football League. All I know is he was a tough, hard-nosed secondary guy, but a beautiful person, too. There aren't that many good head coaches. As a head coach, Dick didn't win. I was rooting for him to succeed in Cincinnati. As a head coach you are only as good as your players and your assistant coaches.

Bill Walsh was a genius when he was at San Francisco. If he didn't have Joe Montana and those guys he wouldn't have been a genius.

"His life after football was kind of sad."

I felt very sorry for Mike Webster when I heard what he was

going through.

I coached against him at Cincinnati. I coached the defensive line, so I was always studying film of our opponents, looking for things that might help us. Mike was a tough guy. They called him Iron Mike. I have great admiration for offensive linemen. Webster was Terry Bradshaw's center. He never gave up. He was like an old-fashioned ballplayer. His life after football was kind of sad.

When I watched game film, I tried to find some weakness in Webster. I had a hard time finding anything with him. He's one guy I couldn't get hardly anything on.

I especially enjoyed coaching early on. But toward the end I had to cuss more. You had to go to confession every day. You had to get on the players more than you once did. The talent is diluted now. I feel sorry for some coaches trying to coach players who can't play.

Looking at the Super Bowl, I believe Tampa will win if they put pressure on Rich Gannon. The pass rush is critical. If Gannon gets time to check his receivers, then Tampa is in trouble against Oakland. I'd like anybody to try and stand back there and defend against pass receivers who can run the 40 in 4.4 if the quarterback gets time to throw. See if you can stay with him.

I coached for Blanton Collier in Cleveland and I learned so much from him. One day he addressed me, "Son, are you going to be a coach or a teacher. You study film and you teach these players how to pass rush. And I became a teacher. I know Chuck Noll always thought of himself as a teacher, and he came up under Paul Brown at Cleveland. They thought you should never stop learning how to play the game right.

The whole key to me on defense is to have an effective pass rush. You don't have to tackle the quarterback, or get a sack, you just have to get him out of his rhythm. I like Warren Sapp. I'd love to have him on my team. His motor never stops. He's got a big mouth, but he never stops coming at you. He moves all the time. I wish to God somebody would teach those defensive backs how to tackle.

There aren't many guys like Ronnie Lott, Mel Blount or Erich Barnes who know how to hit and tackle ballcarriers anymore. These guys today are afraid to tackle. They think they get paid just to cover. Look at DeWayne Washington of the Steelers in the playoffs. It was ridiculous how badly he got burned, and how he missed that tackle. It cost them the game. With Paul Brown, we did our calisthenics and then we practiced tackling. Nobody practices tackling anymore. They're afraid somebody's going to get hurt. It's a shame.

You take Deion Sanders. I'd have him cover your best

receiver. That's how good a cover guy he was. But his heart was the size of a pea. Mike Ditka said he wouldn't have him on his team because he didn't want to hit.

I still pay close attention to the Steelers. They're still the hometown team. And I played for them. I have a lot of respect for Tommy Maddox. Look what happened to him, how he get stretched out in Tennessee. He came back in two weeks and plays far better than the other guy. He's the reason they make the playoffs.

I always had great respect for Chuck Noll. He won all those Super Bowls. Four out of four. I was in Cleveland his first year on the job when the Steelers went 1-13. I think we had more people in the stands from Cleveland than the Steelers did when we played at Pitt Stadium. The Steelers got booed at Pitt Stadium.

I have great respect for him. You have to rate him right up there with Vince Lombardi and Tom Landry and Paul Brown as great coaches in pro football history.

I worked in the steel mill early in my pro football career. I worked back home at Allegheny Steel, which became Allegheny Ludlum. My father had worked for Allegheny Coal and Coke for 32 years. I sold Duquesne and Iron City beer back home for $75 a week. I worked at LaRuse Beer Distributors on 8th Avenue in West Tarentum. I went from bar to bar, trying to sell them some of our beer.

My wife Dottie is the love of my life. She's from Natrona, too. We've been married 49 years. She still sings in the choir. I might bark loud on the football field, but I always peeped close to the house.

"They got this skinny-ass quarterback..."

I remember when I was at the Steelers' training camp at St. Bonaventure in the summer of 1955, and a buddy of mine called me from the Calgary Stampeders in the Canadian Football League. He wanted to know if the Steelers had any quarterbacks they were going to cut who could help his team. They needed a backup quarterback. I said, "They got this skinny ass quarterback I think they're going to cut, but he's not worth a damn." I don't think I ever saw him throwing the ball.

And, of course, in 1958 it was Johnny Unitas who led the Colts to victory over our Giants team in the first overtime game — the championship game that was called "The greatest game in pro football history."

They had a reunion of the guys who played in that game and my wife, Dottie, told Unitas that story about what I'd said

172

about him when he was a rookie with the Steelers. He just smiled. He became a good friend. He was one of the nicest people I've ever known.

It was terrible the way his hands were so riddled with arthritis late in his life. His fingers were all misshapen.I was at a signing with him a few years back and he had to sign his signature with his little finger and his thumb. He couldn't use the other three fingers they were so bent. It was a pity.

You know, I had three sacks in that championship game with the Colts in 1958. I was going for my fourth sack when I got fooled real good. The Colts had the ball on a third and 17 in the overtime. I rushed hard and thought I was going to get Unitas. I was going to nail him. Then I knew I was in trouble. I recognized he was running a trap play to Alan Ameche. No one calls a trap on third and 17. That was a stupid call, but it worked. Ameche breaks through and runs 18 or 20 yards for a first down. Three or four plays later, Ameche is going in from the two-yard line for the game-winning touchdown. One thing Kiesling and I had in common. We both under-rated Johnny Unitas.

We lost that game, 23-17, in sudden death overtime. I didn't realize the impact that game would have on NFL history. Football was very good to me, and if I had to do it all over I'd still want to be a football player.

Dick Modzelewski is flanked by Sam Huff and Rosey Grier as he sings his "Kielbasa Song" at outing in their heyday with New York Giants. They made several national TV appearances, including one with Walter Cronkite.

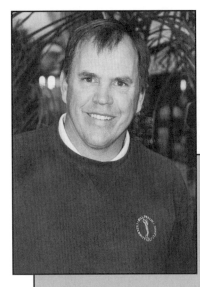

Jim O'Brien

Matt Bahr
Placekicker for two seasons
with Steelers (1979-1980)
And 16 seasons (1979-1995)
in the National Football
League

*"I'm still a Steeler. But I'm also a Giant. I'm a
Brown. I'm an Eagle. I'm a Patriot. I kicked for
and was paid by all of them. I was also fired by
all those teams. I live in Pittsburgh, so I pull
for the Steelers and Penn State.*
*"Kevin Brown was in a no-win situation here.
The field had gotten into his head. The Steelers
certainly weren't going to get into a bidding
war for him. They ended up with Jeff Reed and
he's done well for them.*
Sometimes you get lucky.
*"Webby was always the go-to guy for me. If I
needed some reassurance, I went to Webby. He
was always so down to earth and he had sound,
sensible things to say. Jack Lambert was supportive when I really needed it. I remember him
telling me the team believed in me. That meant
the world to hear that.*
*"The first professional athlete I ever heard
speak was Chuck Bednarik of the Philadelphia
Eagles and he left an impression on me for life.
That's why it's important for athletes to think
about what they're going to say to kids at these
summer instructional camps."*

Snapshot:

Marvin Lewis
He earned his way

"It's about hard work."

Marvin Lewis realized a long-time dream when he became a head coach in the National Football League on Tuesday, January 14, 2003. Some say it was a shame it had to be with the Cincinnati Bengals, a franchise that had long floundered in the standings and had been a bit of an embarrassment in recent seasons, but Lewis didn't look at it that way.

He preferred to remind critics that the Bengals had been to the Super Bowl twice in their history. Lewis didn't say it but, for the record, they also got there sooner than his hometown Steelers. It took the Steelers 41 years to get to the promised land, while the Bengals, founded by the legendary Paul Brown, got there in 13 years.

"They're one of 14 teams to play in multiple Super Bowls," allowed Lewis, "so it can be done in Cincinnati."

The 44-year-old Lewis would like to lead the Bengals back to the top again. He was starting at the bottom. He was all too aware that Steelers' broadcaster Myron Cope had been calling them "the Cincy Bungles" for years.

"This is about hard work," Lewis said at the announcement of his hiring in Cincinnati. "I have a plan to get the little things done to bring the performance of our team up, to cultivate the guys we have and to add players to it."

He signed a five-year contract with the Bengals, believed to be worth $1.5 million a year.

Lewis was hired to replace Dick LeBeau, who had coached the Bengals to a 2-14 season in his third year on the job. It was the worst record in team history. The Bengals' record during LeBeau's three seasons as head coach was a dismal 12-33. LeBeau had been a defensive coach with the Bengals in both of their Super Bowl seasons. They lost both championship games to the San Francisco 49ers.

Lewis and LeBeau had a lot in common. They had both coached on the staffs of Bill Cowher with the Steelers in Pittsburgh, and they were both two of the most decent and classiest competitors you could ever meet. During the holiday season, for instance, when LeBeau was going through a difficult time, I received a Christmas card from LeBeau in which he wrote, "I hope your Steelers go all the way."

LeBeau had been a mentor to Marvin Lewis on the Steelers' staff, and Lewis remains an admirer.

Leo Durocher, one of baseball's feistiest competitors, once said "nice guys finish last." Lewis was out to prove him wrong.

Lewis would be the third black head coach in the NFL, joining Tony Dungy of the Indianapolis Colts and Herm Edwards of the New York Jets, and the eighth in league history. Dungy had played for and later coached on the staff of Chuck Noll with the Steelers. Following a disappointing playoff loss at the end of the 2002 season, Dungy had been rapped, along with his quarterback Peyton Manning, by Colts place-kicker Mike Vanderjack for being "too soft and too nice" for their own good. Steelers' president Dan Rooney headed an NFL committee aimed at setting up guidelines for league members to hire more minorities in coaching and front-office positions. Rooney had interviewed former Steelers star Joe Greene for the head coaching vacancy when Noll retired, but chose Bill Cowher instead. When there is an opening, NFL teams are now required to consider minority candidates in the interview process. Lewis was the Bengals first black head coach.

For the first time since owner Mike Brown took over the team in 1991, he looked outside the organization for a head coach. Brown also interviewed Steelers offensive coordinator Mike Mularkey and former Jacksonville head coach Tom Coughlin.

In late April, the Bengals chose Carlson Palmer, a quarterback at Southern Cal who won the Heisman Trophy as the best college football player in the land, with the first pick in the National Football League draft. The Bengals were given high grades for their entire draft class. It signaled a good start under Lewis.

In late June, Tom Tumulty of Penn Hills, who played under Lewis as a linebacker at Pitt in the early '90s and then with the Cincinnati Bengals, told me, "I still go to Cincinnati a lot, and Lewis is changing things. When I was there, I was one of five or seven guys working out there in the off-season. Now there are 50 or 60 guys there."

"I've been battling something here."

Marvin Roland Lewis Jr. hails from McDonald, Pa., in Washington County. He was an all-conference quarterback and safety at Fort Cherry High School, the same school that produced NFL coaches Marty and Kurt Schottenheimer. Lewis was an assistant coach who tutored outside linebackers on Paul Hackett's staff at Pitt in 1990 and 1991. Marty Schottenheimer was an All-East center and linebacker at Pitt in the mid-60s. During his days at Fort Cherry High School, Lewis also earned letters in wrestling and baseball.

His high school coach, Jim Garry, retired after the 2002 season after 44 years at Fort Cherry. "He always had the attitude and desire," Jim Garry said of Marvin Lewis. "Once, when he was playing for me, he injured his shoulder. I thought he was out for the season.

"Shoot, no. He was out that night. But the next week he taped it up and played. He wants to be the best at whatever he gets into."

Lewis says his boyhood sports hero was Pittsburgh Pirates Hall of Fame outfielder Roberto Clemente. He likes to read books that provide guidelines for success, and has a strong spiritual bent and work ethic he learned from his parents.

> **"Marvin Lewis has turned things around in Cincinnati. It's no longer a cadaver. Now some people want to play in Cincinnati."**
> **— John Clayton, *ESPN***

He was the first youth Sunday school superintendent in the history of McDonald's First Baptist Church.

Lewis directed the NFL's fifth-ranked defensive unit during the 2002 season with the Washington Redskins, serving as assistant head coach and defensive coordinator on the staff of Steve Spurrier. He was thought to be one of the highest paid defensive coordinators in the league. He had signed a three-year contract for $2.5 million. That's more than $850,000 per season. He went to the Redskins after being disappointed by the Tampa Bay Buccaneers. Lewis was led to believe he would become the head coach of the Buccaneers, but the owners nixed a decision reached by team management. They hired Jon Gruden instead and he led the Bucs to a Super Bowl title the first time out. They didn't second-guess their choice.

Lewis had been offered the head coaching position at Michigan State in mid-December of 2002, but turned it down because he said he had spent too long in the pros to settle for a college job. That's a loss for the college game. Lewis would be a great college football coach, a tremendous model and influence for young people.

"I've been battling something here in the NFL," Lewis said at that time. "We've got things to do here. I'd like to be a head coach. I'm not sure where at. I just felt like it wasn't the time."

When questioned about his role as an African-American coach, Lewis said at his first press conference in Cincinnati, "It comes back to hard work, whatever color you are. I think I represent coaches who came up as I have come up, that's from (Division) 1-AA, small college graduate assistant all the way through all levels. Hopefully, I represent those guys, guys who work hard and have a passion for this game."

He began his 22-year-coaching career working with linebackers at his alma mater, Idaho State (1981-84). He was on the staff as a linebacker coach at both Long Beach State (1985-86) and New Mexico (1987-89), and then Pitt (1990-91). Then Cowher came calling.

Lewis gained a reputation as head coaching material as a defensive coordinator on Brian Billick's staff with the Baltimore Ravens. In the 2000 regular season, his defense set an NFL record for fewest points (165) allowed in a 16-game season, 22 points less than the previous record. The Ravens went on to defeat the New York Giants convincingly in the Super Bowl. That defensive unit gained notoriety as one of the best in NFL history. There was even talk that they were superior to the Steelers' "Steel Curtain" defense of the '70s, a claim rebuked by fans in Pittsburgh.

"Wait till they win four Super Bowls," was the usual battle cry in the 'Burgh. (For the record, the 1976 Steelers surrendered only 138 points in a 14-game schedule. That's 9.85 points per game versus 10.31 for the 2000 Ravens.)

Lewis has always taken pride in his family. He and his wife, Peggy, have a daughter, Whitney, 17, a high school senior at the time of his hiring in Cincinnati, and a son, Marcus, 12, a seventh-grader and devoted lacrosse player. Lewis has always been active in his community off the field. He was named "Man of the Year" in 2001 by the *Washington (Pa.) Observer-Reporter* newspaper in his home area.

He said he expected to assume a leadership position in the community at large in Cincinnati, which has had more than its share of racial problems. "I think that's important for the head coach of the Bengals to do," he said. "We'll be judged as we do as a football team on the field, but, as we bring quality people to Cincinnati, hopefully, we all need to be involved in the community."

"Mr. Hayes helped me a lot when I was a boy."

I was surprised to bump into Marvin Lewis at the funeral of Jewett E. Hayes at the Bogan-Wolf Funeral Home on Washington Avenue in Bridgeville in the second week of the 2002 NFL season. "Mr. Hayes helped me a lot when I was a boy," allowed Lewis. "He coached me, and taught me how to swim at Trees Pool at Pitt."

Lewis looked resplendent in a sharp dark blue suit that day. It looked like his suit had just been pressed. I was impressed that he came from Washington, D.C. to attend the funeral. It was Monday, September 9, and the Redskins had opened their regular season the day before with a victory over the Arizona Cardinals. Redskins owner David Snyder and head coach Steve Spurrier didn't strike me as men who'd want a coach to go home for a funeral of someone outside the family during the regular season. It might have helped that Spurrier's son, Steve Jr., had previously coached with Jonathan Hayes on the staff at the University of Oklahoma.

"It worked out because our second game was on Monday night, and we had an extra day for preparation," explained Lewis. "I was at meetings later that afternoon. Usually, I have not been able to come home for funerals like this. It just wasn't possible. So I am glad it worked out this way." Art Rooney, the late owner of the Steelers, would have been proud of Marvin Lewis for making the effort to return home to be with boyhood friends at a difficult time. No one went to more funerals than Art Rooney. He thought it was more important to attend a funeral when a friend loses someone more than it was to attend the funeral of that friend. I live about two miles from the funeral home in Bridgeville, and thought I should pay my respects. The ghost of Art Rooney was still riding on my shoulder and telling me it was the right thing to do.

Lewis was a good friend of the three sons of Jewett and Joy Hayes, who lived in South Fayette, a neighboring community of McDonald. He had maintained ties with Jeffrey, Jay and Jonathan, all top-notch athletes in their heyday. The boys were all at the funeral

"All you need in the world is love and laughter. That's all anybody needs. To have love in one hand and laughter in the other."
—August Wilson, Pulitzer Prize-winning playwright from Pittsburgh

Courtesy of Cincinnati Bengals

Marvin Lewis appears above at his first press conference as the new head coach of the Cincinnati Bengals. Below, Jay and Jonathan Hayes, left to right, join their boyhood friend when they were all associated with the Steelers in the mid '90s.

Photo courtesy of Joy Hayes

home. So were teachers from their grade school days, all testifying to what fine young students they had been, and how involved their parents had been with school activity. One gentleman who grew up in South Fayette said that the neighboring kids called the Hayes family the Huxtables because they appeared as perfect as Bill Cosby's TV family by that name.

"He was a big man," said Marcus Davis, a district manager for McDonald's Corp. "We feared and respected him at the same time. He had nicknames for all of us, too. He was a real influence in our lives."

Within a week of his hiring in Cincinnati, Lewis named Jay and Jonathan Hayes to his coaching staff. Jay was hired away from the Minnesota Vikings, where he was the special teams coach for one season. He was hired to be a defensive line coach at Cincinnati. He had been fired by Bill Cowher the year before, soon after the Steelers' disappointing loss to the New England Patriots in the AFC championship game. Special teams were pointed to as the main culprit in the defeat, surrendering two touchdowns. Jay Hayes was looked upon as Cowher's scapegoat.

As I watched Jay Hayes standing over the coffin of his father, straightening his father's tie, and touching his folded hands, I wondered how that scene might register with those who were so critical of Jay, or called for his head when the Steelers' special teams played so poorly. Writers are always watching, always witnessing. Sometimes it makes one feel like an intruder. But it made Hayes seem so human, not a villain.

Jonathan Hayes had played tight end for Cowher when the Steelers last played in the Super Bowl, and was a popular member of the team. He gave me a big hug when he saw me. He had the same huge smile and warm aura that made him so special in the Steelers' clubhouse.

Mark Bruener credits Jonathan Hayes for teaching him the ropes when he came in as a rookie. Hayes had been serving as an assistant coach at the University of Oklahoma when he got the call from Lewis to join his staff in Cincinnati to coach the tight ends. "I have special respect for them," said Lewis. "I think Jay got into coaching because of what I was doing. He's smart and diligent and wherever he's coached he's been successful. I want people who have great teaching skills. You know how they're going to react under pressure. Jon is younger in coaching, but he's vibrant in his approach. He gets people's attention and respect."

I got to know the Hayes family when I was working on some earlier books about the Steelers. Jewett Hayes had been a patient in the Cancer Center at Allegheny General Hospital, where my wife, Kathie, has worked as a social worker for 12 years. She had tipped me off about the Hayes family, and what a wonderful, caring family they were. Mrs. Hayes always asks me to remember her to my wife.

As a child growing up in McDonald, Lewis never left the house without first making his bed and straightening up — or redding up —

his room. Vanetta Lewis, mother of the Bengals head coach, can't remember her son ever being not prepared for anything in his life. "He always did his homework," Mrs. Lewis said. "He always did his chores without a reminder."

Hard work and success were expected in his boyhood home. His mother went back to school to become a nurse practitioner. It took her eight years, but she did it. His father, Marvin Sr., was a "chipper" who worked his way up to be a foreman during a 28-year work stint in the Shenango Steel mill. His youngest sister, Andrea, now 38, was an Allegheny County police officer. His other sibling, Carol Joy, had a degree in electrical engineering and lived outside Akron.

Young Marvin spent one summer during his college years working at the coke ovens at Shenango Steel. Lewis said the temperature in those coke ovens reached 2,800 degrees. Once, he got too close to the coke ovens, and his plastic safety goggles began to melt. "That was nine weeks of hell," he recalled. "I knew I didn't want to do that. My dad didn't think I'd fare that well as a coach, but I told him I wanted to do what I enjoyed doing. I said, 'Daddy, you go into that mill every day and you hate your job. I want to do what I love to do.' "

A man familiar with housecleaning and dealing with heat on the job had some credentials for the task that awaited him in Cincinnati. The Bengals were playing in a new stadium named for their founder. Lewis wanted to revive a team so that it met the high expectations of Paul Brown, one of the pioneers of pro football.

Marvin started playing football at age 9, and showed leadership skills right from the start. "The coaches always said he was like a little coach on the field," Vanetta Lewis said. "He knew all the plays and where everybody else on his team was supposed to be."

Lewis played baseball in the summer and worked for a neighbor's garbage-collecting company. He'd work all day and would have just enough time to change in the truck on the way to practice or a game. There was no time to take a shower.

His teammates always greeted him by saying, "Oh, Marvin, you stink, man."

Lewis spoke over the telephone from his office at Paul Brown Stadium on February 11, nearly a month after he'd taken the job.

Marvin Lewis:

My parents did everything they could to provide the best environment for us. From my dad rotating shifts to my mom going to work and going to school. They made sure one of them was always home. They had to really go out of their way to manage things. It was a good upbringing.

The best thing that I can tell you lately about my parents is that during my six years in Baltimore and my one year in

Washington, they only missed three home games in the last seven years. They have been tremendous fans of mine, all along the way.

They taught me so much. They're the reasons I'm here. They showed me the way: how hard they worked, their determination, so we could have things when I was growing up. I hope my children have the same appreciation for what my wife and I try to do. They've grown up under totally different circumstances.

This is a job I have been preparing for all my adult life. I invested so much time in the pros. I thought everything was great about Michigan State, but when I got back on the plane to return to Baltimore I wanted to know what happened in the NFL. That was my mindset.

It's been good here so far. I have a plan. I don't think the Bengals' job is an impossible situation. I wouldn't have come here if I thought that way. This is no more difficult than Tampa was. They had never been to the Super Bowl before this year. Look how the Philadelphia Eagles have come back. They had their struggles, but they've become a winner.

You have to do these things right. You have to work hard. I've been hearing from people back home, and they're happy for me. They were all set to celebrate when it looked like I was the choice for the job at Tampa Bay, so they've been on hold for a year.

I'm happy to have Jay and Jonathan Hayes on my staff. Their mom and dad grew up with my mom and dad. Mr. Hayes taught me how to swim at Trees Hall. He took us into Pittsburgh all the time for sports events. If you got out of line, he slapped you on the back of your head and called you "Fathead."

My high school coach, Jim Garry, just retired last fall. Marty Schottenheimer was in his first class. Coach Garry is a first class, tremendous person. He was also one of my coaches my first year in Little League. He was an assistant coach on that team; his son was on the team.

Bill Cowher was with Marty in Cleveland, and I know what they both said about your relationship with your players. They said, "They don't care what you know until they know you care." It's the same way you deal with your children. They'll listen when they know you really care about them.

I was lucky to break into pro football with a team like the Steelers. Mr. Rooney was such a calming force as an owner. I enjoyed my dealings with Bill Cowher and Tom Donahoe. I was with Bill in his first year as a head coach in the NFL. He was able to lead the team right from the start. Ron Erhardt, his backfield coach, was a great influence. He kept things on an even keel. He had been a head coach (with the New England Patriots), and I think he was a big influence on Bill.

There was a newspaper strike going on when Bill took over that first season. That was something we didn't have to deal with the first five or so games. We had Dick LeBeau and Dom Capers who were such great guys and great coaches. You had a guy like Dick Hoak who was such a calming force. I learned a lot from him. I didn't take some jobs that came along in the NFL because Dick always spoke about the advantages to his family of coaching his entire career in one place. I was just surrounded by such great people. Tom Donahoe, Dick Haley and Tom Modrak headed up the player personnel and scouting department. I've been lucky to have good people around me right from the beginning. With my first baseball coach, we went 1-17, and the next year we won the championship. I've seen, from the start, how to turn a losing situation into a winning situation.

I like the kind of people you have in western Pennsylvania. They have a good work ethic. I think they have substance to them. That makes a difference. I'm thankful. I have a sense of gratitude.

Bill Cowher was the second youngest coach on the staff when I joined the Steelers. I was the youngest at 31. I would characterize Bill as sound and aggressive. I learned something from all the coaches I've been associated with along the way. Now it's my turn to show I am ready to run my own program.

Photo provided by Joy Hayes.

Marvin Lewis Sr., Christian Okoye of the Kansas City Chiefs and Jewitt Hayes were all in attendance at wedding reception when former Chiefs and Steelers tight end Jonathan Hayes was married.

A letter from Florence Joy Hayes:

"Marvin is a fine young man who comes from a good family."

Florence Joy Hayes offered a reflective essay on a mother's role in one of our earlier books about the Steelers called "Keep The Faith." One of her sons, Jonathan Hayes, was a tight end on the Steelers at the time. Another son, Jay Hayes, later coached on Bill Cowher's staff. She sent me a letter six months after the death of her husband, Jewett, It was about her family's relationship with the family of Marvin Lewis Jr.

Marvin Lewis' family and my family have been friends forever. My grandfather and grandmother were Virginians, as were Marvin's paternal great grandparents. His paternal two aunts were my mentors at church. All of them were educators and professors.

His great grandfather as well as his grandfather were photographers. The "Lewis Studio" was a well-known business in McDonald. Mr. H. J. Lewis took all the pictures of the people in the area, black and white. He also took the school pictures until big business moved into the mix.

Matthew Lewis Jr. is a Pulitzer Prize-winning photographer. I don't remember what year that was.

Marvin's Aunt Doris, Uncle Matt and his father all attended school together.

There was a strong connection with the First Baptist Church of McDonald. The Hayes boys — Jeffrey, Jay and Jonathan — attended church and Sunday school with the Lewis kids — Marvin, Carolyn Joy and Andrea.

The church had a group for the youth, namely "The Boys Club." My husband, Jewett, was one of the sponsors. He did, indeed, take as many kids as he could get transportation for to Trees Hall (on the Pitt campus) for swimming. He would get tickets for basketball games, football games, etc., and take the kids.

Marvin tells us often about Jewett's mentoring and he always talks about him teaching him to swim.

The boys were in different school districts. Our boys were in South Fayette, and Marvin and his sisters were in Fort Cherry. When Marvin and Jay went to college a year apart the rivalry continued. Marvin was at Idaho State University, and Jay at the University of Idaho. When Marvin was at Pitt, Jay was at Notre Dame. When Marvin was with the Steelers, Jay was there on an internship. When Marvin was with the Baltimore Ravens, Jay was with the Steelers.

What can I say? If you live in western Pennsylvania you bleed black and gold. My husband grew up in Muncie, Indiana and he wanted his boys to play basketball and be a "Hoosier" like him.

My husband was a graduate of Virginia Union University and a veteran of the Korean War, serving in the U. S. Army. He was a retired supervisor for the Pa. State Parole Board and served as chairman of South Fayette Parks and Recreation, a past president of the South Fayette Kiwanis Club and South Fayette High School Quarterback Club. He was also a past member of South Fayette Municipal School Authority and past Commissioner of South Fayette Boy Scouts. He worked closely with St. Vincent DePaul Society and the House of Hospitality organizations. He served in many capacities at the First Baptist Church of McDonald. He was a 1997 recipient of the Allegheny County African-American Pioneer Award. His legend will live on. I was always proud of him.

By the way, the First Baptist Church membership included Ray Kemp, who came out of Cecil and Duquesne University to play for the Steelers (then the Pirates) in their first season of 1933. He was the only black on the team. He was a fine man, too.

Marvin Lewis Jr. is a fine young man who comes from a good family. His parents were always there for their children. They were all well raised and educated.

Marvin Sr. and Vanetta still work in our church. He ushers and he's a good cook, though he's slowed down because of health problems. Vanetta — a nurse practitioner — takes our blood pressure and is a support for all of us with health problems.

The members of our church are a proud people. Parents worked hard to educate their children. Members who are as old as 93 are college graduates. The people will give you as much support as you need. Our church motto is "Saved to Serve."

Last year, on Father's Day, my husband and I presented each of our boys with a plaque that had a picture of the three of them. It read this way:

HAYES

You got it from your father; it was all he had to give.
So it's yours to use and cherish, for as long as you may live.
If you lose the watch he gave you, it can always be replaced.
But a black mark on your name, son, can never be erased.
It was clean the day you took it, and a worthy name to bear.
When he got it from his father, there was no dishonor there.
So make sure you guard it wisely, after all is said and done.
You will be glad the name is spotless, when you give it to your son.
Anonymous

Robin Cole
Building bodies and character

"I've known hard times."

Robin Cole always stands out in a crowd. He loves to wear bright colors. He shows up for most social events wearing a suit or sport coat unlike any other in the room. He has a bright smile to go with his costume. It disarms anyone in his path.

When Cole came to see me on Friday, January 24, 2003 at Applebee's Neighborhood Grill and Bar in Peters Township he was wearing a colorful Coogi sweater. "It's made in Australia," said Cole when I asked him about it. "No two alike."

We got together again at the same site, one of 14 Applebee's in the region owned and operated by two of Cole's former teammates on the Steelers, Larry Brown and J. T. Thomas, on Wednesday, February 19. Once again, he was resplendent in a bright green sweater. There was snow on the landscape, so he was appropriately attired.

Sometimes, when he speaks to elementary school kids, he might show up wearing his No. 56 Steelers' uniform. Hey, it gets their attention. Robin Cole has always subscribed to Chuck Noll's mantra — "Whatever It Takes."

Robin Cole is in constant search of his "life's work," and he has taken a fling at many pursuits. He has sold cars, suits, coal, and sports and fitness equipment. He served as an analyst on Steelers' football on KDKA-TV. He's taken a fling at coaching on the collegiate level at both Washington & Jefferson College and Robert Morris University, and even in politics in Washington County where he lives. He worked at W&J with John Banaszak, one of his former teammates, and at RMU with Joe Walton, who had been his head coach when he completed his NFL career with one season with the New York Jets in 1988. He's been heard on the radio promoting Red Dawgs Restaurant, Arnold Pontiac and Bradley Physical Therapy.

"Hey, I'm just chasing dollars," claimed Cole, with a roll of his bright dark eyes. "You do what you need to do at the time."

When we spoke, he was working for Clinton Sports International, offering state-of-the-art weightlifting and physical fitness equipment, and delivering motivational speeches. He has lent his name and services to so many worthwhile causes in the community. Wherever he could be of help, Robin Cole could be counted upon to show his smiling face.

Through the years, he had been associated with Big Brothers & Big Sisters, March of Dimes, The United Way, the Arthritis Foundation, National Safety Program, and The Salvation Army. He was a lifetime member of the NAACP and a member of the McMurray chapter of Rotary International.

He had been named a Most Valuable Person in Pittsburgh, Miller Lite Beer Man of the Year, YMCA Man of the Year and was inducted into the University of New Mexico Hall of Fame.

He smiled when I told him he reminded me of Ben Vereen, the dancer/actor. "Yeah, I've heard that before," said Cole with a nod.

He and his wife, Linda, have lived in Nottingham, near 84, Pennsylvania, since 1984. They have four children, Robin Jr., 24, Jeremy, 21; Lacy, 14 and Logan, 12.

He had served for several years as the president of the Pittsburgh chapter of the NFL Alumni. He had scheduled a meeting of its members for Froggy's on Tuesday, February 18. He called a day before to make sure everything was in order, and learned that Froggy's had been closed for renovations and was not scheduled to reopen until August. Steve "Froggy" Morris had been hospitalized with emphysema. That didn't surprise anyone who knew Froggy. One of Pittsburgh's most popular restaurateurs, Morris always had a cigarette pressed to his lips. He was one of those guys who lit a new cigarette with his last cigarette.

His bar and restaurant on Market Street had attracted the stars of the sports and business world for several decades. Pictures and posters and artwork depicting local sports stars decorated every room in his expansive three-story complex. He was Pittsburgh's answer to Toots Shor. I spoke to him soon after his hospital stay and he said he had stopped smoking and felt better. He said he'd be re-opening in the fall.

The NFL Alumni would have to look elsewhere for a meeting spot for a few months. They landed at Ruth's Chris Steak House, just a block away from Froggy's. I stopped by such a meeting on Tuesday, April 22, 2003. I parked my car near Froggy's. It was eerie-looking to walk by the place, and peer through the windows, seeing the familiar setting in a dimly lit bar area. It was only nine o'clock at night and not a soul in sight.

"Success is a journey, not a destination."

Robin Cole looked in great shape. He was always an impressive individual, a lean and mean 6-2, 220-pound linebacker. He sometimes lined up at defensive end and held his own.

Cole had played for the Steelers for 11 seasons, from 1977 to 1987, and then one year with the New York Jets. He was a No. 1 draft choice out of the University of New Mexico. From the start, he was a standout on special teams as a tackler and as a blocker.

His philosophy could have been adopted by the present-day Steelers who had problems on special teams in recent years. "When you're on special teams," points out Cole, "you have a job to do. If you're out there going half-speed, you're sure to get hurt. It's a one-

187

shot thing and you owe it your best shot. I like to tackle people, and that's easier than throwing a block, but I know how to block and I've always taken great pride in that."

He played alongside Jack Ham and Jack Lambert, splitting time at first with Loren Toews as an outside linebacker. Before he became a fulltime performer, Cole was used mostly when the other team figured to run the ball. He was the Steelers' player representative in 1981. Cole contributed to two Super Bowl championship seasons with the Steelers.

He was born in Los Angeles on September 11, 1955, and grew up in nearby Compton. He learned a lot in the mean streets of LA and Compton, learning mostly how to stay out of trouble. He said he learned a lot as a newspaper delivery boy. Street gangs were common in Compton, but Cole kept away from them, joining sports teams instead. Steelers' receiver Charles Johnson (1994-1998) grew up under terrible conditions in the same community.

"Too many kids I know who went to high school with me don't have much going for them these days," Cole once told me when he was still playing for the Steelers. "One of the ones voted most likely to succeed didn't succeed at anything. Simply because of lack of discipline. Throughout my life, I wanted to work. That was something I wanted to do. You won't find success in the street. It's a dead end, believe me."

Back in September, 1980, I interviewed Cole's high school coach, a man named Ted Williams, who was then coaching linebackers at UCLA. Williams talked about Cole as a scholastic star.

"He was aggressive," said Williams. "He didn't ever want to tackle kids; he always wanted to put on a show. It was a production when he got through with it. He tackled a kid, and he'd start on our 30 and end up 20 yards out of bounds at their 10. Then we'd get penalized for unnecessary roughness and they'd have the ball at our 15.

"He'd grab a kid by the jersey and sling him down and pick him up and throw him. I remember a tackle he missed once, too, and that really teed him off. We were playing the best high school team in the area, and Tony Hill, who's with the Cowboys now, was their quarterback. He was a nifty runner. He ran an option and kept the ball, and was out in the open. Robin sized him up for a tackle. He lowered his head and tackled nothing but air."

Cole had a different recollection of that game. "Tony Hill didn't want to go down once, and I ended up shoving him out of bounds onto the cinder track that surrounded the field."

Williams said he caught Cole on TV playing for the Steelers, and he said, "I have to smile. I tell my wife . . . one thing about Robin . . . he hasn't changed. His idea of football is physical violence. He has a style all of his own."

Cole defended his way of doing things by saying, "I like to throw a back down hard. I'm sort of saying, 'Don't come this way again.' You want to impress that on him."

"Every payday is a good payday."
— Rocky Bleier

Robin Cole

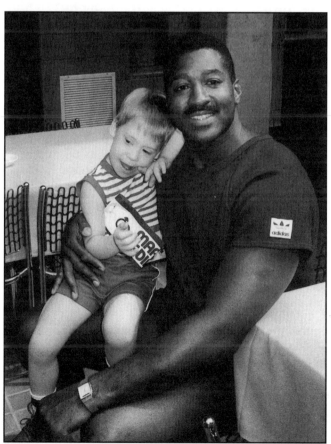

Robin Cole was a big hit with Derek Ross at March of Dimes event.

Robin Cole:

I speak about leadership and teamwork at schools and churches. I think I have some good ideas and philosophies that are good to share. I have found out the hard way that life is not all roses. Without a test there is no testimony. I've known good times and I've known hard times.

My whole message is based on character building. I tell them how those values will serve them well as we walk through our everyday life.

I talk about respect, responsibility, accountability, and how important those things are. These are things I used to get when I was young. Even when I share it with my kids I know they've heard it before.

Some kids are getting it at home, but not enough of them. I'm helping them become a better person from inside out.

I believe that we are all born to win, but conditioned to lose. If we change the input, we can change the output.

My dad's name was Obediah, right out of the Bible, the brother of Abraham. My dad was the baby of 17 children. He and my mother moved to Los Angeles from Shreveport, Louisiana in 1951, when she was pregnant with her sixth child. I was the seventh of her ten children. He did auto-body work and painted cars in Los Angeles. The combination of inhaling all those paint fumes and smoking cigarettes ruined both of his lungs. He died at age 49.

I learned to work from my dad. When I was in elementary school I used to sand cars and do some body work in my dad's shop. I used to go through parking lots and approach people and tell them I could knock out a dent in their cars for $50. I was always hustling, always chasing money. I was never afraid to work. I started making money on weekends.

You've got to get a balance in your life. You've got to recognize the needs and the importance of your family. You have to be involved. You have to remember what's really important.

When I look back at my days in the National Football League and my contract negotiations. I didn't understand the business. I thought it would always work out at the end. I told my agent to get things done so I could report to camp when it opened. I didn't want to be coming in late.

I probably left a lot of money on the table.

You trust people. That's Robin Cole. Then you end up not trusting anybody. You have to be protective.

Bob Hope got his start as a stand-up comic in New Castle. He also worked in McKeesport and Belle Vernon. Asked if he ever played Turtle Creek, Hope said, "Nobody played Turtle Creek."

I wasn't a guy who spent a lot of money. I liked to look nice, and I think I always dressed well. I didn't buy the nicest car. I was a family man and I wanted to make sure my family was taken care of. Everything was to my family.

I got burned by some bad investments. I was part of the group of players who got tied up with Greg Lusteg. He was Jack Lambert's guy, an agent who talked a big game. I know Mike Webster and Cliff Stoudt relied on him for financial advice, and we all lost a lot of money in limited partnerships and other investment vehicles. Lambert got involved in things that made money. I lost most of my savings. I lost somewhere between $450,000 and $500,000. Then I had to pay taxes on phantom income for ten years, money I didn't have. I knew we had a problem when I saw Lusteg sitting around hotel bars, drinking and playing the role. He wanted us to hang out with him, but I'm not a hang-out guy.

These players today are still trusting somebody to handle their money, and they better make sure they're placing their trust in trustworthy people.

I've gone through the same thing, as far as my finances are concerned, as Mike Webster went through. They changed the tax laws after those limited partnerships were created, and a lot of people got burned in the process. They all ended up busted. I heard Kareem Abdul-Jabbar said he lost $19 million in limited partnerships. I lost all my investments. I thought I was being conservative. But it still went bad. It makes you sick. It hurt a lot. I stayed busy, though, and mounted a comeback.

I remember some little saying that Chuck Noll used to use. If a guy got knocked down a few times, Noll would quote from the Bible: "The meek shall inherit the earth." He used it a little different from the way it was meant in the Bible. You can't get knocked down and stay down and make a habit of it. You have to spring back to your feet and start all over again. Don't let anyone defeat you.

Getting knocked down is a part of life. A few years ago I tried to get into coaching. I thought I'd like to get into the NFL. I went to the North-South Game in Mobile. I ran into a lot of people I knew. I had some contacts in Indianapolis. They were going to give me a chance to come in as a coaching intern on an NFL minority-development program. My wife had a seizure and I couldn't go. Things happen.

I thought I'd get into politics. I ran for political office here in 1999. I was on the ballot for county commissioner in Washington County. It was a good experience. I learned some things.

I try to count my blessings. God is continuing to be a part of my life.

My son, Robin Cole Jr., was a graduate assistant coach at Robert Morris University. He's now working to earn a PhD.

When I look at all the challenges I've got through, some tough times, I have to give my wife credit for helping me. Some of our financial problems led to emotional problems. We're still together. We're stronger today than ever. Linda is a full-time operating room nurse at Washington Hospital.

Our son, Jeremy, 21, is playing football as a safety at the University of Findlay, Ohio. He just finished his sophomore year. We have two other children, Lacie, 15, and Logan, 13. Lacie is a ninth grader at Ringgold High School and Logan is a seventh grader at Central Christian Academy.

When I count my blessings my wife and kids are at the top of the list. I owe everything to my wife for hanging in there. I've seen so many guys where as soon as they go through challenges their wives are gone. I've seen so much of it.

"It was an important time of development."

Ted Petersen played one season with the Cleveland Browns and they send him information all the time. They ask him if he wants to attend any games as their guests. They have a booth reserved for their former players. It's a great marketing tool. I'd like to see something like that with the Steelers. I know the Pirates have a booth like that for their alumni at PNC Park. But the Steelers may not see any benefit in that.

They call when they need us for some special promotions. We represent them at certain functions. I'd like to see them do more things to utilize us. The players today make so much money and they don't want to do any appearances unless they get big money. It opens opportunities for us former players to make some extra money. We're still Steelers.

What happened to friendships that Mike Webster had, prior to going through the challenges he went through. It was good to see all the guys who came to the funeral, to see them support the family. It was good to see the guys I had spent a lot of my life with as a young man, from the time I was 21 through 34. It was an important time of development.

I started to realize how quickly life flashes by and you never know when your time is up, when you're going to get called.

I'm sitting there, taking it all in. I'm looking at Pam, the family, and wondering what was going on, what had happened in their lives since Mike and I were teammates. And I wondered where are all the people that you spent so much time with as a young man.

At the age of 27, I got involved with the March of Dimes. I was doing my part to give something back to the community. I knew I had to get really involved. It was time for me to do that. I wanted to meet people and not be a stranger. I got into too many things. I just overdid it. I should have been spending more time with my wife and my family. I was Mr. Charity. It was time for me to become Mr. Cole.

At the funeral, I thought it was time for me to slow down. We've got two kids in college now. All I want to do now is pay the bills. Linda and I have been married for 18 years. I'm always sitting back and analyzing. My brain will be somewhere else. Some one else is in the moment and I'm on the moon.

I looked around and wondered who was going to miss me the most when I'm gone. I figured it was my family. If they're going to miss me the most that's who I should spend my time with. I went to pay my respects in the afternoon the day before the memorial service was conducted at the funeral home. Seeing Webby like that gave you a lot to think about, all that he went through, what went wrong. Maybe he felt ashamed and didn't want anyone to see how far he'd fallen. Maybe his pride got in the way. People are afraid to tell anyone they need some help. Sometimes when you run into challenges you have to tell someone, "I need your help."

I know that everything hasn't gone the way I wanted it to go the last ten years, but I have fought back. I have always worked for myself. I see myself as an entrepreneur of sorts. Sam Davis was like that, too, and look what happened to him. It shows you how quickly things can turn bad for someone. It's a shame what happened to him.

We didn't make big money in the beginning. There were guys in the steel mills making more than me when I first came here. We were all trying to be something we weren't, and we spent what we made in those early years.

"I should have been a Pro Bowl player."

If I had come here after Ham and Lambert had left, I'd probably be in the Hall of Fame. Players have told me I should have been a Pro Bowl player. But I always performed in those other guys' shadows.

I learned from Lambert and Ham. Ham had gone to Penn State — Linebacker U. — and he had us doing some things defensively that weren't in the Steelers scheme of things. We just did them because they worked.

As a player, when I played, I had to put myself aside. We all like the accolades. I wanted to go to the Pro Bowl. I wanted to be a Hall of Fame player. When I came to Pittsburgh, I had to put that aside. The team had to come first. My personal ambitions weren't as important as the team's goals. I could have gone elsewhere. I was making about $70,000 by my fifth year in the league, and I might have made more money somewhere else. I stayed because of the team. There was a history here. It was going to be talked about for a lifetime. If I had known they were going to cut me, I'd have gone elsewhere earlier. I thought I still had something to offer.

I think I have a knack for relating to people. I think I was blessed with that. I've never been afraid to sell a newspaper or a pencil. I wasn't afraid to hustle. I could swallow my pride and go out and sell stuff. I used to sell suits to the guys at golf outings. I bought suits at a discount and took them with me to golf outings. I'd have those suits in the back of my car.

"I was the candy man."

I never had a fight when I was a kid. Maybe some pushes on the football field, but I never had to fight. If I could avoid it, I'd avoid it. I was always busy, working to earn some money. I had no time to get into trouble. Some of the kids I grew up with got into trouble, some bad trouble. That's where my grandmother came into play. She kept us all on the straight and narrow. We always went to church on Sunday. I thought stealing was the worst thing you could do; that you'd die and go to hell for it. I had to work for things.

When I was about nine, I used to ride in a car with my brother and help him deliver newspapers. Then I got my own route later, with the *L.A. Times*. I'd get up at two in the morning, and deliver the papers. We went through some tough neighborhoods.

My route went through an area called Taco Flats. Even I was afraid to go there. It was a Spanish-American community. You learned what you had to do if you were going to go in and out of there. It was the kind of place where you'd have to pray before you went in. If the kids didn't get you, the dogs would. I got a couple of dog bites on my ankles and worse.

I liked to play basketball back then, too, and baseball. Sandy Koufax of the Dodgers was my favorite player. I liked Don Sutton, Wes Parker. I was good at sports, and I stayed out of trouble.

I was good at public relations and dealing with people. I was the candy man. I could sell more candy than any of the other kids at school. I'd sell chocolate bars for 50 cents to raise money for our basketball team, or for Little League. I won a gift certificate; I sold more than 300 other kids. That was the first time I ever won anything. I figured out I had to work to win. I can sell; I'm a hustler.

I'm friends with anybody who wants to be friends. Heck, I was friends with guys on my team who weren't interested in being friends. That's my nature. I know I can direct and manage people to be successful, to work as a team.

I'm like a lot of people who played in the NFL, looking for what kind of work they can do now that they are finished playing. Where do I go from here? That's what you ask yourself when you retire as a player. When you were playing ball, or when you're in the entertainment business, people put you up on a pedestal. Now you've got to get back on level ground again and begin from the bottom to build something else. Some people think you made so much money playing ball that you don't need to work. I want to work. I want to be productive at something else.

You've changed and you've grown since you first came to the Steelers. You should have learned something along the way to help you. Life is about struggles. That's the way it should be. If you're not struggling, you're not working. Success is a journey, not a destination.

Jim O'Brien

Robin Cole checks out former teammate Sam Davis' jersey during visit to Applebee's Neighborhood Grill & Bar in Peters Township that is owned by Steelers' Alumni Larry Brown and J.T. Thomas.

Cliff Stoudt
Still ready in reserve

"Pittsburgh fans just hate quarterbacks."

Cliff Stoudt is a funny man, a terrific stand-up comic. As a kid, he panicked when he had to get up and speak in school. He'd take an "F" for the assignment rather than say anything to the class. He's come a long way since those days. Now, he seems like such a natural with a microphone in hand.

A backup quarterback most of his 13 years in the National Football League, starting out behind Terry Bradshaw with the Pittsburgh Steelers (1977-1983) and finishing up behind Troy Aikman with the Dallas Cowboys, he had time to work on his act.

He was a star during his two years as a quarterback with the Birmingham Stallions of the United States Football League somewhere along the way. In any case, Stoudt saw a lot, and developed a sense of humor along the way — it helped keep Stoudt sane and made him more popular with the crowd — and he's a good storyteller.

It's a bit of a shocker to realize that Stoudt put in 15 seasons in professional football, one more season than Terry Bradshaw. Mike Webster holds the Steelers record with 15 seasons, and then put in two more with the Kansas City Chiefs.

Stoudt didn't get beat up much, except by the fans in Pittsburgh when he tried to succeed Bradshaw during the 1983 season, and when he returned a year later as the quarterback of the Birmingham Stallions of the outlaw USFL. He played against the Pittsburgh Maulers at Three Rivers Stadium and was badly abused by the fans for cutting out on the Steelers. They threw stuff at him from the stands and verbally assaulted him from start to finish.

He must have been penciling in jokes on those clipboards he carried with him on the sidelines all those years.

"I can tell Kordell Stewart the Pittsburgh fans didn't hate him because he's black ," said Stoudt. "Pittsburgh fans just hate quarterbacks."

Thinking better of that, Stoudt added, "I like to go back to Pittsburgh now. They treat me great. I've gotten better in their eyes. Guys like Kordell and Neil O'Donnell and Bubby Brister have made me look better." Stoudt smiles when he says that.

He can provide inside stories, with a little bit of embellishment for comic effect, and Stoudt's style — he knows when to smile, when to frown, when to go with a straight face, and his timing is impeccable — gets a lot of laughs. Stoudt has good stories about Bradshaw, of course, and the likes of Jack Lambert, Chuck Noll, Franco Harris, Rocky Bleier, Gary Dunn, Steve Courson & Co.

Ted Thompson

The Steelers were solid at quarterback position when Terry Bradshaw was backed up by Cliff Stoudt, the team's No. 5 draft choice in 1977 out of Youngstown State.

George Gojkovich

"I was happy for Tommy Maddox.
I was sad for Kordell Stewart, who's a friend of
mine. I think America loves a good story.
Tommy Maddox was a good story and a good
guy. He appreciates more than anyone will ever
know this opportunity, and he won't mess it up."
—Terry Bradshaw At Dapper Dan Dinner
February 9, 2003

Most of all, Stoudt pokes fun at himself. "I was the first player to qualify for an NFL pension (with 3½ years of service) without playing a single down in a regular season game," says Stoudt.

"The back-up quarterback is always the most popular player on the team. I'd have been smart to stay on the sideline. But I wanted to be a starter."

I had recommended Stoudt as a speaker for the Pittsburgh Club of Columbus for their annual "Beat The Winter Blues" dinner. Steelers center Jeff Hartings was originally scheduled to speak but he backed out of the commitment. I had spoken to Stoudt on the telephone several times in previous weeks, and thought he had good stories, and I just had a sense about him that he'd do a good job.

Plus, he was living in Pickerington, a suburb of Columbus, and he wouldn't require travel expenses. I would be the opening act for Stoudt. The previous year I was the lounge act for Rodney Bailey, an engaging young man who had just played his rookie season with the Steelers and had come out of Ohio State. He had graduated in three-and-a-half years, unique in most major college football programs, unheard of at Ohio State. Cliff Stoudt started off by explaining how he came to be speaking to the Pittsburgh Club of Columbus on Saturday, March 1, 2003.

"When Paul Cynkar called me and asked me if I'd fill in for Jeff Hartings, I said, 'That's what I do! I'm always a fill-in.' And so I'm here," said Stoudt in his introductory remarks at La Scala Italian Bistro on West Dublin-Granville Road in Dublin, Ohio.

An eight-course meal just kept coming, and so did our stories. About 80 Pittsburgh ex-patriots seemed to be enjoying themselves immensely. "Do these people have a better time than we do?" my wife Kathie asked me at one point. Yes, they do. They let themselves go more easily.

Stoudt signed 8 x 10 glossy photos of him that were provided by one of the club members — they were great photos — and I signed copies of my books. It's a fun group. The dinner the year before provided me with an introduction to Rodney Bailey, and we became good friends the rest of the year. Bailey plays for the Steelers basketball team managed by Tom O'Malley Jr, and I get to see him in action in area gyms as well during the winter.

Stoudt used to play for the Steelers basketball team. He was listed as 6-4, 218 pounds in the game program. He had lettered for four years in basketball in high school back home in Oberlin. He was also one of the best scholastic golfers in the state.

When Stoudt was competing in a celebrity driving exhibition at Point State Park, golf pro Lee Trevino told him, "If I could drive the ball like you no one would have ever heard of Jack Nicklaus."

One of the schools that offered Stoudt a scholarship was Baldwin-Wallace in nearby Berea. "I didn't want to go there because the quarterback was the coach's son," said Stoudt, pausing for effect. "The kid's name was Jim Tressell."

That same Jim Tressell had coached Ohio State to the national college football championship in 2002. Before that, Tressell had won national championships on a Division 1-AA level at Youngstown State. "I think they're the only father-son combination to both coach national championship football teams," added Stoudt. "Jim once told me that he'd have been happy to stay at Youngstown State all his life, unless he could get the job at Ohio State."

Stoudt looked sharp in his charcoal gray sweater and dark slacks. He's built powerfully in the chest and has a commanding presence. He has green eyes, a sharp nose, and has always borne a certain resemblance to Joe Namath. "I just wish I'd have had his career and his money and fur coats," says Stoudt.

"I wish I could have stayed with the Steelers."

Cliff Stoudt said he would be a late arrival at the dinner because he had a previous commitment. He wanted to watch his daughter Cydnei, a 16-year-old sophomore, play for Pickerington High School in a post-season playoff game. She is a 5-11 center for the Lady Tigers. They won. They would later lose in the regional final.

Cliff was living in Pickerington with Laura, his wife of 21 years, and Cydnei, and their sons, Zackary, 13, a quarterback (of course) for his eighth grade football team, and Cole, 10.

Their home in Pickerington is their 15th in 21 years, said Stoudt. My wife Kathie and I had breakfast with Cliff and Laura at Bob Evans' Restaurant in Pickerington the morning after the sports dinner. Cliff was wearing a black NFL Alumni jersey.

He grew up in Oberlin, Ohio and attended Youngstown State University. He started as a freshman and rewrote many of the school's passing records set by Ron Jaworski, who went on to the National Football League where he starred for the Philadelphia Eagles. Jaworski has since become a respected NFL analyst on ESPN.

At Youngstown State, Stoudt served as team captain and earned MVP honors. He won the MVP award in the Ohio Shrine Bowl.

Stoudt was selected in the fifth round of the 1977 NFL draft, the same round as Steve Courson.

Among the quarterbacks Cliff competed with in Pittsburgh were Bradshaw, Neil Graff, Mike Kruczek and Mark Malone. He was the backup to Bradshaw for six seasons.

He had his own Cliff Stoudt Financial office in Pickerington, allied with K.W. Chambers & Co., a national financial advisory service headquartered in suburban St. Louis. He continued to serve as an analyst for the East Carolina University Pirates.

Several of his former Steelers' teammates were sports announcers and analysts, including Bradshaw, Lynn Swann, Jack Ham, Mark Malone, Merril Hoge, Tunch Ilkin, Edmund Nelson and

Craig Wolfley. Rocky Bleier was still making a living delivering motivational speeches at college and corporate seminars around the country.

Cliff jumped to the Birmingham Stallions of the USFL before the 1984 season. They were coached by Rollie Dotsch, who had been a popular offensive line coach with the Steelers in their salad days.

The Stallions were one of the few success stories in the short-lived USFL. They were the most loved and best-supported team in the league. Stoudt threw for 3,121 yards and 26 touchdowns in 1984 and for 3,358 yards and 34 touchdowns in 1985. He was team captain and team MVP.

He returned to the NFL and played for St. Louis, Phoenix, Miami and Dallas.

"If I had to do it over again, I wish I could have stayed with the Steelers in Pittsburgh," said Stoudt. "If I had known Terry wasn't going to be able to play in 1984 I'd have stayed. But I wanted to be a starter. I was tired of seeing my name in the Did Not Play listing."

"It was great playing here."

Cliff Stoudt says he began saying funny things as the Steelers were preparing for Super Bowl XIV, when they played the Los Angeles Rams at the Rose Bowl in Pasadena. Everyone, including the equipment guys, gets interviewed at the Super Bowl site, and Stoudt wanted to be ready. So he thought up some funny lines beforehand. He said it helped ease the pressure he was feeling. I remember seeing Stoudt shining as he stood around being interviewed at the Steelers' practice site at Cal-Fullerton near Newport Beach.

I revisited those southern California sites while visiting my younger daughter, Rebecca, to celebrate her 26th birthday and Mother's Day for my wife Kathie, in early May of 2003. Rebecca was working as a manager at California Pizza Kitchen in Tarzana, about an hour's drive northwest of Los Angeles.

Stoudt said that the Super Bowl brought out the ham in him. "Before that, I kept my mouth shut," said Stoudt. "It was starting to get to me. I was worrying myself sick about not playing. One day out there I just started joking about it. It took some of the pressure off."

He told people he had gone 56 straight regular season games without playing. "I tied Joe DiMaggio's record," he said.

Asked what his threshold for pain was, Stoudt smiled and said, "Standing on the sideline when it's very cold. I worry about getting frostbitten feet. My dream is just to get a bruise on my body so I can show it to my buddies back at Youngstown."

Soon, Stoudt had nearly as many newsmen chasing after him as Bradshaw. He was a tall Billy Crystal with a clipboard.

200

Cliff and Laura Stoudt

Zackary Stoudt, 13

Cole Stoudt, 9

Cydnei Stoudt, 16

Cliff Stoudt recalls Mike Webster:

*"He was always ready to go.
He was like a gladiator."*

Stoudt's first start with the Steelers almost realized a boyhood dream. It came against the Browns at Cleveland Stadium. Stoudt had a strong performance before more than 80,000 fans, but the Steelers came up short, losing 27-26. With the Steelers leading, 26-14, Matt Bahr's conversion attempt hit the goal post and bounced back. No one sensed at the time that this would prove fatal.

Stoudt had completed 18 of 37 passes for 310 yards, including a 72-yard touchdown pass to Theo Bell.

"It was great playing here," said Stoudt afterward. "Hey, 80,000 people . . . that's four years' worth of crowds at Youngstown State."

After Super Bowl XIV, Stoudt had more one-liners than Henny Youngman. "They say pro football is such a tough sport," he said, "but I have two Super Bowl rings and I've never suffered a scratch."

When his good friend Mike Kruczek was traded to the Washington Redskins and Stout moved up from No. 3 quarterback to No. 2 quarterback on the Steelers, he said, "Well, I'm going from clipboard to headset on the sideline."

Reflecting on his second-string status, Stoudt once said, "At this rate, I could last forever. I'm big and strong and I've never been hurt since I broke into the National Football League."

During the 1980 season, Chuck Noll chewed out Terry Bradshaw on the sideline during a setback in Cincinnati. "Noll even said something to me during the game," recalled Stoudt, with tongue buried deep in his cheek. "He said, 'Move back!' It's the first time he'd talked to me during a game."

Joe Gordon started sending Stoudt out to sports dinners. "Stoudt is hot stuff on the banquet circuit," gushed Gordon. "He's in great demand."

Stoudt hasn't forgotten Gordon's help. "Joe Gordon is a great guy," says Stoudt.

Back in those days, Stoudt used to start his dead-pan delivery by saying, "Hi, I'm Cliff Stoudt. I'm a quarterback for the Pittsburgh Steelers."

That was always good for a few laughs. Like Rodney Dangerfield, Stoudt was simply seeking a little respect.

Fred Rogers — TV's Mister Rogers — had died the day before the "Beat The Winter Blues" banquet in Columbus, and Stoudt remembered seeing him once.

Ray Mansfield on sizing up Terry Bradshaw:

"I could always look at Terry before a game and tell you what kind of day he was going to have. If he was a little glassy-eyed — you'd be talking to him and he'd look through you like you weren't there — I'd know it was going to be a long afternoon."

Meeting Mister Rogers and Arnold Palmer

Cliff Stoudt:

When I was 12 years old, I first started playing golf. As a youngster I used to come over from Cleveland with my dad and he did business in the Latrobe area. That's where Fred Rogers grew up. I got to see his home. I took Laura to see it a few years back, and when we were coming back down the driveway, a car was coming the other way.

It was Mister Rogers. He passed and waved to us. I think he said, "Hi, Neighbor!"

When I was 12, I played golf with my dad at the Latrobe Country Club, which is Arnold Palmer 's club, and at Ligonier Country Club. When I was with the Steelers, I got to play in one of Andy Russell's celebrity tournaments at the Latrobe Country Club. Arnie was our host that day. I always wanted to play Laurel Valley, just down the road.

Once, I was there when they had a Pennsylvania Open, a 36-hole tournament for golf professionals from all over the state. I saw Arnold Palmer and followed him over the course. I've wanted to play it ever since. Thinking of Latrobe brings back a lot of memories.

When I think of the Pittsburgh Steelers, the first person who comes to mind is Jack Lambert. He's the image of the Steelers.

I remember he used to go out in a boat on a small lake at St. Vincent's College and do some fishing. We used to tell people that Jack would just light up sticks of dynamite and toss them in the water and before you knew it there'd be fish floating on the surface. And he'd just scoop them up with a little net. Just kidding. No, Jack loved to go fishing, and he knew what he was doing.

I remember one night at camp that Chuck Noll let the quarterbacks out early. Usually, we were the last players to leave the campus.

I went to a bar where the players liked to go called The Intermission down on Route 30. I go into the place, and there's only one guy at the bar. It was the biggest bar you'd ever see, and there was Jack, in his usual spot, sitting on a stool behind the cash register so you couldn't see him that well. He had his dark blue Pennsylvania Highway Patrol cap on, with the bill down over his eyes.

I thought, "Oh, no, I've got to go sit with him! He's the only one here. What am I going to say?" In short, I was scared of Jack Lambert. He intimidated everyone. I went over and sat with him and tried to make small talk. What are you going to say to Jack Lambert. "Did you kill anyone today, Jack?"

Just then, four guys came into the bar who'd been at the Steelers' camp that afternoon. They were Steelers fans. They sat down at the far end of the bar.

Then I see one of them making a move in our direction. Jack goes, "Ah shit." Then he says, "Watch this."

As the guy gets near us, he says, "Jack, I don't want to disturb you, but . . ."

And Lambert lets him have it. "Then get the hell outta here!"

The guy runs back to his buddies. He must have told them what Lambert did. The next thing you know the four of them are raising their fists to the ceiling triumphantly and chanting "Lambert! Lambert! Lambert!" He had done just what they were looking for Lambert to do. That's what they wanted. They loved it. He made their day. If I had done something like that, they'd have cut off my legs at the knees. "I can't believe you did that," I said to Jack. And Jack is just laughing.

Jack was afraid of snakes, and we used to scare him at training camp by leaving empty cages in his room, stuff like that. He'd come running down the hall, cursing out everybody. He'd be pissed. Tom Beasley once put a five-foot rubber snake under Jack's pillow. He came out of his room screaming, and jumping up and down. He must not have liked snakes.

There were games when Lambert called time out just so he could yell at our guys in the huddle. Chuck Noll would go crazy when he'd do that. Chuck would be on the sideline asking, "What's he doing out there?"

I remember the first time I heard about Jack Lambert. We had a player named Ferris Scott, who was a big defensive lineman, when I was at Youngstown State. He had been picked to play in this Ohio College All-Star Game. It was for seniors from colleges throughout Ohio. Hey, it was a big deal to us. I played in it later on.

Ferris agreed to call us guys back at the dorm at Youngstown State and give us a report on how things were going. After the first day, he called, and we're listening to him over a conference call speaker. "There's a kid here who's about 6-5, weighs about 190 pounds and has this long blond hair. He gets up at a meeting to introduce everyone and tells us he's a middle linebacker. That got a laugh."

Ferris called back the next night, and says, "Forget everything I said about that guy from Kent State. He's the best damn football player I've ever seen. He was killing everybody today at practice."

$\rightarrow$

Latrobe's gift to the golf world, Arnold Palmer, receives his own Steelers' jersey in tribute at Heinz Field during 2002 season, as Pittsburgh Mayor Tom Murphy looks on.

Mike Longo

Jack was one of my beloved teammates, but there was always that little barrier because of his stern front. We had a lot of leaders on that football team. We had our share of fun. But we all had to answer to Jack. If I wanted to please anybody on the team it was him.

We played hard off the field. No one played harder than Jack. But when you went out to play you better get the job done. Jack was the epitome of that. Jack was the guy you wanted to please.

A look from Chuck Noll was worse than getting yelled at. So was a look from Jack Lambert. I never had a cozy, warm, fuzzy relationship with Jack, but I always liked and respected Jack. I felt I had to earn his respect. The year I started at quarterback, Jack always backed me up.

I remember I was having a tough week midway through the 1983 season. My father-in-law had died, and the fans were giving me a rough time even though we were winning. Jack gave the fans a tongue-lashing in the newspapers prior to our game with San Diego at Three Rivers Stadium. The fans gave me a standing ovation when I was introduced before that game. We won that game, 26-3.

In the next-to-the-last game at New York, I threw the last two touchdown passes ever thrown in an NFL game at Shea Stadium. We beat the Jets, 34-7. A little defensive back for the Jets, Jerry Holmes, was twisting my leg, like he wanted to break it, when they had me at the bottom of a pile on our sideline. Jack came over and yanked him out of the pile, and chased him all over the field. It was like what he did to Charley Waters of the Cowboys for tapping Roy Gerela on the helmet after he'd missed a kick in the Super Bowl. It was nice to have Jack in my corner. It was a tough year.

"You've never arrived."

I've had ten conversations with Chuck Noll in my life and my wife started eight of them. I'll never forget one conversation I had with him at St. Vincent.

I'd had this really great showing against the Falcons in a pre-season game. I was like 12 of 17 passing. I threw for two touchdowns and I scored a touchdown. I was feeling pretty good about myself. I came out of the dorm and I saw Chuck waiting there. I thought, "Oh, no, I'm going to have to talk to him!" He still scared the crap out of me.

He said, "How did you think you played the other day?"

I tried to muster all the confidence I could, so I'd impress him, and I started telling him that I thought everything was

Cliff Stoudt at summer training camp at St. Vincent College in Latrobe

George Gojkovich

like in slow-motion, and the receivers looked so open, and I felt so confident when I was calling the plays and throwing the ball. "I think I'm really catching on and finally getting all this," I said.

And he said, "So why don't you just quit?"

I felt like I'd been kicked in the groin. "Huh?" I said, or something even less intelligent. I'm thinking, "Hey, thanks a lot, Coach."

And he says, "If you feel like you've arrived then you should retire. Because someone else is going to come along who is more ambitious and is going to work harder to bump you off. Somebody is coming behind you who wants it more. You've never arrived in this league."

I never forgot that. I've talked about that at a lot of sports banquets and in interviews I've done. My daughter's basketball team, the Lady Tigers, has its own web-site and I checked it out recently and under her picture there was a little bio. There was a line that had her favorite quote, and it was, "You've never arrived." I thought that was great, to see how 20-some years after I played for the Steelers Chuck Noll still has an impact on my family.

I wrote him a letter thanking him for what he taught me. He gave me a shot; he kept me around after I broke my hand. There must have been something he liked about me. I owed him a huge debt of thanks. I never heard back from him, but when I ran into Chuck and his wife, Marianne, at a golf outing, she told me that letter meant a great deal to him. She said that few people ever took the time to let him know something like that. I felt good about that. She said it really touched him, and I could see a tear or two forming in her eyes when she told me that. I've seen Chuck at a couple of golf outings in recent years, and he just wants to talk. Now he's talking like a warm, fuzzy Chuck. He's like a second father to me. That's the way I feel about the guy.

If somebody told me I had one day to live, one day left on this planet, I'd have to talk to Chuck Noll. If I could talk to him for two hours that would be a godsend. I'd love to pick his brain. Some day Terry has to sit back and realize the genius of Chuck Noll. He molded us into a family. He treated us all the way he thought we had to be treated. Terry's ego needed to be stroked more than Chuck was willing to oblige.

Robert Stewart, father of Kordell Stewart:

"He is going somewhere where he has another chance. He gave it all he had in Pittsburgh, and it didn't work. I'm glad he's out of there."

"Terry's rules are you keep playing till Terry wins."

Terry Bradshaw and I had a great relationship. I have a lot of great memories. I was a backup. I stroked his ego, too.

Terry was nervous and anxious before some of the big games, but I think Terry and all of us go through a little bit of anxiety until you get knocked on your ass or complete a pass.

I could listen to Terry go on and on about what was wrong in Pittsburgh and I'd say, "Damn, I wish I had those complaints."

It was difficult to follow Terry in Pittsburgh. Since I played there, I have told him he owes me for what I endured trying to take his place. If I were Terry Bradshaw I'd be living in Pittsburgh. I'd set up my castle there and enjoy all the adulation and opportunities that would present themselves.

I see him on TV, and that's Terry Bradshaw. If he were sitting here right now, he'd still be on stage. He'd be doing some dramatics, patting you on the back, making sure he had your attention. He's the same way on the golf course. I don't mean that in a bad way. He needs to be the life of the party. He's very competitive that way, too.

He had punting contests and passing contests after practice. You had to play by Terry's rules. Terry's rules are that you keep playing till Terry wins.

He commands the limelight. He loves the limelight. I think that's one of the things that makes great people great, the need for attention. I think a lot of us athletes have a lot of insecurities.

When I was in high school and in college I couldn't get up in the front of the class and speak. It wasn't until Super Bowl XIV. I was being interviewed by Bryant Gumbel and I was cracking him up. Soon as I cracked the first joke I felt better. Once you get people laughing you feel like they like you. After that, Joe Gordon got me a lot of engagements. I started being funnier in interviews, and people like John Clayton kept coming back for more.

I love the Tommy Maddox story. I met Tommy at a couple of golf tournaments a few years back. He probably came out too soon from UCLA. I love his story. I love watching him play. It's like Kurt Warner a few years ago, coming out of the Arena Football League and starring for the St. Louis Rams the way he did, being the MVP in the Super Bowl. I like to see a fresh face on the scene.

It was great the way Maddox responded to the opportunity he got in Pittsburgh, and the way the city took to him. I think they showed great patience with Kordell Stewart. There were times when I thought they'd have been better off with Mike Tomczak in there.

I think Tommy's biggest assets are that he's cool and he's an accurate thrower. If I'm a receiver or an offensive lineman on that team I have to love Tommy Maddox. He reminds me of Joe Montana the way he recognizes situations and just delivers the ball on the mark. He brings such confidence into the huddle. That has to be comforting. He's a team player. They know he's not out there for Tommy Maddox.

"Everybody wants to be the guy everyone loves."

When I was a player, we all wished we had the relationship with Chuck Noll that Terry Bradshaw had. I saw him down in Daytona recently where he had a racecar in the competition. I got to talk to him for about an hour. He was telling me about going back to Pittsburgh, and how he and Chuck had made up, and how great it was to be back with him at this dinner and luncheon in Pittsburgh. He said everything was cool now. I told him he was full of crap. I told him that he was always the fair-haired boy with Chuck. "The rest of us would have died to be treated the way you were treated," I told him. Hey, everybody wants to be the guy everyone loves.

Somebody asked me about my relationship with Terry. They said, "Did you get along because you weren't a threat?" Every athlete has a sense of insecurity. Terry and me got along well and we had a good relationship. But he didn't ever want to miss a snap.

I have read all of Terry's books. In the earlier ones, some of his animosity toward Chuck came out. He was put off by some of the things that had happened to him in Pittsburgh.

I was never that close to Chuck, but I always admired him. After I was done playing, I realized how much Chuck had taught me. Ninety percent of what I teach my kids came from Chuck. Now I realize why he treated us the way he did.

I got a chance to start for the Steelers in 1983 when Terry Bradshaw had an injured elbow. Everybody thought he'd be back the next season. During that season, Rollie Dotsch told me he was going to Birmingham, and he told me I'd be his starter if I signed on there. We didn't know Terry was going to miss the whole next season, that he couldn't play anymore. I told Rollie I would join him. I ended up getting several offers from the USFL teams. People forget, but we were 10-6 with me as a starter and we won our division title. We lost to the Raiders in the playoffs and they went to the Super Bowl that year.

I signed with Birmingham a three-year one hundred percent guaranteed contract. After the 1985 season the USFL sued the NFL and Birmingham protected me and they had to pay me. Pittsburgh still had the rights to me in the NFL. Robert Friday was representing me. He's the guy who was with Payne Stewart when his plane went down. Robert and I flew in to Pittsburgh. Mr. Rooney sent a limo to pick us up at the airport. We sat in his box with him. We signed the next day with Jim Boston and Dennis Thimons, who handled the negotiations. They offered me a two-year deal for $250,000 a year. It was half as much as Mark Malone and David Woodley were making. They ended up giving me a one-year deal, with a ten percent raise. They had to do that when I returned to the NFL according to the league's collective bargaining act. They came back to us with Dan Rooney and he told me I'd been traded to the St. Louis Cardinals. That's how my days with the Steelers came to an end.

I try not to look back with regrets. Before things went sour for me in Pittsburgh, I was pretty popular there. The two years with Rollie in Birmingham were great. I wouldn't trade them for anything in the world. I played some good football there. I dusted off the rust from six years on the bench in Pittsburgh.

I hope Tommy Maddox doesn't lose that relationship he has with the fans in Pittsburgh. I hope he continues to do well.

It's a great town. For years I didn't want to go near the place. I thought there were people at the border there waiting for me to turn me back. I go here now, though, and I get treated well. I'm happy about that. My wife's from Youngstown, but I met her in Pittsburgh, so I have to be thankful to the town for that, too. I think Laura was four or five months out of high school. I laid eyes on her and I was gone. It was love at first sight. She was 18, going on 30. I was 25, going on 12. It's the greatest thing that ever happened to me. I had been married before, but that didn't work out.

Pittsburgh was a great place to play pro football. The organization, as I would learn later, was better than it is in many NFL cities. I didn't realize what we had until I played for Dallas and Miami and St. Louis and Arizona. We had something really special there in Pittsburgh.

"We thought Webby was indestructible."

We all knew Mike Webster was having problems. We were at the Ray Mansfield Memorial Tournament in September, (2003) playing golf at Diamond Run in the North Hills and I was mixing with the guys in the clubhouse during dinner afterward when Bill Hurley came in and said, "Webby had a heart attack."

211

That wasn't the first time he'd had a heart attack. Once before, he had a heart attack and was found at the side of a road by a passerby. They got him to the hospital in time to get him proper treatment. We figured Webby would get through this scare, too. We thought Webby was indestructible.

The next day, Hurley called me and told me Webby had died. It was a shock. As football players and athletes, we all feel bulletproof. He had been such a strong leader. Nothing could hurt him. Thinking of all the problems he experienced after football, I'm glad he's finally at peace.

Whatever the problems were that haunted him, maybe this provided relief. It hurt, though. He meant so much to all of us. He had been such a calming influence on me in the huddle many times. There'd be a situation in which I came in, and maybe I said something wrong in my nervousness. Webby would say, "Start over. You can't do that." Larry Brown was that way, too. They were among the guys who were going to fight for me. Webby was our anchor. In the middle of a cadence, he would turn around to me and give me an audible if he didn't like the way the defense was lined up against us.

One time he called an audible and we lost five yards on the call. He came back to the huddle laughing. "Sorry, wrong audible, Stoudter," he said. "Yeah, he called me Stoudter. All the guys called me that. It started with Gary Dunn.

"Bubba" was our nickname for Larry Brown. One time, during the 1983 season, we're playing the Raiders before 92,000 in the Los Angeles Coliseum in the AFC playoffs. I got in the huddle and called a play we worked on all week. We knew how the Raiders would react to this particular pattern. I told the guys in the huddle that this play was going for a touchdown. Then Lester Hayes, a defensive back for the Raiders, did something he had never done in the film we'd seen, and he stopped instead of continuing across the field on a certain pass route. I tried to hit Stallworth, but I hit Hayes right in the chest and he ran the ball in for a touchdown. He ran it 90 some yards for a touchdown. As we walked to the sideline, Bubba said, "Hey, Stoudter, you called that right. It was a pass for a touchdown all right."

The one thing I'll always remember about Webby was his routine of sprinting out of the huddle. He did that at mini-camp in May. The ballcarrier is no sooner down and Webby has his hand up to form the huddle.

When I was with Miami, we went up against the K.C. Chiefs when Webby was playing there. I told our guys to watch him. He was 38 and in his 17th year and he's sprinting out to the ball to start every play, and running back and forming the huddle. He was always ready to go. He was like a gladiator.

I remember another year that Chuck was big on having us running up and down the stairs at the stadium. He had us running in the upper deck up to the roof. We'd all do about eight to ten sets of those, and jog back down the ramps. Our legs were shaking. Webby wouldn't stop. He went around the stadium until he'd run up all the steps. He'd come into the locker room and retreat to the weight room and work out for another hour. He was just a machine. He was like the Energizer bunny.

He had a high-pitched voice, but I never heard him raise his voice. You had Stallworth and Swann competing every day at practice to prove who was the best pass-catcher on the team. You had Franco putting moves on imaginary tacklers and running the distance on every carry.

Bradshaw didn't want to leave the field. He'd be the last one off. He was like a little kid. It was like playing street football with him around. That's one thing I miss, fooling around with Bradshaw like that. We had a great group of guys, and they all loved to play the game. We had at least 15 bona fide leaders.

I hated the Friday walk-through practice session in the locker room because I always ended up as a defensive end. Jon Kolb would be across from me. He got a kick, for some reason, out of punching my arms. He'd never crack a smile. He was like a Cro-Magnon man. He'd never let his shield down, though he was probably laughing on the inside. I'd be black and blue.

I can't believe I miss that sort of stuff, but I really do.

Kent Smith

"THE STOUDTERS" — Former Steelers quarterback proudly poses with his family in Pickerington, Ohio, from left to right, Cydnei, Cole, Cliff, Laura and Zackary.

Andy Russell
Still the student

"I'm the rookie writer."

A ndy Russell would rather talk about his favorite writers more than his favorite football players. Russell was sitting at a round table in his spacious office on the 31st floor of Dominion Tower, talking about Pat Conroy and Robert B. Parker. They are also two of my favorite writers so it was something we could discuss as comfortably as Jack Ham and Jack Lambert. Russell and I had read most of their books.

Russell, age 62, is the Managing Director of Laurel Mountain Partners, merchant bankers, and is involved in other investment ventures.

Few Steelers have been quite as successful in their "life's work." He is usually one of the first mentioned when anyone discusses how well former Steelers are faring in the business world.

Russell was a superb linebacker for the Pittsburgh Steelers for 12 seasons (1963, 1966-1976), playing in the Pro Bowl seven times. He had written two books in recent years, *A Steeler Odyssey* and then *An Odd Steelers Journey.* I had read his first book over a few nights earlier in the year, and found it full of good stories and reflections, adventure stories that were easy to read. Russell has lived an interesting life and recognized a good story when he saw one. I called him when I finished the book to tell him how much I enjoyed it. He sounded pleased to hear from me. He doesn't take good reviews for granted either.

He said he had recently read Pat Conroy's personal story, *My Losing Season,* about Conroy's basketball playing days at The Citadel, and loved it. "When he writes about how he felt as a bench-sitter," related Russell, "it was exactly how I feel as a writer. I'm the rookie writer. I feel out of my league with veteran or established writers."

After reading the book, Russell felt compelled to send a long letter to Conroy with his thoughts about their respective positions in the world of athletics and authorship. Conroy, of course, is best known for novels such as *Lords of Discipline, The Great Santini,* and *Prince of Tides,* which were all made into movies. Russell also invited Conroy to play in his annual summer golf tournament. "He loves to play golf," said Russell. "I hope he'll come."

He had also written to one of his writing instructors at the University of Missouri, Paul Doherty, who was now teaching at Boston College. He regarded Doherty as one of his mentors. Doherty told Russell that he knew and spent time with Robert B. Parker in Boston. Russell asked him if he thought it would be possible to set up a meeting with Parker if he'd travel to Boston.

"I wish I could write metaphors and similes like Pat Conroy and dialogue like Robert B. Parker," said Russell. Who wouldn't?

He showed me a letter he had written to Conroy. In it, he wrote, "I realize that me talking to you as though I'm a writer is something akin to you telling Michael Jordan that you have also played basketball." He went on to tell Conroy that "I couldn't carry your jock, excuse me, your pen." Conroy had to enjoy Russell's confession. They would enjoy each other's company.

Russell was always popular with the writers who covered the Steelers. He confesses that he enjoyed the company of writers like Phil Musick and Pat Livingston and liked to talk to them. In that respect, he reminded me of Jim Bouton, the Yankees' pitcher who wrote "Ball Four." I knew Bouton when I covered the Yankees in the early '70s, and he often kept company with writers covering the club.

When Roy Blount Jr. of *Sports Illustrated* spent the 1973 season with the Steelers to write the celebrated insider's book, "About Three Bricks Shy of a Load," Russell recalls that he and his buddy Ray Mansfield visited Blount in his apartment atop Mt. Washington. (Many people credit me for writing that book, and Rocky Bleier's book, *Fighting Back*, but I have to inform those folks that Roy Blount Jr. and Terry O'Neill are the respective authors.)

"I thought I could learn something from these writers," said Russell, "and I guess I was always interested in writing."

Russell also corresponded with Pete Gent, the former Dallas Cowboys receiver known best for his controversial tell-all novel about life in the NFL, *North Dallas Forty*. In that one, Gent populated his stories with homosexuals and drug addicts. "That was never my experience," said Russell, "but I loved the book just the same. We drank lots of beer and cheeseburgers in my day. That's how we got our highs." Russell said Gent embellished every aspect of what goes on in pro football. He said Gent told him he should write a novel about things he experienced in pro ball. "You have to write fiction in order to tell the truth," Gent told Russell. "You just give the characters different names."

Russell was wearing a pale blue dress shirt, open at the collar, which brought out the blue in his bright eyes, and went well with his close-cropped white hair. He had ordered lunch from a deli shop in the lobby at Dominion Tower, and his receptionist, Farrell Manuel, was gracious enough to bring it to us. Russell's significant other, Cindy Ellis, also stopped by to say hello. It was March 17, 2003, and I was spending lunchtime on St. Patrick's Day with a Scot. I had a turkey sandwich. Russell was eating fresh cut fruit and cottage cheese. No wonder he's trimmed down so much from his playing days. He hardly touched the plateful of potato chips in the center of the table.

> *"When given an assignment, I carry it out to completion, my five senses lit up in concentration. I believe with all my heart that athletics is one of the finest preparations for most of the intricacies and darkness a human life can throw at you."*
> — **Pat Conroy, author**
> ***My Losing Season***

When we had finished eating, he brought a huge reference book that contains profiles of every player in the history of pro football. It's called *Total Football: The Official Encyclopedia of the National Football League*. It had data on my good friend Bill Priatko, of North Braddock, Pennsylvania and Pitt, who played as a reserve for the Steelers in 1955, and went to camp with the Browns and Packers. That was it; but he's in there. "Everybody's in there," related Russell.

He also disclosed that he was taking Gent's advice, and was at work on a novel, more about his adventures away from football, rather than about his life with the Steelers. "Did you know there was a story making the rounds in town that I met Osama bin Laden in one of my early business dealings in the Mideast?" said Russell. "It's possible. I know for a fact that bin Laden was a student intern with one of the companies we dealt with over there. I went to a party at one of the owners' homes, and it's possible that bin Laden might have been there. Maybe I can work something like that into my book."

"Frenchy and I were in the trivia section."

Only the day before, Russell had appeared at an autograph signing session at a shopping mall in Chantilly, Virginia, a suburb of Washington, D.C. He was there with six other Steelers, Terry Bradshaw, Joe Greene, Franco Harris, Jack Lambert, Rocky Bleier and Frenchy Fuqua. Those seven Steelers were *the* show for that Sunday. Russell picked up $2,000 for his services, and his contract called for him to sign 500 autographs. "Lambert keeps track of how many he signs," joked Russell. "He gets a bonus if he signs more than he contracts for." Russell said he and Fuqua were on the low end of the pay scale for such gatherings. "They had already sold out all the tickets for Bradshaw when I got there," said Russell. "Frenchy and I were in the 'trivia section' of the lineup. He was the other guy involved in The Immaculate Reception and I was the other linebacker who played with Ham and Lambert."

Russell also took advantage of the opportunity to visit his brother, Will, in Washington D.C. while he was in the neighborhood.

Russell was intrigued with the idea that the Steelers were such a draw in Washington, D.C. "Can you imagine having seven Redskins signing autographs at South Hills Village?" he asked. "How do you think that would draw? They had lines for three hours for us."

Earlier in the month of March, Russell had rounded up some former Steelers for a dinner for members at the Duquesne Club in downtown Pittsburgh. Russell has belonged to the Duquesne Club, frequented by the city's business leaders and CEO types, for over 20 years. It's only two blocks from his office.

> *"Athletics provide some of the richest fields of both metaphor and cliché to measure our lives against the intrusions and aggressions of other people."*
> — Pat Conroy, author *My Losing Season*

Photos by Jim O'Brien

ndy Russell and Chuck Noll meet at Mel
lount Youth Home Celebrity Roast to
onor Joe Greene.

Jack Ham, above, doesn't have a bigger
booster than Andy Russell, who helped
mentor him when he first reported from
Penn State in strong 1971 draft class.

Two of the regular participants in Andy Russell's Celebrity Golf Classic for
Children are former teammate Glen "Pine" Edwards, left, and former Kansas
City Chiefs' Hall of Fame linebacker Bobby Bell. Russell and Bell went on a
UFO-sponsored tour of Vietnam during the conflict there.

Among those in attendance at that dinner were Mike Tomczak, Randy Grossman, Tunch Ilkin, Craig Wolfley, Mike Wagner, Todd Kalas, Bruce Van Dyke, Edmund Nelson and Louis Lipps. My wife Kathie and I had been to a party hosted by Russell at the Duquesne Club the month before to treat patrons for the 27th Annual Andy Russell Celebrity Classic. That two-day event was set for mid-May at The Club at Nevillewood and Chartiers Country Club. Some of those same Steelers were in attendance that night, too.

"I tried to get some other Steelers for that reunion at the Duquesne Club," said Russell, "but Lynn Swann, Franco Harris, Joe Greene, Rocky Bleier and Jack Ham all had speaking engagements somewhere that same night. Those guys are still in great demand.

"If somebody had told me back in 1976 that I'd be going to a sports memorabilia show and signing autographs in 2003 I'd have thought they were absolutely out of their mind. I wasn't even invited to them in 1976."

Russell believes, by the way, that the Steelers' best team was the 1976 edition, even though they didn't win the Super Bowl. Too many of the Steelers' offensive stars were sidelined when they lost to a very good Oakland Raiders team 24-7 in the AFC title game. Russell says it's also important, when comparing clubs, to talk about the teams before the rules were changed that dramatically changed the way players could function on defense. The Steelers recorded five shutouts in their last eight games in 1976, and surrendered only one touchdown in their last nine games of the schedule.

Some believe that Russell is one of the former Steelers who rate inclusion in the Pro Football Hall of Fame. He and defensive back Jack Butler would have to be voted in by the veterans' committee that considers players from an earlier period. L.C. Greenwood and Donnie Shell are still under consideration by the Hall of Fame media selection committee.

Russell says there are several other linebackers that merit membership, but have been overlooked as well. He cited Chris Hanburger of the Redskins, who played in nine Pro Bowls, Chuck Howley of the Cowboys, who was in six Pro Bowls and was a Super Bowl MVP, Maxie Baughan of the Rams and Redskins, who played in nine Pro Bowls. Randy Gradishar of the Broncos is on the current ballot. Russell has endorsed his candidacy. Russell remains one of only 75 players in NFL history who went to seven or more Pro Bowls. He made it before the Steelers got good, and that's even more of an accomplishment.

He spoke about the decline in players' ability to make tackles. He said they don't want to scrimmage or practice tackling because they don't want anyone getting hurt that way. "People should watch film to see how Mike Wagner made tackles," he said. "He wrapped his arms around people's legs and held on for dear life. He knew how to bring them down. Now they're trying to get on Sports Center or that night's highlights with a big hit. They're trying to take out people rather than tackle them."

We also spoke about some of the Steelers who dominated the news over the past year, namely Tommy Maddox, Terry Bradshaw and Mike Webster. The comeback stories of Maddox and Bradshaw delighted all Steelers' fans, and the tragic tale of Webster, who died at age 50, saddened all.

As much as the death of Webster was worrisome, the death of Sophea Spanos Zaccharias of Mt. Lebanon during the previous Christmas season hit home even harder with Russell.

She was the wife of Sam Zaccharias, a long-time friend and partner in many ventures with Russell. She was 60 when she died. I had seen her in the Dominion Tower a week before she died. I was there to sign copies of my books in the lobby during the holiday season. She entered the lobby looking so great. She was dressed so nicely; she looked so vibrant. She gave me a kiss on the cheek and a holiday greeting. We had been in some of the same English and Spanish classes during our student days at Pitt. She had been the valedictorian of her class at Braddock High. Coming from Braddock she could appreciate a guy from Hazelwood. She always made a fuss about what I was doing as a writer. Moments later, I spotted Sam coming through the same lobby. I told him that Sophea was already upstairs at Russell's office, looking for him. A few days later, she died of an aggressive infection. It hurt. It could happen to anyone; it could happen to my wife. That's why it was so difficult to accept. "She always watched what she ate," related Russell, "and she took good care of herself. She didn't smoke or drink, or anything like that. She was such a good person. It was unreal. This was a tremendous blow for Sam. He's been like a brother to me, so I feel his pain."

Andy Russell:
I watched with great surprise when Kordell Stewart was struggling early. After a Pro Bowl and team MVP season, you didn't expect this to happen. You thought he'd continue to play well. You didn't think he'd be replaced unless he was hurt. Then he throws three interceptions in a quarter and you knew that was unacceptable. I could have done that well. Then, after they lost their second game, Bill Cowher announced that if Kordell had difficulty in the next game he'd have to turn to Tommy Maddox. And that's what he did when Kordell bombed again. It was courageous of Cowher to make the switch, all things considered.

When Maddox came in, he had nothing to lose. He just started throwing the ball. He moved them in for a touchdown, and he looked good. When you're an old-school defensive player like I was it's hard to watch what they do today. It's so different now. They let the offensive linemen use their hands,

> *"One thing leads to another."*
> **— John McPhee on writing stories**

instead of making them keep their fists folded to their chests, and they won't let the defensive backs bump and run anymore. Even so, the defenses are so good, the quarterbacks don't have a lot of time to throw the ball.

That's what worries you about Maddox over the long haul. He's not as mobile as Kordell, and he can't escape a good pass rush. Plus, there's concern about his ability to take the big hits. But he's a more accurate thrower than Kordell, for sure, and he hits the receivers on the break. They've got a good corps of receivers in Plaxico Burress, Hines Ward, Atwaan Randle El, Terance Mathis and Lee Mays. They don't throw the ball much to the tight end, but Mark Bruener and Jerame Tuman can both catch it. They seem to prefer Maddox because he gets the ball to them faster and more on the mark. It had to be a difficult situation, though, because I'm sure some of them liked Kordell, too, and wanted to see him in there.

Sometimes Maddox throws the ball up for grabs, hoping his receiver can go up and get it, but Bradshaw did that, too, when he had Swann and Stallworth. And it worked. Maddox can look bad, too, when he gets intercepted too much.

Maddox seemed like one of those classic coming-out-of-nowhere stories. He had been a high draft choice, No. 1 with the Denver Broncos, coming out early from a high profile program like UCLA. He was supposed to replace John Elway. There were unbelievable expectations.

It didn't work out there, and he bounced around the NFL. Then he was in the Arena Football League, and the XFL, and he never gave up. He was out of football for a few years, selling insurance, but he jumped at the chance to come back. He never gave up on himself. It's one of those unbelievable stories about a guy hanging in there.

He was still chasing his dream even though the odds were stacked against him. He had a great attitude. He still loved the game. It wasn't about the money. I liked his comments. He always seemed to know how to deflect ego issues. I thought Kordell did a great job in that respect after he was replaced in the starting lineup. I thought he was very supportive of Tommy.

I'll be interested to see how Tommy Maddox does next year. It will be interesting to see how much time he has to throw now that they've lost some offensive linemen. You get one hole and you can be in trouble. The opponents will all attack that spot. In the '70s, we didn't have any holes.

"I hope I run out of breath and money at the same time."
— Bobby Layne, Hall of Fame
Pittsburgh Steelers (1958-1962)

"I'm glad Terry did this."

My reaction to the "Terry Bradshaw comes back to Pittsburgh" story was that I thought it was a genuine mea culpa. We're all getting older. As you get older, you realize you have to make amends, and ask people to forgive you, and you have to forgive them. I'm glad Terry did this. I thought his remarks were heartfelt and genuine.

When he came back for that Monday night game with the Patriots at Heinz Field I heard the concessionaires lost about $250,000 in sales at halftime. No one left their seats. They all stayed to see Terry take the field. It was great. I thought it was cute that he took his daughters out on the field with him. He said he didn't think the crowd would boo them.

I saw him a lot during the weekend when he was in town for the Dapper Dan dinner and luncheon. I felt the need to apologize to him as well. I had dressed him down a few times in the locker room after games. I came up with guys like Ernie Stautner and Myron Pottios and they didn't think you should ever take your helmet off, or play to the crowd. You never got carried off on a stretcher and came back in the same half to throw a touchdown pass. Terry did that sort of thing too much to suit some of us veterans.

After one instance when we thought he had flagrantly played to the crowd, I announced in the locker room afterward that Terry Bradshaw deserved an Oscar for the acting performance of the year. I know I embarrassed him. What did I know about what to do? We were always lecturing those young guys, but, with the exception of my first year (1963) with the Steelers, we never had a winning team. Bradshaw got back at me by saying he couldn't learn anything from us guys, that we were all a bunch of drunks. Yeah, he said that. We had this old-school philosophy that you played hurt, and you never played to the crowd. And yet we weren't winning. I think I was insensitive to his feelings. I think I hurt his feelings as a young player.

Terry makes about $35,000 an hour now. (He made $50,000 when he came to Pittsburgh to speak to Hoddy Hanna's group at Hanna Real Estate Services shortly before he came in for the Dapper Dan dinner.) So I don't expect him to come back here too often. I've invited him to come to my golf tournament, but he declined. I think it's good if he comes back on occasion, when his schedule permits.

"He became very reclusive."

As for Mike Webster, I think it's a tragedy that Mike had the problems he had. I don't know the cause for his problems, and I don't know what caused him to be angry with the Steelers.

221

He came in here one time seeking capital for one of his projects. He brought in his partners with him. We turned him down. We see a lot of people looking for money to underwrite their business plans, and we didn't think his venture was going to be a winner. We thought his partners were nice enough people, but we didn't think they had the business background to succeed. We may have misjudged a good business opportunity. But I heard he lost all his money. That's not being judgmental. A lot of smart people around this country are losing money these days.

I don't know what caused him to adopt a negative attitude toward a lot of us. He became very reclusive and did not participate in team reunions. He put off people like Tunch Ilkin and Craig Wolfley who wanted to help him. They wanted to support him and help him.

I was in my 12th year when he came in to training camp the first time. I recognized that we had this young stallion who was going to take only two years to take away my buddy's job. Ray Mansfield was our starting center, but he saw it coming. He knew he couldn't hold off Webster very long.

I thought he died so young. He was so unhappy with his lot in life, after all those hours and so many people in Pittsburgh who loved him.

It's hard to know how much his head injuries figured in what became of him. I had ten concussions in my career. I filled out some interview forms for the NFL for a study they are doing about that. Concussions are regarded as a much more serious matter these days.

In our day, guys used to joke about them. They talked about getting dinged, and you were expected to get back in the lineup sooner than later. It was like being a fighter. You took tremendous blows to the head. If you put your head in front of Jim Brown's knee when he was running the ball there was no punch that explosive.

As far as players running into problems with their money, I used to be asked by Dan Rooney to come in each year and talk to the players about how to manage their finances and stuff like that.

But the players didn't like what I had to say. I told them to get rid of the fancy cars and fancy clothes and not to open a restaurant. They stopped having me. No one wanted to hear what I had to say.

> *"There are teams named Smith, and teams named Grabowski . . . we're Grabowskis."*
> — Mike Ditka, during his days as coach of the Chicago Bears

Jack Lambert followed my advice, and now he can do whatever he wants to do, and he's got a young family. He was careful with his money. No matter how much money you make — and they're making so much more money now than what we did — you still have to be careful with it.

Mike Webster was making big money compared to what we were making. Yet he lost it all. That's a shame.

> "There is no teacher more discriminating or transforming than loss. The great secret of athletics is that you can learn more from losing than winning . . . If I could bring us a national championship, I would not do it . . . My team taught me there could be more courage and dignity and humanity in loss."
> — Pat Conroy in *My Losing Season*

Jim O'Brien

Andy Russell is host to Coach Chuck Noll and Chuck Puskar at Andy's annual golf outing at The Club at Nevillewood on May 16, 2003. Puskar was a partner with Russell's dear friend Ray Mansfield for many years in a Canonsburg-based insurance firm.

Mike Wagner
Watchful eye on North Shore

"This town treats us well."

Mike Wagner always looks like he has just come away from the barber shop or a hair styling salon. He always looks like he's dressed for a job interview. In short, his hair and tie are always perfectly in place, along with his smile and sense of humor. His mustache is always trimmed just so. He favors pale blue shirts that set off his bright blue eyes. He's handsome and smiles like he knows it.

No matter how he dresses, however, people who are meeting him for the first time can't believe he once played ball for the Pittsburgh Steelers. He doesn't look big enough or rugged enough. He's quick to point out that, at six feet and a half-inch, 200 pounds, he is bigger than all of the contemporary Steelers' defensive backs, save Chad Scott. They're the same size. He's taller than Troy Polamalu, the 5-10, 206-pound Samoan safety from Southern Cal the Steelers selected with their first pick in the 2003 draft.

"They always say, 'You must have been much bigger when you played,' but I haven't dropped that much weight," said Wagner.

Wagner was considered one of the best and smartest defensive backs during his ten-year stint with the Steelers (1971-1980), and he has four Super Bowl rings in his collection. He played strong safety and weak safety.

He was more of a hard-hitter and sure-handed tackler than any one of the present-day DBs. His friend and former teammate Andy Russell says today's Steelers' defensive backs ought to study film of Wagner to see how to wrap up a ballcarrier's legs with proper tackling technique. Wagner was tough, too. He made a tremendous comeback in 1978 after fracturing three neck vertebrae in the third game of the 1977 season against the Cleveland Browns. He also overcame painful hip ailments and surgical procedures to return to play.

When he talks about those glory days when he was a knight in shining armor he does so with a wink and whimsical comments. Yet the pride and assuredness in his ability is always there, firmly stamped with black and gold italic type. This is a man who never doubted he would make the team in the first place, and he started from the first game of his rookie season and couldn't be displaced.

He appreciates pals who want to promote him for induction in the Pro Football Hall of Fame, but knows his place, maybe a notch or two below Mel Blount and Donnie Shell. He also knows that he and Ron Johnson, John Rowser, Glen Edwards and J.T. Thomas, along with the linebackers and linemen made their contributions to the success of "The Steel Curtain" defensive unit. J.T. Thomas thinks their

Mike Wagner is flanked by Marianne Noll and Becky Bolden at black-tie Mel Blount Youth Home Celebrity Roast at Pittsburgh Hilton on May 30, 2003.

Two of the Steelers' all-time greatest defensive backs, Glen "Pine" Edwards and Mike Wagner, are reunited at Andy Russell's Celebrity Classic for Children at The Club at Nevillewood.   **Photos by Jim O'Brien**

names ought to be mentioned on some of those other guys' Hall of Fame plaques. Chuck Noll always spoke of the Steelers' synergy — that the whole was greater than the sum of its parts.

It's easy to be comfortable in the company of Michael R. Wagner, the pride of Waukegan, Illinois. He's smart, for starters, so he has something worthwhile to say. He was nearing his 55th birthday, so he was old enough to reminisce. The gray in his hair certified that. He's thoughtful, and pauses to reflect on a question before he answers it. He's generous with his opinions — and admits to having plenty of them — but he also knows when to keep quiet. He'll smile off a question he doesn't want to answer. Coach Noll would be proud of his wisdom and wit and knowing when to say nothing. He'll discuss some issues off the record. Noll never does that.

"It would be heresy for any ex-Steeler to say anything critical of their experience here," said Wagner for openers at one meeting. "This town treats us well. I like being a loyal ex-player."

Becky Bolden, his significant other, is a personal trainer and she makes sure that Mike looks good in every respect before he leaves their home in Sewickley. She makes sure his colors are coordinated. When I've seen her, at Andy Russell's get-togethers at the Duquesne Club or The Club at Nevillewood, she always looks splendid as well.

Mike Wagner and I had meetings in January and March of 2003 at his offices on the seventh floor of the historic D.L. Clark Building on the city's North Side, now promoted and known as the North Shore. It's the building where they once made Clark Bars, a candy that was as much a part of Pittsburgh as the pickles and ketchup of the nearby H.J. Heinz Co. along the Allegheny River.

The Clark Building once had the famous Clark Bar sign atop its roof. That has been replaced by a *Trib* sign, as the *Pittsburgh Tribune-Review* offices are now housed in the renovated office complex. The Clark Bar sign is now on view above a parking lot across the street from the building.

Mike's office is on the seventh floor. You have to take the elevator to the sixth floor and walk up a flight of stairs to the seventh floor. He works for the H.T. Capital Markets division of Hefren-Tillotson, Inc. His boss, Bill Tillotson, is a big fan of the Steelers and all things Pittsburgh. You're as likely to find Bill at Heinz Hall or the Duquesne Club as Heinz Field and PNC Park.

Mike Wagner has a degree in accounting from Western Illinois University in 1971, the year he was an 11th round draft choice of the Steelers, and an MBA from the University of Pittsburgh, which he obtained in 1988. He has the credentials and carriage to play the part in the world of high finance. Martindale Street doesn't resemble Wall Street, but Wagner can walk both with equal aplomb and confidence.

Both of our most recent interviews were conducted at the end of a long table in the even longer conference room that faces toward the downtown Pittsburgh skyline. It's quite a view from there. The Clark Building overlooks a large parking lot where Three Rivers Stadium once stood. When Wagner looks out the windows, he can still see Three Rivers Stadium. To the right is Heinz Field. To the left is PNC Park. Like Dwight White, Wagner believes it was the Steelers' success in the '70s, and the Pirates' success during the same span that is responsible for the new sports venues being in place on the North Shore. "It will be exciting to see what this place ends up looking like," ventured Wagner.

The Clark Building is located between those ballparks and near other North Side landmarks such as St. Peter's Church — the Rooneys' house of worship — West Park and the Pittsburgh Aviary, the venerable ice ball stand of Stella and Gus Kalaris, Children's Museum, Divine Providence Hospital, Allegheny General Hospital and Community College of Allegheny County. The appearance of that ice-ball stand signals that summer is coming nearly as much as the opening of Kennywood Park.

The Steelers and Pirates are responsible for developing the area around their ballparks. That task has been turned over to Continental Real Estate, the Columbus-based development firm responsible for The Waterfront complex along the Monongahela River in Homestead.

There were plans on the drawing boards for a 5,600-seat open-air amphitheater for concerts, apartments, offices and shops. The amphitheater was scheduled to open May 1, 2004, according to Art Rooney II, vice-president of the Steelers. It will be a "destination point" in the jargon of civic planners.

All of those things were already in place on the city's South Side, but that didn't seem to deter anyone from duplicating such a complex. Some civic leaders who were part of the think tank process thought the best plan would be to leave the area as it is, with much-needed parking space. There is office space available in the Clark Building and the Cardello Building near the West End Bridge, yet there's a belief that more office buildings are needed in that neighborhood. No one appreciates a consultant who says the best plan would be to leave well enough alone. When it comes to the South Side and North Side or North Shore, some sound as if they're talking about South Dakota and North Dakota or Braddock and North Braddock.

Then again, based on conversations I have had with many sports enthusiasts, I think the majority of Steelers' fans would be happier and contented in their same seats in a renovated football-only Three Rivers Stadium, and Pitt fans in a renovated Pitt Stadium on the campus of the University of Pittsburgh. That's my sermon for this chapter.

The park along the Allegheny River was being spruced up, and bars and restaurants and office buildings were appearing on their own. Alcoa had moved its headquarters to a new building on the North Shore and more were expected to follow. The Carnegie Science Center was being expanded and renovated.

The new David L. Lawrence Convention Center and Renaissance Hotel were among the beautiful buildings in sight from Wagner's window. Andy Russell had a view of the same area from across the river from his office on the 31st floor of the Dominion Tower.

Dwight White and Randy Grossman both were doing well in high finance/investment related businesses as well in Centre City Towers and Oxford Centre, two other midtown skyscrapers.

Wagner is proud of their successes. "It's your family; you might fight to defend them to the outside," said Wagner. "Sportswriters are always trying to find out what really happened behind closed doors, but I believe some of that stuff is best kept behind closed doors. The media love people who talk. There are some Steelers who will speak out on any subject you might want to introduce. The media loves those guys. I prefer to remember all my teammates at their best."

Wagner and Russell both believe that what they were doing was so complex, yet so simple, that they often confused their own coaches. It's too deep, they think, for any mere sportswriter to comprehend or appreciate. At least they smile when they say things like that. They didn't have me in mind anyhow.

Wagner and I also had lunch at Legends of the North Shore, a wonderful restaurant on North Avenue next to Allegheny General Hospital. There are pictures on the walls of many local legends. The restaurant is patronized by Pat and Dan Rooney, among other North Side legends. The Rooneys brought Marianne and Chuck Noll there to dine in early May, 2003. Wagner presented owner Dan Bartow with a signed portrait of himself for his Hall of Fame collection. The photos of Joe Greene, Jack Lambert, Mel Blount, Terry Bradshaw and, of course, Art Rooney inspired story-telling. North Siders honored there include the late Baldy Regan and Tom Forster, Dan McCann, Jerry Bergman, Richie McCabe, Don Graham and Bill Baierl.

"Real fans don't leave games early."

Mike Wagner:

All of us former Steelers, especially those from the '70s, are treated as treasures in this town. This community treats us well, and the Steelers treat us well. There's an employer-employee relationship that remains and you respect it. Overall, it has all turned out well.

We're role models now, for the players and for the fans. I'm a tough fan, a demanding fan myself now, but I don't want to get up on a pedestal and tell today's players what they ought to be doing. The fans have been great, but sometimes they are too demanding. Real fans should stick with their teams, no matter the outcome of a contest.

Real fans don't leave games early.

228

Some of our fans used to get upset with us, and say nasty things, even when we won. If we didn't beat the point spread they were upset with us. They invested more money than they should have in a bet and now they're mad at us for letting them down. Now you're a jerk. You can't believe some of the things I overheard fans telling Terry Bradshaw when we'd be out somewhere after a game. Now that we're older, and not playing anymore, the fans are kinder when they see us. Now we can do nothing wrong in their eyes.

I have little patience with people who are just as critical when they go to their own children's sports contests. People have to learn to step back and be fans. Too many people try to be coaches, referees and parents at the same time. It's impossible to pull that off well. Too many fans think they are participants in sports events these days, and the media — mostly television — encourages that. Everybody wants to be up on the big screen. There I go getting myself in trouble with the media. . .

I'm a big believer in the importance of sportsmanship. And that's been absent in too many games that go on these days. That's what I talk about when I'm invited to speak at sports banquets or luncheons. At the end of the game, the game is fought and won or lost on the field. It's not about what town is best and what town sucks. When it's all over, fans from Cleveland or Baltimore or Buffalo should be able to mingle with Steelers' fans in the parking lot and have fun in each other's company. They shouldn't be shouting at or insulting one another. That's not what sports are supposed to be about. I'm very serious about this.

The fans might be surprised to see how us ex-Steelers enjoy seeing and spending time with guys who used to play for the Raiders, the Browns, the Colts and all of those teams. We see them at golf outings and social gatherings, and it's always great to see them. Coaches and players sit around yukking it up with these guys they used to go up against. We see them in a different light today than we did when we were fierce rivals. I always loved to play against the Bears, my boyhood team, but I don't see it that way anymore. I go to all kinds of games. It can be Pitt vs. Notre Dame, or some high school or grade school games, and I just enjoy them as sports contests. My message is that a true fan loves the sport.

If you're going to be the City of Champions you have to be champions in every respect. Going to a game should be an exciting experience. A minority behaves in an ugly manner and look at going to a game as an excuse to behave badly or to

> *"That's the function of enlightened journalism,*
> *to lead, to put in what ought to be."*
> — Henry Luce, Founder of Time-Life, Inc.

be rude to those around them. It should be good fun. I know Dan Rooney has talked to league officials about getting players to be more respectful of one another, on and off the field.

Jack Lambert used to say, "Nobody intimidates the Pittsburgh Steelers." We believed that. We strutted our stuff whenever we came out on the field in those days. But that attitude shouldn't carry over into the stands and the parking lots. The contest should be contested on the field.

I try to teach kids how to compete, and not to give up. To me, that's still fundamental. But I stress sportsmanship; that's important, too We were a comeback team when I played for the Steelers. Noll would not let us give up, or think that a game was over, that we weren't good enough that day. You have to respect that approach.

It's hard to determine how players are performing. Who's overachieving? Who's underachieving? Who's good enough to determine that? Noll did not believe in pep talks to motivate people. We had people who were driven. He taught us ways to do it better.

"Noll was trying to put together a team."

Quarterbacks have always been the most marked men among the Steelers. I'm sure it's that way in every city. People love quarterback controversies. In our day, you had Terry Hanratty, Joe Gilliam and Terry Bradshaw, and you had Neil O'Donnell and Bubby Brister, and more recently you had Kordell Stewart and Mike Tomczak and then this year you had Kordell Stewart and Tommy Maddox.

When Hanratty came here, he was an instant favorite. He was from Notre Dame and nearby Butler. It was like having Joe Montana or Danny Marino playing for the Steelers.

Noll was trying to put together a team. He's thinking here's a guy who has brains and athletic ability, and he comes from Notre Dame. He was a winner; he had led Notre Dame to a national championship during his college career. He had a wonderful pedigree. He was a good guy, a leader. All he needed was some tools around him.

Then the Steelers drafted this Bradshaw guy. Bradshaw was better physically. He's the Golden Boy as far as throwing the football and running over people. When Noll picked Bradshaw to be the quarterback, he struggled. Bradshaw had all the raw ability, like Kordell, but he struggled just the same. Maddox has come in and showed that he could be more successful in getting things accomplished than Kordell did. So you had a split among the fans as to who should be the No. 1 guy.

Terry Hanratty fell behind, but he couldn't go elsewhere. We were slaves, indentured servants in those days. You couldn't sign with another team if that was in your best interest. Joe Gilliam got a chance, too. We had three quarterbacks who all had great ability. You had fans, players, coaches, the Rooneys all thinking one of the three should be the main guy. Quarterbacks come under a great deal of scrutiny. Some of the struggles Joe Gilliam had later on, some believe, can be traced back to his disappointment in Pittsburgh. Who knows?

"Players don't want a reason not to play."

I liked the Tommy Maddox story. I wasn't surprised he came back to play so soon after he was knocked out in Tennessee. That's the way athletes are. There's no pain involved most times after you've recovered from a concussion. You just get knocked out. It's not like the pain you have when you suffer a separated shoulder, for instance. You wouldn't play football if you weren't a risk-taker. If you get hurt you're going to get back in there as soon as you're able. Sometimes sooner.

Players don't want a reason not to play. Some are told they should quit because the risk is too great. That's what happened to Tim Lewis, the Steelers' defensive coordinator, when he was playing for the Green Bay Packers. He suffered a career-ending neck injury (in the fourth game of the 1986 season). That's what happened to Al Toon in New York, and Merril Hoge in Chicago and Troy Aikman in Dallas.

It's difficult for doctors to determine whether you should or should not continue to play football. Everybody played hurt when I was with the Steelers. Tommy's not really playing hurt.

I used to spend my off-seasons tumbling down ski runs in the mountains of Colorado. That was a risk, too. But I knew when it was time for me to step aside. The Steelers wanted me to continue playing, but the injuries had started to pile up on me, and I knew it was time to walk away.

If you're a fan of football, Tommy Maddox is a great story. This is role model stuff. He's a poster boy for persevering, hanging in there. His story is the stuff of movies and books.

I'm not an expert anymore. I get to sit up in one of the boxes and watch the offense and defense perform. I think Tommy believes in himself. He's not the athlete that Kordell Stewart is, but he seems to understand the game better. Some guys are great athletes, and some guys are smarter than others, and it's nice if you can have a guy who is both. That's rare. Maddox is more of a drop-back quarterback, and he can put the ball on the money. I'm sure the receivers like the way he hits them on the break, and just as they get open. The ball's there. He's not nearly as mobile as Kordell, and he can be vulnerable to a good pass rush. The Steelers' offensive line will have to hold their blocks and keep Maddox healthy.

All quarterbacks make mistakes. I played in the defensive secondary and we did a lot of things to screw up a lot of quarterbacks. We disguised our defenses, and our blitzes.

Tommy has good targets. Plaxico (Burress) has tremendous tools, it's obvious. Plaxico could be a superstar. He just needs to be a tougher player and more consistent. Harold Carmichaels and Kenny Burroughs were both big receivers who used their size to their benefit. Hines Ward doesn't have that size, but he's willing to do anything to win. He'll run across the middle and make the tough catch. He'll block people. He tears up some defensive backs. He'll do anything to win. He's enjoying himself. They can go to Randle El. They're looking for mismatches. Randle El is an exciting player. He not only can catch the ball, but he's a threat to break a long run every time he touches the ball. He can make tremendous big plays. He can't weigh more than 175 pounds, though, and people could hurt him. On the other hand, Hines Ward looks like he's really strong.

Tommy Maddox is really good at reading defenses. He's more like a Brian Sipe or a Kenny Stabler in that respect. If you didn't put pressure on those guys, they'd pick you apart. They're so accurate. Tommy Maddox can really throw a football.

When I was playing, we were always trying to beat up the quarterbacks. They'd be bleeding from the chin by the end of the game.

"It's all about performing."

I think this team has been humbled from time to time. Sometimes they have to eat their own words. We came out of the school that we beat people on the scoreboard, not in the media. Maybe it's been a good experience for this team to lose some of these big games.

We had a sufficient amount of players who thought they were really, really good. But they kept it under wraps for the most part. I hate to see a Rooney team not win, but it reminds people of what a tremendous thing we accomplished in the '70s. We won four Super Bowls in six years. We never lost a Super Bowl.

232

They spent a lot of money here in recent years to put a lot of firepower out on the field in coaching and in players. It's kind of a curse. The Rooneys know what it takes to put a winner on the field. That's what they want. They are not satisfied with anything less.

Leadership is important. I think the concept of leaders is really incorrect. The media identifies certain guys as being leaders. The captains are not necessarily good leaders. Most people thought Jack Lambert was the leader of the defense. Jack was an emotional guy, for sure, and he was very expressive. He was always hollering at somebody. Joe Greene was considered a leader. But Dwight White was a leader, too, just by the way he played. And don't tell me that Jack Ham — who never said anything — wasn't a leader. Donnie Shell was a leader. Whoever the leader was he was leading a bunch of leaders. Sometimes Ernie Holmes was the anchor of the defensive line. In other words, there wasn't one guy we were all rallying around. We fed off each other. Players get in trouble, looking for something to say. Sometimes they point fingers, and that's never productive. At the end of the day, it's all about performing. Some people are motivated by screaming, some by pats on the butt. Some don't need motivation.

"Mike was always working harder."

I remember Mike Webster going into the weight room after games and lifting weights. You could hear the clanging through the walls. We were thinking about where we were going for dinner or a party. But you could tell Mike wasn't worrying about that. He'd come in the locker room and he'd still be wearing his weight-lifting belt.

You have to think about what you want out of life. Mike was always working harder, always striving harder. Mike had a hard time separating himself from football.

I don't know if that gave us an edge or what. We weren't the only team lifting weights. There were big guys on other teams. It's part of the legend. It's a good story. We have this reputation for being one of the first teams to really stress weightlifting and conditioning.

Our offensive linemen cut off their sleeves and taped their jerseys to their shoulder pads. It allowed everybody to see how big their arms were. They did it so defensive linemen couldn't grab and hold them by the jersey. Nobody in our defensive line was in on that, and look how strong they were.

> *"The journey of life is not paved in blacktop;*
> *it is not brightly lit, and it has no road signs.*
> *It is a rocky path through the wilderness."*
> — Scott Peck,
> *Further Along The Road Less Traveled*

We had a weight coach and a weight program. The offensive line made it their thing. It gave them an identity. If I had to do it all over again I wouldn't have lifted weights any more than I did. I even had a rack of weights in my house in Colorado. Most of our defensive backs did what they were asked to regarding weightlifting, but they weren't crazy about it. There were different views about its effectiveness.

Chuck Noll was against bodybuilding. If he saw anyone was doing bodybuilding he'd put a stop to it. Hey, football is not all about strength. Chuck thought leverage was more important. Chuck would tell players how he wanted them to lift weights.

"When Terry threw the ball, it came in whistling."

Terry Bradshaw was an ugly duckling when he first got here, but he's a beautiful swan now. Terry was just a country boy when he came here. Look at him now. There were great expectations for him, and he struggled to live up to them in the beginning. People were picking on Terry for a while. This can be a tough sports town.

This is a winner's town. Whether Terry burned bridges here or not, it is time to forget that. Pittsburgh has learned how important he was to our team. Terry's a funny guy; he's as silly as can be. People all over the United States think he's a real hoot. He loves being silly? Who is Terry close to on our team?

I know he's had some difficulties in his family life, going through three marital break-ups. I'm familiar with how difficult a divorce can be. If Terry's your friend, though, he's your friend for life. I think it's important for Terry to come back and to make amends.

Terry has proven himself. He's accomplished so much, and he's surprised so many people. No one — except Terry and his dad perhaps — ever thought this guy was going to win four Super Bowls. And I don't think we do that without Terry. That's all anyone should care about. It's the same way with Chuck Noll. He didn't get the same respect as people like Vince Lombardi, Bill Parcells, Hank Stram, Tom Landry, but he directed his team to four Super Bowl victories.

Terry threw the most beautiful passes I ever saw. He may not have always called the right play or did the right thing, but there were not many quarterbacks who threw the ball as beautifully as he did. Danny Marino may have had a quicker release, and Joe Montana and John Unitas did some special things — you see all the highlights — but none was better than Bradshaw at throwing the ball. I can see the ball floating through the air, those tightly thrown spirals, whistling down the field. Yes, you could actually hear the ball whistling. I hated to face Roger Staubach of the Cowboys, but I had to go against Terry Bradshaw every day at practice during training camp, and I loved it. During the season, the first team offense usually ran its plays against the second team defense. During the season, at the stadium, I usually played against Cliff Stoudt, Joe Gilliam and Mike Kruczek.

I've got just wonderful memories of Terry Bradshaw. He's the only quarterback I ever played against that when the ball came in it was whistling. It amazed me the way Swann and Stallworth were able to hold onto his passes. Lynn and John never wore gloves. Jim Smith wore rubber gloves, and he could hold his passes, too.

In my mind, I still see Terry Bradshaw throwing the best passes in the league. I can still hear them whizzing by.

George Gojkovich

Strong pursuit is demonstrated by Steelers' Jack Lambert (58), Jack Ham (59) and Mike Wagner (23) against Tampa Bay Buccaneers.

John Banaszak
Always a Marine

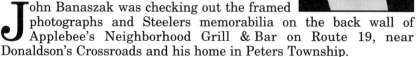

"I've never been a quitter."

John Banaszak was checking out the framed photographs and Steelers memorabilia on the back wall of Applebee's Neighborhood Grill & Bar on Route 19, near Donaldson's Crossroads and his home in Peters Township.

This was one of 13 Applebee's Restaurants in western Pennsylvania owned and operated by his former Steelers teammates Larry Brown and J.T. Thomas. Steelers from different eras were memorialized on this black and gold wall, with a Terrible Towel as a centerpiece. There was a framed No. 57 jersey, once worn by Sam Davis, who worked in sales at H.J. Heinz Co. (57 varieties) when he was with the team. Banaszak noted that jersey and pointed to a publicity montage that included Mel Blount and Gabe Rivera, among other Steelers.

"How can I think of Sam and Gabe and feel sorry for myself?" said Banaszak, his dark brown eyes shooting upward to punctuate his observation.

Sam Davis, who played guard on four Super Bowl winners, was in a rather modest personal care home somewhere in McKeesport. He was brain-damaged, a shadow of his old self. Gabe Rivera, who was left paralyzed by a head-on auto accident during his rookie season of 1983, was in a wheelchair somewhere in San Antonio. Rivera was intoxicated and driving in the wrong lane when he crashed into an oncoming car that had a STEELERS license plate on the front bumper. The fan survived the crash.

"Sam was such a beautiful guy," said Banaszak. "He was an inspiration for all of us free agents. Rivera was going to be a great defensive lineman. He had natural strength and speed. He could run. He was going to be a great player, I'm sure of that."

John Banaszak was merely between jobs. At age 52, he was trying to figure out what he wanted to do next. He had been unceremoniously fired in mid-December, 2002 as the head football coach at Washington & Jefferson College. He had a crew cut, looked in great shape, and could have passed for a Marine drill sergeant if he were wearing khakis.

His firing at W&J befuddled anybody who knew Banaszak or followed his football team. "He's been a winner in every way," said his friend and former teammate Mel Blount. "Somebody must've had it in for him." It was even stranger to the casual reader of the sports page. Banaszak had coached W&J to four championships in the Presidents' Athletic Conference (PAC) and a 38-9 record. He was respected as a former Steelers defensive lineman who had three Super Bowl rings in his jewelry box. He had not only been a big winner at W&J but had represented the school in a first-class manner. He was popular with his players and had been a positive influence on many of them. It seemed a shame, a loss for everyone. I always thought that W&J and Banaszak were a perfect pairing.

But Banaszak didn't want anyone feeling sorry for him.

Banaszak also recalled how he feared that he might lose a leg, even his life, back in the summer of 1995 because of a rare staph infection that flared up during a stay at Canonsburg Hospital. He checked in for knee surgery that he thought was a routine maintenance procedure and nearly died.

"It was the most pain I've ever experienced in my life," he said. "I'm telling them it's okay if they have to take off my leg if the pain would stop. They darn near did. So I've been a lucky man for a long time. When it was all over I was thankful to God that I was alive and able to walk on my own two legs. I was fortunate my body fought off the infection. It also points up that I'm a fighter. I'm going to fight for every last breath I take."

I had interviewed Banszak for an earlier book, "Steelers Forever," before his final season at W&J, and the handwriting was pretty much on the wall that his days at the Washington, Pa. campus were, indeed, numbered. There has been a change in administration at W&J and Banaszak wasn't on the same page, for whatever reasons, with the new president and new athletic director.

Because of this predicament, Banaszak had investigated other coaching opportunities, at Mercyhurst, California (Pa.) and Eastern Michigan, his alma mater. It was a Catch-22 situation. He loved W&J, but he knew his job was in jeopardy so he looked elsewhere just in case he needed a position.

"I went to Mercyhurst as a favor to a friend in Erie," said Banaszak. "I wanted to see what W&J's reaction would be."

As it turned out, his job search was cited by school officials as cause for his dismissal. "It created instability in our program," said W&J athletic director Rick Creehan. "His job searches the past couple of years left a cloud of uncertainty over the program. This allows us to gain control of the future of the program."

One of Banaszak's assistant coaches, offensive coordinator Mike Sirianni was named as his successor, signing a two-year contract.

Banaszak got off on the wrong foot when Creehan first came to W&J. Creehan had left behind a mess at Allegheny College, where a close friend of his had to be fired as the football coach for behavior unbecoming a college administrator. As they shook hands, according to a reliable source, Banaszak said to Creehan, "Don't come in here and screw up our football program like you did at Allegheny College."

It was hardly diplomatic of Banaszak to greet his new boss that way. He kept his distance during the remainder of his stay on the campus. But the handwriting was on the wall that he wouldn't remain long on the job. He was fired at season's end.

Banaszak thought there were two situations in the Pittsburgh area where he might fit in. His former boss, John Luckhardt, had been hired during the off-season as the head coach at California (Pa.), and would welcome John as a part-time assistant coach on his staff.

Banaszak said another possibility was joining Joe Walton and Dan Radakovich as a part-time assistant at Robert Morris University. Radakovich had coached Banaszak during an earlier stint as a Steelers' line coach under Chuck Noll. Walton, who had been a head coach with the New York Jets, also served as an assistant head coach to Noll in 1990-91, but Banaszak was gone by then.

Banaszak had worked in the business world prior to joining John Luckhardt as an assistant coach for four seasons, serving as defensive coordinator. Banaszak had started working with Luckhardt for two years as a volunteer assistant at W&J.

Several months after our initial interviews, Banaszak told me in a telephone conversation that he had taken a position in promotion, marketing, and sales with Iris Technologies in Greensburg.

"Somewhere, some day, I will be back on the sideline again," he said, assuredly. You hoped his confidence about landing such a job would be realized. In July, he said he was going to coach with Walton. Things were looking up at Robert Morris. They were building a new football stadium.

He wanted to stay in the area because his wife, Mary, was the executive director at Greenbriar Treatment Center, a personal reha-bilitation facility in Washington, Pa. She had been working there for 18 years, the last ten as CEO. That's why W&J College was the per-fect place for John. He seemed such a good fit for anyone assessing the situation from a distance. He said on several occasions that he would have been happy to remain coach at W&J for the rest of his career.

He believed in the school, its tradition, its academic reputation, its promise for young people. He didn't have a hard time selling W&J to anyone. New academic buildings were going up, more were on the drawing boards.

When things soured for him with his bosses, he also inquired about openings at the University of Pittsburgh and West Virginia University. Banaszak would seem to be an asset to either program. Walt Harris told him he chose another candidate instead, and told John he could understand how difficult that becomes. "You know how tough it is when you're down to two guys," Harris told him. John spoke to Rich Rodriguez at WVU, and expressed disappointment that Rodriguez never got back to him.

"Sports do not build character. They reveal it."
— Haywood Hale Broun

John Banaszak checks out Steelers' display at Applebee's Neighborhood Grill & Bar near his home in McMurray. The restaurant is one of 13 units owned by former teammates J.T. Thomas and Larry Brown.   Jim O'Brien

John Banaszak appears at Coaches Corner luncheon at Riverwatch Room at Boardwalk Complex in The Strip along with Pitt head coach Walt Harris and Steelers' linebacker Clark Haggans. Banaszak is now at Robert Morris University.

John Banaszak and I met for lunch at Applebee's on Monday, March 10, 2003, and three days later for breakfast at Eat'n Park Restaurant on Rt. 19 in Peters Township. At least that was the idea. John had nothing to eat at either place, saying he wanted to lose a few pounds. He was a cheap date. I never felt more in the spotlight when I was eating a meal. I felt guilty eating eggs, strips of bacon and some biscuits. Whenever John looked across the table at me, I felt like he was looking at me through a microscope.

We talked about his career situation. We talked about Terry Bradshaw and Chuck Noll and their much-ballyhooed reunion. We talked about Mike Webster and Steve Furness and their unfortunate premature deaths. We talked about our fathers and mothers.

Our fathers seemed to have a lot in common. Both were mill-workers. Both worked hard and drank hard. Both had died years before. In between our interview visits, John had gone back home to Cleveland. He had driven his wife Mary to the airport in Cleveland to take advantage of cheaper airfares available there versus departing from the Pittsburgh International Airport. He had taken his mother to see her doctor while he was there. "She was showing me off to all the nurses," said Banaszak.

He visited a good friend of his family, Pat Catan, who came from McKees Rocks, and has been a big success in Strongville, Ohio. "He started a wholesale arts and crafts business with $250, and now has over 2,000 employees," said Banazak. Catan is one of John's heroes, too.

On the Tuesday Banaszak was driving to Cleveland with his wife to see his mother, I was driving to Wheeling with my wife, family and friends to bury my mother, Mary O'Brien. She had died, at age 96, that weekend at Asbury Heights, an assisted-care senior complex in Mt. Lebanon, just four miles from my home in Upper St. Clair. My mother had been born and grew up in Bridgeport, Ohio, just across the Ohio River from Wheeling. As a teenager, my mother had worked at a funeral home in Bridgeport.

She had been telling me the month before she died that she'd seen my dad at Asbury — he had died at age 63 back in 1969 — and that she wanted to go home. I told her it was okay if she wanted to go home. And that's what she was doing.

John was proud of his family. He and Mary had been married for 32 years and had three adult children, Jay, Carrie and Amye. Two of them were getting married in the coming summer. Jay was going to marry Tara Saccamango, and she already had a five-year-old boy named Angelo. "We're instant grandparents," said Mary Banaszak, "and we couldn't be more excited. Angelo is a real joy for us." Amye was scheduled to get married June 7 to Matt Raffaele. "So we have lots to be happy about, and lots to look forward to," said John. "So I'm not about to go in the tank. I've never been a quitter."

John spent the winter and spring doing remodeling jobs around his home. "I haven't had to empty the dishwasher since he left W&J," reported Mary. "We've spent so much more time together, and John seems to be his old self again. He was not happy all last season because of the tension at school. When he first took that job we thought he'd be there for life. I'm going to miss him when he goes back to work. This is an obstacle for us to overcome. But it's not the end of the world."

"It's a new chapter in my life."

John Banaszak:

Life is good. I don't feel like it's the end of something. To me, it's the beginning of something, a new chapter in my life. I feel like I did when I first came out of college, looking for new challenges, new opportunities. What happened to me wasn't the worst thing in the world. My work is done at W&J. I'm tougher than letting this defeat me. I'm proud of the work I did there. I will always be proud of it. That can't be erased from the books.

I've always had a positive outlook on life. That's just the way I am. I passed that down to my children. My son Jay has gone through a very difficult experience in recent years, and he battles every day. That's what the Banaszaks are about. If I were to go in the tank now everything I've been taught and everything I've been preaching would be fraudulent.

That's not my style. I'm fighting. I can build on what we did the last four years at W&J. I know I can coach. I know I can motivate young people to accomplish their goals.

You've got to be able to deal with disappointments. It would be easy to give up on everybody. That's why the divorce rate is so high. People give up on commitment too easy. We're no different. Mary and I have had our difficulties, but we fought hard to keep each other, to love each other. When you're 52 you better have somebody you can always count on. I feel that way about Mary. I feel sure Mary feels the same way about me. I lost my job, but I didn't let her down.

So I am not going to allow getting fired to affect my life in a negative manner. I knew my environment at W&J had changed, so this didn't come as a surprise.

I could have gone to California (Pa.). I was made to feel I was their No. 1 choice. And John wasn't going to apply if I was going to take the job. But I felt I owed it to my seniors — my first recruiting class — to see it through at W&J. I have no regrets in that respect. Look at what John Luckhardt did at W&J. And he had to leave, too. They didn't want us around anymore. We both got pushed aside.

I was also told that maybe they didn't like my demeanor on the sideline. That's ridiculous. I know I was quite animated. But my behavior on the sideline was not a problem. Not one time was I penalized for anything I said or did. We never had a bench penalty in four years. Do I rant and rave? You bet. But I'm never vulgar; I never use profanity. Am I more like Chuck Noll or Bill Cowher? I think I'm somewhere in between.

I received about 40 letters from my players and their parents expressing their disappointment that I had been fired. I have to remember all the positive experiences I had with my players and their families. I just heard from a young man yesterday, telling me how grateful and thankful he was for my influence on him.

It is gratifying to know I was more than a football coach to these guys. That was my goal. I wanted to be a mentor and a teacher, a counselor. When you have 19 and 20 and 21-year-old kids they are going to have problems. Their parents might be breaking up. They might be breaking up with their girlfriends. They're having some other problems. I think it's important to them that they have somebody they can lean on. You're there to help them. When the new athletic director came in, one of the things we were required to do was write a self-evaluation and a program evaluation. OK, I thought, I can do that. After reading it, I realized there was an awful lot I did there above and beyond the job description.

I took the kids to Children's Hospital. We helped build homes for Habitat for Humanity during the summer. I took them to sports banquets. I brought many of my former Steeler teammates to talk to my guys.

Football-wise, what more could they want? We won four conference championships and went to the national playoffs four years in a row. We were 9-3 my last year. I coached the girls' golf team at W&J and we won back-to-back conference titles. That wasn't because I could teach them how to play better golf. But I could help them when it came to competing in sports. It was fun. I coached the baseball team here before that. I was convinced the school was the ideal place for anybody I recruited to go there. I believed it and sold it. I was loyal to the school and to the administration. Two of Dan Rooney's kids went to W&J and Dan has strong ties to the school, but I didn't go running to the Steelers, saying they should intervene on my behalf. He and I talked after I lost my job. He was surprised at what happened. I don't expect the Steelers to solve my problems anymore. Mary and I have had some challenges, but we both believe that nobody owes you anything. That's the way I was brought up.

> *"I'm a pretty simple, straighforward person.*
> *I like to compete. I say exactly what I think*
> *and I guess that threatens some."*
> — George Blanda

George Gojkovich

John Banaszak (76) and Jack Ham (59) put the rush ~~on~~ former teammate Terry Hanratty when the ~~B~~utler High and Notre Dame star was quarterback~~in~~g the Tampa Bay Buccaneers. Ham blocked ~~H~~anratty's pass.

Jim O'Brien

John Banaszak wears his Eastern Michigan alma mater's jersey during interview at Applebee's Neighborhood Grill & Bar near his home in McMurray.

John Banaszak

From the Banaszak family photo album

The Banaszak Bunch gathers one last night as a family on the eve of Jay's wedding in June of 2003. From left to right, there's Jay, Carrie, Mary, John and Amye. A few weeks later, Amye also got married. It's one of life's transitions.

"You had to take your lunch pail to work everyday."

My father worked at Lincoln Electric, and they made welding equipment. At one time, that company was the No. 1 manufacturer of welding equipment in the country, maybe the world. It was a non-union shop, and they worked on a piecemeal basis. The more work you completed the more you got paid. You had to take your lunch pail to work everyday. That's what I learned from him. I was just talking to my mom about that.

She asked me if I found work yet. She used the word "work." I told her I was the luckiest guy in the world. I said I never looked at what I was doing as "work" — I just didn't see it that way.

I was part of a special group when I played for the Steelers. I learned a lot from all of them. It reinforced all I had learned from my family. Just look at the success of my former teammates.

It never ends. You became part of that family. That is certainly one of the greatest things I've experienced. I was a part of something special. There is a unity . . . that love for each other.

A lot of times you get so hung up in your daily life. You don't think about what you have, what you've been through. I'm grateful. I look upon my teammates as friends and family.

My background gives me a point of view as a motivational speaker that is different from some of the other speakers out there. I'm a blue-collar guy. I know I can't demand the same kind of fee as Fran Tarkenton, but maybe some people can't relate to Fran Tarkenton. Maybe the supervisor or foreman can relate to me.

I'm a product of watching my dad get up every morning, and watching him put his game face on in the car. He drove me to school for four years when I went to a Catholic private school that didn't have bus service. I went to Holy Name in the city. I can still remember him. It's not easy to go to work every day. Here's some help in overcoming those days when you don't feel like going to work.

There's always been a sign in my office that reads: Life is tough, but I'm tougher. That was the attitude my dad had. Guys like that are real MVPs in the workplace.

"Nobody's perfect."
— Joe E. Brown

"I'm in pursuit of happiness."

I was a roommate for several years with Mike Webster. I only really know the Mike Webster who was my teammate. I don't know what became of Mike Webster, or what went wrong in his life. I've heard all the stories, but I don't know it on a first-hand basis. I can't tell you why he played all those years, or what it did to him. I knew him as a teammate for seven years. He was a tremendous football player and a good man with a good family. That's the Mike Webster I know. What happened to him in the 15 years or so after his retirement as a player, I can't even comment on it. I don't know the extent of the situation. So I don't want to go there.

I run the risk of hurting somebody if I said anything, and I don't want to do that. It wouldn't be fair.

Tunch Ilkin, Craig Wolfley and Ted Petersen and I tried to get Webby some help. He knew he was having a problem with prescription drugs. I wanted him to talk to my wife Mary and get some help with his addiction to (pain-killing) drugs. He was staying with Steve Courson down around Uniontown. When he caught wind of what we were trying to do to help him he left Uniontown. It all fell apart after that. Six months later he gets arrested for passing bad (forged) prescriptions for painkillers.

We tried. Webby was not going to accept anyone's help. He was too stubborn. He was trying to handle it himself. He was a big strong macho guy. He thought he could handle it himself and find a way to work it out. When he was playing there was no injury that could keep him out of the lineup. He approached his serious problems after football the same way. He was a victim of his own toughness probably.

I think Mike was the victim of his own obsession, his compulsive behavior. He was so intense. Always working out. Maybe his family paid the price for that. There has to be balance. I'm in pursuit of happiness.

It's in the Constitution. That's good enough for me. That's right . . . the pursuit of happiness.

A lot of people have problems facing life after pro football. That was Mike's situation.

Lifting weights and working out so much paid off for Mike Webster. I worked out, too, but never to the same degree as he did. There's more than one way to skin a cat. I always felt that way. No matter what I've done. I did what I could to be the best football player I could ever be. Sure, Mike wanted us all to do more. But I told him enough is enough.

When I was playing for the Steelers toward the end, I was also starting my own business. When it's time to go home, I put the Steelers aside. I didn't want to go home and watch another game tape.

I hit 50 and I'm OK now. I try to take care of myself. I watch my diet. I get an annual physical. I just came away from another reality check. That is what funerals are. It's a basic reality check. I was more affected, frankly, by the death of Steve Furness because we were closer, and had seen a lot of each other just before he died. Furny looked good when I last saw him. His death was a real shocker. That really bothered me.

Steve and I played next to each other, and we often rode to and from the stadium together. We spent more time together at meetings for defensive linemen. Webby's death wasn't a surprise at all. Steve's was out of nowhere. He was at W&J the Friday before he died. He went to lunch with me and John Luckhardt. He had sold us a new field surface, and he seemed real happy with what he was doing. We were supposed to get together for lunch the following week.

He was really down after he was fired by Bill Cowher a few years earlier, but he bounced back from that. It was tough for him for awhile. But he was joking and laughing the last time we were together. He was back doing something he really enjoyed doing.

I worked out with those guys on occasion at the Red Bull Inn in Washington, but I wasn't one of the regulars. Their schedule was different from mine. I was downtown more often, and it was just as easy to work out at Three Rivers Stadium. I was somewhere between L.C. Greenwood and Joe Greene when it came to being enthused about weightlifting, but I worked out. I did what was laid out for me by the team trainers. I was comfortable with it. It suited me just fine.

I still go down to the restaurant for a meal from time to time. I liked the people there. I'm a pretty easy guy to get along with. I've always taken pride in my job, and I always did it to the best of my ability, and I've done that in all three phases of my life

I'm still a Marine at heart. I believe that we should defend our freedoms, whatever it takes. It does upset me that people have such short memories. Have they forgotten what happened in this country on September 11th? We lost 3,000 or so of our citizens. There were a lot of foreigners in those buildings, too. Maybe that's why some of the Europeans, especially the British, are behind us.

Saddam Hussein is not a good person. He's full of hate. He's tortured and killed his own people. History will prove he's not a good man. War is tough, but our freedom is a direct result of what we've won in wars. I'm proud of the people who serve. I have a 54-year-old brother-in-law, Bob Redig, who is an Air Force reservist, and he just got called up. So this has affected my family and we're very proud of him. We're proud of all the young men and women who are serving our country.

I went to the Marines for two years between high school and college. I didn't feel like I was ready for college right away. I benefited by that time and the discipline it entailed. I think we needed to do something. I think the world needs to do something to put an end to terrorism. I wish more people would recognize that France and Germany are in bed with Iraq. They have short memories, too.

My mother taught me to have pride in my family. My grandparents came over from Poland. They came over here like a lot of people to build a better life. My grandparents worked so their children could graduate from high school. When my grandfather retired from the mill, he opened a bar. He was the bartender. I grew up within walking distance of that bar, and spent time there as a child. My parents wanted to provide an even better opportunity for their children. They wanted us to graduate from college.

My daughter Carrie, my middle one, told me that whatever job I found she was confident I would be happy. They enjoyed me coaching so much. I'll take a job and be competitive at whatever I do. That's just the way I am. When I was working in the business world, I knew that eventually I was going to get into coaching. And I know I'll be on the sideline again. I have some serious challenges in front of me, I know, but I feel up to the challenge. I don't know whether I want to work for some company, or work for myself. My family has been very supportive. They're behind me all the way. That helps.

"We just didn't invite him anymore."

Terry Bradshaw was a good teammate. He made some decisions that affected his relationship with his former teammates. I think he missed a lot of good times that we enjoyed in the years since we played. He missed out on a lot of great outings. I think this whole thing wasn't really a problem. I think it started up when he wrote his first book. They had to be controversial. If there had been a real problem between Terry and Chuck, or with his teammates or the town, it would have come out sooner.

He's apologized. I accept his apology. He knows that he missed out on quite a bit. He was the reason he hasn't been asked back in recent years. Invitation after invitation drew no responses from him. So the NFL Alumni stopped sending invitations. We just didn't invite him anymore.

Terry treated me very well when he was on the team. He was, as I said, a good teammate. We went out and played golf

---

"Life is difficult."
— Scott Peck
The Road Less Traveled

together. As a rookie, he took me out during training camp. I always appreciated that.

He's like anybody else. He got into his life's work and it didn't happen to be in Pittsburgh.

I think Terry Bradshaw was genuinely excited about being back in Pittsburgh. Hey, he sold out the Dapper Dan Dinner in record time. If he comes more often, he'll continue to bring some excitement back to the city. His schedule is so busy, but it will be nice if he can fit in some stuff here. It would be great if he'd come here for the NFL Alumni golf outing. That would sell a few more foursomes. He said he was going to try and come back for the Mel Blount Dinner. Joe Greene is going to be honored at that dinner. That raises money for Mel's place, so he can take care of the kids at his ranch. That's a good cause. If you have Terry Bradshaw you can sell a few more tables. We want Terry to get involved. Andy Russell will try to get him back for his golf outing. If Terry Bradshaw wants to be welcomed back that's his role now. Our city needs him. We're going through some tough times, as a city, as a nation. Terry Bradshaw can revitalize some things around here.

I loved going out and representing the Steelers. I loved doing it for the Chief because that's what he wanted us to do. I learned a lot from Mr. Rooney, the way he treated disadvantaged and less fortunate people. Joe Gordon used to set us up with a lot of appearances. And he'd tell us what to wear and what to do, what was expected of us. I see some of these Steelers today and they show up in T-shirts for a luncheon appearance. No one tells them what they ought to do. There's no guidance.

I had a great quarterback during my days at Washington & Jefferson. His name was Brian Dawson. He threw only six interceptions all year, and he threw seven interceptions in the final playoff game. They all weren't his fault. He stood out in the center of the field all alone after the game, and he was just feeling so bad, like it was all his fault.

Soon after, I asked him to go with me to Children's Hospital. I was going there with the Steelers' Alumni, and I wanted him to join us for our Christmas visit. He was busy getting ready for tests, and he tried to beg off but I told him I wanted him to come. T.J. Srsic, another kid from Thomas Jefferson High School, came with us. Andy Russell, Todd Kalas and Robin Cole were Steelers Alumni who were there that day. Our kids loved that. We saw some kids on the first floor, and then I got him to go up with me to the 8th floor. There were young guys, 17 and 18 years old, who couldn't come down to the first floor. They were battling for their lives. They had tubes and bandages everywhere.

A week later, Brian was sitting across from me in my office. He said, "Coach, I want to thank you for what you did for me. I want to thank you for showing me that thinking seven interceptions in a playoff game was the end of the world. I have to be thankful to be able to play in a playoff game."

We learn from all these experiences. That whole story . . . that's my record, too. It gave me such a great feeling so see my kids making a contribution to that visit to Children's Hospital.

When you have kids that are 18, 19 and 20 years old they are going to have problems. There better be somebody they can talk to about disappointments in their life. I've learned some lessons the hard way, or through other people's bad experiences.

I think about Gabe Rivera. If he had been wearing a safety belt he wouldn't have shot out the back window of his car upon impact like he did.

Ever since his accident, I never enter my car that I don't put my seat belt on. If Gabe had done that he would have continued playing pro football. He'd be able to walk today.

I think he would have been an exceptional football player. From what I saw at training camp and in the early part of the season, he had the strength and cat-like quickness and speed to be a special player. I played with Joe Greene and then Reggie White (with the USFL's Memphis Showboats) and I know a great defensive lineman when I see one.

Look at a guy like Pete Duranko. Here's a former NFL player who's fighting for his life. He's in the biggest battle of his life. He's got Lou Gehrig's disease. That's a tougher situation than getting fired at W&J. I have so much respect for these guys. They never give up.

"I've come a long way since then."

Going back to see my mother always brings back a lot of memories. I see the playgrounds where I played as a child. I remember going to the Browns and Indians games at old Cleveland Stadium. I have six brothers and one sister. My mother had five boys in seven years. I'm the third.

I still visit Sal Menarcore, one of my boyhood neighbors, who was like a seventh brother. I see Greg Muczka, who went to Bowling Green to play football and was a year behind us. We played against each other in college. He's one of the guys who calls me "Jack." When anybody calls me "Jack," I know they're from my old neighborhood in Cleveland.

Chuck Noll played for the Browns I first knew as a child. I remember Vince Costello and the Modzelewskis — Ed and Dick — and Dick Schafrath and Bill Glass. I remember how disappointed I was when they traded Bobby Mitchell to the Redskins. They traded him for the draft rights to Ernie Davis of Syracuse. He never played a down for the Browns. He died of cancer. I met Lou "The Toe" Groza at the Pro Football Hall of Fame in Canton, and had a chance to talk to him. He was a great guy. You remember names like Dante Lavelli and — speaking of names — Fair Hooker. Now there's a name you can't forget.

I remember going to the Indians' games, starting when I was 12 or 13. I remember Rocky Colavito. I hated it when he was traded to the Detroit Tigers for Harvey Kuenn. I remember Tito Francona — he was my hero — and I see him now at golf outings around here. He's from Aliquippa. And I loved "Sudden Sam" McDowell, and he's from Pittsburgh. He's still active with the Pirates Alumni around here and I've had a chance to talk to him about those days.

That's how I grew up. We used to ride our bikes to play sandlot football against older guys who drove to the same fields in their cars. I've come a long way since then, I guess, but I didn't think about how far I've come. I just did it.

I remember when I was looking at the home we live in now, back in the spring of 1976, I found out that one of our coaches, Lionel Taylor, lived in a house four doors away. "Lionel said they weren't going to let a Polack like me move into the neighborhood. I reminded Lionel that he was half black, part American Indian, part white, so that he shouldn't be concerned about a Polack moving into the neighborhood. We had some fun with that. His daughter ended up baby-sitting for us. We were one of the first Steelers in the neighborhood. After we bought our home, Loren Toews moved to Peters Township from Bethel Park. Steve Furness moved from Washington to Peters. Then Mike Webster moved in. Jim Boston, who was the business manager of the Steelers, lived nearby, too.

That's when so many pro athletes lived in the South Hills. Now they all live in the North Hills. It seems so long ago.

"I was a big Cleveland Browns fan. I grew up two miles from Hiram College where, at that time, they had their training camp. I used to ride my bike up there every day. I've still got autograph books at home filled with Jim Brown and Milt Plum and Jim Ninowski and Leroy Kelly and all those guys."
— Jack Lambert Hall of Fame linebacker

Dr. Joseph C. Maroon
Checking on concussions

"I was the smallest football player in the Big Ten."

D r. Joseph C. Maroon is one of this country's most-respected neurosurgeons. Since 1999, he has been vice chairman and professor of the Department of Neurological Surgery at the University of Pittsburgh School of Medicine. He has been the team neurosurgeon for the Pittsburgh Steelers for 23 years and, along with neuropsychologist Dr. Mark Lovell, has developed innovative studies and programs for the management of athletes with cerebral concussions.

Their ImPACT (Immediate Post-Concussion Assessmemt and Cognitive Testing) is the first computerized evaluation system relating to concussions and has been adopted by the National Football League, National Hockey League, some teams in the National Basketball Association, and over 200 high schools and colleges throughout the country, including many in western Pennsylvania.

Dr. Maroon has cared for Tommy Maddox and Myron Cope, as well as two of my neighbors in Upper St. Clair, Joe Irwin and Pete DeWalt. He was the doctor who cared for Maddox, when he was knocked out in a game at Tennessee during the 2002 season, and he performed back surgery for Cope, Irwin and DeWalt.

He's about the same size as Cope, at 5-6, but he's a giant in his field. He's been a fiercely competitive individual since his school days. He's 63 and still competing in world-class triathlons.

Joseph Charles Maroon was born in Wheeling, West Virginia, but grew up in Bridgeport, Ohio, just across the Ohio River. Bridgeport is my mother's hometown, so I know it well. His father, Charlie Maroon, of Lebanese descent, was the kingpin of pinball machines in the Ohio Valley, controlling such action in bars, restaurants and gaming rooms throughout the area.

Joey, as he is known to old friends back that way, was a bright and talented athlete, small in stature, but with a big heart. He was determined and ambitious and did his homework. He kept his nose clean and was admired for his excellence in sports and in the classroom. He was educated in parochial schools in nearby Bellaire.

He went to Indiana University of Bloomington on an athletic scholarship. Not bad for a 5-6, 165-pounder. "I was the smallest football player in the Big Ten," he boasts with a smile. He was a running back in the mold of Buddy Young, the legendary Illinois scatback. He was an even better student, and gained national Academic All-American honors at IU.

Following his undergraduate education, Maroon obtained his medical and neurosurgical training at Indiana University,

Georgetown University, Oxford University in England and a microsurgical fellowship at the University of Vermont under the highly respected R. M. Peardon Donaghy.

He began his practice at the University of Pittsburgh in 1972 and was promoted to Professor and Director of Neurosurgery at the University of Pittsburgh-Presbyterian University Hospital.

In 1984, he joined Allegheny General Hospital as Chairman of Neurosurgery and in 1995 he assumed the additional role as Chairman of the Department of Surgery at Allegheny General Hospital/Medical College of Pennsylvania. In 1999, he rejoined the Department of Neurosurgery at the University of Pittsburgh Medical Center (UPMC). He was designated the Dennis and Rose Heindl Scholar in Neurosciences.

"Legends of the North Shore."

I invited Dr. Maroon to meet with me for an interview over dinner at Legends of the North Shore, then a relatively new restaurant on East North Avenue, next to Allegheny General Hospital. We met at 6:30 p.m. on Monday, March 24, 2003. There was a large mural on the wall in the dining area that I wanted Dr. Maroon to see. On an earlier visit, having lunch with former Steelers' star Mike Wagner, I had spotted two pictures of Dr. Maroon from his football-playing days at Indiana University. The mural was a montage of large black-and-white photos of the likes of such Steelers as Terry Bradshaw, Mel Blount, Lynn Swann, Joe Greene, L.C. Greenwood, et al. Wagner and I sat next to it. Dan Bartow, the owner of Legends of the North Shore, asked us to identify the players in the mural. Wagner recognized everyone but this one fellow who appeared in two of the photos. There was an IU on the player's helmet. I'm pretty good at faces and I suggested it might be Joe Maroon, the Steelers' team doctor. I felt like I had just unearthed the tomb of King Tut.

It turned out that Dr. Maroon had given that mural to someone who looked after one of the apartments he owns near the hospital. Dr. Maroon owns much real estate in that neighborhood, some of which is utilized by Allegheny General Hospital.

Dr. Maroon told Dan Bartow he'd like to have the mural. He said he had wondered what happened to it. I thought he'd like the idea of having it displayed where doctors and staff members at Allegheny General often have lunch and dinner. After all, he was in great company, with other legends of the North Shore. But, no, he took it to his home in Fox Chapel. A high-ranking official at Allegheny General Hospital told me that Dr. Maroon was now a legend of Oakland.

While we were eating, Dr. Maroon was hailed by Dr. Gerald Pifer, who was dining with his wife at a nearby table. Dr. Pifer said he was going over to KDKA Radio to do his weekly "Medical Frontiers"

Photos by Jim O'Brien

Dr. Joseph C. Maroon checks with Dan Bartow in the kitchen of his Legends of the North Shore Restaurant, and studies mural that Dr. Maroon created with photos of the Steelers' great players of the '70s. Dr. Maroon has been one of Steelers' team doctors for 23 years.

show. He and Dr. Maroon exchanged pleasantries. For the record, Dr. Maroon picked up our dinner tab. This is a busy man, and I was grateful for his time and attention. He was quite serious about most of the topics we discussed. He had his OR mask on, in a sense, most of the time.

We talked about Tommy Maddox, Terry Bradshaw and Mike Webster, as well as Dan Rooney, Chuck Noll and Bill Cowher. Bradshaw had a new book out called *Keep It Simple* and was telling everybody who'd listen — like Don Imus, Bryant Gumbel, Jay Leno and Bob Costas — about the difficulties he had dealt with as a quarterback for the Pittsburgh Steelers, and in ensuing years as a TV sports celebrity. Terry was telling stories about how unhappy he'd been for so long, through three marital breakups and other personal setbacks. Dr. Maroon matched Bradshaw's marriage total. "It's no fun," said Dr. Maroon.

Bradshaw, who has an image as a light-hearted sonofagun, who'd do anything for a laugh, confessed to suffering from depression most of his adult life.

It was known that his center, fellow Hall of Fame member Mike Webster, had suffered brain damage, and had bouts of depression and memory loss as well.

"I had my own dealings with depression during my first stay at Pitt," disclosed Dr. Maroon. "It was a bad time. I was going through a divorce from my first marriage, my father had just died, and I quit my job as a doctor and went back home to help my mother sort out my dad's business affairs and estate. I took a job while I was with my mother in Bridgeport loading trucks. I just wanted a change in my life. I was feeling that bad. Here I was loading trucks back home a week after I had performed brain surgery in Pittsburgh. Like I said, it was a bad time. But I came out of it and came back to being a doctor. Medicine is a demanding field, and a lot of doctors go through tough times emotionally. Doctors dealing with serious stuff hit a wall sometime in their career. I wasn't alone. Now I feel fine."

Dr. Maroon consulted with me at our dinner meeting on what he would need to do to get a book published. He wanted to write about his own experiences. He has quite a success story and much to share.

"The spinal cord is pristine."

Dr. Maroon had been in the spotlight back on Tuesday, November 19, 2002 when he appeared at a press conference at the Steelers' UPMC Sports Complex on the city's South Side to explain what had happened to Tommy Maddox, after he was temporarily paralyzed that Sunday from a hit on the last play of the third quarter against the Titans in Nashville.

"As far as I am concerned," declared Dr. Maroon, "he is back to a normal state after suffering both a cerebral and spinal concussion."

Dr. Maroon brought medical bone structure models with him in a show-and-tell presentation for the sportswriters. For a day, they had some idea of what it was like to be a student at the School of Medicine of the University of Pittsburgh and most of them were completely lost. Much of the presentation was, let's say, over their heads. I remember Dr. Freddie Fu, another famous sports medicine doctor, doing a similar seminar on a hand injury suffered by a football player during my days as assistant athletic director for sports information at the University of Pittsburgh. Most team doctors I've met like the limelight.

I remember Dr. Alan Levy, the team doctor for the New York Nets in the days of Dr. J — my favorite team doctor of all time — telling me, "I consider every operation in which I don't cut myself a success." Dr. Maroon didn't come up with any lines quite that memorable. But he did provide real insight for sportswriters into what was wrong with Tommy Maddox, and how it might affect his future.

"On studying the film," said Dr. Maroon, "there is absolutely no evidence of any spinal column or disc problem. The spinal cord is pristine in terms of its depiction on the MRI."

He said there was no narrowing of the spinal column or stenosis. He said the ImPACT test Dr. Maroon and Dr. Lovell had pioneered to measure the effects on the brain of a concussion had come back normal. Dr. Maroon and his staff take a baseline test of every player before there is a problem, checking many aspects of brain activity, and when there's a head injury they re-test the player. They measure the reaction time, memory, orientation, processing speed of the brain and other symptoms. The test, which he first used with the Steelers, is conducted throughout the NFL, NHL, NBA, NASCAR, colleges and 250 high schools. "Looking back on my career," said Dr. Maroon, "I've written over 250 medical papers, and the ImPACT test is my greatest accomplishment.

"I also should say that when doing these baseline studies, it is interesting to say that Tommy scored among the highest out of over 5,000 athletes that we tested, in terms of reaction time and his processing of information," added Dr. Maroon. "Maybe this came from Arena Football, too."

Dr. Maroon talked about the time he had spent with Maddox, going over his tests, talking to him about his condition, and what recovery time might be required before he could resume playing football. Dr. Maroon said there could be psychological side effects to taking such a hit to the head. They might be gun-shy at the start, and that was perfectly natural. So Maddox, understandably, was "Tommy-Gun Shy" early in his comeback start. After a few completions and taking a few hits, Maddox was fine. It was a remarkable return, and a relief to all his fans who'd been so worried about his condition.

"If you are lying on a football field unable to feel your arms and legs and are unable to move," continued Dr. Maroon, "I can't imagine a more frightening experience. I have seen this in quite a few athletes, and they haven't returned to function. There is a major psychological factor, and he needs to consider this as well, but this is his decision.

255

"I will be very candid with you. It is amazing to me that we don't see this every game. When I looked at the replays of the hit, it wasn't any more violent or severe than any of the other hundreds of hits that we see in an average game."

"Hoge had it right."

There was a report called "The Cutting Edge" that appeared in *Pitt Magazine* by Kris Mamula on this subject that was provided by the UPMC public relations department. An excerpt follows:

"A jarring of the brain is what causes concussion. For players, 'getting your bell rung' has always been part of team sports. Blows to the head can shear the microscopic fibers that are the body's main switchboard wires. Unconsciousness can occur when these tiny fibers break. If the hit is severe, the tearing of the tiny fibers can disrupt the electrical signals that regulate heartbeat, breathing, and blood pressure, resulting in shock and even death.

"Unfortunately, severe hits are not unusual — touch football doesn't sell. Dr. Maroon says that between 50,000 and 150,000 high school athletes suffer concussions each year. Most heal well. Others don't.

"Mood swings, memory loss, and attention-span problems are among the possible long-term effects of a concussion. After a series of concussions, some professional football players have hung up their cleats. In 1994, former Pittsburgh Steeler Merril Hoge retired at age 29 after his second concussion of the season as a running back with the Chicago Bears. Even 10 days after the hit, Hoge said he was dizzy and sleepy and having trouble remembering things. Hoge said he returned too soon after the first concussion, making the second concussion much more serious than it otherwise might have been.

"Hoge had it right. Treating a concussion successfully depends on gauging its severity, then allowing enough time for the brain to heal. But how do you know when it is safe to allow a player to return? Dr. Maroon and Dr. Lovell, with help from Steelers' athletic trainer John Norwig, developed a pencil-and-paper test called the Steelers Battery that the NFL and NHL have used since 1991 to evaluate concussions. Returning too soon to the game — as Hoge's experience suggests — leaves the player more vulnerable to another, more serious head injury, according to Dr. Maroon.

"The Center for Sports Medicine provides training services for athletes at 41 area high schools and seven colleges. Test results are being used to build the country's biggest database of concussion injuries, Dr. Maroon says. The database will be tapped for research, meaning fewer athletes may have to take it on the chin — or noggin — for years to come."

Jim Murray of the *Los Angeles Times* on the Steelers:

"A Supreme Court Justice once played in their backfield. So did a lot of guys whose cases would come before him."

In a later UPMC-sponsored seminar in which Hoge took part, Dr. Lovell allowed, "We all want to be on the same page." Whom does that sound like?

"Everything was quite blurry."
— Mark Bruener

Among the more famous NFL players who were forced into retirement by a series of concussions were quarterbacks Troy Aikman of the Dallas Cowboys and Steve Young of the San Francisco 49ers, and receiver Al Toon of the New York Jets, who was represented by Pittsburgh sports attorney Ralph Cindrich. Toon had suffered at least ten concussions. Charlie Batch, the Steelers' backup quarterback, suffered a concussion when he was playing for the Detroit Lions.

Mark Bruener, the Steelers' tight end, wore a new football helmet during the 2002 season that was designed to reduce the risk of concussions. It was part of a league-wide experiment with protective equipment. Bruener had suffered a concussion two years earlier. "I can remember getting up and looking at the sideline," Bruener recalled of his knockout. "Everything was quite blurry."

He mentioned how it had affected his good friend Merril Hoge. "He's still feeling the side effects," said Bruener. "There was a story he told me where he didn't remember how to get home after a game to a house he lived in for several years."

That happened in 1994. Dazed and lost in the hospital after he was injured, Hoge didn't know his wife, his brother or that he had a 14-month-old daughter. His phone number? He didn't have a clue. Hoge told reporters, "I couldn't find my way home. I was two blocks from my house and it was like I was in the Mojave Desert. I was lost in my own neighborhood."

Dave Wannstedt, then the coach of the Bears, was upset about what happened to Hoge. The Baldwin-bred and former Pitt player and coach said of Hoge: "From the day we signed him, he was the first one here every morning at 6 a.m. In training camp, he was the first guy on the field and one of the last guys to leave."

Hoge said, "I remember Dave Wannstedt said to me, 'No one will think less of you as a player — they know how tough you are.' And I thought, why would anyone think less of me? But the mentality in the early '90s was that head injuries didn't end careers."

In the summer of 2000, Hoge successfully sued former Bears team physician Dr. John Munsell for $2.2 million, and was awarded a $1.55 million settlement by an Illinois jury.

Hoge had spoken at a seminar on the subject of concussions in athletics at a UPMC Sports Medicine-sponsored project, and in a panel discussion on ESPN TV. "I am the poster boy for all concussion stories," said Hoge, a popular guy in the clubhouse and pressbox.

"Hoge came to see me after he retired," said Dr. Maroon. "He said he felt great, 'Why can't I play?' he asked. I told him the risk of further injury was greater because of the concussions he had incurred."

Two of the Steelers' most famous fullbacks, Fran Rogel, who has since died, and John Henry Johnson, suffered dementia in their senior years. Johnson had moved from an apartment in Cleveland to an assisted-care facility in the Los Angeles area. Both Rogel and Johnson were touted for their toughness and hard-hitting style. Ernie Stautner, a Hall of Fame inductee like Johnson and regarded as one of the toughest players in pro football history, was suffering from Alzheimer's Disease. "Concussions are serious injuries," said Hoge. "They're not sissy injuries."

Chad Brown, a former Steelers linebacker who left Pittsburgh in 1997 to sign as a free agent with the Seattle Seahawks, suffered a severe concussion that first year in Seattle and again in the 1999 schedule during a game at Three Rivers Stadium, and in 2000 in Carolina. "A lot of guys lose track of what's going on or where they are," said Brown. "I lose control of my emotions. I can usually tell how severe my concussion is by how much of my emotions I lose. Am I angry? Am I frustrated? Am I crying? Each one is different."

Brown said he probably returned from one concussion before he was fully recovered. In the 1997 concussion, Brown not only returned to play, but recovered a fumble that he returned for a touchdown. He couldn't even remember the play after the game.

When Chad Brown returned to the field following the halftime break, he was spotted by a club official practicing fielding punts when the punters were warming up. The official called the Seahawks' sideline and told them to keep Brown out of the game.

It has been my experience that old ballplayers who are plagued by Alzheimer's Disease or dementia still have the ability to discuss their glory days with credibility. They can remember their heyday; they just can't remember yesterday. Or what they had for breakfast.

Dr. Maroon told me that is not unusual. "Their difficulty is with short-term memory," he explained. "They like talking about their best days. Those memories get encoded. They're much deeper; they were intense when they were registered."

"Why are you telling me he can't play?"
— Coach Chuck Noll

Dr. Joseph C. Maroon:

When I finished my residencies, I came to Pitt. I was the team neurosurgeon under Jim McMaster at Pitt. I was there during the (Tony) Dorsett years. I was very interested in the problems

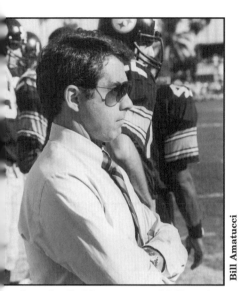

Bill Amatucci

. Joseph C. Maroon on sideline for
eelers' AFC championship game at
iami on January 6, 1975.

Indiana University Sports Information

Joe Maroon was an Academic All-American
running back at Indiana University in
Bloomington back in 1960.

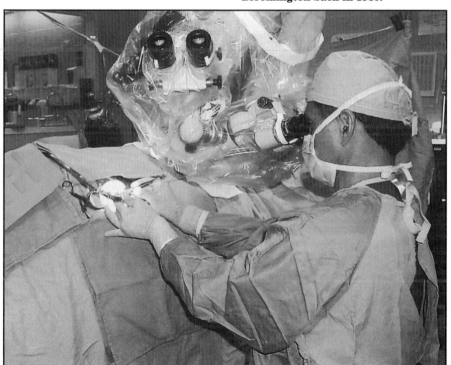

Courtesy of UPMC

Dr. Joseph C. Maroon performs back surgery at UPMC.

caused by head and neck injuries. I had a neck injury myself. I also worked with Dr. Paul Steele, who was one of the Steelers' team physicians at the time. He'd check with me when one of the Steelers had a concussion.

I remember checking out Lynn Swann after he'd been dealt a severe blow. They wanted to know whether he should sit out a game or two. After serving a year or two as a consultant, I was asked by Dan Rooney to be one of the team physicians for the Pittsburgh Steelers. That was in the early '80s. There was very little medical literature on the subject of head and neck injuries for athletes at the time. Everything was experimental and anecdotal. I remember that David Woodley suffered a concussion when he was playing quarterback for the Steelers in the mid-'80s. We had different grades for concussions, and kept players out of action for a length of time depending on what grade they had. There were Grade 1, Grade 2 and Grade 3 concussions.

Grade 1 was a ding and you'd be out for a week; Grade 2 was for no loss of consciousness and that required a two-week layoff, and Grade 3 involved a loss of consciousness and required a three-week layoff. We arrived at that strictly in an arbitrary way. There was no science behind it.

I recommended that Woodley be held out for at least two weeks. Chuck Noll called me and asked me why Woodley couldn't play. He wasn't complaining. He just wanted me to explain how I had reached that determination. I didn't feel good about not being able to give him the kind of information he sought. Noll said, "Why are you telling me he can't play? Are you just trying to protect yourself? Is there really objective data you can show me? Look, I'll listen to you, but I think this is not a very scientific way to approach this."

I was chagrined. I wasn't upset with Noll. He never gave me a bad time. No one associated with the Steelers ever gave me a bad time. That's when I called Mark Lovell and asked him if we could develop something so I'd have the answers to Noll's questions in the future.

We put together a series of cognitive tests so we could determine what was normal for an athlete so we'd have something to measure them by when they suffered a head or neck injury. Noll was right. We needed better information. We needed to gather objective data. We just never thought about it. We never thought we'd be challenged like that. That tells you a lot about Chuck Noll, too, and why he was successful.

Boxing, by the way, is the only sport in which the goal is to deliver a blow that will cause brain damage to the other

"The mind swims, binding itself to whatever flotsam comes along, to old driftwood faces and pieces of the past, to places and scenes once visited, to things not seen or done but only dreamed."
— Bill Nack, author
My Turf

person. Every knockout is a concussion, usually a severe concussion. In boxing, it was mandatory to stay out of action for three weeks after suffering a knockout. So this guideline, strangely enough, was adopted by football as well.

Mark and I came up with this screening process and now we had to sell it to the Steelers. It required baseline testing. We had to convince the NFL Players Association that it was a cognitive test, not an I.Q. test. They were concerned about what information we were seeking. We wanted to know their ability to do certain tasks under normal conditions. We wanted to know what's normal. We convinced Chuck and Dan Rooney to do that. We treated them at 24 hours and 72 hours after a concussion. We found that rather than keeping them out of sports sometimes we could get them back (to playing) faster. Some people we kept out longer. That's because they couldn't remember what they had for breakfast.

It was thought that head injuries weren't that serious if the player didn't lose consciousness. But that's not true. It can build up. Merril Hoge never lost consciousness, for instance. Mike Webster never lost consciousness. We checked the team's medical records and there were no indications that Mike was ever knocked out, or carried off the field. We never saw Mike Webster for a head injury. If you have amnesia that's a more sensitive indication of brain malfunction than the loss of consciousness.

I saw Terry Bradshaw that time he was literally spiked into the turf by Turkey Jones of Cleveland. His neck had a tremendous degree of degeneration. Given his age, it was significant. It's common for football players to suffer degeneration in their bone structure. Studies have been done at the University of Iowa in which they took x-rays of college football players and found that 34 percent of them had significant degeneration.

"Do what is best for Tommy."

Dan Rooney has been extremely supportive. He went to Paul Tagliabue, the NFL commissioner, and helped get our ImPACT program into the NFL. In my 23 years with the Steelers, I've never had my recommendations or suggestions challenged, unless you're counting the time Noll asked me to give him a basis for holding out a player for two weeks who's suffered a concussion. That wasn't really a challenge. He just wanted to know the background for my determination.

And Noll did it in a correct way. Bill Cowher is the same way. If you say a guy can't play then Cowher accepts that. He can't play.

261

It's the same with the Tommy Maddox episode. Dan Rooney and Bill Cowher both said, "Do what is best for Tommy, whatever the outcome. We can live with whatever that might be."

So we did all the scans with the Steelers' blessing. He suffered a brain-stem concussion. It happens when the brain is shaken violently. He shut down. That was his brain stem. He was unable to move. We did all the tests that were appropriate for his brain and spinal cord. We did what they call neuro-imaging. We did psychological testing. We stimulated the nerve endings in his arms and legs. We did an impact test. We determined that there was no structural damage. Psychologically, everything was normal. It came down to what is the likelihood of him having some kind of permanent injury if he's hit again?

It's not like you have a series to go to for the answer to that question. It became a clinical judgment, the best I could weigh the facts. I didn't think he was at any unusual risks. He was astute himself in discussing his situation. We asked him if he saw any abnormality. He said, "There's nothing abnormal."

I told him it was my professional opinion that he was not at any increased risk, but stressed that this was merely an opinion. It was based on experience, not a case series or purely scientific evidence. I told him to get another opinion. Tommy was able to take the information I gave him and feel confident about his own decision.

I have taken care of players who've had quadriplegic injuries. I can't imagine worse injuries. If there are structural abnormalities, you are at risk. How much? Only God knows.

We monitored Tommy on the sideline when he returned to play. I don't know how many times I asked him, "How are you?" when he came out of the game. It was probably the most difficult medical decision I've ever made in sports medicine.

If he had gone back and had another injury, regardless of my stating that everything was okay, there clearly could have been a lot of repercussions. I felt pretty involved.

Tommy Maddox was a great story and I'm happy that he still has more chapters to write. It would make a great book.

George Blanda of Youngwood, Pa., speaks up:

"They called me a castoff quarterback and they called Len Dawson a castoff quarterback. The NFL gave us both a raw deal; we went to the new league where we did well and they call us castoffs. Hell, Johnny Unitas was released by Pittsburgh before he became what he became with Baltimore. Would anyone have guts enough to call him a castoff? Isn't that what he is? I mean, if we are, isn't he?"

Rick Druschel
One super season

"Those days at St. Vincent were very special."

The 1974 draft class of the Pittsburgh Steelers is regarded as the greatest in the team's history. It has to be one of the best in the history of the National Football League, though an argument might be waged that the Chicago Bears' class of 1965 might be better. That's when the Bears grabbed Gale Sayers of Kansas and Dick Butkus of Illinois with their first two choices. The numbers favor the Steelers.

Mel Kiper says the 1986 draft by the San Francisco 49ers, who didn't even have a first-round pick, was the best in NFL history. It produced eight starters for the 49ers. I don't think that class compares with the Steelers' draft classes of 1974 or 1971

The Steelers were picking 21st in that 1974 draft because they had posted a 10-4 record and were a wild-card playoff team. Their first five choices were: 1) Lynn Swann, wide receiver, Southern California; 2) Jack Lambert, linebacker, Kent State; 3) Choice to Oakland; 4a) Jon Stallworth, wide receiver, Alabama A&M (choice from New England); 4b) Jim Allen, defensive back, UCLA; 5) Mike Webster, center, Wisconsin. Four of those players — Swann, Lambert, Stallworth and Webster — are in the Pro Football Hall of Fame. Allen was with the Steelers for four seasons and gave them great depth in the defensive secondary. Fourteen first-year players, including free agents Donnie Shell and Randy Grossman, made the roster during that summer training camp in 1974 when the veterans reported late due to a player strike. Team rosters were expanded by three players because of the late start.

Though he doesn't come into the conversation when that draft class is discussed, Rick Druschel, an offensive lineman from North Carolina State, was selected by the Steelers that same year. The Steelers had two sixth round choices. Jim Wolf, a defensive end from Prairie View A&M, was taken first with a choice obtained from Denver, and he made the team and stuck with the Steelers for one season. Druschel also made the team and played on special teams and as a backup guard. He was 6-2, 250 pounds, and wore jersey number 73. He got to play in the Steelers' 16-6 victory over the Minnesota Vikings in Super Bowl IV. Druschel has a Super Bowl ring to show for his one season with the Steelers, and his one season in the National Football League. How cool is that?

Druschel grew up in Greensburg and was a second-team all-state selection during his schoolboy days playing for Bill Abraham at Hempfield Area High School. He served as athletic director at

Hempfield for seven years (1995-2002) and during the school year when we met he was the director for alternative education. He dealt with 35 students in Hempfield who had a poor attitude, or had problems of other kinds. "I try to motivate them," he said when we spoke on Friday, March 28, 2003 over lunch at Mr. P's Restaurant in Greensburg. "These are kids who are at a crossroad in their lives. You hope you can help them find their way."

Earle Edwards was the head coach at N.C. State when Druschel showed up, and then retired after that one season. Al Michaels took over for Druschel's sophomore season. In his junior year, they went after Lou Holtz at William & Mary to be the coach.

Now Druschel is involved in college football.

Druschel has served as a line judge as a collegiate football official, and worked games involving local schools such as Duquesne, Carnegie Mellon, IUP, Shippensburg, Grove City, Washington & Jefferson, Edinboro and California. He had been an official for eight years in college ball, and before that he worked high school games for 15 years. "I've worked a game where I had John Banaszak hollering at me on one sideline, and Jon Kolb complaining on the other sideline," recalled Druschel.

Druschel had suggested we meet at Hoss's Restaurant in Greensburg, and that we meet at 11 a.m. on Friday when they put out fresh clam chowder. Rick wanted it when it was good and hot and full of clams. I pushed for Mr. P's, located at the Westmoreland Inn, because Jack Perkins has been a long-time patron of mine, and because I love the food and atmosphere at his supper club. I was relieved when Jack's daughter, Jacque, told me that the soup of the day was Manhattan clam chowder. I didn't want to disappoint Druschel who seemed to have his heart (and stomach) set on clam chowder. I invited a friend, Bill Priatko, to join us. Priatko was retired from a position as athletic director at Yough High School in Westmoreland County. Priatko's photo is among those on the Wall of Fame at Mr. P's. Oldtime sports luminaries from the area have a monthly luncheon session there.

Druschel's brother, Bill, was an offensive tackle at North Carolina State when Bill Cowher was a linebacker for the Wolfpack. When the fields at St. Vincent College were too wet for the Steelers to practice there a few years earlier, Druschel had extended an offer to Cowher to bring the Steelers to practice on the artificial turf at Hempfield High School. Cowher accepted the invitation.

An education major at N.C. State, Druschel was named to the all-ACC Academic team.

"You've got to have a life after football.
You can't play all your life."
—Donnie Shell, Former Steelers' safety

Jim O'Brien

Rick Druschel is joined by proprietor Jack Perkins and Bill Priatko at Mr. P's Restaurant in Greensburg. Mr. P's is the home base for the Westmoreland County Athletic Association. Druschel and Priatko are former Steelers and athletic directors at Hempfield High School and Yough High School, respectively.

STEELERS ROOKIE CLASS OF 1974, regarded as the best in pro football history, includes, left to right bottom row: Richard Conn, Frank Nester, Donnie Shell, Tim Hornish, Leo Gasienica, Greg Pemberton, Nate Hawkins, Lynn Swann, Jesse Taylor, Billy Joe Releford, Bruce Henley, Marv Kellum, Reggie Garrett. Second Row: Mark Green, Bobby Huell, Jim Allen, Randy Grossman, Jim Larson, John King, Octavus Morgan, Mike Webster, Rich Arrigoni, Mark Gefert, Jack Lambert, Larry Moore, Jim Wolf. Top Row: Jerone Hodges, Richard Fowlkes, Rick Druschel, Dave Reavis, Hugh Lickliss, Charlie Davis, Allen Sitterle, John Stallworth, Gary Pinkel, Dave Davis, Scott Garske, Chuck Dicus.

"Ah, God, these guys are legends."

Rick Druschel:

I was Mike Webster's roommate that first year. I remember we'd sit in our room at St. Vincent College and worry about whether or not we were going to make the team.

The veterans missed most of the first five weeks of the camp, so we were never quite sure where we stood. You just wondered what was going to happen to you when the vets came in. When they first started coming in you saw the difference in the level of playing ability. No one realized just how good that first-year class would turn out to be.

Mike and I originally met in Lubbock, Texas where we were playing for the East team in the Coaches All-America Bowl. Our coaches were Johnny Majors and Jackie Sherrill of Pitt. My college coach, Lou Holtz, selected me to represent North Carolina State. Johnny Majors said some things to me that were special, and meant a lot to me at the time.

Mike was a workaholic, right from the start. No question about it. After our first practice in Lubbock, Webster said to me, "Let's go to the weight room and work out." Everyone else went off to lunch. It was like he had just gotten up out of bed. We worked out for an hour and a half. I wasn't prepared for that. They had some nice activities lined up for our entertainment in Lubbock. I knew Webster was something special and unique. But I knew I didn't want to spend so much time in the weight room.

Mike and I were both married, and our wives were there with us. Webster's wife was named Pam, the same as my wife. So they hit it off right from the start, and spent time with each other in Lubbock while we were practicing and lifting weights. We had a great time. Mike was playing right guard and I was playing right tackle.

It hit me hard when I heard he died. It was similar to my father's death. It was the end of an era. We had a fond relationship through the years. When I was waived during my second camp with the Steelers, I fell back into my little world, and Webster went on to a long and great pro career in the NFL. I had a chance with the Canadian Football League, but I got injured in the last exhibition game. I was with the Winnipeg Blue Bombers and I was covering for a punt and the guy who broke through for the Calgary Stampeders hit me. That was it for me. Ironically, the guy who hit me had been cut by the Steelers at the 1974 training camp.

Even though I grew up in Greensburg, I had never gone to the Steelers' training camp in Latrobe. The first practice I ever saw was one in which I participated. It's like Fort Ligonier. It's so close you don't think about going there. I participated in sports, but I wasn't a big sports fan.

I was with the Greensburg YMCA for a year, and I was a probation officer for four years in the community. My father was involved in local government, so I had good connections.

That one year I spent with the Steelers was a special year in my life. I'm thankful to the Rooneys and to Chuck Noll for giving me that experience for one year. Bruce Van Dyke was traded to Green Bay while I was at camp, and that opened a spot for me. Noll wanted to start Gerry Mullins at guard and dealt Van Dyke so he could do that. When that happened, my brother-in-law, Joe Kemmerer, said, "You have made an NFL team." That still means a great deal to me to have achieved that. I couldn't believe I was playing for the hometown pro team. I had gotten about two or three calls from the Dallas Cowboys, but I didn't know the Steelers were going to draft me.

Joe Gilliam was our starting quarterback at the beginning of 1974, but they settled on Terry Bradshaw before we got too far into the regular season. After a loss to Oakland (17-0) in Pittsburgh the third game of the season, they switched quarterbacks. We had Terry Hanratty, too, and they were all good quarterbacks. They were all tremendous athletes. It's hard to comprehend how good they were.

We'd go in on Tuesdays and watch film of our last game, and then we'd play a touch-tag football game. When they threw a pass it was difficult to catch it. The velocity was unreal. They were all unique in their own right. They were all very personable.

Ray Mansfield, Jim Clack and Moon Mullins were always joking with us. Gordy Gravelle came in early that year because he didn't want to lose his job on the offensive line. He was on the bubble. The veteran I admired the most was Sam Davis. My personal experience with Sam Davis helps explain that. We had played two pre-season games on the road and now we were playing Chicago in Pittsburgh. It was the first time I'd be in the starting offensive line for the Pittsburgh Steelers in front of a home crowd. A strained ligament put me out of the game. I had missed the third and fourth exhibition game when Gordie Gravelle rolled onto my leg at the end of one practice, and I hurt some ligaments.

Sam Davis had broken a bone in his hand. He had it well bandaged, and he had a huge claw as a result of that. He had broken his hand in the first quarter in a game at Washington. I was his backup. He refused to not play. He wanted to play no matter what.

267

In the second quarter, I asked him how his hand was. "It has to be hurting you," I suggested. "That hand has to be hurting you." He just shrugged. Finally, I said, "This is probably going to be my last game. I expect to get cut. I'd like to play one more time before I go."

Sam said, "I'll tell (trainer) Ralph Berlin it's bothering me."

So I got into the game in the second quarter. I did some good things on traps, and Noll must've liked what he saw. I made the team that game.

In the final exhibition game, I started alongside Mike Webster against the Cowboys in Dallas. We were lined up against Jethro Pugh and Bob Lilly. I'm thinking, "Ah, God, these guys are legends, you've been watching them on TV for years."

On the first play, Joe Gilliam goes back and takes those three extra steps before he throws. Lilly and Pugh jumped over us and sacked Gilliam. You just didn't realize the caliber of these guys.

The same goes for the Steelers I was playing with. You're playing with Swann and Stallworth and Lambert — they're rookies, too. But they're not like you. They're better than everybody else. There's nothing to compare it to.

I've always been grateful to Sam Davis for giving me that chance. I didn't realize until I ran into him in 1999 the scope of his physical problems. I saw him at a reunion of the team at the David L. Lawrence Convention Center. It hurts to see him diminished by his injuries. He was such a great guy.

I wasn't sure I should go, but my wife urged me to go. I felt in awe of all the people in the room. I'd only been on the team for one year, and I wondered how I'd be accepted. I was sitting with Andy Russell and Mike Wagner and I felt at ease, very much at home. Every player got up and said something and it was just great to be among them. I'm just so thankful.

I was part of the greatest team that ever played in the National Football League. They were the best in the NFL. I have a ring. What's to complain about? I never envied their success after I left the team. Two days ago I got a letter from a gentleman in New Jersey and he wanted to know if I wanted to sell my ring. I told my wife, "I could get that truck I wanted." She said, "Over my dead body."

I have a football autographed by everyone who was on that 1974 team. That means a lot to me. That's not for sale either. I wear my Super Bowl ring from time to time. I'm not big into jewelry or flashy stuff.

But I can still remember flying to New Orleans for that Super Bowl, knowing I would be on the kicking or receiving team at the start of the game. That was absolutely surreal.

At the time, you're hoping you can stick for five years. That's what all the guys were saying. Back then, you had to be in the league 4.7 years to qualify for an NFL pension.

At first, I stayed with my parents, Albert and Alberta Druschel, in Delmont. We stayed a couple of months with them. Then we found these two apartments over a four-car garage in Delmont. We lived in one apartment and the Websters lived in the other apartment. Pam and Pam became good friends. Mike and I were fifth- and sixth-rounds picks, so we seemed to have a bond. The next year they cut the squads from 47 back to 43, and about seven guys who'd been on the team lost their jobs. You had to get on with your life's work. But it was great while it lasted. I showered with the greatest football players in the land.

Rick Druschel of Greensburg with Steelers in 1974

Merril Hoge
Determined to whip cancer

"I'm on the road to victory."

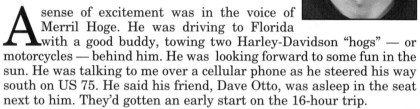

A sense of excitement was in the voice of Merril Hoge. He was driving to Florida with a good buddy, towing two Harley-Davidson "hogs" — or motorcycles — behind him. He was looking forward to some fun in the sun. He was talking to me over a cellular phone as he steered his way south on US 75. He said his friend, Dave Otto, was asleep in the seat next to him. They'd gotten an early start on the 16-hour trip.

It was mid-morning, temperatures were rising from 65 to 85 degrees during the drive — 20 degrees higher than it would get in Pittsburgh — and Hoge was even more high-spirited than usual. He was 38 years old, and he had learned five weeks earlier that he had cancer. He was given the diagnosis on Valentine's Day that he had stage two non-Hodgkins lymphoma. Cancer of the lymph nodes at an advanced stage can kill you.

The doctors and Hoge are hopeful the cancer was caught in time, and that he can be cured. He had already had two chemotherapy treatments and had lost his hair. Being bald wasn't so bad, he thought. He said it's even fashionable these days. Hoge has always looked at things from the bright side. His mother raised him to look at obstacles as opportunities, just like Lance Armstrong's mother.

His enthusiasm for life will serve Merril well. He was talking about his situation the way he once approached games as a confident running back for the Pittsburgh Steelers for seven seasons (1987-1993). He finished up with one season with the Chicago Bears and was forced to retire during that 1994 season because he had suffered two many concussions. He had persistent headaches, bouts of wooziness and was told by doctors that he was susceptible to more head injuries.

He had sued one of the Bears' team doctors a few years earlier for allowing him to play too soon after he had suffered a concussion, and had expressed concern in an interview we had a year earlier about the lingering effects. "I have memory lapses, my eyes twitch," he said then. "I've had six concussions and I'm a poster boy for NFL concussion stories. Sometimes my eyes go black, and sometimes one of my eyes is an inch higher than the other one."

When I asked Hoge this time around about his concussion-syndrome concerns, he said, "I don't even care about that now. That's on the back burner."

During his playing days, Hoge put up good numbers for the Steelers, and was one of their most popular players. He and Franco Harris are the only two backs in Steelers' history to rush for 100 yards in consecutive playoff games. He has always been one of my personal favorites. He's always been approachable, affable, accommodating and considerate, willing to share. A journalist can't ask for more than that. Talking to Hoge had the same empowering effect as attending a revival meeting. He was always good for the soul, and for a smile. Even so, I hated to hear that Hoge was being challenged by cancer.

As he headed for Florida, humming "On the Road Again" by Willie Nelson, he took time out to call me in Pittsburgh, as promised. He said if Dave were awake they'd have sung aloud with Willie. Hoge was talking a blue streak and sounded like a college kid on spring break, or a kid who'd had too many spoonfuls of sugar with his cereal that morning. He may have been trying to drive the demons out of his body with sheer bravado.

"I'm on the road to victory," he had told me the night before when we touched base about doing an interview, "and I'm halfway there!"

He was on the road to Sarasota. He said he had a condo there on Long Boat Key, and he couldn't wait for him and Dave to be driving their "hogs" along the roads along the shore. "Then we'll have a good dinner," he said, "and settle in to watch Pitt play in the NCAA tournament."

I, too, was looking forward to watching Pitt play Marquette in the Sweet 16 Round at Minneapolis. On the poll I played at Atria's Restaurant & Tavern I had picked Marquette to beat Pitt. It was one of those picks I didn't want to be right about. I often root against my own picks once a game starts, and an underdog has a chance to knock off one of the big favorites. I wanted Pitt to prevail, but I just thought something would go wrong. There was no joy when it did. Marquette didn't permit Pitt to play its best game, something Pitt had been doing to teams all during a wonderful season in which they ranked in the Top Ten most of the way.

Some times things don't work out the way you want. (For the record, I ended up finishing second by a mere two points in the Atria's poll and collected $146. The winner took home just over $1,000.)

Hoge had left his home in Fort Thomas, Kentucky, a suburb just south of Cincinnati. His wife of nearly 11 years, Toni, and their two children, Kori, 10, and Beau, 6, stayed behind. This was a challenging time for them as well, but they believed the main man in their lives would be okay. "It has no chance to win," Hoge said of his cancer. "I'm destroying it. I'm halfway there. In the end, more good will come of this than bad."

Hoge was looking forward to the National Football League's college draft April 26-27, when he would be co-hosting 17 hours of live coverage on ESPN television.

He had been thinking of wearing each team's ballcap prior to their pick, or just wearing one of his own caps, or just going au natural. "I don't look that bad bald," he said. "I'm sorta getting used to it."

He was scheduled to have his third chemotherapy treatment on April 7 and his fourth two days after the NFL draft. He would have all six of his prescribed treatments near his home in Kentucky.

Hoge does his homework, as do Ron Jaworski and Mark Malone, two former NFL quarterbacks known for watching lots of game tapes of NFL action. Hoge and Malone, who once quarterbacked the Steelers, are among the many former Pittsburgh players now seen regularly on television, or heard on the radio.

Hoge is always canvassing coaches around the league to get more inside information. Coaches like Bill Cowher and Brian Billick will tell Hoge stuff they wouldn't share with each other. They trust him; that's the secret. Lots of writers call Hoge to find out what he's found out. Only a week earlier, Hoge had visited Marvin Lewis, a former Steelers assistant who was the new head coach of the Cincinnati Bengals, to get his take on the draft. The Bengals had the first pick in the draft. Lewis, from McDonald, Pennsylvania, had been on Cowher's staff, looking after the linebackers, in Hoge's last two seasons (1992-93) with the Steelers.

Hoge had been an 11th round draft pick out of Idaho State in 1987. As a 6-2, 220-pound running back, he had set all sorts of records on the Pocatello campus. Pocatello lies in the fertile Snake River Valley in the foothills of the Rocky Mountains in southeastern Idaho, just above the western wing of the Caribou National Forest. He was a real country boy, just as naïve about big city ways as Terry Bradshaw had been 17 years earlier. When Pat Hanlon worked in the Steelers public relations office, he once assigned Hoge to represent the Steelers at a midget football banquet. I shared the dais with Hoge at another dinner soon after, and Hoge confessed to the audience at St. Agatha's Church smoker in Bridgeville, "I knew football was big in western Pennsylvania, but I couldn't believe they had a league just for midgets."

Hanlon was now the vice-president of communications for the New York Giants, and remained a big fan of Merril Hoge. "I call him Brick Head, but I love him," said Hanlon. "I'm rooting for him."

"The ability to help others is great."

As it turned out, Hoge appeared bald for the 2003 NFL draft show on ESPN-TV. A few days in advance of the 17-hour show, he explained why he decided to do that. "I don't want to wear a hat that says I'm afraid to be bald," he told Chuck Finder of the *Pittsburgh Post-Gazette*. "I don't want that message to be sent. Cancer hasn't taken my hair; the treatment took it. Seventeen hours of me being bald, you'll get used to it. I've been bald long enough to realize I look good. I'm excited about it. I just think there's tremendous power in these things. The ability to help others and strengthen others is great.

"My doctor called me. A 19-year-old kid here was just diagnosed with non-Hodgkins lymphoma, and he and his family are just devastated. If you've had cancer, if you've just been diagnosed, or if you know somebody who has cancer . . . my instincts are to destroy it

and to win and to accept nothing but that. People have that in them.
I had it in me from football."

"You gotta believe!"

Steelers' fans first learned that Hoge had cancer in an exclusive report
by Ed Bouchette, who covers the Steelers' beat for the *Pittsburgh Post-
Gazette*, and is one of the most respected reporters on the NFL scene.
It was in the Friday, March 21, 2003 edition of the *Post-Gazette*.
  There was a scary story in the same section about Tug McGraw,
58, who had been a terrific and fun-loving relief pitcher for the New
York Mets and Philadelphia Phillies when they won the World Series.
He'd become even more famous as the father of Tim McGraw, the
country singing sensation. It was revealed that Tug McGraw was
recovering from surgery in a Florida hospital to remove a brain tumor.
Doctors said they wouldn't know until they operated whether or not it
was cancerous.
  What was going on? That's what I was wondering. I had met
McGraw and gotten to know him when I covered the Mets for the *New
York Post* during the 1972 season. It was McGraw who started the
rallying cry for the 1973 Mets — "You Gotta Believe!" He threw a
wicked screwball and he was one himself.
  He was on a team with Tom Seaver and Nolan Ryan and Ron
Swoboda, and in a town with Joe Namath of the Jets, Fran Tarkenton
of the Giants, and the Knicks of Willis Reed, Walt Frazier, Earl
Monroe, Bill Bradley, Dave DeBusschere and Dick Barnett, and held
his own. He once wiped out the audience at a Dapper Dan Dinner in
Pittsburgh with his off-color remarks. Like Hoge, he always had time
to mix with the media. Like Hoge and Terry Bradshaw, McGraw was
a hoot. But a brain tumor, cancerous or not, was no laughing matter.
  "If you look around," said Hoge, "you'll see that there are a lot of
people with challenges as great or more so than mine."
  He said he had discussed his situation with Mario Lemieux, who
overcame stage-one Hodgkin's disease and returned to play on a high
level for the Penguins. He said others had offered him support.
  Dr. Stanley Marks, a renowned oncologist at UPMC's Hillman
Cancer Center in Shadyside, was treating Hoge. He talked to
Bouchette about Hoge's situation. "He has a pretty good chance," said
Dr. Marks. "He probably has somewhere in the range of 75 to 80 per-
cent chance of prolonged remission and, hopefully, cure."
  Dr. Marks explained to Bouchette what lymphoma is all about.
Oncologists rank lymphoma in stages, from 1-4, four being the worst.
They also attach a letter grade, A or B, depending on whether a
patient is losing weight and feels sick. Dr. Marks listed Hoge's condi-
tion as 2-A, the best possible condition.

> *"A winner is somebody who has*
> *given his best effort."*
> **— Walter Payton in his autobiography**
> ***Never Die Easy***

"It is destroyable," Hoge told Bouchette. "It is beatable. You have everything in you to do it. The mind is a powerful thing. There is no doubt, come May, I'll be cancer free; five years after that, I'll be cured. Fifty years or whatever time I have left after that, it will be the platform I stand for. I'll be a better man. This has been a blessing."

When Hoge was talking to me en route to Florida, I asked him, "Do you look like Mel Blount?"

"No," he answered, and I could picture his lopsided grin, "I'm better looking than Mel Blount."

He may have lost his hair but he hadn't lost his sense of humor.

Before I interviewed Hoge, I read Lance Armstrong's book about his victory over cancer, and his success as a world-class cyclist.

"I know I'm going to beat it."

Merril Hoge:

This cancer is the biggest challenge of my life. I firmly believe I have the right mind-set and spirit to beat it. Having a good attitude about any challenge is one of the most empowering things. It's funny when you've sharpened your spirit there's nothing you can't overcome in this world.

I had to have that kind of attitude and spirit in order to play the game of football at the level I was playing the game. The knowledge that I have cancer has forced me to sharpen things that had been dulled.

I know I'm going to beat it. I've never been surer about something in my entire life. I've got a more positive attitude about this than I had with any game I ever played.

I read Lance Armstrong's book (*It's Not About The Bike*) a few years back. I learned how he dealt with and defeated cancer and became the greatest bicycle racer in the world. He wouldn't be denied. You always draw strength from other people.

There's one thing that book doesn't give you. It doesn't give you the ability to handle the word "cancer" when they're talking about you. I remember when I read the book that I thought aloud about what I'd do, or not do if I were in Armstrong's situation. That's not what I did when I was told I had cancer. I didn't react the way I thought I'd react.

Yes, all the air went out of me. But I think I bounced back in a hurry. I always loved General Patton, and I loved reading his books about World War II (1940-45). I loved his outlook on

Photos by Jim O'Brien

Former Steelers' defensive back Carnell Lake visits with, at left, Dwayne Woodruff, who helped show him the ropes when he reported from UCLA in 1989, and with Coach Bill Cowher who called him one of his "all-time favorite players," during outing at Southpointe Golf Club.

Mark Bruener welcomed sportscaster Bill Hillgrove and Geyer Printing Co. sales rep Keith Maiden at Celebrity Golf Classic for Children. Proceeds go to the Western Pennsylvania Caring Foundation. This event is coordinated each year by Judd Gordon.

"The disease doesn't discriminate or listen to the odds — it will decimate a strong person with a wonderful attitude, while it somehow miraculously spares the weaker person who is resigned to fail. Why me? Why anybody?"
— Lance Armstrong, from his book,
It's Not About the Bike

war, and it's ironic now that we're in a war. I loved the movie, too. He said he didn't want anybody to call him and up and say "We're holding our position." He said, "You will attack and you will attack and you will attack"

He reminds me a lot of Chuck Noll. The more I read of Patton the more he reminds me of Chuck Noll.

For me, to play in the NFL, I had to be a physically, mentally and spiritually strong individual. I never had a greater challenge in my life than the NFL — until this.

I've been forced to sharpen my attitude and outlook, and live in less fear. I'm more powerful, I'm happier, and I'm enjoying life more. If my head weren't bald you wouldn't have a clue about my condition. I'm still playing in all my basketball leagues, I'm still working out regularly. I'm healthier than I was the day before I learned I had cancer. There are poisons in my body, but I'm going to get rid of them.

I will be a changed man. Lance Armstrong talks about changes, and I want mine to be all for the better.

I'm a health fanatic. I've never needed drugs. I get high on life. I feel so good when I'm out hunting, just to be out there. I'm in the mountains, or I've gone up 4,000 feet and look out over the Continental Divide, and it doesn't get any better. No, I don't need drugs to get high.

Physically and mentally, I've been able to maximize my potential. I'm in my own war. There's nothing a person can't accomplish with a positive attitude. Some people shut down when they hear they have cancer. They stop working out. I haven't stopped a thing. They've done autopsies on people who were thought to have died from cancer and they discover that they are cancer free. They died because they gave up on life. The disheartening thing is when people hear they have cancer they just give up.

None of this is a day at the beach. I have peaks and valleys, and I get tired more than I used to. I have to sneak away for midday naps. The toughest days are the seven days after you've had your chemotherapy treatment. That steals a lot of steam from you.

I was talking to a nurse the first day I was receiving my chemo treatment, and she said, "Eighty percent of this is up to you, and 20 percent is up to what I'm doing for you right now." I've kept that in mind. I thanked her for telling me. It set me on the right path.

Nobody will ever tell me when I'm going to live and die. Only a higher power can determine that.

You've got to get your butt out of bed, and get going each day. I refuse to lie around. My family has been great about this. Toni, my wife, has been like a rock. I feed off her and she feeds off me. We know I'll be cancer-free. The tough part was telling my kids.

We had a five-day get-away week together at our cabin in Idaho. I got a call when I was there with my family, and that's when I found out that I had a malignancy. I had to tell my kids we had to leave. I bawled like a baby when I explained it all to my kids. Corie, who's 10, was taken aback. She's older and understood it better. Beau, who's six, listened and then he asked us, "Can we go to Wal-Mart now?" I had to smile. He was saying, in his own way, we've got to move on. Let's move on.

I told them I was going to be bald, and this bothered them at first. Then, soon after I went bald, they started bringing their friends around the house and had me show them my bald head. Like I'm a show-and-tell deal at school. I'll get my hair back, and I'll be all right.

I've always told my kids that you have to find a way to win, or find a way to get something accomplished. You have to find a way to get it done. I've always preached that, so now it's my turn to live by that.

"It looks like lymphoma."
— Dr. Stanley Marks

I found out about my situation by visiting Dr. James Bradley, one of the Steelers' team doctors. He started the miracle. I went in to see him as a follow-up examination for a shoulder injury I suffered a year earlier in a car accident

While I was there, I told him that when I'd stoop getting in the shower in the morning I had this sharp pain in the middle of my back. It was nothing big, but when he asked me if there was anything else going on I thought I should tell him.

I had an x-ray and then an MRI because there was something he wasn't sure about that showed up on the x-ray. Dr. Bradley called a radiologist and told him to check out a certain spot. He thought there was something there in the lymph nodes of my back. I followed that with a CAT-scan. Dr. Bradley sent me to see Dr. Stanley Marks, one of the best oncologists in the region. He put the MRI negative up on one of those lit-up boards. I could see it in his face that something was wrong. Soon as he put it up there I could tell he knew something was amiss. "It looks like lymphoma," he said. He told me he wanted to run some further tests. But he knew what it was. He's been around long enough to know what he was seeing. He had to confirm it.

This was about two months ago, during the big snowstorm. That storm was indicative of what I was going through in my life. It was one storm after another. I'm doing all I can to combat this. I've been doing my chemo treatments and I'm into some holistic stuff.

Cancer doesn't care who you are, or what you are, what color, what ethnic group, what religion, or how much money you might have.

The cancer was confirmed when I was on that five-day getaway with my family at our cabin in Idaho. I found out on Valentine's Day, 2003. Here I'm telling my wife I love her and that she's my Valentine, and I get the word that I have cancer. We'll never forget Valentine's Day. We'll celebrate it more joyfully the next time around when I'm cancer free.

I was in Pittsburgh for a biopsy at the Hillman Cancer Center at UPMC in Shadyside. I was there from 3:30 to 4:30 p.m. and then I drove to Monroeville for an appearance at the Travel & Outdoor Show at the Expo Mart. It was a most surreal thing. It was the most memorable autograph signing session I've ever done in my life. I had taken a local anesthetic before the biopsy. So I was feeling a little off when I got off that table to go to Monroeville.

People are showing me pictures of myself as a Steeler rookie, and telling me they couldn't believe I was 38 because I looked so young. I was thinking if they only knew about my cancer they wouldn't think I was in such great shape. I was there for two hours and it was a weird experience.

Someone showed me a picture I had posed for with a baby 12 years earlier. Now the 12-year-old is standing there next to me. It was the most memorable autograph session I've ever gone through. I said to myself that I'll be standing here next year, too. I'll be a changed man, an even better man.

I had been worrying about some of the lingering effects of all the concussions, but I don't even care about that now. One thing I've found out through all these tests is that my organs are all in great shape. One of the doctors said my vertebrae were evenly spread, much better than a football player normally has. In another six months, I'll be cancer free. Then I'll be in great health, and I'm going to do all I can to stay that way.

I'm not going to lose this battle. I'm going to heal whole. My spirit will be much stronger.

One of the most overwhelming things is the people I've heard from since the word got out that I had cancer. Marianne and Chuck Noll called me and that meant so much to me. All I can say to everyone is "Thank you." The Nolls care about their players.

My friends have been there for me. I'm blessed from that standpoint. Cancer is always a mortality check. And my experience has humbled me to my knees. I feel humiliated in some respects.

Steelers who have spearheaded the annual Celebrity Golf Classic for Children for a decade are, left to right, Hines Ward, Mark Bruener, Carnell Lake and Merril Hoge at Southpointe Golf Club.

Photos by Jim O'Brien

Brothers Marty and Merril Hoge have some business interests back home in Pocatello, Idaho. Marty is bigger than his older brother and gets around on a Harley-Davidson motorcycle.

I trusted one of my friends with the information early on that I had cancer, long before I went public with it. He told me what I was going through. He said, "You lived the first 38 years of your life for yourself, and now you're going to live the next 38 years for other people."

"I was like a kid in a candy store."

One of my great experiences in my sports career happened when I was playing for the Bears in Chicago. Walter Payton used to come to our practices on Wednesday. He wasn't playing for the team anymore, but he was on the board. He motivated me as a kid. He was my idol when I was a kid out in Idaho. I watched him on TV, and he inspired me.

I want to do for others what Walter Payton did for me. Payton would play pass and catch with me on the sideline. During our special team practice drills, I'd hang out with Walter on the sideline. I wanted those special teams to stay out there forever. I was going into my ninth year in the NFL, and I was like a kid in a candy store. I'm playing catch with my boyhood hero.

Another great thing is that he turned out to be a worthy idol. He was everything you wanted in a hero. He was the genuine article. I think we all need idols. I try to remember that. You never know what kind of an impression you leave on people. I've always done my best to be at my best for everybody.

My brother Marty runs our company out in Pocatello. We rent furniture and appliances and all kinds of stuff. A police officer came by recently to make sure everything was OK, and he told my brother a story. He said that years earlier his wife was dying of cancer. He said that he and his son, who was eight years old at the time, had met me at a program when I was involved with Children Against Drugs.

I heard about what the family was going through. When I got back to Pittsburgh I sent this kid a care package. I sent him a jersey and signed some stuff for him. The guy said his wife had died in the interim and that my gift had helped them both get through a difficult period. He said it meant a lot to them. You like to hear that maybe you helped somehow. That was 16 years ago. Now the kid is 23 and he hasn't forgotten that.

"I'll always be a Bear. That's a fact of life."
— **Mike Ditka**

"You have to finish every game."

When the Pittsburgh Steelers won four Super Bowls from 1974-1980, no player epitomized the Steelers' offense more than Mike Webster. I played with Mike the first two years of my career and he taught me more about how to win in the NFL than anyone else.

During my second year in 1988, we were losing 28-7 in the fourth quarter to the Cardinals in Phoenix. At the time, I was the third-down back, but they put me and the rest of the second string into the game to play all the downs the rest of the game.

The only starting player who would not leave the field was Mike Webster. The plastic had been stripped off his facemask. His hands were taped and bleeding. His jersey was ripped. He had deep, huge gashes in the front of his helmet. He had grass stains everywhere and dirt in his face.

And as we were standing on the field during a TV timeout, he said, "Men, one thing you can never do in this league is quit. You have to finish every play and finish every game. We're going to take the ball and go down the field."

We didn't win the game, but his words left a permanent mark in my mind about what it takes to be a champion, to win every Sunday and to win the Super Bowl.

Mike was also my roommate my rookie year. At first, the idea of rooming with him was a little intimidating. I thought the Steelers may have paired Mike with me to groom me. I needed a lesson or two coming from a small school like Idaho State. But after the first few hours, he became just a teammate. I tried to absorb everything I could from him as a professional, as a future Hall of Fame center and as a player I had watched and idolized.

During our first night as roommates, at around 10 p.m., he asked if I wanted any dessert or if I wanted to watch a movie. After I said no to both questions, he got out of bed, locked the door, put the chain on and bolted it. I said, "What did you do that for?" I thought, "He's Mike Webster; he can't be afraid of anything."

He said, "The last time I was here, I was rooming with Lynn Swann. And some hookers (who had been in the room earlier) took the keys from the previous occupants, and they came in and ransacked the room and stole our wallets and everything." I never forgot that. Now, when I'm on the road, I always lock the door when I go to bed.

I remember another time we were playing a pre-season game against the New York Giants at the New Jersey Meadowlands. One of the nice things during training camp is that you get to sleep in on the day of these games. I was

281

rooming with Webby at this hotel overlooking a swamp in the meadowlands.

He gets up at 5:30 in the morning and pulls the curtains back all the way on the window. It was like rooming with your dad. He says, "Now there's a real cesspool. Who'd want to live here?" Then he turns back to me and says, "What do you want for breakfast?"

Everybody else is going to sleep in till noon, and we're up for the day. Webby was ready to go.

There's a lot to be said about the Tommy Maddox story. I think it shows Bill Cowher's maturity as a coach. It shows his ability to change with the game. They changed their philosophy around this past year. Cowher turned over the offense more than he ever did before when he named Mike Mularkey the offensive coordinator.

Tommy Maddox and Kordell Stewart have different strengths and weaknesses. From my research, more players fear Kordell, and more coaches fear Maddox. The players have to be fearful that Kordell can beat you running or passing. There are different dynamics at work when he's in there. Maddox is no threat to run. The coaches fear Tommy Maddox more because the Steelers can use more formations with him in there. As a coach, you're forced to deal with more options. Tommy can run a high-low combination where you have to read a bunch of things, or he can have his receivers running complementary routes, and he's able to handle that. He gets rid of the ball quicker than Kordell, and hits guys more on the break. A lot of young quarterbacks wait for a receiver to get open before they throw the ball. But the receivers don't stay open that long. You've got to be able to anticipate them getting open. Otherwise, you'll throw a lot of interceptions. Maddox gets intercepted because he's so confident he can get the ball in there and that his receivers are going to come away with the ball.

From a schematic standpoint, Maddox gives you more to think about. He can frustrate coaches. The year after I left the team, the Steelers started to slip. One of the reasons was they lost John Jackson at left tackle. They moved Justin Strzelczyk over from right tackle. By doing that, they weakened two offensive line positions. That left tackle position is important because he has to handle the outside rush from the blind side for a right-handed quarterback. Now they've lost Wayne Gandy and they're talking about moving Marvel Smith over into that slot. The same thing could happen again, and that will hurt Maddox. He's not as good at avoiding the rush.

The key for the Steelers is their offensive line. You have to have a cohesive group. You need time and the same personnel to establish that.

I don't know what's going to happen to my buddy, Mark Bruener, but I'd hate to see the Steelers let him go. They could use two tight ends at the same time and be awesome. Mark is the best guy you'll ever meet.

The other story I liked was the Terry Bradshaw story. I would hope that he's at peace with Pittsburgh and the Steelers now. After what I've gone through in the last few weeks, I can see more clearly now about these things.

There's one thing in life you can never get back and that's time. It's so precious. Why waste it on negative thoughts or animosity? You have to put those things aside and get on with your life. Both Terry Bradshaw and Chuck Noll were pivotal guys to everything that was achieved in Pittsburgh during those Super Bowl years. I think Terry Bradshaw made Chuck Noll a better coach. He had to baby-sit Terry because Terry demands a lot of attention. Without Chuck, Terry doesn't become the player he became. Everybody who's ever played for Chuck becomes a better player and a better person.

Terry Bradshaw is one of the best in our business. He lights up any stage he's on. He loves the camera and the camera loves him. I can't be like him. You have to be who you are. But you can learn some things from him. I have a better shot at being like Terry now that I'm bald-headed, too. Right now, Terry actually has more hair than I do. That's scary now that I think about it.

Jim O'Brien

Merril Hoge still wears Steelers outfits while visiting Atria's Restaurant & Tavern in Wexford, not far from a home he keeps in Pittsburgh.

Pete Duranko
West End Story

"I don't feel sorry for myself."

Todd Kalis was attempting to call a meeting of the Pittsburgh chapter of the NFL alumni to order. Pete Duranko had it in disorder. This was in a dining room on the second floor of Bruschetta's Restaurant on East Carson Street, the main drag on the city's South Side.

The room was dimly lit and it looked like the scene at the Last Supper. About 13 men once associated with the Steelers or some other National Football League team had gathered for one of the group's occasional get-togethers. They were seated around a long dark table. Kalis wanted to talk business now that they had eaten a wonderful dinner served to them by restaurateur John Lewis. Duranko wanted to keep the table entertained. He had been telling one joke or bawdy tale after another.

Duranko had driven the farthest for the meeting, all the way from his hometown of Johnstown in Cambria County, and he wanted to get his money's worth. I could see that Steve Fedell, a former Steeler, and Gerry Hart, a former member of the Detroit Lions and NFL officiating staff, were getting a kick out of Duranko. Bob Milie, a former trainer with the Steelers, was chuckling as well. My friend Bill Priatko, who enjoyed brief stints with the Steelers, Browns and Packers, was blanching because Duranko was a little too X-rated for his straight-arrow tastes.

Duranko's dark hair and mustache framed his bright, dancing eyes. He's a big guy with a big, hearty laugh, the life of every party. He was like Zorba the Greek. He meant no harm.

Duranko was reined in by Kalis, eventually, and Kalas began to outline some planned activities for the Alumni Chapter, such as visiting the patients at Children's Hospital in Oakland once again, or building houses for families down on their luck. Duranko can't do any heavy work, but he was there handing out wiring when they were building homes for disadvantaged people.

Duranko had been a star fullback at Bishop McCourt High School, an All-American lineman on a national championship team at Notre Dame in the mid-60s, and a star lineman for the Denver Broncos from 1967 to 1975. No one enjoyed reunions with his old teammates and fellow pro football players any more than Pete Duranko. He's a legendary Pennsylvania football star. He ran for 3,168 yards in two seasons as a Crusher fullback. "I was a damn good fullback," he recalled proudly.

I had no idea that night, sitting across the table from him, that Duranko had Lou Gehrig's disease. Or that he was dying. I learned

His whole family surrounded Pete Duranko at his home in Johnstown when he signed a letter-of-intent to accept athletic scholarship to attend the University of Notre Dame.

Boy Scout Pete Duranko receives medal for saving schoolmate Delsien Herman after she was swept away in a swift-flowing stream in Cambria City. Young Duranko held out an old Christmas tree that she was able to grab and get to shore. Ceremony was held at St. Mary's Byzantine Church.

Photos provided by Duranko Family

that later while speaking to some of the former Steelers who had gotten to know him. They were worried for him. ALS, or Lou Gehrig's disease, is nothing to laugh about.

It's a disease named after the great Lou Gehrig, the first baseman of the New York Yankees who was known as "Ironman" because he established the record for most consecutive games played that Baltimore's Cal Ripken Jr. broke a few years back.

There's an irony there. Mike Webster of the Steelers was known as "Iron Mike," and he ended up dying of a heart attack at age 50. "That was a real tragedy," said Pete Duranko. "That was a real shame."

So was what was happening to Pete Duranko. The disease undoes the nerve endings from the extremities and moves inward. In time, Duranko would lose the use of his hands, then his legs, then his voice, then the organs that feed the brain, which never loses awareness until the last blink. Some people last a year following diagnosis and some last 20. When we spoke, Duranko said he needed both hands to lift a cup of coffee.

Duranko doesn't get down in the dumps about his dilemma in public, and refuses to seek pity. That's not his style. He takes pride in being from the West End of Johnstown. That was a tough neighborhood, full of tough guys like Pete Duranko.

"I don't know if I'm hiding it or what," declared Duranko in an interview he had with Dennis Roddy of the *Pittsburgh Post-Gazette*. "You know what I worry about more than anything? What's my wife going to go through?"

In a later interview, Pete Duranko told me he's been married to Janet for 37 years. "I tell people we've been married for 74 years," said Duranko, always with the funny line. "Thirty-seven years for her, and thirty-seven years for me."

They have two boys, Nick, 36, and Greg, 32.

"I'm 59 years old, I act like I'm 12 and I feel like I'm 85," Duranko was fond of saying. "Now I'm the child and my kids are the parents."

When I spoke to Duranko on Thursday, March 20, 2003, he had just returned from Florida, where he had spent several days playing golf and having fun with several of his former teammates from his days at Notre Dame. He's a serious Notre Dame alumnus. His birth name is Nicholas Peter Duranko, but he had it changed to Peter Nicholas Duranko so his initials would be PND. To him, ND means Notre Dame.

And Notre Dame means tradition. He looks like Tevye, the milkman from the musical *Fiddler On The Roof*, when he says it. Tradition is important to Pete Duranko. He loves the tradition of Pennsylvania schoolboy football, Touchdown Jesus and the Golden Dome at Notre Dame, the Broncos and the Steelers.

In the movie "Seabiscuit," Tom Smith, the trainer stops a guy from killing a lame horse: "You don't throw a whole life away just 'cause it's banged up a little."

Laughead Phortographers

Pete Duranko in publicity photo at
Notre Dame in 1966

Duranko is flanked by sons Greg, age 10, and Nick,
age 14, in front of their home in Johnstown

Pete Duranko gives victory salute to crowd as he joins his coach Ara
Parseghian for reunion at Notre Dame.

He loves to talk about Rocky Bleier and Terry Hanratty, his teammates at Notre Dame, about Dave Hart, who tried to recruit him to go to the University of Kentucky, about Johnny Unitas, Jack Ham, Steve Smear, Mike Ditka, Leon Hart, Johnny Lujack and Johnny Lattner. It doesn't take much to set off Pete Duranko. He has stories and more stories, jokes and more jokes. "I love that stuff," he says with a broad smile. He tells you he almost went to Penn State and Pitt, but a priest at Bishop McCourt kept after him and pointed him to Notre Dame. It was the right choice, according to Duranko.

He loves to tell stories about the days when he chased after and took down Terry Bradshaw in the backfield when the Broncos were playing the Steelers. "I never lost to the Steelers," boasts Duranko. "I get on those guys about that. I don't let them forget that. We beat them twice and tied them the other time I played against them."

The Notre Dame get-together was hosted by Angelo Schiralli, a second-team guard at South Bend in the mid-60s. Schiralli has a palatial home in Palm Beach. He's done well selling insurance to business executives, Duranko said. Duranko mentioned that among those in attendance were Larry Conjar, George Goeddeke (also a teammate at Denver), Kevin Hardy, Bob Kuechenberg and Bill Zloch. "We had a great time," declared Duranko.

He said many of those same fellows had attended a dinner held in his honor by the Notre Dame Club of Central Pennsylvania at a hotel in Johnstown on March 1, 2003. Pete "Diesel" Duranko had been a powerful fullback who gained Big 33 and All-Pennsylvania honors during his days at Bishop McCourt High School, class of 1962.

Ara Parseghian, the new head football coach at Notre Dame, switched him to being a defensive lineman and then a linebacker. Parseghian was a master at making such personnel switches and directed a dramatic turnaround in Notre Dame's fortunes during his tenure there.

Duranko was Notre Dame's defensive lineman of the year in 1966 when the Fighting Irish won their second national championship under Parseghian. He was named to the Bishop McCourt Alumni Association Hall of Fame on September 9, 2000.

"I'm a professional bullshitter."

Pete Duranko:

I moved back to Johnstown in 1976 when I finished playing football for the Denver Broncos. I also went to St. Francis College in nearby Loretto and gained a master's degree in industrial relations and administration. I got involved in the steel industry right after a flood in 1977, and right before the collapse of the local steel industry. I worked for a time as a middle manager at a rail wheel plant and, when that ended, I sold insurance. I think I made $10,000 that year. You have to get started in the insurance business when you're younger and build up a clientele. I was 53 when I got started. A friend asked me to do it, and I gave it a try.

I know why Tommy Maddox was willing to give up selling insurance to get back into pro football. It's not easy. I tried it for about three years. On the other hand, one of my former teammates, Dave Casper, who went from Notre Dame to the Oakland Raiders, has been a big success selling insurance. But he got started earlier. It's something you have to build up.

I thought the Tommy Maddox story was a great one. Anyone could appreciate his comeback story. He has a special mentality; he wouldn't give up.

I've been involved with the NFL Alumni since 1983. I got in touch with Ray Mansfield, who was running things for the Pittsburgh chapter back then. I asked him why I never got invited to any of their functions and golf outings. He said he didn't know I was in the neighborhood. After that, Ray and I got to know each other pretty well and I went to Pittsburgh for a lot of their activities. I've spent a lot of time with Andy Russell and attended his golf event.

It doesn't matter who you played for at this stage of the game. We're all in the same boat. We're all dealing with the same problems. We're all getting older and better. Like the Steelers, we hated the Raiders, but now we enjoy getting together with those guys. Phil Villapiano, who played for the Raiders, is a good friend of mine, for instance.

Phil had me come to an NFL Alumni affair in New Jersey. I went. As long as I can talk I enjoy seeing those guys, and gabbing about the old times. I bullshit a lot. I'm a professional bullshitter. That's what I am now. After all those years at Notre Dame and in the NFL, I have lots of stories to tell. Everyone has a story. I just tend to be louder than most of the guys. I've heard many of the stories before, but I still enjoy hearing all those stories. They had a big dinner for me here about two weeks ago, on March 1st, and about 45 guys from Notre Dame, 30 guys from that 1966 team, showed up for my dinner. They all had different stories.

About three years ago, I had trouble doing push-ups. Hey, I used to be able to walk on my hands. I did that at a few parties. So I was worried about what was going on. A doctor ran me through some tests, and told me I had ALS. I said, "What the hell's ALS?" The doctor said, "That's Lou Gehrig's disease." I was scared, and relieved at the same time. For awhile, I was afraid I was a schizophrenic. I was talked into applying for a disability pension so Medicare could take care of my medical bills. I came from a family that wouldn't take welfare, or anything like that, so I wasn't looking for anybody to take care of my responsibilities.

I also do motivational talks. I learned about public speaking from some of the best, like Ara Parseghian, Johnny Ray, another of our coaches at Notre Dame, and Stan Jones and people like that in Denver. I can talk. I haven't lost that ability yet.

"They called me Little Pete."

My dad was Pete Duranko. He was a big Slovak. They called me "Little Pete." My dad owned a tavern for 40 years called Duranko's Bar & Grill. It was on the corner at Baron Avenue and Stackhouse Street in the West End of Johnstown. That was the tough end of town, near the steel mills. I used to go there when I was six years old and the guys would buy me pop and chips, and I learned all the bar tricks. It was a shot and a beer trade. I learned all those tricks in high school, college and pros. I learned to entertain people.

Notre Dame was great. I got to meet Frank Leahy's family. I got to meet Ralph Guglielmi and Paul Hornung. Those guys were my heroes. I met Leon Hart and Johnny Lujack and Johnny Lattner. It was like being in a movie.

I met Jimmy Brown at one of those NFL Alumni golf outings. When I was in high school, and I was a running back I loved Jimmy Brown. I got to talk to him and he was a nice guy. I met Johnny Unitas, and I was in awe of him. He ended up not being able to use his hands, either. He had arthritis so bad, and his fingers were all bent up. He couldn't do simple tasks, either. It happens to the best of them.

I'm involved with the Big 33 Game and all that goes with it in Hershey, Pa., and I've been an honorary chairman for the game. They've had Joe Montana back, and Danny Marino is the honorary chairman this time around. He's going to speak at this year's dinner. I love being with those guys. We talk about our high school coaches and how they had more of an influence on us than any of our other coaches. That's why high school coaches are so important in the lives of young people. Mike Ditka is always praising his high school coach at Aliquippa. You know Dan Devine didn't like Joe Montana, but he put him in during the fourth quarter when he needed to win the game.

"I pay people to listen to me speak."
— Pete Duranko

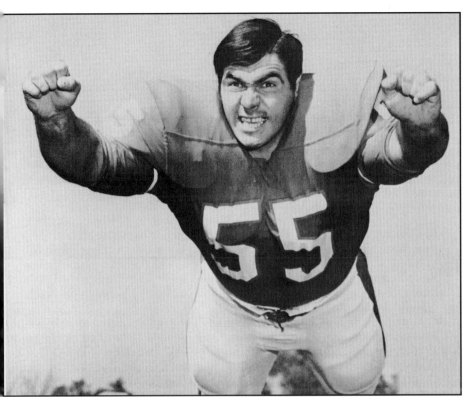

Pete Duranko dives through the air for photographer during his days with Denver Broncos (1967 to 1975), and dives through the line for real in pursuit of New York Jets quarterback Joe Namath. Duranko hailed from Johnstown and Namath from Beaver Falls.

"The Steelers were really America's Team."

I thought it was wonderful that Terry Bradshaw came back to Pittsburgh, and kissed and made up with Chuck Noll. Everybody was pissed off at Terry because he had stayed away for so long, and he stayed away from so many Steeler reunions. He had this thing about Pittsburgh because people had booed him and thought he was dumb, and stuff like that. He had to grow up, that's all. He's a great guy.

What he did for the Steelers and for Pittsburgh was fantastic. Sometimes you don't click with a coach, but later you both realize that you were good for one another. As you get older, you have to learn to forgive and forget. Sometimes people don't understand you, but you have to get over that. It's great that Terry Bradshaw is back. He should have been back a long time ago.

He's funny as hell. I see him on TV. He came to Johnstown and did a motivational speech, and he had them laughing in the aisles. He's got that southern accent, and a real knack for show business.

He and Tommy Maddox were both good stories. Then you have Mike Webster, and that was sad. He was a tough guy. He worked his butt off. He had a blocking dummy in his backyard when he was playing for the Steelers. That shows you how dedicated he was to the game. But he had a mental illness, and he had too much pride to get or stay with the people who could help him.

I've dealt with mental illness in my own family. I know what schizophrenia can do to people. (Schizophrenia is a psychosis characterized by withdrawal from reality and by behavioral and intellectual disturbances.)

I serve on the board of directors in Pennsylvania for NAMI, the National Alliance of the Mentally Ill. Did you see the movie "A Beautiful Mind"? (It was the story of a college professor who was a mathematical genius, yet he thought he was receiving messages from interrestials. He went positively mad for a period.) Sometimes you just don't know or understand what people are dealing with from a mental standpoint. They're doing a study now in the National Football League about the long-range effect of head injuries.

I've gotten to know a lot of these Steelers through the years, and they're a top bunch of guys. The '70s were unbelievable. The Cowboys liked to boast that they were "America's Team," but the Steelers were really "America's Team."

I got to know them real close, through Rocky Bleier and Terry Hanratty. I love their tradition, their ethnic followings and all that. I loved Franco's Italian Army, Gerela's Gorillas, Ham's Dobre Shunka. That's when football was a lot of fun.

You hear so much about football players getting involved with alcohol and drugs, and beating up their wives. But the Steelers have a lot of good guys in their ranks. They go up to see the kids at Children's Hospital, and so many good things in the community. I can let my hair down with those guys, and talk off the cuff with them, and have fun.

"It's hard for me to button my shirt."

I've had a lot of ups and downs lately. It takes me an hour and a half to get dressed. I drop a spoon when I'm trying to fix my coffee. It's hard for me to button my shirt. I see a psychologist twice a month, and I try to look at things from the bright side. I try to think of a cup being half full instead of half empty. If you give me lemons I make lemonade. That's the way I am. Things happen for a reason.

At Notre Dame, I was ready to leave in 1964. I had been starting, and I got injured early in the season and couldn't play the rest of the schedule. I got red-shirted. Someone talked me into staying. Someone helped me through that.

People help me now. I have a hard time raising my hands to comb my hair. Johnny Unitas ended up having problems doing stuff like that. And look what a great athlete he was.

I'm not a millionaire. I didn't make big money that would carry me through my post-playing days. The most I made was $45,000 in my eighth year with the Broncos in 1975. I've tried to get a job in recent years, but it's hard to do in this economy, at my age, and with my ailment.

So I deal with it. Sometimes people see me laughing and think I'm OK. My wife sees me on the floor when I am pissing and moaning. I've broken down a few times and I'm hollering and swearing and getting real ugly. My wife has toughed this out with me. I'm no day at the beach, but she's there for me.

I don't know what happened to Webster, but he obviously had his own demons. It's like what happened to that center for the Oakland Raiders this year, the one who missed playing in the Super Bowl. The public didn't know he was mentally ill. He had failed to take his medication. He wasn't himself.

My grandparents looked old before their time. That's the way it was back then. My grandmother wore a babushka and she always looked old. Now I'm the old one before my time.

> "We're all hanging in there from day to day.
> That's the best we can all do."
> — Janet Duranko

Bob Milie
A man for all seasons

"I always loved being around sports."

B ob Milie parlayed a boyhood enthusiasm for sports and some street savvy into a lifetime in the world of fun and games. He truly rated the label as a man for all seasons. A popular and agreeable guy, Milie never met a sport or job and few people he didn't like. He's not as famous as the football players and athletes he looked after through the years, but he's one of the behind-the-scenes guys who's got great stories to share.

Milie is a man who has put his time to good use, doing something he really enjoyed. He was an assistant trainer with the Steelers for 15 seasons from 1965 to 1980, while juggling two or three other jobs at the same time. It's a point of pride that he tended to the needs of four Super Bowl championship teams.

As Beano Cook, who has also held a few jobs in the sports world, would say, "He's had more jobs than *The Fugitive.*"

Bob Milie grew up in the East Liberty section of Pittsburgh. He's 5-8, 175 pounds, but he played most sports at Peabody High School and on Pittsburgh's sandlots. He chased after boxing champion Billy Conn as a gym rat and followed the Pirates, Steelers, Hornets, Pitt and Duquesne teams. He was a good-looking guy, with dark wavy hair, and he always dressed well, in my mind.

Conn, a neighborhood hero in Pittsbrgh's East End, became the light-heavyweight boxing champion of the world in 1939, and nearly upset heavyweight champ Joe Louis in 1941 in the first of their two famous fights in New York. There was a boxing ring in the balcony at the Sacred Heart Church complex in East Liberty, and Conn worked out there and attended church services on Sunday as well. Milie would catch Conn at both places. It's difficult to appreciate it now in this mega-communication world, but Conn was truly as popular a civic hero as Pittsburgh ever boasted.

Kids like Milie and his boyhood buddy John Cinicola couldn't get enough of Conn and other Pittsburgh sports heroes. Cinicola would later coach the Duquesne University basketball team and recommended Milie to Red Manning when they needed a trainer for the men's basketball team up on The Bluff.

Billy Conn and Art Rooney, Terry Bradshaw and Franco Harris, Rocky Bleier and Jack Lambert, Willie Somerset and Norm Nixon, Garry and Barry Nelson are only some of the names that Milie might mention in a casual conversation. He punctuates most of his stories with a broad smile framed by a gray mustache. Milie is one of those people who have been a big success in life, though he never made much money at any of his tasks. He keeps in touch with Nellie King, who lives nearby in Mt. Lebanon. King, a former Pirates pitcher and broadcasting sidekick to Bob Prince, succeeded Milie as sports information director at Duquesne University. Their children all attended Duquesne University tuition-free while their dads were employed there. It was a nice perk.

"I hustled so much because I was raising a family," said Milie. "I traveled to so many cities with so many different teams that there were times when I'd wake up and I didn't know where I was."

Milie can talk knowledgeably about Pittsburgh sports because he was a close-up witness to much of what happened. He not only rubbed shoulders with sports stars, but, as a sports trainer on a collegiate and pro level, he rubbed the shoulders and taped the ankles and wrists of many of the city's sports stars, giving them lots of tender loving care along the way. He patched up their wounds, whether they were bleeding or brooding. Several Steelers insisted that Milie do the taping of their ankles and, to hear Milie, this may have helped them get to the Pro Football Hall of Fame.

I visited him at his home in Mt. Lebanon on several occasions from January through April, 2003, and had lunch with him at DeBlasio's Restaurant in nearby Scott Township, once with Rocky Bleier and another time in the company of former Steelers defensive end Lloyd Voss.

Voss was having a challenging year. His wife, Dianne, had died of kidney failure. His dad was ailing, and would die in early May. Both were buried back home in Minnesota. His wife, a former nurse, had looked after Lloyd and his dad. Lloyd had his share of health challenges, too, and I wondered how he'd fare without Dianne.

Nobody ever hosted me in a more caring and first-class manner than Dianne Voss. Every time I came to talk to her husband Lloyd for my last book, *Steelers Forever*, she set out a nice spread, complete with candles and a glass of white wine. In fact, Milie's wife, Maureen, called Dianne to ask her what I liked, and maybe what I was like, before she hosted me in her home when I came to interview her husband for this book.

Milie likes to keep in touch with the Steelers he served for 15 years as an assistant to head trainer Ralph Berlin of Bethel Park. Berlin was a little gruffer with the Steelers than Milie, but that was part of his act, too. They were like the good guy-bad guy tandems to be found in police stations and boxing ring corners. Milie serves as secretary for the Pittsburgh chapters of both the NFL Players Association headed by Robin Cole and the NFL Alumni Association headed by Todd Kalas. "I enjoyed those guys so much," said Milie, "and this enables me to keep in touch with them. Otherwise, I wouldn't see them." Milie, at age 76, is retired now. Officially. He lives with his wife of 47 years, Maureen, and their two bishon frise dogs, Bogie and Gigi. I had not noticed on my initial visit that Gigi got around on just three legs. Her front left leg was amputated when she was a puppy because she was hit by a passing auto.

Maureen is a blonde pixie who immigrated to America from her native Ireland. She reminded me of Mary Martin in her portrayal of "Peter Pan." Maureen's Irish eyes are always smiling and a visitor feels comfortable in her company. I wanted to take the Milies out to lunch, but Maureen insisted on preparing a meal for us at her home. She's a wonderful hostess, in the fashion of Dianne Voss. The former Maureen Ward was a favorite of the late Art Rooney for obvious reasons. The Milies managed to raise four children in their cozy four-bedroom home. It has one bathroom and a powder room. The powder room is on the first floor with a galley kitchen, a dining room and a living room. I had no problem finding the Milie Manse on Dixon Avenue, in the northeast tip of the South Hills community, because there was a 1999 model silver Cadillac Deville in the narrow driveway with the license plate MILIE facing the brick-paved street. Milie says he's had Cadillacs all his life, and wishes he still had his first one, a 1941 model. "That would be worth something today," he said.

"I had a '41 convertible when I was at Miami. Imagine that. It was a real beauty. It was dark blue with a white top and a spotlight and all. I bought Cadillacs new when they were under $10,000. Now I get them used from Tony Farina. We went to kindergarten together, so I trust him."

Making enough money to afford Cadillacs and four kids may help explain why Bob Milie was so busy most of his adult life. At one time, back in the mid-60s, Milie was an assistant professor in the physical education department at Carnegie Mellon University (known then as Carnegie Tech), and a defensive backfield coach on the staffs of Eddie Hirshberg and later Joe Gasparella. Hirshberg played at the University of Pittsburgh and owned WEDO radio station in McKeesport. From Vandergrift, Gasparella played quarterback at Notre Dame and with the Steelers and was a much-respected architect as well as a football coach. One of the assistant coaches on the defensive side for a brief period was Richie McCabe, the former Pitt and Steelers defensive back, who would later coach in the National Football League. McCabe played football in the same backfield as Dan Rooney at North Catholic High School and was a waterboy with the Steelers in his youth. Milie mixed with all these local stars.

Starting on a part-time basis in 1969, Milie was a trainer for the men's basketball team at Duquesne University as well as with the Steelers, while working the $10 pari-mutuel window at The Meadows, and as a lifeguard at a summer camp at Shadyside Academy. He was a longtime scout for the University of Miami and sent a lot of kids from Western Pennsylvania to Coral Gables. Somewhere in there he worked for 13 years as a bartender at Lou Grippo's Original Oyster House at Market Square until 1997, and worked at Neighbor Care, a pharmacy warehouse, from 1997 until 2003. That's when he left his last job, in between my visits. He worked at one of the pari-mutuel windows at The Meadows from when it opened in 1963 and stayed for over 20 years. In late June, 2003, Milie attended a 40th anniversary celebration at the Meadows.

Bob and Maureen Milie enjoy their bichon frise pets, Bogie and Gigi, at their home in Mt. Lebanon. Maureen refers to her husband's basement office/workshop as "Bob's Dungeon" — where many Steelers are pictured in every available space.

Photos by Jim O'Brien

There was a period when he was the sports information director and the trainer for the men's basketball team at Duquesne University. He had to be the only one with such dual duties at any Division I college in the country. "I don't think there are many people doing what I'm doing," he said, humbly, at the time. Sportswriter Russ Franke once described Milie in an article in *The Pittsburgh Press* as "the world's only trainer-sports information director."

Milie only smiles at the memories. He was a high-speed radio operator in the Pacific Theater in the U.S. Army during World War II, but didn't see any combat action. He served with Headquarters Company, 19th Infantry, 24th Division South Pacific and occupation of Japan. He points out proudly that he was one of the first GIs to see Hiroshima and Nagasaki after they had been bombed in World War II. His oldest brother, Jack, was stationed in Okinawa, and an older brother, Lou, was in the South Pacific for four years. So three Milie boys were all serving in the South Pacific at the same time.

When Bob Milie returned home from the military service, he played football for the East Liberty Bombers. He then went to the University of Miami on the G.I. Bill and graduated with a B.A. degree in physical education in 1955.

"There were a lot of Pitt guys who helped establish the University of Miami. Bowman Ashe, who had been the Dean of Men at Pitt, was the first president of the University of Miami. He was the grandfather of Gary Dunn, who came out of the University of Miami to play for the Steelers. Gary's dad, Eddie Dunn, held many of the rushing records at Miami, and later served as a backfield coach for Andy Gustafson. Jack Harding, who had been a running back at Pitt, was the first athletic director, and he hired Gustafson, a Pitt guy, as the head football coach. They played in the same backfield at Pitt. Gustafson had been an assistant coach at the U.S. Military Academy. I remember Gustafson was a big fan of Glenn Davis and Doc Blanchard of Army, and he had a picture of them in his office. I was hoping to play football there, but I got hurt and it just didn't work out."

While at Miami, Milie worked as a student trainer and then an assistant trainer for the Hurricanes. He also helped out with the Baltimore Orioles during the spring training stay in Miami. He worked as a lifeguard in Miami during the summers.

He recalls how he once rubbed down the right arm of Orioles' pitching coach Harry "The Cat" Brecheen before a ballgame. "Now that you've done that," Brecheen said to the kid trainer with a smile, "how about doing my left arm? That's the one I'll be using when I'm pitching batting practice today."

Milie even took a turn at bat against Brecheen one day at Flamingo Park. Milie was brazenly swinging a bat on the sideline when Brecheen asked him if he wanted to bat against him. "Sure," said Milie, a little of that East Liberty background getting the best of his good sense. He looks back on it now as one of the shining moments in his life.

"How many guys can say they were struck out by Harry Brecheen?" asks Milie. "He did it on four pitches. He threw the first one at my head and scared me. I swung at the next three pitches. But he was a good guy." Then again, Milie might say the same thing about Genghis Khan.

Milie still has a press guide for the Orioles from that 1955 season. It includes some ticket information for Memorial Stadium in Baltimore. Box seats cost $2. It was $1.25 for reserved seats, and bleacher seats were 75 cents that season.

He was offered a job by Jack Dunn to be the assistant trainer for the Orioles at $2,000 a year, but turned it down to take a job at Carnegie Tech for $3,000 a year as an assistant professor of physical education with football coaching duties. He had been a head trainer for two years (1954-1955) in the North-South Shrine Bowl in Miami, working with the South and then the North the next year. That tells you all you need to know about Milie's approach to gaining a paycheck. Milie later got a master's degree in education at the University of Pittsburgh.

"We call the basement Bob's dungeon."
— Maureen Milie

Bob Milie took me down a wooden stairway to a small, cluttered basement. Maureen Milie calls it "Bob's dungeon." It serves as an office, workshop and Wall of Fame for her husband. There are tools scattered about, sports memorabilia, photography equipment. It once served as a dark room when Bob developed and printed his own pictures.

There are photographs taped to the beams and more photographs pinned and taped to every inch of wall space. Bob is in many of them. Whenever he's busy in the basement he's surrounded by some of his favorite people. He's shown in a tuxedo alongside, left to right, Terry Bradshaw, Mike Webster and Steve Furness at a Steelers' reunion. He's shown helping L.C. Greenwood and Bradshaw off the football field when they were injured. He's smiling next to Sam Davis in one photo and in another with Lynn Swann. He's taping or teasing the likes of Dwight White, Andy Russell or Jack Lambert in other photos. He's shown during his days at Duquesne, chatting with Nellie King. Milie has a long cigar in his mouth in many of the photos. His buddy Berlin liked to smoke cigars, too, especially the ones Art Rooney offered his favorites.

There's a photo that Milie took and developed of Princess Grace Kelly of Monaco when she was given an honorary degree at Duquesne.

There's a great color photo showing the Pro Football Hall of Fame induction when Lambert and Harris were honored in 1990.

His daughter Patty put together a scrapbook for her dad and gave it to him as a Christmas present in 1981. My favorite part of that scrapbook, which included newspaper clippings, photos, notes, you name it, were the personal notations Patty made on some of the newspaper photos. There are notes in the margins pointing out "Dad's hand" or "Dad's back" or "Dad's leg" whenever those portions of Bob Milie's body would be shown as he assisted some injured Steeler. The scrapbook was definitely a labor of love.

Patty, age 40, was a nurse at Children's Hospital in Oakland before her marriage to Greg Genevro. They have three children and live in New Jersey, where Greg is a regional vice-president at Enterprise Rent-A-Car. At the outset of 2003, Milie's son, Bob, then 44, was a government agent for Naval Investigative Services (NIS) and a former FBI agent. Daughter Valerie, 42, was a detective for the City of Pittsburgh. Another daughter, Maureen, 35, was an assistant news director for UPMC. She was married to a cardiologist, Dr. Ken McGaffin, and is the mother of two children.

"Two former Steelers played a prominent role in our lives," said Bob, nodding toward Maureen. "Walt Kichefski was our best man and was also a godfather for our Patty. He played and coached at Miami. He was with the Steelers in the early '40s, left for the military service, and came back to play for the Pitt-Cards, when the Steelers and Cardinals combined forces. When Kichefski came to Pittsburgh for a visit he'd always have me stop to see Mr. Rooney at the Steelers offices.

"Our Val used to baby-sit for Molly and Gordon Gravelle when they were with the Steelers. Joe Gasparella was Maureen's godfather and also stood for Bob when he was confirmed. If you ever ask Dan Rooney, he will tell you that Joe Gasparella was the only player that came to see him when he was in the hospital."

I sat next to Milie during the funeral service for Mike Webster. We were sitting directly behind Lynn Swann and Terry Bradshaw, who both spoke during the service in September of 2002.

Bob Milie:

I was all alone when I went to the casket to pay my respects to Mike. It reminded me of how his hands were so big. He was a big guy, but his hands were even big for a guy his size. I still can't believe all these guys are dying. Like Mike and Steve Furness. So young. And Ray Mansfield and Joe Gilliam. It's mind-boggling. I'm 76. I'm the one who should be dying. It doesn't seem right.

I spoke to Mike's younger son, Garrett. God, he's a giant. He said, "My Dad talked about you." It was good to hear that.

I remember Mike came to the Oyster House when I was working there as a bartender a few years ago. His son ate two fish sandwiches and Mike ate one. Mike gave me a $20 bill.

When Steelers attended a team reunion at David L. Lawrence Center in 1999 Bob Milie was joined by Terry Bradshaw, Mike Webster and Steve Furness.

Franco Harris held a 30th anniversary party to celebrate his "Immaculate Reception" and invited Bob and Maureen Milie to join the fun at Sheraton at Station Square in December, 2002. **Photos from Bob Milie collection**

I knew he was having some financial problems. I said, "It's on me." He refused to accept it.

It shook me up when I heard that he was living in his car, or sleeping in the bus station. I couldn't believe he was having those kinds of problems.

I remember that I'd go into the locker room after a game was over, Mike didn't look for the cameras. The media didn't come his way much. Guys like Sam Davis and Jon Kolb and Mike Webster never drew a crowd. It was that way with offensive linemen. They weren't glamour guys. Mike kept to himself. He didn't talk much.

I remember watching him as a rookie at the training camp at St. Vincent's. Chuck Noll liked to test guys with the "Oklahoma drill" on the first day of camp. It was a one-on-one deal, and Webster was going up against Jack Lambert, who was also a rookie. Webster was so strong.

Webster got the best of Lambert a few times, and I remember telling Tony Parisi, "This kid made the football team right here." No one could move him.

So many stories of those guys come to mind. I remember once that Terry Bradshaw broke off a tooth while eating a T-bone steak. Terry takes the tooth and wedges it back where it belongs. In a game, he's calling out signals and his tooth flies out and bounces off Ray Mansfield's helmet. He had to call time out to look for his tooth. Everybody was laughing, and I was wondering what they were laughing about. The referee found it. He gave it to Terry and he came to the sideline and tossed it to me. I kept a sanitary pouch to put stuff like that in such emergencies.

My leg feels like it's on fire!"
— Jack Lambert

Jack Lambert was one of my favorites. For some reason, he liked having me tape him. But you couldn't touch him on the field if he was bleeding. He'd holler at you, "Don't touch me!" We thought he liked having blood on his uniform. He was probably the biggest intimidator we had on the football team.

I remember Lambert going after Cliff Harris when Harris patted Roy Gerela on the helmet after he missed a field goal attempt in a Super Bowl.

When we played the Rams in Super Bowl XIV, Wendell Tyler had the biggest run of the game. He came near our sideline and Lambert had him pinned down. Lambert was screaming into his face, "I'll kill you! I'll kill you!" He intimidated people with stuff like that. Tyler wondered what was going on.

So many stories come to mind when I sit down and think about it. I remember Lambert cramping up in this pre-season game we were playing at Tulane Stadium. It was Lambert's first game in a Steelers' uniform. We had left the regular analgesic in the locker room at halftime. So we put some "Red Hot" salve on his leg. Lambert came over to me on the sideline in the second half, and said, "What the hell did you put on my leg? My leg feels like it's on fire."

At our home games at Three Rivers Stadium, Jackie Hart used to fill two garbage cans with ice and fill it with beer cans. That was put in the trainers' area. Lambert would go in there right after the game and have a few beers before he'd go out into the locker room.

Jack enjoyed his beer. I'd join him on occasion at the Touchdown Club or the 19th Hole on Rte. 30 near the training camp in Latrobe. He'd get two Budweisers and he'd be finished with them before I'd go through one can. Of course, he worked up a bigger thirst at practice in the sun.

"Terry loved to play cards with us."

A few days before our first Super Bowl game with the Minnesota Vikings at Tulane Stadium I was playing catch with Terry Bradshaw. I had good hands, and I enjoyed warming him up. I forgot to take my watch off.

He started throwing the ball to me and, like he normally did, he started throwing the ball a little harder as he went along. He could really zip that ball. I noticed later that my watch had stopped. When we got back to Pittsburgh, I took the watch to a jeweler I knew who had a shop on Banksville Road. When I returned to pick up my watch, the guy said, "Hey, Bob, did you throw your watch off a cliff or something? Everything is loose inside your watch." When I told him I was catching Bradshaw he just raised his eyebrows in disbelief.

(I mentioned to Milie that maybe his story about his watch was what happened to Mike Webster. Though he never suffered a concussion, perhaps the parts inside his head were all knocked loose. "Maybe," said Milie, shrugging his shoulders to indicate he wasn't sure what happened.)

When we traveled to road games, Bradshaw played "Hearts" on just about every trip in the front of the plane with me, Jackie Hart and Tony Parisi. One time, when Terry was wearing a wig, Parisi took it off his head and passed it around and we all tried it on. We did stuff like that on every road trip. Terry loved to play with us. It was a good way for him to relax and get football off his mind.

There was one game at Three Rivers when he got hurt, and the crowd cheered. I took him back to the locker room and the crowd started booing him as he left the field. When we were inside the hall, out of sight, the tears just burst out onto his cheeks. He was crying like a baby. He was that upset. That really hurt him. I think that was one of the slights he never forgot. That's one of the reasons he stayed away from Pittsburgh for so long.

They were rough on him some other places, too. Remember the game in Cleveland when Turkey Jones turned him upside down and literally spiked Bradshaw into the ground? We knew he was hurt bad. He had spinal shock. The ambulance came on the field and Bradshaw had to be put on a board, and lifted into the ambulance. Dr. Best and Dr. Huber were treating him and they told me to ride with Bradshaw to the medical room in the stadium.

We were going up this ramp, and some kid threw a plastic cup full of beer, and the driver had to put the window wipers on in order to see. Someone hollered out, "Bradshaw, I hope you die!" Terry was just coming around at that time, and he looked at me and said, "Can you believe someone would say that?" He came around and got the feeling back in his body soon after. Following the game, Turkey Jones came in to see him, and said he was sorry.

We had a game in Houston where Bradshaw suffered five interceptions in the first half, and hurt his shoulder. "Can you believe I threw five interceptions?" Terry kept saying as we were heading for the locker room. He couldn't play in the second half. Terry Hanratty was supposed to be our backup quarterback, but his elbow was swollen. Joe Gilliam didn't make the trip. So we had to turn to Tony Dungy to play quarterback, which he hadn't done since his college days at Minnesota.

There's a good trivia question from that game. Dungy intercepted a pass in the first half, and threw an interception in the second half. Not too many Steelers can say that.

I remember when Bradshaw came to his first training camp at Latrobe. The rookies were in by themselves for about ten days back then before the veterans would report.

When the veterans reported, Kent Nix and Terry Hanratty, who were our quarterbacks, took me to the 19th Hole, and they were peppering me with questions about Bradshaw. They wanted to know how he looked at camp. They wanted to know if he was as good as the sportswriters were saying in their stories. I told them, "This kid is fabulous. He's even better than what you read." The Steelers ended up trading Nix to the Bears before the season began.

I remember, after Bradshaw had been with the team a few years, he came to training camp and he was in such great

Bob Milie, at left, assists L.C. Greenwood off the field and, above, enjoyed working with veteran team physician Dr. John Best in his early days with the Steelers.

Photos from Bob Milie collection

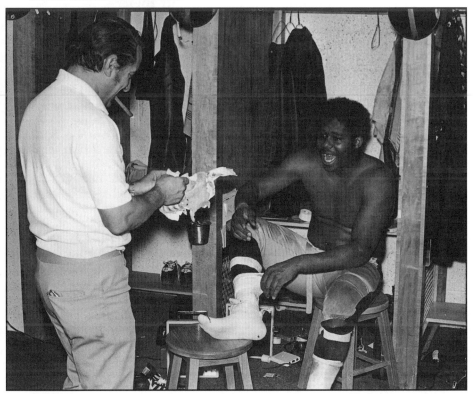

Bob Milie, assistant trainer to Ralph Berlin, checks in with Dwight White after game.

shape because he had been working hard during the off-season. After the players ran the mandatory 350s — runs around the outline of the practice field — we'd check their pulse rate. Terry's pulse rate was lower than mine, and I hadn't run anywhere.

"I am still a big fan of Rocky Bleier."

I remember we were playing a game in Cincinnati, and Rocky Bleier was returning punts. He fielded one and came up the field and got hit hard and fumbled and lost the ball. He was bleeding over his eye. He came off the field and he wanted to get back in when we regained possession of the ball. He was hollering to me as I was working on his wound. He hollered, "Hurry up!" After the game, Ralph and I were putting all our stuff back in these four trunks we traveled with. Rocky was standing in the doorway, looking a little lost. He came over and put his arm around me and said, "I want to apologize for hollering at you on the field." I was not sure what to do. I told him it didn't really bother me; I was used to it. That's the kind of guy he was. I am still a big fan of Rocky Bleier.

Clendon Thomas, one of our best defensive backs when I first came to work for the Steelers, was like that, too. I first met Clendon Thomas when he was playing for Oklahoma in the Orange Bowl, and they worked out at the University of Miami when I was working there. Clendon Thomas was one of the finest individuals I've ever met in my life. He was such a classy guy. Dick Hoak and Rocky Bleier were both good players and good guys. So was Franco Harris. It was funny when Frenchy Fuqua would get mad about something on the field because he'd start complaining and he spoke with a lisp, and it just came out funny.

I remember seeing John Madden, the Raiders' coach, sobbing in a hallway after we beat them in a game. I'd seen college coaches crying, but never pro coaches. Not that there's anything wrong with that; I was just stunned to see Madden so upset.

I recall another day at St. Vincent. This was shortly after Fats Holmes had gotten into trouble, shooting at a police helicopter somewhere in Ohio. A helicopter was hovering over the practice field, and Tom Keating, who'd come to us in a trade with the Oakland Raiders, shouted to Holmes, "Easy, Fats. Easy, Fats." It cracked up everyone.

Ron Shanklin just died and that brought back a memory, too. He suffered the same sort of injury that Bradshaw had, and it happened right in front of our bench at Three Rivers Stadium. It was a spinal shock injury. He went to Divine

306

Providence Hospital. That was the Steelers' hospital, near the stadium. It was right behind St. Peter's Church, where the Rooneys went to church. I went to check on him the next day, and he had one of those halos around his head to keep his head stationary. I think that kept him from playing in the Pro Bowl.

We had some great receivers back then, even before we signed Swann and Stallworth. Frank Lewis and Shanklin were both good, and before them we had Roy Jefferson. But Jefferson was always a problem, and Chuck Noll did not appreciate his attitude. I remember one time we were in the dining hall at St. Vincent's, and Jefferson was complaining about his back. He said, "I don't know if I can play. My back is killing me." Then he repeated it a little louder. Chuck Noll was nearby with Dan Rooney. They were talking over dinner. I'm sitting with Dick Hoak at another table. Hoak heard what was going on. Hoak said, "He's gone."

We were playing the New York Giants in an exhibition game in Montreal, and Jefferson missed the bed check. Noll heard about that and he told Jim Boston to meet him in the lobby when he came in and have a ticket ready for him to return to Pittsburgh. Jefferson got in around 2 o'clock in the morning. Jefferson was sent back to Pittsburgh before the game.

Before long, Noll traded Jefferson to Baltimore. He wouldn't put up with that sort of stuff, no matter how good the player might be. Jefferson was probably the best player we had at the time. He was also fined $1,000. Before long, he was traded to the Washington Redskins. Noll got rid of him before the start of the 1970 season.

He got rid of Ray May, too. And he was a great player. They ended up with Baltimore. They came into our locker room after a game once to show everyone their Super Bowl rings that they'd won with the Colts in 1971.

I remember the time I had to patch up Art Rooney Jr. He got into a fight with Jackie Hart in the clubhouse. Jackie jumped him and punched him when he was wearing glasses. They cut his nose pretty good. Art got the best of it, though. He shoved Jackie into a Coca-Cola cooler and he got all wet. I don't know what that fight was all about. But those sort of things livened up the locker room. When I asked Art what happened, he said a fan hit him.

Governor Milton Shapp came to our locker room after we won Super Bowl IX in New Orleans. He wanted to congratulate Mr. Rooney. I was always the last one in the locker room because one of my jobs was to make sure that everyone was in after a game. When I got to the locker room door, Governor Shapp was telling the guard he was the governor of

Pennsylvania and the guard told him, "Sure, and I'm the President of the United States!" I told the guard, "He really is the governor." The guard apologized and let him in. The Governor thanked me and got in to talk to Mr. Rooney. I never mentioned that to the media because I thought it might embarrass Governor Shapp at the time.

I had a great view of "The Immaculate Reception" catch by Franco. I was on the sideline and Franco caught the ball about ten yards from me. He picked it off his shoetops; it didn't hit the ground. As far as whether the ball hit Frenchy Fuqua first, or that Raiders' defensive back — Jack Tatum — I don't know. I watched it over and over again on film, and I couldn't tell. It looked like it may have hit Frenchy's shoulder. If it hit him and deflected to Franco, then it wouldn't have counted. They've changed the rules, but back then a thrown ball couldn't touch two successive players from the same team.

Franco had a dinner last season to mark the 25th anniversary of the "Immaculate Reception" and Maureen and I were invited to attend. It was at the Sheraton at Station Square. It was a real nice party, and I had a great time seeing those guys again. I remember Franco, as a young player, going out to dinner with the trainers, equipment and ground crew guys at an Italian restaurant in Miami when we went there to play the Cowboys in Super Bowl X. It's always been fun to be around those guys. It's still great to get together and I'm honored that they include me.

From Bob Milie photo collection.

Three days before Super Bowl X in Miami, Steelers' star Franco Harris, left, joins the support team at an Italian restaurant in South Florida. Bob Milie, Frank Sciulli and Jackie Hart were happy to break bread with one of their favorite Steelers.

Nellie King and The Immaculate Reception

Nellie King is never without a story. He can't help himself. At 75, he was supposed to be retired as the sports information director (and golf coach) at Duquesne University, but I called him to check on some names in my chapter on his good friend, Bob Milie. This was mid-May, 2003.

"He was just a quiet guy who loved what he was doing," recalled King. "He had no ego at all. And he was trusting as hell. His wife, Maureen, is a wonderful woman. She just bubbles."

Then King couldn't let me go without a good inside story I'd never heard before. The mention of Joe Gordon, whom I had spoken to earlier in the day, was his cue.

"I remember Joe after the Immaculate Reception," said King. "The game wasn't on television here — it was blacked out in Pittsburgh — but it was on TV monitors throughout Three Rivers Stadium. There were about eight of us down in the Pirates' clubhouse. Hully (equipment man John Hallahan) had the game on the TV in his office and we had beer and sandwiches. It was great. And we had a better view of what happened when Franco caught the deflected pass than just about anybody in the stadium.

"When the game was over, we came out of the clubhouse and caught the Steelers as they passed down the hallway. We were congratulating everybody. I saw Joe Gordon and I said, "It was just like Maz hitting the home run!"

"Gordon shouted back at me in disdain. 'There's no comparison!' I always kid him about that when I see him. Hey, Maz hit a home run to lead off the last inning in the seventh game of the World Series. Franco caught that ball in a playoff game."

Well, the "Immaculate Reception" has been deemed the greatest play in the history of the NFL, but I concur with King that Maz's home run was the most magic moment in Pittsburgh sports history. Everyone knew what had happened. No one knows for sure to this day what really happened in "The Immaculate Reception."

King corrected me in an earlier conversation about something I had said in a radio interview at halftime of the Pitt vs. Duquesne basketball game that officially opened the Petersen Events Center in November, 2002. I told George Von Benko about the basketball opener of Mellon Arena (then called the Civic Auditorium) back in 1961. I said it was a double-header featuring Duquesne and Carnegie Mellon (then Carnegie Tech) in the opener, followed by Pitt playing the Ohio State team that had won the national championship the year before with Jerry Lucas and John Havlicek leading the way.

"There was a triple-header that day," noted Nellie King. "The first game was between the Pirates and the Steelers. I know because I played for the Pirates. So did Dick Groat."

There's one for trivia fans.

Nellie King

Ron Shanklin
Another star from North Texas State

"Shanklin was a terrific player."
— Dan Rooney

A fine rain was falling and it could be heard on the windowpanes as I spoke to Mel Blount on a Monday morning, April 21, 2003, the day after Easter. It was a good day for a funeral.

Blount was packing his bag at his home and ranch in Taylorstown, just south of Washington, Pennsylvania. He was catching an airplane to Dallas later in the day to pay his respects to the family of Ron Shanklin.

A star receiver for five seasons (1970-1974) with the Steelers and a Pro Bowl performer in 1973, Shanklin died at age 55 the previous Thursday at his home in suburban Dallas. He had been battling colon cancer for 2½ years, according to his wife, Linda.

Blount, a Hall of Fame defensive back for the Steelers when they won four Super Bowl championships in the '70s and '80s, had shared an apartment in Pittsburgh with Shanklin in their rookie season of 1970, and for four years on the road. "We were like brothers," Blount said. Shanklin was a speedy 6-2, 210-pound pass-catcher, born in 1948 in Hubbard, Texas.

"Shank was a good guy and an outstanding receiver," said Blount, who turned 55 earlier in April. "We're at that age where people we know are dying around us. I've been going to too many funerals lately."

It was late in September of 2002 when I saw Blount embracing Terry Bradshaw and other former teammates and friends outside a funeral home in Robinson Township when Mike Webster, another Hall of Fame performer on those four Super Bowl teams, died at age 50.

Steve Furness and Ray Mansfield had died earlier. Once they had all lived near each other, and their coaches, in the South Hills when Pittsburgh was called The City of Champions.

Blount was making plans for his 5th annual Mel Blount Youth Home All-Star Celebrity at the Downtown Hilton. He would be a host for a roast of former teammate Joe Greene at that gala black-tie affair. Many Steelers stars were scheduled to attend.

Blount preferred to see his teammates at those kinds of reunions rather than at funerals. He and Joe Greene were going to be pallbearers at Shanklin's service and both would offer eulogies on behalf of an old friend.

The Steelers were making final preparations that week for the annual college draft April 26-27. It's unlikely they would do as well as they did in the 1970 draft, the second for their young coach, Chuck Noll.

From Steelers archives

Ron Shanklin

STEELERS

RONNIE SHANKLIN • WR

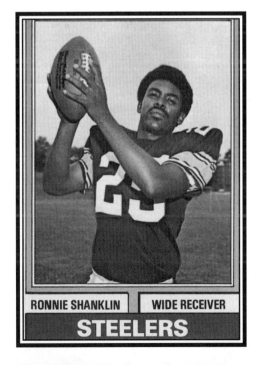

RONNIE SHANKLIN   WIDE RECEIVER

STEELERS

In 1970, the Steelers first three draft picks were Terry Bradshaw, a quarterback from Louisiana Tech, Ron Shanklin, a receiver from North Texas State, and Mel Blount, a defensive back from Southern University.

Bradshaw was the first player picked in the draft that year. The Steelers had won a coin flip with the Chicago Bears to get that pick. The Steelers were surprised when Shanklin was still available on the second round. He'd come from the same school in Denton, Texas, where they had found Joe Greene the previous year.

Shanklin led the Steelers in receiving as a rookie, and for his first four seasons with the team. In 1970, they also drafted two other fine receivers, Jon Staggers of Missouri and Dave Smith of Indiana University of Pennsylvania. That same year Noll kept a 1968 16th round draft choice named Rocky Bleier despite the fact that he had been wounded in Vietnam and didn't look like a top prospect as a running back. Art Rooney had urged Chuck Noll to give Bleier a chance to recuperate from his injuries.

It wasn't apparent at first, but Noll was building a dynasty.

Shanklin was Bradshaw's pet receiver along with Frank Lewis before Lynn Swann and Jon Stallworth showed up in 1974. Swann and Shanklin split time that year at wide receiver and the Steelers went on to win their first Super Bowl.

In his 1989 book, "Looking Deep," written with Buddy Martin, Bradshaw recalled visiting Three Rivers Stadium in August of 1987. Bradshaw said he checked out the stadium scene before the game, but left early because he didn't feel comfortable being there. He said when he surveyed the field he saw the corner of the end zone where he threw his first touchdown pass as a Steeler in 1970. It was a 56-yard TD pass to Shanklin. Bradshaw said it was the first touchdown pass thrown in the new stadium.

Shanklin caught 166 passes for 3,047 yards (18.3 yards per catch) and 24 touchdowns during his four-year stint with the Steelers. Going into the 2003 season, Shanklin stood 15th in franchise history in receptions, 10th in yards and tied for eighth in touchdowns. His best season was 1973, when 10 of his 30 receptions were touchdowns and he led the NFL with a 23.7-yard average. He caught at least one touchdown pass in six consecutive games and was voted most valuable player and earned a spot in the Pro Bowl. A neck injury kept him out of the game. His final NFL season was 1976 with the Chicago Bears.

Shanklin once caught an 81-yard touchdown pass from Bradshaw against the Cleveland Browns

Shanklin was survived by his wife, Linda; two daughters, Ronda and Veronica; his mother and stepfather, Rose Marie and Mervyn Davis of Fairfield, California; eight brothers and three sisters.

"Ron Shanklin was a terrific player," said Steelers president Dan Rooney when he learned of his death, "and he was one of those players who helped us make the transition from the late '60s to the Super Bowl championship teams of the '70s."

Mel Blount called when he got back home from Dallas and the funeral service for Ron Shanklin. He said he saw three of his former teammates there, namely Joe Greene, Ernie Holmes and Chuck Beatty. The latter was a defensive back for the Steelers (1969-1972), who had been a teammate of Greene and Shanklin at North Texas State. After his retirement from the NFL, Shanklin coached at his alma mater for ten years and then at the University of Houston for three or four years, according to Blount.

"Ron got hurt here," recalled Blount, "and he wasn't of much use to the Bears when he got to Chicago." He said Greene started weeping when he opened the funeral service program and saw a picture of a smiling Shanklin staring out at him.

Blount said the Steelers had great receivers before they even landed Lynn Swann and John Stallworth in the 1974 draft. They had Frank Lewis and Shanklin, whom they would trade to the Buffalo Bills and Chicago Bears, respectively, after Swann and Stallworth became starters. Lewis had a Pro Bowl season in Buffalo and several productive years. Lewis led the AFC in pass-catching with 70 in 1981.

"That's one of the reasons we were so good," recalled Blount. "We just had such deep talent at so many positions. We had linemen like Ray Pinney and Steve Courson who weren't full-time starters, and they were so good. I had to go up against guys like that every day in practice. It made us all better. Joe Greene was going up against Jon Kolb and Sam Davis. Larry Brown was going up against L.C. Greenwood. It was like that all across the line. I'm trying to cover Swann and Stallworth and every day they were trying to outdo one another. That's when John felt he was playing second fiddle to Swann and wanted to show he was just as good, if not a better receiver.

"They made me better. That's one good thing about going up against such great talent at practice. We had that luxury. Practice was harder than the games sometimes. They had to pull Ernie Holmes out of practice sometimes because he was so brutal. He loved to beat up on people. By the time we got to Sunday it was easy."

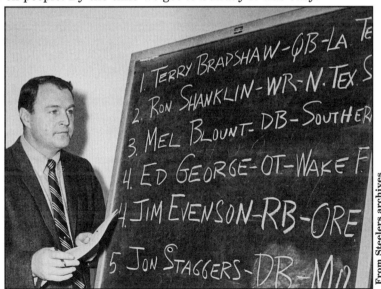

Second-year coach Chuck Noll checks the Steelers' top selections in the 1970 NFL draft of college players.

Life's work
Looking to the future

*"It gives our guys a chance
to check out life after football."*

The Pittsburgh Steelers make an effort to educate their players about the real world. They conduct seminars and have guest speakers and former players come to the UPMC Sports Complex a couple of times each season to meet with players who choose to attend such gatherings. They bring in priests and ministers to make sure their spiritual needs are met as well.

Anthony Griggs is the guy in charge of player development. "My job," said Griggs, "is to give our guys a chance to check out life after football."

Griggs made this statement, as part of his introductory remarks, during a session entitled "Here's My Story V" on Tuesday evening, April 22, 2003. The program followed a social time in the dining area of the Steelers' side of the training complex on the city's South Side.

Such events are much easier to hold there than they were in the dressing rooms at Three Rivers Stadium.

It featured a fine doubleheader: Richard B. Fisher, chairman of Federated Securities Corporation, headquartered in Pittsburgh, and J.T. Thomas, a former Steelers' defensive back in the team's glory days of the '70s, who is an owner/operator of Applebee's Neighborhood Grill & Bar Restaurants, headquartered in Edgewood, just east of Pittsburgh. Thomas is a partner with Larry Brown, a former teammate, in owning and operating 13 Applebee's from Pittsburgh to State College.

Through the years, former Steelers were invited to come back and talk to the current players about business prospects. They included the likes of Andy Russell, Randy Grossman, Mike Wagner, Dwight White, Thomas and Brown. Russell said some of today's players, who make so much more money than his contemporaries, started tuning out the old guys. As a rookie, Casey Hampton explained his bored behavior by saying, "That was then; this is now."

Griggs, with a little help from Mark Bruener, succeeded in convincing about 20 contemporary Steelers to show up for the affair, but several of those left after the social hour. They passed on the actual program. It's the old adage about being able to lead a horse to water, but not being able to make it drink.

The 2003 season would be the 13th at his position for Griggs, who also assists conditioning coordinator Chet Fuhrman with the strength and conditioning program for the players. In his main role in player development, however, Griggs is to provide information regarding continuing education, internships, investment information and counseling services for the players.

314

Anthony Griggs, in charge of player development for Steelers, checks in with Charlie Batch, left, and Marvel Smith at information session at UPMC Sports Complex on South Side. One of the guest speakers, former Steelers' defensive standout J.T. Thomas, talks to businessman Ed Hwang, one of his customers at Applebee's Neighborhood Grill & Bar in Peters Township.

Photos by Jim O'Brien

He became a friend of head coach Bill Cowher in stints as a reserve linebacker with the Philadelphia Eagles (1982-1985) and Cleveland Browns (1986-1988). Griggs was a No. 4 draft choice of the Eagles out of Ohio State. He's a 43-year-old native of Lawton, Oklahoma. He and his wife, Beth Ann, live in Pittsburgh with their two daughters, Alexiss, 5, and Aaryn, 4.

Griggs knows he has an even greater challenge today with so many players making millions of dollars to get them to take a serious look at their future needs. "We'd warn them not to buy all those big cars and flashy clothes, and NEVER to buy a restaurant," related Russell, "but they don't want to hear that."

Griggs said the Steelers have had a high percentage of players who've gotten their college degrees and finished their education during their stay with the team. Kendrell Bell was returning to Georgia to pursue his degree. Griggs also tries to tie them up with Pittsburgh business executives who might open doors for them. "They need to see people like you," Griggs told his audience of Pittsburgh business types.

"They should be asking themselves, 'What do I want to do when I finish this game?' They've got to take an earnest look at their prospects. They need mentorships. They need face time with people like you."

He knows many of the former Steelers are real success stories, but he also knows that retired players run into problems when it comes to getting business careers established. For every Paul Martha and Dwayne Woodruff, who went to Duquesne Law School and became successful attorneys, there are players in impoverished circumstances.

Griggs has heard all the horror stories about how some players lost all their money in bad investments or business deals gone awry. The tragedy of Mike Webster was fresh in everybody's mind, about how a guy who made good money could lose his family, his faith and his finances all in one big swoop, and end up among the homeless citizenry of the city.

"You have to enjoy what you're doing."

Thus the need for a program like "Here's My Story," which was started by Griggs with the help of some friends in the business community. The series is meant to bring together business leaders in the greater Pittsburgh area with members of the Steelers to enjoy an evening of entrepreneurial enlightenment and inspiration on a regular basis while supporting charitable organizations such as the Western Pennsylvania Caring Foundation. Mark Bruener has been allied with that organization for years as a speaker, and one of the hosts — along with Merril Hoge and Hines Ward — at an annual fund-raising outing at Southpointe Golf Club.

Past speakers at the "Here's My Story" sessions were I: Mel Blount of the Mel Blount Youth Home, and Willard J. Tillotson of Hefren-Tillotson; II: Dwayne Woodruff, an attorney with Woodruff & Flaherty, and Bruce Reed of Bruster's Ice Cream; III: Andy Russell of Laurel Mountain Partners, LLC, and James Broadhurst, owner of Eat'n Park Hospitality Group; and IV: Rocky Bleier of Rocky Bleier Inc., and Tom Rooney, then of Team Lemieux LLC.

Mark Bruener offered a few remarks. "I've learned," he told his teammates, "the more you give the more you get back." He talked about the good that is accomplished by the Western Pennsylvania Caring Foundation, which he had been involved with since 1995. To the assembled business leaders, he said, "We wanted you to meet us with our helmets off."

I was invited to attend the event by Jay Simon of Hefren-Tillotson, Inc., located in their building on Seventh Avenue. Simon, a member of the National Football League Alumni organization, has been selected as a registered player financial advisor available to serve the players of the NFL. Since 1989, Simon and his two partners, Brad Dishart and Fred Clerici, have built a successful financial planning service. In the year 2001, they broadened their efforts to develop a special service for professional athletes. They point out that the average stay of the NFL player is only 3.5 years, so there's a need to preserve and grow wealth with a managed financial investment program.

Richard B. Fisher, a graduate of Central Catholic High School and Holy Cross College, began his business career in May, 1951 by selling mutual funds door to door. In October, 1955, he and two associates, Jack and Tom Donahue, also Central Catholic alumni, founded Federated Investors. They are now one of the world's largest fund investment management firms. "We were just trying to make a living," he said of the company's modest beginnings.

He said one of his partners had 13 children, and that he and the other one each had seven children. "So we had a lot of motivation to make money," he said. Jack Donahue, he continued, had 84 grandchildren.

He said there were a lot of similarities between the economic picture in Pittsburgh in 1951 and today. "Back then, people had lost money in the stock market crash and Mellon Bank was paying one percent interest on savings accounts. Today we have the same atmosphere. After what's happened the past three years in the market it's tough to get people to pay attention to what they need in this regard. But it's more critical than ever," offered Fisher.

He said they have a rule at Federated Investors for their employees: "If you don't enjoy coming to work here, then don't come".

"To be successful in business, you have to have tremendous belief in what you're doing. You have to enjoy what you're doing." He said there were 130 mutual funds when Federated Investors was started, and there are now 7,000 mutual funds.

"It's about relationships."

J.T. Thomas talked about how he and Larry Brown got started in the restaurant management business. His experience in the food service business began in 1983 after he retired from playing football, operating a number of Burger King Restaurants, before he and Larry Brown got involved with Applebee's in 1987. He and his wife, Deborah, a librarian/reading specialist teacher in the Gateway School system, have two children and one grandson.

He said he took great pride in being an entrepreneur. He spoke of his humble beginnings in a racially-divided community of Macon, Georgia. He remembers segregated restaurants, movie theatres, having to sit in the back of a public bus, and being a part of the civil rights movement. At age 14, he was among the first black children to enter an integrated school situation in Macon. He credited his mother and father with forging the proper self-esteem, the courage to go after what you wanted, and spoke of a strong religious bearing that has served him in good stead all his life.

He was the first black football player at Florida State University. "I wasn't just playing for myself," he said. "I was playing for everyone in the South."

He said it was difficult breaking into an all-white lineup, and playing in a full stadium. "I was like a fly in a bowl of milk," he recalled. "When I entered the game there was complete silence."

He said that he and Larry Brown believe their background with a successful sports team has helped them considerably, not because they're celebrities, but because they learned the importance of teamwork, and the value of having good people on your side.

He says they stress taking good care of their own people and their customers. "We're not in the restaurant business," he said. "We're in the service business. Some people don't know what business they're in. We try to make sure people who come to our restaurants have a pleasant experience in every way. That's what makes me click. We want to create a good experience and environment. We treat our guests as a valuable asset. We try to do the same with the people who work for us.

"You can't manage people anymore. Kids today don't want to be managed. It's about relationships. We work hard to have great relationships."

He said he learned a lot from Chuck Noll and his staff about making wise personnel decisions and getting the most out of everybody on the team. "Larry and I find ourselves using a lot of things we heard in football to get our people on the same page. There I go again."

"Nobody ever lives their life all the way up except a bullfighter."
— Ernest Hemingway,
The Sun Also Rises

Steelers from '50s
Bubble gum cards come to life

Gary Glick wasn't such a bad pick

I spent the last weekend of April 2003 with the Pittsburgh Steelers from the 1950s and it sure beat watching the NFL draft for 17 hours on ESPN TV. I'm sorry, but I could never get excited about the NFL draft, even when I was reporting on it for *The Pittsburgh Press.* I'll get excited about Troy Polamalu, the Samoan safety from Southern Cal and the Steelers' No. 1 draft choice in 2003, when he proves he can play like Mel Blount, Rod Woodson or Jack Butler.

Butler was a defensive back, and sometimes an end, for the Steelers in the '50s and he deserves to be in the Pro Football Hall of Fame as much as Woodson. Butler heads up the Blesto scouting service that helped teams like the Steelers prepare for the draft. He broke away from that activity on Saturday eve to join some of his old teammates to sign autographs at a sports card and memorabilia show at Robert Morris University in Moon Township.

There were 25 Steelers from the '50s at the show, which also featured Hall of Fame baseball pitchers Juan Marichal, Jim Bunning and Gaylord Perry. There were 15 Steelers who were good enough to have played in Pro Bowl games. Butler, who lives in Munhall, was in four Pro Bowls.

Ernie Stautner, a defensive end from Boston College, was in nine Pro Bowls during a 14-year stint (1950-1963) with the Steelers and is also in the Pro Football Hall of Fame. It was great seeing Stautner, Bill Walsh, Jerry Shipkey, Dale Dodril, John Reger, Mike Sandusky, Frank Varrichione, John Nisby, Joe Krupa, Dean Derby, George Hughes, Johnny Lattner, Lynn Chandnois and Ray Mathews. They were all Pro Bowl performers.

Walsh, who later coached at his alma mater, Notre Dame, was a terrific center, probably third in team history behind Mike Webster and Dermontii Dawson. He was a third-round draft choice in 1949, after the Steelers had taken two running backs, Bobby Gage of Clemson and Harper Davis of Mississippi State, on the first two rounds. The Steelers selected Joe Geri, a triple-threat back from Georgia, on the fourth round. Geri, Walsh and Shipkey all represented the Steelers in the 1951 Pro Bowl. Those three, along with George Hughes, played in the 1952 Pro Bowl as well.

"I thoroughly enjoyed my stay with the Steelers," said Walsh (1949-1955), who brought his family with him to Pittsburgh for this reunion.

"The draft wasn't as big a deal in those days," recalled Walsh. "I remember that another center, Chuck Bednarik, was the first player picked in the draft that year. He played at Penn, and the Eagles got him as a bonus choice, sort of a territorial pick. I remember I stayed at the William Penn Hotel when I first came to Pittsburgh. It was a good city for me, and I played with some terrific people."

Pat Brady, one of the Steelers' greatest punters, was also there, along with George Tarasovic, a big defensive end, John "Bull" Schweder, a tough center, and Dick Alban, a defensive back. These were all my first Steelers, the Steelers of my childhood. I collected their bubble gum cards, first in black and white, and then when they came out in color editions.

Also in attendance were Sid Watson, Ed Beatty, Darrell Hogan and Leo Elter. The Steelers had only one winning team in the '50s, 7-4-1 in 1958 under Coach Buddy Parker. They were 6-6 in three of those seasons in that decade, and usually flirted with a .500 record. But those Steelers were special. They played at Forbes Field and later Pitt Stadium and we loved them.

I had breakfast at the Embassy Suites, where these Steelers stayed over the weekend, with Lynn Chandnois and his wife Paulette. I had met them years ago, and it was like it had been yesterday. Chandnois, the Steelers' No. 1 draft pick in 1950, remains one of the great backs and kick-off-return specialists in Steelers' history. He was a sales representative for years with Jessop Steel in Washington, Pennsylvania, and recalled that Dick Groat of the Pirates worked in a similar position during the off-season. He also remembered Carl Moulton, an executive at Jessop Steel, who befriended him.

Lattner (1954) and Varrichione (1955), both out of Notre Dame, were also No. 1 draft choices. Chandnois returned kickoffs for 93 yards against the Giants and the Eagles. Actually, he returned a kick-off for 97 yards against the Giants in October of 1953 but it was called back because a Steeler was off-sides. The Giants kicked off again and Chandnois returned it 93 yards for a touchdown that counted.

I reminded Chandnois of our first dining experience. About 20 years earlier, Jerry Nuzum invited my wife Kathie and me to join him and some of his Steelers teammates for dinner at the Pittsburgh Athletic Association. Also at our table were Bill Dudley and his wife, Libba, Joe Gasparella and Fran Rogel. "I remember we had to borrow a tie for Rogel at the front desk that night," said Chandnois. "Otherwise, they wouldn't let him in."

He said it was a nice deal to be invited to the card and sports memorabilia show. He said each Steeler was paid $500, plus travel expenses and rooms at the Embassy Suites. Ray Mathews came out of Port Vue to star at McKeesport High School and Clemson University and was a terrific receiver for the Steelers. He's still in their record book listings.

Anyone under 60 who saw them in the hotel having breakfast or loafing in the lobby might have mistaken them for an Elks' convention or bowling league members, or maybe an AARP group. They're all in their 70s. Most were gimpy, Shipkey was in a wheel chair, and they were complaining about arthritis and rheumatism, and comparing knee replacements and shoulder surgery.

Mike Sandusky was a starting guard from Maryland from 1957 to 1965. The Steelers' No. 1 choice in 1957 was Len Dawson of Purdue. They also selected four Pitt players: Ralph Jelic, Herman Canil, Corny Salvaterra and Bob Pollock.

Lynn Chandnois, one of the Steelers' all-time kick-returners from Michigan State, stands behind another Big Ten product, offensive lineman Joe Krupa from Purdue. Krupa was a scout for the Steelers for many years.

Frank Varrichione was Steelers' No. 1 draft choice as an offensive lineman out of Notre Dame in 1955 and was a perennial Pro Bowl performer.

Bill Walsh, a third round draft choice out of Notre Dame in 1949, was one of the Steelers' all-time best centers.

I took my wife Kathie with me when I returned on Sunday to see these Steelers. She couldn't believe what people were paying for sports stuff that she's seen in my office at home. I'm in trouble now.

The Steelers have had the first pick in the overall draft on three occasions in their history. They took "Bullet" Bill Dudley of Virginia in 1941, Gary Glick of Colorado A&M (now Colorado State) in 1956, and Terry Bradshaw of Louisiana Tech in 1970. Glick was certainly the most controversial choice.

They got him as a "bonus pick" to start the 1956 draft. He was a defensive back and place-kicker. The Steelers were often criticized for that choice, but he was a decent player. He lasted four seasons (1956-1959) with the Steelers and eight years in pro ball. The 72-year-old Glick proudly showed me two gaudy rings on his fingers. One was for playing for the San Diego Chargers when they won the American Football League title in 1963. The other was for playing on the championship team in the national senior softball championship in Overland Park, Kansas in 1995.

So Gary Glick was a good pick after all. And he's still kicking.

"To me, he was indestructible."

Frank Varrichione was the Steelers' No. 1 draft choice out of Notre Dame in 1955, and he played six seasons in Pittsburgh. In five of those, he represented the Steelers in the Pro Bowl.

Buddy Parker traded him in 1961 to the Los Angeles Rams in exchange for Lou Michaels, a defensive end and place-kicker, who stayed with the Steelers from 1961 to 1963, before being swapped to the Baltimore Colts.

I had a chance to speak briefly with Varrichione when he was sitting with Ernie Stautner in the lobby of the Embassy Suites. I called him a few weeks later at his retirement residence in Alton Bay, New Hampshire. "It's in the middle of the state," said Varrichione, now age 71. "We have two seasons here — winter and the 4th of July."

He says he and his wife, Mitzi, are taking it easy there, helping out their daughter, Lauri, who owns and operates a dog agility school. Lauri's husband is a sea captain, and he was over in Japan, hauling U.S. Marines around the Pacific Ocean ports. "He's away for long periods," offered Frank, so we keep Lauri company.

"I really enjoyed seeing all the guys in Pittsburgh. That was tremendous. I was terribly disappointed to see Ernie in his present physical condition. He's got Alzheimer's and that's a darn shame. To me, he was indestructible. He was like an iron horse. Seeing him like that made me feel sad. It was great to see the guys, though. I haven't seem some of them in 45 or 46 years.

"When the Steelers traded me to the Rams, Buddy Parker told me he hated to do it. He said they needed a guy like Lou Michaels, and

FRANK VARRICHIONE
TACKLE   PITTSBURGH STEELERS

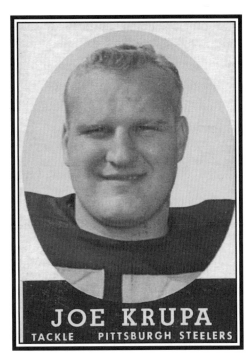

JOE KRUPA
TACKLE   PITTSBURGH STEELERS

MIKE SANDUSKY
GUARD   PITTSBURGH STEELERS

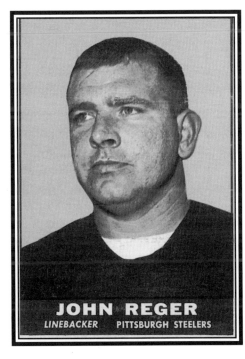

JOHN REGER
LINEBACKER   PITTSBURGH STEELERS

that the Rams wouldn't accept anybody but me in the trade. I put in five more good years with the Rams, so it worked out fine."

Lattner had visited Pittsburgh a few months earlier to participate in an autograph signing show at the ExpoMart in Monroeville. Lattner won the Heisman Trophy in 1954 and was taken as the No. 1 draft choice by the Steelers. Art Rooney always had a soft spot for players from Pitt, Duquesne and Notre Dame. With their eighth selection that year, the Steelers took another running back, Paul Cameron from UCLA, just ahead of Joe Zombek, a big defensive end from Pitt and Scott High.

Lattner and Cameron were both All-American performers, but they played only one season with the Steelers. They both suffered career-ending injuries, as did Zombek. It was different in those days. Such knee surgeries are routine these days, and players are sidelined a month or so. Players had options to make more money in the business world, and they often walked away while they could still walk.

Lattner remembers those days with the Steelers. "I was on the College All-Star team that year and we played the Detroit Lions on a Friday in Chicago," allowed Lattner. "The next day I went to Pittsburgh to play against the Bears. I didn't get time to change my pants.

"Later, at camp — it was at St. Bonaventure — I was rooming with Cameron. I guess the rookies stayed together. Anyway, I got a pulled hamstring right away and the veterans were saying, 'There goes the greatest phony of them all.'

"Well, one day I got a good shot at Dick Flanagan and after that they respected me. But the next year I went to the Air Force and played ball for Bolling Field in 1955 and 1956, and then I got hurt again and had to have a knee operation.

"By the time I got back to the Steelers, the ligaments were torn so bad my knee felt like it had a tire around it. We had an exhibition game with Detroit but Buddy Parker wouldn't dress me for the game. It was then that I saw the handwriting on the wall. I might as well call it quits, so I did."

"An old-time Steelers' fan is familiar with the guys from the '50s. Those were the days when they didn't win too many games, but they were so tough on the opposition that even if they lost they so thoroughly beat up the other team that it often lost the next game."
— Frank Haller, Mt. Lebanon

Johnny Lattner of Notre Dame and Paul Cameron of UCLA, left to right, were promising rookie running backs with Steelers in 1954.

From the '50s

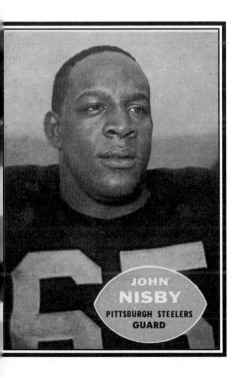

JOHN
NISBY
PITTSBURGH STEELERS
GUARD

Dale Dodril was outstanding middle linebacker from Colorado A&M with the Steelers from 1951 to 1959.

Steelers from the '50s were reunited at sports card and memorabilia show at Robert Morris University. Among the 25 in attendance were, above left to right, Dale Dodril, John Reger and Gary Glick. Frank Varrichione and Ernie Stautner, left to right below, were both former Pro Bowl performers.

Photos by Jim O'Brien

Joe Greene
Enjoys the reunions

"I'm one of the old people now."

Joe Greene may be the greatest Steeler of them all. Certainly, Greene was the building block upon which Chuck Noll and the Steelers built their dynasty, the still-celebrated Steelers of the '70s, the Team of the Decade.

Like the 1960 Pittsburgh Pirates and, to a lesser degree, the Penguins of the early '90s, those Steelers of the '70s are a "forever team." Those guys will never be forgotten by their fans. Greene, the team's No. 1 draft choice out of North Texas State in Noll's first season of 1969, was one of the main reasons for the Steelers' success. It all started with Noll and Greene.

Greene was invited to be the honored guest at the Mel Blount Youth Home 5th Annual All-Star Celebrity Roast at The Pittsburgh Hilton on Friday, May 30, 2003. Blount was one of his best friends on those Steelers teams. Both were remarkable physical marvels. Teammate Mike Wagner believes those two and Terry Bradshaw were in a class all by themselves as once-in-a-lifetime athletes.

Nearly 1,000 fans turned out for the dinner at the Hilton, and they gave Greene, as well as Coach Noll, a standing ovation when they were introduced by emcee Rocky Bleier. Bleier, by the way, stood out in his white tuxedo, looking like a nightclub singer.

One of the highlights of the introductions was when Bleier introduced Tommy Okon, a name in the program that must have puzzled everyone at first glance. When did he play for the Steelers? But Okon was the kid who gave Greene a bottle of Coca-Cola in that memorable TV commercial that won awards, and is rated by *TV Guide* as one of the Top Ten TV ads of all time.

Okon, now 33, returned that towel that Greene had given him as a child — remember how gruff Greene was when he spoke to that kid as he came limping through a dark tunnel after a disappointing game? — and gave Greene a big hug. Okon, once a cute kid, is a handsome man. "That's very warm and fuzzy," said Bleier, but warned the audience that this event was a "roast," and that Greene would get roughed up pretty good. In time, Greene did get roasted by his son, Charles Major Greene; Lynn Swann, the Hall of Fame receiver; Andy Russell, of Laurel Mountain Partners, a former linebacker and teammate; Ralph Berlin, the team trainer in those days; and Randy Grossman, a tight end from those days. Grossman got the highest grades for his performance.

Greene's older son, by the way, was 34 years of age, the same age as Joe Greene when he retired in 1981 after playing 13 seasons with the Steelers. Charles Major is a sales agent for Cen-Tex, a realty company in Dallas. His other son, Edward, 33, works for Southwestern Bell, and his daughter, JoQuel, 28, is a recent graduate of Arizona State University. "She's looking for a job," said her father. Joe's wife of 35 years, Agnes, also accompanied her husband to Pittsburgh, and was happy to be reunited with so many old friends.

There were about 33 former Steelers present for the Blount dinner, enough to field a team in the early days of the National Football League. Among those in attendance were fellow Pro Football Hall of Fame members Franco Harris and John Stallworth, to share the spotlight with Swann, Greene, Blount and Noll.

Some of the personalities have changed since their playing days. Swann refused to sign autographs for children at a special V.I.P. pre-dinner reception. He has done that at other Pittsburgh events, including one where he was the host at Heinz Field. Marketing executives at H.J. Heinz felt short-changed when Swann snubbed some of their guests who sought his autograph. Swann even turned down requests from some of the kids who were staying at the Mel Blount Youth Home. That seems like strange behavior for the national chairman of Big Brothers & Big Sisters and the chairman of the President's Council on Physical Fitness and Sports. At the same time, Greg Lloyd, who was always so gruff and difficult with the media during his days with the Steelers, couldn't have been more gracious and generous with his time with anyone who approached him at the V.I.P. session in the Kings Garden. Lloyd looked like he could still play for the Steelers, as buff as ever.

Three of the boys who asked Swann to sign footballs were there because a friend had given their family tickets for the Blount dinner. Their dad died three years ago after suffering a heart attack at age 34, and friends have held an annual golf outing and sports auction to raise funds for their college education. Then again, Swann had no way of knowing that. Maybe he should rethink his strategy before people begin thinking less of Lynn Swann. I think Lynn Swann shouldn't worry about what someone might do with his autograph. It won't diminish his lifestyle. I did see Swann pose for pictures for people who asked.

Greene obliged everybody, as he had done a week or so earlier at Andy Russell's 27th Annual Celebrity Classic for Children. Greene greeted everyone who approached him with a toothy smile. He signed autographs for anyone who asked, and he obliged everyone who asked if he would be willing to pose for a picture with them. Greene would pause before responding to the request, and then said, "I would be honored." If the individual had a drink in his or her hand, Greene would gently remove it and put it on a table, out of sight. Greene was looking out for their image as well as his own.

Greene participated in a sports card and memorabilia show at the Expo Mart in Monroeville on Sunday afternoon of the same weekend as the Blount dinner. He was there with his friend "Fats" Holmes, Bleier, Stoudt and Jack Lambert.

> *"No one knows another man's pain."*
> **— Joe Greene**

Joe Greene cracks up while exchanging pleasantries with former teammates Mel Blount and Roy Jefferson at Andy Russell's Celebrity Classic for Children at The Club at Nevillewood. Mark Malone, Greene, Randy Grossman and Bill Hurley caught up with each other's activities at same function in May, 2003.

Photos by Jim O'Brien

Other Steelers who showed up for the Blount Youth Home fund-raising event, a black-tie affair, were John Banaszak, Greg Best, Craig Bingham, Emil Boures, John Brown, Mark Bruener, Jack Deloplaine, Alan Faneca, Steve Fedell, Ernie Holmes, Todd Kalis, Jon Kolb, Mark Malone, Gerry "Moon" Mullins, Ted Petersen, Donnie Shell, Cliff Stoudt, J.T. Thomas, Mike Wagner, Dwight White, Craig Wolfley and Dwayne Woodruff. Tony Parisi, the team's equipment manager, and Paul Uram, a strength and conditioning coach, were there in tuxedos as well. They never looked better. Joe Greene was 56 and he would turn 57 on September 24 of the 2003 season. He was looking forward to his eighth season as an assistant coach with the Arizona Cardinals. He began his coaching career as an assistant to Chuck Noll with the Steelers for five years (1987-1991) and the Miami Dolphins for four years (1991-1994). He was with the Dolphins when another Pittsburgh favorite, Danny Marino, was the quarterback.

Joe Greene was always a good interview. He was honest with his emotions, thoughtful, considerate, absolutely charming at times. I still love to hear his voice, not quite as deep as L.C. Greenwood's, but rich in tone. There is a positive joy in his voice. I like the way he tugs at his beard sometimes when he's considering how to answer a question. He was nicknamed "Mean Joe" because he played in a fierce manner for the Mean Green of North Texas State. "I just want people to remember me as being a good player and not really mean," he said.

Chuck Noll said of him, "He's the best I've seen. He set the standard for us . . . There will never be another Joe Greene. Joe will always be something special."

When he had completed his weekend appearances, Greene pronounced his Pittsburgh visit one of his best since he left the Steelers after Noll retired. "Being in public sometimes is a pain in the ass," explained Greene, rather frankly. "Nowadays, people can't see you on the street that they don't stop you and want an autograph. It wasn't always that way. There was a time when Clemente and Stargell could go down the street, and someone would just say, 'Hi, Roberto," or "Hey, Willie!" That's changed in most places.

"Pittsburgh's always been better than most cities in that regard. I always appreciated that. They let you be yourself here; they give you some space. Sometimes in sports today genuine respect and admiration get lost. That's been lost for sports figures."

When I asked Greene to pose for a photo with Lambert at the card show in Monroeville, Greene said, "Get this in one shot. You know how crusty he gets." He said it so Lambert could hear him.

Later, I told him that Lambert did everything I asked him to do, but that interviewing him was still difficult. I'm still not relaxed or at ease with Lambert. There's always some tension. Lambert likes that, I think.

"The hole is never where it's supposed to be."
— **Franco Harris**

Joe Greene and L.C. Greenwood were glad to see each other.   Jim O'Brien

Joe Greene and his wife, Agnes, pose with Art Rooney Jr. and Bill Nunn Jr. of Steelers' player personnel department in early '70s.

"Thanks for the memories."
— Bob Hope on his 100th birthday

"He's a little different than I am," said Greene, "but in some ways we're alike. You're careful about who you let into the space you live in. You don't invite in a lot of people. Today, some people are trying to take advantage of you. I understand why Jack is sometimes the way he is."

"It's more meaningful now."

Joe Greene:

When I sit down with the guys I played with, I am back at Three Rivers Stadium and at summer training camp at St. Vincent College. It comes back so quickly. We are young again. Those were the good ol' days.

Yes, it's more meaningful now, much more meaningful. I know I'm not young anymore. I see the gray in my whiskers and in the hair on my head. I can't kid myself about that. The mirror tells me every morning that I've gotten older. My children are as old as I was when I was wrapping up my playing career with the Steelers.

Sitting there, with the guys at Andy's golf outing, I had a little melancholy moment. I was looking at L.C. Greenwood, Glen Edwards, Andy and Moon Mullins, Gordon Gravelle and Wagner. We started reminiscing. When I got sad, I looked at all the years that have gone by. I'm one of the old people now.

I'm glad to have those kinds of memories.

As a coach with other teams, seeking that Holy Grail, I've got a better idea of how difficult it can be to win a championship in this league. What we did — winning four Super Bowls in six seasons — was a tremendous accomplishment. I realize that more than ever now. The enormity of our accomplishment has been validated.

We were in a good place at the right time. We had outstanding leadership. I was with an outstanding group of guys. Chuck Noll's leadership made it all mesh.

I was headstrong when I first came to the Steelers, and thought I knew everything. He got rid of players I liked, and I wondered what he was doing. I was in my second year when he traded away Roy Jefferson, for instance, and that upset me. What did I know? At the time Chuck was building. When a team is in a building process, sometimes it's difficult to comprehend what's happening, and why. You don't see the big picture.

The things he was teaching us, I hadn't seen a lot of evidence that it was working (the Steelers' record was 1-13 his first year). Now I think it was correct. Enough time hadn't passed by for me to understand the wisdom of it back then. It's simply a matter that enough time has passed to properly evaluate that he knew exactly what he was doing.

I thought Terry Bradshaw was quite a quarterback when we were teammates. That's been verified, too. I've talked to Terry from time to time and I know he cherishes his Steelers' experience. I remember that Terry told us, "You can lose with me, but you can't win without me." He said it mostly in jest, but he was right.

He was there when we needed him. He was a big game player. I've seen other teams with championship quality, but they couldn't win again and again as we did. You look at the Chicago Bears (of Mike Ditka in the mid-80s) and they had an outstanding team for five years. But they won one Super Bowl. They didn't always have the same quarterback. Jim McMahon wasn't always the quarterback the way Terry Bradshaw was always our quarterback. Terry was there for us . . . all the time.

That's the incredible thing. You mention guys like Swann and Stallworth, and they were always there, too. You never mentioned dropped balls when you talked about those guys. They pulled in everything, especially in the clutch. They were champion receivers.

Terry struggled at the start, as we all did. He had some rough times. Outside of Pittsburgh, there was talk that Terry wasn't real bright. Terry threw a lot of interceptions for awhile. But it wasn't true that he wasn't bright. Terry had so much confidence in his arm, sometimes he did things that came back to haunt him.

People in Pittsburgh know what he meant to our team. That's why I was glad that he got the reception he got last year when he came back to Pittsburgh as an honorary captain. He deserved that. I talked to Brad about that, and he said, "I was amazed. I didn't know they liked me so much."

It's the same everywhere. When things don't go well, the quarterback is an easy target. Terry had a rocky start in Pittsburgh. The day he got hurt and they cheered as he was coming off the field stuck with him. I know that hurt him badly, and he never really got over it. He never forgot it, anyhow. That had to be painful.

I always liked to say that no man knows another man's pain. That's why we shouldn't be too quick to judge other people when they're having problems.

What I understand better today, as a coach, is how difficult it is to make decisions. Maybe what you think is right goes against the tides. No one may know it's the right decision but you. But you have to do the things you believe in.

Chuck Noll being a young guy — he was 33 to 40 years old — when he first had us. He lived an awful lot in a short time. He made some great decisions. If I could say there was one failure — and I use that word guardedly — we were slow to change once we fielded the finest team in the league. None of us wanted to leave. No one was happy when they were cut or traded away. Some guys were kept one year too long. I might have been one of them.

But look at the good decisions he made. He picked Terry Bradshaw over Terry Hanratty and Joe Gilliam. Believe me . . . that was not an easy decision when it was made.

Look at how he traded away Bruce Van Dyke to open up a position for a young Gerry Mullins. Mullins was a college tight end, yet Noll took him to play guard. What about moving Larry Brown from tight end to tackle? How about taking a college center and turning him into the outstanding offensive tackle of his era. I'm talking, of course, about Jon Kolb.

Being a coach these many years, I know how difficult it is to get 45 to 50 guys to work in unison. But Chuck Noll did that. That's why we're still being remembered.

You asked me what it was like to be with the Dolphins and watch Danny Marino. He and Bradshaw both had overwhelming confidence in themselves. Growing up in Pittsburgh, Marino had to be a big fan of Bradshaw. How could a young quarterback not be a fan of Bradshaw in his hometown?

Terry threw the ball 15 or 20 times, and Danny threw the ball 40 times a game. He had a gift and he could get rid of that ball so quickly, and on target. He could throw that ball. So could Bradshaw, but he didn't have to do it so often. He had more weapons than Marino around him. On both sides of the ball. Things were different back then when Bradshaw was our quarterback. We had a strong running game. Bradshaw had a big game when he threw for 200 yards or more. But he came up big in the biggest games. That's how he's in the Hall of Fame.

The comeback of Terry Bradshaw was a good story, and so was the comeback story of Tommy Maddox. It goes to prove that Dan Reeves was right about him, even if it's so late in the process. Sometimes you see something in guys and no one else can see it.

It's fortunate for Maddox that he had the time and the opportunity to prove himself. He wouldn't give up on himself. He kept trying things to resurrect his career. He's still healthy, and his mind has caught up with his football abilities. That's coming from a fan. I'm still a players' person first. I root for guys like Tommy Maddox. I still root for the Steelers. I still root for the Rooneys.

Joe Greene and kid actor Tommy Okon were featured in award-winning Coca-Cola TV commercial during glory days of the '70s.

Chuck Noll and defensive coordinator George Perles provide instruction for Joe Greene during game at Three Rivers Stadium. Offensive line coach Rollie Dotsch can be seen in background.

"We're playing a kids' game and getting paid a king's ransom."
— Warren Sapp, Tampa Bay Buccaneers

"It's like a piece of you goes with them."

The death of Mike Webster was difficult for all of us to deal with. It's just sad. When your teammates die it's like a piece of you goes with them.

Last night, when I saw L.C. Greenwood I was so delighted to see him. I got so sentimental. It wasn't something I planned. It's just where we are these days.

When I first came to Pittsburgh, I had no idea I'd be received with an appreciation that would have much of a timeline to it, or that I'd have so much success. These guys are a big part of that. Seeing them brings out some emotions.

When I went to the funeral of Ronnie Shanklin it really hit home. We all talked about Ronnie last night. We all saw him in the same light. He was a sensational athlete. His challenge always was to make people laugh. He had a great smile. There was something impish about him.

It was good to see Roy Jefferson here. He was a big-time player for us. He helped me get started on the right foot in this league. I hated to see him go, but Chuck probably knew what he was doing right along. He didn't want a young quarterback to deal with Roy's independence. He sent Ray May away for the same reasons and Ray was a fine linebacker.

What could you do about that? You couldn't do anything about it. I never saw them being a problem in the locker room or giving the coaches a bad time.

Mike Webster was never a problem for anyone. Mike was a very quiet, unassuming guy. He took his work seriously. When Mike first came here, Ernie Holmes and I had to beat him up in practice every day. And he never said a word. He set his teeth that it wasn't going to continue.

Mike was the first player I told I was going to retire. Why was it Mike? Maybe it's because he was there. I felt comfortable sharing that with him. It seemed that I should tell him.

You say people have told you there are other Mike Websters out there, former players with problems, who need help. That might be. I don't want to bury my head in the sand, but I don't want to stir up any ghosts.

I'd rather have positive thoughts about Mike and my teammates. I'd rather think about them at their best. Those teams of ours in the '70s will remain in the minds and hearts of Steelers' fans forever. A lot has to do with longevity, but I think a lot more has to do with the style.

After a game in which the Steelers played poorly, but won, Joe Greene was asked how the Steelers managed to win. He replied, "Because we're the Pittsburgh Steelers!"

Art Rooney Jr.
Has the magic name

"It's a fat man's sandwich."

A rt Rooney Jr. tucked a white linen napkin between his buttoned-down shirt collar and his Adam's apple. He told Shawn, the waiter, what he wanted for lunch. For starters, he wanted a glass of cranberry juice and a fruit cup. Then he said he wanted a turkey sandwich on whole wheat bread, with lettuce, tomato, mustard and pickle. "It's a fat man's sandwich," he told me with a mischievous wink. "Don't let me hold you back, though. You order a hot meal if you'd like. I bring a friend or a priest here from time to time and I always tell them to go ahead and order a hot meal."

I get a kick out of Art Rooney Jr. He just says things like that, like no one else I know. He later said he owed Garrett Webster, the son of Mike Webster, a steak dinner. Not just a dinner, mind you, but a steak dinner. There is something splendidly common about Art Rooney Jr. He is like his father, the founder of the Steelers and a Hall of Fame performer, in that regard. It's part of his charm. He had the same gritty complexion, the tough guy jaw, the street fighter's spirit.

"If this guy kept giving Dad a tough time, I thought I'd have to punch him," he said more than once. So he has a bit of Billy Conn in him, too. He has a lot of time on his hands and, like his father, he uses it to spread good cheer. He's thoughtful, and drops a friendly line to a lot of friends and associates on a regular basis. Former Steelers players, in particular, are pleased to hear from him.

Arthur Joseph Rooney Jr. was wearing a well-worn dark blue sweater and a dark gray glenplaid sportscoat. Outdoors, he wore a cap and sunglasses, and looked like an Irishman fresh off the boat from Dublin. He's about 6-4 and still a broad-shouldered guy. Like Jerome Bettis, he guards his weight. It's not for public disclosure. The late Dick Schaap told me that Art Rooney looked like Pittsburgh. In that respect, the second son looked like Greenfield or Garfield.

This was a Wednesday, April 23, 2003 and we were seated at a table in the middle of a sun-splashed dining room at the St. Clair Country Club, about two miles from my home, and two miles from Art Rooney Jr.'s office in the Southmark Building. His office was about three miles from his mansion home in Mt. Lebanon. His home is a stately mix of Georgian and Tudor elements. We were surrounded in the dining room by well-turned-out women and elderly men, none in an apparent hurry, most speaking in hushed tones.

I confessed to Art Jr. that I felt like I was loafing, even though I was interviewing him for this book, because of the grand manner in which we were dining. My napkin couldn't wipe away the guilt. I used to feel the same way when I was chatting with his dad on the sideline at a Steelers' practice at Three Rivers Stadium.

The first time I was ever at the St. Clair Country Club, back in the early '80s, I was a guest of Bob Prince, a legend at the club as well as a Hall of Fame broadcaster for Pirates baseball for 28 years. I remember he kept ordering Screwdrivers (vodka with orange juice), but he told the waiter to write something else down on his tab every other drink. "Ol' Bets checks these, and I don't want her to know how many Screwdrivers I had to drink," snapped Prince. I had been there more recently, along with my wife Kathie, as a guest of Betty Prince, the wife of the late "Gunner." Bob Prince picked up the tab wherever he went, the P.A.A. or the Field Club or Park Schenley. Prince liked playing the role of a big shot, much to Betty's chagrin.

Dick Young of the *New York Daily News* once explained why he chose to be a sportswriter. "I don't want to be a millionaire," said Young, "I just want to live like a millionaire."

The Rooneys have always had more money than most people in Pittsburgh, but they always acted like they didn't. The Rooneys never realized they were rich. They never subscribed to *Esquire* or *GQ*. Art Sr. liked keeping a low profile, and forbade his kids from driving Cadillacs. He drove a loaded Buick instead, from a dealership owned by his father-in-law. And he remained in the family home on the North Side, even after the neighborhood had declined. That remained a large part of their appeal to the average sports fan in the city. I know a common man when I see one because I see one in the mirror each morning when I am shaving. His father's favorite phrases were "kiddin' on the square" and "you're brand new" and "he's come a long way." One of his phrases that has stayed with Art Jr the most is this one: "Treat everyone as you would like to be treated, but don't let people confuse kindness for weakness."

Art Jr. is a veritable storehouse of information on his father and the Steelers. He was working on a book (for family distribution only) with 88-year-old Roy McHugh, the gifted writer and former columnist with *The Pittsburgh Press*. He was also assisting Rob Ruck, a Pitt history professor, with a book on the Rooneys that the family had commissioned. Ruck's wife, Maggie Patterson, an instructor in the journalism department at Duquesne University, was helping on the project. Ruck had already written some fine books on black baseball history in Pittsburgh. Art Jr. was a patron for my book on his dad called "The Chief: Art Rooney and his Pittsburgh Steelers." He said, "That was a wonderful celebration of my father's life. Everyone I gave a copy to loved it."

Art Rooney Jr. wanted to be an actor when he was in college, at St. Vincent's in Latrobe, and even went to New York to get started. But his first love was football, and he liked being involved in his dad's business. So he quickly abandoned his ambition to become a Broadway star. A one-man play about his dad, called *The Chief*, had been written by Gene Collier and Rob Zellers for production at the Public Theater. Pittsburgh-born actor Tom Atkins was going to play the part of Art Rooney. I thought his second son would have been a

Art Rooney Jr. has drawings of Mike Webster, Lynn Swann and Terry Bradshaw on the wall of his Upper St. Clair office. Below, Rooney visits St. Clair Country Club nearby for luncheon interview.

Photos by Jim O'Brien

smart choice. He was best suited for the part. Everybody who knew him thought Artie was the son most like his father.

"I always liked him," said Bob Milie of Mt. Lebanon, a former assistant trainer to the Steelers. "He is a good-hearted guy, and he had a great deal to do with assembling those great teams of the '70s. He deserves a lot of credit for all those Super Bowls."

"I still have a hole in my heart."

Art Rooney Jr. did odd jobs behind the scenes for the Steelers in his youth, and was named the player personnel director in 1964. "It was a job in name only when it came to my first draft in 1965," related Art Jr. "Buddy Parker had traded away five of our first six picks in the draft."

The Steelers selected Roy Jefferson, a receiver from Utah, on the second round, however, and he turned out to be an All-Pro performer. Not a bad start for the head scout.

Art Rooney Jr. has been working hard to keep his weight under control. He had lost over 100 pounds ten years earlier on a crash diet and training regimen. I think he regained some of it, which seemed to suit him. "It's a constant battle," he confessed. "I win sometimes, lose sometimes."

There was a time when he didn't look good, when his mottled skin was sagging, but he looked good now, comfortable in his body at age 67. He said he would be 68 on October 18, 2003. He volunteered that his brother Dan was 71 and had some health challenges.

There was a golf tournament going on at the highly respected golf course we could see from our table. The head pro was the popular Phil Newcamp. "It's a beautiful course," said Art Rooney Jr. "It looks just like the Masters course at Augusta." And, indeed, bright pink azaleas could be seen on a hill in the distance. Temperatures were in the mid-50s. It would dip into the 40s for a baseball game between the San Francisco Giants and Pirates at PNC Park that night.

Nick Perry, a popular Pittsburgh broadcasting pioneer, had died the day before at age 84. He had become famous as a host for "Bowling For Dollars," and had gained infamy and jail time when he was linked to the rigged "666" Daily Lottery scheme. He hosted the drawing at the WTAE-TV studios and got into trouble in 1980.

Ron Shanklin, a star receiver for the Steelers in the early '70s, had died from colon cancer a week earlier in Dallas at the age of 55. Art Rooney Jr. headed the Steelers scouting department when the team drafted Shanklin of North Texas State on the second round in 1970, right after they selected Terry Bradshaw of Louisiana Tech with the first pick in the entire draft. Shanklin had come from the same school as Joe Greene, the Steelers' No. 1 pick the previous year in Chuck Noll's first season as the head coach.

Art Jr., the second of Art and Kathleen Rooney's five sons was head of the Steelers' scouting department for 22 years. He was fired by his brother Dan, the oldest son and the team president, in 1987. It upset his father and his three other brothers and their families. Their father retreated to his horse farm in Maryland to mourn the decision. "I still have a hole in my heart," related Art Jr. And he left it at that. He is reluctant to talk about his dismissal, or his feelings about what his brother Dan did. He doesn't want to upset his brother. He remains a vice-president of the Steelers and retains 16 percent interest in the franchise. The five Rooney boys own 80 percent of the team's stock, and Jack and Rita McGinley, the children of Art Rooney's one-time partner Barney McGinley, each own ten percent of the franchise. Jack, who is Art Rooney Sr.'s brother-in-law, and Rita are silent partners, and two of the nicest people you'd ever meet. So is Art Rooney Jr. Art Jr. is often confused name-wise with Art II, the oldest son of Dan Rooney, and now a vice-president and heir apparent to the Black and Gold throne.

"I was told I was obstinate," related Art Rooney Jr. "You asked me why I wasn't reassigned to another position in the organization. I don't know. I still ask myself why I wasn't given other duties."

There was a belief for a time that Rooney was removed from his position as player personnel director because he annoyed Chuck Noll, but that story has been put to rest. I am told by others that it was strictly Dan's decision to make the change. He told his father, "It's him or me." He thought his brother had become too autonomous. Normally, Dan likes what corporate types call "creative tension," with department heads challenging one another. But there was also some sibling rivalry.

"The thing that you miss is the camaraderie with the players," said Art Jr. "I had a reputation for being anti-coach, but that wasn't true, and I miss working with some of the coaches."

There was a time, in the years after he was dismissed, that Art Jr. continued to go to college football games and take scouting notes, and to review game films. He sent his scouting reports to the Steelers' offices, but he didn't know whether anyone reviewed them or not. He quit doing that a few years ago. "I just lost interest," he said. "That was amazing, but I'm just not interested anymore."

He keeps a low profile, working out of a handsome suite of offices on the border of Mt. Lebanon, Upper St. Clair and Bethel Park. His office is much nicer than the one he had at Three Rivers Stadium. When I visited his office earlier that morning, he had the window shades drawn to the ceiling on all three windows, allowing much natural light to stream across his dark cherry desk. The offices at Three Rivers had no windows. It was like working in a bomb shelter. You never knew what time of day it was, or whether it was sunny or raining outside. "I like this," said Art Jr.

> *"Going into your past is a gamble because you never know what you'll find."*
> — **John Feinstein, sports author**
> *Forever's Team*

He doesn't use his name to gain favors, and he seldom strays into the city. He's seldom seen at any public affairs. He still goes to the Steelers games and has a family box, but he definitely keeps a low profile.

His friend and former co-worker Bill Nunn Jr. keeps in touch with him. Nunn is a former sportswriter so he's smarter, of course, than most pro football scouts. Those two, along with Dick Haley, headed up the Steelers' scouting staff in the glory days of the '70s. Nunn had named a Black College All-America team when he was the sports editor and columnist for *The Pittsburgh Courier*, and he had great contacts at the black colleges. He was thought to be a real asset to the Steelers in building their empire.

"Noll wanted more weapons."

The National Football League draft of 2003 was only three days away when Art Jr. and I met. He had done a telephone interview earlier in the day with Rich Emert, a stringer for the *Pittsburgh Post-Gazette*. "He told me I was always the easiest and best interview in the Steelers office during the drafts," said Art Jr. with a smug look. I nodded in agreement.

The story would appear in the "Where Are They Now?" section of the next day's newspaper. Art Rooney Jr. was back in the news. The story was available on the Internet, and even Art Rooney Jr., who is all fat thumbs at the computer keyboard, knew how to call that up on his screen.

In his Q. and A. article, Emert wrote a preface that included this reflection on Art Rooney Jr.: "He is still highly thought of by many player-personnel people and has been nominated twice for the NFL Hall of Fame." Rooney dismissed that mention. "It was nice because it came from outside the organization," said Art Jr. "I enjoyed it. But when you consider that L.C. Greenwood and Donnie Shell, who are much more deserving, aren't in the Hall yet, it didn't bother me that I didn't make the final cut. It's just nice that one of the working stiffs was nominated."

This was once the busiest time of the year for Art Rooney Jr. Now he was having a leisurely lunch at a country club, enjoying the good life.

"Bill Nunn told me I should get out more," said Art Jr. "He said, 'You look like a football guy, you dress like a football guy, you talk like a football guy, and you *are* a football guy. You've got the magic name!'"

Yet, somehow, down deep, Art Rooney Jr. doesn't feel like a football guy anymore, or anyone significant in the Steelers' picture. That's a shame. He tends to some family business. Dee Herrod is his secretary and office receptionist. Maureen Butler Maier is in a room between Art Jr. and Herrod. Maureen is the property manager and bookkeeper for Rooney interests. Maureen is the daughter of Art's best friend, Jack Butler, a one-time Steeler star, coach and scout, who still looks after the Blesto scouting organization from what Rooney termed a "bare-bones office" in downtown Pittsburgh.

There are a half-dozen art renderings of his father, Art Rooney Sr., lining the wall where Herrod has her desk. It's like a Wall of Fame for his father. There are familiar Pittsburgh scenes, sternwheelers on the rivers, smoke over the steel mills, all portraits of Pittsburgh's past. There's a framed full-page from the *Pittsburgh Post-Gazette* of story about the famed Steelers' 1974 draft that appeared a year earlier. It was written by Ed Bouchette, the Steelers' beat writer and one of the most respected journalists on the pro football front. It lauds that 1974 draft class as the best in Steelers' history and one of the most productive in the history of pro football.

The Steelers were picking 21st overall that year, which makes the quality and depth of the draft even more remarkable. They had finished with a 10-4 record the previous season.

In 1974, the Steelers selected Lynn Swann, Jack Lambert, John Stallworth and Mike Webster in the first five rounds. They are all in the Pro Football Hall of Fame.

When I was doing some research on the Steelers prior to my interview with Art Jr. it struck me that the Steelers already possessed some outstanding pass-catchers in Shanklin and Lewis, along with Dave Smith and Jon Staggers, when they drafted Swann and Stallworth. So why did they draft Swann and Stallworth with their early picks? Nowadays, with 24-hour sports talk radio stations and cable TV outlets, surely the Steelers would have been strongly criticized for drafting two receivers with high draft choices when they already were strong there.

"Noll wanted more weapons," said Art Jr. "He always talked about the need for weapons. You never had enough weapons. Yeah, we had great receivers in Shanklin and Lewis, but we got even better ones in Swann and Stallworth. When you look at that class and see the four Hall of Famers and then consider that we signed Donnie Shell, who has been nominated for the Hall of Fame, and Randy Grossman, who ended up starting for us in a Super Bowl, as free agents, it was remarkable." The 1971 class was pretty outstanding, too, with Frank Lewis, Jack Ham, Steve Davis, Gerry "Moon" Mullins, Dwight White, Larry Brown and Mike Wagner. It may be the second best draft class in NFL history.

Before Art Jr. and his staff could consider themselves geniuses one has to review the 1975 draft, just a year after their 1974 bonanza. The Steelers took Dave Brown, a defensive back from Michigan, on the first round and he was the only player to distinguish himself. He stayed one season with the Steelers and went to Seattle in the expansion draft. "Bud Carson gave up on him," said Rooney, "but he went on to play about a dozen seasons in the NFL. He was a class guy on and off the field. He became an NFL coach."

There are beautiful art renderings of Webster, Swann and Bradshaw by Merv Corning on the wall nearest the desk of Art Rooney Jr. There are other artworks by Corning on other walls. There are plaques that were presented to Art Jr. for various tributes.

He loves Corning's lifelike images. He's commissioned the California-based artist to create bubble-gum-like cards of his father and some of his favorite Steelers, such as Webster. Art Jr. has postcards with ink sketches of Steelers favorites like his dad, Chuck Noll, Elbie Nickel, Ernie Stautner, Whizzer White, "Bullet Bill" Dudley, Armand Niccolai and Johnny "Blood" McNally that he passes out to friends. They are wonderful postcards and bookmarkers. You can't buy them anywhere.

Like his dad, Art Jr. is quick to send out handwritten postcards to family and friends. He is thoughtful in that regard. They are keepsakes for all that receive them. He's quick to offer praise and positive thoughts that can make the day for the fortunate recipient. Always, Art Jr. takes the time to brighten other people's lives.

Pat Hanlon, the vice-president for communications for the New York Giants, called up the article about Art Jr. on the Internet the same day it appeared and made copies that he passed on to Wellington Mara, one of the Giants' owners, and Ernie Accorsi, the team's general manager. Both are long-time friends and admirers of Art Rooney Jr. George Young, who had died the previous year, was GM of the Giants before Accorsi and a great friend of Art Rooney Jr. They had first met when they were both young scouts, and kept company on the road when checking out college prospects.

Hanlon had been my right-hand man in the sports information office of the University of Pittsburgh when I served as assistant athletic director in charge of publicity and promotions from 1983-1986, and he later worked as an assistant publicity director to Dan Edwards with the Steelers. He had always liked Art Rooney Jr.

Hanlon sent an e-mail message to Art Jr. after reading the article about him that read: "Glad to hear you are doing well. James P. O'Brien gave me your e-mail address. It's funny that I received a long e-mail from Jim last night and it mentioned that you two had lunch yesterday and how much he enjoys your company. Then I got a phone call from Pete Abitante of the league office this morning and he tells me that there are a couple of nice pieces in the *P-G* this morning — one on Merril Hoge and one on you. I made a copy of the piece on you for Wellington and Ernie Accorsi, who both enjoyed it.

"It's another draft weekend. You are right. The dynamics of this thing have changed considerably in recent years. I like the way Ernie and our coach work the system, though. I think George Barnard Young would be proud. "Take care of yourself. I don't need to tell you this, but you are one of the favorite sons of this league. People continue to talk about you, and I have always appreciated your thoughtfulness and consideration."

I had sent Art Rooney Jr. two interns to work in his office when he was still scouting and writing reports on prospects, mostly for his own amusement. One was Paul Roell, a student of mine at Robert Morris University. He wanted to be a pro football scout. I had Art Jr. speak to my sports management class and then linked him up with Roell, who is now a scout with the Indianapolis Colts. I also got Art Jr. to mentor Fred Schaefer from nearby Bridgeville, whom I had first met when he was a poster boy for the Leukemia Society, and had spent a few days as Foge Fazio's guest at the Pitt football camp at Edinboro University. Schaefer got well enough that he played football at Chartiers Valley High School, and wanted to become a pro football scout.

Schaefer was running Pittsburgh Total Scouting Service to help high school athletes get scholarships. He also rated pro prospects on his own. Art Rooney Jr. gave me a copy of Schaefer's ratings for the upcoming draft. "He's pretty good at this," said Art Rooney Jr. He still knows a good scout when he sees one.

Art Jr. said he was still wintering in Florida when Terry Bradshaw came back for the celebrated reunion with his coach, Chuck Noll. Art Jr. was at Heinz Field for the Monday Night Game with the New England Patriots when Bradshaw came back with his two daughters to serve as an honorary captain and received a thunderous standing ovation from a full house.

"It was terribly moving," said Art. "I'm a little skeptical, so I thought some of it was showbiz, too. His daughters are gorgeous. I thought it was very good, showbiz or not.

"When they had the last game at Three Rivers, they played a tape-recorded interview with Terry that I did see. He spoke about his love for my father, and he thanked Dan and Art Rooney Jr. I appreciated that. He's the only one that mentioned me like that. I wasn't close to Terry, or anything like that, but I got along with him. I'm glad he remembered me."

Art Rooney Jr.:

Mike Webster was one of our all-time best draft choices. Mike was not a computer football player. He wasn't one of those guys the computer rankings would place high on a list. We were starting to get more sophisticated about scouting and rating players in the '70s. Gil Brandt and the Dallas Cowboys, who were big on computers, were getting a lot of attention for that. We got into it, too.

The Blesto (scouting service) guys thought Webster was a great college player who had already reached his potential. He had the minimum height and weight. If you went below that you waited until the later rounds to take a chance on the guy.

He was listed as 6-1, 235, but that was probably with a dumbbell in his jock strap. He was timed at 5.2 in the 40, nothing great there, either.

There was an assistant coach at Wisconsin — I can't remember his name — who was a friend of one of our assistant coaches, George Perles. That guy was an Irishman. I can't believe I can't remember his name. Something like McSwain or McSwigan maybe. Perles had been an assistant coach at his alma mater, Michigan State, and he knew a lot of guys in the Big Ten. Michigan State's head coach at the time was Hank Bullough (later the coach of the Pittsburgh Maulers of the United States Football League).

This assistant at Wisconsin kept calling Perles and pleading with him to pick Webster. He said he had a special guy for him. This guy sent us film of Webster. You watched it and liked what you saw. But this guy didn't have the measurables to match some other prospects. George and I weren't real tight, but he kept coming in my office and promoting Webster. George was our defensive coach, and Webster wasn't even on his side of the ball. He'd come in my office like a little kid who cried until he got the candy he wanted. He just kept after me. He kept pushing for him. He really pushed it.

So we watched the film on Webster once again, just to quiet George. It was film then; that was before you had tape. Webster was dominant against Big Ten competition. That spoke well of him. Then he went to the bowl games and he played against some good guys. He had great leverage. He tucked his tail and he'd get right up into their numbers. He'd strike a rising blow. Noll was always urging our guys to strike a rising blow. He was strong in the legs. Noll thought that was important. My coach at North Catholic High School, Don Graham, used to say the same thing. Well, Webster showed real football intelligence as a college player.

In time, we had him rated higher than where we drafted him.

He impressed on the first day at camp. Noll liked to use the "Oklahoma drill" on the opening day. A back would line up behind a blocker and there'd be a defensive player going one on one against the blocker. The field guys would have two blocking dummies lying on their side, and they were about three yards apart. The players had to run between those blocking bags. It was a small chute. They would clash head on.

I was standing there watching the drill, with Phil Musick, the sportswriter, at my side. We had been talking, and I told Musick how I sat next to this little old grandmother in the stands at a football game at the University of Minnesota, and she told me that I had to get Carl Eller. "See, I said, even little

346

old grandmothers can spot a great football player when they see one. You don't have to be a pro football scout."

So Webster takes his three-point stance across from Jack Lambert. Now Lambert is at a big disadvantage, standing there alone, without a nose guard in front of him to clear the blockers. Webster went at him twice and tore him up both times. Lambert didn't look good in the exchange. Webster just crushed him, and then he did it again. Webby made Lambert look bad.

"And what little old grandmother told you about that guy?" asked Musick, looking at Lambert.

Noll said it was a good hitting drill, and he liked it to assess the strength of his players. Webster was so strong, right from the start.

Little did we know that we were looking at two future Hall of Fame football players. (Others who were looking on that day, including equipment man Tony Parisi and assistant trainer Bob Milie, said they knew right then and there that Webster was going to stick with the Steelers.)

He was just a super human guy. The story of Webby is a real tragedy. He just never handled it well after the final gun went off.

As a player, he had the intangibles. It made him a different guy.

"Dad said you're a pretty good guy."

I was a little afraid to go to Mike Webster's funeral because his son Garrett was saying all that negative stuff in interviews. So my wife Kathleen accompanied me to the funeral home out in Robinson Township. As soon as we pulled into the parking lot, we saw my brother, Dan, and his wife, Pat. I suggested we should hook up with them and go into the funeral home together.

Kathleen told me to hold on. She said, and I have to laugh about this now, not to go in yet. She said, "Let's wait and let them go in first. If they get kicked out we'll know we're not welcome. If they come out head over heels, we'll go home."

So they went in first, and we followed a few minutes later. Garrett wasn't in the funeral home when we arrived. Neither was Mike's wife, Pam. I had met her before. I was going to mention my friend Fred Schaefer to Garrett because I knew they were working together. I guess I was nervous about how he'd accept me.

I went in and I saw Colin, the one that's a Marine. I was in the Marines, and I mentioned that to Colin when I introduced myself. I said, "You're a real Marine, of course, and I was just a reservist. But I did training at Camp LeJeune, where I know you're stationed. And he said to me, "What's your name again?" And I said, "Art Rooney Jr." He smiled and he said, "Oh, yeah, my dad talked about you. Dad liked *you*." So we chatted awhile, and he pointed out his sisters to me.

I went over to the younger girl and offered my condolences, and then I went to the other one. She was wearing a strange hat, down over her eyes. I said, "You're such a beautiful girl. You should let people see you." When she heard my name, she said, "Dad said you're a pretty good guy." Then I pointed to my brother Dan, and identified him. She said, "Oh, I know about *him*."

Then Pam came into the room and I talked to her for awhile. It was a real tragedy. I later sent her 220 copies of the card I'd had made of Mike. That's how many games he played for the Steelers to set a team record in that regard. I gave each of the kids 25 copies of the card. I sent them enough stamps for all of them because I figured they didn't have a lot of money for that stuff. After I sent all of them cards, they all wrote me the nicest letters.

I didn't go to the Hall of Fame when Mike was inducted (in 1997). I should have gone. I know you chastised me for that. That was a matter of phony pride on my part. Our team was in Ireland for a pre-season game in Dublin against the Bears, and no one else from the organization was in Canton for the Hall of Fame festivities except for Ed Kiely. Yeah, I should have been there. Kathleen got on me about that, too.

Mike Webster needed help. I think everybody regarded him as The Man. I told Mrs. Webster that things might have worked out differently if my Dad were still alive. I don't know. I know that Dan and Joe Gordon did so much for them. At a minimum, Mike should have had a life like Jack Butler and Dick Hoak (two other former Steeler ballplayers), and he should have had a life somewhere in pro football.

I wrote Mike some letters, and I tried to boost his spirits. That wasn't enough. The Webster family was nothing but nice to me at the funeral home. I saw Garrett in the parking lot. He was coming in when we were leaving. I talked to him and introduced myself. He was nice to me. I told him I'd like to take him out sometime for a steak dinner. I still owe him a steak dinner.

"Art Rooney is the finest man I've ever known."
— Justice Byron White
Former Steeler on Supreme Court

Mel Blount
Still riding the range

"You have to guide boys and steer them straight."

Ileaned against a corral and watched Mel Blount maneuvering his quarter horse, Yuno's Smart Doll, a paint breed with distinctive white and tan color pattern, cutting back and forth. Blount said the horse had championship bloodlines. I always said the same thing about Mel Blount.

At his direction, Yuno's Smart Doll danced back and forth, following a mechanical cow, an inflated make-believe animal that moves back and forth on a wire. Blount held a rein in his bare left hand and a remote-control like one uses to change channels on the TV in his right hand, and darted back and forth to follow the image in front of him.

He had a good seat in the saddle, his legs were loose and extended from the horse's flanks, to keep out of the way of the horse, as he explained, and darted this way and that, in unison with the mock cow, kicking up the soft dark dirt in the round pen. It was a good show.

He said a bystander would have no idea how difficult this exercise was without being in the saddle. I said I would take his word for it. When he removed his cowboy hat after his matinee performance I could see beads of sweat on his clean-shaved head, shining in the midday sun, so I knew Blount had been working hard.

Melvin Cornell Blount (pronounced Blunt) was showing me how he performs with a cutting horse in competitions across the country, at rodeos and horse shows. He adds to his trophy collections and he's brought home some significant prize money in competitions conducted by the National Cutting Horse Association (NCHA). Someday he might be a Hall of Fame performer in the cutting horse world, in addition to having his bronze bust on display at the Pro Football Hall of Fame in Canton, Ohio.

There were smells I wasn't familiar with, and I had to watch where I walked because even a life-long city boy could see that large animals had crossed these paths prior to my visit. Hey, they don't call this neighborhood Buffalo Township for nothing.

This was on a Monday, April 28, 2003, out behind a horse barn and watering hole on the 263-acre spread that is the Mel Blount Youth Home in Taylorstown, a little town in Washington County. The mailing address is Claysville. It's the next exit on Rte. 70 West after you pass Falconi Field where the Washington Wild Things play their baseball games.

Mel Blount had been matching that make-believe cow stride for stride, this way and that, in the same marvelous manner in which he once covered receivers for the Steelers in the National Football League. Few were better than Mel Blount at staying stride for stride and muscling would-be receivers. He was so dominant at the bump-and-run that the league changed the rules to favor receivers. Blount was one of the mainstays of the Steelers of the '70s, one of the principal reasons they won four Super Bowls over a six-year stretch from the 1974 through the 1979 seasons. He and Joe Greene and Terry Bradshaw were a cut above the rest, just athletic marvels.

I thought about how Blount had played ball before hundreds of thousands of fans in Super Bowls, hundreds of millions more on telecasts of those games. Some of those Super Bowls still have some of the highest audience ratings in TV history. I thought about how fans still smile and marvel whenever they catch sight of him. He is still a head-turner. And here he was performing just for me, just so I'd better appreciate what he was telling me. Athletes don't come any more agreeable than Mel Blount in my book.

"You always did like me," he said with a bright smile. That was a no-brainer. Blount was the best in many ways.

The "Steel Curtain" defense featured Joe Greene, Jack Ham, Jack Lambert and Blount, all in the Pro Football Hall of Fame. The offense featured Terry Bradshaw, Franco Harris, Lynn Swann and John Stallworth, all honored at the sport's shrine in Canton as well. The team's leaders, Art Rooney, Dan Rooney and Chuck Noll, are there, too. Blount believes a few others, like L.C. Greenwood, Donnie Shell and Andy Russell, belong there, too. Like riding a horse in competition, it's a team thing.

"I'm making a reputation for myself in horse-riding competitions just like I did in football," said Blount as we toured his ranch in a Dodge pick-up truck. "Whatever you do, to be successful, you have to put in a lot of time and effort. You have to have dedication. It's like a football team . . . you have to be in synch with your horse. I can't play football anymore, but I can still compete. And I can still make a contribution."

The Mel Blount Youth Home is testimony to his all-consuming spiritual desire to make a difference in the lives of young men who need to be steered in a positive direction. He has room in cabins on the campus to house at least two dozen youngsters, and he wants to raise funds so he can expand the enrollment. The youngsters are sent his way by the Allegheny County Family Court (Juvenile Division). Their stays vary in length, but Blount believes he's helping these kids straighten out their lives, and teaching them values that will serve them well the rest of their days.

They are values he learned growing up on a farm — his family had a 2,600-acre spread — in Vidalia, Georgia. His great-grandfather was a slave. His grandfather, Charlie, bought parcels at 50 cents an

Jim O'Brien

Dan Rooney, Steelers' chairman:
From preface for Mel Blount's book,
The Cross Burns Brightly:

One day, Mel, by then an ex-Steeler, showed up at training camp wearing his warm-up clothes. I noticed him walking down the hill and waved to him. He walked over and stood beside me on the sideline. I looked at him, then at the guys practicing on the field.

"Listen, Mel," I said, "you better get out of here."

"Why?" he asked.

"Because you're making those little kids look like they don't belong here. You're retired, and you look better than all of them."

Mel laughed. He thought I was kidding. I wasn't.

acre. Vidalia is best known for its sweet onions, but it's also known as the hometown of Mel Blount, one of the sweetest cornerbacks in NFL history.

It's no easier operating this ranch than riding cutting horses in competitions or covering NFL receivers, but Blount welcomes the challenge. Some of his neighbors out in Washington County weren't too crazy about him establishing a home for troubled youth in their backyard, so to speak.

There are constant challenges from regulatory groups, ever-changing guidelines, critics, and the financial maintenance of such an ambitious program. Mel Blount is always chasing financial backing and support to keep his dream alive.

In Mel Blount's book, *The Cross Burns Brightly*, subtitled *A Hall of Famer Tackles Racism and Adversity To Help Troubled Boys*, he detailed his experiences on and off the field. It's a worthwhile read.

Blount has no background in social work for his task. He's just a country boy who wants to do good. He wants to save some of these kids from themselves and their often-hostile environments. "You have to guide boys," he says, "steer them straight. You have to lead them in the proper direction, teach them discipline, or they'll be wild their whole lives." He listens to a voice that has always been in his ear, the voice of his father, James Blount, telling him if you work harder you can do even better.

It's not easy, it's never easy, but it's worth the work. Blount still believes that.

"We will make it work."

I spent an entire afternoon with Mel Blount that Monday. He showed me his offices in a large log cabin that resembles a retreat at a ski resort like Seven Springs, his fields, five watering holes, a new utility building financed by the Hillman Foundation, and we went bump, bump in the afternoon across his fields. My notes during that tour are hard to read because it was difficult to keep a steady hand as we kept bouncing. I felt at times that I was on a bronco rather than riding in a Dodge pick-up truck.

His immense pride showed through. He introduced me to Luke and Tuffy, two barnyard dogs, both with Australian shepherd blood-lines, though Tuffy is a mixed breed. Tuffy was the black one that kept rubbing against my right leg, eager to be petted and scratched. There were hay strands sticking in their shaggy coats. I also met five of the eight geldings he keeps on the farm. They showed their heads above the barn door, competing for attention, perhaps hopeful of finding a sugar cube in the palm of my hand.

"You know what a gelding is?" Blount asked me.

"Yes, it's a horse that's been castrated," I replied. "That can't be fun."

"No, but it makes for a better-behaved horse," Blount came back. "These are nice horses."

I saw cows and black angus, five or six buffalo, birds of all kinds. Blount says he lives in God's country. He and his wife TiAnda and their three children share a white brick farmhouse. TiAnda kept coming to Mel during our discussion in his office, asking him what he wanted to do about details for this trip or this excursion. Blount keeps a busy schedule, crossing the country for speaking engagements, to lobby for funds and support for his Boys Home, to visit his 96-year-old mother Alice Blount back on the farm in Georgia. You get the idea.

He was making plans to take the family to an NBA playoff game in New Jersey. George Karl, a Pittsburgh native who coaches the Milwaukee Bucks, asked Blount to speak to his team before a game with the Nets.

"I wasn't brought up that way."

In 1983, his last year in pro football, Blount and his brother Clint opened a licensed youth home 200 feet from his mother's back door. Juvenile agencies began sending neglected and abused kids, many with criminal records, to Mel's farm. It was a last refuge before sentencing.

Then, in 1989, Blount bought another farm, this time in Taylorstown, next to Claysville, about 35 miles southwest of Pittsburgh on the way to Wheeling, West Virginia and Bridgeport, Ohio. My mother, who had died in March at age 96, grew up in Bridgeport and was now buried across the Ohio River in Wheeling. So it was a familiar road. My wife Kathie and I had traveled it many times in recent years to visit our younger daughter Rebecca, when she was attending school at Ohio University in Athens and then, after graduation, working in Columbus, Ohio.

I thought about Mel Blount every time I saw the road signs to Taylorstown while traveling that route. I had visited Blount there 13 years earlier. We had lunch at a local restaurant, and I recall how all eyes in the place turned to Blount when he came through the door. That's not unusual, though. He was 42 then and now he had just turned 55. To me, he looked much the same except he had some gray whiskers on his face. He had just returned from attending a funeral that weekend in Dallas where he was a pallbearer along with Joe Greene for a former teammate and roommate on the Steelers, an outstanding receiver from North Texas State named Ron Shanklin. He had died after a long illness with colon cancer at age 55. Same age as Blount. Mel didn't miss that. It got personal.

> **"I learned a long time ago that you don't get anything accomplished by pounding your fist on the grass."**
> **— Mel Blount**

Back in 1970, the year after they had gotten Joe Greene with their first pick with Chuck Noll as the new coach, the Steelers selected Terry Bradshaw with the first pick in the NFL college draft, Shanklin with their second selection, and Blount in the third round. The Steelers under Noll's direction were building a dynasty and probably didn't know it at the time.

Shanklin's death reminded Mel of his own mortality, as did the earlier deaths of Ray Mansfield, Steve Furness, Dan Turk, Tyrone McGriff and Mike Webster and coaches Rollie Dotsch and Dennis Fitzgerald. Another former Steeler, David Woodley, would die of kidney failure at age 46 a few weeks after my visit. I had seen Blount at Webster's funeral service. He stood out in the crowd, as he always has. He's 6-3, and weighs a little more than his 205 playing weight. "I watch my diet when my pants don't fit right," he said. He always looks even bigger because he wears cowboy boots and a cowboy hat. He looks even better when he's wearing a tuxedo, as we all do.

"So many have died," said Blount, "and so many marriages have broken up." He shook his head at the thought. He was among those who had been divorced from their first wives. He had been married to an airline stewardess, Leslie, and they had a daughter, Tanisia, who was now 33. "If you had told me I'd be divorced someday, I wouldn't believe you," he said. "I would never have thought that was possible. I wasn't brought up that way. Not me. No way. I'm not proud of that. But things happen. I realized I had some problems with my personal life." TiAnda was also divorced from her first husband.

The staff at the Mel Blount Youth Home always knows when Mel Blount is coming their way because you can hear the clink-clink jangling of his spurs. Yes, he wears spurs, too. They make a distinctive sound as he crosses the wooden floors in the main offices, or comes up the wooden steps of the cabins where the boys reside during their stays at the Mel Blount Youth Home. He introduced me to some of the boys, and some of the work staff. The ones I met and spoke to briefly came from The Hill District, Polish Hill and Penn Hills. Everybody is busy at the Mel Blount Youth Home.

TiAnda has done a great job of decorating his office with plaques and photos from his glory days with the Steelers. He has an impressive collection of tributes. He didn't frame or post any of the hate mail he received regarding his boys home. Mel Blount knew from the beginning that it wouldn't be easy to establish his youth home in Taylorstown, but even he didn't anticipate the resistance he would meet. It's diminished through the years, but it rears its ugly head, much like a horse that has a mind of its own, every so often.

At first, ugly warnings appeared in mailboxes throughout the area. A so-called "concerned citizens" group lobbied local parents to protest having a boys home anywhere in their neighborhood. The racist flyers kept coming. Harsh words were scratched into one of his

> *"If farmers possess humility, endurance and perspective, it is because they must if they are to survive their wars."*
> — **Victor Davis Hanson, author**
> *The Land Was Everything*

Jim O'Brien

TiAnda and Mel Blount are an attractive couple that appear at many of Pittsburgh's fund-raising events. Mel is seen below competing in horse cutting competion where he's an award-winning performer.

From the Mel Blount collection

fences. It wasn't exactly a welcome-to-Taylorstown greeting. Blount had pointed it out to me on my previous visit.

A township supervisor had said, "It's very possible this could be a great program, but it's also very possible that it could be a great harm to the community."

On August 4, 1989, the day before Mel Blount joined Terry Bradshaw to be inducted into the Pro Football Hall of Fame, two youths steered their automobile up the driveway of the Blount home and fired shots from a .44 Magnum. That was scary stuff. The next day, in his Hall of Fame acceptance speech, Blount spoke about his desire to provide a home for wayward youth, to give kids a "second chance." He revealed the racial problems he was facing, the resistance to his plans, but he steeled his spine and announced proudly, "The Mel Blount Youth Home is going up. We will make it work."

A month afterward, hundreds of "concerned citizens" filled a high school auditorium for a hearing to debate the pros and cons of okaying an operating permit. Blount sat quietly as he heard ranting and raving about why it wasn't such a good idea. Then a minister rose to his feet and declared his support for Blount's project. Then a local businessman boosted the idea, and then a local homemaker got up and offered her support. The tide turned. Within a few weeks, the local supervisors granted the go-ahead permit.

Through the years there have been other challenges, ups and downs, difficult days, but Blount has managed to make his way through the storms, like the long-rider he appears to be when he shows up in his cowboy attire, chaps and all. He still reminds me of Lou Gossett Jr., an actor I admire and enjoy, every time I see him.

Blount remains one of my favorites. He offers a warm hug and a pat on the back whenever I see him. He always offers his time, his talents and his thoughts. His heartfelt reflections are always worthwhile, worth writing in books. There's real substance to Mel Blount. "You've done us a great service to chronicle our achievements," he has said. "We don't want the fans to forget us."

More importantly, Blount has the ability to count his blessings, and put things in their proper perspective:

"Football challenges the total individual — spiritually, physically, mentally, morally, and emotionally. The game exemplifies life. It's a true test of manhood. I think that's one reason the proudest moment of my life, as far as accomplishment, was when I heard the news that I had been selected for the Pro Football Hall of Fame. That was great news. I remember all the people I played with and met while I was in the league. I love the game."

Cynthia Sterling, co-author
Of Mel Blount's book, *The Cross Burns Brightly:*

"Mel Blount is God's rainbow, giving a home to discarded children, and starting them on an adventure that will forever change their lives. Mel is a football star turned hero."

"They call me Supe —
that's short for Superman."

I remember the first time we met, back in July of 1970 at the Steelers' training camp at St. Vincent College in Latrobe. There was a scrimmage that first day. Blount missed a tackle when Jack Deloplaine ran an end sweep to his side. I had a head-on view of Blount bouncing off the turf as Deloplaine deftly moved past him, running behind a block by guard Steve Courson.

Other defensive backs came up behind Blount, forcing Deloplaine to hunt and seek an opening and this delayed his charge. Suddenly, Deloplaine was leveled hard by a tackle from behind. It was Blount who made the hard tackle. Blount had gotten off the ground and given chase, the old second-effort.

Afterward, I asked Blount about what he had done. Here was a man assured of a spot on the Steelers' roster, a star in three Super Bowl victories, a Pro Bowl performer three times already, and yet he was still out to prove himself on the first play of the first day of practice. I asked him why he did it.

"I learned a long time ago," said Blount, "that you don't get anything accomplished pounding your fist on the grass."

Right there, I knew Mel Blount was going to be a good source on the Steelers, someone I'd want to stay close to, someone who had something to say. And his play backed up his bold talk.

"They call me Supe," he'd tell newcomers. "That's short for Superman." Then he'd smile broadly.

Later that night, I was walking through the dark halls of Bonaventure Hall, a student dormitory where the Steelers and sportswriters covering the team used to stay at St. Vincent. (Now the Steelers are housed in a newer dorm named in honor of Art Rooney across the way. It's off limits to the sportswriters who remain housed at Bonaventure Hall. It's not as easy to get to know and interview the players, coaches or scouts these days.) I saw two formidable figures coming through a door into the stairway and I couldn't make them out at first. As they got closer, I could see that it was Mel Blount and his buddy Joe Greene.

They both smiled and said hello. They were two of the greatest players who ever played for a Pittsburgh sports team. Thank goodness they were good guys, too, quick to smile and say hello.

Nothing's changed in that regard. Kathie and I were happy to be invited to the Fifth Annual Mel Blount Celebrity Roast at the Downtown Hilton on Friday, May 30, 2003. Joe Greene was honored at this dinner. It was good to see them back together again when they weren't attending a teammate's funeral. Chuck Noll was there, too, and he couldn't have been prouder.

"I knew I couldn't play football forever," recalled Blount. "I wanted to do something worthwhile with the rest of my life."

He recalled sitting in the locker room after a particularly tough contest late in his pro career, and feeling weary from his afternoon's efforts. He recalled something Noll said in a locker room address to the team. "Football isn't everything," Noll declared. "What will be your life's work?"

Blount said that question stayed with him. He said that a trip back home to the farm, where young fans often visited him, gave him his inspiration. He wanted to do something to help young people.

He thought about his humble beginnings, the hard times growing up on a dirt farm. He went barefoot at times, and the family home was without plumbing and electricity in his earliest days. The Blounts got by, though. "You may resent the way I push you," James Blount would tell his 11 children, "but hard work is the only way not to be poor all your lives."

All the Blount kids had chores, as soon as they were big enough to walk. Mel was the youngest of seven boys and 11 children. He remembers his first job was stacking tobacco leaves. He remembers wanting to stack the most, and setting goals for himself. The tobacco leaves were stacked on a wagon in the golden light of a kerosene lantern. He did that every morning, real early, long before school started. His reward was a few words of praise from his father. "Fine job, Son. Fine job." That was enough. Mel remembers how the family would kneel on the living room floor on Sundays, before everyone went to church, and how his father led the family in prayer. "He'd remind us that good will always prevail in the face of evil, and that God helps those who help themselves," recalled Blount. Even as a young boy, he knew that hard work, pride and responsibility were values to live by. He was lucky, he says, to have that kind of start.

He made a name for himself at the local high school as being quite the athlete, a tall, skinny kid who could play. He landed a scholarship to play football and go to school at Southern University in Baton Rouge, Louisiana. He went there and had a great college career.

He was drafted by the Steelers, then the sorriest team in the NFL. Their record was 1-13 the year before they came up with the trifecta of Bradshaw-Shanklin-Blount in the college draft. He thought he'd get a chance to play in Pittsburgh, that the team needed help, and he stayed for 14 seasons and helped make Pittsburgh the City of Champions. He was named the NFL's Most Valuable Defensive Player and the Steelers' MVP in 1975 when he set a team record with 11 interceptions. He was the first Steeler to lead the league in interceptions since "Bullet Bill" Dudley did it in 1946. Blount had interceptions in Super Bowl games in critical situations that saved the day. He had 57 interceptions in the regular season games in his career, surpassing Jack Butler (52) as the team's all-time leader. He was one of the team's all-time best kickoff-return men.

> *"If you can learn this simple trick, Scout, you'll get along better with all kinds of folks. You never really understand a person until you consider things from his point of view — until you climb into his skin and walk around in it."*
> **— Atticus Finch in Harper Lee's**
> *To Kill A Mockingbird*

Mel Blount loves his farm in Claysville where he practices horse-cutting maneuvers in the corral.

Photos by Jim O'Brien

The city could claim him and Roberto Clemente and Willie Stargell and then Mario Lemieux and all those great Steelers, and none stood taller or prouder than Mel Blount. Only Mike Webster played more seasons with the Steelers than Blount, and only by one year.

Others who played 14 seasons included Bradshaw, Ernie Stautner, Larry Brown, Donnie Shell and John Stallworth. You can't keep better company than that. Blount knew that was a secret to his success as well. It was something he could suggest to the kids he keeps on his farm.

I remember my mother telling me so many times that you'll always be judged by the company you keep. I'm sure that Mel's mother, who was the same age, told him the same thing.

"You're hoping you have more life."

Mel Blount:

I have a lot of memories of the men I played with during my 14 seasons with the Steelers. I miss them, and it hurts when one of them passes. I was very close to Ron Shanklin, for instance. Ron had this big smile; I can see him smiling right now.

I met Ron at the College All-Star Game practices at Northwestern College in Evanston, Illinois. We were there to get ready for the All-Star Game in Chicago. We were playing the Kansas City Chiefs, who had won the Super Bowl the year before. They had beaten the Minnesota Vikings at Tulane Stadium in New Orleans.

Otto Graham was our coach. Ron and I roomed together at the All-Star Game, and at our first summer training camp with the Steelers, and during his four seasons with the Steelers. We were roommates all four years. He and I shared an apartment in Pittsburgh in the beginning. He was like a brother. So I am saddened more than you can appreciate by his passing. I was caught off guard by his death. I knew he was sick (he was challenged for 2½ years by colon cancer, according to his wife), but I didn't realize it was so serious.

I didn't know Mike Webster as well, or Steve Furness, but we were a special team and we accomplished so many wonderful things, and we were together for quite a long run, so it hurt to see them die as well. They were all too young. Your teammates will always have a special place in your life and in your heart. They are always with you. None of us knows when our time is up. It's hard to get someone to understand what we had. We grew up together and became men together. Like Mike Webster and Steve Furness. Your mind starts rewinding and you go back to when you were all young and strong. We had a bond. That period meant something to all of us.

I saw Merril Hoge on TV during the college draft weekend, and he was bald because of chemotherapy treatments he has received for cancer. Merril Hoge? You just never know. My prayers are with him that he can beat this.

I'm sorry to hear about your mother dying. My mother is also 96. I've got to get down and see her. I saw her last month, but I'm hoping to get down to see her this Thursday.

Ron was so young. Just 55. Now I'm 55. I feel so young. You're hoping you have more life. I have always been an ambitious person. I never had a fear of not being able to achieve what I wanted to do, on and off the field. I have plans and aspirations I hope to realize in the future. A lot of it has to do with your mindset. Staying active is important. There is power to positive thinking.

I never let being black hold me back. There is a feeling, especially in black society, that there are barriers out there. So many people think there's only so much you can do. To me, I think it's a plus.

Look what is going on out here, and the history of this program at my boys home. Look at all I went through to get this place up and running, and to maintain our programs. The scrutiny and adversity . . . That's what it's all about. That's when you find out what you're really made of. I welcome those challenges. I always have.

Some of my friends say, "Why are you doing this? You could be on the speakers' circuit, making easy money. You could be out playing in all those celebrity golf tournaments, having a good time."

I see no satisfaction in that alone. I would rather try to get other people on board with what I'm trying to do to help these kids. I get satisfaction from that.

It's amazing what our society sees as being successful. We define success so often by how much money someone makes, or how famous they are. I know a lot of people who are supposed to be successful, but they're not too happy. They're drinking, or on drugs. Their lives are messed up. I'd rather be poor and rich internally.

"I believe the real challenge in writing history is to resist the tendency so prevalent today — to label, stereotype, expose, denigrate — and instead to bring empathy and understanding to our subject so the past can really come alive in all its beauty, sorrow and glory."
— Doris Kearns Goodwin, author
Pulitzer Prize winner

"It is the conquering of fear that makes one great."
— Mel Blount

The Mike Webster story is a sad one. I've been to a lot of funerals over the years, but this one got to me more than most. I felt badly in a lot of ways. This wasn't just another funeral of a friend. This was more. I was feeling sorry on several levels. I was angry. There were a lot of questions I have that aren't answered. I don't know what happened to Mike.

We held him in such high standards until he started to get in trouble regarding drugs and the problems that followed. I didn't think it was going to get to the point where it was the death of him. That's why it bothers me. Mental toughness is all part of being a champion.

You have to keep things in proper perspective. Nothing is too bad that you start taking substances that steal your health, and years from your life. I heard he got addicted to pain-killing medication. And he obviously was having some mental problems. I'm told he suffered brain damage; that might explain everything.

You have to be smart enough to go to people and say, "I need help." You have to have inner peace. Mike always seemed to have a strong spiritual side. You have to know who you are and whose you are. We are all children of God. If you're a committed Christian you can understand that. If you're connected that should give you strength to survive the challenges. He professed Christ as his savior, I know that.

Nobody has come out with everything. He stayed 17 years in the league, and maybe that was too many years. He should have had money. He was making good money the last few years. I don't know what happened to his money. Sometimes you think you know people and you really don't know them at all.

I don't know why he ended up with the people he did. There were so many support systems out there, starting with your family. I knew we talked about Mike at a few get-togethers, and we said, "Let's reach out to help Mike." We'd hear things, and we wanted to find out how we could help. But he didn't want anybody's help.

His funeral was a little strange. I couldn't see why Lynn Swann was asked to speak about him. He and Lynn weren't that close. I thought some of the offensive linemen, especially the guys who tried to help him in recent years like Tunch Ilkin and Craig Wolfley, would have been better choices. They're used to getting up in front of people and speaking, too. They don't have the national name that Lynn has, but they were more closely involved with Mike, and they might've provided some insights we were all curious about.

Everybody liked Mike and everybody had the highest regard and respect for Mike. I always admired Mike. He was a good guy, a likable guy. You'd think he'd have been the last guy on the team to pass. He appeared to be the kind of guy who'd transition into coaching. He'd have made a great football coach.

Players on other teams respected Mike. I remember seeing Harry Carson of the Giants at Mike's funeral. I told him, "I always admired you as a player, and this lifts my respect for you even more."

I don't know what happened to Mike. It's disturbing. It's critical whom you surround yourself with. I think I have a good support system. It would be hard to find a person who's having more fun that I am. I created this. This is mine. I knew when I was playing for the Steelers that it was only temporary. I'm a country boy. I love working with these horses and working with these kids. I'm showing these city kids a whole new way of life. You don't have to be gang-banging to feel good about yourself. You can't be hurting people and yourself. You have to have respect for yourself, your family, your friends and your church and community.

I see all this land out here, and I see room for growth. We can give guidance to even more kids. My dream is to one day have more buildings out here so we can house more kids.

There's a school at the bottom of the hill — Blaine-Buffalo Elementary School — that's been abandoned and I'd like to see us get hold of that, and put it to good use. You see the animals out here. They love the kids and the kids love them. It's good therapy. We have an old school bus out here. I want to paint it black and gold — Steeler colors — so we can make more trips with the kids.

The whole place appeals to me. Every time I come back here I feel comfortable with my surroundings. I get a good feeling when I'm out here. It's nice to get out and enjoy some of God's creations. We raise beef right here on the farm to feed these kids. We stock some of these lakes so the kids can fish. You can see the ducks out there.

"You need to have meaning in your life, a sense of purpose, and other mountains to climb."
— Andy Russell

"I thought it was long overdue."

I'm glad to see Terry Bradshaw back in Pittsburgh, and making peace with Chuck Noll, the Rooneys and the fans here. I thought it was long overdue.

I thought it was a crazy situation. The fans here have always loved Terry Bradshaw. Yeah, they booed him, but there were games they booed me, too. That's just fans being fans. When I got beat for a touchdown I might have heard booing, too. That goes with the territory.

As far as his trouble with Chuck Noll, that's another story. Nobody ever knew or would have thought there was friction between Chuck and Terry. Hey, Terry got more special attention than anybody on the team. And it still wasn't enough. He was the most loved athlete on the team. Terry took a lot of stuff personally early in his career. He was a real talent. This guy was something. I don't know what kept him and Chuck from having a better relationship. Knowing Chuck, he probably didn't think there was a problem.

I liked that story of Terry's return, and I liked the Tommy Maddox story. I think it was an intriguing and fascinating story that could be made into a movie.

The guy was just out there, selling insurance. I don't know how the Steelers found him. It's all a made-for-TV movie. He came into that Cleveland game when we were getting beaten badly by the Browns and rallied the team and wins in overtime.

He moves in to replace a quarterback who just happens to be black. He leads the team downfield and wins the game. Then, a few games later, he gets hurt and he could have been paralyzed for life.

The thing I like about Tommy Maddox is that he is humble. I think he handled his situation well when he was behind Kordell Stewart and when he was playing ahead of him. A lot of that has to do with leadership and the coaching staff. They didn't let it get out of hand.

It's a credit to Kordell and Tommy, too. Some of the call-ins on the sports talk shows wanted to create controversy and trouble between the two. It shouldn't be that way. I didn't like some of the things Kordell did earlier in his stay with the Steelers. You don't tell people you're going to be in the Hall of Fame someday. You play your way into that. You don't talk your way in.

Kordell could strike more fear into a defense because they never knew whether he was going to pass or run the ball. Tommy isn't that kind of threat. But he's more of a pure passer and he's a rhythm thrower. I didn't think Kordell ever accepted the role of the quarterback on and off the field. If you make commitments and you're supposed to be somewhere you'd better show up. Kordell missed a lot of engagements and left people high and dry. I don't think he really sold the rest of the team that he was the leader who could take them all the way.

The quarterback has to be like a politician. You have to keep selling people on why they should like you and it's the way you carry yourself in the community.

Maddox realized what that's all about, and what kind of message that sends. That's leadership. You say, "This is my fault." These guys wouldn't have been around him with a long face. Kordell has to learn that. It will be tougher for him in Chicago. The media will be greater in size and far more critical. The Pittsburgh press has always been more patient, as I see it. That may have changed in recent years, though, since I stopped playing.

I don't think teams had a lot of film, or tape, on Tommy Maddox last year. You could see late in the season that they were better prepared to defend against what he does best. He's a timing quarterback. He can't improvise that well. If he has a problem it's his lack of mobility. Defenses will better understand what they have to do against him. I look for them to rush him up the middle, and force him out of the pocket. They'll be trying to disrupt his rhythm. I hope he can stay healthy. I'd have concern there.

I'll be rooting for him. I'm still a Steeler and I'll always be rooting for him. Hey, I was rooting for Kordell Stewart, so I want to see him succeed as well. If he continues to mature he'll be fine, too. He's one of those guys who saw our four Super Bowl trophies when he first entered the Steelers' offices. By now, he should see how difficult it was to win them, and what we had to do as a team to claim them. I'm proud of that.

"I'll never forget the first time I saw Mel Blount. I was at my dressing stall in the locker room, and I saw the guy in the doorway talking to someone. I asked the guy next to me, 'Who's that guy?' He said, 'That's Mel Blount.' And I said, 'That's can't be Mel Blount. He's too big to have been a defensive back.' He looked like he could still play."
— Carnell Lake, Former defensive back
Pittsburgh Steelers, Jacksonville Jaguars

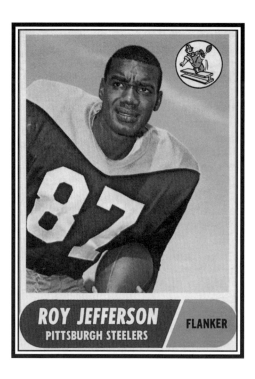

ROY JEFFERSON
PITTSBURGH STEELERS
FLANKER

JON KOLB
STEELERS

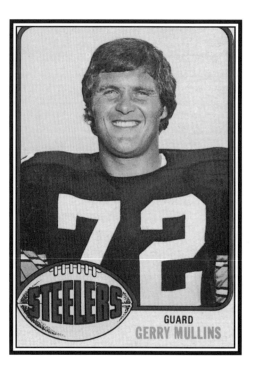

STEELERS
GUARD
GERRY MULLINS

MYRON POTTIOS
PITTSBURGH STEELERS LINEBACKER

Roy Jefferson
Still loves Pittsburgh

"He was our best player my first year."
— Joe Greene

R oy Jefferson is still No. 1 in one of the listings in the Steelers' record book. As a wide receiver, he caught the most touchdown passes in a single game — four against the Atlanta Falcons on November 3, 1968. He caught 11 passes altogether that day, still among the top five for the Steelers in that category, for 199 yards, the fourth best effort.

So Roy Jefferson won't just go away.

He played five seasons (1965-1969) with the Steelers and caught 199 passes. That's only three fewer than Benny Cunningham caught in ten seasons with the Steelers. Jefferson caught passes for 1,079 yards in a 14-game schedule in 1969, and 1,074 yards over a similar stretch in 1968. Those are still in the Steelers' Top Ten in that listing, and everybody ahead of him with the exception of Buddy Dial in 1963 did it in a 16-game schedule. It's still a big deal when someone surpasses 1,000 in receiving yards these days with a 16-game schedule. Jefferson was the Steelers' leading receiver with 58 and 67 catches in 1968 and 1969.

Jefferson, still handsome at age 59, hails from Los Angeles and was a second-round draft selection of the Steelers in 1965 out of the University of Utah. He was born in Texarkana, Texas, but considers himself a Californian. That's where he grew up. He was 6-2, 195 pounds, a good-sized receiver in those days.

He represented the Steelers in the Pro Bowl and was the team's MVP in 1969 and a year later was representing the Baltimore Colts in the Pro Bowl. Chuck Noll traded Jefferson to the Colts, his former team, before the 1970 season.

Jefferson was constantly challenging Chuck Noll's authority, he admits as much today, and Noll was not happy about that. Noll wanted to build his own kind of ballclub and regarded Jefferson as a threat to the sort of attitude and environment he wanted to create. Steelers insiders say that Jefferson had an attitude problem, and was trying to mold the young players in his own image.

Jefferson was a member of the Colts when they won the Super Bowl after that 1970 season — thanks to a game-winning field goal by a guy named Jim O'Brien — and was traded to the Washington Redskins after one season when he had a falling out with Colts' owner Carroll Rosenbloom. So Jefferson wasn't any day at the beach in Baltimore, either. He went to the Redskins and represented them in the Pro Bowl.

He remained with the Redskins for six seasons. He is credited with 12 seasons in the National Football League.

So he could play. "He was our best player my first year, and a good friend, so I was upset when he was traded," recalled Joe Greene. "But, looking back on it now, I guess Chuck knew what he was doing. You can't criticize what he accomplished here."

Joe Greene and Roy Jefferson, as well as John Stallworth, were three former Steelers I was surprised to find when I attended the 27th Annual Andy Russell Celebrity Classic on May 15-16, 2003, at The Club at Nevillewood in Presto, Pennsylvania. That's about five miles from my home in the South Hills of Pittsburgh. Russell usually has an all-pro cast for his outing, but none of these three had been there the previous year.

I was just out of college when I first met Roy Jefferson. He hadn't forgotten. "Jim, you're old, but I can still see your face," he said when he saw me. When I told him about that line over the telephone a few days later, Jefferson joked, "It was just that gray hair that was different. But I could still see your face from back then."

Jefferson's hair was as black as ever, but I don't believe that he and Frenchy Fuqua have found the Fountain of Youth. Just some good hair dye. It works for them.

I checked through the archives to see whom the Steelers got in exchange for Jefferson. He was traded to the Colts in exchange for receiver Willie Richardson and a fourth-round draft pick in 1971. Richardson refused to report to the Steelers, so he was sent to the Miami Dolphins for a fifth-round draft pick in 1971.

The Steelers had a terrific draft in 1971, maybe second only to their 1974 draft, and with the Colts' pick the Steelers selected defensive end Dwight White from East Texas State and with the Dolphins' pick they selected defensive back Ralph Anderson from West Texas State. White was a stalwart for four Super Bowl championship teams, and Anderson played two seasons as a reserve for the Steelers. They were members of the "Steel Curtain" defense. In the end, Noll got good value for Jefferson.

Jefferson was introduced at the Russell Classic as "the best player Chuck Noll ever traded away," but Jefferson was doing his best to dispel any ideas that he was any kind of bad boy when he was with the Black & Gold. "I'm not so bad," he said with a winning smile. Anyone who met Jefferson at this outing would have been surprised to learn that he had been regarded as a clubhouse problem.

He was wearing an all-black outfit, however, like the bad guys in the old cowboy movies. He looked in good shape, and confessed that he had been working out for the previous four months. He was working as a mortgage consultant for Carteret Mortgage Corporation in Centreville, Virginia, a job he had taken earlier in the year.

He was proud to say he had been married for 40 years to Camille or "Candie" Jefferson, and they had three children: Marshall, 38, a high school football coach and house painter; Michelle, 36, with Chase

Roy Jefferson was all smiles when he saw so many old friends at Andy Russell's Golf Classic for Children at The Club at Nevillewood. Above, he is flanked by former St. Louis Cardinals' stars John David Crow, left, and Charley Johnson. Below, he joins Joe Greene, whom he mentored in Greene's rookie season of 1969. Crow was a real favorite of Paul "Bear" Bryant during their days at Texas A&M.

Photos by Jim O'Brien

Manhattan Mortgage; and Damion, 25, whom he said had just moved to Hawaii and hoped to get reestablished in the mortgage business as well.

The Steelers weren't that good when Jefferson played for them, but their fans and the media were much less critical of them back then than they are today when the team turns out winning records nearly every year and is usually in the playoffs.

Today's media would have loved Roy Jefferson. He always had something to say, and he didn't mince words. He was like Donn Clendenon of the Pirates in that respect. Both were considered clubhouse lawyers. Ironically, Clendenon became an attorney after his playing days. Roy Jefferson was Lee Flowers before there was a Lee Flowers.

"They tried to make a bad guy out of Roy Jefferson."

Roy Jefferson:

They got everything from me when I went on that field. No one can say Roy Jefferson didn't give the Steelers his best effort every time out. The old-school coaches liked to demean you. They'd talk down to you, something my upbringing wouldn't allow. I had to say something. They didn't appreciate that.

I had no use for Bill Austin, the coach when I first came here. Chuck Noll was not as bad as Bill Austin. I had no use or respect for Bill Austin whatsoever. He was a real jerk. He tried to be like Vince Lombardi and everybody saw right through that. I didn't have the same feeling about Noll that I had for Austin. Chuck Noll was being Chuck Noll.

I didn't dislike Chuck Noll. I just always reacted to him if I thought he was getting on me too much. They tried to make a bad guy out of Roy Jefferson, but he was not such a bad guy. I wanted to have some fun. I didn't like dictatorial coaches.

Chuck Noll certainly proved that he was a good football coach. You can't argue about that. We had a situation where we were often at odds, so he solved it by sending me to Baltimore. That wasn't so bad because I got a Super Bowl ring that year in Baltimore with Don McCafferty. Neither McCafferty nor George Allen in Washington was like those old-school coaches. I liked the way they treated me better.

I saw Chuck Noll at Bobby Mitchell's golf outing at the Landsdown Resort in Leesburg, Virginia a few years back. I came up from behind him and patted him on the back. I shook his hand and flashed a big smile, and I made a big fuss about him, telling him how great it was that he was in the Hall of Fame, and how successful he'd been, et cetera. He must have said to himself, "Who the hell is this man in front of me? This isn't the Roy Jefferson I know!" I'm sure I confused him, but I really was glad to see him again. Hey, time heals all wounds. I respect the man and what he's done. I bear no grudges toward him.

It's great being here with so many old friends at this golf outing. I left Pittsburgh in a rush when I was traded to Baltimore and I never really got a chance to tell my story. I never really talked to anybody about it.

Andy Russell seemed so genuinely happy for me to be back there. I was with the Steelers when Andy Russell returned from two years in the military service to rejoin the team. We were teammates for four years. I have so much respect for him; that's why it meant a great deal to be invited to participate in his tournament.

I was a very good friend of Joe Greene when I was with the Steelers. I felt like I was one of his mentors, and showed him some things that I think helped him. There was a period, however, when I was working with the NFL Players Association and the Steelers were one of 14 football teams I was responsible for. I came here for a meeting with the Steelers and it was quite a chaotic meeting. I said some things. I thought maybe I had harmed our relationship somehow. I wasn't sure about that.

That was just not the case when I saw Joe this time. You can't imagine how warm and genuine he greeted me. We were sitting around talking and he told the guys, "This was a guy who took care of everybody. Anything you wanted, you went to Roy Jefferson. You needed a place to eat, a place to hang out, you went to Roy's home. You could talk things out with Roy."

I lived in Point Breeze, on the edge of Homewood, back then. I knew everybody within two blocks of my home. For him to say those things, considering his stature in Steelers' history, meant so much to me. He was so open. It was eerie.

It was good to see J.R. Wilburn, too. He led the Steelers in receiving the year before I did it for the first time. I've seen him more recently, though, because I played in his golf event in Richmond. He lost a son three years ago, and he has a golf tournament in his memory. I've been to all of them. He just wanted to do it for three years, so this was the last one.

It was good to see Myron Pottios, too. He was my teammate in Pittsburgh and in Washington. Athletically, he was no Jack Lambert, but he did more than his share of hell raising off the field. He was a handful. I think the Rooneys wanted to get rid of him. I can only imagine what he must have been like in a bar.

Brady Keys was a guy I credit for my success with the Steelers. I credit him for getting me ready before I reported for my first camp. He lived in Los Angeles, and he worked out with me, and told me how to recognize defensive setups and what I needed to do in response to them. Brady was a sharp dude. He knew his stuff.

I remember Ben McGee, Chuck Hinton, Lloyd Voss, Paul Martha, Andy Russell, Joe Greene, Bill Nelsen, Ed Brown, Fran O'Brien, Gary Ballman, Marv Woodson, John Henry Johnson — he was my man; we used to go bowling together — and Big John Baker. They were all great guys. Baker just lost an election after being the sheriff in Raleigh for 24 years. I ran into some people who go to church with him, and they told me about that.

I have good memories about Pittsburgh. The people in Pittsburgh were truly concerned about me. I have yet to have the same kind of relationship with a community as I enjoyed in Pittsburgh. They have the greatest fans with the Redskins in Washington, but I didn't have the kind of personal relationships I had in Pittsburgh.

I did so much more in the community here in Virginia, but that's because of maturity.

We didn't have a lot of success as a team when I was in Pittsburgh, but I didn't realize that at the time. It wasn't as debilitating as it should have been. We had some of the best people. We needed an offensive line and, offensively, we were short-changed. We had defensive people. We beat up people, but we'd often come up short on the scoreboard.

My relationship with Noll was strained. He wasn't sensitive to the players' emotions. He was like the captain of a ship. He'd say something and they'd jump. I didn't jump. But I did what I was supposed to do.

It just burned me up sometimes. I was an intelligent guy. I knew the offense. I knew it cold. When I made a mistake I was the first one to know it. I'd come back and they'd harp on it. I'd say, "OK, you made your point!" And they'd keep it up.

Other than stuff like that, I totally enjoyed the people in Pittsburgh. I enjoyed my five years there. I had some strained relationships with Chuck Noll and Dan Rooney, but the Old Man, Mr. Rooney, was great to me. I was a great friend of Art Rooney.

For years after I was gone, he sent Christmas cards to me and Candy, and birthday cards to my kids. He was great. I really have positive things in my mind about the city of Pittsburgh.

"Most of us run pretty well all day long on one compliment."
— Mark Twain

Ernie "Fats" Holmes
Fatter and sassier than ever

"He seems to be on the right road."
— Joe Greene

Ernie "Fats" Holmes is one of the most storied Steelers in team history. They have been telling stories about his shenanigans and strange behavior for a long time. He was one of the most effective and fiercest of the "Steel Curtain" foursome that included Joe Greene, L.C. Greenwood and Dwight White. They were on the cover of *Time* magazine when the Steelers were winning Super Bowls in the '70s and were voted the NFL's "Team of the Decade."

For two or three seasons, Holmes might have been the best of the bunch. Chuck Noll thought Holmes lost his focus and got into too many diversions outside the game. He had substance-abuse problems. He went haywire after his wife left him. He even fired a shotgun at a police helicopter that hovered over him alongside a highway in Ohio. One of the bullets struck a police officer in the knee.

Dan Rooney and Chuck Noll went to bat for him as character witnesses and managed to get him off without having to do any jail time. Imagine what would happen if someone did that in these post 9/11 terrorist-scare times. It's still unbelievable that the Steelers could have gotten Holmes out of that jam.

Shows you how powerful and popular the Steelers were then, and what persuasive oratory gifts Rooney and Noll possessed.

Once, when he was upset with a teammate at practice, he threatened to bring his "piece" to practice and settle things the next day. Ernie may have been the only Steeler who scared Jack Lambert.

Holmes had his head shaved once with an arrowhead on the top. He said it pointed him in the right direction.

"Fats" Holmes is fatter than ever. He has to weigh over 400 pounds. He must require two seats on an airplane, or he flies with the luggage. He came to Pittsburgh in late May of 2003 to appear at the Mel Blount Youth Home Celebrity Roast that honored Joe Greene, and he stayed over at the Pittsburgh Hilton for a week to visit with old Steelers friends. He moved about with the aid of a walking cane.

He also appeared at a sports card and memorabilia show at the Expo Mart in Monroeville on Sunday, June 1, joining Joe Greene, Rocky Bleier, Jack Lambert and Cliff Stoudt on the dais. When Holmes smiles, and he does so often, his eyes are mere slits. There's an Oriental look about him. He's the one who bangs the gong.

He enjoyed holing up in Room 917 at the Hilton for a week when someone else was picking up the tab. I had visited with him in that same hotel about ten years earlier. I remember his mother telling me she used to cook steak and eggs for breakfast every morning for her Ernie. Imagine what that did for his system. He was trying to get his act together back then and, it appears, he is still searching for the answers a decade later.

"He seems to be on the right road," said Greene, perhaps a tad optimistic because he genuinely cares about his former linemate and soulmate. "You hope things will go well for him."

"I felt betrayed."

Ernie Holmes:

I talked to Mel Blount about coming out and seeing his ranch. I know Joe is going out there to see him. I'd like to see Mr. Rooney while I'm here, maybe Joe Gordon and some of the guys. I'm trying to re-learn my way around Pittsburgh. I fell in love with this place when I was here, and it's changed a lot. There are a lot of buildings down here, a lot more things. It's amazing what they've done with the riverfronts, and with the new stadium and ballpark. It's impressive. I've got quite a view from my room.

It reminds me more of Houston, where I spent a lot of time in my youth. I'm living on a ranch in southwest Texas now. I have a home by two lakes. It's a nice place to relax. I've got some livestock, but not much. I've got multiple places around the country, but I still call Texas home.

I agree with Walt Garrison who played for the Dallas Cowboys. He said you need cattle for a tax write-off when you're working and making money. When you're retired, you don't need tax write-offs. You need money; you need an income. I heard that Mike Webster had money problems. He grew up on a farm, just like I did. He was a good man. It was sad to hear what happened to him.

I remember when Mike Webster first came to the Steelers. He was muscular, but he got even more muscular while he was with us. Joe and I used to beat up on him pretty good at practice. But that didn't last too long. You could see his intensity. He wanted to get even with us. Working out with him and Jon Kolb and Gordon Gravelle and guys like that kept us honest. They got us ready for Sunday.

Chuck Noll was one of the first coaches to work military-like conditioning into our program. He'd have us run, and then check out oxygen intake, our pulse rate, our heart beat.

374

George Gojkovich

rnie Holmes takes a breather.

Bill Amatucci

Ernie Holmes and Joe Greene at St. Vincent College

Ernie Holmes

Ernie Holmes signs
photos at autograph
show in Monroeville.

Photos by Jim O'Brien

They checked us out the same way they checked out astronauts.

One of the guys I admired was Rocky Bleier. Seeing him working so hard to get in shape so he could play football again was inspirational for everyone.

We ran before and after practice. That Noll nearly killed us.

I worked very hard. For three years, I thought I was the best defensive lineman.

There was a lot I had to overcome. I had to get over a lot of setbacks in the beginning. Chuck and I never had a bad relationship, but I didn't think I got much credit. I thought I should have been in Pro Bowls. I could have been bitter about some of the things that happened. It affected me in a most serious manner. I never felt like I was asked what I thought about anything. When we talked about strategy, I never had a say in things. That was part of my inner struggle.

I never received any credit. I was trying to regain my balance on and off the field. I went to a psychiatrist. I got some religious help. I was looking for the community to embrace me. It was too much to take to be on the outside looking in.

The community never took me seriously. The team forgot what I'd done. I felt betrayed. I don't want to get too much into this. I'd like to do a book about it someday.

I never was really a bad person. Somehow I just lost my way here.

I never felt I was too big of a drinker, but I guess I had a problem.

I took on some of the older guys when I got here. I didn't like their attitude. I didn't like being a part of a loser. I'd be going to meetings, and the older guys were laughing about getting beat. I complained about that to Lionel Taylor, one of our coaches.

I wasn't ready when I first got here. I'd been in a small college program at Texas Southern and I didn't know as much as the guys from the big-time schools. They wanted to put me on the taxi squad that first season. I went home instead, and was planning on going back to school. Art Jr. came after me and brought me back to Pittsburgh. They let Chuck Hinton go, and there was an opening for me.

The Rooneys helped me greatly. They were my family.

Chuck was like a father to me. He had so much input in my life. I had so much respect for the Rooneys. Dan was more like a father to me and his father, Mr. Rooney, was like a grandfather to everyone.

The guys on the team were like brothers to me. I started having problems with my legs. They started giving way on me. I wasn't sure what was going on. Before I knew what had happened, I was out of the mix. Before you knew it, I get traded to Tampa Bay. That hurt.

I'm seeking more religion now. My pastor at my hometown church has been helping me. The Rev. James Gifford is the pastor of the Iron Wheel Baptist Church in the Lone Star Association. I've been studying with a young preacher named Rev. Lyons. That's in Jasper, Texas.

My hips and my knees are hurting. I've had some medical work done on this old body. But it's still causing me great pain. I take some Celibrex, and it makes me feel so good it scares me. Some of my knees are just bone on bone. That's why they hurt so much. I'm more aware of pharmaceuticals now. I feel like I'm in the middle of a pills war. I get headaches on one side of my head one day, and then headaches on the other side the next day. It can get real bad.

I take my pills and I pray a lot. I think I'm turning the bend in the river.

> *When Randy Grossman asked former teammate Ernie Holmes what he was doing these days, Ernie said he was studying to be a Baptist priest. "I'm not of the persuasion, Ernie," said Grossman, "but I don't think Baptists have priests."*

Jim O'Brien

SIGN OF THE TIMES — Travelers on Rte. 19 (Banksville Road) could smile during persistent April showers that drenched Pittsburgh.

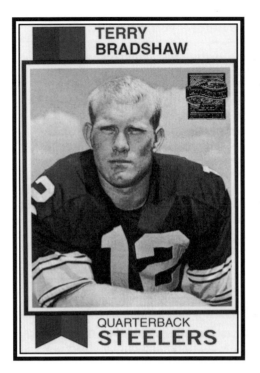

TERRY BRADSHAW

QUARTERBACK
STEELERS

JACK LAMBERT

58

AFC PRO BOWL

Topps

Steelers

STEELERS

ILB

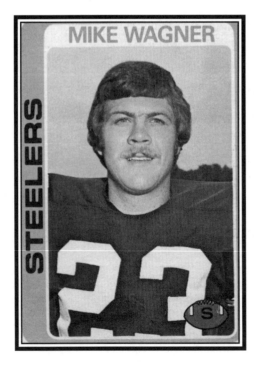

MIKE WAGNER

STEELERS

23

S

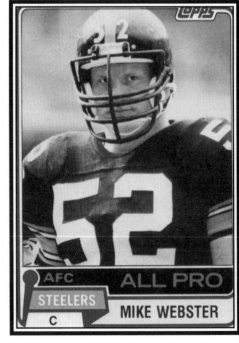

Topps

52

ALL PRO

AFC

STEELERS

C

MIKE WEBSTER

Jack Lambert
Still the one

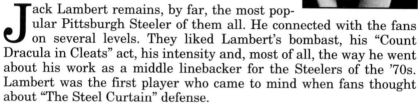

"He's a cult figure."

Jack Lambert remains, by far, the most popular Pittsburgh Steeler of them all. He connected with the fans on several levels. They liked Lambert's bombast, his "Count Dracula in Cleats" act, his intensity and, most of all, the way he went about his work as a middle linebacker for the Steelers of the '70s. Lambert was the first player who came to mind when fans thought about "The Steel Curtain" defense.

There were more blue-collar workers in Pittsburgh back then and they thought Lambert was their leader. They saw him somehow as a guy who took his lunch-pail to work with him. He was a butt-kicker and they liked that, too. He wouldn't take guff from anyone.

It' s no different these days. Joe Greene and Jack Ham and Mel Blount are other Steelers from that unit who have been similarly inducted into the Pro Football Hall of Fame, but Lambert seems to symbolize what Steelers' football was all about in those glory days. During the past dozen years, when I've done signings at shopping malls throughout the tri-state area, I often asked fans to name their favorite Steeler. I kept score. Lambert won in a landslide.

Lambert and his wife and four children live in Worthington, Pennsylvania, in the northwestern section of the state, on the way from Pittsburgh to Erie. He likes his privacy these days, and seldom strays into Pittsburgh.

When I first attempted to contact him, Lambert said he didn't want to do any interviews. "We've got to get on with our lives," said Lambert. "Do you think I've changed any in the last 30 years?"

I told him I was sure he had changed. I also told him that I knew the fans were still interested in his whereabouts, and what he was up to these days, and I reminded him that he still got paid handsomely to sign autographs at sports card and memorabilia shows. So he hadn't completely moved on, either.

He limits his appearances to about three or four shows a year, and commands an appearance fee of $20,000 per show. "We don't want him overexposed," said his agent, Curtis Boster, a bespectacled redhead who also lives near Erie. "Jack Lambert is a cult figure and we want to keep it that way."

Curtis Boster accompanies Jack Lambert when he makes such an appearance and keeps score of what he signs. Jack gets paid a certain fee for signing a flat item, a little more if he signs a football or a helmet, or some other memorabilia.

Lambert made such an appearance on Sunday, June 1, 2003 at the Expo Mart in Monroeville. He was on the same program as former

Steelers teammates Joe Greene, Rocky Bleier, Ernie Holmes and Cliff Stoudt. Tommy Maddox had been one of the current Steelers who were there to sign autographs the previous day.

There was a long line to get Lambert's autograph, longer than anyone else's line. Anyone wanting his autograph had to buy a ticket for $75 to do so. That was for a flat item. Maddox had been a big hit the previous fall at the Expo Mart when his autograph cost $20. The price had been hiked to $35 for this second appearance and, according to insiders, there was some resistance among the autograph-seekers. Maddox didn't see that much business on Saturday, according to reports by some of the vendors. It was good to learn that Maddox is turning over whatever he makes at such shows to his Tommy Gun Foundation for Children.

Frank and Mark Caputo of Caputo's Sports Cards had booked Lambert for a Sunday appearance several months earlier and drew long lines. I was there that day and thought they were doing tremendous business. Caputo admits he lost money on that show, however. He had spent a lot of money to promote it and had committed to several significant guarantees for the likes of Maddox, Kendrell Bell, Joey Porter and especially Lambert. Caputo likes having Lambert signing in his shop at Century III Mall in West Mifflin. So does Ed Nuttall of Pittsburgh Sports Store at The Mall at Robinson Township. "Lambert is a big draw for shows like this," noted Nuttall. Art Thurau of Tri-State Productions, who hosted the Expo Mart show, believes Lambert is the best draw among Pittsburgh sports stars. Thurau booked about four shows a year at the Expo Mart.

Caputo credited his 26-year-old son, Mark, for recognizing that Maddox would be a good draw, booking him for a show when he was still the backup quarterback with the Steelers. By the time he came to the show, he was the No. 1 guy. "He relates well to the fans, and he talks to everyone," commented the elder Caputo. "My son saw the potential in him. I got a picture of Tommy with me."

Lambert's agent, Curtis Boster, said he screened what card shows he'd let Lambert attend. "This can be a slimy business," he explained, "so we only work with people we know we can trust."

Lambert said he had done a show in suburban Washington, D.C. earlier in the year that was a first-class affair all the way, and he was pleased with the big turnout. Joe Greene, Jack Ham, Terry Bradshaw, Frenchy Fuqua and Andy Russell were there as well.

Lambert consented to an interview when I saw him at the Expo Mart. He was busy signing helmets and other stuff that was sent in by mail-order customers. I dropped my notebook at his shoes before I asked my first question. "You still make me nervous," I told Lambert. "Good," he said with a mischievous sneer, pleased as a safecracker that he hadn't lost his touch.

Lambert looked great. He said he weighed 218 pounds, three more than when he was playing. "I weigh about the same," he said, "but the weight has shifted to my rear end."

Jack Lambert signs away at everything placed before him at sports card and memorabilia show at Monroeville Expo Mart as his agent Curtis Boster, at right, keeps track of Lambert's autographing activity.

Photos by Jim O'Brien

When I asked him if he was still working part-time as a ranger in the forest near his home, Lambert scolded me. "Damn it, Jim, I told you five years ago that I wasn't doing that anymore." When I told him one of my neighbors bumped into him while fishing, Lambert snapped, "Probably never happened."

When I related this to Bleier, he smiled and said, "He looks great, and he's still as ornery as ever. You gotta love him."

"I always liked Terry."

Jack Lambert:

I thought it was great that Tommy Maddox had such a great season. I'm happy for him. I've seen him on TV and I think he handles himself well. He seems like a really sincere guy. I hope he has another year like he did last year. I root for guys like him and I'm happy for him.

The Mike Webster story, on the other hand, was a tragic story. The people I felt sorriest for are his family. They had it tough. Things should have been better for them.

You say that some of our guys think that maybe Mike gave too much of himself to football. Is that possible? I wouldn't agree with that statement. Mike, to me, was having health problems before he ever retired from football. He's one of those guys who played with a lot of injuries. It took its toll. We knew guys like that, right? I wasn't like that. I'd sit for a few weeks if I had a hangnail. Right? I'm a guy who sat out for the littlest thing.

I can understand why Terry Bradshaw felt the way he did about Pittsburgh. Some people down there weren't real nice to him early in his career. He remembers that time when people cheered when he got hurt. They were cheering to get him out of there. You don't forget stuff like that.

After all this time, though, it's good that he came back the way he did. You mention about Terry's comeback . . . is he coming back to play in the National Football League? That would be a real comeback.

Hey, I like Terry. I always liked Terry. But I don't get it. It's always something. I don't know. We're all getting to the years when things start to happen. This is life. Just because we're a Pittsburgh Steeler doesn't mean we're not going to have the same problems as everyone else. I try to limit how many of these shows I do. You can do too many of them.

I'm not playing hockey anymore. I played one shift last year in Kittanning, and it didn't go well. I think my days of hockey are over, unless it's a father-son game. I'd like to do that. Otherwise, I'm retired. Unless Craig Patrick wants me to come down to help the Pens out.

I still like to go fishing, and I do a little hunting. My wife and I both manage ball teams. We've got four kids playing on four different teams. We're either at a baseball game or a fast-pitch softball game. We've got two boys and two girls and they're all playing in some league. That keeps us busy. It's something we enjoy doing. Can you picture that? Jack Lambert, Little League manager?

Jack Lambert and Joe Greene, two Pro Football Hall of Fame members and the pillars of Pittsburgh's "Steel Curtain" defense of the '70s, appear in same autographing lineup at sports card and memorabilia show at Expo Mart in Monroeville.

Photos by Jim O'Brien

David Roderick, former president and chairman of the board of U.S. Steel, presents Steelers' MVP Award to Jack Lambert, as defensive coach Woody Woodruff, Andy Russell and Jack Ham look on in Steelers' locker room at Three Rivers Stadium. Note football on display in background that Mel Blount intercepted from Jets' Joe Namath.

A Jack Lambert fan forever

"I used to go up to St. Vincent every summer to see the Steelers. One time, I spotted Jack Lambert coming up from the field to the locker room by a different path than the rest of the players. It was lunchtime. This old man was trying to chase him, but he was out of breath and he sat down on a bench to rest. Lambert saw him and went over and sat down next to him. Lambert gave him something. I don't know what. He treated him like he was his grandfather.

"Another time, he was standing at the top of the hill, signing autographs to everyone on the other side of a restraining rope. This woman was pushing these kids. One fell. Jack reached down and picked the kid up and patted him on the behind. Then he looked at the woman and said sternly, 'Don't ever push your kids!' With kids and old men, he was terrific. I thought he was insensitive, aloof. But, for the way he treated the old and young, he was my favorite football player on the Steelers."

— Linda Ademetz, a fan from Shaler
At Ross Park Mall, February 8, 2003

Rocky Bleier
Still paying back

"Why do I know that name?"

Rocky Bleier paid a visit to Asbury Heights, an assisted-care facility about a mile from his home in Mt. Lebanon, about five miles from Heinz Field. He was there in October of 2002 to discuss plans for a dinner appearance there the following month to raise funds for benevolent care to support residents who needed some financial assistance to pay for their stay.

My mother, Mary M. O'Brien, was nearing her 96th birthday at the time. She was suffering from dementia, and her once-wonderful mind wasn't working so well anymore. She was in her fourth year at Asbury Heights after residing at the St. Augustine Plaza Apartments in Lawrenceville for over 22 years.

She would turn 96 on Christmas Eve and she would die — she just got tired — in early March. She died in her sleep, as she prayed she would. The last picture I took of her was with Rocky Bleier.

I was on the board at Asbury Foundation and had been asked by John Zanardelli, an old friend from our Rotary Club days who was the director at Asbury, to host an annual fund-raising dinner on the campus. We called it "Keeping The Faith" and had former Steeler lineman Tunch Ilkin as our first speaker, and former Pirates manager Chuck Tanner for our second dinner.

During his initial visit, Bleier toured the building complex and said hello to staff and residents alike. It caused a buzz in the building. He sat and spoke with my mother for a few minutes.

"Rocky Bleier . . . Rocky Bleier . . . why do I know that name?" my mother asked aloud.

Then she turned to me and observed, "He's a cute guy."

Bleier blushed. He posed for some pictures with her and other people at Asbury who approached him. Rocky Bleier has time for everybody.

He was a big hit as a speaker when he returned in November. Zanardelli, Cheryl Turner, the director of development at Asbury, and their staffs raised $65,000 with Bleier as the main attraction for "Keeping The Faith — III." His friend, Andy Russell, had agreed to be the main speaker for the edition of the series scheduled for October of 2003. Russell also knows how to relate to people.

Russell's parents had both been residents at Friendship Village in Upper St. Clair, prior to their deaths only a few years earlier.

Bleier participated in the 27th Annual Andy Russell Children's Classic at The Club at Nevillewood in May and served as the toast-master for the 5th Annual Mel Blount Youth Home Celebrity Roast in June where Joe Greene was honored.

"One of the things I talk about when giving speeches is what we all need is hope."
— **Rocky Bleier**

Bleier appeared in a white tuxedo with black trim that evening, and was a big hit.

"Your problem is that you believed them."

Rocky Bleier has been telling his own story of a courageous comeback from wounds suffered in combat in Vietnam, and making a good living as a motivational speaker on the national circuit ever since he retired as a Steeler following the 1980 season. He had a brief stint as a sportscaster at WPXI-TV before he concentrated entirely as a speaker.

He tells his story well and, better yet, he invests time and effort to making sure that everyone associated with every appearance he makes gets the best of Rocky Bleier. One of his talks is titled "Be The Best You Can Be," and Bleier walks the talk. He gets high grades wherever he goes, and everybody speaks about his interaction before and after the program with those involved in the program.

I was talking to Bleier after his appearance at Asbury, and I was looking him directly in the eye when I said, "Rocky, I'm only 5-8½ and I'm as big as you are. All my life football coaches told me I was too small."

Bleier didn't blink. He stuck a stiff finger into the center of my chest and kept tapping me on the sternum to make his point. "Your problem," he said very precisely, "is that you believed them!"

Bleier makes that kind of point routinely in his talks. He tells the story of a young man who wasn't particularly big or fast who overcame great odds to play and captain a championship football team at Notre Dame University, and to go on and become a vital contributor to the Steelers winning four Super Bowls. One season he and Franco Harris both gained over 1,000 yards for the Steelers.

"We weren't bosom buddies."

Rocky Bleier:

I don't know why all these teams have gone to a single back offense. The Steelers have a great inside runner in Jerome Bettis, for instance, and a great outside runner in Amos Zereoue. Why don't they have them in the same backfield? In today's game, I wouldn't be in the lineup. I think certain kinds of backs can complement one another, and I think they cause the defense to wonder which one is carrying the ball next.

Photos by Jim O'Brien

Jan and Rocky Bleier are thrilled with their two daughters, Rosie, 4, in Rocky's lap, and Elly, 5, at their home in Virginia Manor section of Mt. Lebanon. Both girls were adopted three years ago from the Ukraine. Rocky is joined below at Andy Russell's Golf Classic for Children by Mark Malone and Emil Boures.

I'm just talking as a fan now, but I do talk about those things. Sometimes I think the coaches are too close to the situation to see what the fans sometimes see and speak about. I don't like situational substitution much, either. I want my best players on the field as much as possible.

I buy season tickets and I still go to most of the games. I still enjoy the games and my wife Jan and her family all like going to the games.

I see a lot of my former teammates at all these reunions and golf outings, and it gets more meaningful, especially if it's soon after one of our guys dies. That hits home and it hurts.

Mike Webster was one of those situations. When all is said and done, maybe you only knew Mike as well as he allowed you to know him. Maybe you didn't really know him at all. Mike was a teammate. We played together for a lot of years. But it's not as if we were bosom buddies. He came from Wisconsin and, of course, I was from Wisconsin. That was a bond. But I didn't keep as close to Mike once we were done playing. We were teammates for seven years, but we didn't socialize much together away from the stadium.

Then Mike played for Kansas City for two years and that took him away from Pittsburgh. There was a period of ten or 15 years, maybe longer, when I lost track of Mike. That happens. Then I heard he was having some problems with pain-killing drugs. I heard that Pam had left him, or had asked him to leave. He was kinda floating around and then he stopped in Pittsburgh.

Some of the players here got together with Mike to see what he was up to. He was always talking about some deal, about something he was selling. There was always something happening.

He had anger issues about lost money and people screwing him. Then you found out he was having a difficult time. Stories would circulate about him sleeping in his car or in a bus station.

His friends held a press conference for him to clear up some matters. Andy Russell, Mel Blount, I think, Randy Grossman and I and some of the other players in town came to the press conference and supported him. It was held at a hotel in Moon Township, out where he was living with his son, Garrett, who was going to school there and playing football for the high school team.

He had his doctor and an attorney and some of this friends there with him. We were helping him out. We sat behind him when he was at the microphone. He read a statement. We thought he was getting some help. Then Mike had a heart attack and died. I was out of town when that happened. I was in shock when I heard the news. I had

Rocky Bleier was a standout performer as emcee at the Mel Blount Youth Home Celebrity Roast at Pittsburgh Hilton. There were about 35 members of the Steelers' family present to pay tribute to Joe Greene. Bleier, by the way, is the one in the white tuxedo. In photo above, Rocky swaps stories with former trainer Ralph Berlin, at left, and Steelers' chairman of the board Dan Rooney.

Photos by Jim O'Brien

commitments out of town and was not able to attend his funeral.

I didn't think Mike had those kinds of health problems. It's indicative that, hey, we can all go out at any time. Who's to say when our time is up? This was not like Ray Mansfield where you knew he was out of shape, and that his family had a history of heart disease. This was more of a surprise to your system.

I guess we thought Mike Webster was indestructible.

We wondered what part steroids played in his declining health and his memory problems. It was too easy to tag it on them. Maybe he just had a heart attack.

"What's he promoting?"

As for the comeback story of Terry Bradshaw, my first thoughts were flippant, of course. "What's he got," I asked the other guys, "another book coming out? What's he promoting?"

You could see an agent at work in there, telling Terry this was a good idea, something he should do. And Terry was well advised, if that's what happened.

Then he talked about his depression thing, and how he was never really happy. Who's really to say when it comes to stuff like that? Most of us, when we think of depression, have an image of people hanging their head. From what I've gleaned, some people are good at covering up for how miserable they might feel. You might see a guy and wonder what he has to worry about. It might not make sense to you. But it's real for him. I didn't see his interview on Bryant Gumbel's show, but I heard about it. I don't understand depression or what kind of problems it causes.

I'm told he said he was always trying to please people, that he wanted everybody to like him. Hey, I've always been that way. I worry about what people think of me, too. I'm always trying to win approval. Who knows what that stems from? That was always a driving force to succeed and to treat people the same way you wanted to be treated.

To a degree, we all have that problem. That's one of my issues. I was always trying to please my parents, and trying to please my coach, the fans, the writers, my teammates.

Maybe some of his behavior comes into a clearer picture. He was a loner when he was on our team, I remember that. He didn't have any close friends on the team. We were a part of the team, and Terry was the star. From a teammate's point of view, he wasn't really close to anybody, really. Tony Parisi, our equipment manager, was telling me that after a Super

Former members of Steelers' support cast, equipment manager Tony Parisi, conditioning coach Paul Uram and head trainer Ralph Berlin were looking sharp at Mel Blount Youth Home Celebrity Roast.   Photos by Jim O'Brien

Former Steelers, left to right, Cliff Stoudt, Dwight White, John Stallworth and Dwayne Woodruff, appear at Pittsburgh Hilton gala.

Bowl, it was just Tony and Bradshaw in Bradshaw's hotel room, smoking cigars. Tony brought that up to me. It's kinda interesting. Makes you wonder.

"And it all fell into place."

Tommy Maddox is a great story. It shows you that he just found himself in the right situation. Has his ability changed? No. He did what he had to do here. Tommy needs to stay in the pocket. Tony worked on technique. He couldn't run out of the pocket. He's like me; he has no speed. He's not a big, lumbering quarterback, so he can't overpower people like Terry could.

He has good instincts and he has a nice touch on the ball. That's his game. He's got a great receiving corps. He has the people to throw the ball to and they catch the ball. His maturity and experience are assets now. He has an offensive line that gives him protection and he can read defenses and it all fell into place.

I was selling insurance and thinking about giving up football early in my career. But I didn't like the insurance business. That's no reflection on the people who make it their career, and are good at it. You find out what you don't like. It was something I didn't like and something I could not do. That's not to take away from the insurance business or anyone in it, but it was not for me. Tommy's dad did well in the insurance business, but Tommy didn't like it, to hear him talk. It's important to learn what you can do and what you can't do. He's never going to be a Kordell Stewart. But sometimes Kordell's athletic ability didn't allow him to refine his skills to be a drop-back quarterback. When you have his kind of physical skills, you know you can always get out of trouble with your legs. Now Tommy has to do it again. He has to do it the same way if he's going to have any kind of success.

"I'm not good at ad-libbing."

I'll tell you something about what I do these days. I may have appeared relaxed when I was emceeing Mel's dinner for Joe Greene, but that dinner took eight weeks out of my life. I couldn't socialize with my teammates and their families because I was working. I had to remember what I was doing.

I can't go out there and just speak. I have to be prepared. I have to have everything down on paper. I'm not good at ad-libbing, and I know that. I have to think of a theme, how I'm going to paint this to Joe Greene. For two months, I'm thinking about it. This is not my usual motivational talk.

It's a relief when it's over. I don't enjoy the evening. I can't really talk to players, or relax. My mind is working overtime. I was in that V.I.P. Room before the dinner, but I didn't see my wife, Jan, all night. I'm glad to see the guys, but I'd rather see them when I'm not working. It was more fun at Andy's affair for me. When you're emceeing, it's not like seeing guys when you're sitting there fishing. You're just talking, and checking to see if there's anything on your line.

But this is what I do for a living. Where am I going next? Where am I now? I'm going to Las Vegas tomorrow, then Phoenix and then Fort Lauderdale. Then I'll be back home on Saturday for the weekend. I'll have to check my calendar to make sure.

Jim O'Brien

Rocky Bleier joins former assistant trainer Bob Milie for lunch at DeBlasio's Restaurant near his home in Virginia Manor section of Mt. Lebanon. Don DeBlasio's restaurant is a favorite with many sports luminaries such as Jim Leyland, Walt Harris and his Pitt coaching staff, Foge Fazio and Joe Gordon.

Looking after the children
Steelers support good causes

"You'll know you're getting old."
— L. C. Greenwood

I was like a kid in a candy store. I was surrounded by Steelers from past and present, stars from other pro football teams and former local baseball and hockey standouts. This was at golf outings in the South Hills over a five-day stretch. I don't play golf, but no one was having more fun.

The 27th annual Andy Russell Celebrity Classic for Children and the 10th annual Hoge-Bruener-Ward Celebrity Golf Classic for Children are as good as its gets for fund-raising golf outings in the Greater Pittsburgh area.

Russell and his sidekick Sam Zacharias of Mt. Lebanon rounded up over 70 former star athletes and raised a record $300,000 playing at The Club at Nevillewood and Chartiers Country Club on Friday, May 16, 2003, and Merrill Hoge, Mark Bruener and Hines Ward highlighted the lineup of Steelers at an outing sponsored by Highmark Blue Cross Blue Shield to raise funds for the Western Pennsylvania Caring Foundation. That was held three days later on Monday, May 19 at the Southpointe Golf Club in Canonsburg.

On Thursday at a dinner to kick off Russell's roundup, I sat at a round table during a social hour. Sitting left to right were Mel Blount, John Stallworth and Joe Greene — they are all in the Pro Football Hall of Fame. Then came Roy Jefferson and Myron Pottios, two Steelers' stars from the '60s, then Charley Johnson and John David Crow, two stars from the St. Louis Cardinals of that same era. King Arthur didn't have as many good knights at his Round Table.

Jefferson, who was introduced by Zacharias as "the best player Chuck Noll ever traded away," surprised me by his recognition. We had not seen each other since 1968. "Jim, you look old," he said, "but I can still see your face." I liked that line.

I hadn't spoken to Johnson since the fall of 1965. I was stationed at the U.S. Army Home Town News Center in Kansas City, Missouri and doing some stringing for *Sport* magazine and *Newsweek*. I was asked by John Lake, the late sports editor of *Newsweek*, to go to St. Louis one weekend to interview Johnson. I remembered he had played at New Mexico State, John David Crow at Texas A&M. They had gotten old, but I could see their faces as I first knew them, too.

I had last seen Pottios, from Van Voorhis, Pennsylvania, near Charleroi, at a party a few nights before the Steelers won their fourth Super Bowl in January of 1980. I went to a party held by some Steelers' fans from Pittsburgh's North Side at a hotel in Seal Beach, California, and Pottios, who played for the Steelers from 1961 till

Joe Gordon coordinates annual Ray Mansfield Memorial Golf Tournament at Diamond Run that features likes of former Steelers, left to right above, Cliff Stoudt, Mel Blount and Frenchy Fuqua, and, pictured below, Emil Boures, Craig Wolfley, Bruce Van Dyke and Lloyd Voss. They were there in September, 2002 when they learned that Mike Webster had a heart attack. He died the next morning.   Photos by Jim O'Brien

1965, then the Rams and Redskins, made a surprise appearance. He played his college ball at Notre Dame and was a tough linebacker with the Steelers. Like Jack Lambert later on, Pottios got into more than his share of skirmishes.

Other Steelers favorites present at Russell's golf outing were Frenchy Fuqua, L.C. Greenwood, Rocky Bleier, Lynn Swann, Glen Edwards, Frank Lewis, Bill Hurley, Mark Malone, Gerry "Moon" Mullins, Robin Cole, Craig Bingham, Cliff Stoudt, Ted Petersen, Edmund Nelson, Mike Wagner, John Banaszak, Gordon Gravelle, Jerry Hillebrand, Dwayne Woodruff, J.R. Wilburn, Randy Grossman, Larry Brown, and Rod Woodson. Two of the Steelers coaches, Tommy Clements and Dick Hoak, were there as well.

I took a photo of Blount with Woodson, and told them they were the Steelers two best defensive cornerbacks. "I only wish I made the kind of money he's making," said Blount.

Fuqua said he would be retiring at year's end from his job in the circulation department of the *Detroit News*. Fans were still asking him at Nevillewood to give them the lowdown on what really happened when he was in the middle of the "Immaculate Reception" sequence, the greatest play in NFL history. Fuqua has a lot of fun with that.

Hall of Famers present from other teams were Willie Lanier of the Kansas City Chiefs and Tom Mack of the Los Angeles Rams, as well at Mark May, the former Pitt star who was Pro Bowl performer for the Washington Redskins. Russell said that Mack had caught a "red-eye special" to get to Pittsburgh on time to play in the golf outing.

Greene said he got emotional when he embraced L.C. Greenwood. "I didn't expect that to happen," said Greene. Mean Joe had been a pallbearer along with Blount for Steelers receiver Ron Shanklin two weeks earlier in Dallas. Greene and Shanklin were teammates at North Texas State and with the Steelers. "I think Ronnie was still on my mind," explained Greene.

Yes, these Steelers are getting older. "They're like family," said one Steelers' fan. "They are linked to our lives, whether we like it or not. They gave us so many thrills, and we went through so many ups and downs together."

Greenwood, who wore flashy black and gold adidas golf shoes, and showed up in resplendent attire for dinner both nights, was laughing about the getting-old business. He told Bingham, who's quite a bit younger, "Wait till you start telling stories and you stop and say, 'Now what was I talking about?' and you'll know you're getting old."

Greene was great with the sponsors in attendance. He was repeatedly asked if he would pose for a picture with someone. Greene would give them his best grin, hesitate a moment, and say in that warm voice of his, "It would be my honor."

Then he would take a drink or beer out of their hands, place it on a nearby table, so it wouldn't be in the picture.

Andy Russell's Celebrity Classic for Children drew all-pro lineup to The Club at Nevillewood in spring of 2003. Left to right above, former Steelers include Robin Cole, Louis Lipps and John Stallworth. Two of Steelers' all-time greatest defensive backs, seen below, are Rod Woodson and Mel Blount.

Photos by Jim O'Brien

"I'm still a Steeler."
— Carnell Lake

Pierre Larouche, the best Penguins' scorer before Mario Lemieux came along, was there, too, as was Bob Friend, the most reliable pitcher in Pirates' history. They appear at so many of these charity functions, still lending their name and time to worthwhile causes.

Bill Cowher competed in both of these golf outings, and was joined by Chuck Noll at the second one at Southpointe. "I'm either hitting them real good or real bad," said Cowher. "There's nothing in between."

Everyone was pleased to catch up with Merril Hoge, who showed up bald. He's been undergoing chemotherapy treatments in his battle with cancer, and reported that he was presently cancer-free.

Hoge delivered a stirring talk about his challenge, how it had changed his perspective on things, and how he hoped to turn it into a positive aspect of his work. Dr. Ken Melani, the CEO of Highmark, spoke of how Hoge had awed him with his approach to his health challenge, how he remained committed to helping children. He said Hoge was a true hero.

"This is a hard way to learn something," Hoge said, "but I've learned to appreciate everything more than I used to. I've met a lot of wonderful people. I have received so many phone calls and cards from great people, and I wonder whether I deserve that."

Mark Malone, who still keeps a home in Bridgeville, was there, too, along with Tommy Maddox, who's quite a golfer as well as the Steelers' starting quarterback. Dick Anderson, a former defensive back with the Miami Dolphins Super Bowl teams and a regular at Russell's golf outing, had said that all the guys on the Celebrity Golf Tour were rooting for Maddox because he was so popular with the guys.

Some of the current Steelers who played in the event were Charlie Batch, Josh Miller, Deshea Townsend, Brent Alexander and Antwaan Randle El. Former Steeler, Carnell Lake, who lent his name to this same event when he was with the Steelers, came back to town for the outing. He had retired after the 2002 season after four seasons with the Jacksonville Jaguars.

"I'm still a Steeler," allowed Lake. "I made so many great friends during my ten seasons with the Steelers. "I was very involved in the community and made a lot of friends here. We had great support. It wasn't just about business when I was with the Steelers. When you get old, though, you gotta go where you can get the best deal."

Bill Cowher spoke to Lake at length. Later Cowher confided, "Carnell is a class guy. He is still one of my all-time favorite players."

Cowher said something about "the business of pro football" when he spoke with Lake. That's why they parted company. There was more than a hint that the same thing could happen with another of the

398

Louis Lipps and Bryan Hinkle, above, were in celebrity cast at Ray Mansfield
Memorial Smoker during 2002 season.   Jim O'Brien

Former Steelers wield hammers to build a home in Habitat for Humanity
Greene County project in Waynesburg: Todd Kalis, Dave Moss, Bryan Hinkle
and Rocky Bleier.

Steelers' most popular players who was so active in community causes and that, of course, was Mark Bruener.

Bruener's wife, Traci, was there, pregnant with their fourth child, and not knowing where that child might be living when the 2003 season got underway. The Steelers had signed some high-priced tight ends and Bruener had been sidelined with injuries in the stretch run the previous two seasons.

Bruener had been a good citizen with the Steelers, on and off the field. On at least three occasions, according to his count, he had taken adjustments in his salary so the Steelers could get under the salary cap. He said they didn't owe him anything for that, though, and that he had been treated well during his eight years with the Steelers.

The Steelers would start two weeks of so-called "voluntary work-outs" the next day at their UPMC Sports Complex on the South Side, and many in the media were asking Bruener about his status.

"I'm approaching this off-season program as I've approached the last eight — that's to try and find a way to help this club and organization win a championship," said Bruener, still a Boy Scout. "I still believe I can contribute to a football team. I hope it's here. But we'll cross that hurdle when it comes.

"I don't think I need to (know) right now. I feel this organization will be straight with me when the decision is made. I haven't had a reason to change my approach. I'm going to show up for work every day with the same attitude that I've had.

"If that has to change, then I'll have to adjust. But I feel that I shouldn't worry about things I can't control. I have to worry about things I can control. What I can control is my approach and how I show up for work every day."

Bill Cowher couldn't ask for anything more. Cowher has always been one of Bruener's biggest fans, often calling attention to his contribution as a blocker who's contributed to the success enjoyed by running back Jerome Bettis. A ten-year veteran, Bettis was also under the microscope at the Steelers' training facility. Bruener and Bettis made a lot of fans and a home for themselves in Pittsburgh, and the thought of them not being with the Black and Gold was difficult to consider. If Bruener left who'd help Bettis get up after each of his runs? Their distinguished service wouldn't matter, my wife Kathie kept reminding me, when it came down to finalizing the lineup.

When I caught Clements at the Southpointe Golf Club, I kidded the Steelers' quarterback coach that he was on the celebrity golf tour. "It all ends today," he said. "Tomorrow it's back to work."

I knew his father, Doc Clements, who used to drive over from McKees Rocks to Baldwin-Whitehall to drink in the company of Bobby Layne, Ernie Stautner and Myron Pottios, among others, at Dante's, a great gin joint owned by Dante Sartorio. That was back in the early '60s. That seemed so long ago.

These golf outings, luncheons and dinners are reunions for the celebrities who participate in them, and a great opportunity for fans

PMC Health System

Sports Training Center

Pittsburgh Steelers Football Club

University of Pittsburgh Panthers Football

UPMC Sports
Training Center
is home on South Side
to Steelers and Panthers.

Photos by Jim O'Brien

to mix with their sports favorites. The staff and volunteers and sponsors are critical to the success of these events. "This is a tough economy," reported Russell, who knows something about money markets, "and yet we set a record this year. So we were really pleased, and grateful for everyone's participation."

And it's all for kids who need some help.

Photos by Jim O'Brien

Hall of Fame cast at Andy Russell's Celebrity Classic for Children included, left to right, Mel Blount, John Stallworth and Joe Greene.

MYRON POTTIOS

FRANK LEWIS

Tom Clements
Still a hometown hero

*"I was just hoping I could be
another Tommy Clements."*
— Joe Montana on his
ambitions at Notre Dame

A light rain was falling most of the morning. It was a fine mist for the most part, good for greening the grass. It was Wednesday, May 28, 2003. The Steelers were conducting "voluntary" coaches' sessions over a three-week span and all the Steelers showed up. Voluntarily, of course. It was a preliminary workout in advance of the official mini-camp. In truth, there is no off-season for football players on any level these days. It's a year-round activity.

That suits the Steelers' fans just fine. They can't get enough of their beloved Black & Gold.

Tom Clements, the team's quarterback coach, had just come away from an indoor session at the UPMC Sports Complex the Steelers share with the University of Pittsburgh football program on the city's South Side. His dark hair was damp, and he dried it somewhat with the sleeve of his black windbreaker. Tom Clements looked good in black, with a *Steelers* signature over his heart.

It was another mostly gray day on the Pittsburgh calendar. April showers overstayed their welcome, and summer was in no hurry to get to Pittsburgh. The Pirates couldn't win in Pittsburgh, and poor weather on too many home dates and poor play in too many respects were keeping the crowds down at PNC Park. Road construction and detours didn't help. Sports fans were already turning their attention to the Steelers for some relief.

Neither the Pirates nor the Penguins offered hope of being a contender any time soon, whereas the Steelers, under Bill Cowher and his staff, were nearly always in serious contention. Cowher kept saying the Super Bowl was the team's ultimate goal. Not just getting to it, but winning the Lombardi Trophy — getting that ring, the elusive one for the thumb, at least for owner Dan Rooney and running backs coach Dick Hoak. They were the only ones at the office with four Super Bowl rings in their jewelry collection.

When the Steelers were at Three Rivers Stadium, they would have practiced there on the artificial turf in such a light rain, or maybe even at the short grass field tucked between a building and neighborhood streets nearby on the North Side. If it rained harder, they'd commandeer some buses and go practice in the bubble at the Arthur J. Rooney Field at Duquesne University, or at the Charles L. Cost indoor practice facility at Pitt. Neither was an ideal situation. Such days were difficult, especially if they had to deal with heavy traffic. Cowher was known to cuss mildly on such days. The Steelers were spoiled even then. None of them would believe how primitive the facilities were at the Fair Grounds in South Park when Buddy Parker was coaching them in the early '60s.

"You had to be there to believe it," says Rocky Bleier, looking back to his rookie season of 1968. "Coming from a first-class situation at Notre Dame it was quite a shock to the system. The weight room was a Universal gym on the porch. It was pretty pathetic."

The players had to dress in a moldy basement of a white concrete-block building. There were a few working shower stalls, and some of the toilets didn't even have seats. It was just short of an outhouse. There were two rooms upstairs where they'd stuff the offensive units and defensive units into under-sized rooms to watch film. If the players had gone out to lunch at nearby restaurants, and had a few beers to wash down the cheeseburgers, they might fall asleep and be heard snoring during the film sessions. This was another era.

That's where I first met Art Rooney, the team owner, standing with him on the sideline during my days as a student sportswriter at Pitt. The Steelers may have practiced in the shabbiest surroundings in the NFL back then. Keeping company with Art Rooney, however, was always a good day. Following that first meeting, I remember he sent me a post card at Pitt, apologizing if he'd come off as a know-it-all when he was relating stories to me about his favorite sportswriters in New York.

That was a tip-off as to the quality of Art Rooney. He was apologizing to a punk Pitt sportswriter when he was the owner of the Pittsburgh Steelers, and one of the NFL's most respected pioneers. It was the beginning of a beautiful relationship, and a string of such postcards, whether I was working in Miami, New York or Pittsburgh.

Nowadays the Steelers and Pitt have some of the best facilities in the country on an NFL or collegiate level. They are good neighbors. They are supposed to be separate but equal, but some of the Pitt people stray over to eat in the dining area on the Steelers' side of the state-of-the-art complex. Clements had just gotten a Styrofoam cup of Coca-Cola there.

Later, I saw Cowher and Kevin Colbert, the team's director of football operations, coming across the parking lot from the indoor facility. Both were sweating profusely, probably coming away from a personal workout. They like to play racquetball when they get some free time. They have to love the UPMC Sports Complex. It's unlikely Art Rooney would have approved a move to the South Side from his native North Side, but he'd have been impressed with the place. "This is nice, too," he'd have said. He always said the Steelers weren't a first-class operation until they moved into Three Rivers Stadium in 1970. Rooney was right about that.

"Cheer, cheer for ol' Notre Dame."
— Irish fight song

404

Tom Clements shined at Notre Dame as quarterback with Coach Ara Parseghian, as an assistant coach with Lou Holtz, and in contest, below, with arch-rival Purdue.

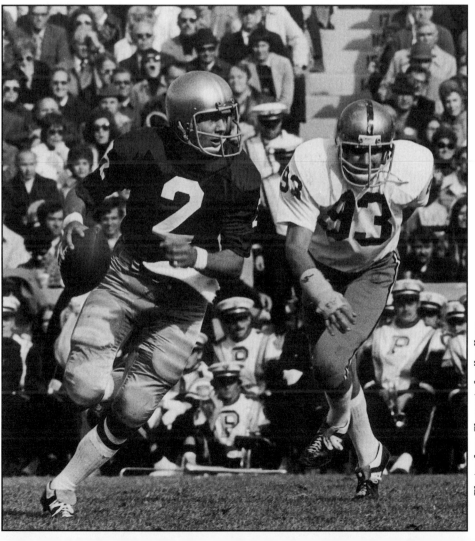

Photos from Clements family album

Clements comes home again

It's hard for me to write Tom Clements, or to think that he was nearing his 50th birthday. He would celebrate his 50th birthday — it made him shake his head, too — the next month. I had always known him as Tommy Clements, a multi-sports star at Canevin High School, and a terrific quarterback at Notre Dame and in the CFL and NFL.

"I am Tom," he said, when I asked his preference. "But I still get Tommy."

He became an attorney and worked in Chicago, but gave that up to go coach at Notre Dame. He was there when Lou Holtz was the head coach and Joe Moore of Mt. Lebanon was the offensive line coach. Clements was later the quarterback coach for Mike Ditka with the New Orleans Saints, all sorts of western Pennsylvania connections. When Ditka gave up the ghost, and Clements was available, Cowher came calling. It was a good fit. Tom or Tommy Clements was coming home again.

I remember hearing Joe Montana of New Eagle and Monongahela when he was inducted into the Pro Football Hall of Fame along with Steelers' president Dan Rooney at ceremonies in Canton, Ohio in the summer of 2000. During his remarks, Montana said, "When I went to Notre Dame I was just hoping I could be another Tommy Clements." High praise, indeed.

Clements is a handsome fellow, with dark wavy hair to die for, and he is still a hometown hero. He grew up in Stowe Township, just northwest of McKees Rocks, a storied slice of Greater Pittsburgh. He was a schoolboy star at Canevin, the best all-around athlete the Crusaders had claimed since Frank Gustine Jr. When he went to Canevin, Clements may have just wanted to be another Frank Gustine Jr. Clements stood 5-11½, and was a right-hander. He played basketball and he also played baseball his first two years in high school.

Clements was the first quarterback coach the Steelers employed since Vito "Babe" Parilli, the old pro NFL and AFL star who was the pride of Rochester, Pennsylvania, held the job under Chuck Noll in 1973. Clements' influence was dynamic. Clements was credited with helping Kordell Stewart reestablish himself as a productive passer and leader of the Steelers during the 2001 season — he was the team MVP and a Pro Bowl selection — and for helping Tommy Maddox make a dramatic comeback as a pro a year later.

Stewart strangely slipped and faltered at the start of the 2002 season, and had to be replaced in the starting lineup. Clements was in the middle of what could have been an unsettling quarterback controversy, but he and the coaching staff, with big assists from both Stewart and Maddox, made it work peacefully and productively. Stewart bounced back to play well when the Steelers needed him, and he kept his feelings mostly to himself about his reduced role.

After the Steelers released him at the outset of 2003, Stewart signed as a free agent with the Chicago Bears. Now Charlie Batch was the backup quarterback behind Maddox. Clements was comfortable having two proven pro passers to work with.

Clements has come a long way from Stowe Township. Now he lives with his family in Fox Chapel. He and his wife, Kathe, have two children, Stephanie, 24, and Tom, 21. His mother, Genevieve, 88, was still living in Stowe Township.

Room with a view

Tom Clements was looking forward to his 20th year in professional football. He took me to his office on the second floor of the Steelers' side of the complex. It's a large, nicely furnished corner office with big windows on two of the walls. There were x's and o's in red and black on a whiteboard on another wall. Clements can look down the Monongahela River to the Ohio River and, on a clear day or at least in his mind, see McKees Rocks. Or, he can look the other way and, as I pointed out to him, see where Frank Thomas of the Pirates and Danny Marino of Pitt and the Miami Dolphins grew up on the hillside across the river. I told him that Bruno Sammartino and Andy Warhol — this might be the first time they were mentioned in the same breath — grew up in the same neighborhood in South Oakland. Joe Gordon, the former Steelers' publicist, lived there near the Holmes Elementary School. You could walk from there to Forbes Field or Pitt Stadium. Farther up the river was my hometown of Hazelwood.

The Jones & Laughlin Steel Mill had part of its plant on the South Side where the Steelers now practice, and where something akin to The Waterfront in Homestead was coming up on the site of the former steelworks, and the rest of it across the river in Greenfield and Hazelwood. They held good and bad memories for me.

It was a great view. Clements never worked for the Steelers at Rivers Stadium. There were no windows there, until Gordon got mehow late in his stay with the Steelers. He might have gotten ndow in lieu of a pay raise. The coaches and players never knew as raining or snowing outside, or whether the sun had made a ppearance in Pittsburgh. It was like working in a bomb shelter. Noll might have liked it that way as it was easier to focus on ll, football and football. Noll might have regarded sunlight as a tion. I told Tom Clements how lucky he was, and how pleasant roundings were. It would be a wonderful office for a writer as

lements had a great 12-year playing career in the Canadian Football League with Ottawa (1975-1978), Hamilton (1979, 1981-1982) and Winnipeg (1983-1987). He was inducted into the CFL Hall of Fame in 1994. A seven-time divisional All-Star, Clements led two teams — Ottawa (1976) and Winnipeg (1984) — to Grey Cup championships, and was the Outstanding Offensive Player in both of those contests. When the similarly-sized and dark-haired John Congemi of Pitt went to the CFL in the mid-80s, he hoped he could be another Tommy Clements. Congemi, also a favorite son of the western Pennsylvania chapter of the Italian-American Sports Hall of Fame, did quite well there, too.

During his career, Clements completed 2,807 of 4,657 passes (60.3 percent) for 39,041 yards and 252 touchdowns. He was the league's Rookie of the Year in 1987. He also served as a backup quarterback for the Kansas City Chiefs in 1980. He later returned to serve as an assistant coach with the Chiefs in 2000, where he was credited for improving the play of Elvis Grbac, who enjoyed his finest year as a pro and earned a trip to the Pro Bowl.

Clements was accorded All-American honors at Notre Dame in 1974. Notre Dame had a history of having great quarterbacks from western Pennsylvania such as Johnny Lujack and Terry Hanratty. Clements started three seasons for the Fighting Irish (1972-1974) and led them to a 29-5 record during his tenure, including an unbeaten national championship season in 1973. He finished fourth in the Heisman Trophy balloting as a senior in 1974. Archie Griffin of Ohio State won the award.

A licensed attorney, Clements was with Bell, Boyd & Lloyd, a Chicago-based law firm, from 1988 to 1992, and in 1996 he worked in the law department of Republic Industries, Inc., a public company owned by Miami Dolphins owner Wayne Huizenga. Clements went to law school during his playing days in the CFL, and graduated magna cum laude from Notre Dame's School of Law in 1986. So he's a smart cookie this Clements kid.

"Doc" Clements was proud of his boys

Stowe Township and McKees Rocks share a great sports tradition. Their high schools still turn out terrific sports teams. When I was a kid, growing up in Hazelwood, and reporting on the J.J. Doyle's football team in *The Hazelwood Envoy*, I remember them playing in championship games and coming up short against the Rox Rangers and the Sto-Rox Cadets.

Those were two of the storied sandlot heavyweight teams of all time. Toby Uansa, a former Pitt backfield star, coached the Rox Rangers, and John "Pokie" LaQuinta, the uncle of former Pitt lineman Bernie LaQuinta, coached the Sto-Rox Cadets.

When I served as the public relations director for the Pittsburgh Valley Ironmen of the Atlantic Coast Football League in 1963 and 1964, we had two terrific players from McKees Rocks, namely Clem Smarra and Mike "Hotsy" Olander. They were both characters. Smarra was once pictured in the newspaper walking a rat on a leash

my Clements is congratulated by his father, Dr.
ry Clements, and brothers Dave, left, and Frank
wards ceremony during his Canevin High
ol days.

Bishop Wright presents MVP
award for Diocesan Grade School
basketball league.

With CFL's Hamilton Tiger-Cats

ents in Canevin High days

From Clements Family Album

As Canevin shooting star

down the streets of McKees Rocks.

I remember taking a trip with the Ironmen to Hazleton. We chartered a small plane in the Allegheny Airlines fleet; back then that was known as "Agony Airlines." Olander, who'd been in the Air Force, kept saying there was something wrong with the right engine on the two-engine plane. This did wonders for the spirits of some of the white-knuckled travelers who were used to traveling to road games on buses when they played at Slippery Rock, Edinboro or California.

As we were boarding the plane for the return trip from Hazleton, Olander noticed that it was a different plane. He said something to one of the pilots. "Oh, we had to get another plane," the pilot responded. "There was a problem in the right engine on the one we came up on."

When I served as the assistant athletic director at the University of Pittsburgh in the mid-'80s, the Panthers had a center named Tony Magnelli, who hailed from McKees Rocks. His father, "Toodles" Magnelli, was a dear friend of Foge Fazio, the Pitt coach. Fazio often visited a barbershop in McKees Rocks and had his hair cut by Joe Panucci or his brother Vince. Vince has owned and operated that barbershop for years. There are sports photos and memorabilia are over the walls. John Williams, a friend of mine who has been a banking executive in Pittsburgh, always went back to McKees Rocks to get his hair cut at Panucci's Barber Shop. The sports talk there was enthusiastic and intoxicating.

McKees Rocks turned out Ted Kwalik, who was an All-American at Penn State, and a Pro Bowl performer for the San Francisco 49ers and Oakland Raiders. The community turned out more than its share of fine quarterbacks, such as Chuck Burkhart, John Hufnagel and Chuck Fusina. Joe Panucci pointed out that Burkhart never lost a game when he was quarterbacking at Montour High School or Penn State. Bob Phillips, who coached at Montour, later joined Joe Paterno's staff at Penn State.

McKees Rocks sent Pitt some good quarterbacks in Davey Havern, Bob Medwid and Billy Daniels. I remember when I was working in Miami in 1970, I did a sports commentary each morning for WEEP Radio in Pittsburgh. I sneaked away one weekend with my wife Kathie to a retreat in the Florida Keys. I didn't even tell my mother back in Pittsburgh where I was going. One morning, I got a phone call from Joe Panucci and his buddies in McKees Rocks. They wanted to give me an exclusive that Bob Medwid was going to go to Pitt on a football scholarship. I couldn't believe those guys had tracked me down in the Florida Keys.

McKees Rocks has more characters per square inch than any other community in western Pennsylvania. When I was a student at Pitt, I loved to go there to spend a weekend evening at Mancini's where they had live and outstanding music entertainment. One of the musicians was named "Cincinnati" and the other "Collard Greens." The singer reminded me of a later diva, Diana Ross. When the wind was blowing hard, you could also smell the bread from the bakery of the same name. The smells and memories are still as keen as Tom Clements.

I knew his dad, Dr. Harry Clements, known to his friends as Doc Clements. He used to frequent Dante's, a bar-restaurant favored by Bobby Layne, Ernie Stautner and other Steelers, as well as sports media like Pat Livingston, Bob Drum, Myron Cope, Dave Kelly, Ed Conway, Tom Finn, Tom Hritz, Doc Giffin and Tom Bender, and characters with names like Funny Sam, in the Brentwood-Whitehall business corridor. It was owned and operated by Dante Sartorio, and his brother Bruno Sartorio. I still bump into the waitresses, Helen Kramer from Bon Air, and Hilda Phillips from Dormont, and we reminisce about those days at Dante's.

Doc Clements always showed up looking terrific. He was truly one of sportswriter Al Abrams' Dapper Dans. He favored dark suits, shiny ties, silver tie-bars on well-starched white dress shirts, a fluffed up handkerchief in his breast pocket, and sparkling cuff links. I was there, as a 19- and 20-year-old aspiring sports writer, to keep company with Cope and Drum more so than Layne and Stautner. It was part of my education, as much as my English writing classes at Pitt. There's nothing like it today.

Doc Clements was always boasting about his kids. He was so proud of them. They were Michael, Dave, Frank and Tommy, all standout schoolboy athletes. Frank was a better basketball player than Tommy when he starred at Stowe High School, and a good quarterback prospect as well. Frank suffered a disabling knee injury at the start of his senior year in a football game against rival Langley High School, and was never the same after that. Pitt honored its scholarship offer, but Frank never lettered at Pitt. He's now a Pittsburgh attorney. I bump into him and his brother Dave from time to time at Atria's Restaurant & Tavern in Mt. Lebanon. We swap stories about their dad and their kid brother, Tommy. They are as proud of him as their dad was. Whenever I'd go to the Primadonna Restaurant in McKees Rocks, the owner, Joe Costanzo, would always boast about the Clements as well. They are still hometown heroes.

"He's a good leader."

Tom Clements:

It's been great. It's nice to be back. We've had some good years since I've been here, and we hope to have some more. Tommy Maddox has an opportunity to prove that he's a first-rate quarterback in the NFL. It was Bill's decision to make the change from Kordell to Tommy. He made the final decision. The rest of the coaches can make recommendations and offer their suggestions, but the final call belongs to the headman. Some of the suggestions may be criticized, but you want to do what is in the best interest of the team. Last year it worked out very well.

When Tommy got hurt, Kordell came in and did well. Both handled it well. It was a lot harder for Kordell. He had been our team MVP and a Pro Bowl player the year before. It had to be a blow to his ego. He handled it like a true professional.

Our offense isn't a great deal different when Tommy's in there. Maybe 15 percent might be different. You still have the same core of plays. When Kordell is in there, you might do some things to take advantage of his running ability. With Tommy, there are some plays he likes better. You try to give him what he does best.

Tommy's intelligent. He's decisive. He has a quick release. He's accurate. He's a good leader. Those are good traits to have if you're going to be a successful quarterback in any league.

He can look at a defense, size it up, and get the ball out of his hand quickly. The openings aren't there long. You have to anticipate quickly to get it in there. Sometimes the receiver isn't open, but you have to put it where he can get it. You have to know your receivers' capabilities.

He does it fairly well. Sometimes he gets locked in on a receiver, like all quarterbacks do. Sometimes you have to throw it when the guy doesn't appear to be open. Terry Bradshaw was confident that Lynn Swann and John Stallworth would get the ball somehow. That gives a quarterback great confidence.

In general, Tommy doesn't force the ball. He throws a lot of interceptions on third downs. He's trying to keep the ball moving downfield. He knows that. He knows he can't always go for broke on third down. He learned as he went along.

On the field, the biggest thing is to be productive. That is a great way of getting people to accept you. As long as he gets the ball to the right people at the right time, they'll be happy. They don't care who's quarterbacking the team if the offense is working and the team is winning.

They saw him be critical of himself. He'd let them know it was his fault if he made a mistake, or did something he shouldn't have done. He's a good locker room guy. Before he was starting, he was helping a lot of the receivers, telling them things that could help them. He's a good team guy. He had a great year. We hope he can duplicate what he did this time around.

Tommy is what they call a rhythm passer. He goes back so many steps, turns and throws. The defenses will try to do something to break up his rhythm and that of his receivers. If they want to bring more pressure by bringing one or more extra rushers, that can also work in Tommy's favor. That means our receivers will be in single coverage. Our protection for the passer has been good the last two years. Tommy can make quick decisions and get it out of his hand quickly. His Arena Football experience helps him in that regard. You had to deliver the ball in a hurry in that game. Generally, he's an accurate thrower. If they blitz him, he's smart enough to know how to combat that.

He's a great guy to work with, a good team guy. He's receptive to what you try to do. He offers ideas, but Tommy does what he's asked to do, and he does it well.

We're solid with Charlie Batch as a quarterback, too. Charlie has started a lot of games in this league, and he has a lot of talent. He's been in playoff games as a starter. He has a good feel for the passing game. He has a good touch, and is a smart quarterback as well. He's a take-control kind of guy. Charlie is probably more of a classic drop-back guy, more similar to Tommy in that respect.

He knows how everyone should be running his routes. He's good at communicating with his receivers. He's an accurate passer as well. We've added a tight end or two, and we lost a wide receiver in Terance Mathis, and we've got some new guys. We should have a good group of receivers.

Everybody wants to be No. 1. That's understandable. That's the way it should be. At the same time, a backup has to accept that role and be prepared to play when called upon. You can't be disruptive. What you've got to do is prepare each week as if you're the starter.

Now the backup doesn't get to run our plays during the week. The backup runs the opposition's offense with the scout team. The starting quarterback gets the majority of reps at practice. The backups will get some, but not many. Most of his physical work is with the scout team.

We are fortunate to have the kind of multi-talented players that you can run some gadget plays. That's what makes our special plays so good. Hines Ward can catch the ball and run with it and block. Randle El can get open and catch the ball anywhere, and he can throw and run with it. He has done a lot of things. Plaxico is a big target. It gives us a lot of flexibility.

We may practice those gadget plays two or three times a week. But other teams have to spend a lot of time on those plays to be properly prepared for them. There's only so much time for practice each week, and if you can make teams spend time preparing for those special plays it's a real plus. It makes it harder for teams to prepare for us.

I was 33 when I gave up being an attorney. I have no

regrets at all. I had a lot of fun while it was going on. I was with some championship teams in college and in the pros. I was practicing as a lawyer for four-and-a-half years and I just decided I missed football. I missed the week-to-week excitement of getting ready for the game. I missed the competitive aspects of sports. I missed the instant feedback from what you did. I had great highs and great lows. Sometimes you have to try other things before you realize what you ought to be doing.

"He was the best bad-weather quarterback."

I was a big fan of Terry Bradshaw, so I enjoyed being there when he returned to town. It was great to have him come back and see how the fans reacted to it. When he was playing here I always thought he was a great player.

He was the best bad-weather quarterback I ever saw. He could throw perfect spirals in rain, sleet or snow. I was always a big Steelers fan and I got to see them become the best.

Tommy Maddox is a great story. It's kind of unbelievable when you think about it. He was a No. 1 draft choice, but he might not have been ready for it when he came out of UCLA after his sophomore season. He went to the Broncos when John Elway was still at his best. So Tommy struggled.

He got back into pro football at a lower level, and he regained his game and got an opportunity to get a second chance at the NFL. He was able to work his way back into a situation that was perfect for him. He got back in with a good team. It shows what perseverance and hard work will do for you.

It's always shocking when somebody as young as Mike Webster dies. He was very young. Anytime something like that happens it has an effect on people. He had been around this team for so long. There are a lot of people here who've worked here a long time. You have the same owners — the Rooneys — and that's unusual around the NFL these days. So the loss was still felt throughout the building.

Pittsburgh is a football town and such people are important in everyone's daily life. They were a part of your life.

Bill Cowher is a fine coach. It's good to work for him. He handles players very well. Players like playing for him. He is energized and prepared. He's successful. It's always good to be with a successful coach and a successful organization.

I like it. I have one of the better jobs in the league. Sure, I'd like to be an offensive coordinator and a head coach someday. Most everyone in the profession wants to advance.

I'd like to move up. I had an offer to be the offensive coordinator for Tom Coughlin with Jacksonville. I turned it down. As it turns out, I would have been there one year and I'd be out of work.

When Mike Mularkey was being interviewed for head coaching jobs this past year, I thought maybe I might move up here if Mike moved on. But we're a better team with Mike remaining on the staff. We have a better chance to win. I've got time. I'm happy with what I'm doing for the Steelers. My time will come.

Jim O'Brien

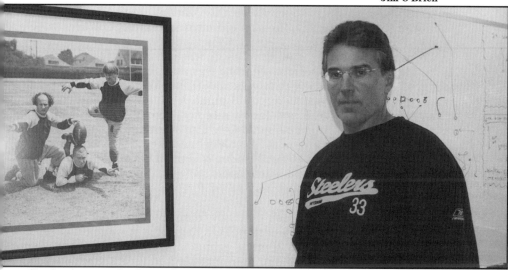

Steelers' quarterback coach Tom Clements is comfortable in his corner office at UPMC Sports Training Complex. Photo shows former McKees Rocks football team in action. Yuk, yuk, yuk. . .

Bill Cowher on a formula for winning football:

"You have to play good, smart situational football in this business if you want to become consistent and you want to win close football games. Part of winning close football games is not beating yourself and being able to be a good situational football team — showing poise, being smart when the game is on the line, making third downs, stopping them in the red zone, holding them to field goals, scoring when you get down there, not turning it over, not beating yourself and make them beat you. And if you do that with a degree of mental toughness and a degree of physical toughness, I think you've got a pretty good football team. And that's what we're in the process of getting our football players to try to understand."

Tommy Maddox
He cares about children

"My family is what my life is all about."

Tommy Maddox is a movie waiting to happen. Some of the scenes might have been shot on a perfect May day at the Southpointe Golf Club in Canonsburg, Pennsylvania. It's a picturesque setting, especially on this Monday, May 19, 2003. The sun was shining brightly, the sky was clear blue, temperatures were in the 65-72 degree range — perfect for a golf outing — and Tommy Maddox never stopped smiling when he was out on the course.

He looked more serious when he was standing tall in a banquet room afterward, listening to stories about The Western Pennsylvania Caring Foundation, sponsored by Highmark Blue Cross Blue Shield. It's a place for children and families to find counseling and comfort when they are grieving a personal loss. The stories were the sort that seize one's heart. Several of the Steelers had taken off as soon as they were finished playing golf, but Maddox remained behind for two hours of socializing with those in attendance.

He signed autographs and posed for photos with anyone who asked, and did several TV and radio interviews. Maddox couldn't have been more obliging. He's been that way from Day One since he signed with the Steelers two years earlier. He's just more in demand.

Maddox, all 6-4, 225 pounds, prides himself in his concern for children. He was listening and learning. He had recently announced the formation of his own Tommy Gun Foundation to raise money for children's charities. Most of the activities will be in Pittsburgh, and some in his hometown of Dallas.

Maddox was the headliner at the 10th annual Hoge-Bruener-Ward Celebrity Golf Classic for Children. He was there with Merril Hoge, Mark Bruener and Hines Ward, who all serve on the Caring Foundation Board and make appearances on its behalf. So was former Steeler Carnell Lake, whom Ward replaced when Lake left Pittsburgh to sign as a free agent with the Jacksonville Jaguars in 1999. These are some of the classiest individuals ever to dress in the Steelers' black and gold uniforms.

Maddox played with a foursome from Federated Investors and they were in the hunt all day and finished third in the best-ball tournament. He said he'd be coming back in two weeks to play in the Mellon Mario Lemieux Celebrity Invitational. His name appeared in the newspaper ads and highway billboards boasting the Lemieux line-up, right up there with such marquee names as Lemieux, Michael Jordan, Charles Barkley, John Elway, Stan Mikita and Dan Marino. Maddox had to like seeing his name alongside Elway and Marino. Both are sure bets for the Pro Football Hall of Fame.

George Gojkovich

George Gojkovich

Tommy Maddox is a lot happier as a Pittsburgh Steeler than he was during his struggling days with the New York Giants.

Courtesy of Pat Hanlon and New York Football Giants

I rode in a golf cart with Maddox at the wheel, and went 11 holes with him from No. 8 to No. 18 at the Southpointe Golf Club, and left his group when they still had four holes to go after a "shot-gun" start. Maddox was a most entertaining companion for everyone in the foursome he played with, as well as the foursome that followed.

He was the same good ol' boy he appeared to be during his previous two seasons with the Steelers. He agreed to allow me to accompany him without hesitation even though we had never talked before. We were together for 2½ hours — "my longest interview since I've been in Pittsburgh," he said. I didn't talk to Maddox once he got out of the cart to hit or talk with his foursome. He chipped in a 6-iron shot for an eagle on a par 5 hole on the first hole where I was watching him, the No. 8 hole. "You play well with a sportswriter watching," I told him.

After six holes in this scramble — everyone taking a turn at the best ball — his Federated Investors team was six under par and they didn't have a birdie. They had three eagles and three pars to their credit. It was a good start. I had hooked up with a winning team. Bill Cowher captained the foursome in front of us, and kidded with Maddox during delays.

When I related my experience with Maddox to another former Steeler quarterback, Cliff Stoudt, he said, "I'm glad to hear he was what you thought he would be. I met him several years ago at a golf outing and at a skiing event, and I was very taken with him. He just seemed exceptionally real, and I'm glad to see him in the position he's in."

Mel Blount had said that Maddox understood better than Kordell Stewart what it took to get the team and fans behind him.

It was an idyllic day to start with as the sun came out early and stayed the rest of the day. Like me, Tommy Maddox thought it was a nice way to spend a Monday. A lot of folks dread going to work on Monday.

I bumped into Bob O'Connor of Squirrel Hill and Greenfield, one of my favorite Pittsburgh politicians. I had seen him at Andy Russell's golf outing as well. "Don't you have a job?" he said, somewhat sarcastically, the way guys from Greenfield talk to guys from Hazelwood.

"This what I do for a living," I reminded O'Connor. "I do what I want to do. It sure beats the J&L."

"He epitomizes what this team is all about."
— Bill Cowher

Tommy Maddox was a magnificent story in the Steelers' 2002 season. His comeback captured the nation's attention and the hearts of Black & Gold fans. The 31-year-old Maddox was named the National

Photos by Jim O'Brien

Tommy Maddox is at ease holding 9-month-old Gabriel Costain, grandson of sports equipment representative Carl Dozzi, and in company of one of his favorite receivers, Hines Ward. Below, Mike Logan of McKeesport and Tommy's roommate Mark Bruener are honored at Thompson Run AA Sports Awards Night in West Mifflin.

"I think the Steelers have been very loyal to me. I don't think they owe me anything for what I've done before to help them with the salary cap."
— **Mark Bruener**

Football League's Comeback Player of the Year. And that was an understatement. He was the first Steeler ever to be so honored. The Tommy Maddox Story was the ultimate Feel Good Story. In mid-July, he won an ESPY award as the Comeback Athlete of the Year. Whereas Carmelo Anthony thanked himself when he was given an award, Maddox thanked his teammates.

His story would get a Hollywood flack fired for turning out such an unbelievable script. Maddox was a sports star with tremendous appeal in all respects. He was Hollywood handsome, resembling George Clooney, and humble, the way Pittsburghers have preferred their sports heroes. The combination made him the most appealing guy in town. Tommy Maddox was a stand-up guy, something critics of Kordell Stewart thought he wasn't.

One day, during an appearance on Dan Patrick's syndicated ESPN Radio show, Patrick asked him, "You've told your story so many times now. Do you ever embellish it a bit . . . just for fun?" Maddox came back, "The nice thing about my story is I don't have to."

And then he did. He got knocked out in the Steelers' seventh game of the season, at Tennessee. He lay unconscious on the field. Steelers teammates held hands and prayed when he was rushed from the Coliseum that day to Nashville's Baptist Hospital. He couldn't move his legs. Three weeks after suffering concussions to his head and spinal cord, Maddox was back in the starting lineup. Unreal. Maddox dismissed those who kept telling him he was writing a fairy tale story. "It's just a story," said Maddox. "Everybody has a story."

After missing two games, he returned to lead the team to a 3-1 finish and the AFC North championship. He got the Steelers to the second round of the AFC playoffs where they disappointed their fans by losing to the Titans in Nashville, 34-31 in overtime. That would have been so great if Maddox could have returned to the scene of his frightening collision and come away a winner. Steelers fans felt the team was good enough to get to Super Bowl XXXVII in San Diego.

Despite this disappointment, Maddox had made a lot of friends and followers for himself during the 2002 season, and offered hope for the future. He replaced Stewart on the regional covers of all the preseason football annuals.

"This whole year has been like a story-book tale," said Steelers offensive coordinator Mike Mularkey. "This will make a best-seller."

Terry Bradshaw of Fox Sports said it was the pro football story of the year. Bradshaw had made a comeback in Pittsburgh himself, showing up as an honorary captain for a nationally-televised Monday Night Football game with the Indianapolis Colts at Heinz Field on October 21, 2002. Bradshaw came back again, in early February of 2003, to kiss and make up with Coach Chuck Noll, the Rooneys, Steelers, the City of Pittsburgh, at a Dapper Dan dinner.

It's a toss-up as to which comeback stirred up Steelers' fans the most, but they were both positive stories that went down well with everybody. Fans, especially the women, were so concerned when Maddox was hurt in Tennessee. Fans, especially the women, were so pleased when Bradshaw, the self-professed Prodigal Son, was coming back to Pittsburgh to make peace with everyone.

Maddox made his first start at home in that same game against the Colts. He and Bradshaw exchanged pleasantries on the field. Maddox thought that was great.

"I'm happy for Tommy," said Bradshaw. "I saw when he came in for Kordell, and he made quick decisions and moved the ball around pretty good. Tommy's one of those kids everybody gave up on. He's revitalized himself. I love the way he's playing. He had a big arm and he's throwing the ball around, moving it around. I feel badly for Kordell because I like him, too."

Maddox had started his NFL career ten years earlier, leaving UCLA after his All-American sophomore season to sign with the Denver Broncos as their first round draft choice. He was to be groomed to replace John Elway at the helm in Denver.

Maddox was always a hot prospect. He was a standout quarterback in suburban Dallas, and a two-year starter at UCLA, indeed a first-team All-American his second season. He was born Thomas Alfred Maddox on September 2, 1971 in Shreveport, Louisiana.

It's amazing, when you think of it, how many Steeler quarterbacks have come out of Louisiana. There's Terry Bradshaw, David Woodley, Bubby Brister and Kordell Stewart. Brett Favre of the Green Bay Packers is from there, as is Peyton Manning of the Indianapolis Colts. Bert Jones of the Colts came out of Louisiana, too. Must be something in the water down there. A lot of great quarterbacks have come from Western Pennsylvania as well, so fans there appreciate a good quarterback when they see one.

High hopes were held for Maddox when he came to the NFL. It didn't work out that way, however. Maddox played for six different teams since then, two minor leagues, and was out of football for over three years, trying his hand at operating his own insurance agency in Dallas. He had short, but unsuccessful stints, with the St. Louis Rams, Atlanta Falcons and New York Giants. Dan Reeves, who drafted him at Denver, gave him chances to come back at both Atlanta and New York. Maddox couldn't stick with any of those teams. He had some horrible outings.

During his stint with the New York Giants, when he replaced Kent Graham on the roster, there was a headline in a New York City newspaper that read: "Maddox awful; Giants crumble." In a 37-27 loss to the Ravens, he was five-for-ten passing for 42 yards, with one TD and one interception, and he fumbled two snaps. In a 17-14 loss to the Philadelphia Eagles the year before, Maddox completed just six of 23 passes for 49 yards, and was intercepted three times. He took only one more snap the rest of the season, and he fumbled the exchange.

In 2000, Maddox made his return to football with the New Jersey Red Dogs of the Arena Football League. The following year, he joined the Los Angeles Xtreme of the XFL. He was the league's MVP in its only season. Bill Cowher gave him a chance that same year, and he made the team as a backup to Kordell Stewart. Cowher signed Maddox after seeing him throw just ten of the twenty passes he threw at a workout at the team's training facility on Pittsburgh's South Side.

Stewart won Pro Bowl honors and was the Steelers' MVP that season, and Maddox stood on the sideline with the clipboard in hand, helping as best he could. Stewart stunk out the joint at the start of the 2002 season, and was relieved by Maddox in the third game. Maddox led the Steelers to an overtime victory over the Cleveland Browns. If it were not for Tommy's heroics, the Steelers would have started the season with an 0-3 record and the season would have been over. Cowher made the dramatic decision to start Maddox in the fourth game at New Orleans. It was Maddox's first NFL start since Dec. 12, 1992.

I recall how Maddox had made an appearance on behalf of the Steelers in his first season with the team at the Coaches Corner luncheon series held at The Riverwatch Room of The Boardwalk Complex off Smallman Street in The Strip. The Steelers seldom send their top stars to this monthly get-together for sports fans co-promoted by the Pittsburgh Brewing Company and KDKA-TV.

Maddox was more prepared than most of the team's contemporary representatives at this luncheon. He was dressed appropriately, was well spoken, and had something to say. Maddox had a message. He was impressive. He was genuine, thoughtful, and appealing. I remember telling Dan McCann of Pittsburgh Brewing how impressed I was with Maddox, and how he was the sort of guy you wanted to see succeed. But he was a second-stringer and didn't stir the kind of response such an appearance would have had during the 2002 season. Even the ever-optimistic Maddox had no idea of what lie ahead for him and the Steelers a season later.

He was a happy camper, never complaining about his backup status. It beat selling insurance. His father had worked for AllState for 30 years. "Everybody knew it was not making me happy," Maddox said of his insurance business efforts. "But it was an eye-opener. You have to work for everything, then enjoy the ride; enjoy life.

"One day I was sitting in my office listening to a song by Steve Curtis Chapman called 'The Dive,' which talks about just diving in, having a leap of faith." After that, he attended a staff meeting, and found himself thinking, "What am I doing here?"

That got him thinking about a return to pro football. "I just remember thinking, man, I don't want to be doing this when I'm 45. It's nothing against the industry; it's nothing against them. Some people really have a knack for doing it and they love doing it. I just wasn't one of those guys." But his status was still shaky with the Steelers after that first season back. He didn't have many opportunities to show his stuff in 2001 as Stewart was having a great season.

The Steelers signed former Detroit Lions and Steel Valley High star Charlie Batch during the off-season. Maddox had to battle just to be the No. 2 quarterback. Personally, I thought Batch was the best of the bunch from what I observed at the Steelers' summer training camp at St. Vincent College and in some of the pre-season games. But Batch didn't get to play during the regular season schedule.

Maddox wasn't nearly as mobile as Stewart, but he seemed to see more on the field, found his receivers sooner, on the break, and gained the respect of the receivers because he made them more effective. He took the blame when he played badly, something Stewart wasn't good at doing, and he minimized his starring role. He said all the right things. He set all sort of Steelers' passing records.

"It's been a good year, but we still have a lot of work to do," he said after being named the league's Comeback Player of the Year. "I'm very excited about the opportunity Pittsburgh's given me, not only to be part of their organization, but also to go out there and play.

"I've said all along, early in my career, early in anybody's career, you worry about individual things and what comes your way. Really, at this point, the only thing that matters to me is making a successful run at the Super Bowl."

Cowher became his biggest booster. "The thing I like about him," Cowher said, "he has a good perspective on things. He doesn't get caught up in it, maybe because of where he has come from. I can't say enough about Tommy. He epitomizes what this team is all about."

"I'm just rooting for Tommy."
— Kordell Stewart

The Steelers released Kordell Stewart at season's end, and he signed with the Chicago Bears. Stewart was wearing a Chicago Bears' No. 10 jersey and singing the National Anthem before a Cubs' game at Wrigley Field the night before I was writing this chapter. Batch had been re-signed as a backup, but pledged to do his best to challenge for the No. 1 QB job. The Pittsburgh media made a big deal out of the fact that Batch would be making more money — with his $1 million-dollar contract — but Maddox never said anything about it. Batch had made a lot more starts in the NFL, and Maddox knew that it was unlikely he'd have sold enough insurance to make $800,000 or more for a year's work. Plus, now he has seven years credit toward an NFL pension that will be quite substantial. It's a nice insurance policy.

To his credit, Stewart said the right things when Maddox moved ahead of him in the Steelers depth chart. "Tommy's a good guy," said Stewart before Maddox made his first start in their native state of Louisiana. "He was supportive of me when I was in there, and even through the tough times, he was still supportive. So it's my opportunity to give back to him what he's been giving to me because he's been really genuine about it all. I'm just rooting for Tommy. I just really want him to go out and do well."

Hines Ward was supportive of Stewart and Maddox. Of Maddox, Ward said, "What does he have to lose? No one gave him a chance anyway."

For the record, here's what Maddox accomplished during the 2002 season:

Maddox completed 234 of 377 passes for 2,836 yards, 20 touchdowns, 16 interceptions and an 85.2 passer-rating. He set team records for pass attempts (57) and completions (30) for 325 yards in one game.

Maddox set a Steelers record with 473 yards passing in Week 10 versus the Atlanta Falcons, one of his former employers. He also set a career-high with four touchdown passes. With that game, Maddox broke the Steelers record of 409 yards passing in a game, set by Hall of Fame quarterback Bobby Layne on December 13, 1958, against the Chicago Cardinals. The Chicago Cardinals! That tells you how long that record has lasted. In Week 8, Maddox completed his first 11 passes, including two touchdown throws, in a 31-18 victory over the Baltimore Ravens.

The Steelers publicity office provided an interesting perspective on Maddox's comebacks. Maddox broke into the NFL in 1992. That was Bill Cowher's first year as head coach of the Steelers, and now he's the longest tenured coach with one team in the NFL. Rookie wide receiver Antwaan Randle El was 13 years old. Thirteen-year veteran receiver Terance Mathis was the only player on the Steelers roster who was in the NFL during Maddox's rookie season.

When he returned to play after suffering temporary paralysis at Tennessee, Maddox dismissed those who cited his courage by saying, "I don't want to make that seem less important, but it was another thing added to everything that's happened over the years."

"Just keep fighting and good things will happen."

Tommy Maddox:

The great thing about my story is that I don't have to embellish it. If I had written the script I'd have sold myself short. It's been unbelievable and a fun story, for me and my family.

The media has made a big deal out of me making less money as the starter than our backup Charlie Batch, but that's never been an issue with me. It's not something I'm comfortable talking about. I don't want to talk about it a whole lot.

No, I never instigated one conversation with anyone in the media about that. I've gone through too much stuff to worry about that. Charlie and I get along, as we did with Kordell Stewart when he was here.

Tommy Maddox looks reflective following practice session at Steelers' training camp at St. Vincent College in Latrobe.

Photos by Jim O'Brien

I'm excited about my opportunity to play quarterback for the Pittsburgh Steelers. I've talked to Mr. Rooney and to Bill Cowher and I know they'll do what's right. With all my special incentives, I'll make plenty of money.

I appreciate what you told me about what Mel Blount said about me, and why he's behind me. That's a huge compliment coming from a guy who's done as much as he has in his career. I'm just excited about being here. When you go through the things I've gone through you realize how fortunate you are to be in this situation. I try to live my life to let people know how excited I am.

You mentioned that Derek Jeter of the New York Yankees said the big money would not change him because his dad would kill him if he did. That's the same way with me. I was brought up the same way. I was taught to respect my coaches, respect my elders. That's the way I was raised. I'm excited about my future.

I've always had dreams. I have dreams about plays, about making big plays. Throwing a touchdown pass or throwing a touchdown pass late in the game. I don't worry about the story itself, and whether I can keep the dream alive.

You never know when your last day is going to be. You've seen the stories about Steelers and other star athletes dying just since I've been here. Early in my career I worried about the wrong things. I don't worry about things I can't control anymore.

I may not be as mobile as some quarterbacks, but I'd rather be a guy who can read defenses, and deliver the ball on the money to the right receiver. I love it when teams try to blitz me to get me out of my rhythm. They want to put pressure on me. They tried that in our last few games last year with Carolina, Tampa Bay, Baltimore, Cleveland and Tennessee. We averaged 31 points in those games and won four of them.

When they do that it means that Plaxico Burress, Hines Ward and Antwaan Randle-El are in single coverage. I love it when those guys are in one-on-one situations. I'll take pressure all day if I can get those match-ups.

I don't do anything out of my normal character to be a leader on this football team. Anything I do is heartfelt. I don't think about what to do to lead the team. You can't stage being a leader. It's who you are. I don't have to go out of character to accomplish that.

Last year I heard from guys who wouldn't return my calls the year before. Now they're saying, "I always knew you had it in you." So I can see through that stuff, and know how transparent that can be. Last year everything was in place for me to be successful.

John Elway was always an outstanding quarterback. But he was there in Denver for so long without winning a championship. Then they get Mike Shanahan in there, and they get Terrel Davis and a running game and they get back-to-back Super Bowls. Now Elway is respected as one of the great ones. Super Bowl rings can certify your greatness.

"I was excited the night Terry Bradshaw came back."
— Tommy Maddox

I'm a big fan of Terry Bradshaw. Terry and I live about two miles apart in Dallas. We were both born in Shreveport, Louisiana and we have the same birthday (September 2, 1971 for Maddox, September 2, 1948 for Bradshaw). I talked to him from time to time. I'm more of a Texas guy because our family moved there when I was five, almost six, years old. That's home. I know about some of the quarterbacks who've been with the Steelers, like John Unitas, Lenny Dawson, Bobby Layne, Earl Morrall, Bubby Brister, Neil O'Donnell and, of course, Bradshaw. I played golf with Morrall at Neil Lomax's golf tournament a few years back. He's an impressive guy. I'd like to stick around as long as Morrall did.

I was excited the night Terry Bradshaw came back to serve as our honorary captain when we played the Colts in a Monday Night football game at Heinz Field. That was my first start at home, so I'll never forget it. That was some response by the crowd to Terry's appearance. It was great to see him in that setting, to see him come back and get the kind of ovation he received. It was exciting for me. I threw a touchdown right before that. To talk to him on the sideline during the game was great. In the first half, one of the linemen tipped a pass I threw and it was picked off. As I came off the field, Terry grabbed me and said, "There's nothing you can do about that. You're playing great. Just keep playing that way." To hear that from a quarterback who's in the Hall of Fame and has four Super Bowl rings means a lot to me. It was real encouraging.

I know the great things that team accomplished.

I like playing in Pittsburgh. I tell people all the time it's more like a college atmosphere on a pro level. They live and breathe Steelers' football. They're so passionate. It's like college football in the South or Southwest. It's something that's unique about this city.

"It could be tricky at Three Rivers Stadium when the wind blew in off the lake."
— Bubby Brister

"You could feel it throughout the building."

I didn't know Mike Webster, but his death affected everyone associated with the Steelers. It was a real sad day for all of us. Even guys who didn't know him know what he stood for. Talking to Tunch Ilkin about him, I know that it was obviously a tough day for Tunch to lose such a good friend and someone who had been a mentor. Yes, it was a sad day. You could feel it throughout the whole building.

You say that Mike Webster never suffered a concussion, or was carried off the field like I was at Tennessee, but maybe he just never told them when he had a concussion. Years ago, you'd get knocked silly, and you might not know where you were during the next series, and then you'd come around and be okay. Back then you didn't tell people when you were hurt. That's like saying Muhammad Ali didn't lose many fights. He got hit in the head in every fight, though, and often in most of his fights. Mike took more shots than most. Taking that pounding at center, taking one head shot after another shot, is tough.

I tell people all the time that when you look at quarterbacks who are in the Hall of Fame you usually find that one or two of his receivers are in there, too. I'm fortunate to have five or six weapons to work with. We not only have a lot of great receivers, but we have good backs who can run and catch the ball. Now we have a good group of tight ends, too. The key to our success is that we have a great offensive line. So I'm at the right place at the right time. That's very much a blessing on my part. Terry Bradshaw always credits his supporting cast. He was surrounded by Hall of Fame football players.

I grew up with a great family. My parents are still together, still in love, still having fun. I have an older brother who was very athletic, and I got to follow him around. So I learned a lot from him and my parents.

Expectations were high in our home. My parents believed in discipline and they were strict about some things. But I didn't mind.

My dad, Wayne Maddox, was a senior vice president with Allstate Insurance Co. He'd done great.

My mother's name is Glynda. She's a homemaker . . . best cook in the South. I grew up in a great home. I didn't overcome a lot of odds. There was a lot of sports and a lot of love in our home.

My dad preached that you should work as hard as you can. He worked hard and he was an honest man. He grew up fighting the odds. He grew up in a log cabin in Laurel, Mississippi, and worked in the fields. He's the one who had to overcome adversity.

I always had an earlier curfew than all of my friends. I was urged to do the right thing and to stay out of trouble. I think parents are too concerned with how their kids are going to view them. I respected my father. I loved him then and I love him even more now. He's my best friend now. He wasn't my best friend when I was growing up. Growing up he wasn't a best friend figure. He was a father figure. We go golfing just about every Saturday when I'm home. My brother and a friend of ours go out together. We're too worried about whether our kids are going to like us. When we do that we're doing them an injustice.

"Someone is going to see you."

I try to help where I can. I'm trying to help Brian Dawson, for instance, who played quarterback at Washington & Jefferson. I've talked to him. He wants to play pro football, but he didn't get drafted. He's frustrated. I told him to keep playing. I told him to just play anywhere he can. Sooner or later, someone is going to see you. If I made a mistake, it's that I should have insisted on playing somewhere during my three years with the Denver Broncos. John Elway was our quarterback and I didn't get to play. I wanted to play in the NFL European League, but the Broncos wouldn't let me. I should have pushed for it. I was just sitting for three years. You get rusty. Arena Football and the XFL got me going again.

Since last season my world has changed quite a bit. Obviously it's been a little more hectic. But people closest to me know that my wife and our two kids are still the most important people in my life. I do what I can for good friends of mine. I try to accommodate as many requests as I can possibly do, but I don't want to be away too much during the off-season. I don't see enough of my wife and children during the season, so I want to make up for lost time. We have a home here in the North Hills and we have a home in between Dallas and Fort Worth. It works out good. My little girl went to school here in the fall, and in Texas in the spring. She seemed to like that. We have 12 homes on a cul-de-sac here, and there are 26 kids living there. So we have a lot of fun.

I was lucky here, too, to be paired with Mark Bruener as a roommate during my first two years here. We have a really good relationship. There aren't enough kind words I could offer about Mark Bruener. No one is more giving of his time than Mark, whether it's for charity causes or guys in the locker room, or with his family. He and his wife, Traci, are expecting their fourth child soon, and they're a great couple.

As great as Mr. Rooney is as an owner, it's a business. So I don't know what's going to happen to Mark as far as his future with the Steelers is concerned. We seem to have more tight ends than we need and there's a lot of money tied up in tight ends. A lot of people, including Mr. Rooney, don't want to see him go. But he'll be all right no matter where he goes because of what he's all about. He has a good future.

Anybody who's been successful has been in the right place at the right time. I came to Pittsburgh when they were looking for an extra quarterback. I threw to a tight end — ah, I knew you were going to ask me his name, but I don't remember — and I threw him about ten passes in each of two pass-and-catch sessions and then I talked to Mr. Cowher, Coach Cowher, in between.

I hadn't started a game in the NFL since 1992 when I got my first start here last year. I was away from the game so long they're going to have to rip my jersey away from me.

Have I pinched myself yet? Not really. I don't want to pinch myself . I might wake up. I hate to say this — I don't want it to sound like I'm boasting — but every time I go out on the field I expect to do well. If you talk too much about what's happening you might get distracted.

We didn't go to the Super Bowl last year. That's the ultimate goal. That's why you play. So I didn't achieve everything I wanted. So we'll try again. Someday, sooner or later, this will all be over, and they'll stop asking for me. I may as well enjoy it while it lasts. When I was selling insurance no one asked me for my autograph. So I tell these guys on the team not to complain about signing autographs

One thing I want people to know. I'm just a normal guy with a wife and two kids and I want them to grow up and be successful and love their parents and love their Lord. This is it. It's a blessing to have what we have. I have a strong feeling for children, my own as well as other children. That's why I have formed the Tommy Gun Foundation. Everyone knows how much I love the game of football. After all I've been through I know better than most that it's just a game. My wife and my children are most important to me.

"Obviously, every team has its own philosophy, but in Pittsburgh the football is what counts — football is what's king. I'm not against teams that have mascots, but that's not our philosophy. People get on me sometimes because we don't have dancing girls or mascots at our games. My response is we don't need those types of things. Good, entertaining football is what people come to see."
— Dan Rooney, Steelers chairman

"I don't want to go anywhere else."

Why has it jelled now? If I ever figured that out, I'd probably screw it up. So much of it is being in the right place at the right time.

So many times you see quarterbacks who are in the right situation and they sign somewhere else maybe for a million dollars more. And it's not the right situation and they don't play well, and all of a sudden they find themselves out of the league or not starting or whatever. I'm very comfortable here with the system. I don't want to go anywhere else. I've moved around enough already. I've done that before.

It's taken ten years to get here, and I'm going to enjoy it and savor every moment I can. I've seen the other side. That's why I enjoy this and appreciate this a lot more I'm going to play this game as long as I can.

Every time you put the uniform on, it's big. I went a few years and didn't get the opportunity to put a uniform on. I still get the same chills I got when I put my high school uniform on.

I've always enjoyed being the quarterback. I've always enjoyed playing the position. I like when guys are looking at me. It makes me feel good as a quarterback to know they are looking at you.

I've had a lot of people tell me when I get on the field, I'm a little bit different person than I am off the field. I think that's part of playing the game. You have to have a little bit of that in you. I don't do it for show, just whenever I feel the team needs a lift. Sometimes you do it for selfish reasons to kind of get yourself going.

The great thing about this team is that there are a lot of leaders in the locker room. Everybody at one point or another stands up and has something to say, and everybody respects everybody else.

"Sometimes I try a little too hard."

I never had anything happen to me like what happened in Tennessee. Sure, it was scary to get knocked out like that. I have played this game my whole life and never had anything like this happen before. You look at the odds, because this happened, does that mean it can happen again easier?

If I was worried about that to begin with, I shouldn't be playing this game. We've been a football family our whole lives. After I felt better after my setback in Tennessee, my dad told me to take it slow, to see what I could do and then to get back out there.

I have been through a lot to get to this point, so I am eager to continue to play here. Sometimes I try a little too hard to make the big play. That's something where you have to be patient and take what they give you and not feel like you got to win the game on every play.

We were successful being very aggressive for a little while. And I am probably aggressive by nature and I don't want to take that out. I don't want to get to where I'm passing up things, trying to be patient. You just got to know when to take down your shots, when to dump it down or when to punt.

I don't think if you talk to Bill Cowher that he wants me to alter my style. It's just two or three plays. Instead of making a bad decision you make a good decision. It might not look like a great decision because of the results, but, in the long run, it will be a good decision.

I think if you do your homework and you can pick up tips and see they're coming from this side or that side, I think it's an advantage for the offense. If you're on top of your game and they blitz, it's one on one. If your guy beats their guy and you can get him the ball, it's a big play.

I think about John Elway from time to time. It was a privilege to play behind John Elway in Denver. I learned a lot from him. You have to have the mentality that no matter what happens, just keep fighting and good things will happen. I would hope that he would be proud of me.

People have made a big deal about what I did in our overtime victory in Cleveland, but that was a team thing. It's always a team thing. I can't tell you everything I said in the huddle. But basically, I just told the guys that if there's anyone who doesn't think we can win, just go back in the locker room. "We are going to find a way to win," I told them.

I'm telling you, when a team sticks together it's a huge momentum lift. This team has done a good job of sticking together and not pointing fingers and finding a way to get it done at the end. That's what being a team is all about.

We have good receivers here who make me look good. Plaxico (Burress) is a very talented receiver. Hines Ward will catch everything near him, and he'll block for me, too. Antwaan (Randle El) is an exciting young talent who understands what I'm doing. He's been a quarterback. If the play doesn't work, he'll find a way to get open and he'll make something happen.

Plaxico has made some unbelievable plays for us and he'll continue to make some unbelievable plays for us. He's a game-breaker. So is Hines and Antwaan. You want to get the ball in their hands as much as you can.

> *"Tommy is a rebel, a real gunslinger.*
> *That's why we call him Tommy Gun."*
> **— Hines Ward**

"I always knew I had the talent to play."

I think that everyone wants to talk about the past and I've said all along that the past is the past. I mean ten years ago seems like another lifetime ago. This is kind of my second career and I plan on being here as long as I can.

I believed in my heart that I could still do it. In my heart of hearts, I always knew that I had the talent to play and still had the ability to play, so I wanted to keep giving it a shot. I tell people all the time that earlier in my career, if I had gotten a chance to start for two years and it didn't work out, it would have been easier to walk away. But I just never felt like I had that opportunity.

Anybody in any profession learns more from the times they are down than the times they are up. I wouldn't want to go through it again, but the things that I've gone through have definitely helped me. If not football-wise, then being a better person, a better man, a better husband.

I've got a great wife. I've got two kids at home — that's my life. When I leave here and go home, the kids don't care what I do. They just want me to play with them and ride bikes with them. My wife wants me to be a good husband. They help me keep things in perspective.

If it wasn't for my wife, I wouldn't be able to do this. She's packed the kids and the family up and moved across the country three or four times. When I came here and was going to give it another shot, I know there was a part of her that probably didn't want me to, because she had seen all the ups and downs. And she didn't want me to go through that again, but she said, "If that's what you feel like you want to do then I'm OK with it, and I'll support you and let's go." To have that kind of confidence and stability at home really helps.

I think I've learned how to be a better person, a better husband and a better father. I respect things more and I don't take things for granted.

Everybody keeps trying to make me an old man. I've been around a long time because I started when I was 20. I have a lot of football ahead of me. I'm going to play this game until somebody kicks me out and tells me to go home.

Bill Cowher commenting on Tommy Maddox's future prospects:
"Tommy, my God, you look at his age!
But selling insurance must not have taken a
whole lot out of him.
He may have a lot more years left."

Jim O'Brien

Snapshot:

John Elway, Retired Denver Broncos quarter-back who was a teammate of Tommy Maddox when Maddox came into the NFL in 1992, President and CEO of Colorado Crush of Arena Football League interviewed at the Mellon Mario Lemieux Celebrity Invitational at The Club at Nevillewood, June 7, 2003

"Tommy Maddox is a good kid. I'm happy for him. Sometimes it's a matter of being at the right place at the right time. That's why I think the Arena Football League is good for young quarterbacks, and to develop receivers and players who need some seasoning. He's a great athlete. I don't think people realize what a great athlete he is. He's quite a basketball player and a good golfer, too. A lot of it is maturity. Some quarterbacks don't mature until they're 26, 27 or 28. Everyone's excited for Tommy because of the kind of guy he is. It wasn't easy for him coming to Denver and tak-ing my place. It was the same for anybody here taking Terry Bradshaw's place behind center."

Charlie Batch
Hometown hero in Homestead

"You are never guaranteed tomorrow."

I started working on this chapter about Charlie Batch back in February of 1999. At least that was the idea. I was writing a book called *Hometown Heroes* and Batch seemed like a good fit. He grew up in Homestead, Pennsylvania and had been a star quarterback at Steel Valley High School. He went off to rewrite the passing records at Eastern Michigan University and was drafted by the Detroit Lions. The Lions traded three draft choices to the Miami Dolphins to move up in the second round of the 1998 draft to nab Batch. He became a starter in his rookie season.

I had read about Batch in stories written by my buddy Norm Vargo in his sports column in *The Daily News* in McKeesport, just across the Monongahela River from Homestead and Duquesne, as well as in Batch's hometown weekly, *The Valley Mirror*, where I write a column.

He was 6-3, 220, handsome, with a strong arm and he carried himself in a noble manner. I was rooting for him. I had already interviewed two other great quarterbacks from western Pennsylvania for *Hometown Heroes*, Johnny Lujack of Connellsville who had won the Heisman Trophy at Notre Dame in 1947, and Dan Marino, who grew up in South Oakland, about two miles from the University of Pittsburgh where he gained All-America honors. Lujack and Marino both went on to star in the National Football League.

Marino had been a boyhood hero of Batch. Now he'd be in a book with Marino and Lujack, and Tony Dorsett and Arnold Palmer and Billy Conn, some of the area's all-time superstars. At least that was the idea.

I had seen a story about Batch that was written by Amy Whitesall in *The Detroit News*. It was encouraging. She wrote that Batch "is cool, smart and a quick learner. And, as a bonus, he's a truly decent human being. That shouldn't be an issue, but it is in pro sports these days."

I telephoned Jack Giran, who had been Batch's football coach at Steel Valley High School and was now the school's activities director, following in the footsteps of another old friend, Lou "Bimbo" Cecconi, the pride of Donora who had played and coached at Pitt and was an assistant on John Michelosen's staff when I was a student at Pitt in the early '60s.

I could talk to them about Batch. That would be easy. I was explaining to Giran what I had in mind. Giran gave me a phone number for Batch's mother, Lynn Settles, who had recently moved to Roberta Street in Munhall to a home her son had bought for her. She was a secretary at Filtech in Homestead.

435

As I was talking to Giran, a good guy who had always been most friendly with me, I said I needed some background on what was going on in Homestead and the Steel Valley during Batch's schooldays, so I could provide some insights into what Batch had sidestepped on the way to sports stardom.

"I remember a teenage girl getting caught in the crossfire of some young gang members," I said to Giran, "and getting killed just by being at the wrong place at the wrong time."

There was silence on the line . . . for a long time.

"That girl," began Giran, slowly, "was Charlie's sister."

Now I was silent. That was unbelievable, that by accident I'd come up with the connection. I was also more eager than ever before to have a conversation with Charlie Batch. At least that was the idea.

I later learned that in 1995, several months after Charlie Batch had a breakthrough season at Eastern Michigan that his 16-year-old sister had been shot and killed in a gangland crossfire while walking down the street with school friends. She was an innocent bystander. Her name was Danielle Settles, so I wouldn't have linked her to Charlie Batch. A 14-month-old boy was shot in the head and killed in a drive-by shooting incident at a gasoline station in West Homestead in early January of 1997. That stayed with me, too. Another errant shot. It happens in my hometown of Hazelwood these days, too. It happens in Homewood, The Hill, Greenfield and Garfield.

With the support of his mother, Batch stayed in school and continued working toward his dream of playing in the NFL. It was a good story. His father had abandoned the family when Charlie was just two years old. Charlie suffered kidney damage while working a summer painting job before his sophomore year at Eastern Michigan. Treatment forced him to miss the season. He had overcome that setback as well.

The NCAA granted him a rare sixth season of eligibility because he missed that season with an illness. During that sixth year, Batch was able to take classes in a master's program for social work at Eastern Michigan.

Asked what caused his kidney problems, Batch disclosed, "It was a summer job in 1993. I was working for a painting company and whatever it was in the paint we were using really messed up my kidneys. There were three other people who had similar problems. One of them required a kidney transplant, and the other required dialysis. This was serious stuff. I was lucky to have my problem detected early, and the medication cleared up my problems."

He had to sit out his first year because he was a Prop. 48 recruit. His SAT scores were substandard. Pitt had recruited Batch ardently, but backed off when his test scores didn't improve to a passable state. He wasn't the first quarterback Pitt backed away from because of poor test scores. They had turned away Johnny Unitas back in 1950, letting him go to the University of Louisville. The Steelers would cut Unitas from their training camp squad in the summer of 1955.

Batch became a starter with the Lions in the third game of his rookie season, replacing Scott Mitchell in the lineup for Coach Bobby Ross. Batch became an instant star. He was named the NFL's Player of the Week and NFC Player of the Month honors in October of 1998.

I knew Bill Keenist, the vice-president of communications, sales and marketing with the Detroit Lions. Keenist came from Pittsburgh and had worked in public relations once upon a time with the Penguins. He said he would speak to Batch about doing an interview with me. For some reason, it never happened. Keenist later apologized when I said I'd been unable to link up with Batch. He said he'd speak to him again. I thought I'd write about Batch in a followup book.

A year later, I tried once more. Batch had been back home and had spoken to students at his old elementary school. He read from a Dr. Seuss book, *All The Places You Will Go*, at Barrett Elementary. I knew his roots were important to him.

I got hold of his mother, Lynn Settles, and she said she'd help me. In fact, she said that Charlie was coming home soon for a visit. She'd get back to me. Within a week, Mrs. Settles called me and told me she had spoken to her son. He would see me when he came home the following week.

She told me to meet him at Damon's in the Southland Shopping Center along Rte. 51 in Pleasant Hills, near the Century III Mall in West Mifflin. She said he'd be with some of his boyhood friends who had been with him out in Detroit. She said he'd have time to talk to me then. It seemed that everything was set.

I showed up at the appointed hour at Damon's. It's a sports bar-restaurant that prides itself in its barbequed ribs and steaks, as well as the abundance of TV monitors and big screens showing sports events all across the country. I checked out some of the framed photographs on the wall and took some notes. I don't have those notes anymore, but remember that Stan Musial and Roberto Clemente and Mario Lemieux were among those pictured on the wall. There were other sports stars as well.

Batch and his buddies were down front, right below the biggest movie-size screen in the dimly-lit joint. They were eating an early dinner. It was around 4 o'clock. I had never spoken to Batch before, so I approached him at his table, and introduced myself. He didn't smile or say much. He didn't introduce me to any of the other four fellows who were with him. They weren't looking to be introduced. Their eyes were on the barbequed ribs on their plates. You can bet that Batch was picking up the tab.

Batch didn't ask me to have a seat. In fact, he hardly spoke to me at all. I told him I'd wait for him. I sat down at a seat at the next table. A few minutes passed, and he paid me no mind. I was uncomfortable as hell. I got up and told Batch I was going to the back of the room, and would wait for him there.

I took a seat near the bar so I could keep an eye on Batch and his buddies. Then his mother came into the room with a gentleman friend. I introduced myself to him, and shook Mrs. Settle's hand. I told her I had spoken to her son, but that he hadn't joined me. I said I needed to speak to him alone.

Mrs. Settles went down to see her son. She spoke to him briefly. Then she returned to the table where I was sitting, making small talk with her friend. She said, "Charlie's tied up with his friends for dinner," she said, somewhat apologetically.

"Can you do this some other time?" she asked.

I told her I had made this trip specifically to see her son and to interview him. I couldn't understand why he wouldn't talk to me since it was a scheduled meeting.

Mrs. Settles seemed displeased with my inquiry. She got defensive, saying her son simply couldn't do it that day.

I showed her a copy of *Hometown Heroes* I had brought with me. I had already signed it to Charlie, mentioning that he was going to be keeping good company in a sequel to be called *Glory Years*. I was upset and it showed. So was Mrs. Settles.

Now she was unhappy with me. "I don't like your attitude," she said. She had no sympathy for my plight.

I turned to leave, and then I realized that I had this signed book for Charlie Batch. I made a U-turn and went down to his table. I handed him the book and expressed my disappointment. I had never had an experience quite like this in a lifetime of interviewing sports personalities. Charlie could have cared less. He made no attempt to change my mind about leaving Damon's.

I departed Damon's with the worst feeling in my stomach. I felt as though someone had just kicked me in the groin. If Charlie Batch wanted me to feel bad, he had succeeded and then some. It was an awful experience. Charlie Batch had blown me off. I couldn't understand what had gone wrong. There must have been some miscommunication about what I was seeking in whatever Mrs. Settles told her son beforehand.

I had been turned down for an interview by Kordell Stewart because it wasn't Wednesday, the only day he did interviews with the Pittsburgh media, but that was a different matter. This was a scheduled interview. Batch had told his mother he would do it.

I like to root for hometown heroes, but Charlie Batch had just lost a fan. He was on a short list of sports personalities I wanted to see fail. Hey, I grew up in Hazelwood, just across the Monongahela River from Hays and West Homestead. My father, brother — both named Dan O'Brien — and two uncles, Rich and Robbie O'Brien, had all worked at Mesta Machine Company in West Homestead. Some of my boyhood friends worked there, too. This was personal. This hurt. Have you ever heard of Irish Alzheimer's Disease? You forget everything but a grudge.

It didn't seem to sidetrack Charlie Batch. In 2000, he signed a contract with the Lions that included a signing bonus of $10 million. Not bad for a suspect student out of Steel Valley High School. It sure

During his days as a Detroit Lions' quarterback, Charlie Batch came back to Munhall to visit his mother and paid a visit to his old school, Barrett Elementary School, to kick-off "Read Across America" program. Batch read from the Dr. Seuss book *All The Places You Will Go.* He said hello to, left to right below, his football coach Jack Giran, Steel Valley High School principal Aldine Coleman and former Barrett principal Doris Hyde.

Photos courtesy of Tony Munson and The Valley Mirror

beat working in the mills of Homestead, but then Mesta Machine Company and U.S. Steel were long gone. There were no mills along the Mon anymore.

Nowadays the young people have to settle for mostly minimum wage jobs at all the eateries and stores at The Waterfront.

"I was behind the eight ball."

In June of 2002, the Lions released Charlie Batch. Good, I thought at the time. That serves him well for what he did to me. The Lions were going with Mike McMahon and Joey Harrington, two recent draft picks. Batch was released in part to save money under the salary cap, and there had been a change in management. The Lions waited until after June 1 in order to divide up the hit between the 2002 and 2003 caps. It was good for the Lions, but limited Charlie's chances of catching on with another NFL team at favorable terms.

"I was behind the eight ball," said Batch.

Kevin Colbert, the Steelers general manager, had come to the Steelers from the Lions where he was the director of pro scouting. He had known enough about Batch to believe he could help the Steelers in a backup capacity. Kordell Stewart was the Steelers' starting quarterback and Tommy Maddox had been one of his backups. Tee Martin was still in the Steelers' fold as well. The Steelers looked solid behind center. Colbert had been with the Lions when Batch was the third quarterback picked in the 1998 draft, behind only Peyton Manning and Ryan Leaf. Remember Ryan Leaf?

Bill Cowher had seen enough of Batch up close to be impressed as well. In a nationally-televised Thanksgiving Day game, the rookie Batch led the Lions to a 19-16 overtime victory against his hometown Steelers in 1998. He threw for 236 yards while extending the number of throws without an interception to 94. Hundreds of Charlie Batch and Steelers fans from Homestead had made the trip to watch the game in the Pontiac Silverdome. Batch was big at Joe Chiodo's bar and restaurant at the end of the High-Level Bridge.

His mother was among those who made the trip. She attended the Lions' home games and many of the team's road games.

That meant a great deal to Charlie Batch. "It was just the two of us for a long time," Batch said. "We always shared everything and I'm glad we can share this.

"The things that happened in our family inspired me to work harder. You can't take anything for granted. You are never guaranteed tomorrow so you better make the most of today."

Batch had met and shaken hands with Dan Rooney and Bill Cowher at the scouting combine workouts in Indianapolis prior to the 1998 draft and ranked it as a major thrill.

"He's a mobile quarterback," Cowher had commented about Batch before that Thanksgiving Day meeting with the Lions. "He's throwing the ball well, making good decisions. I've just been impressed with the way he's handled himself, the poise he's shown in the pocket, his decision-making process, the accuracy of his throws. He does have a strong arm."

Soon after Batch became a free agent, the Steelers signed him to a one-year contract as a backup quarterback for a million dollars. It was a bargain basement price for a quarterback with his background.

So now Charlie Batch was a Steeler. What was I to do now? I saw some TV interviews of Charlie Batch and liked what I saw and heard.

I went to the Steelers training camp at St. Vincent College in Latrobe late in August, 2002. I had an up-close view of Batch doing some TV interviews and liked what I was seeing. He handled himself well. So I thought it might be a good idea to kiss and make up with Charlie Batch. Hey, if Terry Bradshaw can come back to Pittsburgh to kiss and make up with Chuck Noll and everybody else, so could I make peace with Charlie Batch.

I introduced myself to Charlie Batch on the football field, told him about the difficulty and disappointment of our first meeting. I could tell right away that the day had stayed with me longer than it had with Batch. But he agreed that a fresh start would be fine with him. We made a date to talk on August 23, the last day of training camp.

Since then, Tommy Maddox took the starting assignment away from Kordell Stewart, and at season's end the Steelers released Stewart and allowed him to sign elsewhere as a free agent. He ended up catching on with the Chicago Bears. Batch signed another contract to stay with the Steelers at $1 million for the year, a little better than Maddox was making. Batch had a lot more NFL starts under his belt than Maddox, though, and had worked his way up the salary ladder over a longer and more rewarding period of time. It should not have factored into any quarterback controversy, but the local media made an issue out of it just the same. They wouldn't let the issue die.

Now Batch was a backup to Maddox, but more in the chase than ever before to realize a dream to be the starting quarterback for the Pittsburgh Steelers. He didn't play in any regular season games in 2002, but that would probably change in 2003. When we spoke a year earlier, Batch was saying all the politically correct things about his backup status with the Steelers, but I knew that deep in his heart he wanted to be No. 1.

One summer later, Batch said of his bid to start ahead of Maddox, "Right now, he's the guy, and I have to actually try to get him out of there."

While visiting good friends Ruth Ann and Ralph Papa — he's the regional president of Citizens Bank — at their beautiful home in the Gray Oaks development in Franklin Park, a suburb to the north of Heinz Field, my wife Kathie and I saw the palatial home of Charlie Batch.

Let's just say it's a nice neighborhood and a long way from his humble boyhood home in Homestead. Charlie Batch should count his blessings every day. I asked him if he had ever heard about Bobby Layne, and he had. I should have asked him if he ever heard of Tobin Rote. Now there's a great name for a quarterback.

"You always want to compete to be the guy."

Charlie Batch:

This was always the dream. When you grow up in Homestead and you dream of playing in the National Football League someday, it's playing for the Pittsburgh Steelers.

I saw them play at Three Rivers Stadium. Even when I was in Detroit, I was still a Steelers fan. I still followed them to keep up with what they were doing, how they were coming along.

When I was in high school, I was a big fan of Dan Marino. He had come from the same Pittsburgh area. Just being able to watch him and knowing he came from a nearby neighborhood was an inspiration for me.

I believe in myself. When I go in the huddle, I just want my teammates to believe in me, that I will get the job done.

After being a starter for most of my four seasons in Detroit, this was different to be in Pittsburgh as a relief pitcher. When I step on the field here, all the starters are looking at me. I have to prove to these guys that I can play. You're going through training camp and you're doing everything, but those guys are thinking, "Yeah, we knew you played in Detroit, but you didn't do it here." In that sense, I have to prove to these guys, as well as the coaching staff, if I'm put in that position, you can trust me on that field.

I have to know what all 11 guys are doing. Not only do I have to know my assignment, I have to times that by 10 because I have to know everybody else's assignment. That part is going to come a little slower: I've been able to absorb the majority of it.

You already know how to play the game, now you want to minimize the thinking part of it and your natural instincts take over. With me, it's kind of like the defensive coverages are the same, you may call it different, but it's all the same thing. You go out there, try to pick it up and compete and do it that way.

I'm happy just to be here. Considering my family's history, you just don't let the outside world confuse you. A lot of things can make you go down the wrong road. You are

Courtesy of Bill Keenist and Detroit Lions

Charlie Batch was starting quarterback with the Detroit Lions. Batch muses over his situation as reserve with hometown Pittsburgh Steelers during their summer stay at St. Vincent College in Latrobe.

Jim O'Brien

never guaranteed tomorrow and that is the attitude I take, and I am going out there living every day to the fullest.

Obviously, the Steelers were not looking for somebody to come in and compete with Kordell for the No. 1 job. I came in with that understanding. But there's no reason for me to be here if I'm not going to compete at my best. That's what I'm about. That's how I got here in the first place.

In your mind, you know what you have to do. I only know one way to compete, or to prepare, and that's as a starter. You always want to compete to be *the* guy.

You shouldn't be out there unless you want to be the starter. I want to be the next guy to go in. I understand, from the offensive standpoint, that there's only one ball. Only one guy can have it at a time. It's no different from what Shaq and Kobe go through with the Lakers in the NBA.

When it comes to running the ball the guy on this team is Jerome Bettis. Everybody understands that. Given an opportunity, if Kordell or Jerome get hurt, you want to be ready to do the job.

I do know the situation. It was that way when I first reported to the Lions when the starter was Scott Mitchell. I'm not used to having to take a back step to anybody. I'm leaving it to everybody else to worry about it.

When I'm in there, I behave like a starter. What can I say? You can't talk to everybody the same way. You can't do it.

I understand that injuries happened. I got hurt and lost my job because of injuries in Detroit. I want to stay healthy here and be ready when it's my turn, whenever that comes.

I know the name Bobby Layne. I know he played for the Lions and then came to the Steelers. He's the last quarterback to win a championship for the Lions. That I know. They still talk about him in Detroit, the way they still talk about Terry Bradshaw here. They're both in the Hall of Fame, so you can understand why the fans are so fond of them.

I don't know a lot of history, but I know about that.

Charlie Batch has always been in sports, always competing. As a kid, I loved the Steelers. So this is great to be with them.

I knew about Danny Marino and I knew about Randall Cunningham in Philadelphia. Marino had the arm and the quick release and could pick you apart, and Cunningham could keep you guessing. No one ran any better than him. Now they have Donovan McNabb and he does the same thing.

The Steelers tell everyone I was brought here as a backup. I know they have to say that. But it's hard for me to accept it. You have to keep your own goals and you have to stay out of trouble. As long as you play sports, you want to be a winner. There's no reason to approach it any differently.

My first concern is how can I help this team win. If I can do that then I will have a purpose here. I missed the mini-camps this year (2002), so I am playing catch-up to learn the system. But I know how to play in this league and I'm not worried about that.

I know I can play.

I was cut in Detroit because of the salary cap. I knew back then that I was going to be released, but I couldn't talk to any other team about a move.

The Steelers' history is important to me. I grew up as a fan. For years, as a Lion, I was still a Steelers fan. It was hard for me to break that. It was hard to change unless we were playing the Steelers.

I liked Joe Montana, too. I liked the way he played calm under any situation. I didn't emulate him, but I liked the way he was going to get the job done. We all have our own unique style. It didn't matter whether it was the first or fourth down, Montana would make the play.

With Marino, I liked the way he threw the ball. He had a different style. He wasn't that mobile, but he knew how to slip the rush. He said, "I'm not going to beat anybody with my feet." His release was special. The ball was in his hand and then it was in the hands of the right receiver. Bam. Like that.

With the brand of football that's been played here, the running game is more important that it might have been with Miami, or with San Francisco. But I think I can run this offense, which is more balanced, and run it well.

The quarterback should expect to be the marked man. You get to take the ball every play. I'm playing for the Steelers, not for Charlie Batch. When I was younger it might have been the other way, but I'm going to try and please Bill Cowher now. I'm not playing for personal praise anymore.

I enjoyed my time in Detroit. I was treated well. The only disappointment was not being able to lead the Lions to a championship. That's one of the reasons I came here. I thought this team had a chance to win a championship.

"I know the power of a dollar."

When you're not playing much, you have to push yourself to stay sharp, and to be properly prepared. I'm making good money to do what I do. I went through most of my life without much money, and I still see myself as not realizing I have that much money. Just because I have a lot of money now doesn't mean I have to spend it. I know what I have and I want to keep it. I've taken good care of my mother and I'm taking care to make sure I have a good life. I bought my mother a house she wanted in Munhall.

I know the situation where I grew up and I don't want to go back to that. I know the power of a dollar. When you start asking for a lot of stuff you run into trouble. I knew what I could ask for. I never asked my mother for too much because I knew how hard she worked to make the money she had. She always did her best by us.

I remember one day I went to Century III Mall and I didn't have any money. I saw something I really liked at Kaufmann's and I wanted it. She said, "No." I knew she had just gotten paid so I couldn't understand why she wouldn't get it for me. I didn't always get what I wanted.

I think I spent half of my first paycheck on my mother. I asked her, "What do you want?"

I wanted to show my sense of gratitude.

Our relationship is very close. We've done a lot together. I don't feel like I'm talking to my mother, but to a friend or a sister.

When I'm on the phone talking to my mother, nobody knows I'm talking to my mother.

I like to go back to my hometown. I like what Bill Campbell has done to clean up the football stadium for Steel Valley High School. I think it's named in honor of his father. He was the school superintendent in Homestead, I'm told, and his kids, Bill and Jim, did well in football and in life. I feel the same way about The Waterfront.

To see it now is amazing. I saw it all torn down, when the mills were leveled. That caused a lot of sadness throughout the community. But this is better than abandoned steel mills like they still have in McKeesport. My grandfather, Robert Bolden, worked at U.S. Steel.

When I saw the mills closing up and being torn down, I said, "Damn, I'm getting out of here." It looked like the death of a town, but instead it has been the birth — after a long dry spell — of a new town.

You're always thinking to yourself about the dream, and how exciting it is to play in a stadium. You also know at some point that it all comes to an end.

So I want to take advantage of this opportunity. I always wanted to play for the Steelers. It's up to me to show Coach Cowher that he can count on me, that I can do it. My mother was happy that I came here.

What do you want people to say about you? It's one thing to be as great as Marino as a quarterback and yet have people say you couldn't have been that great because you never won a championship. That's what they said about Jim Kelly. I think they were wrong.

446

Will they say you didn't have a strong arm? Or that you weren't the toughest guy? How do you want to be remembered? I don't want personal stats to measure me or my contribution. I want to be remembered as a winner, in every way. The ultimate dream would be starting for the Steelers and leading them to another Super Bowl victory. That would be a dream. Will it happen? I don't know. I don't have to prove I can play. I just have to prove I can play with my new teammates.

I don't have anything negative to say about my situation. I want to live my life to the fullest, that's all. When the word got out that I had signed here, Kordell was one of the first to call me. He said, "Welcome aboard!" So far here, everybody has been trying to help everybody out. I have to help the Steelers get ready for every game by giving them the best possible look at what the other team's quarterback will do, and what their offensive schemes will look like.

I think the fans are spoiled here. They have had so much success. Compare what's happened here to what's happened in Detroit. We had one of the greatest runners ever in Barry Sanders, but the Lions couldn't win a championship. The fans here have a sense of arrogance about them because they expect to be winners. Like we know we're good.

In Detroit, they were hoping they'd be in the playoffs.

In Pittsburgh, they're still not satisfied unless you win the Super Bowl.

Jim O'Brien

Charlie Batch works hard at Steelers' summer training camp at St. Vincent College to compete for top quarterback position.

Antwaan Randle El
Triple-threat delight

"Do you believe in yourself?"

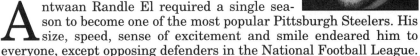

A ntwaan Randle El required a single sea-
son to become one of the most popular Pittsburgh Steelers. His
size, speed, sense of excitement and smile endeared him to
everyone, except opposing defenders in the National Football League.

He's 5-10, 185 pounds, so more fans can identify with him than,
say, Plaxico Burress, one of the biggest receivers in the NFL at 6-5,
230 pounds. All of a sudden, a lot of young Steelers' fans started showing up at the shopping malls wearing an official black Steelers jersey
with RANDLE EL across the shoulders. His name was different and
catchy.

He was a triple-threat back, a throwback to an earlier era, a
modern-day Bill Dudley, who could run, pass, catch and, if necessary,
even punt the ball. Surely, he'd be a fast learner if there were ever a
personnel shortage in the defensive secondary. He can do all these
things, and he does them with great zeal. Like Hines Ward, watching
him is fun because he seems to be having such a great time. He is
intelligent and pleasant, two pluses.

Randle El put pizzazz in the Pittsburgh offense. Mike Mularkey,
the team's offensive coordinator, went to bed at night dreaming up
new schemes for employing Randle El. It was a mutual admiration
society. Randle El is, indeed, a coach's dream. He was an outstanding
quarterback at Indiana University in the Big Ten, so he's a quick
learner, and he loves to play the game. Playing in the NFL is a dream
come true. He put excitement in the games, as when he returned a
kickoff against the Cincinnati Bengals for a 99-yard touchdown on
October 13, 2002. It was the second longest in Steelers' history, behind
Don McCall's 101-yard scamper in 1969. He ran and threw passes
from reverses. As the Steelers' slot receiver — the third receiver in
multiple-receiver alignments — he caught 47 passes for 489 yards and
two touchdowns. He averaged better than seven yards a carry on 19
runs, mostly end-around plays. He returned kickoffs and punts with
equal abandon.

He wasn't perfect. He committed some costly fumbles, and that's
something he was hoping to avoid in his second pro season.

He's an outstanding representative for the Steelers in public
appearances. He dresses appropriately for a business luncheon, and
he comes prepared. I caught him in October of his rookie season as the
featured speaker at a Coaches Corner Luncheon sponsored by the
Pittsburgh Brewing Company and KDKA-TV at the Riverwatch Room
of the Boardwalk Complex in the city's Strip District.

He delivered a message in a talk entitled "Faith, Family and
Football," directed some of his remarks to local high school players

Photos by Jim O'Brien

George Gojkovich

Antwaan Randle El proved to be one of the Steelers' most exciting and popular rookies in team history. He was a big hit when he appeared at a Coaches Corner luncheon emceed by sportscaster John Steigerwald at the Riverwatch Room at the Boardwalk Complex in The Strip. The monthly sports luncheon series is sponsored by the Pittsburgh Brewing Company and KDKA-TV.

seated in the audience, and stayed late to sign autographs for every-one who approached him. He stood next to John Steigerwald, the KDKA-TV sportscaster, to show everyone that he was a little taller than Steigerwald. Apparently, Steigerwald had suggested on one of his shows that he was just as tall as Randle El. Maybe even taller.

Everyone should measure up to Randle El. One of his big boosters was Merril Hoge, the former Steelers and Bears running back who serves as an analyst on ESPN TV and Radio. "He's one of my favorites," said Hoge. "I love that kid. He's got tremendous spirit." Hoge said that Randle El was going to serve on a panel discussion at an NFL-sponsored rookie orientation in the summer at West Palm Beach, Florida. Randle El had something to offer to help first-year players make the transition from college to pro ball.

"Coach Knight and Coach Cowher are similar."

I was among those critical of the Steelers when they selected Randle El on the second round of the draft, and bypassed Antonio Bryant of Pitt. The Steelers have a history of bypassing Pitt players through the years, from Danny Marino on down to Curtis Martin, and it seemed like they were repeating their act. Bryant, after all, was bigger (at 6-2) than Randle El, and was a proven pass-catcher. He had won the Biletnikoff Award as the nation's outstanding receiver in his sopho-more year. He left Pitt following his junior season to turn pro. I have a preference for tall quarterbacks and receivers.

Bill Cowher chose Randle El because the Steelers' scouts were so high on his versatility and promise as a pass-catcher and kick-returner. Plus, he could pass and punt. He also bypassed Bryant because the South Florida import had a string of problems with Pitt coaches, and was regarded as a disciplinary problem. Cowher had an up-close appraisal of Bryant's behavior because the Steelers share a duplex practice facility with the Panthers as well as Heinz Field. He already had two problem receivers in Burress and Troy Edwards and didn't want a problem trifecta at that position. Burress has gotten better as he's matured in three years. When Bryant got drafted by the Dallas Cowboys, he said, "It would have been nice to be picked by the Steelers. I know where all the parties are in Pittsburgh." And, if he didn't, Burress could tell him where they were. That comment only confirmed Cowher's concerns about Bryant's liabilities.

Bryant became a starter for the Cowboys, and was drawing early raves from the team's former star receiver (and problem child) Michael Irvin. So perhaps both teams are happy with their selections.

The Steelers were taking a chance on Randle El as a receiver candidate. Most NFL teams felt he was too small to play quarterback in the pros, but most liked his athletic skills. He finished at Indiana University as the most statistically productive triple-threat quarter-back ever.

Randle El is the only player in Division I-A history to pass for 7,000 yards and rush for 3,500 yards, and he is the only one to throw 40 touchdown passes and score 40 touchdowns. In 44 career games at IU, Randle El passed for 7,489 yards and 42 touchdowns. He rushed for 3,895 yards and 44 scores. He caught seven passes for 90 yards and one touchdown. He punted 17 times for a 33.5 yard average. He returned 16 punts for 149 yards, a 9.3-yard average. He gained 11,384 all-purpose yards and averaged 258.73 yards per game in total offense.

He played a little baseball at Indiana — he was good enough to be drafted by the hometown Cubs when he completed high school — and he played two seasons of basketball under Bob Knight. "It was fun," Randle El said of that experience with the legendary fiery Knight. "Interesting. Interesting. I got to know Coach Knight, still know Coach Knight. Know him as a friend, as a person, not only as a coach.

"Coach Knight and Coach Cowher are similar. They want it this way, and this way, you get it done this way. We've been getting it done this way for a long time, and we're going to stick with it. That's how Coach Cowher is, too. I'm lucky to have had the opportunity to play for both of them."

Randle El spoke about his first season when he came off the field following a workout in late May, 2003 at the UPMC Sports Complex on the South Side. He was pointing toward getting married the coming Saturday and the 2003 season. Tunch Ilkin came over and asked him if he was interested in doing a training film in the near future. There was a payday involved. Randle El expressed interest and said he'd like to talk to him more about it. He wanted more information. Randle El is in demand. We sat on a bench in the shade, and talked about some things near and dear to his large heart.

"Tommy throws a crisper ball."

Antwaan Randle El:

When I am talking to young people, I try to start off with some stories about my background. I tell them where I came from and how I got to where I am today. I tell them about my faith, my family and football, and how they all play such a big part in my life.

If you don't have all three intact it's going to be a hard road.

I have faith in God and it's a source of great strength. I love my family and everyone in my family has been so supportive. It's most important that you care for your family.

If you are going to play football then I feel like you have to give it everything you've got to be successful. Why do it if you don't give it everything you have?

All my life people have underestimated my ability to accomplish things. They've been telling me, "You're too small. You can't be good at this. You're too light." I've heard it all.

How do you take it? That's the important factor. How do you respond to those doubters? What do you believe? Do you believe in God? Do you believe in your family? Do you believe in yourself? You have to know yourself, and what you're all about. What are your personal beliefs and standards? No matter what comes your way, what are you going to stick to?

We've got lots of guys on this team who have demonstrated great courage to overcome adversity or doubters to succeed. Especially Tommy Maddox. He tried to leave football alone, but it kept calling him back. For some reason, he couldn't give it up. He kept coming back, to other teams in the NFL, to the Arena Football League, to the XFL. He wouldn't stay down. His heart still wanted it. He still believed he could be the best quarterback in the league.

I hadn't been with Kordell Stewart as long as some of the other receivers. You could see the switch from Kordell to Tommy was difficult for some of them. Some of them wanted to stick with him. They wanted to see him turn things around. Then Tommy Maddox moved into the lineup, and they said, "Wow!" They were happy with the way things were going.

It all came down to that we were winning. We played well as a team. A lot of people were hurt that Kordell wasn't playing because they liked him, too. But, with Tommy in there, we didn't miss a beat. It wasn't a race thing, either. No one cared what color the quarterback was. They just wanted the ball in their hands and they wanted us to win.

Tommy throws a crisper ball. There's a little more spice to it, or pop. That's not to say Kordell can't throw the ball with some steam. They're just different. Both of them have different attributes. Kordell has legs and he can get out of trouble, and run on his own. Tommy can't do that.

I'm just glad we're not playing the Chicago Bears this season. Kordell is hungry now, and he wants to prove something. I wouldn't want to go up against him.

Tommy slowly sold himself to the team during the mini-camps and the training camp. We got more and more comfortable with him. We could see how he threw the ball, and how well he threw the ball.

When he came into the huddle during the Cleveland game early in the season, he had the look of a man who was in charge. He said some things we didn't expect to hear from him, about what he wanted from us. Everybody said, "OK, let's go!"

From that point on, they were saying, "Let's roll."

When I was a kid, I wasn't small for my age, but I always played with older kids, so I was small with them. I had two brothers, Curtis (now 25) and Marcus (16), and I used to play ball with my older brother. I always thought I was the best player. Nobody could stop me.

I played on an outstanding basketball team in high school. We played in the state finals three years in a row. We also lost three years in a row, to the same team. Peoria Manual High School beat our Thornton Wildcats. Two of our guys are in the National Football League now. I'm here and Napoleon Harris was a starting middle linebacker as a rookie with the Oakland Raiders. Melvin Ely is with the Los Angeles Clippers in the National Basketball Association.

I had lots of scholarship offers to play basketball in college. I played two years with Coach (Bobby) Knight when I was at Indiana. And I loved baseball. I was a big Cubs fan, and I was drafted by them in the 14th round out of high school.

"You have to be consistent."

I'm glad I was able to come in and contribute here last year. I didn't realize all my personal or team goals, though, and I'm always hungry to get better. I want to come back and play well. Year to year, you have to be consistent. I don't want to hear anything about a sophomore jinx. I want to pick up where I left off and build on it. That's why I'm working so hard in the off-season to improve my skills.

I think we've got a great group of receivers here. I love them. We've got some real playmakers. You've got Plaxico, so big and elusive. You've got Hines, and he's such a fighter, whether he's catching the ball or blocking. He takes hits. You're gonna know he's out there. I'm a finer ingredient. Time and time again, I want to get the ball in my hands, and make something happen.

I love the way Coach Mularkey is always trying new things. I love that. It doesn't matter whether I'm catching the ball, running the ball or throwing the ball. I was nervous when he was being interviewed for head coaching jobs elsewhere. I was saying, "Oh, no, we might lose Coach Mike." I didn't want that to happen. He's a person you can talk to. He understands your ability, and he wants to make the best possible use of your talents.

My favorite player in the NBA was M.J. Yes, of course, Michael Jordan. Hey, I'm from Chicago. I liked the total Michael Jordan, the way he carried himself, the way he cared

453

about kids, the way he worked with them at summer camps. I liked his love for the game, his love for the kids. His team struggled at the start, but then they got him the kind of supporting cast he could lead to championships. He cared about his family, for the kids. He was not a standoffish person.

I'm not a star like he was, but I think I have a lot of his qualities. He was a good role model. I like to spend time with the kids. I take the time to sign autographs.

I'm excited for what's to come. I think Tommy Maddox is going to get even better. I think the best is yet to come. He's still hungry. He hasn't had a big one yet. He was with Denver when they had John Elway. And Elway went without a championship for a long time; then he got two. Tommy was behind him. Now it's Tommy's turn.

It's important to me to be well thought of in Pittsburgh. I think the fans have been great, and I try to give back to them. No one should be against me. I'm not going to do anything to hurt them. I love and care for my fans. I like to spend time with my fans. I want to keep my family intact. My mother, Jacqueline, has her own day-care center in Chicago. My dad, Curtis Randle El, was a dock worker, but now he's selling insurance. I'm happy about that. That dock work was hard work, dangerous work.

My parents had high standards for us. We were expected to respect our elders. We were expected to be loving God. You were always representing your home when you went out, and you weren't going to do anything to bring disrespect upon your home and your family. They didn't have to say it; it was just understood. We were expected home earlier than any of our friends. When the streetlights went on you were expected to be home. Mom and Dad looked after us real good.

Having parents who stayed together was a real advantage. They will be celebrating their 25th anniversary this October. I realized the importance of an intact family when I left high school. I met different people at college who didn't have a mother and father who cared.

My dad and I are best friends. I love my family. I love my children. I love my Mom and Dad and my brothers, my grandparents and my cousins.

I'm getting married this Saturday. Her name is Jaune. We went to the same church in Chicago, the Church of God in Christ. We have two children, Dijon, who is 9 and is her child, and Ciara, who just turned 2 on May 10, and is my child. I also have a nephew, Marcus Randle El Jr., who will be 1 in June. He's special in my life, too.

> *"We don't know the millionth part of one percent of anything."*
> **— Thomas Edison**

Kendrell Bell
The fire still burns

"I'm never satisfied with my game."

Kendrell Bell is a bull of a man. He's the strong, silent type, almost sullen. One fully expects him to snort flames from his flared nostrils at the snap of a football. He often looks like he's glaring at you, checking you out with narrow dark eyes. Bell, a tautly built 6-1, 255-pound linebacker and defensive end, is one of the Steelers' most talented and fiercest performers.

Once you crack that shell, and speak to him at any length, you have to like him. You like what he's all about, and what he stands for. He's got quite a comeback story, and he may have more to write.

As a rookie in 2001, Bell was a big reason for the Steelers' successful season, going all the way to the American Football Conference championship before bowing out of the Super Bowl chase. In his second season, plagued throughout the schedule by a nagging ankle injury that wouldn't heal properly, Bell was a big reason the Steelers didn't get so far in the playoffs.

The 2002 season was a bummer for Bell. He suffered what is termed a high sprain on his right ankle. He missed four games altogether, saw limited play in a half dozen others, and was never quite the force he had been the year before. He had hurt his left ankle at the outset of his first season, but it didn't prove to be as disabling an injury.

Bell bounced back late in the 2002 season to show flashes of what had been routine in his rookie season. He re-injured his ankle in the last regular season game against Baltimore, but surprised everyone by coming back the next week for a wildcard playoff game with the Cleveland Browns. He finished with nine tackles (eight solos), including 2½ tackles for losses totaling six yards. He started the next game against Tennessee, but had to come out early in the game and never returned.

As he worked out at the UPMC Sports Performance Complex on the South Side in the summer of 2003, Bell was optimistic that he might still enjoy a full season of good health, so he could really show his true self. He and Jerome Bettis and Mark Bruener were among those out to show Bill Cowher they could still contribute to a championship season.

Cowher wouldn't expect anything less from any of them. He knew what they were all about, and hoped they would bounce back and be a big part of the Black & Gold gridiron machine once more.

Bell believes in himself, yet is never boastful. It's a quiet confidence, built on his success at Laney High School in Augusta, Georgia, where he was a late bloomer, and at the University of Georgia in

Athens. He was the undisputed leader of Georgia's defensive unit. Dick Bestwick, a long-time friend of mine who worked as an administrator in the athletic department at the same time, tipped me off to watch Bell as well as Hines Ward. He thought they were both terrific young men who worked hard to realize their dreams and aspirations. Bestwick was right on the mark about both of these young Steelers.

During his first two seasons with the Steelers, Bell shared an apartment with Rodney Bailey on Pius Street on the city's South Side in a building that used to be St. Michael's High School. Teammate Clark Haggans lived in the same complex and came to their apartment to hang out from time to time. During the off-season prior to his third season, Bell got an apartment of his own in Oakland, equally convenient to the team's training complex.

He continued to take home-study classes in sports business to complete his degree at Georgia. Bailey, who was an outstanding student at Ohio State, getting his degree in $3\frac{1}{2}$ years, keeps after Bell to do his homework. Bailey is a bright-eyed, bubbly sort, a real contrast to Bell. Their close friendship helps certify the belief that opposites attract. Visiting with them is always a good experience.

Bell was a second-round pick in the 2001 college draft, the 39th pick overall. He quickly impressed with his ferocious hitting and tenacity. He was named the National Football League's Defensive Rookie of the Year, the first Steeler to earn the award since Jack Lambert of Kent State in 1974. He was selected by *Sports Illustrated* as the NFL Rookie of the Year, and was an alternate to the Pro Bowl, and was added to the AFC squad for the all-star game in Hawaii because of a roster need. He could have been added to the Pro Bowl after his second year, but was thought by league officials to be injured.

It had been a banner year for Bell. I learned some interesting things about his childhood and how he'd overcome a tremendous setback as a youngster. It prompted me to approach him to talk about it at the Steelers' training camp in Latrobe on August 22, 2002. It was the next to the last day of camp. He was riding a golf cart about the campus, and when he got off he'd hobble around with the aid of a crutch. He'd hurt his ankle again.

We sat on a bench in the shade, under an archway near the dining hall at the St. Vincent College campus. Out of habit, he had his left hand clasped over his right wrist, as if to soothe it or perhaps hide it. The dark skin there was gnarled, a scar and souvenir from a childhood accident.

> *"My mother had a great deal of trouble*
> *with me,*
> *but I think she enjoyed it."*
> **— Mark Twain**

Photos by Jim O'Brien

endrell Bell covers his burned right wrist ut of habit.

Bell gets around St. Vincent on crutches after injuring his ankle.

George Gojkovich

Rodney Bailey and Bell are buddies.

Bell wants to excel in NFL wars.

"I'd get into fights and I'd go home and cry."

Kendrell Bell:

I got burned there when I was six years old. My mother was burning some trash in the backyard. And I had an aerosol paint can and I was spraying everything in sight. I threw the can in the fire. It blew up. It came back at me. The paint just hit me. I got it on both of my arms and my face. My right arm got the worst of it. It hurt real bad. I spent two weeks in a burn unit at a hospital at the Medical College of Georgia.

My right arm got infected. My mouth hurt. I couldn't talk for awhile. My parents were really, really scared and sad.

The worst problem for me came afterward. Kids said some things about my scars. They made fun of me. It was difficult to deal with that when you're only six years old. I wore a glove sometimes. It kinda humbled me.

I think it had a lot to do with the way I am now. I get upset when I hear people making judgments about people because they have a physical defect. I know what it was like when I went through my trials and troubles, people picking on me. That's a terrible experience. I'd get into fights and I'd go home and cry.

I got to the point where I became the aggressor. Nobody was going to make fun of me anymore. People thought of me as a bully in school.

I quit school for awhile. Everybody gave me a hard time.

Now it's my ankle I have to worry about. But it's coming along. It's fine now. It will be all right. Really. I know it's not the end of the world. It's an injury. I can't do anything about it.

People in other situations go through a lot more turmoil than my sprained ankle. I know me. I know I'll be back. Yes, I'll be back.

I remember another setback when I was a kid. My grandfather got sick. He had a stroke when I was 11 years old. He had been sick a long time. I spent a lot of time with my grandparents when I was young and they were so important to me. I think things like my scars and what happened to my grandfather humbled me a lot. When he was left paralyzed it affected his mood. He was grouchy a lot, complaining. He was very frustrated.

My grandparents had spoiled us. They took care of us. My parents both lived nearby, but my grandparents adopted us.

458

When he got sick it changed me. One time when I went to the movies, I took a couple of dollars. Just picked it up and took it. I got caught. That totally changed me. I never, never stole anything in my life again. I had learned my lesson the hard way.

My grandfather, we were so close. His name was Henry Booker. He was like my real father. Every aspect of me came from my grandfather. He gave me that true desire to be something.

When he was paralyzed on his left side, though, it changed him. He had always been happy and always joking and having fun. All I know is that, after his stroke, he got real mean. He didn't want to talk to you. He'd snap at you. It wasn't fun being around him anymore. But he was still my grandfather. I hadn't forgotten how much fun he'd been.

So I'm used to taking care of people. My grandmother's name was Barbara Booker — I called her Mom. I stayed with them my whole young life. Both are still alive, still married. My dad, Cliff, and my mother, Pam, are still there for me, too. We're survivors. That's why I know I'll come back strong.

"I'm still looking for that perfect practice."

I don't get too excited about practice. I try to go through a day without making a big mistake. I haven't accomplished that yet. I'm still looking for that perfect practice. Even if I had it, I still wouldn't be satisfied. I'm never satisfied. I always know I could do better.

I'd never been to a camp till I went to college. Camp last year was longer, and horrible. If we have to spend every week like this, I thought, I'll die. This is like being back in college, living in dorm rooms.

Rodney Bailey and Clark Haggans are my real good friends here. I can talk to them about sensitive things. Rodney has a real sensitive side. When I first came here, we expressed some things, and he'd listen. He'd talk to me about certain things, how I had to finish my schooling at Georgia, get my degree, lots of things. I tried to help him, too, in different ways.

When I came in here I just wanted to make the team. I didn't have any false thoughts about myself, being a big deal, or anything like that. I had to make the team. I wanted to put the fear of God in everybody. If you come in thinking you're just better than everybody else you're in real trouble. You have to prove yourself . . . every day.

I got real high standards and I'm not going to let anybody out-hustle me. If I get cut for not hustling, shame on me. I can't explain why I'm like that. I always go hard. When I watch film, I'm highly critical of myself. I'm flying out there. I'm not going to get caught with my pants down. I'm going to be ready on every down. I'm coming after you.

Clark Haggans is like that, too, as a linebacker. I'm not saying that just because he's my friend, either. I truly believe that if he were playing for somebody else, he'd be starting in a minute. We have two Pro Bowl outside linebackers (Bell and Jason Gildon), and I'm always telling him how good he is even though he doesn't get to play much.

I just went to Coach (Tim) Lewis and told him about my concerns. They've been trying me at defensive end. I'd rather be an outside 'backer. I don't like experimenting at another position. I need to focus on the position I'm going to play. I don't need five coaches telling me five different things. I only need one coach.

Coaches make or break a player. Players look at them as a father. But you can't please five of them, or even three of them. I want to learn the system I'm going to play. I have a hard time when I have to learn more than one system.

I've been able to go to Mike Archer and talk about the problems I'm having. I'll tell him, "Let me work on this. Right now, I'm trying to do too much. I'm having trouble with this." At least I can talk to him. I will miss having him as our coach.

I don't like to be yelled at. Let's have some respect. I don't want anyone chewing me out. If a coach yells at me, I'm going to tell him, "Don't talk to me like that." I go to him all the time to make sure we're on the same page, and that we understand one another. They don't have to worry about me. I'll give them everything I have . . . every game.

George Gojkovich

Kendrell Bell was named the NFL's Rookie Defensive Player of the Year as a second-round draft choice out of Georgia in 2001.

Amos Zereoue
From A to Z

George Gojkovich

"I'm lucky to be living in the greatest country in the world."

If Jerome Bettis has been the beef in the Steelers' running game, then Amos Zereoue has been the sizzle. Not-So-Famous Amos was not satisfied with that as he prepared for the 2003 schedule. He was eager to elevate his game, get more consistent, stay healthy, have a breakthrough campaign, and make a name for himself in the pro game.

Zereoue had breakaway speed and quickness, and could run outside better than Bettis, but had to demonstrate that he could also get those tough yards inside as well as Bettis, a likely future Hall of Fame honoree. Bettis had missed the stretch run of the previous two seasons with leg injuries and, at 31, was being evaluated with a more critical eye by Bill Cowher and his staff at this summer session. There might be an opportunity for Amos to go after Jerome's job as the featured back in the Steelers' attack, and to do so in earnest.

Zereoue took over the starting position when Bettis was injured the previous season, and led the team in rushing with 762 yards on 193 carries, to become the only other player besides Bettis to lead the team in rushing since 1996. Amos also caught 42 passes for 341 yards.

His best outings were in back-to-back games at midseason at Cleveland and with the Atlanta Falcons at Heinz Field when he rushed, respectively, for 111 yards on 29 carries and for 123 yards on 37 carries. He finished the regular schedule strong, gaining 104 yards on 26 carries in a home game against the Baltimore Ravens.

He reminded me, in stature and skills, of Mercury Morris, a young man who had come out of the city's North Side, where Three Rivers Stadium once stood, and became a vital part of the Miami Dolphins' juggernaut of the early '70s. Morris was the outside threat that complemented the inside running power of Larry Csonka and Jim Kiick. I covered those guys and that team for *The Miami News* in 1978, when the Dolphins weren't very good. Zereoue isn't nearly as glib or light-hearted as Morris, but he may be even more determined to succeed.

During his three seasons at West Virginia University, Zereoue rolled up numbers as good as any running back in the nation, and drew All-Big East recognition and All-America mention. He set school records in rushing and total yards. The Steelers drafted him after his junior season on the third round of the 1999 college draft.

They weren't scared off by the fact that two previous WVU running backs that had been drafted by the Steelers, Dick Leftridge and Larry Krutko, couldn't cut it in the NFL. Leftridge, the team's No. 1

461

draft choice in 1966, was a total bust. His agent, believe it or not, was Pirates' broadcaster Bob Prince. Leftridge lasted one season; Krutko managed three mediocre campaigns. As Zereoue looked forward to his fifth year in Pittsburgh, he was optimistic that the best was yet to come for a Mountaineer with the Steelers.

"I can't believe I'm here."

I like interviewing Amos Zereoue because, at 5-8½, I am actually about an inch taller than he is. He's listed at 5-8, 207 in the Steelers' media guide, but that may be a tad generous measurement. He might have been wearing cleats when the tape was stretched to the top of his head. His furrowed brow makes him appear older than his 26 years. He would be turning 27 on October 8, 2003. There were beads of perspiration in those furrows as we sat on a bench in the shade of the Steelers' training facility at the UPMC Sports Complex on the South Side.

One could hear his teammates grunting and groaning, shouting to one another, in a glass-enclosed weight room behind us.

He's a quiet guy who doesn't seek the spotlight. Mark Bruener, who dresses alongside Zereoue in the clubhouse, is fond of him. "Good luck," Bruener told me when I told him what I wanted to do. Bruener volunteered to endorse me as someone Zereoue could trust. Bruener stopped by during our interview to say hello, and to reassure Zereoue that he was in good hands.

When the Steelers were going through an hour-and-a-half "voluntary workout" session, a woman sat next to me with her teenage son, a Down Syndrome child who was there to meet some Steelers and get some autographs. "I can't believe I'm here," the woman said excitedly as she studied the green expanse before her. Any fan would feel that way.

Amos Zereoue might have expressed similar sentiments. He said he still had work to do to get in playing shape for the 2003 season — "so I'm not winded after running a few laps" — but he admitted he felt a lot better than he had during the same time period a year earlier. This was Thursday, May 29, and the Steelers had just finished the final workout of a training session that had stretched across two weeks, interrupted by a break for the Memorial Day weekend.

Amos Zereoue — I have to check the spelling every time I type his name — made quite a comeback from a serious health scare in the spring of 2002. It's a comeback that didn't merit as much attention as the comeback of Tommy Maddox or the comeback of Terry Bradshaw, but it was noteworthy just the same. It wasn't the first time in his young life that Zereoue had overcome adversity.

His story is a good one. It's one that should provide inspiration for youngsters thought to be too small for sports like football and bas-

Photos by George Gojkovich

Amos Zereoue

Courtesy of Holy Family Institute

The Holy Family Institute's 10th Annual Arthur J. Rooney Sr. Courage House Awards Luncheon was chaired by Greta Rooney, at left, and hosted by Sister Linda Yankoski, Holy Family Institute president. Amos Zereoue of the Steelers was presented the Ed Block Courage Recognition Award for overcoming personal challenges, and, at far right, Holy Family Institute alumna Pam McWhorter, a USAirways flight attendant, received the Arthur J. Rooney Courage House Award.

ketball, for youngsters challenged by the field mines that are out there as numerous as the sewer lids in the city streets. He was born in the Ivory Coast of Africa, more famous as a French colony where they killed elephants for their tusks, than producing pro football players. He grew up with his father and sister in Hempstead, located in the heart of Nassau County, Long Island, New York.

Amos Zereoue has been one of the lucky ones. He has a beautiful home in Wexford, and he drives a late model pale green Land Rover. He makes more than $2 million a year to play football when he could just as easily be in jail or in a hospital or worse. The best part is he knows how fortunate he's been. "I wouldn't be here if it weren't for my father looking out for me when I was a teenager looking for trouble," he said with a smile, "and I'm lucky to be living in the greatest country in the world."

"I wasn't thinking about my football career."

The previous April, Zereoue was suffering stomach distress and he didn't know what was causing it. Doctors found a cyst on his liver the size of a tennis ball. "At first, I was afraid it would impact my career," Zereoue said. "When we didn't know whether it was cancerous, I wasn't really thinking about my football career."

Zereoue offered this reflection when he received the Ed Block Courage Recognition Award for overcoming a personal challenge. It was presented at the 10th annual Arthur J. Rooney Sr. Courage Awards Luncheon of the Holy Family Institute at Heinz Field. I was at this luncheon on Tuesday, October 29, 2002 and saw Dan Rooney, the president of the Steelers, and his son, Art Rooney II, the vice president of the Steelers, in attendance. Bill Cowher offered his thoughts about the courage exhibited by Zereoue in the face of his scary health problems. Cowher, who presented the award, added that Amos was "a genuinely good guy." That's important, too.

Zereoue spent a month in a hospital on medication to shrink the cyst and was not allowed to work out until June. He had to fight his way back from fatigue and got a late start getting in shape for the 2002 campaign. "I had to do what I had to do to get where I needed to be," Zereoue said at the awards luncheon. He also related how he had lived in a group home on Long Island from the time he was 13 till he was 18. "It definitely gave me perspective on what life is going to give you, some good and some bad," he recalled.

> *"The Pittsburgh Steelers are an organization that tries to do it right. Doing it right is important to us. We want to be something special to our people. That's how we view the Steelers; they are special."*
> **— Dan Rooney, Steelers chairman**

"I was out of control."

It was a good day for football practice. The sun peeked out every so often — Pittsburghers can pinpoint the days this happens — and temperatures rose to the low 70s. The scale of the UPMC Sports Complex is still mind-boggling for anybody who remembers what the Steelers' facilities were like at Three Rivers Stadium. It's even more unbelievable if you go back to their days at Forbes Field and Pitt Stadium, when they practiced at the Fair Grounds in South Park.

As I drove down South Water Street, on the south side of the Monongahela River, I spotted two friends who are neighbors in Upper St. Clair. Bob Junko and Tom Freeman, two of the most trusted assistant coaches on the staff of Walt Harris at Pitt, were walking briskly in my direction on the sidewalk. I used to see these two walking or jogging through the streets of Oakland. I see Junko walking by my house at least once a week. I stopped to check in with them.

As I pulled into the parking lot where the Steelers and Pitt football operations occupy equal halves of a huge building— it's like a duplex home the size of twin airport hangars — I saw the Panthers senior quarterback Rod Rutherford approaching the entrance to the James Duratz Athletic Complex. Rutherford was talking to someone on a cell phone as he walked through the parking lot.

I caught the tail-end of the Steelers' workout, and waited for Amos Zereoue to join me on the black bench near the door to their locker room and weight room. Few NFL teams have a complex that can rival this one. There are four green, green fields — two for the Steelers and two for Pitt — plus an indoor facility, where the J&L Steel Mill once stood.

Zereoue and I started off talking about his hometown of Hempstead, New York. I knew that town well. When I moved from Miami to New York in the spring of 1970, I got an apartment in East Rockaway, not far from Hempstead. Three years later, my wife Kathie and I bought our first home in Baldwin, about four miles on a direct shot to Hempstead.

I had to be in this location for two reasons. At first, I was covering the New York Nets, with Rick Barry as the star forward, and Lou Carnesecca as coach, at the Island Garden in West Hempstead. Then the Nets, with Julius Erving, and the newly formed New York Islanders of the National Hockey League, moved into the Nassau Coliseum in Uniondale, next to Hempstead. The Islanders won only 12 games in their first season, but started to draft the players that would lead to four Stanley Cup championships. I had to be near Hempstead because it had the only 24-hour Western Union office on Long Island. I had to send my copy via Western Union to the *New York Post* offices many evenings. It's a lot easier to transmit stories these days. So I know what Hempstead looks like. Al Skinner, the basketball coach at Boston College, grew up in neighboring Malverne and later played with the Nets. His hero, Dr. J, grew up in nearby

Roosevelt. The accountant who prepared our tax filing had an office in Hempstead. So I knew the neighborhood that nearly devoured Amos Zereoue. Hempstead was a lot like our Homestead.

Hempstead is also the home of Hofstra University and the Weeb Ewbank Training Center on Fulton Avenue. That's the home of the New York Jets. I used to go there to interview Joe Namath when he was the quarterback of the Jets in the early '70s. Zereoue went there often to watch the Jets practice. The Jets were his team. He remembers watching Freeman McNeil and Al Toon. He knows all about Curtis Martin, the former Pitt sensation who is the star running back of the Jets, and one of the Top Ten all-time running backs in NFL history. I pointed up the Monongahela River toward my hometown of Hazelwood to show Zereoue where Martin came from. He went to Allderdice High School before he went to Pitt, the same as I did.

I had to look in the World Book to find out a little about Zereoue's birthplace. The Ivory Coast borders Guinea and Liberia on the west coast of Africa. It was colonized by the French. Francs are still the local currency. Liberia was in the news in July when the U.S. was asked to intervene in political unrest there.

Besides elephants, it's famous for its bananas, coffee, cacao, oil refineries, pineapples, rubber and tobacco. Amos's mother, Ercilia, remained behind when her husband, Bonde Jean Claude Zereoue, immigrated to America, taking their son and daughter, Regina, with him. Regina is now 24. Bonde Jean Claude Zereoue made his living as a free-lance photographer. Amos visits his mother in Ivory Coast each off-season. George Vecsey of the *New York Times*, a colleague of mine during my nine-year stay in New York, wrote a wonderful column about Zereoue during his days at West Virginia University, just before he was drafted by the Steelers.

It began: "Amos Zereoue was furious when his father sent him to a group home where the lights went out at 11 p.m. He was used to running the streets at that hour, drinking and fighting, dangerous pursuits for anybody, particularly a boy of 13."

Vecsey interviewed Amos and his father. "I was out of control," the younger Zereoue confessed to Vecsey, recalling his walk on the wild side as a schoolboy. The group home was aptly named Hope for Youth.

"We live in Hempstead where people get shot all the time," the father had said. "I would tell him that I didn't want him on Terrace Avenue because that's where they deal drugs. But he wouldn't listen to me and I couldn't control him. And that's what I told the courts."

His father still lives in Hempstead and comes to Pittsburgh to see his son play. It's the same route he used to take to see Amos in action in Morgantown. Amos said he had an eight-month-old son of his own, Amos Jr., living with the baby's mother on Long Island.

According to Vecsey's report in *The New York Times*, young Zereoue was picked up by the police for picking a fight with strangers, and the family court recommended Hope for Youth in Bellmore, a few towns away on Long Island. The home had rooms for seven boys who needed a place to live.

He also entered Mepham High School in Bellmore. Zereoue groused about the nightly meetings he had to attend at the group home, the strict curfew, the rules, the chores, but he stuck it out. He didn't realize at the time that this demanding routine was good for him. He tried out for the soccer team in high school, and then switched to football because his classmates challenged him to "get with a real sport."

Zereoue became the first double winner of the Thorp Award, as the best player in Nassau County, an honor that Jim Brown from Manhasset and Matt Snell from Carle Place had won only one time apiece. He also took a course for the Scholastic Assessment Test (ACT) and, on his last try, skyrocketed past the minimum of 700 to 1020. West Virginia had a scholarship waiting for him.

"We won't forget him," said head football coach Don Nehlen when Zereoue left WVU a year early. "All we have to do is open up our record book and Amos is everywhere."

When Vecsey asked Amos Zereoue where he might be if his father hadn't checked him into Hope for Youth, he paused and said, "I probably wouldn't be sitting here talking to you."

"I count my blessings every day."

Amos Zereoue:

Hempstead was tough. It was a lower-to-middle class type of neighborhood. I had some rough times, but I had a lot of fun, too. I was in one of those situations where you're young and you want to go out and have fun and do what you want to do.

I didn't agree with my dad's decision to send me to a group home. As I've gotten older, I realize it was for the best. My sister and I were just too much for my dad to handle on his own. If he hadn't done it, I might have been lost to the streets. When you see stories about what happens to some young people it makes you realize what could have been. I count my blessings every day.

I'm a lot better this year than I was last year at this same time. I have to be more careful this time around. Last spring my situation was very scary. I was in trouble mentally, physically and emotionally. I had a lot of support from my teammates, coaches and the training and medical staff of the Steelers.

My morale was down. When someone suggests cancer it's not a word you want to hear. Being an athlete, you don't feel those things can happen to you. You think you're invincible. Cancer . . . when I first heard the word I didn't know what to think.

467

I'm young. How can this happen? It may have been a blessing that I went through what I went through, so we could take care of the problem, and nip it in the bud. I started having stomach pain. I had started to work out with the team, but the abdominal pain became unbearable. I went to our trainer, John Norwig, and he sent me to one of our team doctors. That was Dr. Tony Yates. He had me on those purple pills — Nexium — for awhile, but they weren't doing me any good. Nothing was happening; nothing had changed. They're for acid reflux.

I started to have night sweats. Now I was really concerned. I ended up in the hospital in late April and early June, and finally got things taken care of. I'm not to where I want to be even now, but I am trying to get back in shape. I want to be able to run a few laps without feeling like I'm going to pass out. Yes, I am hoping to have a breakthrough season. That's the way I'm approaching it. If you're a competitive person you never want to settle for second. To me, the sky's the limit.

I need to get out more and tell my story. That's a flaw with me now. I should do more of that. I think I could help young people find their way, too. I didn't even start playing football until I was in the 9th grade. I went out for the team as much on a dare as anything else. My friends kept telling me, "Why are you over there with those soccer boys? Why don't you try a real sport?"

I have a message for young people. If you really believe in something and you really want to do it, you can accomplish it. One thing is not to talk about it. Go out and do it. Maybe I should be more like Mark Bruener in that way.

I get inspired by some of the people on this team. The Tommy Maddox Story was a good one. That's amazing. How often do things like that happen? He has a unique story.

I was there the night Terry Bradshaw came back, and remember what a great reception he received. I didn't really know the whole story, or what had happened to him when he was here, but it seemed like his coming back was really a big thing. I got caught up in it myself.

Throughout my life I've had to overcome challenges — on the street and on the field. My dad is a very strong-minded individual. Everything we did was a big deal. Any time a family comes from as far away as we did, and comes to a different country, it's going to be a real challenge.

This is a long way from the Ivory Coast of West Africa. My mom — she's 52 — still lives there and I go to see her during the off-season. She may not like it that I told you her age.

The first thing I would tell young people is that have all the opportunity they could ask for, being from the greatest country in the world. If a guy like me can come from the Ivory Coast, be of small stature, to overcome things I went through in an urban setting, going to a group home, and then go to college, and then have an opportunity to play for the Pittsburgh Steelers . . . well then, they can accomplish great things, too. To be in the National Football League is a dream I didn't dare to dream. But it's an example that you can definitely accomplish anything you want to accomplish. I hope I have a big year. I'll do whatever it takes to accomplish that. I want to show what else I can bring to the team.

"It was definitely a sad day."

I was here during a bad time for the team last year, too. Yes, I remember what it was like the day we all learned that Mike Webster had died. It was definitely a gloomy day that day. We just sensed that they lost a family member. Anytime anyone passes it's difficult, but this hit close to home for a lot of people here. He had been a Steeler. Being a member of a professional ball team, we all felt like we lost someone who meant something here. It didn't matter that we didn't know him personally. We had heard about him. It was like the whole city of Pittsburgh had lost a family member. It was definitely a sad day. At first, the Steelers' history didn't mean that much to me. Once you get into your third and fourth year, though, you start to become more aware of it. You see the pictures and the trophies, and the former players tell you stories. You start to feel like a part of it.

One thing I'd like people in Pittsburgh to know about me. I have a hard shell, but I'm soft hearted. I'm learning things all the time that help me. Mark Bruener dresses next to me and he's one of the nicest guys you'll ever meet. It's not a front; it's genuine. He's very intelligent and respectful of everyone. He's just an all-around great guy. It's definitely a plus for me to know him. I can't believe all the things he does. You sit back and ask yourself, "Is this guy for real? Can anybody be that nice all the time?" But he really is. It makes my life a lot easier around the locker room.

I don't know what's going to happen to him here. There are a lot of tight ends all of a sudden. We don't have to worry about Mark. He's going to be a successful guy wherever he goes. He'll be a big plus for whatever organization he might go to. We hope he'll stay, but Mark is one of those guys you don't have to worry about.

Amos Zereoue was eager to get into shape for 2003 season by working out regularly at Steelers' training facility on Pittsburgh's South Side.

George Blanda, a Hall of Fame quarterback from Youngwood, Pennsylvania, returned to his hometown in mid-July, 2003 to attend the funeral of his older brother, Mike. George would celebrate his 76th birthday in September. A friend remarked that he looked as young as ever. Replied Blanda: "That's because I've been old-looking all my life."

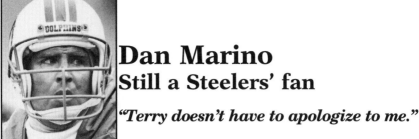

George Gojkovich

Dan Marino
Still a Steelers' fan

"Terry doesn't have to apologize to me."

Dan Marino looked as tall and handsome as ever as he practiced tee shots prior to starting play in the Mellon Mario Lemieux Celebrity Invitational at The Club at Nevillewood on Friday, June 6, 2003. He looked good in his beige golf shirt and cream-colored slacks. He'd wear a dark blue golf shirt the next day. He still has that great smile, those liquid blue eyes. One guy shouldn't have so much going for him in this world.

Emil Boures, a former teammate of his at Pitt and a versatile lineman for Chuck Noll and the Steelers for five seasons (1982-1986), was at his side, serving as his caddy. His son, Emil Boures, Jr., was caddying for another former Pitt quarterback, John Congemi. Marino's son, Michael, was also with him.

Danny and his wife, Claire, who is from Mt. Lebanon, have five children: Daniel, Michael, Joseph, Alexandra and Niki. They live in Weston, Florida, near Dan's parents, Dan and Veronica Marino.

Marino was entering his fourth year as host of HBO's *Inside the NFL* and his second year as a studio analyst for CBS' pre-game *The NFL Today*. Marino retired after the 1999 season. He holds NFL records in four major categories: passing yards, pass attempts, completions and touchdowns. He holds more than 40 Miami Dolphins and 25 regular season NFL records. He led the Dolphins to the divisional playoffs in his last season. He threw for a record 5,084 yards and 48 touchdowns in 1984 while directing the Dolphins to Super Bowl XIX. He was named the NFL's MVP that season.

He grew up in South Oakland and starred in football and baseball at nearby Central Catholic High School. He earned All-America status while leading the University of Pittsburgh to four bowl games. His jersey is among those that have been retired at his alma mater.

He was asked what he thought about Terry Bradshaw coming back to Pittsburgh to kiss and make up with Coach Chuck Noll:

"Growing up in Pittsburgh, I was a huge fan."

Danny Marino:

Was it a long kiss? If it makes Terry feel good to do that it's okay with me. For me, a fan who grew up in Pittsburgh following the Steelers when he was their quarterback, he doesn't have to make up to me. I thought he was great and I

thought the fans here felt the same way about him.

Tommy Maddox is a great story. I did an interview with him for our HBO show. I like him. It shows you how if you work hard and keep following your dream that things can turn out right for you. He did a great job of handling himself under the circumstances — taking over for Kordell Stewart and all that — and what he said in all his interviews.

I didn't know David Woodley that well. I was with him only one season in Miami, and then they traded him to Pittsburgh, where he played for two seasons (1984-1985). We knew he had some health problems, and that he had a liver transplant, but we never saw him after he left Miami. I guess we didn't realize how bad off he was. You hate to hear about someone dying that young.

People always think it would have been great if I'd gone to the Steelers. Sure, it would have been nice to go to the hometown team, but there would have been a lot more pressure. Following Terry Bradshaw would be like following Bob Griese in Miami. The expectations are greater because of their success. Those are the guys you get compared to.

My dad used to say, sure, he wished I had gone to the Steelers because he missed taking all those vacations on the North Side. He never thought it was so bad to come down to Miami to see me.

David Woodley had a lot of pressure in Miami because they'd gone to the Super Bowl and won before he joined the team. Not that I couldn't deal with it, but it was just easier to go in the way I did. That's why I enjoy our team reunions. I enjoy seeing guys like Mark Clayton and Mark Duper, my two great receivers. As you get older, you appreciate more what we accomplished together.

I'm sure it was tough for Tommy Maddox to come in behind John Elway in Denver. They went to the Super Bowl five times with John, and won the last two times they were there. So expectations were great.

When you grow up in Pittsburgh you know all about Mike Webster. I was a huge fan, so I was very aware of Mike Webster. He'd come out to our Pitt practices to see Joe Moore from time to time. He'd show our linemen how to do it right.

It's a sad story. Guys like him were such a big part of the city, winning all those Super Bowls. You wonder how it happened.

> *"Terry Bradshaw is a very special person.*
> *He was a great leader and was able to take us*
> *to four Super Bowl championships."*
> *— Chuck Noll*

Photos by Jim O'Brien

Dan Marino, with son Michael, was a big hit at the Mellon Mario Lemieux Celebrity Invitational at The Club at Nevillewood on June 6, 2003.

Dan Marino is flanked by two of his long-time friends from his Pitt and Oakland days, police officer Patsy DiTommaso and former Panthers' and Steelers' lineman Emil Boures. DiTommaso lives in Oakland and Boures in Edgewood. Boures caddies for Marino each year and DiTommaso offers him security assistance.

Art Rooney and Terry Bradshaw
They had a special bond

*"Mr. Rooney was one of the nice
human beings in the game."*

Bradshaw on Rooney:

If there were a contest to elect the most popular owner in the
National Football League, Art Rooney of the Pittsburgh Steelers
would have won in a unanimous voice vote. It was no secret that
for years insiders around the league rooted for the Steelers out of
great affection for their owner. On provocative issues laid before the
lords of professional football, Art Rooney wanted only to know what
was right. Well into his seventies before his team ever won as much
as a divisional championship, Art Rooney was celebrated only mod-
estly for his team's accomplishments in the '70s, when we won four
Super Bowl championships in six seasons.

Around the league, there was great jubilation for him. To say
that he was one of the nice human beings in the game is to suggest
tacitly that other owners were not so nice. So be it. He did not need
the ownership of the club either for self-gratification or as a tax-
shelter. He owned the Steelers because he loved them. He was in his
office each morning, but only after attending church services.

He had the same friends he did years ago, and while he was
uncommonly successful and uncommonly influential, he was truly a
common man. And I mean that as a compliment.

He was as much at home — perhaps more — with scruffy old
codgers down on their luck and looking for a fast twenty as he was
with giants of the political world and titans of industry. And players
who suggest that the professional game is a dehumanizing thing
never met Art Rooney. His love for his players was a real thing, and
he particularly loved Terry Bradshaw.

**Hoisting Super Bowl trophy high at celebration in "The City of Champions"
are, left to right, Steelers' president Dan Rooney, Coach Chuck Noll, team
patriarch Art Rooney Sr. and Pittsburgh Mayor Richard Caliguiri.**

Hoddy Hanna introduced Terry Bradshaw who was a big hit at Hilton luncheon for Hanna Real Estate agents and office personnel. Bradshaw was there to pump up the troops to make good on company's "The Best Is Yet To Come" battle cry.

Rooney on Bradshaw:

(These comments were made in an interview in 1980)

You know, the Steelers had a history of bad first draft choices. We'd either draft wrong or something. Anyway, we wound up discarding them, the way we did Johnny Unitas. We missed so many good players over the years. We agreed that Terry was going to be our number one draft choice and we made up our minds that we were going to go with him. He was going to be our quarterback. We got tremendous offers to trade Terry, but we weren't tempted.

We got him on a coin flip. The Chicago Bears had tied us as the worst team in professional football. We won that toss and we took Terry. They took Bobby Douglass of Kansas with the next pick. My son. Artie, who was in charge of our draft, followed Terry's college career and we felt he had everything: size, ability, the arm, durability — everything. It took time, but it all finally came together.

In the early years, there were difficult times. I'd kid Terry a lot and sit with him on the team bus. So often he'd be sitting by himself. He seemed to be down. I didn't give him much advice — I try to stay out of people's way — but I remember telling him to have patience and things would work out. It's awfully tough for a young person to have patience. I guess you acquire patience when you get older.

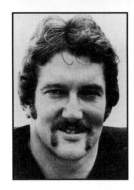

Jim Clack
Another comeback

"It's been tough on my family."

Jim Clack's voice kept cracking, and it dipped so low a few times that I had to ask him to repeat what he'd said. His voice was raspy, like he had a bad cold, as he spoke over the telephone from his office in Rocky Mount, North Carolina. I'd been to Rocky Mount a few times, visiting the mother of Steelers' receiver Yancey Thigpen in nearby Tarboro the last time I was there. I could picture the community in one of my favorite states. I could picture Jim Clack, too, or at least the one who had played center and guard for the Steelers for eight seasons (1970-1977) and four years with the New York Giants (1978-1981),

"Do you know I have cancer?" he asked, when he knew I figured something was wrong with his voice, when he had to stop at mid-sentence a few times, like he was catching his breath.

"Yes, I know," I said. "I was sorry to hear that."

This was in mid-May, 2003. Clack said he had lost a lot of weight because of his illness, going from 245 to 195 pounds. He said he was starting to put some weight back on, and was hopeful he'd be back to normal soon.

My pal Bill Priatko had told me that Jim Clack had cancer, throat cancer, to be more specific. Priatko had played one season as a linebacker for the Steelers back in 1957, and took great pride in being an active member of the Steelers Alumni. He had seen Clack and Johnny Lattner and Bill Dudley, among others, when they were in Pittsburgh for a sports card and memorabilia show in March, 2003 at the Expo Mart in Monroeville, not far from Priatko's home in North Huntingdon. Those former Steelers were signing autographs and Priatko, who turned down an invitation to join them because he didn't think he was important enough as a Steeler to draw that kind of assignment, had gone there just to say hello to old friends. Priatko had played ball in the Air Force with Lattner, a Heisman Trophy winner at Notre Dame in 1953.

Jim Clack had forged a successful career as a motivational speaker, telling his own comeback story in the same way that Rocky Bleier has been making his living following a short-lived sportscasting career after he retired as a running back with the Steelers.

And now Clack was having a hard time having a conversation on the telephone, let alone being heard by an audience in a hotel ballroom, or in an auditorium. It reminded me of the cruel manner in which legendary Pirates' broadcaster Bob Prince was stricken and died from head and neck cancer, mostly in his mouth of all places.

Like Merril Hoge, another former Steeler who learned he had cancer in February of 2003, Clack was doing his best to be positive about his situation. He'd been telling people for years about the importance of a positive attitude, and now he had to once again heed his own words. It wasn't easy.

"Career-wise, it's set me back as far as speaking," commented Clack, "I'm not doing all-day seminars, that's for sure. It's been tough on my family, especially my wife, but we're working our way through it. I'm doing my best to battle it."

Still a hometown hero

Jim Clack has always been a highly motivated, competitive person. He competed in three sports in his student days at Wake Forest University, lettering in football all three varsity seasons. He is a member of the Wake Forest University Hall of Fame.

He entered the National Football League in 1969. He signed as a free agent with the Steelers and was the last player cut. He played for Norfolk of the Continental Football League that season, and was re-signed as a free agent by the Steelers for the 1970 season. He was a standout offensive lineman for the Steelers, and was a starter in two Super Bowls for them. He was the recipient of several awards. He was nominated for NFL Man of the Year, and served as offensive captain of the New York Giants for three years.

After retiring from his NFL career in 1981, he turned to business and launched into a successful career as a commercial and residential real estate developer, restaurant owner and retailer.

In addition to his many business ventures, Clack found time to champion a long list of charities as both a volunteer and board member. He has been active with the American Lung Association, The American Heart Association, Hospice, Multiple Sclerosis, the Boys' Club as well as with the YMCA, not to mention hosting his own charity golf tournament.

Although his list of accomplishments is impressive and long, success did not come easily. Clack was faced with and conquered incredible obstacles from devastating athletic disappointments and defeats to crushing business failures. His greatest victory, however, was overcoming a grinding automobile accident that almost took his life in 1985.

His story has touched thousands of people and encouraged them to achieve and continue to strive in spite of their own personal obstacles. His inspirational and heart-warming messages were celebrated in the motivational speaking world. Jim Clack was considered one of the best in the business, someone that could get an audience's attention in a hurry. He could touch their hearts and their minds.

"He had a fire in his belly."

Art Rooney Jr. remembers Jim Clack well. "Now you're asking me about a guy I can really talk about," said Rooney, at his office in Upper St. Clair, when I checked in with him in mid-June, 2003. "He's my guy! I signed him. People tell me I have a great memory. Others tell me I'm not consistent. But this is a guy I know.

"We signed him as a free agent. I was down at Wake Forest for spring ball in 1969, getting a head start on scouting seniors for the following season. The football coach at Wake Forest told me, 'You know the best football player on our team didn't get drafted or signed.' He showed me films of Jim Clack. I was impressed with what I saw.

"He was tall enough at 6-4, but he weighed about 215 or 220. He had what they call a chicken breast frame, like Jack Lambert. But he was dominant in the film I saw. He had good strength, leverage, quickness and, according to the coach, intelligence.

"I got to talk to him when I was there. I liked him. He was respectful, but you could tell he had a fire in his belly. I think I signed him right there on the spot, on the roof of a rent-a-car, but that would be overly dramatic, and I'm not sure that was the case.

"Chuck Noll had come in in 1969, and he was big on getting under-sized guys if they had the right physical skills, quickness and intelligence. He thought we could build them up. He'd been with the San Diego Chargers of the American Football League, and they had to sign a lot of guys the NFL had passed over in order to fill out rosters. They started their own strength programs to build up their ball-players. That was Noll's background.

"He had been a center himself, and he was an under-sized guy, even in his day. He was also intelligent, and he liked smart football players. Jim Clack was tall and raw-boned. Noll brought in Lou Riecke, who had been a silver medalist in weightlifting in the Olympics, and he had Riecke set up a strength development program in Pittsburgh. Jon Kolb was one of the guys who was a small center when he came in, and was turned into a top-flight tackle. Those centers were smart. Mike Webster was one of those guys. He wasn't a computer guy, but he had the heart and desire to do what had to be done to become a great football player.

"Jim Clack was one of my favorites. A lot of times we didn't get to see a guy we drafted. We might be going by reports from Blesto (the scouting service), or from some of our regional scouts. We didn't personally see everyone. But I saw the film on Clack and had a chance to talk to him, and I liked what I saw and heard. As a scout, you get too much credit, and too much blame for these guys, but sometimes you don't see a lot of them yourself. Jimmy Clack was one of those guys I really scouted myself.

"We got caught in a numbers game, however, and we were hiding him. I shouldn't tell you this stuff, but it's funny now. We were playing an intra-squad scrimmage in Jeannette that Aldo Pallone and

Tony DeNunzio promoted up there every year. My friend George Young, who was then a scout with the Baltimore Colts, but later became the general manager of the New York Giants, was there that day watching us.

"He pointed to Clack — I don't remember what his number was, but let's say it was 50 — and Young asks me, 'Who's that No. 50?' I said, 'Oh, he's nobody.' And Young says, "Like hell, you're hiding him, aren't you?' We were good friends, so he let it go. But that was something that we had one guy there who wasn't supposed to be there, and Young spots him. George was an observant guy. After Jimmy played for us, he later played for the Giants. Young didn't forget him. George and I always had a thing about him.

"The Vietnam War was going on at the time, and I think Jimmy had to do some service time at the start. So he was on our 'hideout' squad, so to speak.

"I always took great pride in him. He started two Super Bowls for us. He may have been my best find. I'm glad you called and asked me about somebody I can honestly say was my guy."

"I'm happy to be alive."

Jim Clack:

We just raised about $35,000 at my golf outing for the Hospice of Nash County and the Boys and Girls Club of Nashville. I wasn't able to play because I'm not up to full strength, but I hit with everybody off a par 3 hole.

I'm in my 16th year with The Brooks Group, but my career has been set back a little as far as speaking. I'm not doing all-day seminars right now.

I just thought I had strep throat or something. My cancer was so developed that they just about burned up my throat to kill the cancer cells. The doctor said I had cancer on my tonsils. Upon further studies, they found cancer in my neck. They removed a large tumor. It's level 4 cancer. I had between 36 and 40 radiation treatments on my neck in 24 days. That's usually done over a longer time period. I went from 245 to 195 pounds. It was difficult to eat my throat hurt so much.

There were a lot of things I couldn't eat. There are still some things I can't eat. It was diagnosed on June 4th of last year (2002). It has been a really tough time since then. The Lord has allowed me to live. Nothing compares to cancer. Psychologically and physically, it really does you in. Every fifth day my throat felt like it was on fire.

I couldn't work up any saliva. I was hoarse most of the time. It was tough on my family, especially my wife, Susan

Joseph. Her daughter and my step-daughter, Linzi, went away to school in Australia. So I bought Susan a silky terrier called Lizzie. That silky terrier turned out to be a blessing in disguise. I love to take Lizzie for walks. She's been good company. Linzi had graduated with a 3.5 GPA at UNC-Wilmington. My daughter said, "Big Daddy, do you mind if I took a year off and go see the world, and just take a break?" I think she deserved a break. I also have a son, Joseph, who's 19.

I love my kids and I love my wife, and I want to enjoy them. I'm looking to back off. If my 401 retirement plan hadn't turned into a 104 I'd be thinking about retiring. I'm more connected with my family.

I went through some serious tough times. I'd be asking myself, "Am I going to die?"

You hear that big C word, and it's enough to scare the hell out of you. It's tough to get over. I know a lot of people have it a lot worse than me, but it's been difficult for me. (His voice sounded more strained here.)

Excuse me, I'm going to drink some water.

I have to be so attentive to my physical needs now, or it causes worse problems. I was working in the office, even if I couldn't do speaking engagements like I'd always done. It was the first time I beat Bill Brooks in sales, and I was working part-time. I was giving myself my best motivational speech. I'm 56 years old, and I have obtained a certified professional speaker certificate, something I've been wanting to accomplish. I hope I can put it to good use.

The first couple of times after I'd had the treatments I'd get up in the morning and look in the mirror, and I looked like a refugee, or like I'd been in a prison camp. My bones were pushing through. My ribs were showing.

I always had some meat on me. I played at 6-4, 248 or 250 pounds. I hope to start putting some weight on my frame again.

I'm happy to be alive. I'm happy to be able to talk to you, or anyone else. I love being called. I love hearing from old friends.

Mr. Art Rooney Jr. sends me cards and letters. He sent me a collection of cards about his father and some of the Steelers' early great players. He calls me, too. Joe Gordon has called me and checked to see how I'm doing.

Jim Clack, I'm happy to say, has had time to reflect on how good we were and what a great bunch of guys we assembled in Pittsburgh. No matter how long it's been since we were together and playing football, we're going to take care of each other.

480

Former Steelers and Giants center Jim Clack's family includes son, Joseph, 19, wife Susan and daughter Linzi, 21. They make their home in Rocky Mount, North Carolina.

Lance Armstrong, upon learning he had cancer, from *It's Not About the Bike — My Journey Back To Life:*

"Athletes don't tend to think of themselves in these terms; they're too busy cultivating the aura of invincibility to admit to being fearful, weak, defenseless, vulnerable, or fallible and, for that reason, neither are they especially kind, considerate, merciful, benign, lenient, or forgiving, to themselves or anyone around them. But as I sat in my home alone that first night, it was humbling to be so scared. More than that, it was humanizing."

The Dinosaurs of "Lost Pittsburgh"

There were dinosaurs on display throughout the streets of Pittsburgh in the spring and summer of 2003. Chicago had cows on every corner, some cities had pigs, and Pittsburgh had its dinosaurs, and they were not all politicians and sportswriters. The idea was to portray Pittsburgh as an international port, an artistic undertaking of Pittsburgh's Carnegie Museum of Natural History.

One in particular that caught my eye — my wife Kathie's eye, in truth — was one created by the faculty of the Pittsburgh Art Institute. We saw it during the final day — Sunday, June 22 — of the Three Rivers Arts Festival. This dinosaur's exterior was tattooed with photographs and newspaper clippings of things that are missing from the Pittsburgh scene, sort of like dinosaurs. It was in a plaza of the PPG Complex, near Market Square. It's called "Lost Pittsburgh."

Pictured are two former mayors, David L. Lawrence and Richard S. Caliguiri, Steelers' founder Arthur J. Rooney, Tony Dorsett in his Pitt days, Roberto Clemente, Andrew Carnegie, Rege Cordic, Frank & Sedar, Gimbel's, Horne's, Boggs & Buhl, Isaly's, Pitt Stadium, Three Rivers Stadium, Forbes Field, Motor Square Garden, Loew's Penn Theater, Donahoe's Cafeteria, 1960 Pirates, a Feb. 1, 1956 edition of *Pittsburgh Post-Gazette* showing front page story about a B-25 crashing into the Monogahela River between Hazelwood and Homestead. There are other Pittsburgh icons such as Billy Eckstine, Errol Garner and Gene Kelly. The Homestead Grays, admission tickets for The Beatles in the loge section of the Civic Arena for $5.90, millworkers coming out of work at the U.S. Steel plant at the Amity Street Entrance in Homestead.

Then, too, there is a picture of the Steelers' Mike Webster — ol' No. 52 — blocking for Rocky Bleier. Webster, sadly enough, was also a part of "Lost Pittsburgh."

* * *

Only one day earlier, Pittsburgh Steelers' president Dan Rooney donned a white ballcap with the team's logo on it and took a symbolic ride in a large canoe on the Monongahela River. It was a photo opportunity for the local media for a "Corps of Rediscovery" trip that 36 Rooneys would take the following weekend to retrace the steps of explorers Meriwether Lewis and William Clark.

Only the month before, I had read the book, *Undaunted Courage*, by Stephen Ambrose, about the Lewis and Clark Expedition. I did it while traveling to and from the West Coast to visit our younger daughter, Rebecca, who had moved to southern California at the start of 2003. Lewis had picked up boats and supplies in Pittsburgh just prior to the official start of the search for the Northwest Passage.

The Rooneys were going to travel part of the route on a two-week vacation in July. The family planned to collect botanical specimens and water samples that would be displayed at the Lewis and Clark bicentennial exhibit at the Senator John Heinz Pittsburgh Regional History Center.

Art Rooney II, the son of Dan Rooney and heir apparent to the presidency of the Steelers, expected the trip to be arduous. "We'll need another vacation by the time we get home," said Art II. He was named team president when the Rooneys returned from their expedition. "We just thought it was time to do this," said Dan Rooney.

Jim O'Brien

Mike Webster is portrayed in the belly of this dinosaur that was discovered in a walkway near Market Square in Downtown Pittsburgh. This dinosaur, that depicts "Lost Pittsburgh," was the work of the faculty of the Pittsburgh Art Institute.

Sudden death overtime
Revisiting some Steelers and friends

"Find a way."
— Merril Hoge

Presto! It's a snappy word, a magic word. A magician says it and rabbits or doves or multi-colored scarves appear from nowhere. Presto is also a patch of Collier Township that abuts Bridgeville on its western border in the South Hills of Pittsburgh. Where there was once the extensive grounds of Woodville State Mental Hospital there is now a Jack Nicklaus-designed championship golf course and a surrounding, ever-growing community of mansions, townhouses and apartments, all up-scale pads.

The Club at Nevillewood is the centerpiece. One of its better-known members, Mario Lemiuex, is mostly responsible for attracting some of America's most celebrated athletes and showbiz stars to its doorstep each June. The Mellon Mario Lemieux Celebrity Invitational has become one of Pittsburgh's proudest productions. Mario and his staff do a super job.Where else can you see Michael Jordan, Joe Pesci, Dan Marino, John Elway, Tommy Maddox, Jerome Bettis, Mike Schmidt, Emmitt Smith, Gary Carter, Rick Rhoden, Brett Hull, Charles Barkley, Stan Mikita, Bill Cowher and Jack Wagner, the soap opera star, all in one Nike swoop?

Joe Pesci, by the way, is a little guy with a big sense of humor. He's a Hollywood version of our Myron Cope, and even smaller in stature. Both of them can talk their way around any golf course.

It's a fun four days, dodging rain drops, seeing the sun break through the clouds, seeing some very good golf and some very bad golf, getting autographs, getting photographs, seeing some of our favorite people up close. Imagine if Ray Romano had been able to come as he had planned. Everybody loves Raymond, right?

Apparently, everybody loves Mario Lemieux, too. "I'm here because of Mario, and all the good things his foundation does for children and cancer," explained Elway, when asked why he comes back each year. "I love the way the fans in Pittsburgh treat me," said Barkley. "That's why I come back every year."

Jerry Lucas, one of the greatest basketball players on every level in the history of the game, was there, too, one of those sports greats who are taken for granted because of the appearance of so many marquee figures.

Lucas had lots of riddles for the kids who wanted his autograph. "I have two coins in my hands," he said, showing two fists before their young eyes. "They add up to 30 cents. But one of them is not a nickel. What are the two coins I have in my hands?"

Photos by Jim O'Brien

Mario Lemieux, Michael Jordan and Jerry Lucas were among the competitors at the Mellon Mario Lemieux Celebrity Invitational at The Club at Nevillewood. Many of the Steelers and other NFL stars were in the field.

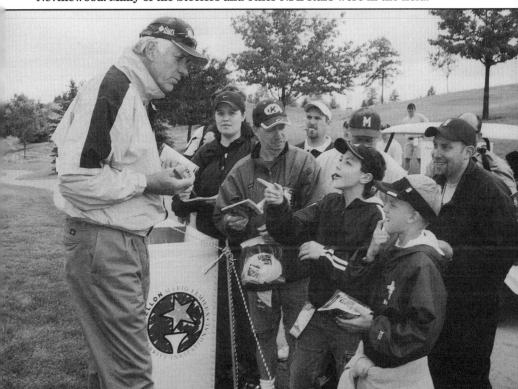

Ivan Lendl, the Czech tennis star, had a joke about every country you can think of on the other side of the ocean. "How many Frenchmen does it take to defend Paris?" he asked the members of his foursome.

Lucas let his question sit there for awhile . . . you have time to think about it, too . . . before he answered, "A quarter and a nickel. See, one of them — the quarter — is not a nickel."

Lendl let his question sit there for awhile, too, before he added the punch line. "No one knows. They've never done it."

Lucas and Lendl, who were so serious on different courts when they were competing on the highest level, have fun when they are playing golf, though both are quite good at the game.

I'm not for building Mario a new arena for his Penguins to play in it, not with the National Hockey League having so many financial problems, not with TV ratings so dismal, not with the prospects of playing without a star of the magnitude of Mario or Jaromir Jagr. I'm not convinced Pittsburgh would support such a team in these times. But I'm for building a statue in his honor. He's had that kind of impact on this town.

He's done more for this city than any other single athlete.

The Club at Nevillewood was under contract to host the Mellon Mario Lemieux Celebrity Invitational again in the summer of 2004 and it would be a date for every sports fan and golfer to put on their calendar.

It's a patch of green that gets even greener when Mario and his staff succeed in raising more than a million dollars for UPMC and Children's Hospital at each outing.

"It doesn't last long."
— Tommy Maddox

Tommy Maddox was up there on the marquee with Mario Lemieux, Michael Jordan and some great NFL quarterbacks like Danny Marino and John Elway, as well as John Congemi, Stan Humphries, Jim McMahon, Mark Rypien, Joe Theismann and Billy Joe Tolliver.

Quarterbacks can play golf, too, most of them anyhow. Maddox was quite a good golfer the year before, too, but he was a backup quarterback in those days, and not in demand on the celebrity golf tour. What a difference a year makes. Now he was one of the draws. Kordell Stewart had participated in the Mellon Mario Lemieux Celebrity Invitational the previous June. Bettis said he was traveling south to play golf with Stewart after he departed Nevillewood. Indeed, what a difference a year makes. Stewart was now with the Chicago Bears.

Wherever Maddox moved on the golf course at The Club at Nevillewood there were crowds following him. He was more obliging than most of the celebrities when it came to signing autographs for the fans. He had to beg off a few times because he was holding up his foursome.

He waved to the crowd at the start of every hole. He was having a good time. If Mario smiled as much and waved as much as Maddox he could be mayor of Pittsburgh, or at least get that new arena he was seeking. Maddox walks and talks like a guy with great appeal in Pittsburgh.

Asked by Gerry Dulac, who writes about golf and the Steelers for the *Post-Gazette*, why quarterbacks were such good golfers, Maddox said, "We're used to relying on our eyes and trusting our eyes." Maddox, a member at Nevillewood, is a 2-handicap golfer.

"As a quarterback, if you don't trust your eyes, you're not going to be very good — making the ball go to a spot. Sometimes it's easier hitting to a spot than throwing to a spot."

In his Saturday outing, Maddox played with Marino and Congemi, two former Pitt quarterbacks. It was a trio that was popular with the crowd, and Maddox heard his name called out from the crowd quite a bit.

"I enjoy it," said Maddox. "I learned that the hard way. It doesn't last long, so you might as well enjoy it. I enjoy talking to them. Whether you play four years, six years or 10 years, one day it's going to be over. That's a hard thing to go through, and I've already had to go through it once. I don't understand it, but if I can make their day by signing their piece of paper, I'll do it. It's funny, I never really understood autographs."

Maddox was back at work with the Steelers the following week, participating in a four-day mini-camp. The team was set to open its training camp at St. Vincent College on July 25.

Once more the media put the rush on Maddox on the subject of his compensation. They were hell-bent on making an issue of the fact that Maddox would be making less money than his backup Charlie Batch in the coming season. This time, Maddox, who had told me he'd never introduced the subject, expressed some concern about the situation.

Maddox was set to earn $650,000 — a lot more than he would have made selling insurance, no doubt — and a possible $75,000 in bonuses compared to a million dollars for Batch. "It's an unusual situation," said Maddox. "I don't know if it's ever happened before in the NFL. I think sometimes, if you start thinking about it and let it get to you, it starts bothering you."

The average pay of starting quarterbacks in the NFL is $5,387,000. It would be such a change of character for Maddox to make an issue out of this situation. Hopefully, he will remember where he came from. If he can produce another season like he had in 2002 surely the Steelers will rectify the situation. They can't be blamed for wanting to wait another year. Many fans felt the Steelers should be paying Maddox more money for what he meant to them.

"I just keep saying that all that I've been through and all the things I've had to go through, I'm still — over everything — excited about the opportunity to be the starting quarterback of the Pittsburgh Steelers. So, I try real hard not to let any of that interfere with it, and just realize that I'm in a fortunate situation and go out there and try to capitalize on it."

"Nothing makes you happy."
— Terry Bradshaw

Terry Bradshaw told Dan Patrick and Sean Salisbury of ESPN Radio that the most money he ever made for quarterbacking the Pittsburgh Steelers was $300,000, and that was after winning four Super Bowls. He signed initially for $26,000. He said he would have signed for $15,000 if that had been the going rate. He also said he made $2,500 in endorsements the year after the Steelers won their first Super Bowl. That was it.

Sean Salisbury told Terry that the most he ever made was $1.1 million, and that ruined Bradshaw's breakfast.

"It's all a joke what these quarterbacks are making," Bradshaw said on the nationally syndicated radio show. "I think it's crazy. Dante (Culpepper) is coming off a bad year and he's getting a $16 million signing bonus. Thank you for the bad year. Then there's Carson Palmer at Cincinnati. Carson, we know you beat Cal, so here's $10 million. Sure hope you can beat Cleveland."

He also discussed the depression that has haunted him throughout this life. "I had permanent depression," Bradshaw said. "The worst time in my life were the Super Bowls. You're never satisfied, nothing pleases you, you're never happy. I always thought I'd be happy if we won a Super Bowl. But nothing ever pleases you. Your depression is your motivation. You have to fight it. You have to overcome that before you can overcome anything else. I take Paxil now. As long as I take the medicine, I'm okay.

"I don't have the burdens now. I make better decisions. If I could do anything over again I wouldn't have been married three times. But that comes from depression. We're never satisfied. Nothing makes you happy."

"You can go home again."
— Thomas Wolfe

My wife Kathie and I traveled to Los Angeles at the outset of May, 2003. We were visiting our daughter, Rebecca, who would be celebrating her 26th birthday on May 7. She had moved from Columbus, Ohio to Woodland Hills, an hour's drive northwest of Los Angeles, in

January to work as a manager at a California Pizza Kitchen Restaurant in Tarzana.

I read the book *Undaunted Courage*, about the Lewis and Clark Expedition, by Stephen Ambrose that week. I thought it was fitting for a trip to and from the west coast. I visited the UCLA campus, checked out buildings named after John Wooden and Arthur Ashe, two of the Bruins' best, and knew within five minutes why Ben Howland had left Pitt to take over the basketball program at UCLA. It was back home and he had to go. It was a shame that his dad took a bad fall and died a few months after he moved there.

During our visit, I was retracing some of the steps I had made during my first and last visits to Los Angeles. I first went there with the New York Knicks basketball team in late April and early May of 1970. They won their first NBA championship that season, defeating the Los Angeles Lakers in seven games. I had been in L.A. on the same date exactly 23 years earlier. I had also been there in January of 1980 when the Steelers defeated the Los Angeles Rams, 31-19, in Super Bowl XIV at the Rose Bowl in Pasadena. I was also there, reporting for *The Pittsburgh Press,* when the Washington Redskins defeated the Miami Dolphins, 27-17, in Super Bowl XVII at the same site.

Covering the Knicks for *The New York Post* and the Steelers' fourth Super Bowl victory were two of the highlights of my sports-writing career, ranking right up there with the Muhammad Ali-Joe Frazier "Fight of the Century" in 1974.

I have always had a soft spot in my heart for the Dolphins because I covered that team for *The Miami News* in 1969, and because Pittsburgh's Dan Marino would become their quarterback. But I hadn't given any thought to seeing them play at Pasadena on January 30, 1983 until I saw an article in the obituaries section of *The Los Angeles Times* on Wednesday, May 7, 2003.

The headline read: **David Woodley, 44; Former Dolphin Quarterback Was in 1983 Super Bowl.** Woodley started for the Dolphins in that Super Bowl, but lost his job to Dan Marino the following season. He was traded to the Steelers and became their starting quarterback in 1984. It was reported in his obit that he replaced Terry Bradshaw in Pittsburgh. That wasn't true. He replaced Cliff Stoudt, who started for the Steelers during the 1983 season when Bradshaw was sidelined with an elbow injury.

I didn't know David Woodley that well. He came to the Steelers the year I left the beat to become the assistant athletic director for sports information at the University of Pittsburgh. He beat out Mark Malone for the starting job with the Steelers and stayed for two seasons. Woodley's first training camp with the Steelers was best known for the final holdout by Franco Harris who ended up with the Seattle Seahawks for half a season.

Woodley had a drinking problem, and he died of liver and kidney failure on May 4, 2003, at a hospital in his native Shreveport, Louisiana — the hometown of both Bradshaw and Maddox, ironically enough. Woodley underwent a liver transplant in 1992.

His NFL career ended when the Steelers released him before the 1986 season. With the Dolphins, he succeeded Bob Griese, now in the Pro Football Hall of Fame, as a rookie. Don Shula said he knew Dan Marino was special the first time he threw passes alongside David Woodley at the Dolphins' training camp.

Woodley had thrown a 76-yard TD pass to Penn State's Jimmy Cefalo in the first quarter of Super Bowl XVII, but the Dolphins lost that game, 27-17.

No sooner did we get back to Pittsburgh than I learned of the death of Dave DeBusschere. I was listening to Tony Korheiser's show on ESPN Radio and Kornheiser, who grew up on Long Island and wrote for *Newsday*, was talking about DeBusschere's passing.

This was a real bummer. I shared Korheiser's enthusiasm for Dave DeBusschere. I once got into a scuffle at the press table with Happy Fine, later a writer for *The Washington Star*. Fine, a friend of Bob Ryan of *The Boston Globe*, was sitting next to me keeping stats one night at Boston Garden. He kept hollering out at DeBusschere every time he passed us at the press table. Fine called him, "Dave DaButcher!" I asked him to knock it off. He refused, and I grabbed him by his tie and asked him once again to knock it off. This time he did.

In writing about DeBusschere, Mike Lupica of *The New York Daily News* referred to the Knicks team DeBusschere had played for in the early '70s as a "forever team." The same could be said for the Steelers of the '70s or the 1960 Pirates.

I got to New York just in time to be part of a four-man reporting team that covered the Knicks in the 1970 playoffs when they went on to win the first title in the history of the franchise. The Knicks owned New York in those days, their success coming on the heels of the Miracle Mets and the "I guarantee it" Jets of Joe Namath. New York was the best place possible for a sportswriter.

DeBusschere was in a starting lineup with Willis Reed, Bill Bradley, Walt Frazier and Dick Barnett. Three years later, the Knicks would win it again with Jerry Lucas and Earl "The Pearl" Monroe in the lineup. Phil Jackson was with both of those teams.

DeBusschere had died, at age 62, of a heart attack. He collapsed on a Manhattan street and died at the NYU Downtown Hospital. I remembered a time when I saw DeBusschere paired with Dustin Hoffman, the movie actor who was a big fan of the Knicks, as a doubles team in an exhibition tennis match on a court set up outside one of the skyscrapers on one of those Manhattan streets. Hoffman was often seen at a courtside seat, not far from Woody Allen, at Madison Square Garden.

I remembered that DeBusschere was a great friend of Bradley and that they roomed together on the road. I covered the ABA when DeBusschere became the general manager of the Nets and then the last commissioner of the ABA. He had great connections with the NBA and he helped in the negotiations that led to the absorption of four

Photos by Jim O'Brien

Tommy Maddox checks out the auto-graphed jerseys of two Hall of Fame quar-erbacks Terry Bradshaw and Joe Namath at auction for Celebrity Golf Classic for Children.

Jerome Bettis takes a bike ride to begin a fateful evening on next-to-last night of training camp at St. Vincent in August of 2002.

Pittsburgh Steelers publicity photo

19   DAVID WOODLEY   QB   PITTSBURGH STEELERS

ABA teams into the NBA in 1976. The merger meeting took place in Hyannisport, Massachusetts — best known for the Kennedy's getaway retreat — at Martha's Vineyard — because NBA Commissioner Lawrence O'Brien had been a Kennedy aide.

DeBusschere was less than two years older than me so that made the impact of his death even greater. It made me feel vulnerable. Two Davids I knew in sports had died within a week of each other. It made me think.

Jerry West, one of my all-time favorites, said DeBusschere was "one of the really classy people" in the sport. DeBusschere had been in Cleveland at the NBA All-Star Game in 1996 when he was named one of the 50 greatest players in the league's first half century.

Younger fans remember DeBusschere as the GM of the Knicks when he won the first NBA draft lottery and picked Georgetown center Patrick Ewing as the No. 1 overall choice in June 1985.

"It's sad. He's a hero."
— Dr. Fred Jay Krieg

The more people I spoke to, and the more clippings I went through in my Mike Webster file, the more I learned that helped make sense of what happened to the Steelers' Hall of Fame center.

Dr. Fred Jay Krieg, a clinical psychologist in Vienna, West Virginia who served on the staff at Marshall University Graduate College, said in 1999 that Webster was "the football version of punch drunk."

Commenting on Webster's situation, Dr. Krieg said, "It doesn't get any better. You get more and more demented. It's sad. He's a hero. He was the epitome of physical and mental strength, but he's a shadow of his former self. Mike had dementia due to head trauma, a series of blows to the head over a period of time. He couldn't concentrate, he had difficulty focusing, the conversation was rambling."

Webster surprised Terry Bradshaw when he asked him to be his presenter for the Pro Football Hall of Fame in 1997.

"I was blown away when he asked me," said Bradshaw, "because I know how deeply personal that moment is. I would have given anything to have been with Mike last week (before he died) and asked him to bend over one last time and let me put my hands under the greatest center of all time. I'm sure, up in heaven, Johnny (Unitas) is doing it for me." Webster went from being a recluse to sharing a rented home in Moon Township with his son Garrett. There were mattresses on the floor where they slept, and lots of empty pizza boxes about the room. It was a mess, a bad situation for both of them. But Garrett thought it was great.

"Oh, what I would give to put my hands under Mike Webster's butt one more time."
— **Terry Bradshaw**

"When you look at your dad, you see Superman," said Garrett. "He was John Wayne to me. I want people to remember Mike Webster running from the huddle, with biceps bulging and snow falling around him, pointing to the defense with those crooked fingers and his huge forearms. He was Iron Mike. I want him to be celebrated, not mourned."

In Webster's final year, his divorce became final, his health and financial situation worsened. He had to turn over most of the money he had from annuities and his NFL disability payments for alimony and child support, plus he owed the IRS money for back taxes.

His lawyer, Robert Fitzsimmons, helped him win a $115,000 yearly disability award from the NFL for a football-related injury. That payment ended upon his death, but his two youngest children still get $1500 a month.

Webster got in trouble in 1999 when he was arrested for forging Ritalin prescriptions. His doctor had prescribed the drug originally, but Mike made out his own after his doctor moved away.

"Mike changed," his wife Pam said, explaining why their marriage broke up. "I didn't realize he had a brain injury. I just thought he was angry at me all the time."

When I spoke with her at the luncheon held at the Downtown Hilton in her husband's honor, she said, "I talk about Mike pre-brain damage and the Mike post-brain damage. They were two different men. I was glad my children had a chance to hear his friends and teammates speak about him so positively." His friend and disciple Tunch Ilkin said, "He was Webby. He was proud and worked hard. There was a toughness about him that I've never seen in anybody else."

Another disciple, Craig Wolfley said, "He was very big in my life. You are affected by people like that. Anybody who brings the amount of professionalism to his work as he did was a great example."

His coach Chuck Noll said, "Mike Webster was the best center who ever played the game. He was the only position I never had to worry about." Noll and Dan Rooney, and eight other former Steelers, would be participating in Pro Football Hall of Fame ceremonies the first Sunday in August. More than 110 Hall of Famers would be there, but Webster would be among the missing.

Franco Harris was at the funeral. He said it was a reminder to everyone about their own mortality. "All these guys were talking," Harris said, "about how maybe they should get checkups.

"A lot of guys look back and they love the game," Harris told Meryl Gordon, "but there are some who can't walk, who find it hard to do simple things. You can't help but wonder, is it worth it?"

Over the years Dan Rooney, the Steelers' president, often picked up the tab for Mike Webster when he was staying at the Hilton Hotel or somewhere else. He paid for almost all of his $7,600 funeral. He went to bat for him with NFL officials to get him a disability pension. "Everybody gets hurt in football," related Rooney, "but very few

493

players get hurt permanently. He wasn't eligible, to be honest. But we did get it for him."

On the same day that Dan Rooney was relating this to Meryl Gordon for a story on Webster for *Reader's Digest*, Rooney spotted Tommy Maddox in the hallway outside his office.

Maddox was temporarily paralyzed in a game in Tennessee three days earlier. While standing on a sideline later that day, Maddox complained about the Steelers keeping him out of the next game. He wanted to play. He had suffered a serious concussion, and there were people worried that he might never walk again, and 72 hours later he wanted to get back on the field.

"People forget how powerful they are."
— Merril Hoge

Merril Hoge can relate to that feeling. He wanted to get back in action, too, after suffering concussions. When a team doctor for the Bears let him do it, however, he sued and a won his case against him for letting him return to action too soon after a concussion.

It puts the players and the team doctors on dangerous ground.

Hoge returned a call from his home in Fort Thomas, Kentucky, and he told me he was on the way out the door with his six-year-old son, Beau, for a baseball game in the neighborhood. He said he'd call me when he got there. Hoge is one of the most reliable people on the professional sports scene in this regard. He is good for his word. This was on Thursday, June 12, 2003.

When he called back, every now and then he hollered out an encouraging or instructive message to Beau from his seat in the bleachers. "Gotta keep an eye on that boy," said Hoge, excusing himself for a break in our conversation. "It's a coach-pitch league and that boy is on a hot streak. He's hit three home runs in the last three games. My man's got a dangerous bat. He's got quick hands . . ."

Hoge said he was disappointed to hear that the Steelers might get rid of his buddy Mark Bruener. This was before the news broke that the Steelers wanted Bruener to take a big pay cut if he wanted to remain with the team. "Teams are always saying they want good character people," said Hoge, "but they really don't live up to their word."

I had called Hoge to see how he was doing with his cancer treatment. "I had my last treatment yesterday," he said. "I consider myself cancer-free. Now I have to have CAT-scans every three months for the next two years. What I've learned the most is that cancer is such an unfair opponent. I have a deeper driven passion to live more than I ever did before. I want to get the most out of life. I'm not worrying about some of the things I worried about before.

"I see people in a different light. So many people are worried about me, concerned about me, interested in how things are going. I am embarrassed by all the attention. It's made my life easier, simpler. Hey, Beau, don't do that! Sorry about that.

"Cancer is blind. It has no concern for race, color, religion. Nothing. It doesn't care who you are or what you are. It's an equal opportunity employer, in a sense. Cancer. It's a very scary word.

"I've learned a lot from this battle. People forget how powerful they are. We all have great resources to deal with something like this. I've tapped into things I didn't even know I had in me. I played in the NFL, but that was nothing compared to what I'm up against now.

"I wish I were going to training camp this year. I'd have my best camp. Spiritually, physically, mentally I'd be stronger. I'd be the best camper. I told someone the other day it's the best thing that ever happened to me. People say how could you want to have cancer. Hey, no one wants to have cancer. Lance Armstrong spoke about that in his book. But it's been good for me and my perspective on life, I really believe that. I just wonder if I'd have made some of the changes in my life if I hadn't gotten cancer.

"At 38, I have to do over things I used to take for granted. I'm a lucky man. I'm fortunate, blessed. My wife Toni has been great through all of this. You can't change people against their will, but I've truly been changed by what we've gone through.

"Everyone remembers how in junior high you wanted everyone to love you. But you can't make everyone love you. You can't. You get your heart broken. You wanted everyone to think the way you were thinking. But you can't do that, either.

"I don't want to offend anyone. That's important. I'm going to be talking at a rookie orientation for NFL players in West Palm Beach this year. It's something the league started doing six years ago. It's to inform players about things they need to know to get along and succeed in the NFL and in life.

"I feel a little smarter in that regard than I ever did before. Randle El from the Steelers will be on the panel. I like him a lot. He's got a great attitude. I've been thinking about what I plan to talk about. We're going to do a video documentary about what I've been through. I've always had this theme in my talks. 'Find A Way.' That's what I'm thinking of calling it.

"I think when you go through something like this you discover a better sense of who you are."

"I can still drive."
— Pete Duranko

Pete Duranko said he could drive, when I spoke to him on several occasions in June, 2003. "It takes me longer to get dressed these days," he said, "but I can still drive."

Duranko was suffering from ALS, better known as Lou Gehrig's disease. There is no cure for ALS. About 30,000 Americans at any given time are living with the disease.

Duranko had to drive from his home in Johnstown to Pittsburgh three times in a six-day period. Johnstown is located 60 miles northeast of Pittsburgh. "I'm fine with getting to Pittsburgh," he said. "But when I get there I don't know my way around, especially with all the detours and construction."

I told Pete that not too many Pittsburghers were getting around the city too well at this same time. Even natives like me get lost on occasion, or find ourselves going places we hadn't planned on going. Duranko was coming to town on Tuesday and then Thursday for two different NFL alumni chapters. The Tuesday meeting was at Ruth's Chris Steak House in Market Square, and the Thursday meeting was at Bruschetta's on East Carson Street on the South Side.

Then he was coming back to serve as honorary chairman for a Saturday event sponsored by the Western Pennsylvania chapter of the ALS Association at PNC Park. It was a fund-raiser to mark Lou Gehrig's 100th birthday on June 19. The Yankee Hall of Famer left the legacy of a fatal neuromuscular disease, amyotropic lateral sclerosis, which is often referred to as Lou Gehrig's disease. When Gehrig was diagnosed with this disease during the 1939 season, he ended his 2,130-game playing streak (since surpassed by Cal Ripken, Jr.). He gave a moving farewell speech before 62,000 fans at Yankee Stadium on July 4, 1939. In his speech he said, "I consider myself the luckiest man on the face of the earth." Gehrig died two years later at age 38.

Pete Duranko had been doing some speeches himself. He's always loved to talk. He had been to Chicago to speak on behalf of the ALS Association. He had always thought of himself as a terrific motivational speaker. As he looked forward to coming to the second alumni meeting within three days in Pittsburgh, he said, "I haven't seen some of these guys in three months. They'd better be ready for all my stories and jokes. I think some of them are bringing duct tape with them to shut me up.

"Once I get going, I could keep them there till midnight. I hope I can get around okay. Gerry Hart met me the last time and took me to the Ruth's Chris Steak House. I got lost coming home. I didn't know the tunnels would be closed. I'm not a Pittsburgh guy, and I got lost following all the detour signs. I know Route 51 and Station Square and, finally, I found the Smithfield Street Bridge, and managed to get out somehow.

"But I was going round in circles for awhile. It's tough when you don't know the detours."

He said the ALS people had put him up in a hotel overnight after his Saturday appearance. "That will be nice," he said. "I can relax in my room, and drive to Johnstown in daylight. That should be easier."

I asked Duranko about Carlton Haselrig, a former Steeler who'd gone from being a big success story — a 12th-round draft pick in 1989 out of Pitt-Johnstown who became a starter and a Pro Bowl lineman.

He had been an NCAA heavyweight wrestling champion at Pitt-Johnstown. He was Myron Cope's "pick" in the draft that year. Cope pleaded with the Pittsburgh brass to take a chance on him and they took him with their last pick. Haselrig lasted three years before he derailed himself with substance-abuse problems and public intoxication problems. Haselrig had several scrapes with the law. Haselrig, 37, was arrested again on Thursday, May 1, 2003, and held in the Cambria County jail on charges stemming from an altercation with his wife at their Johnstown home. According to police, Haselrig violated a court order to stay away from his wife. His wife told police Haselrig assaulted her and threatened to kill her early Thursday morning.

Haselrig lost his home in Monroeville when it was put up for sheriff's auction because he owed more than $228,000 in principal and interest on it. He was previously jailed in Cambria County after pleading guilty to a third drunken driving charge.

"I've seen Carlton at some sports events and dinners up here," said Duranko. "He's having a tough time. He's a nice guy, but he has this serious drinking problem. He drinks the hard stuff big-time. He gets to drinking and he gets mean. He tends to stay to himself at some of these social functions, so I don't know him that well. But I feel for him just the same. People have tried to help him, but he keeps getting into trouble. I've got my hands full taking care of myself and my family. I stay up late and go to bed when I want to, and get up when I want to. I'm allowed to do that now. I like going to all these different functions to see people, and meet new people. There are a lot of good people out there."

"That's what I went to school for."

Kendrell Bell learned during mini-camp that the Steelers are going to use him at several different positions in the 2003 season to make sure he stays on the field as much as possible. Defensive coordinator Tim Lewis looks to a healthy Bell as somebody who can make a great impact on the team's improvement in that area.

When mini-camp was completed, Bell headed back to the University of Georgia where he planned to take two classes. If he successfully completed these classes, he'd be within six credits of getting his degree. He hoped to accomplish that the following year.

"That's what I went to school for," he said, when asked about his ambitious schedule. "Before I played professional football, I went to school to graduate."

I interviewed Bell at length for this book on the next-to-the-last day of training camp in August of 2002. I took photographs that same day, around dinner time, of Jerome Bettis riding around the St. Vincent campus on his bike. Bettis obliged me, as he usually does, when I asked him if I could snap some pictures of him at play.

497

Later that night, a woman approached Bettis at a bar on nearby Route 30, and let him know she was available for the evening. What Bettis didn't know was that she had been put up to this advance on him by a teacher at Penn State-McKeesport. The woman reported Bettis to the local police and accused him of raping her. She brought a lawsuit against him. The plan called for Bettis to have to surrender money to her for his offense. He was later cleared of the charge. Bettis acknowledged having sex with the woman, but said it was consentual. He had been named the NFL's Man of the Year a season earlier and was easily one of the most popular Pittsburgh Steelers. His fans stuck by his side.

He was told by Bill Cowher that he had to get in better shape during the off-season. Bettis and Mark Bruener were both under the microscope when they came to camp. Both had missed key games the two previous years. "I don't have anything to prove," Bettis said upon reporting for voluntary practices at the UPMC complex. "It's an opportunity for me to come out and show everybody that The Bus still has a little trailer left."

Bruener said he wasn't worried, either, and that he planned to worry about what he could control. "What I can control is my approach," he said, "and how I show up for work every day. I'm going to show up for work every day with the same approach I've always had." On June 25, 2003, Traci Bruener gave birth to their fourth child, a healthy baby boy named Braydon Robert Bruener. A week later, Mark took a 60 percent pay cut to stay with the Steelers, going from over $2 million to about $800,000. "I'll still prepare the only way I know how," he said. "I'll still be the same person I've been for the last eight years. I expect that every one in the organization will treat me the same way." The Brueners were building a new home in the north suburbs of Pittsburgh.

Garrett Webster, the son of Mike Webster, was admitted to Pitt in mid-summer. He was invited to try out for the Pitt football squad as a walk-on. He had poor grades at Moon Township High School, but he received strong support because of extenuating circumstances. Dan Rooney of the Steelers sent a letter of recommendation.

Pam Webster, Mike's wife:

"We tend to forget that football is the be-all and end-all of these guys' lives. It's the father, mother and everything else. It tells you what time to get up, what to eat and where to go. That's a very structured, stabilizing force. I think without the direction that football put in his life — put in our life — it was a very difficult transition."

Sojourns on the South Side
Reflections on life and death

"They think we've got it made."
— Former Steeler Todd Kalis

I traveled to Bruschetta's Restaurant at the corner of East Carson and 19th Street on Pittsburgh's South Side for a meeting of the National Football League Alumni Association because Pete Duranko told me he was driving down from Johnstown. This was Thursday evening, June 20, 2003.

The NFL Alumni would have a dinner meeting on the second floor, like the one I had attended three months earlier at the same venue. Gerry Hart, who had played for West Point and the Detroit Lions, and refereed for many years in the NFL, was there telling the same stories he had told three months earlier. He was talking about a woman who boasted that she was the only woman in America who had been married to two Heisman Trophy winners — Alan "The Horse" Ameche of Wisconsin and Glenn Davis of Army — and how he could have been Howard Cosell's sidekick on "Monday Night Football" instead of Frank Gifford, and how he tried to recruit Joe Namath, a quarterback at Beaver Falls High School, for the U.S. Military Academy. Just imagine Broadway Joe as a cadet at West Point. It's my belief that the first thing a coach from West Point would check before recruiting anyone would be his academic record.

Three of the regulars at these alumni meetings, Bill Priatko, Ernie Bonelli, and Bob Milie, sat in silence and listened to these stories. Priatko and Bonelli both played at Pitt and each put in a season with the Steelers and treasure those days dearly. Milie was an assistant trainer with the Steelers over 20 seasons, and serves as secretary for the NFL Alumni. Bonelli, who lived in Mt. Lebanon, played for the Steelers in 1946. Priatko, who grew up in North Braddock and lived in North Huntingdon, played for the Steelers in 1957.

When Hart wasn't talking, Todd Kalis, the group's president, and Robin Cole, the president of the Pittsburgh chapter of the NFL Players Association which had met two nights earlier at Ruth's Chris Steak House, were exchanging their thoughts about whether they should get paid for personal appearances.

"There's a perception out there that we're all millionaires and that we've got it made," commented Kalis, who played most of his pro football as an offensive lineman for the Minnesota Vikings and finished up with one season (1994) with the Steelers.

"I've got to charge," said Cole, who played 11 seasons as a linebacker with the Steelers (1977-1987) and then one season with the New York Jets. "That's one of the ways I make my living. There are exceptions, of course."

Both agreed that they love the group's annual visit to Children's Hospital. "I love to go there," said Kalis, "and I like speaking to kids in schools. I'll do that for free, too. When I'm out having lunch or dinner at Denny's, and someone comes over and asks for an autograph, I'll give it to them. But people don't think they need to pay for something like that. I just do it. They think we made what the players are making today."

They also spoke about a Habitat for Humanity project they would have later in the year, helping to build a home in Carmichaels for a disadvantaged family.

The former players tend to spend a great deal of time talking about how much money the current players make, and wish they had cashed in on the game's popularity and financial riches explosion.

Pete "Diesel" Duranko doesn't think it's worth worrying about. Duranko discovered the previous year that he has ALS, or Lou Gehrig's disease, and few of the players' complaints mean much to him anymore. Then again, they never did. He was 59 and had a frightening future, but he tried to smile through it.

Duranko drowned out most of the conversation among the dozen men and one woman at the NFL Alumni meeting. No one could quiet Duranko. He kept telling non-stop stories, jokes and tall tales.

He told everyone he'd gotten into Notre Dame even though he was mostly a "C" student at Bishop McCourt High School in Johnstown, and scored 850 on his College Boards. "They used to give me a little leeway in my classes at Notre Dame," he said. "A math teacher asked me how many seconds there were in a year. I said there were 12, and named them: January 2nd, February 2nd, March 2nd and so forth. One of our football coaches convinced my teacher that this was a correct response, if you gave it some thought.

"They asked me to name two days of the week that begin with the letter 'T' and I told them today and tomorrow. They gave me credit for that answer, too."

"They think they're going to live forever."
— Pitt football coach Walt Harris

As I entered Bruschetta's earlier that evening, I came upon two of my former classmates at the University of Pittsburgh, both starters on Pitt's 9-1 football team of 1963. Sitting on stools at the end of the bar, waiting for a table, were tackle John Maczuzak and end Al Grigaliunas, who was the captain of that team. Both were engineering graduates and went on to successful careers. Maczuzak had just retired as a top executive at U.S. Steel. He had previously headed the Benjamin Fairless Works in New Jersey. He wanted to move back to Pittsburgh to be close to his grandchild.

NFL Alumni meeting at Bruschetta's on East Carson Street on Pittsburgh's South Side drew likes of, left to right, Bob Norman, Bob Butts, Bill Priatko, Ernie Bonelli, Bob Milie and Tom Averell.   Photos by Jim O'Brien

Two former Pitt football ends from the 1960s are Al Grigaliunas and Dr. Woody Haser.

They were later joined by Ray Tarasi, who had played soccer and football at Pitt, and Walt Bielich, a former Pitt football player who served as director of the Pitt Varsity Letter Club. They were all talking about the death of Billy Gaines, a 19-year-old sophomore wide receiver from Ijamsville, Maryland. He had fallen the night before while walking on scaffolding high above a Homestead church sanctuary and struck a pew below. He suffered spinal injuries and a fractured skull and was taken to Mercy Hospital.

The accident took place at 2:30 a.m. on Wednesday, June 18, when Gaines tumbled off the planks and fell through a false ceiling, a 25-foot fall. At 11 p.m. that same day he was pronounced dead.

It was a strange story with many loose ends at the time. Most thought there had to be alcohol involved, and that was confirmed the following day after an autopsy at the Coroner's Office.

"Billy was a believer, and I know where he is," said Gaines' mother, Kimberly, when she spoke to reporters outside the church on Thursday. "He's in heaven, but I want him with me."

Billy Gaines and some of his teammates had to leave their apartment in Oakland after a fire, and were temporarily housed at a former convent at St. Anne Church. Why? That's what I wanted to know. As a former administrator in the Pitt athletic department, I wanted to know why Pitt football players were living in a convent in a church in Homestead. They had worked in a cemetery there the summer before.

I remembered that three days after I took the job as assistant athletic director for sports information in 1984 one of the football players fell from a high wall in the dormitory complex and was killed. Drinking was involved in that incident as well.

"It is a very, very sad day for all of us," said Mark Nordenberg, the chancellor of the University of Pittsburgh, referring to the death of Billy Gaines. "People think about the University as a big complicated place. They think about it in terms of buildings and programs. But really it is a community of people.

"When something like this happens it really does stop you dead in your tracks and it's a source of great sadness."

Football coach Walt Harris hit home even more, offering a comment that is appropriate to many of the stories in this book. "The players took this very hard. When you are young, you don't have to deal with death and the issues of your own mortality. That's the great part of youth, they think they are going to live forever.

"These are highly conditioned, cream-of-the-crop athletes and they have tremendous confidence in themselves. When one of their peers leaves them through death, it is a real eye-opener to them and it really affects them."

"This isn't really death. We'll be legend.
We won't grow old."
— **Tyler Durden in *The Fight Club***

Pete Duranko took part in an ALS fund-raising project in the parking lot at PNC Park on Saturday night, June 21, 2003, and stayed overnight at the Omni William Penn Hotel. We met for lunch at noon at Fathead's, at the other end of the block from Bruschetta's on East Carson Street the next day.

Duranko was delighted when he learned that Fathead's had raspberry iced tea. We both had a glass. Duranko held his glass with both hands when he took a drink. He had a turkey and ham club sandwich, and I had a bleu-cheese burger. The place was packed and there was quite a din, but I could hear Duranko without any problem as he spoke about his situation:

"Attitude is the most important thing."

Pete Duranko:

What do I know now that I didn't know when I was playing for the Denver Broncos? I know what I feel. I feel a lot more confident. I know people are basically decent. And everyone has a story. I always felt that football teaches you how to deal with life, and I realize that more than ever now.

I went out and enjoyed football. It taught me how to deal with adversity, the failures and successes. Attitude is the most important thing.

I've been blessed with a lot of good fortune in my life. I was shocked when I learned that I had Lou Gehrig's disease and what that was all about. I'm always borrowing phrases from everybody for my talks, and I repeated what Gehrig said when he gave that memorable speech at Yankee Stadium. I said I was the luckiest person on the face of the earth.

I can relate to what's happened to Merril Hoge, when he learned he had cancer. It's gut-check time. I always felt I could play ten percent better. I was always trying to get better.

My teammates used to get angry with me at summer training camp with the Broncos. It'd be hot as hell, and I'd be hollering in the locker room, "I hope it gets to 110 degrees today, that we practice for three hours, and that the coach wants us to run extra laps afterward." The guys would be yelling, and tossing water at me. I'd say, "This is going to be a great day! I hope it gets hotter!"

Hey, I was as miserable as the next guy. I learned that by being upbeat and a little crazy I could get through the day. It made me get through tough times.

I came from a family that loved to sing and dance and have a good time. I used to sing the Notre Dame fight song in Polish words. I'd just make them up, like Sid Caesar used to do in one of his comic skits, and it sounded like the real stuff. My family is from Carpatho-Rusyn, and I belong to the Byzantine Catholic Church. Our religion is important to us, but we know how to have a good time.

These guys today make a lot more money than we ever did, but I feel sorry for some of these players. They don't have the camaraderie that we enjoyed. When I was with the Broncos, we were a young team, and we weren't very good. We wanted to win, and we tried hard. But we had a good time. It was just the best of times.

I was with the Broncos in 1967 when they were still in the American Football League. We had the first black starting quarterback in Marlin Briscoe. We were the first team in the AFL to beat an NFL team when we beat the Detroit Lions. We had a lot of firsts.

I'm proud of what I've done. I'm glad I went to Notre Dame. Dave Hart had coached in Johnstown and he tried to recruit me for Kentucky when he was an assistant coach for the Wildcats.

I'm upbeat when I'm out in public, and some people can't handle that. They figure I should be crying in my beer.

I'm not a religious freak, but I pray to the Blessed Mother and I ask her to look after me and my family.

Sure, I get scared sometimes. I'm afraid I'm going to wake up someday choking to death. I don't know how I'm going to be when I'm in a wheelchair, when I can't get up.

Rocky Bleier was a teammate of mine when I was at Notre Dame. He was a junior and I was a senior when we won the national championship. I have been inspired by Rocky's story. His hard work and dedication were unbelievable. He was very tough at Notre Dame. Even before he got wounded in Vietnam he had a lot of obstacles to overcome to be a ballplayer. He was double powerful. No one knew what he had to go through.

You have to believe in yourself. You have to look in the mirror and be honest with yourself. I like to hear motivational speakers, guys like Lou Holtz. They get me pumped up.

I have sympathy for people who can't rally themselves and who can't be upbeat. Everybody is different. I don't know how I'll be a year from now, but I'm trying to stay positive.

I saw Bruce Edwards on TV last week, caddying for Tom Watson. Now Edwards has Lou Gehrig's disease. He has difficulty speaking. But he's out there, and he's fighting. Tom Watson is going to help the ALS people raise funds. I want to write to him about that.

I got into the Cambria County Sports Hall of Fame along with Jack Ham. Arnold Palmer was there, too. I love to be out with those kind of guys. I like to get my picture taken with them.

Photos by Jim O'Brien

Johnstown's Pete Duranko kept telling one story after another at NFL Alumni meeting at Bruschetta's on East Carson Street. His license plate shows his pride in Pennsylvania and our nation's heroes.

Now that everyone knows I have Lou Gehrig's disease I get invited to golf outings that I didn't used to hear from. My wife says I'm enjoying this notoriety. Hey, I have an ego, sure, and I like being in the center of things. I always did.

But this is serious stuff. Every year, about 5,000 people in this country die of Lou Gehrig's disease, and about 5,000 more are diagnosed. So the number of people affected with it remains at 30,000.

Everybody has a disease they're fighting for.

God gives us certain things to deal with. I don't think he's a mean person, or that he hurts and kills people. People ask how he could have permitted something like 9/11. I don't think you can blame him for that. I'm like everyone else. I enjoy hearing "God Bless America" and "America the Beautiful" more than ever before. I was impressed with the people who refused to allow terrorists to take over Flight 93. Imagine what that must have been like to be up in that plane? Look what happened with the nine miners at Quecreek Mine last summer. That's a case of 70,000 people getting together to save nine miners. I've been doing charity work since 1973, and I do my best to make a contribution, to lend my name to good causes.

I love Terry Bradshaw. He's a good ol' country boy. He's just being himself. He came to Johnstown and spoke to Boy Scouts and he was great. He was funny. He talks from the heart. I try to do that.

My wife says I'm a Narcissist and she says, "You're loving this." No, I'm not thrilled about all of this. But I do enjoy the people. They want to help, and I can still help people.

When I was a kid my heroes were Tarzan and Jim Thorpe and Knute Rockne. I'd seen them all in the movies. I pretended to be like them; I swung from trees as a kid. I loved Johnny Weismuller, who was from Windber, just outside of Johnstown. He was an Olympic swimming champion. I thought I could be like him as Tarzan.

I go to golf outings now and I get to spend time with guys like Mike Ditka and Jim McMahon, or Yogi Berra. These are guys I look up to.

I get to go to Notre Dame reunions. I see people like Paul Hornung and Johnny Lattner. I remember as a freshman at Notre Dame in 1962, when I was still a running back and wearing No. 32, I was standing in a tunnel at Notre Dame Stadium before an alumni game and I got to see Ralph Guglielmi, Johnny Lujack, Johnny Lattner and Leon Hart. Our spring game was against the Old Timers. I ran over Lattner during the game, and knocked him out when my knee struck his helmet. I was upset. I've hurt a Heisman Trophy winner; they won't like that.

506

I played with Paul Martha when I was at Denver. He came to us in a trade with the Steelers. He ran back a kickoff for a touchdown and beat us when I was at Notre Dame. I hated to lose to Pitt. Paul led a charmed life. We called him 'Perfect Paul' when he was with the Broncos.

Tommy Clements is a Notre Dame guy, and he took me to his office and showed me the Steelers' training complex here on the South Side. He's done a great job for the Steelers. When I was there, I also got to meet Walt Harris, the Pitt coach, at his offices next door. I like Walt Harris.

There are so many people I've gotten to know through the years. My wife gets on me, but she's been at my side, helping me through all of this. She has her own problems, but she's been so supportive of my situation. She's the one who told me to make lemonade out of lemons.

Jim O'Brien

Pete Duranko draws a sidewalk crowd when he sings his Polish version of the Notre Dame fight song. "Anything for a laugh," declares Duranko.

*"I consider myself the luckiest man
on the face of the earth."*
— Lou Gehrig, Retirement speech
at Yankee Stadium July 4, 1937

Real ironmen of Steelers
Joe Maroon and Myron Cope
are comeback kids

*"I've only missed one game
in my career."*
— **Myron Cope**

The real ironmen of the Pittsburgh Steelers may be Myron Cope and Joe Maroon. They are both 5 feet 6 inches tall. Cope is 74 and Maroon is 63. They have to look up when they're talking to the Steelers, with the exception of Amos Zereoue, one of the team's scatbacks.

Maroon was a scatback himself when he played football at St. John's High School in Bellaire, Ohio, near his boyhood home of Bridgeport, and at Indiana University in Bloomington. He has the pictures to prove it. Maroon is better known as Dr. Joseph Maroon, hailed as one of the best doctors in the city by *Pittsburgh Business Times*. He is vice chairman and visiting professor of neurological surgery at the University of Pittsburgh School of Medicine. He has been one of the Steelers' team doctors more than 20 years.

Cope, of course, is a member of the Steelers' radio broadcast team. He has the worst voice in any National Football League broadcast booth, yet he is mostly beloved and sometimes reviled by Steelers' fans. It's the kind of love-hate relationship Bob Prince once had with Pirates' fans. Dr. Maroon got a lot of attention during the 2002 Steelers' season for treating Tommy Maddox after the Steelers' quarterback was knocked unconscious in a game against the Titans in Nashville. But Dr. Maroon also performed back surgery on Cope in late September and has been looking out for him ever since.

Cope had been suffering great discomfort for over a year from chronic back pain. Cope is a competitor, though, and it didn't keep him from performing his chores alongside his sidekicks, Bill Hillgrove and Tunch Ilkin. Cope continues to get VIP treatment at UPMC Presbyterian Hospital. Cope was a question mark in regard to his ability to continue on Steeler' broadcasts when the team opened training camp in late July, 2003.

During the Steelers' bye week, Cope bit the bullet and went in for back surgery under the scalpel of Dr. Maroon at UPMC. Dr. Maroon repaired three bad disks in Cope's spine. Cope came back to work in the Steelers' broadcast booth 11 days after the surgery.

Cope growled if anybody offered sympathy. "There are guys playing down there in a lot worse shape than me," he told his listeners on the Steelers' WDVE-FM flagship booth high above Heinz Field.

Dr. Maroon is on the sideline at Steelers' games, helping to tend to injured players. He made a house call before the game started, however, checking on Cope for ten minutes in the media dining room. Cope had been sitting on a new cushy pillow, but spent more time standing and screaming during the game.

Cope said he had missed only one game in his 33-year career as a Steelers' game day analyst, about ten years earlier, when his wife Mildred died. He missed the first quarter of a game to attend his brother-in-law's funeral. It's difficult to keep Cope on the disabled list, though he's had to give up golf, his favorite pastime. The first commentary Cope offered upon his return, ironically enough, was his thoughts about the death the week before of Mike Webster, the Steelers' Hall of Fame center, known as "Iron Mike" because of his physical workouts and his determination to be in the lineup for every offensive play during his career. Cope shares Webster's passion for the game.

"This is the Superbowl of Triathlons." — Dr. Joseph Maroon

I like to watch the TV shows on CNN when authors are interviewed. I figure I can learn something. Bob Woodward, who has written so many books on the power figures in Washington, D.C., was being interviewed on this one show, and he said something that stayed with me. He said, "You've got to go back to your interview subjects from time to time, and interview them again." I did that quite a bit with this book.

Dr. Joe Maroon, for instance, comes from Bridgeport, Ohio, my mother's hometown. People in my neighborhood in Upper St. Clair came from there, too, and they knew him as just plain "Joey" and they knew his family. They said his father, Charlie, owned a little grocery store, had been involved in real estate and the fuel business. Even more interesting, they said Charlie Maroon had control of the pinball and slot machines throughout the Ohio Valley. Others competed for the same action.

Maroon's old neighbors remembered stories and photographs appearing in the *Times-Leader* and *The Intelligencer* about a bomb being left on the porch of the Maroon home. They remembered that a bomb actually went off and caused a great deal of destruction at the home of his uncle Abby, who has owned a restaurant in Bridgeport for over 30 years. The restaurant is still in business. "It's a nice little place that serves honest-to-goodness food and has a steady clientele," said Dr. Maroon. Maroon's dad knew Bill Elias, who ran Wheeling Downs and other shady business interests in the Ohio Valley, and Bill Elias was a dear friend of Art Rooney, the owner of the Steelers. There are so many links here.

I was told that Dr. Maroon's mother, Ana, of Polish origin, was

509

an attractive woman, and that she had two daughters who were both beauty queens in statewide and national pageants. Dr. Maroon was born on May 26, 1940 in Wheeling Hospital, just across the Ohio River from Bridgeport. Bill Mazeroski was born in that same hospital four years earlier and also grew up in Ohio.

Both were terrific all-around athletes who made their mark in the Ohio Valley, a real hotbed for sports. Maroon graduated first in his class at St. John's High School and went to Indiana University of Bloomington on an athletic scholarship.

He played on all-star football and baseball teams with the likes of John Havlicek and Joe Niekro, both Hall of Fame athletes in their respective pro sports. Havlicek was a receiver and Maroon a quarterback for an Ohio all-star football team. Havlicek, who played basketball at Ohio State and with the Boston Celtics, had a tryout as an end with the Cleveland Browns when Paul Brown was the head coach. Maroon captained most of the all-star teams he played on. He was just that kind of leader.

Dr. Maroon is quite the success story himself. His paternal grandparents had emigrated from Jal-El-Dib, in the northern suburbs of Beirut, in 1910. They settled in Bridgeport. Dr. Maroon is proud of his Lebanese heritage.

He's always been a dedicated, ambitious performer in whatever pursuit he adopts. He's a driven individual.

When I last checked in with him in mid-June, 2003, Dr. Maroon told me he had just qualified for the Hawaiian Ironman Triathlon contest, scheduled for Sunday, October 12, 2003. "This is the Superbowl of triathlon competitions," declared Dr. Maroon. It's held in Kailua-Kona, Hawaii. A triathlon consists of three demanding athletic contests: a 2.4 mile swim in the ocean, a 112-mile bike ride through the lava fields of the Big Island of Hawaii, and then a 26.2 mile marathon. Doing one of those would be enough to tax a well-conditioned athlete. It's regarded as the toughest single day endurance event in the world. Imagine a 63-year-old physician doing it. He has run the marathon in Pittsburgh and other places.

Dr. Maroon told me he prepped for the "Ironman Triathlon" by running and biking in Schenley Park in Oakland and also in North Park, and that he did his swimming workouts at the YMCA in Sewickley, not far from his home, and at the Pittsburgh Athletic Association (PAA) not far from the UPMC complex.

"I feel better and I work better when I'm in training," said Dr. Maroon, who added that he was 5-6, 160 pounds — the same as his playing weight in college. "I'm sharper and more efficient in the operating room. Everybody benefits from me being at my physical and mental best. Plus, I enjoy this."

It's a shame Cope couldn't go along for the ride, and do a play-by-play call of the Hawaiian Iron Man Triathlon. It's an Olympic sport now and it deserves an Olympic announcer.

Somewhere Mike Webster is smiling at the thought of all of this.

Joseph Maroon crosses finish line in 1993
nman Triathlon World Championship,

Myron Cope questions Casey Hampton, 6-2,
320-pound nose tackle, during drills at
Steelers' training camp at St. Vincent
College.

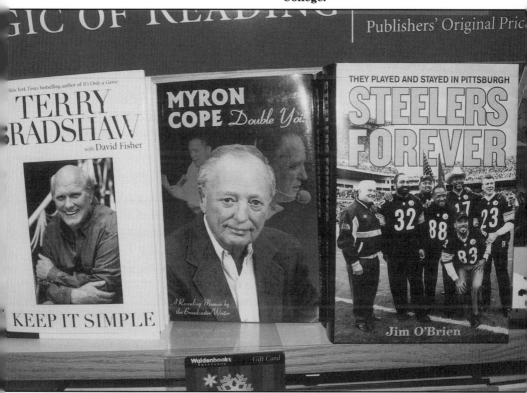

Among the most popular sports books in Pittsburgh during the 2002 holiday
season were by Terry Bradshaw, Myron Cope, Jim O'Brien and Andy Russell

Jim O'Brien was presented a plaque for induction into the U.S. Basketball Writers Hall of Fame by past president Bob Ryan of *Boston Globe* at ceremonies during the NCAA Final Four in New Orleans in early April of 2003.

"They were all quarterbacks for the Pittsburgh Steelers, and don't you think it's intriguing that Terry Bradshaw, David Woodley and Tommy Maddox were all born in Shreveport, Louisiana, or that Bradshaw, Maddox and Bobby Layne all lived in Dallas, Texas at the same time? Or that Maddox and Bradshaw share the same birthday?"

— Jim O'Brien